Forever Patriots

i

Forever Patriots

A Novel

By

Stoney Livingston

Cover by:
Gordon Mustain
&
Terry Del Bene

To all combat veterans of the Viet Nam War. You won all the battles. Someone else lost the war.

"...if people bring so much courage to this world the world has to kill them to break them, so of course it kills them. The world breaks every one and afterward many are strong at the broken places. But those that will not break it kills. It kills the very good and the very gentle and the very brave impartially. If you are none of these you can be sure it will kill you too but there will be no special hurry." Ernest Hemingway. **A Farewell to Arms)**

CHAPTER ONE: THE BEGINNING

The smell of burning flesh and singed hair wafted into young Jesse Langley's nostrils. He shook his head and breathed out quickly, pushing the pungent odor from his nose in a puff of white vapor.

His father smiled down at him from the back of his horse. "It does get a mite strong if you get just the right whiff, don't it?"

Jesse grinned into the cold October air of the Mogollon Rim of east-central Arizona. "This is the last one, ain't it Dad?"

"One more. I saw a maverick in that stand of pines just south of us." He looked down at the bawling steer hog-tied next to Jesse. "You can let this one up. Let's go look for that bunch-quitter."

Jesse unwrapped the rope from the young steer's hocks and stepped back as the frightened animal awkwardly gained its feet and moved into the small herd east of the branding fire. He walked to his horse silently as his father rode slowly alongside. He would be glad when the roundup was over. The sixteen-hour days were hard on him. He was grateful for school during the week, even though he'd had to miss one day during the roundup. He didn't believe he could take a steady diet of this kind of work. Of course, he knew it was only a week or so in October, and once again in the spring – but what a week or so!

Up before the sun and in the saddle, searching for strays, rounding them up, starting the branding fires, pruning, castrating the bulls, branding, earmarking, tick-dipping, doctoring, separating, roping, tying, herding – it was almost impossible for a nine-year-old boy to make it through the day and into the night. But this was his first round-up as a full-fledged hand and he was determined to do as well as the grown men. He hadn't been so sure about some of the Mexicans. A few showed some of the symptoms Jesse felt but those weren't the regular cowboys. The regulars carried on as though they had done nothing more than stroll to the creek for a refreshing drink of water. They didn't even appear tired at the end of the first day or two. Those men seemed like they had been born in the saddle. Jesse felt better when these Mexicans began to show exhaustion on the third day, not because he wanted them to suffer, but because he was beginning to think he was making too much of his own discomfort. It

1

was nice to know he wasn't alone.

Jesse mounted his buckskin and followed his father's chestnut mare into the pines. Pablo, one of the wetbacks, rode on their right flank. The clean, crisp smell of the pines overpowered the stench of the burned hair and Jesse felt better to be away from the branding fire. His buckskin snorted loudly, blowing a cloud of white vapor into the cold mountain air. Jesse folded the collar of his sheepskin jacket tightly around his neck.

Pablo let out a howl and exited the pines on their right, ten feet behind a bawling, frightened steer. Jesse wheeled his buckskin and took up the chase. He worked his rope loose from the saddle horn and adjusted the loop on the run. Pablo threw his loop at the animal's head. Jesse took a shot at the hooves. His loop encircled the rear legs of the fleeing steer and he jerked quickly on the rope. The buckskin sat back on his haunches as Jesse dallied around the saddle horn and jumped to the ground.

Pablo's loop had settled over the small horns on the steer's head and his mare was already on her haunches. Both the man and the boy ran the length of their ropes to the animal struggling on the ground as the two horses pulled in opposite directions, keeping the ropes taut. Pablo pinned the steer, placing his hands on the head and a knee on the neck as Jesse quickly tied three legs with his rope while his buckskin moved in to give him just enough slack to do the job.

Jesse's father sat his horse a few feet away, smiling. "That was a right fine job. Now what are you going to do with him?"

Pablo and Jesse looked at one another foolishly. They had been so taken up with the excitement of roping and tying the steer they had forgotten the fire was out of reach. The branding iron would cool long before they could complete their job.

Pablo looked up at Jim Langley and shrugged. "Senior Jeem, if you ride a faster *caballo*, you could get the iron to us weeth heat to spare."

Jim Langley laughed softly. "Hell, why don't we just cut down a tree and build a fire right here? Save us the trouble of havin' to move the steer or the iron. I've got another iron with me."

Jesse smiled sheepishly at Pablo and undid the bindings on the animal's hocks. They remounted and led the steer toward the branding fire.

Jesse rode next to Pablo, Jim riding behind, keeping the steer in check.

Pablo looked over to Jesse. "Senior Jesse. I have never seen such a young boy throw a rope like you. Someday you weel make one *muy bueno caballero* – like your *padre*."

"I don't think I'll ever be that good, Pablo."

"I don' know. You preety good."

They rode toward the fire in silence, Jesse dreading the thought of the pungent odor that would soon assault his nostrils.

*****

The simmering beans and beef cooking over the open fire was more than adequate to send Jesse's stomach into a loud growl. The sun had long since drifted below the horizon and the air was crisp and cold but, due to the number of men involved in the roundup, his mother cooked outside on a large homemade grill. Once you had the food on your plate you were welcome to go inside the ranch house or the bunkhouse. Everyone knew that. These men had all been here before. They knew they were welcome anywhere Jim Langley ran a spread.

Forever Patriots

Some of the men chose to eat in the warmth of the large fire in the pit behind the main house, their friendly chatter in English and Spanish mixing with the crackle of the fire.

Jesse filled his plate and walked to the house. He sat in the large livingroom near the bright fireplace, next to his father and Pablo. He let his glance drift past the two Model 92 Winchesters hanging above the mantel and meander around the large room, taking in the familiar faces. None of the men wore their spurs. His mother drew the line there. No spurs in the house. There was a stack of them in the sun room, Jesse's among them.

Pablo's voice drifted into Jesse's consciousness. "...but, Senior Jeem, why do you want to leave thees life and move to a beeg city like Tucson? You are a *caballero*, like the rest of us, only maybe a leetle smarter. You are the foreman of a good ranch. You have a nice house and a good family. What more could a man wan'?"

Jim chewed his biscuit slowly. When he was finished, he answered quietly, sadly. "I'm gonna miss this way of life, *amigo*, but I've got Jesse to think about. He needs the education he can get in a bigger town. These ranches won't be here forever. He's got to learn about other things in life. He can't get it here. The new foreman will work with you and the rest of the men."

Jesse knew his father was referring to Pablo's immigration status. His family lived in southern Sonora, Mexico, depending on Pablo's jaunts into the States for the extra money they needed to supplement his income as a mechanic.

Pablo leaned around Jim and took a peak at Jesse, who was wolfing down his pinto beans and beef. "He ees a smart boy, Senior Jeem. He is a good *caballero*. He don' need mush more than he has. He don' need the beeg city."

"I appreciate what you're sayin', *amigo*, but the fact is, this is my last round-up. Someday Jesse will join the service like all of his forefathers did, and when he does, I'd like him to know more than how to throw a loop. We'll be movin' out in the early spring. I've got a job lined up at the airbase down there and I've given Mr. Grant my notice."

"We weel mees you, Senior Jeem."

Jim's eyes moistened as he looked about the room. The fireplace crackled loudly. Tired but happy voices filled the air. He looked back at Pablo. "I'll miss you too, old friend."

Jesse carried his half-eaten plate of food to the kitchen sink. He wasn't hungry anymore. He didn't want to leave the ranch. His world was falling apart. His great-great grandfather on his mother's side had joined the Confederate Arizona Rangers during the Civil War and he had had almost no formal education. Jesse could learn what he needed to know about the military when that time came. He didn't need any special education that he couldn't get right where he was. He couldn't imagine living in a town the size of Tucson. His mother said more than sixty thousand people lived there. He had never seen sixty thousand people before. Jesse was afraid.

His fear of the unknown, coupled with the loss of the horses and dogs and the cowboys, was almost too much for him to bear silently. He wanted to talk to his mother and father and express his feelings but he would wait - maybe sometime in November. Next spring was a long way off. By then maybe things would change and they could stay on the ranch. Maybe.

He walked outside into the cold evening air of the Mogollon Rim. He heard

3

Stoney Livingston

the horses in the corral and smelled the scent of pine carried to him by the gusting wind through the branches as it brushed the smell of the horses to the south. He pulled the collar of his sheepskin jacket closed and buttoned it. One of the four Border Collies belonging to the ranch came near him and sat silently a few feet away.

Jesse walked to the cow-dog and sat next to him. He put his arm around the animal and held him tightly. "They're gonna take me away, Biff. They're gonna take me away." The dog whimpered softly for a moment then sat still.

The sounds of a song emanating from near the large fire pit behind the house drifted to his ears. The men there had finished eating and, as was the custom, someone had dragged out a guitar. He recognized the words: "*When the work's all done this fall*," and listened intently until the song was finished. It was one of his many favorites. If they moved to the city he would probably never hear any of the old cowboy songs again. He cried silently in the night, shivering from the cold and the fear and the loneliness.

*****

The two boys stared cautiously at one another over clenched fists as they circled in a counter-clockwise direction, each hoping he would be the one to strike the victory blow. There were no spectators to this fight, except for Jesse's mother who watched from her kitchen window. Jesse knew she was there. He wished she would go away and let him fight without watching his every move.

Things were different in big cities. Jesse was not familiar with the ways of those his own age who grew up in town. He had endured much in the way of harassment from some of the boys at school and now he was tired of it. For almost two months he had listened to the boys in class and on the playground as they made jokes about his ignorance. He didn't know how to play marbles the right way, or he was too bashful, or they didn't like the way he combed his hair, or something else.

He studied the boy before him. Norman was a year older but about the same size as he. He had followed Jesse home from school, taunting him all the way, teasing him, challenging him. Jesse had ignored him until they were in front of his house. He had stopped at the curb and said, "Will you wait here, Norman? I'll be back."

"Where you going, you big coward?"

Jesse's eyes narrowed. "I'm going in the house and tell my mother that I'm gonna whip you."

"What did you say?"

"You heard me, Norman. I'm tired of it. All I wanted to do was make friends, and all you and your friends want to do is be smart-alecks and make my life miserable. Well, you're gonna be sorry."

"Oh, is that so?" Norman said.

"Yeah, that's so. You gonna wait or not?"

Norman smiled broadly. "You bet I'll wait. If you got the guts, I'll be here."

"Oh, I got the guts all right. I'll be right back. You just stay here." He walked across the yard and into the house.

"Why don't you invite your friend in, Jess?" His mother was just inside the door.

Jesse looked at the floor. "That's what I was gonna talk to you about, Ma. You remember when Biff was only a puppy and the older dogs used to pick on him

4

all the time?"

Betty Langley furrowed her brow. "Yes."

"You remember how I was all the time protecting him from the other dogs?" His mother nodded, a slow smile working its way across her lips.

"Well, anyway, you and Dad said that Biff would eventually have to stand up for himself. Remember the day he stood up to ol' Jeb? How I wanted to step in and break things up?" He continued, not looking up for his mother's response. "And how you and Dad held me back, sayin' it was time for Biff to fight his own battles? And how Biff made a believer out of Jeb?" He looked up into his mother's face.

"I remember, Jess. Now, what are you driving at?"

Jesse jerked his head in the direction of the street. "Well, that's my Jeb out there, Ma. Him and his friends been pickin' on me since the first day I was in school. I gotta go outside and fight him."

Betty put a hand on a hip. "You think your dad would approve of this?"

"I know he would. One time I seen ...."

"Saw."

"....saw him whip one of the cowboys for beatin' up on one of the steers at roundup. He lit into this guy like ...."

"That's enough, Jess. I get your drift." She nodded to the door. "You really think that's your Jeb out there, huh?"

"I know it is, Ma."

"Well then, go do what you have to do."

He knew she was watching as he threw a wild left hook, missing his opponent. He breathed heavily. His arms felt like lead weights.

After almost twenty minutes of sparring and wrestling with neither gaining a significant advantage over the other, Norman puffed, "You wanna quit?"

"You ain't beat me, Norman. I can still whip you. I'll stay out here all night if I have to."

"I didn't say I beat you," wheezed Norman. "I just said 'do you wanna quit?' We could call it a draw. Nobody wins."

"Who loses?"

"Nobody loses either."

That sounded better to Jesse. "Okay, if that's what you want. Just don't be tellin' your friends you won, 'cause it ain't so." He lowered his hands warily, ready for a trick.

Norman dropped his hands. He wiped a small splotch of blood from his lip. "Okay, I'm going now." He backed up a couple of steps, watching Jesse closely.

"So go. Just leave me alone from now on."

"I might."

Jesse put up his fists. "Then let's finish it here and now."

"You already agreed to call it a draw."

That was a fact. He had. He hadn't set any conditions before the agreement. "Yeah, I guess I did. I keep my word." He lowered his fists. "But I promise you, Norman, if you mess with me tomorrow, I'll whip you. And this time I won't quit until the job's done."

Norman picked up his books and walked away silently.

The fact Jesse had not won a clear victory bothered him, not because he wanted to win so much as he did not want his mother to see him not win. His pride hurt. He felt as though he had failed. He wasn't sure who or what he had failed, but he had failed. To continue the fight would have been even more devastating had he been beaten. If it was a victory, it was a hollow one at best. He still wasn't sure what a draw was.

He turned from Norman's rapidly diminishing form and walked into the house, dreading his mother's reaction. She stood inside the kitchen wiping a plate that Jesse was certain had been dry for at least ten minutes. He looked at her silently, waiting for her to speak. He was about to leave the kitchen when she turned.

"Did you take care of business?"

Jesse shrugged. "I ain't sure, Ma."

"Then it don't sound to me like you took care of business."

Jesse felt the tears welling in his eyes. "He's older'n me, Ma."

"You knew that when you started, didn't you?"

Jesse nodded.

"You think he'll leave you alone now?"

"I think so."

Betty Langley smiled. "You did what you could. That's the most important thing."

"Do you think Dad would think that was more important than getting the job done for sure?"

She put the plate and towel on the counter and placed an arm around his shoulder. "Jesse, there's nothing more important than doing your best. That's the most anybody can do. And don't you ever forget that."

*****

Jesse became popular in school with most, but not all, of the students. He was soft-spoken and a natural athlete. Despite this, the fights continued. Though Norman had moved out of state within two months of their fight, there had been others who had wanted to take Jesse on. At first it had been Norman's friends but the circle of antagonists soon spread to anyone looking to enhance his reputation at school.

Jesse fought them one and all, asking no mercy, but often showing compassion when he bested his adversary, as he almost always did. His fighting skills improved with each confrontation and soon those who would challenge him did so in pairs. He tried to avoid every fight. He would do anything to talk his way out of a physical confrontation short of running away. He could never run away. His parents would be mortified. He fought to uphold his dignity and his pride and the pride of his family. He longed to move away from the city and leave the fighting behind. Every time it became apparent a fight was imminent, he was choked with fear, a fear that seemed about to consume him – until the first blow was struck. Once the fight was started his fear became controllable. He never mastered it but at least he was able to manage it.

In high school the fights became less frequent but more violent. After one particularly brutal fight that ended up in the center of a busy intersection during the rush hour, the police arrived en masse.

Several police cars filled the corner service station lot, their drivers in the busy intersection, trying to straighten out the traffic jam. The officer in charge questioned Jesse's opponent. "What started this whole thing?"

Jesse's opponent stared at him from a bloody face, his clothing a dark red

6

as the blood dried on his new shirt. He pointed to Jesse. "That guy jumped me when I got off the bus."

Jesse had been prepared for some kind of lie but nothing so blatant. Unable to control his anger, he lunged at the larger boy and peppered his face with several short, chopping blows. Two officers pulled him away and wrestled him to the ground.

"Calm down, son, or we're going to have to handcuff you," said one of the officers.

Jesse stopped struggling. The officers let him stand but watched him closely. The officer who had been questioning the bigger boy turned to Jesse and said, "I take it you have a different version of the story?"

"Yessir, I sure do. I don't even know who this guy is. He slammed me into a drinking fountain at school today and said he was going to kick my ass when I got off the bus today."

"All right, why don't you have a seat over there in the back of that police car while I talk to this young man?"

"Yessir." Jesse walked slowly to the opened door of the police car and sat on the rear seat, the door open wide, his left foot on the ground, ready to pounce should the larger boy tell another blatant lie, but he could not hear what was being said. He watched as the other boy talked to the officer and gestured at him from time to time. Shortly the larger boy went into the restroom at the rear of the gas station. He stepped outside a moment later, the blood washed from his face, and walked south from the station.

"Where's he goin'?" Jesse asked the officer who had been talking to his opponent.

"Home I guess."

"Home? What about me?"

"I'm going to have to take you downtown."

"Me? For what?"

"Just put your feet in the car and let's get going."

"But, officer, I didn't start the fight."

"Maybe not. But you'll get your chance to tell your side of the story."

"Just like he did?" Jesse nodded at the disappearing figure of the larger boy.

"Look, kid, don't get smart with me. Just get your feet inside the car and let's get going."

Jesse attempted to stand. The officer slammed the door on his leg. Jesse screamed in pain and jumped into the back seat, lunging for the door on the other side. A second officer held it fast. Jesse jumped for the front seat just as the first officer leapt into the car and over the back of the front seat at him. Jesse took a swing at him, grazing his nose. As his fist traveled downward, one of his knuckles snagged on the edge of the officer's badge, ripping Jesse's flesh open.

"You wise-ass punk!" shouted the officer.

Jesse took another swing. This one connected. Another officer came over the back of the front seat from the passenger side. Two others opened the rear doors and joined the fight. Jesse struggled but was quickly overpowered and handcuffed. The officer Jesse had hit, the one with the bleeding nose, slammed the cuffs tight against his wrists, cutting off circulation. He was the officer who had let the other boy go. The officer gave one final push on the cuffs to tighten them further.

"Ow! Take these cuffs offa me and let's find out how tough you really are!"

7

Stoney Livingston

shouted Jesse.

The man made a move to strike him but another officer held his arm. "He's in custody, Jack. Let it ride. He's just a kid."

Jack's face turned red. "Get the paddy-wagon out here. Let the little punk ride in style."

The second officer stared at Jack for a moment then moved to his car to call for the paddy wagon.

Jesse cried silently in the back of the paddy wagon as it slowly made its way to Mother Higgins, the juvenile hall. He cried out of shame and hurt. His father had always told him to be sure he was right, then do it. He had been right. He'd had no choice. The bigger boy had assaulted him as soon as he had stepped from the bus.

He worried what his mother would think. Despite his many fights he had never been in trouble with the law. He was sure she would eventually understand. She would believe him. He didn't lie to his mother and father. They knew that.

At the detention center the officer called Jack removed the cuffs and placed him into a cell with a tall black boy. Jesse ignored the other boy's presence as he sat on the lower bunk and wiped the dry tear streaks from his face, then rubbed his wrists to reduce the numbness in them. He pulled up his pant leg and studied the large bruise forming on his shin caused by the police car door.

"Hey, man, you're sitting on my bed," said the black boy.

Jesse stood. "I'm sorry. I didn't know."

"Shit. Don't gimme that crap, man. You come in here lookin fer a fight."

Tears welled into Jesse's eyes. It seemed everyone in the world wanted to push him. "Leave me alone! I don't want any trouble. Just leave me alone. You have your bed."

"You're standin' in my spot, punk," said the other boy.

Tears streamed down Jesse's cheeks as he faced the other youngster. He considered his options and found his anger left him no choice. He lunged into the other boy, his fists flailing.

They fell into the bars on the door, grappling at each other. Two guards opened the cell door and rushed inside. They yelled something into the hallway as they tried to pry the two boys apart. One of them was struck in the face by a wild swing. He cursed and redoubled his efforts to separate the two boys. Two more men entered the cell. With the added manpower, they successfully separated Jesse from the other boy. He continued to fight until completely overcome. He didn't care who he was fighting. It seemed as though the whole world was against him. He felt totally alone.

*****

A juvenile officer sat behind an old oak desk as two detention officers ushered Jesse into a small office. The man looked up at him and smiled. "I'm Joe Dobbs. Have a seat. Relax." His eyes lingered on the deep red marks on Jesse's wrists and the laceration on his knuckles.

Jesse sat suspiciously in one of the two wooden armchairs facing the desk. Joe sat for a minute, unmoving, studying him. After a while he said, "They tell me you handle your dukes pretty well."

"I get by." Jesse was sullen.

"You want to tell me what happened?"

8

"I must've told ten people already. What good does it do to tell anybody anything? Believe what you want."

"I want to believe what really happened."

Jesse stared at him for a time, uncertain of the man's intentions. After a moment or two, Joe's quiet confidence reached him. He smiled and said. "That other guy didn't leave me much of a choice." He told his story, from the moment he had first seen the large boy in school, to the fight in the busy intersection, then the policeman named Jack, and finally the black boy in the cell with him. When he was finished, Joe looked at him a long while.

"And for that, they brought you here?"

"Yessir. I didn't set out to hit that police officer, but he wouldn't listen. He slammed the door of his car on my leg." Jesse pulled his left trouser leg up to reveal a large purple bruise on his shin. "The others were all right, but that one officer was a jerk."

"I'll look into that. As for Hector, – that's the name of the kid that was in the cell with you – I wouldn't feel too bad about that. I'm sure it happened just the way you said it did. He's on his way to Flo. You shouldn't have been put in the same cell he was in."

"Florence?" Jesse had never been that close to anyone who was on his way to prison. "What did he do?"

"Burglary. Auto theft. Robbery. You name it. He'll be remanded to adult court this time. He likes to push other kids around – especially the younger ones." Joe smiled. "I guess he found one who doesn't push so easy, huh?'

"I don't much take to it," admitted Jesse, matching Joe's smile with one of his own.

Joe waited a moment before continuing. "Your mother has been notified and she's on her way here. You can go home just as soon as we've got the paperwork completed."

"Thank you, sir. I've never been in trouble with the police before."

"You're not in trouble with us now, Jesse. It was a big misunderstanding that, hopefully, we can put behind us. Can you put it behind you?"

Jesse found the lazy smile on Joe's face contagious. "Yessir."

Joe leaned over his desk. "You ever think about boxing amateur?"

"No, sir."

"I'm involved in a program to keep kids off the street. One of the things my guys do is box. From what I heard, you'd make a pretty fair welterweight." He paused. "You can use the facilities of the Old Pueblo Boxing Club. You don't have to join the club, but it would be a nice gesture."

"I don't want to join any clubs."

"Like I said, you don't have to. Mr. Fimbres, the manager of the club, says all of the kids in my program can use his facilities to train with no obligations. How about it? Can I talk to your parents?"

Jesse shrugged. "I guess."

*****

With his parents' permission, Jesse became an amateur boxer, resulting in further improvement to his already potent street-fighting skills. At age fourteen, he was an undefeated contender for the Arizona State Golden Gloves competition. His dark hair, light skin, high cheekbones, and battleship grey eyes, set him apart from the other boxers, all of whom were black or Hispanic. The promoters loved him. He was a good draw. He helped bring in the *gringo* crowd.

Jesse sat in his corner, waiting for the referee to signal him and his opponent to center ring. Gene Stabler, Arizona's pro fighter of the month, was Jesse's second. He'd never met Gene before this night but he liked the quiet-spoken black man from Safford.

Gene whispered in his ear as Jesse kept his eyes on the referee. "Don't worry about this guy, kid. I've seen you fight. You can take him. He may have more wins than you but that's only because he's been doing this a lot longer. Neither one of you have lost a fight. Remember, he walks away with the big 'one' tagged onto his record after the fight tonight, not you. If you lay that left on him, he'll stay away."

"Thanks, Gene."

The referee signaled them to ring center. Jesse stared into the face of Oscar Montiel as the referee repeated his instructions in a monotone voice. Montiel stared back at him fiercely. Jesse let a smile move across his face. He thought he saw Montiel's facial muscles tighten a little. Jesse's smile broadened.

The first round was a testing of the other man's defensive and offensive capabilities. Montiel was good. He was quick and he could hit hard. He was older – seventeen – and more experienced. But he was not unbeatable. He was not used to boxing a left-handed fighter. Jesse sparred with him jab for jab throughout the first round.

Gene spoke softly to him as Jesse sat on his stool between the first and second round. "You're gonna have to go after him, Jesse. He's a big favorite with the judges. Whoever wins this one goes to the Golden Gloves regionals. He's in the Old Pueblo Boxing Club. You're an independent. He's Mexican. You're a *gringo*. The judges are all Mexican. Do you understand what I'm tellin' you?"

"I gotta knock him out?"

"Only way I can see you winnin' this one, Jesse. That's a hard pill, boy, but you're big enough to swallow it."

The buzzer sounded and Jesse stood. When the bell rang, he closed with Montiel quickly. He jabbed and countered and threw rapid flurries. Montiel matched Jesse's energy. The crowd in the Tucson Gardens came to its feet. Jesse landed a hard right, then a left. Montiel went down.

Jesse retired to a neutral corner. He watched Montiel stand and take the mandatory eight count. The ref looked into his eyes and waved the two of them together. Jesse pressed his opponent into the ropes and threw a continuous flurry. The crowd remained standing. Montiel covered himself well, and though it appeared Jesse was beating him to a pulp, his blows caused very little damage to his experienced opponent.

Jesse felt his arms growing heavy. He backed away and waited for Montiel to move from the ropes, lowering his arms to allow blood to circulate more quickly. Montiel came at him with a quick flurry. Jesse parried the blows and countered with a right-left-right. Montiel fell to the canvas. The crowd cheered wildly as he moved to a neutral corner to wait out the count.

Montiel made his feet shakily on the count of eight. The ref stopped the count at nine and looked into his eyes. The bell rang ending the second round.

Jesse plopped down heavily on his stool. He fought for his breath. His breathing came in heavy gasps. Gene wiped his sweating face and shoulders with a damp towel. "You did great out there, kid. You can take him out in the next round."

"I'm too tired, ...Gene. I'm ...gonna have to ...let him wear himself down a ...little bit. The old ... Archie Moore stance."

"That's not good in amateur boxing, kid. If you do that, he gets all the points."

"Not...if I ...knock him out." Jesse was exhausted but, for some reason unknown to him, he was also confident.

Gene smiled. "You got a point there, kid."

The buzzer sounded. Jesse made his feet and waited for the bell. The referee brought the two fighters together in the center of the ring. They touched gloves, indicating both knew it was the last round. The bell rang and Montiel moved in quickly.

Jesse crouched low and crossed his arms in front of him. Montiel's blows glanced harmlessly from his arms and shoulders. Jesse gathered strength as Montiel wasted his in a useless attempt to break Jesse's defensive strategy. The crowd booed. Jesse back-peddled and threw three quick punches. The crowd cheered. Jesse barely heard Gene shouting from his corner. "He's tired. Put him away!"

He's tired? I'm dying out here! Thought Jesse. He went back into the Archie Moore crouch. The crowd booed. He held his position as Montiel continued to bang away on his arms and shoulders. When he guessed there were about thirty seconds left in the round, he came out of his stance swinging. His first left caught Montiel on the chin, sending him reeling against the ropes. But something was wrong. The referee was between him and Montiel, pushing him back. He stepped back and stood, waiting for an explanation.

The ref stepped to Montiel, who had just come away from the ropes. He raised the older boy's right hand. Jesse stared at the referee in mute disbelief. Montiel had scored no solid hits against him in the entire fight. Jesse shook his head. The crowd booed. He realized the fight was over and he had lost on the referee's decision. Anger welled up in him. He stepped close to the referee.

"What's going on?"

"I'm stopping the fight."

"For what?"

"You weren't able to continue."

Jesse spit out his mouthpiece. "What? He never laid a glove on me!"

The crowd booed loudly. The referee looked at him. "The fight's over. Montiel is the winner by TKO."

Jesse punched the referee solidly on the cheek. The crowd roared its approval. Gene jumped into the ring and grabbed him quickly, pulling him away from the fallen referee. "It's okay, kid. We know who won. We'll appeal. It's not over yet."

Jesse looked into Gene's face and said, "It's over for me, Gene." He felt the tears starting down his face. He wiped his eyes with his gloves and hurriedly left the ring. Jesse retired to the dressing room in tears, where he promptly quit organized boxing.

It mattered little to him that within a week, one of the Tucson newspapers exposed a plot by the local promoter and the referee to ensure his opponent's victory. Montiel represented the Old Pueblo Boxing Club. Jesse boxed as an independent, the only fighter in southern Arizona not representing a club.

*****

Early in his sophomore year of high school, Jesse stopped at Will Hunt's house to advise him of a sandlot football game at the nearby park. He and Will had been casual friends for more than a year and most of the time they met in school or at the neighborhood park. It was Jesse's first trip to Will's house.

As he approached the front yard, there was a girl washing a '55 Pontiac. She smiled as she looked up from her work. It was the warmest smile Jesse had ever seen. He guessed she was older than he by a year or two.

"Hi. Is Will home?" He couldn't decide which was prettier, her smile or her golden-brown eyes.

"Hi. I'm Shannon, his older sister. He's in the house." She gestured with her hand, the one holding the hose.

Jesse jumped aside when he saw the stream of water moving towards him but was unable to avoid getting wet. Shannon laughed an embarrassed laugh and Jesse said with a smile, "I was gonna wash 'em but I had planned on doing it *after* the game."

"I'm sorry. I forgot I had the hose in my hand."

"It's time for my Saturday bath anyway."

"What's your name?" Shannon asked, still holding her smile.

"Jesse."

When Will opened the front door Jesse was bent at the waist, leaning forward to keep the cool water on his shirt from touching his body. "What's the matter with you?"

Jesse looked up at him. "It's a long story. You wanna play football? There's a game at the park in about ten minutes."

"Let me change shoes and I'll be right there."

While he waited for Will to change his shoes, Jesse and Shannon made small talk, but Jesse was unaware of what either of them said. He was too busy studying her for his mind to take in anything other than what his eyes could deliver. She was not a classic beauty, nor was she a sex goddess, but Jesse believed she was the most perfect girl he had ever met. She was small, about five feet two inches or so. Her hair was brown with a hint of red when struck just so by the sun. Her eyes were a shade of light brown with flecks of gold evenly distributed throughout the iris. Her lips were neither big nor small and her mouth was perfectly shaped. Jesse wondered what it would be like to kiss her. When she moved, her body seemed light and airy. Her tanned legs looked better-shaped than Betty Grable's – at least the part he could see below the hem of the blue shorts she wore. Her waist was small and her breasts proportioned for her size. He couldn't have drawn her better had he made a blueprint of the perfect girl. And she could speak English in whole sentences, without the use of words like "cool" and "rad". That was most impressive to Jesse. He liked the way she talked.

As they walked to the park, Jesse looked over his shoulder at Shannon. "You never told me you had an older sister."

"You never asked," said Will.

"She's kinda neat. How old is she?"

"She's a senior. Got a college boyfriend. He's a jerk but Shannon says he's more mature than the guys in high school. If that's what she calls mature, she can have it."

Jesse's experience with girls was no more or less than any average fifteen-year-old in 1960, but he felt uncomfortable in a girl's presence unless he was on a

12

Forever Patriots

football field or a baseball diamond. He had been on dates, and often the dates had turned into heavy petting sessions if circumstances allowed, but Jesse wasn't really certain what came after the petting. He knew there was more but he didn't know how to approach whatever it was.

Jesse thought of Shannon often after that first awkward meeting and saw her some of the times when he was at Will's house. Their relationship developed into one of mutual friendliness. He was sure he wanted more but was just as sure he didn't know what it was.

Jesse met Shannon's boyfriend one weekend as the college boy picked her up for a date. He saw the brand new MGA sports car and considered his own old Triumph motorcycle, then thought he understood why college men were more mature.

The weekend after Jesse met Shannon's college boyfriend, he and Will were playing a game of ping-pong at the table on Will's back porch and listening to records when Shannon learned he didn't know how to dance. Jesse didn't remember how the subject came up but he did remember feeling a little embarrassed at his ignorance or inability, or whatever you wanted to call it. Shannon said she thought it was a shame that an attractive young man his age didn't know how to dance. She didn't say it in such a way as to embarrass him, but he never-the-less felt his face heat up. Without much ado, she quickly put on a fresh record and pulled him away from the ping pong table. Will was not happy about the interruption, especially since he was three points ahead in the game, but he smiled at Jesse's awkwardness as he attempted to follow Shannon's steps to the music.

Jesse felt especially uncomfortable with the faster music. He thought it stupid to stand on a floor and wiggle your body and make your feet move in random directions to the beat. The gyrations reminded him of a sorrel gelding who had danced and bucked wildly every morning when his father first saddled him. He wondered what had become of that horse.

Jesse's discomfort turned to fear when Shannon put on a slow tune and held her arms open. He wanted to be near her and to touch her, yet, at the same time, was terrified of such a happening. He carefully held her hands in his and moved nearer to her. She smelled clean.

She didn't step into him but held her distance at not quite arm's length as she explained the steps. The touch of her hands on his was electrifying as they moved slowly about the room. After a while Jesse was unaware of the music. When the record ended he continued shuffling his feet until he realized the music had stopped.

Shannon smiled. "So you like the slow dance better than the fast, huh?"

Jesse felt the heat rise in his face. "It seems a little easier to learn – and I don't feel as stupid."

"You want to try it again?" she asked.

Do I ever! He thought. "If you don't mind," he said, making a conscious effort to sound casual.

Shannon put on another slow tune. Jesse took her hands and stepped a little closer to her than before as he moved to the sounds of his own music. He became aware of her breasts against his chest, touching lightly. He pulled away just enough so they no longer touched. He looked down into her face to see if she was aware of his self-consciousness. She looked at him and smiled. He couldn't tell.

When the song ended, Will said, "C'mon, you guys. Enough is enough. Let

13

me win this game before we have to quit."

The following weekend Jesse was treated to more dance lessons. He knew he would never be a Fred Astaire but he was able to be near Shannon and, for some reason, that seemed very important. He was bothered by her nearness, especially during a slow dance, but it was the kind of bother he looked forward to.

*****

It was the first week of school after the Christmas break. Jesse still wasn't used to writing "1961" on his papers but he was getting better at it. He was sitting in the hall monitor's desk outside of his geometry class. He had been two minutes late getting to the class, and his teacher, Mr. Lincoln, had made it perfectly clear the first day of the semester that he did not appreciate students entering his class after the final bell. As Jesse sat at the desk pondering his next move, Shannon walked slowly down the hallway, her normally straight shoulders drooping slightly as she approached him.

When she spotted him, she stood erect and smiled. "Hi, Jesse. What are you doing out here in the hall? Mr. Lincoln kick you out of class for goofing off again?"

"Naw. I was late. I'm tryin' to work up the nerve to walk in."

"Better you than me," she smiled. Mr. Lincoln's requirements were well known on campus.

"What're you doin' out here?" he asked.

She lowered her eyes. "I'm on the way to the office to drop chemistry."

"I thought you needed that course to graduate," he said.

"I do. Dad's going to kill me." A tear found its way to her cheek. Jesse suddenly felt uncomfortable. He had never seen Shannon cry.

"Hey, I'm takin' chemistry and, if I do say so myself, I'm acein' it. I can come over after school and help you out. You don't have to drop the course." His voice smiled.

She returned the smile weakly. "I don't know. I'm pretty stupid when it comes to balancing those equations. I just can't seem to grasp the concept."

"Aw, that's easy. Don't drop the course, Shannon. You can do it. One or two lessons from Professor Langley and you'll have your chemistry teacher eatin' outa your hand."

"I don't know ..."

"I'll tell you what. If you turn around and go back to your chemistry class, I'll show you real nerve, and I'll go into Mr. Lincoln's class late."

Her smile broadened. "I guess if you can go into *his* class late, the least I can do is give chemistry one more try."

"Promise? I'd hate to walk into *his* class late and find out you dropped chemistry."

"I promise. You first." She nodded to Mr. Lincoln's classroom door.

Jesse shrugged and stood, a smile curling up the corners of his lips. "What you're seein' now is the purest form of bravery." He opened the door and stepped inside with a parting wink to Shannon.

Mr. Lincoln stopped his lecture mid-sentence as Jesse entered the room. The class was deathly silent as all eyes turned to the latecomer.

"I'm sorry I'm late, Mr. Lincoln," said Jesse softly.

Mr. Lincoln cleared his throat. "Does being sorry eliminate the disruption

14

you have caused the class?"

"No, sir."

"Do you think you are someone special who should not have to be on time – that you can just saunter into my classroom whenever you feel like the time is right?"

"No, sir." Jesse slowly moved in the direction of his desk at the rear of the room.

"Where are you going, young man?"

"To my desk, sir."

"No, no. You come back up here to the front of the class. If you wish to remain in my classroom today, you will stand in the front of the room, to the left of my desk."

Jesse thought of his promise to Shannon and wondered if it extended to this level. "Yessir." He moved to the front of the room and took his position next to the large oak desk.

Mr. Lincoln glared at him. "Very well, Mr. Langley. I'm glad to see you have such a desire to learn." He turned to the class. "Now, as I was saying before the rude interruption...."

Jesse stood, his face hot and flushed as he watched Gail Duncan and Janice Huntington whisper to one another in the back of the room. They were cheerleaders, popular with almost everyone at school, and he knew his humiliation would be common knowledge by lunchtime.

*****

Shannon didn't drop chemistry and, true to his word, Jesse tutored her, taking great efforts to be certain she clearly understood each and every concept, feeling unexplainably fulfilled when he saw her eyes light up with understanding of a difficult problem. Sometimes they studied at his house but most often at hers. The two grew closer but it was the closeness of friends. It was good, but it wasn't what Jesse wanted. He felt in command while explaining a chemistry problem but was unable to take that first step to tell her what he felt inside. He wasn't certain what those feelings were but he knew she was on his mind every waking moment.

Shannon improved her understanding of chemistry through Jesse's persistence. When he couldn't show her how to solve a difficult problem, he called his chemistry teacher at home and found a better way to explain the solution. He pushed her when she appeared about to give up on a concept or a problem. Shannon was impressed with Jesse's patience and ability, and told him so.

*****

Shannon and Jesse were studying late. Will and his younger brother and sister were asleep. Mrs. Hunt had retired at eleven and, with Will's father on temporary assignment at Edwards Air Force Base in California, Jesse was all too aware he was alone with the girl of his dreams.

He checked his watch. It was almost midnight. He felt uncomfortable as he often did while in Shannon's presence unchaperoned. He knew if he stayed he would tell her how he felt about being near her. He didn't think he was ready for that. He wasn't sure how to tell her anyway because he wasn't really certain what it was he felt. He knew it was the weirdest thing in the world, whatever it was. Besides, what if she misunderstood his intentions? "It's getting late. I think we've about got today's lesson whipped," he said. "What do you think?" That wasn't what he had

15

wanted to say but that's what came out.

She smiled, her light-brown, almost yellow, eyes twinkling. "It's past late. Thanks, Jesse."

He picked his books from the table and stood to leave. Shannon took his arm and walked him to the door. She had never done that before and Jesse wondered why she was doing it now. She reached to open the door then seemed to change her mind and turned to face him.

"Jesse, Will just told me this evening that you quit your job to help me in chemistry."

"Will is a great guy but sometimes he talks too much," said Jesse.

"Why in the world did you quit your job?"

"I was gonna quit anyway."

She said nothing, but waited for him to continue.

"I can always get another job. You graduating from school is more important than a part-time job."

"To me – but why to you? I would never have wanted you do something like that if I had known," she said.

"Let's just say it was something I wanted to do."

"Why?"

"I don't know. I just did."

"You really are a special guy, Jesse. I don't know what I'd have done without you to help me through this. I only wish you hadn't quit your job."

"I'd do it again in a minute." He smiled but it was a facade. He needed that money to make the payments on his Triumph. He still owed a hundred and sixty dollars to his uncle, who had co-signed the loan.

She put her arms around his neck and kissed him on the lips. He felt her body against his and forgot he was holding his books. They fell to the carpeted floor with a muffled thud as he put his arms around her waist and took in the unfamiliar feel of her. It was a long kiss, and though Jesse had experienced longer and more sensuous, he couldn't remember anything in his whole life that had felt as good. His body tingled.

He didn't know what to say when they pulled apart. He looked down into her eyes and supposed he should say something, but he had no idea what it should be. "Why did you do that?"

"I don't know. It started out to be a good night kiss. I don't know what happened," she answered, a serious expression on her face.

"Let's do it again," he said.

He held her in his inexperienced embrace for several minutes, taking in whatever his senses were capable of capturing. After a while he felt her body quiver ever so slightly as she pulled away.

"You better go, Jesse."

"Did I do something wrong?"

Her lips trembled. "No. You didn't do anything wrong, Jesse. I just think ...Well, I ...It's late and mom might be getting up, and.... Oh, Jesse, hold me." She stepped into his arms.

He stood with his arms wrapped around her as she cried softly on his shoulder.

"What's wrong, Shannon? Are you sure I didn't do something wrong?" He worried that he hadn't kissed her properly.

16

She pulled her head back and looked into his eyes. "I don't know that you're capable of doing anything wrong."

"Say, would you tell that to the dean of boys? I could use the help." He tried to make light of something he didn't understand.

Shannon smiled weakly. "I've got to go to bed now, Jesse. Will I see you after school tomorrow?"

"Do you want to? I don't understand what's goin' on here."

"Neither do I, Jesse. Neither do I." She kissed him lightly on the lips and left the room.

Bewildered, Jesse stood for a moment in the semi-darkness of the livingroom. He picked up his books scattered on the floor and let himself out. He walked the three blocks to his house in a state of confusion, not sure whether he should be ecstatic – which is what he felt – or if he should be fearful that he had done something wrong to cause Shannon to cry. He was certain of only one thing. He was in love with Will Hunt's older sister – whatever that meant.

Jesse spent a sleepless night. His day at school seemed to last forever. When the bell rang dismissing classes for the day he rushed home and paced his bedroom until an hour after supper. He ate nothing.

He feared going to Shannon's house even though they had a standing seven o'clock appointment two nights a week. He called. Will answered the phone.

"Hi, Will. Is Shannon home?"

"Where else would she be on a school night? You know dad's rules."

"Yeah, yeah, but I thought that since he was TDY in California the rules might've got bent."

"No way. She's here all right and I think she's expecting you. You gonna make it, or should I tell her you've got a hot date?"

"I might have. Let me talk to her for a minute."

"Hang on." There was a short pause.

"Hello? Jesse? Are you coming over?"

Her voice indicated nothing out of the ordinary. He said, "I was just checking to see if you still wanted to study tonight."

"Of course I do."

"You do?"

She laughed softly. "Jesse, you slay me sometimes. I've got my book on the table and I'm ready to go."

"I'll be right there."

They had been studying for little more than an hour when Shannon moved away from the table. "Let's take a break. You want to take a walk in the park?"

"Park?" Jesse's heart leapt to his throat.

"Sure, the park. We study every night without a break. Tonight I feel like taking a walk in the park."

"With me?" He couldn't seem to control his mouth.

She laughed. "You should see your expression. Why not?"

"No reason I guess. You think your mom will let you go?"

"With you? She'd sooner let me go wIth you than Bill."

Thoughts of her college boyfriend with his new MGA flashed through Jesse's mind.

They walked to the front door. Mrs. Hunt sat on the sofa reading a book.

17

Stoney Livingston

"Mom, Jesse and I are going for a walk in the park. We need a break from chemistry for a few minutes."

"Okay, Hon, but don't be out too late."

"Thanks, mom."

The park was only two houses from Shannon's – not far enough for Jesse to form a cohesive thought. He was lost. Shannon sat on a small bench and motioned for him to join her. Apprehensively he sat next to her on the cold wooden bench.

The moonlight ricocheted from her eyes. "How old are you, Jesse?"

"Fifteen. I'll be sixteen in about a month. Why?"

"I just wondered. You're more mature than any of the guys I've met at school and that includes the seniors. As a matter of fact you're a lot more mature than Bill ever will be."

"I don't own a new sports car."

"That has nothing to do with maturity."

"I was just kidding. Are you having troubles with your college boyfriend?"

"As far as I'm concerned, you can stop calling him my college boyfriend or even my boyfriend for that matter. I've found someone else that's a real person, not a self-centered egotist like him. I don't know why I was ever attracted to him in the first place. I guess because he was older, I thought he was more mature. I was really wrong on that one."

Jesse searched the ground for his heart. He was certain it had fallen out of his body when she said she had found someone else. "You found someone else? Just like that?"

"Yes. And as a matter of fact, it was 'just like that'."

Jesse held his breath. He dared not speak.

"I've thought about it for almost twenty-four hours and I shouldn't have had to think about it at all. My guy is Jesse Langley. Of course, I don't know much about his private life but I hope he doesn't have a steady girl because I love him like you wouldn't believe."

Jesse felt a thump in his chest. He had never been hit that hard in any of his numerous fights, nor in the toughest football game he had ever played.

"Me?"

"You." Her white teeth seemed to glow in the moonlight.

"Me?" he repeated.

She leaned into him and kissed him gently on the lips. His heart and lungs began to function again. He put his arms around her and returned the kiss. When they broke apart, he held her to him. He said nothing because he didn't know what to say. He was overwhelmed.

"I mean it, Jesse. I love you. I've been so full of myself with this college boyfriend business that I lost track of what's really important. Bill is a spoiled little rich boy. He's not ever going to change. I thought he would but he won't. I've been wanting to call it off for some time now but I kept waiting for something to happen. Well, it finally did. It wasn't what I was expecting but it definitely happened. I love you, Jesse, and I don't know what took me so long to realize it.

"I've gone through high school with the wrong attitude. Bill knew I was in trouble with chemistry. He also knew how important it was to me to graduate. He was too busy playing the role to bother with my problems. And it takes my little brother's friend to get me through it."

Jesse held his silence. He tried to digest what Shannon said but couldn't quite take it all in. He studied the trees in the park, painted silver by the moonbeams. His concentration was broken by her voice.

"Am I too forward, Jesse? You're not saying anything."

He turned his attention from the trees. "I don't know what to say." He knew what he wanted to say but he couldn't bring himself to confess an undying love, even though it was true – at least he thought it was.

"I'm going to have trouble studying but I think we'd better get back to the house. I just wanted you to know how I felt." She squeezed his hand.

In a trance, he stood and walked silently with her at his side, his mind in Never-Never Land, or wherever minds went when they weren't in your head.

"Too cold outside?" asked Mrs. Hunt as they entered the living room.

Jesse hadn't noticed the cool of the evening. "No, Ma'am. We still got a lot of work to cover and it's not getting any earlier." He seemed to have no difficulty talking now.

Mrs. Hunt clucked softly. "I swear, Jesse. I wish you'd let some of that attitude rub off on Will."

"He'll come around." Jesse smiled. Until he had started helping Shannon, he had never studied his chemistry book. School didn't seem all that difficult that one should have to open a book too often if he just paid attention in the classroom

After Mrs. Hunt retired for the evening, Jesse and Shannon moved to the livingroom with their studies. It was farther from the bedrooms than the dining room table where they normally studied. They held hands and exchanged looks more than they studied chemistry. Finally they closed the books and lay on the carpeted floor, all pretense of study abandoned. Jesse pulled her close.

"Are you sure you know what you're talking about, Shannon?" He felt her warm breath on his lips.

"I've always liked you, Jesse. I just thought you were a little on the wild side, and not very grown up. I was wrong. I guess I just had to really get to know you to find out how wrong I really was." She kissed him.

They kissed until Jesse's lips were sore but their physical contact did not go beyond that, though there were times when he thought Shannon expected more. He was uncertain of what he should do and afraid of shattering perfection. When he left shortly after midnight, he fairly skipped home.

*****

Jesse sat in the park, chewing on a blade of grass, as he listened to John Hinterland tell of Melvin Lackey's latest flame.

"I don't know how he comes up with these ideas. Pat Bromly is stuck up," said John.

"Hell, she said hello to me in the hall today," defended Melvin.

"You foo'. She'll play it for all it's worth but when it comes to putting out, she won't."

Rob Preston raised an eyebrow. "Are you talking from experience?"

"Shit, Rob, you know what I mean," said John.

Rob laughed. "Not me. I never have that problem."

Will said, "Ol' Jesse over there is being awful quiet. What about it, Jesse? You think Mel can get into Pat's drawers?"

"I wouldn't know. I barely know her."

19

Stoney Livingston

"You know, I've noticed you haven't had much of an opinion about anything for the last coupla' weeks. Whatsamatter? You sick or something?"

"Nope. I just don't know Pat that well."

"I think Mel's got a better chance with Sylvia." John returned the conversation to the topic of his choosing.

"Yeah, him and everybody else. I'd be afraid to touch that one. She's probably got every form of VD known to man," said Rob.

Not one among them had any personal experience with women but it was fashionable to talk like a man of background, which they often did. They were a close group but no one was certain of the other's sexual experiences.

"Maybe, but you could always use a rubber," said John.

"Who the hell wants to use a rubber? That's like not even doing it," said Melvin with a voice of authority.

"Yeah, I guess you're right," agreed John.

"What about you, Jesse? How are things between you and Shannon?" asked Rob.

"Shannon and I have a different kind of relationship and I don't think it belongs a part of this conversation."

"Shit, man, I didn't mean anything by it. Little touchy about that, aren't you?" said Rob.

"She's pretty special to me, Rob. I didn't mean to be shitty about it but I'd just like to keep that part of my life personal for now, if you don't mind."

Rob smiled and softened his voice. "I think I know what you're saying."

"Here comes Danny and those guys from the other side of Twenty-Second Street. Let's get the game started," Will said, pointing to the far side of the park.

*****

Jesse knocked on Will's front door and smiled as he thought of the past six weeks. Since the first time he had kissed Shannon his life had changed. Everything seemed brighter. He had no worries of any consequence.

Will answered the door.

"Hi, Will. Shannon home?"

Will appeared upset. "I think you better come in, Jesse. Mom wants to talk to you."

The way Will said it, Jesse knew something was wrong, and whatever it was had something to do with Shannon. His heart thumped wildly.

Mrs. Hunt, normally a happy and smiling woman, greeted him without her smile. "Sit down, Jesse."

"Is something wrong, Mrs. Hunt?"

She seated herself next to him on the sofa and said, "Shannon has disappeared. As far as we know, you were the last one to see her last night. Do you have any idea where she might be?"

Jesse felt an emptiness in his chest. He stood. "Disappeared? You mean she's missing? Nobody knows where she is?"

Mrs. Hunt nodded, making a visible effort to hold back her tears. "Mr. Hunt is flying in from California this evening. He should be here at eight-thirty."

Everyone in the room jumped with a start as the telephone rang. Mrs. Hunt answered it before it rang a second time. She nodded into the phone. "Yes." Again she nodded. "Yes." There was another pause. "Shannon, what are you doing?

20

Forever Patriots

Where are you? Your father's on his way home from Edwards Air Force Base. Are you okay?"

There was a long pause as she listened intently to the receiver, nodding from time-to-time, then she said, "But wait. Yes. Yes. I'll tell him." Slowly she hung up the phone.

She turned to Jesse. "She's in California with Bill. He met her at school this morning. They're going to get married."

"Are you sure you understood her right, Mrs. Hunt?" asked Jesse, his heart beating loudly in his throat, a feint ringing in his ears.

She nodded.

"Why?" was all Jesse could muster.

"They're going to call again this evening when Mr. Hunt is home. She asked me to tell you she was sorry."

"Sorry? Why should she tell me she's sorry?" He turned towards the door to hide the tears he knew he couldn't hold back much longer. "I guess I'll be going now, Mrs. Hunt. If I can do something to help, let me know." He left without waiting for a response. He didn't remember walking out the door.

*****

Shannon returned to Tucson three days later. She met with Jesse in his backyard, under the large apricot tree Jesse had planted his first year in town. The late afternoon sun bounced from her light eyes. She had never looked more beautiful.

"I don't understand, Shannon. If you don't love this guy, why are you gonna marry him?"

"I'm ashamed, Jesse. I didn't want to have to tell you, but there isn't any other way – I'm pregnant."

Pregnant was an adult word. It didn't apply to high school kids. Jesse searched for a reply. "You said you didn't love the guy, so why marry him just because you're pregnant? We could get married. I could quit school and get a job. We could make it."

She sobbed. "I could never do that to you, Jesse."

"Do what?"

"Let you marry me after this."

Jesse's footing was unsure. He didn't know how to respond. He said, "Don't marry this guy, Shannon." He wanted to say "*I love you, Shannon. I'd die for you. Marry me and together we can conquer the world.*" He wanted to say it but he couldn't. He didn't know why, but he couldn't and he didn't.

"I stopped having a choice when I found out I was pregnant. I feel cheap and dirty, Jesse. I knew two weeks ago and I still kept seeing you. I kept hoping something would happen and it would go away, or that it was a mistake and you would never have to know."

"Now I know. So what's the big deal? You're still the same person and so am I." He couldn't make his mouth say what his heart felt.

"It doesn't work that way, Jesse. I only wish the rest of the world had your simple solutions for everything. I love you, Jesse. I love your simplicity and your honesty and your goodness. No matter what happens, I'll always love you. Remember that. Always."

21

Stoney Livingston

Jesse sat on the cafeteria steps in the shadows cast by the lights from the stadium and watched Bill open the door to his MGA on the passenger side. Shannon looked beautiful, even in the graduation robe. Jesse was proud of her, proud that she had hung in there and stuck to her guns; proud that her final grade in chemistry was a C. She had almost made a B, but the C was good enough to pull her through. He felt a sense of accomplishment, mingled with a deep sense of loss as Shannon removed the cap from her head and sat in the car. The removal of the cap seemed to symbolize the end of everything for Jesse. It was over and done. Shannon would go to California with Bill and live happily ever after.

He wondered how long "ever after" was. It sure seemed like a long time.

Jesse felt his heart pound in his chest as Bill started the engine. He closed his eyes, squashing a hidden tear from each of them, praying for the little MGA to break down in the parking lot. He wiped a forearm across his eyes to clear his vision then shook his head to rid it of the selfish thought. This was Shannon's day and he would take nothing from her, not even in thought. If she wanted to go to California with Bill, who was he to wish otherwise?

The MGA left the dirt parking lot and pulled onto 5th street, its tail lights growing dimmer and closer together as the distance from the school grew. Jesse forced a smile as the tears rolled silently down his cheeks. "You did it, Shannon. You graduated with your class. I'm proud of you and I love you. I wish you the best of everything there is."

When the taillights disappeared from view, Jesse stood slowly and walked to his motorcycle, tears of joy and pain mixed, blinding his vision. He sat on the Triumph and felt the touch of an old friend. He kick-started it and the bike came alive. It seemed to be the only thing in the world that understood how he felt. Jesse was thankful his mind allowed him the fantasy. He drove slowly from the school grounds, into a dark and lonely world, a world with uncertain futures and memories of a fantasy past. He was already beginning to question the reality of his relationship with Shannon. He wasn't sure whether it had really happened or if his mind had made it up.

CHAPTER TWO: MANHOOD

Jesse struggled through the summer and one more semester of school after Shannon left but his heart wasn't in it. He didn't go out for football that fall nor did he miss the camaraderie of his old teammates. The only thing he missed was Shannon. He missed her smile and the twinkle in her eye; the warmth of her touch and the euphoric feeling he always got when he was near her. It was all he could do to attend classes, which he sometimes didn't. His grades dropped. He made friends with an old bum who, for a small price, bought him liquor. He began to drink in the park on nights and weekends. He started smoking. He drank and smoked and looked at the trees and the park bench where Shannon had confessed her love.

Before the end of the first semester in his junior year, he quit school and left home. His mother cried and tried to talk him out of it but she knew she had lost her son to something more powerful than she could fight. His father was saddened but gave Jesse a hug, a firm handshake and his last hundred dollars. Jesse promised to pay him back as soon as he was able.

Jesse left Tucson and rode his Triumph motorcycle to California. He picked California only because that's where Shannon had gone. He knew he couldn't see her but he felt better just knowing he was closer to her.

*****

He arrived in Los Angeles in the middle of the worst rainstorm in the recorded history of the city – or since the year 1938 – depending upon which newspaper you read. It didn't really matter to Jesse whether it was a record rain or not. It was too much water for a guy on a motorcycle to contend with comfortably.

The Triumph, complete with bedroll and suitcase, stood out of the steady rain, under an apartment awning. Jesse kept an eye on it from the window of a doughnut shop as he drank his coffee and munched on a fresh doughnut. He was hungry for real food but knew he had to stretch what little money he had as far as it would go until he found work. Coffee was a dime and the doughnut was a nickel. He could afford that but not much else if he wanted his money to last.

"You look like a drowned puppy, man."

Jesse turned to look at the heavy-set young man sitting on the stool next to him. He looked a few years older than Jesse, maybe nineteen. A lock of his straight brown hair fell over one eye as he talked. He stuck out his lower lip and blew upward, forcing the wayward strands perfectly back into place.

"Maybe you didn't notice, but it's wet out there," said Jesse.

The older boy laughed a belly laugh. "That came to my attention on the way over here." He pointed through the window to a service station on the adjacent corner. "I work at that station."

"How do you manage to stay so dry?" asked Jesse.

"I didn't say I worked hard."

23

Stoney Livingston

Jesse couldn't hold back a grin.

"Louie Forth." The young man held out a hand.

"Jesse Langley." The two shook hands. At last he knew someone in Los Angeles.

"Where you headed, man?" asked Louie.

"Wherever there's work."

"Oh, man, you'll crash and burn in this town before you'll find work, unless you know somebody."

"Well then, I guess I'm in for a big crash," said Jesse.

"Where you from, man?" asked Louie.

"Arizona."

"You mean you came to L.A. lookin' for work, and you don't know anybody here?"

"Basically."

"You must be one of them crazy cowboys, huh?"

Jesse thought of the Bar X. It seemed like ancient history. "No, not really. I just thought a change of scenery would be nice."

"Things not going so good back on the ranch, huh?"

"They've been better," said Jesse.

"What you drivin'?"

"Motorcycle." Jesse nodded to the Triumph.

Louie glanced out the window. "A buzzsaw? In this weather?" He laughed again. "Boy, I can see right now, you *are* a crazy cowboy."

Jesse wanted to become irritated with Louie but couldn't. Besides the fact that Louie was the only person in California who had spoken to him, his blunt and affable manner was a pleasant change from the standoffish attitudes that had so far marked his trip. "Yeah, maybe I am. But I don't have a car, so I ride my bike."

"Buzzsaw, man. Out here they're called buzzsaws. You gotta learn to talk like the people around here or they'll know right off you're from out of town."

"Buzzsaw?" asked Jesse.

"Yeah, and you know – like – my car is a soupcan."

"A car is a soupcan?"

Louie swallowed his coffee hard and laughed again. "I can see you're *really* green. No, not any car is a soupcan, just Fords."

"What's a Chevy?"

"Stove."

"Stove? Who comes up with these names?" asked Jesse.

"Who knows?"

"What's a Pontiac?"

"Poncho."

"How about a Studebaker?"

"Stud."

"I been here too long already. That one makes a little sense."

"You'll get the hang of it."

Jesse glanced out the window at the driving rain. "Not if I don't find some work."

"You got a union card?" asked Louie.

"A what?"

"A union card. You a member of the union?"

24

"What union?" asked Jesse.

Louie shook his head. "You're gonna have a tough time out here, cowboy. I can see that already. You mean to tell me you expect to find work out here without joining a union?"

"I don't need a union. I'm a good worker."

"That's even worse. You join the union and you get a job. Then you only do what you're supposed to do – nothing more. Unions don't wanna hear none of that crap about you bein' a good worker. What you tryin' to do, put a union boss outa work?"

Jesse took a bite from his doughnut. "Maybe I wasn't cut out to live in California after all."

"Maybe not, but you'll never know unless you give it a try."

"I'm not into joining a union. I don't think a man ought to have to pay anyone to get a job. It's not like I'm looking for one of those big-time, high-paying jobs. I just want something to keep me in beans until I can get settled."

"How old are you, cowboy?"

"Sixteen."

Louie hunched up his shoulders and looked furtively about the doughnut shop. "Sixteen? Jesus Christ, man. You'll never get a job out here. You can't even join a union until you're eighteen," he whispered.

Jesse felt his spirits begin to sag. "I'll get by."

"How? You gonna rob banks?"

"You need a union card for that too?" asked Jesse.

Louie leaned close. "If the lawyers ever found out you were robbin' banks without a card, you'd be a dead man."

Jesse laughed quietly. "So I won't rob banks."

"Where you stayin'?" asked Louie.

Jesse hesitated. "Nowhere yet. I may push on when the rain lets up."

"Damn, man, that may be next month. It's been raining a week already. Where you gonna go? Your chances of finding work aren't any better anywhere else."

"I don't know anybody here."

"You know me, remember?" Louie smiled broadly.

Jesse's hopes picked up. "You know somebody lookin' for help?"

Louie's chest expanded. "As a matter-of-fact, I just might. My boss was sayin' just yesterday that he was gonna hire a part-time man for the evening shift. You know anything about cars?"

"A little. I know about engines."

Louie frowned. "Well, that's a start. Why don't you come on over to the station when you're done here." It was an order, not a question. "See me and I'll introduce you to the man. Give me a few minutes to work on him before you come over. You're eighteen when you talk to him. Remember that." He stood and walked to the cash register.

*****

Dick Warner, the owner of the station, had been reluctant to hire Jesse at first but, within a week, Jesse was promoted to full-time status as a result of his work ethic and quick learning ability. In less than two months he had saved a hundred dollars, which he promptly sent to his father with a brief letter of thanks. He shared

25

Stoney Livingston

Louie's apartment and paid half the rent. That and food was all he spent. He saved everything he could. He wasn't sure when he would have to move on and he wanted to have a grubstake. He was in California but he had neither seen nor spoken to Shannon. It didn't make much sense to him but he had to stay as long as he could stand it.

The weekends, when he wasn't working, were continuous streams of parties and social activities. There were volleyball games with kegs of beer and junk food. If the weather was bad, there were beer and pot parties, and though Jesse didn't smoke pot, he attended the parties for the beer and the company. In bad weather he rode to them in Louie's '49 Ford. The old "soupcan" was held together with clothes hangers and bondo; it rattled and shook like an old wringer-washer; the brakes failed from time to time when Louie forgot to add brake fluid to the master cylinder on a daily basis; the headlights refused to work when there was rain or high humidity, and the seats looked like ground zero of an atomic explosion. Jesse accepted it though, because it was a part of Louie's character and, despite his many faults, Jesse liked him.

Louie had introduced Jesse to Rosanna at the first party he had attended. Rosie, as she preferred to be called, was a thin girl with straight, dark brown hair and small breasts. She had a pretty face and skinny hips and talked very little. Their second meeting came at a party in Newport Beach. She was the only person at the party, other than Louie, who Jesse knew.

He stood outside on the sandy beach, wishing he could leave for the two-room apartment he shared with Louie, cursing himself for leaving the Triumph and riding to the party in Louie's old Ford. The night was dark, except for the light coming from the interior of the beach house where twenty or thirty people drank cheap beer and smoked reefers. Jesse didn't mind the beer but took exception to the marijuana. He wanted to go home.

Rosie stepped up to him in the darkness. "You bored?"

Jesse jumped at the sound of her voice. "Kinda."

"Yeah, I know what you mean, man. These parties get to be a drag." Rosie was nineteen and Jesse knew without being told she had a lot of experience he lacked, even though everyone thought he was at least nineteen or twenty – Rosie included.

"Why do you go to them all the time then?" he asked.

She shrugged. "Free booze. Good weed. And you meet guys." She was high on a mixture of beer and marijuana.

Jesse sipped from his half-full can of Brown Derby beer.

"You don't talk much, do you, man?" said Rosie.

"Sometimes I do."

She giggled. "When?"

"When I have something to say."

"Hey, man, you're a trip. You want a hit?" She held a stub of a reefer to his face.

He lifted his beer can. "No thanks. I'll stick to beer."

She puffed on the marijuana until it was no more than a roach then threw it carelessly into the sand. "Loosen up, man. Relax."

"I am relaxed."

"You wanna go for a walk down the beach?" she asked.

"Sure," Jesse answered almost disinterestedly.

26

Forever Patriots

She took his arm and they strolled at the edge of the wet sand. She staggered into him then swayed away in the opposite direction repeatedly. Neither spoke for almost five minutes. The night air was chilly. Jesse shivered involuntarily.

"You cold, honey?" she asked.

"A little," he answered.

She put her arm around his waist and pulled him to her hip. "I know how to fix that."

Jesse wasn't certain what she meant by her remark. A twinge of fear born of ignorance crept through him but it was an exciting feeling. His heart began to pound lightly in his ears. She was attractive enough, and apparently willing. He turned to face her then put his arms around her awkwardly. He put his lips to hers and kissed her gently. She moved into him and returned the kiss, rubbing the front of her body against his in rhythmic motions. Jesse was instantly aware of his male reaction to the stimulus.

When she broke the kiss, she reached down and touched him in the crotch. "I see you know how to fix it too."

He jerked at her touch. He was glad it was dark. His face was hot and he knew it was beet-red.

She fumbled with the buttons on his Levis. "Why can't you guys wear pants with zippers instead of these damn buttons?"

Jesse could barely speak. He had no answer anyway. He had barely heard the question. He experienced a tingling sensation and looked shamefully up and down the deserted beach, fearful someone might see them. She had his Levis opened and he felt her cool hand touch him. He didn't know what he was supposed to do.

"Oh, baby, you *are* ready!" He felt the warmth of her mouth on him and his body jerked spasmodically. She pulled her mouth away. "Jesus! Are you hot or what?" She stood and lifted her cotton dress over her head. Despite the coolness of the night, she was wearing nothing underneath it. She spread it on the sand and turned to him.

"Are you going to stand there all night?" she asked.

He remained motionless.

"You want some more, is that it?" She knelt before him and took his manhood in her mouth. Her head moved back and forth as she stimulated him almost to the point of explosion. She suddenly pulled away and laid on her dress in the sand. She spread her legs. "Come on, baby. It's waiting for you."

Numbly he removed his shirt and pants, then his underwear. Naked, he slowly and carefully lay beside her on the dress.

She turned on her side to face him. "What's the matter, baby? Too much booze? I can fix that." She rolled him onto his back and lay on top of him.

He felt her flesh against his and forgot the coolness of the night air. He had never experienced what his body was going though. He wanted more but he didn't know how to go about getting it.

She kissed him roughly on the lips, her hands massaging him. He felt himself growing harder. He was aware of her small breasts against his chest. He closed his eyes and took in as much as he could of everywhere their bodies touched.

She pulled her lips from his. "That's better, baby. Now you just relax. I know how to handle things when you guys get too much booze."

She straddled him and moved her pubic hair roughly against him in gyrating

27

motions. He felt her hand guiding him into her. She was warm and wet inside. She began to move her hips over him. He felt a pressure in his loins. His heart pounded in his temples. Rosie moaned and picked up the tempo of her movements. Jesse felt a rush in his loins and surged upward, forcing himself deeper into her body.

Rosie moaned, "That's it, baby. Harder!"

His body jerked and bucked as he forced himself further into her. He felt his release of sperm and his entire body went rigid in a shallow arc as Rosie rocked and ground viciously above him. "Oh yes! Yes! Oh! Oh. .oh. ." Her voice drifted off. She went limp and fell atop him.

He relaxed and lay motionless for a short time then put his arms around her and held her tightly, trying to digest what had just happened, forgetting the cool night air. After a few moments she pulled away from him and stood.

"We better be getting back to the party. You weren't bad. I'd like to try it sometime when you're sober," she said.

Jesse rolled from her dress and moved to his clothes, suddenly embarrassed by his nudity. "Just like that?"

Rosie slipped the dress over her head and walked to him. "How much do want? There'll be other times."

He pulled his pants up. "Why don't you go ahead back to the party? I think I'll stay out here a while."

"Suit yourself." She grabbed at him playfully and walked down the beach.

Jesse finished dressing and sat in the sand. He lit a cigarette and watched a ship offshore as it plowed through the water in the darkness. He felt dirty and ashamed. *What happened? How could she just get up and go back to the party? This isn't how it's supposed to be.* This was not how he had pictured things happening with Shannon. Truth be known, he hadn't quite gotten that far with his thoughts insofar as they pertained to Shannon.

He took off his pants and waded into the cold Pacific until the water reached his waist. He washed his genital area as best he could without soap, then returned to the sand and put on his pants, shivering violently the whole time. The feeling of dirtiness wouldn't leave him. He lit a cigarette.

Staring at the distant lights of a passing ship, he softly said, "What have I done, Shannon? What have I done?"

*****

Louie kicked the bottom of Jesse's foot as the latter struggled to remove the heavy transmission from the Hudson. Jesse looked down the length of his body to see Louie's face peering at him under the frame of the car.

"What's up?" asked Jesse.

"You heard the news lately, cowboy?"

"Can't it wait until I get this transmission out? I've almost got it. I'd've had it out by now if you hadn't tied up the hoist all afternoon with that blonde's car."

"Hey, man, she was a knockout, wasn't she?"

"Yeah, Louie, she was a knockout. I just don't see her under here with me taking this transmission out."

"I'll bet if she was under there with you, you wouldn't be takin' out no funky transmission. You know what I mean?"

"Yeah, Louie, I think I get your drift. So what's so important on the news that it can't wait until I'm done?"

"It looks like we're goin' to war, man."

Jesse rose up slightly, bumping his head on the frame of the car. "Ow! What the hell are you talking about?" He slid out from under the Hudson.

"Laos, man. President Kennedy sent the marines into Laos."

"Never heard of the place," said Jesse.

"Me neither. But who the hell cares? We're gonna have a damn war. This means I could get drafted."

"What did he send the marines into that country – whatever-its-name-was – for anyway?"

"To stop the commies, man," answered Louie.

"Where were they going?"

"I mean, Jesus Christ! What the hell am I gonna do with your funky ass? Don't you keep up with what's going on in the world? The commies are trying to take over the whole continent of Asia."

"If they're lookin' to take over the whole continent, why'n the hell would they start in a country nobody's ever heard of?"

Louie slapped him on the shoulder. "That's the way they do things, man. That's the way they do things. Where you been all your life?"

Jesse wiped his hands on a shop towel. "You got time to help me drop this transmission?"

"I just told you I was gonna be drafted, and that's all you got to say?"

"Are you gonna be drafted before tomorrow afternoon?"

"Probably not."

"Well, this thing's gotta have a new clutch in it by that time. Now, which would *you* say was a priority?"

Louie shook his head. "Ever since you turned seventeen, you been a real butthead, you know that?"

"A butthead?"

"Worse than that, but that was all I could think of on short notice," said Louie.

"Will you help me pull the tranny or not? We can talk about your draft status after work."

Louie shrugged. "You buyin'?"

"If you help me, yes. If you don't, no."

A broad smile covered Louie's face. "I mean, what the hell are you standin' there for? We got a clutch to replace."

*****

They sat on the front steps of Louie's apartment, downing cheap bear and smoking cigarettes, Louie pointing out every article in the *LA Times* and *Los Angeles Herald Examiner* that dealt with the marines in Laos, Jesse not listening, running a war scenario through his mind. He was glad to see some of Louie's friends arrive. On any other night he wouldn't have been remotely interested in Nick or Chubs but on this evening they filled a gap Louie needed filling, a gap which Jesse had no desire to fill.

Despite his liking for Louie, this latest thing with his concern over the possibility of being drafted chipped away at the closeness he felt for his first California friend. At first he had thought Louie had been kidding but, by the time they opened the first can of beer after work, Jesse realized Louie was serious.

29

Stoney Livingston

Jesse studied the can of Golden Gate beer in his hand absentmindedly as his thoughts drifted to his friends in Tucson. He wondered what they thought about a war in Laos. He wondered how they would react if they weren't in school and they were called to serve their country. Melvin and John would step to the front of the line. Will wouldn't wait to be drafted. Rob might not go but it wouldn't have anything to do with fear. Rob had the worst case of asthma Jesse had ever seen.

Everybody had to serve his country. He didn't understand why Louie was openly trying to dodge his duty. The man had no pride.

He turned to look through the open door of the apartment. Louie had the newspapers spread all over the small livingroom. Nick and Chubs each bent a sympathetic ear to his complaints as he pointed first to one section of the paper then another. Nick clucked softly in sympathy as he reached for another can of beer.

Jesse sipped his beer and stared into the cool March evening. Rosie and a friend approached the apartment, the friend almost oozing out of the top of her loose-fitting blouse as she laughed loudly at something Rosie said. Jesse wondered if Rosie had told her about their night on the beach. He hadn't seen her alone since that night and had no desire. He felt only filth and shame at the thought of their romp in the sand.

"Hi, Jesse," smiled Rosie.

He nodded.

"This is a friend of mine, Carol. Carol, this is Jesse. I told you all about him, remember?"

Carol laughed again, shaking her straight brown hair and wiggling her large breasts. "So this is the famous super stud?" She winked knowingly at him.

Jesse felt the heat rise to his face.

"Oh, look, Rosie. He's blushing. That's cute."

"Us super studs don't normally kiss and tell. It's a little embarrassing when we're found out."

Carol raised her eyebrows. "You must be older than you look."

"How old do I look?"

"Twenty, twenty-one."

Jesse smiled. "That's close enough. Don't make me any older."

"You guys got any beer?" asked Rosie.

Jesse nodded to the open door. "In the fridge."

They stepped past him, Carol puckering her lips in a mock kiss as she brushed against him lightly, her breasts touching his t-shirt. That slight touch and the sweetness of her perfume stirred something in Jesse but the feeling didn't linger. It was gone almost as quickly as Carol.

He lit a cigarette and listened, only half attentively, to the voices in the apartment. The sounds of fast-moving cars on Highway 101 entered his consciousness more clearly than what was being said inside. He let his mind race to the freeway and jump into one of the sleeker cars. It was headed south. When it reached San Diego, it would turn east and head for Arizona. Home.

He shook his head and looked into the apartment. Nothing had changed. Louie had them all standing around various sections of the paper. He lit another cigarette and searched for another car heading south.

"You gonna join the party?"

He knew it was Carol before he turned to face her. Her perfume marched before her like a bandleader in front of a marching band. "Not tonight."

"What's the matter? All Louie's talk about the draft got you worried?" She sat on the lounge chair next to him.

"No. I'm not worried about being drafted. If we have a war, I'll volunteer."

"Why in the world would you do that?"

"Somebody's gotta do it."

"Let the other guy do it. There's enough of them out there somewhere." She gestured to the world in general with her can of beer.

"I'd rather earn my own freedom."

She arched her eyebrows again. "I never thought of it that way. My, you *are* a deep thinker, aren't you?"

He took a drag from his cigarette. "I don't think that requires a whole lot of thought. It just happens that way. Wars happen and guys my age fight 'em. Everybody's fought a war: our fathers, our fathers' fathers. Now it's our turn."

Carol shrugged. "It sounds easy from here, but I don't imagine fighting a real war is a picnic. It's sure isn't something I want to do."

"I didn't say I wanted to do it. I just said that everybody has to fight his war. This is just my turn." He looked over his shoulder at Louie. "It's his too. And Nick's and Chubs' and everyone else our age."

Carol shook her head. "You're weird, Jesse, you know that?"

He sat his empty beer can on the grass at his side and stood. "Yeah, maybe I am. Maybe I am." He felt an unexplainable anger rising in him. "I think I'll take a stroll. I'll see you in a little bit."

He smiled at the startled expression on her face as he stepped into the apartment parking lot. She probably wasn't used to someone walking from her company, especially when she was devoting all of her attention to him.

It was almost an hour later when Jesse returned to the apartment. He had hoped the others would be gone since it was the middle of the week and he and Louie both had to work in the morning, but his hope had been in vain. There were even more people crowded into the apartment and several sitting or standing outside the door. He spotted Louie standing outside, the front page of the paper spread wide, nodding at the headline as Carol and a neighbor shook their heads then nodded in unison as Louie continued his running commentary.

Louie looked up from his paper. "Hey, Jesse, man, where you been? Get your funky ass over here and check this out."

Jesse stepped up to him and nodded politely to Carol. "Check what out, Louie?"

"This, man. Just listen to this. President Kennedy says that we're gonna stop communism in Southeast Asia. Period. He says if we let one country fall to communism, the rest will fall like dominoes."

Jesse shrugged. "So? Sounds like a good idea to me."

"Are you nuts, man? We could be the ones doin' the stoppin', if you know what I mean."

"Take it easy, Louie. Nobody's sent you a draft notice yet."

"It's too late when that happens."

"I don't see what we can do about it," said Jesse.

Louie looked at him pleadingly. "You're a pretty smart guy for a cowboy. Can't you think of something in the Constitution – some kind of technicality?"

Jesse wanted to scream; to rip the paper from Louie's hands and tell him to stop whimpering unashamedly, like a baby, in front of all of these people. Didn't the

31

Stoney Livingston

man have even a little pride? "Don't worry about it, Louie. They may not even call you. We got any beer left?"

"Beer? Beer? I'm on the verge of being drafted into a funky-ass war and all you care about is a lousy beer? Yeah, Goddamnit, we got beer left."

"Excuse me." He moved past them, through the doorway and the throng of people – most of whom he didn't know – to the refrigerator.

Outside again, he sipped his beer and listened as Chubs and Rosie talked about Laos and President Kennedy.

"Yeah, I like President Kennedy too," said Chubs. "But this crap in Laos is for the birds. I just got this thing goin' with this chick out in Buena Park, you know. I don't wanna be goin' off to no damn war right now. Things are looking too good."

"If it wasn't the chick, what other excuse would you think of?" It was out of Jesse's mouth before he realized he had said it.

"What'd you say, man?" asked Chubs.

Jesse felt the rage building. "I said, you like the milk and honey but you don't wanna work for it. You love the music but you don't wanna pay the fiddler. You're a bum, Chubs, a bum and a coward. You'd have somebody else go off and fight for you 'cause you ain't got the guts to do it yourself. And my good buddy, Louie, is no better. I hope you get a draft notice in the morning."

"Hey, punk, who you think you're talkin' to?" said Chubs loudly.

Jesse's voice became firmly quiet. "I thought I made it pretty clear who I was talkin' to. But if you want me to repeat it, I'll be glad to. On top of bein' a coward, you must be hard of hearing too."

Rosie stepped between them. "Hey, guys. We don't need this. You guys are friends."

Jesse knew he was letting his last chance go. "He's no friend of mine. He's just another big-mouthed punk."

Chubs pushed Rosie aside and rushed Jesse. Even as Rosie screamed, Jesse punched Chubs in the nose with two quick right jabs. By the time her scream faded into the night, Jesse had finished him with a pile-driving left.

Jesse stood over him. "Get up, punk. Show me who I'm talking to." He clenched his fists menacingly.

Chubs held his hands to his bleeding nose. Rosie stooped next to him and pulled his hands away from his face. "Oh my god! His nose is broken!"

Jesse stepped back. He looked around the crowd. Most of them had not yet reacted. Louie stood, the paper in his hands, his eyes large and round, looking innocently stupid.

"I'm leaving, Louie. I don't want anymore trouble. So all of you patriotic Americans leave me alone." The crowd parted as he made his way into the apartment and his bedroom. No one spoke as he shut the door behind him and began packing his belongings.

Tears ran silently down his face as he stuffed the last of his clothes into his motorcycle pouches. He wiped his face quickly as he heard three light raps on the door. The knob turned and Rosie stepped into the room.

"Can we talk for a minute?" she said.

Jesse dropped his hands to his side. "I don't have anything to say. I said it all out there. I'm sorry it had to happen, but it did."

"But where are you going?"

"Away from here," he answered.

32

"Why?"

"I don't belong here."

"Sure you do. It was just an argument that got out of hand. That's all," she said softly.

He stared into her eyes. "I'd do it again. As a matter-of-fact, I *will* do it again – with any of them, including Louie – if they wanna cry about the honor of defending this country. I've got no use for 'em – any of 'em – and I don't belong here."

"Maybe you don't, Jesse. I knew you were different, but Jesus, I didn't know you were *this* different." She closed the door tightly behind her. "You can stay with me and my roommate, Susie, until you find a place."

Jesse concealed his surprise. "I appreciate it, Rosie, but I think I'll get out of L.A. I can't remember why I came here in the first place."

"You need some traveling money? I got a few bucks stashed. It's not a whole bunch but it might help. You can always pay me back when you get situated."

The tears broke through his resolve. He moved close to Rosie and put his hands on her shoulders. Softly he kissed her on the forehead. "Thanks, Rosie. You just taught me something. Take care of yourself. And keep your money." He turned from her and picked up his bags.

Louie met him in the livingroom. "Where the hell you goin', man?"

"Away from L.A., Louie. I appreciate all you've done for me. I left a few bucks in my room. Tell the boss I'm sorry, but I had to leave."

"What the hell am I gonna tell him you left in such a hurry for? Why couldn't you give him two weeks notice?"

Jesse hesitated as he looked into Louie's eyes. "Tell him I joined the marines."

Carol was doctoring Chubs' face as Jesse stepped from the porch to the parking lot. "So long, Carol. I wouldn't waste my time on him if I were you. Ain't worth it."

He threw the pouches over the rear of the seat on the Triumph and tied his suitcase behind it. He jumped on the kick-starter and the bike came alive. Louie stood next to Rosie silently as the Triumph roared out of the parking lot and onto the street.

*****

Jesse had little trouble convincing his parents to allow him to join the marines. Jim, as an ex-navy man, would have preferred his son join the navy but Jesse was adamant. The marines were in Laos and he wanted to be where the action was.

Within a week of his return to Tucson, Jesse found himself on a Greyhound Bus, headed for Los Angeles to be sworn in. From there he would re-board the bus and continue to San Diego, where he would report to Marine Corps Recruit Depot for boot camp.

As the bus hummed west on the two-lane highway between Gila Bend and Yuma, Jesse visualized himself in full combat gear, a bayonet on the end of his rifle, the enemy all around him. He whipped them all single-handedly. In his next vision, he received the Congressional Medal of Honor. Shannon was there in the crowd. When the ceremony was over, she rushed out of the grandstands and into his arms. At that point his vision went grey and he couldn't find Shannon. He couldn't find anyone. There was nothing but a dense golden fog.

33

Stoney Livingston

The sound of air brakes brought him back to the real world and he looked outside the window at the small bus station in Yuma. He could smell the Colorado River somewhere nearby and he wondered if they had rivers in Laos.

CHAPTER THREE: THE CORPS

Boot Camp, Marksmanship Training, Camp Mathews, California

"But, Sir! Sergeant Williams knew I used twenty-nine clicks of elevation at the two-hundred-yard line." Jesse stood at rigid attention behind the firing line. A small man, Jesse's new Preliminary Marksmanship Instructor, wearing the rank of sergeant E-4, stood before him, his eyes blazing into Jesse's.

Jesse had feared this confrontation when he'd heard of Sergeant Williams' emergency leave this morning. Williams had been Jesse's Preliminary Marksmanship Instructor since the recruit platoon had arrived at the Camp Mathews rifle range.

"I don't give a rat's ass what Sergeant Williams knew. He's not here and I am." Sergeant Cooley moved closer, his nose almost touching Jesse's. "If all of you maggots don't qualify, I don't get promoted. If I don't get promoted, I won't be happy. You don't want me to be unhappy, do you, maggot?"

"Sir! No, Sir!" shouted Jesse.

Cooley smiled. "Good. Then run that rear sight down to ten clicks for the next relay, maggot. We'll get you some new dope and get this thing done right."

"But, Sir, the next relay is rapid fire, Sir."

"I know what the next relay is, maggot. If the dope is a little off, you'll shoot another round in the alibi relay."

"But, Sir. Ten clicks will put me too low on the target, Sir."

"You're starting to piss me off, maggot."

"Sir, I'm left-handed, and Sergeant Williams converted me to shoot right-handed with the M-14." At first, Jesse had resisted the desire of Sergeant Williams to convert him to a right-handed shooter but, after ten rounds of rapid fire at the two hundred-yard line, he was convinced. Unless you had an M-14 or an M-1 Garand that had been converted for a left-handed shooter, the hot brass shells ejected into the right side of the shooter's face, often dangerously close to the eye. "I hold my face right up against the receiver when I shoot right-handed. Ten clicks will put me low on the target, Sir."

"Maggot, you got something wrong with your ears?"

"No, Sir. I was just trying to explain...."

"Shut the fuck up, maggot! And get your dope on that rifle."

"Yessir!"

Cooley moved down the firing line.

"That guy's an asshole."

Jesse turned to Schuyler, undoubtedly the worst shot in Platoon 324. "How you doin', Sky?"

Schuyler looked down at his feet as though they might go somewhere without him.

"That bad, huh?"

35

Stoney Livingston

"We don't need rifles in Detroit. Hell, a zip gun gets the job done."

Jesse knew Schuyler was worried. A marine is foremost a rifleman, and to fail to qualify with the rifle in boot camp was the ultimate sin. It was a transgression against God himself. Every man in the Corps was required to qualify annually, including cooks and clerks. If Schuyler didn't qualify tomorrow, his life would be miserable. The Platoon Commander and the other drill instructors would insure it.

"Just relax, Sky. There's nothing to it. Treat that rifle like it was your girlfriend. Take it slow and easy."

"You don't know my girl. We damn sure don't take it slow and easy."

"Oh. Well, hell. Think of something else then. What was your score in off-hand?"

"Thirteen."

"Thirteen? Jesus! You can't shoot that bad with your eyes closed."

"How'd you do?" asked Schuyler.

Off-hand was Jesse's worst position. "Forty-four."

"Forty-four! Christ! You're gonna be high man. Dress Blues and showers shoes for you, man."

"Hey! You two maggots knock off the bullshit down there."

Jesse glanced down the firing line at Sergeant Cooley.

"Prick," mumbled Schuyler.

Jesse leaned forward, his elbows pressing against the inside of his spread legs, sling taut from the front swivel to his arm. He waited for the loudspeaker.

"All ready on the right. All ready on the left. All ready on the firing line. Watch your targets," said a tinny, treble voice through the loudspeaker.

Jesse watched the target area through his peep sight. His target shot up and bounced as it reached the top of its travel. He breathed deeply and let out half a breath. He fired the five rounds in his rifle magazine then quickly removed the empty magazine and replaced it with another containing five rounds, pulled the bolt to the rear and released it in one swift, fluid movement. He settled back on the target and squeezed off the five rounds, allowing only enough time between shots for his body to recover from the recoil.

He heard Cooley's voice behind him. "What the hell is going on down there?"

Jesse felt his heart beating heavily in his chest as he saw the dust flying from the ground in front of his target, almost obliterating it from view, drifting to the right in the gentle wind. He held his position while the others on the firing line continued to fire, utilizing most of their allotted fifty seconds.

"Cease fire. Cease fire. Clear all weapons. Clear the firing line," said the voice on the loudspeaker.

Jesse removed the empty magazine from his rifle and moved off the line. Cooley was waiting for him.

"What the hell do you think you're doing? You trying to piss me off, maggot?"

Jesse stood at rigid attention. "Sir, no, Sir!"

"You were finished in nineteen seconds. What the hell were you thinking?"

The targets popped up. Jesse didn't have to watch for the marks. He knew he had missed the target with all ten shots.

Cooley looked through a pair of 6 X 30 field glasses. "For Christ sake! Ten

36

Maggies' Drawers! You didn't hit the goddamn target! Not one fucking hit! Not even a deuce!" Cooley pulled the glasses from his eyes and stared at Jesse. "All right, you smart-ass-maggot. Put your own dope on that rifle. You're shooting in the alibi relay, and so help me God if you don't shoot a possible, I'll have your ass doin' duck-walks up Little Agony with the heaviest goddamn seabag you ever lifted. Do you hear me, you fuckin' maggot?"

"Yessir!"

Cooley walked down the firing line, visibly shaking.

"Jesus, what happened up there?" asked Schuyler.

"I told him ten clicks wasn't enough for me."

"Yeah, well, I hope to hell you get all fifty in the alibi, or you'll have frogs popping out of your calves for a week."

Jesse waited nervously for the four relays to complete the sitting rapid fire at the two-hundred-yard line. He ran the rear sight aperture up thirty-one clicks and checked the windage knob to see that it was set at two clicks right. He checked the front sight blade to insure its tightness and cleaned the chamber with a small brush. When the M-14 was as clean as he could get it under range conditions he put a light coat of lubriplate inside the operating rod handle groove and worked the bolt slowly back and forth to spread the lubricant.

The booming treble voice he had been dreading blasted into his eardrums: "Clear the firing line. All marines shooting in the alibi relay, take your positions."

Jesse looked at Sergeant Cooley, who stood at the rear of the firing line. Cooley pointed to the small marker indicating target twelve. At least he didn't have to change targets.

Cooley whispered in his ear as Jesse stood behind the firing line. "I'm gonna have your ass, maggot."

"Shooters to the line. Take your positions. All marksmanship instructors move to the rear. Prepare the relay." Jesse moved quickly to his assigned location and took up the sitting position. The treble voice paused a moment. "Load and lock." Another pause. "All ready on the right. All ready on the left. All ready on the firing line. Watch your targets."

Jesse started shooting the instant his target hit full mast. His second shot was gone before anyone else on the line fired. He squeezed off the next three and changed magazines before half of the other shooters had fired their first shots. When he emptied the second magazine he held his position and waited for the remainder of the fifty seconds to expire. It seemed to take forever before the loudspeaker blared, "Cease fire. Cease fire. Clear all weapons. Move off the firing line."

Cooley waited for him at the bench behind target twelve. "Whatsamatter, maggot? You nervous? You finished in seventeen seconds that time. Hurry your shots a little bit, did you?"

"No, Sir. That's the way I shoot rapid fire. They felt pretty good, sir. I may have jerked one but I think the others were good, Sir."

"Don't get smart with me, you fucking maggot. That isn't the way you've been taught."

"Yes, Sir."

The targets were back in the air. Jesse could see a group of white pasties at six o'clock on the black silhouette. Every shot had felt good except that first one. He wasn't sure about that one. He held his breath as the flat disk on the end of a long handle shot into the air. When he saw the red and white, he knew he had no

37

score lower than a four on any of the shots. He waited for the man in the butts to pump the marker up and down to count his four-point hits. His face heated in anticipation. His body needed oxygen but he didn't dare breathe until he had his count. *What the hell is taking so long for that guy to mark my target?*

Suddenly the disk began to spin as the man in the butts twisted the handle. It was the signal for a perfect score. Jesse exhaled and drew a deep breath. *That first one must have made it into the black.* He turned to Sergeant Cooley. "Sir, Private Langley requests permission to use his own dope."

Cooley glared at him. "Use your dope, maggot, but I expect you to be high man in this platoon." Cooley spun on his heel and walked down the line.

Schuyler looked up at him from the bench. "I don't believe that shit. That was the fastest shooting I ever saw in my life; you get a possible, and that asshole can't wait to burn you for something."

"I don't think he'll bother me. The better I shoot, the better he looks. He's just pissed because my dope doesn't fit within the book."

"Damn, man, your lip is sure puffed up. Looks like you just got hit in the mouth with a Mack truck."

"It's this right-handed shooting. I get my lip too close to the damn receiver. Every time I shoot, I get punched in the mouth."

"Damn, that must hurt like hell."

Jesse smiled, the right side of his upper lip stretching tight and causing a slight pain. "It ain't so bad right now, but by the time we get back to the five-hundred-yard line, it gets my attention real good every time I pull the trigger. I'm afraid I'll start pulling them if it gets too bad."

Jesse wrapped the sling around his arm as he waited for the loudspeaker to order them to the line. He wished he had been sick today. On Pre-qual day, he had fired a 238 out of a possible 250 – highest in the platoon. Today, his offhand score was 41 – three less than Pre-qual day. His two-hundred rapid fire was 50, the same as before, but he was worried about the offhand score. He looked up to see Schuyler's long face.

"How you doin', Sky?"

"Shitty. I'm not gonna make it. I'm scared, Jesse. They'll beat the shit out of me. Maybe even kill me and chop me up into little pieces and hide the bones. Cooley's already planning my funeral. Said he never had anyone fail to qualify before and I'm not gonna 'by-god-be-the-first'."

"What was your offhand score?"

"Twenty-one."

Jesse winced. "How about two hundred rapid?"

"Thirty-four."

Minimum qualifying score to make the marksman badge was 190 out of 250. Sky had already lost forty-five points. If he fired a perfect score on the next three relays, his best possible score would be a 205 – high marksman. Sharpshooter, at 210, and expert, at 220, were far beyond his reach.

The next position was kneeling, slow fire, five rounds at three-hundred yards. It was Jesse's worst position with the exception of offhand. If Sky fired less than thirty-five on the combined kneeling and sitting slow fire he couldn't qualify, even with a perfect score at the five-hundred-yard line prone slow fire and the three-hundred-yard line prone rapid fire.

Jesse liked Schuyler. He was full of laughter and smiles, a hard thing to come by in marine boot camp – until they had hit Camp Mathews. The rifle training had changed him. Even now, as Jesse studied Schuyler's face, he could see the fear.

Jesse ran through the numbers in his mind. He leaned close to Schuyler. "If I put three on your target in the kneeling position, can you at least get me a few deuces?"

Relief spread across Schuyler's face. "They'd bust you out if they caught you."

"You just watch me. When I fire on your target, you fire on mine."

"First relay. Three-hundred-yard line, slow fire, kneeling, five rounds, take your positions."

Jesse stood and moved to the line. "The first three shots, Sky. Got it?"

Schuyler nodded nervously and moved to his position on target seventeen.

When the command to watch the targets was given, Jesse sighted down the barrel of his rifle. At three-hundred yards it would be difficult to determine he was shooting at a target five numbers to his right but it could be done, especially if Cooley were to stand directly behind him.

The rifle bucked into Jesse's shoulder. He glanced down the line to Schuyler and saw that he was loading another round. He looked at his target. It was still in the air. So was Schuyler's. *What happened? I'm sure I was on seventeen. It was a good shot too, damnit.*

Cooley stood behind him, waiting for the target to come down. He turned to one of the recruits sitting at the field phone. "Tell them to mark twelve and seventeen."

Jesse watched as his target was lowered into the butts. Schuyler's target was the first of the two to reappear. It was followed shortly by the red disk. A bull's eye. Jesse's target raised into view. He felt his stomach turn as the red flag was passed in front of the target from left to right. Maggie's drawers.

Damn! Sky missed the whole target.

Jesse reloaded and glanced down at Schuyler, who had a big smile on his face. *That's it, Sky, smile you dummy. Now, try hitting the goddamn target this time.* Jesse aimed in on target seventeen. He squeezed the trigger until the heavy M-14 slammed into his shoulder and the receiver smashed into his lip. Again, neither target was pulled down.

Jesse turned his head to see Cooley standing directly behind him, staring at him intently. "What the hell are you doing up there, Langley? You got your head in your ass?" He glanced at Schuyler's target standing motionless, Schuyler reloading. "Goddamnit! What the fuck's goin' on around here?" He turned to the field phone operator. "Tell them to mark twelve and seventeen."

Jesse watched a rerun of the last scene: another bull's eye for Schuyler, another miss for him. *Goddamn, Sky, I was counting on at least two points per shot.*

Cooley shouted to him from the rear of the firing line. "I'm watching you, Langley, you fucking maggot. If you pull any shit, I'll have your ass in front of the old man quicker'n you can say 'horseshit'. Do you hear me?"

Jesse was grateful no one but shooters were allowed on the firing line during a relay. "Yessir," he said over his shoulder. He looked at Schuyler, five targets to his right. Schuyler's eye's met his and Jesse shook his head slowly. Schuyler gave him a knowing nod. Jesse aimed in on his own target.

Schuyler hung in there. His qualification came down to his last shot at the five-hundred-yard line. It was that close. He needed a bull's eye. Everyone in the platoon was rooting for him. His final shot was a four and his score of 189 was one point short of qualifying.

Jesse fired a 226 - second highest in the platoon – not good enough to get the free Dress Blues and the automatic promotion to private first class.

Jesse realized that the targets weren't pulled on those two shots he threw onto Schuyler's target because the angle was just enough, even at three-hundred yards, to cause the bullet to strike the butts behind the target to the right of Schuyler's, and to the left of his. He had wondered why the man on his left and the man on Sky's right were both allowed to shoot in the alibi relay. Jesse knew Sergeant Cooley had figured it out too, but Cooley never said a word. Maybe he figured Jesse suffered enough by not getting the high score. But for his two lost bull's eyes, his score would have been 236. The high man for the platoon fired a 232. The high man for all four platoons in the series fired a 235.

In the squad tent later Jesse reflected on what he had done. He knew he didn't deserve to be the high man and get those dress blues and the automatic promotion. He had cheated – not for his benefit – but that didn't matter. He had cheated just the same.

They packed their seabags for the trip back to San Diego and Jesse returned to M.C.R.D. just another expert rifleman. It didn't seem to matter as much now. There would be no war in Laos. They got the news upon their arrival at M.C.R.D.. Jesse felt like a man trapped in hell for the duration of his three-year enlistment – and it was just beginning. *What a helluva mess. No war. No heroes. Just some of the stupidest bullshit I've ever seen.*

Camp Pendleton

Gunnery Sergeant Pickering looked at him solemnly. "Decided to come back, huh?"

"It was only a week, Gunny. And there wasn't a mount-out when I left."

Pickering shook his head. "Get into your tropicals and report to the company office in ten minutes for office hours. The Skipper is still here but that's about all. Everyone else is already down in San Diego."

"I'll be there in five minutes," said Jesse as he rushed to the barracks to change into the summer dress uniform. It was October but the Southern California weather was warm and balmy. Only the hint of a cool breeze passed between the barracks at Camp Marguerita as Jesse ran back to the company office, his tropical dress uniform pressed and clean.

Jesse stood at rigid attention in front of Captain Eldridge's desk, allowing his eyes to wander to the wings on his company commander's blouse. He conjured up all kinds of reasons a pilot might be commanding an infantry company but couldn't come up with one that seemed plausible.

Eldridge was blond and tall, a square-shouldered man with a straight back and a handsome mustache. Jesse thought he looked like Errol Flynn.

"You made PFC out of I.T.R. so you must have something on the ball,

Langley. What in the hell were you thinking when you went over the hill?"

Jesse stared straight ahead. "I don't know, sir. I joined the marines to go to war. There wasn't any war ..."

"So you figured you'd just go home until we had one?"

"Almost, Sir. Well, not exactly. I don't really know what I was thinking."

With his peripheral vision Jesse saw Eldridge shake his head. "I don't know what you were thinking either, marine. Well, you came back pretty damn quick so I guess you mean business. You plan on staying around this time, Langley?"

"Yessir."

"Very well. In view of the fact that you made PFC out of I.T.R. and this is your first time for Office Hours, I sentence you to six days E.P.D."

Jesse waited for the rest of his punishment. He knew he wouldn't get off with only six days of extra police duty. He waited for the fine or the restriction to quarters.

"That'll be all, Langley. Get out of here and get your gear together. The last truck to North Island, San Diego leaves in about thirty minutes."

"Yessir!" Jesse did an about-face and marched briskly through the open door.

Outside the captain's office he confronted Gunny Pickering. "I don't get it, Gunny. He only gave me six days E.P.D."

Pickering smiled a knowing smile. "Captain Eldridge was a bit of a rebel in his early days. He was in the air over Seoul, Korea, when they announced the armistice. He flew under the high-power lines near the capitol in a Panther, then did a victory roll. The Crotch grounded him. He's been in the infantry ever since, waiting for a chance to get back into a fighter jet. He's all right. Just don't get in front of him a second time."

"I don't intend to."

"You'll start your E.P.D. tonight at eighteen-hundred. Two hours a night for six nights. Report to me at eighteen-hundred. Now get out of here and get your gear. Report here in twenty minutes ready to mount out."

"Thanks, Guns." Jesse rushed from the office.

San Diego

"Where the hell you been?" PFC Manning met Jesse at the top of the gangplank as he stepped aboard the U.S.S. Noble. Jesse saluted the flag blowing in the light breeze under floods on the fantail, then turned to the officer of the deck and saluted him crisply. Only when he completed the ceremony did he turn to Manning.

"Damn, Bergie. Let me get aboard before you give me the third degree fer cryin' out loud." Jesse couldn't remember why everyone called him Bergie. His first name was Harold, and between that and Manning, there didn't seem to be a connection to the nickname but it didn't really matter. He was Bergie now. It fit him well. Besides, almost everyone in the Corps ended up with a nickname before he got out. Jesse hadn't been tagged yet but he knew it would come in time.

"Well damnit, you're on board now. Where the hell you been?" Bergie took Jesse's seabag.

"I was in Arizona."

Bergie waited. When it became apparent that Jesse was through with his

41

explanation, Bergie said, "No shit. What the hell were you doing there? I mean were you gonna stay over-the-hill or what?"

They walked slowly toward the fantail. "I don't know. I just got tired of this stupid military garbage and needed a break. I don't know if I ever would've come back if I hadn't seen the news on TV that the marines were leaving Camp Pendleton. I was havin' a good time – visitin' with my high-school buddies and lookin' up a few girls that I ignored when I was goin' to school, and all that kind of stuff."

"So why'd you come back?"

Jesse smiled. "You didn't think I'd let you guys go off somewhere and have all that fun without me, did you? By the way, where in the hell are we going?"

Bergie entered a hatch. He struggled with the seabag while Jesse managed to get through the it without striking his rifle against the bulkhead. "Hell, nobody knows. Our best guess is someplace in Central America but we ain't all that sure." Bergie dragged the seabag down the steep ladder, allowing it to bounce off each step on its way down.

"You mean nobody knows where we're goin'?"

"Say, you're real sharp. You pick up on shit real fast."

"Somebody's gotta know."

"Yeah, somebody. But whoever it is ain't tellin' us."

A chorus of salutations greeted them as they stepped onto the steel deck in hold D. Jesse shook hands and exchanged remarks with nearly every man in his platoon before he was informed the only rack left was the upper cot near the hatch.

Jesse arched his neck back until his face was almost parallel to the overhead in the narrow passageway between cots. Only then was he able to see the top rack. He turned to Bergie. "Jesus Christ. Seven high? I'll get nose bleeds up there."

"Hey, man. That's what you get for goin' over-the-hill."

Jesse turned to the voice. It was Tony Carratta, one of his better friends in the outfit. He rushed to Tony and shook his hand, an over-sized smile on his lips. "Wop. How you been? I can't believe they let you on this tub. This must just be some kind of exercise. If it was for real, they'd've left you at Pendleton."

Wop shook his hand and hugged him tightly. "It's for real all right. I was talking to one of the swabbies and he says we got nothing but live ammo on board and we'll be loading a bunch more." Wop was the kind of guy who could meet and be friendly with almost anyone immediately, even sailors.

"Yer kiddin'?"

Wop crossed his heart. "So help me. I swear on Stacy's life." Stacy was his girl. She lived in Stockton, California.

"Did this swabbie say where we were goin?" asked Jesse.

Wop smiled. "He says we're going to Formosa. Chiang Ki Chek and the reds are having problems. They need us to settle 'em."

"No wonder there's so damn much activity down here." Jesse shuddered. "I hope he's wrong on that one. There's more Chinese than there are bullets."

"We'll just have to make more bullets." The soft voice came from behind him.

Jesse turned. It was Dave Boomer. Dave was a quiet, soft-spoken, redheaded, freckled-faced man from Utah. At age twenty-two, he was five years older than Jesse, but because of their partial rural up-bringings they had much in common. "Dave. It's good to see you, man."

"It's good to see you too, Jesse. I didn't think you were going to make it there for awhile."

"So where do you think we're goin'?"

Dave shrugged. "I haven't got the foggiest. Wherever it is I don't think it's very cold. The only cold weather gear we've got is our field jackets." Dave would think of something like that. He was logical.

"Hell, that don't mean nothin'. It probably means we're going to Antarctica," said Baby Huey from between two of the lower cots.

Jesse settled into the top rack and after only a few tries, learned to make the precarious climb without much disturbance to the men in the six cots below his. He also learned that his was one of the best cots in the hold. On the pipes directly overhead, he hung his cartridge belt and pack, helmet and rifle. There was a large cubbyhole created by the curve of the ship's hull and the placement of the deck above him – the perfect size for his seabag. Few could stretch out on a cot clean of gear, for there was no place to store it. He found the climb from the deck below wasn't necessary if one climbed the ladder to the hatch and stretched a leg from the ladder to his cot. Jesse was quite happy with his new bunk.

Jesse put his gear in place then glanced at his gold Wittnauer dress watch. It was time to report to Gunny Pickering for his first day of E.P.D. He made the descent to the deck from his rack and searched out the gunny. He found him topside barking orders to a working party.

"Guns, I'm reporting for my E.P.D."

Pickering looked him up and down then glanced at his watch. "Stand by. There'll be a twenty-man working party here in about five minutes. You'll be going ashore to unload trucks."

They unloaded trucks all right. One after the other – semi's full of ammunition and explosives. Jesse hadn't known there were that many trucks in the world. They were everywhere. When a loaded truck pulled into position it was swarmed over by one of the many working parties. They covered it like bees cover a hive. In less than ten minutes the big trailer was picked clean. It pulled away from the unloading zone even as the last pallet of ammo was lifted from its innards. Another replaced it immediately.

Jesse's working party stayed at it until daylight when it was replaced by another group. When he returned to the *Noble*, he found his hold and crawled tiredly to his cot. His head was about to hit the canvas when he heard his name called.

"Langley."

"Yo." He answered quickly.

"Carretta."

"Yo." Wop's voice came from the next aisle.

"Report to the fantail. Gunny Pickering wants to see you."

They mumbled as they stepped to the deck and made their way aft.

Gunny Pickering held out a black thing. It looked like some kind of space-age weapon but neither Jesse nor Wop was sure exactly what it was.

"Langley, you and Carretta have been assigned this gun. Langley, you're the gunner, Carretta the A-gunner."

They stared at the weapon.

"Well, goddamnit, are you gonna take this thing or do you expect me to stand here all day holding it out in the wind?"

Jesse grasped the odd-looking weapon by the forearm stock and the butt.

43

Stoney Livingston

He looked at the gun then at Pickering. "What the hell is it? It looks like a ray gun from some science fiction movie."

"That, Mr. Langley, is the Corps' newest machine gun – the M-60."

"That's a machine gun?" asked Wop.

"What's the matter with the A-4?" asked Jesse.

"This thing will shoot rings around the A-4. It's lighter, has a faster cyclic rate, quick-change barrel, no adjusting head space, lighter tripods," he picked up a set of grey tripods and handed them to Wop. "... shoots the same ammo as the M-14, uses link-belt feed, requires little help from an A-gunner, can be field-stripped in half the time of an A-4, has its own bipod legs built onto the barrel for quick set up, can be fired by one man in the standing position in a pinch, and it's not as prone to malfunction as the A-4."

Jesse looked from the M-60 to Wop then to Gunny Pickering. "So why are you giving it to us? We're not in the weapons platoon. We're mortarmen. Why do we need a machine gun?"

"You're new, Langley. Neither of you know much more about an 81 mortar than you do about this M-60. Eighty-ones is being issued a machine gun. You and Carretta here figure to be as easy to train as any of the new men. You'll still be in eighty-ones, and you'll still train as mortarmen, but you'll also be responsible for the M-60. Since you're both last ammo carriers in your respective squads, you aren't assigned a piece of the mortar to carry and clean. Now you've got something to take care of."

"But, Gunny what the hell do we know about taking this thing apart?" asked Wop.

Pickering looked at him sternly. "We don't want this gun disassembled beyond a very basic field-strip. We don't have any spare parts. You have a class at 0800 on the fantail. Now, secure the gun and get to chow. Report to Sergeant Milliken of the weapons platoon right here at 0800. Got it?"

The Pacific

Jesse and Wop learned the basics of the M-60 and by the time the *U.S.S. Noble* sailed from San Diego that evening they were already stripping the gun to its smallest component part for cleaning. By daybreak the newness of the machine gun had worn off and the big question in their minds was their destination.

The following day everyone on the ship attended a class in Spanish at some time during the day. So much for Wop's theory of a landing in China.

The *U.S.S. Noble* was an APA, an amphibious troop ship, the kind marines used for landing on beachheads. The entire thirteen-hundred man, 3rd Battalion, 5th Marines was embarked aboard the old ship with all of their weapons and gear, ammunition, and many of the battalion's vehicles, crowded into a space about one-third the size of a standard cruise ship. When they had stepped aboard the *Noble*, the 3rd Battalion, 5th Marines had disappeared and they had suddenly become the 1st Battalion, 7th Marines. Everybody was the same but they were a different outfit on paper.

Speculation about their destination grew almost hourly.

"You got any more great scoop on where we're goin'?" asked Jesse. They sat amidships on the starboard side, cleaning the machine gun, which Wop had

44

named "Lucy".

Wop shook his head. "Hey, man. I can't help it if I was given some bum scoop. Maybe they speak Spanish in some parts of China."

"Hand me that bipod retaining pin, will you?" Jesse glanced out to sea. "Well, wherever we're going it must be south of here. We been sailing south since we left San Diego."

Jesse pushed the bipod pin against the spring as he tried to slip the retainer into place. His thumb slipped from the edge of the pin and the force from the spring shot the pin into the air. Both he and Wop made a desperate lunge at it but both missed. They watched helplessly as the black pin disappeared over the rail and into the Pacific Ocean.

They looked at each other foolishly. "Now what?" Jesse asked. "We're dead. We weren't supposed to strip the gun down that far. We've got an inspection this afternoon."

Wop hunched his shoulders up. "How long do you think we'll have to spend in the brig?"

"Who else has got an M-60? We'll borrow a pin. I'll get it back to him after the inspection."

Wop shook his head. "The whole weapons platoon is getting inspected at the same time."

"Damn. I guess I'll just have to tell Gunny that I lost the pin."

"Wait a minute. They've got a machine shop on the ship."

"So?"

"So I met one of the swabbies that works there." Wop grinned.

"You think he might make us a pin?"

"He might."

*****

Jesse and Wop stood by the machine gun as Captain Eldridge inspected the weapon thoroughly. "This is one of the cleanest machine-guns I've ever seen, Langley."

"Thank you, sir," said Jesse, at rigid attention.

"I'm curious about the pin in the right bipod leg. I find it odd that it has no parkerizing." Eldridge paused. Neither Jesse nor Wop spoke. The captain turned to Gunny Pickering. "Well, we can't have a machine gun with a shiny silver pin in it. Besides rust, it will give away your position. See to it these men get some M-nu."

Pickering arched an eyebrow at Jesse. "Yessir."

Jesse smiled quickly at Pickering as the gunny followed Captain Eldridge to the next gun

*****

"Goddamn. Did you see the water this morning? It looked like a damn mirror." Bergie polished his bayonet below decks.

"Yeah," answered Jesse. "It almost looked like you could walk on it."

"Yeah? Well, I wouldn't try it. I heard they crucified the last guy that pulled that shit," said a muffled voice.

Bergie and Jesse looked up at Wop, who stood with his toothbrush in his mouth, wearing nothing but a pair of skivvie shorts.

"Jesus, Wop. You ain't at home. Why don't you use the head for brushing your teeth?" asked Jesse.

Around a mouthful of dry toothpaste, Wop said, "Hell, man, there's no room in there. As a matter-of-fact, there's no room anywhere on this iron bucket."

"No shit. They can't keep us on this thing much longer. Christ, we could've sailed around the world by now," said Bergie.

"Not quite, Bergie," said Jesse.

"Where the hell are we going? Why don't they tell us? What's the big deal? Who the hell are we going to tell?"

"You write letters home don't you?" asked Jesse.

Bergie shrugged.

"Yeah, well, I'm with Bergie. We're the ones gonna hit the beach. The least they could do is tell us which beach," said Wop.

"So why pick on me? If I had any idea where we were going, I'd put it over the p.a. system," said Jesse defensively.

Bergie looked at him. "What's your guess?"

"If I had to guess, I'd say Korea or Japan, or somewhere else where it gets colder'n hell."

"Why'd you say that?" asked Wop.

"Cause we don't have a stitch of cold weather gear and that's how the Crotch does things."

"Damn good point," agreed Wop.

There was a moment of silence. Jesse said, "Wherever we're going to end up is anybody's guess, but I think we're goin' through the Panama Canal."

Wop stopped brushing his teeth. Bergie looked at him without moving. Wop spoke first. "Why'd you say that?"

"We been headed generally south since we left San Diego. Sure, we zig and we zag. But we end up south of where we started every day. Not west and south – but almost due south. There's nothing going on down here that I'm aware of that would cause this big a ruckus. It's gotta be east of the Canal."

"Makes sense to me," agreed Wop jovially as he moved down the crowded passageway to the head to spit out a mouthful of toothpaste.

Panama Canal

Jesse stood on deck almost the entire trip through the Panama Canal. About midway, the ship anchored in a lagoon while the marines were taken ashore in Peter boats for their first feel of solid ground in more than a week. They were given physical training exercises for an hour then returned to the *Noble*. When the last platoon was aboard, the ship continued her journey to the east end of the canal.

Jesse marveled at the huge locks and the rapid rate at which the water levels equalized on both sides of the man-made mini-dams.

"You still up here, man? You're gonna fry your brains if you don't get outa this sun."

Jesse smiled at Wop as his friend lit a cigarette. "We may never get to see this place again. It's one of the prettiest places I've ever seen."

Wop exhaled a puff of smoke. "Yeah, It's pretty all right. It's got twenty million different kinds of poisonous snakes. How's that for pretty?"

"I didn't say I'd wanna spend the rest of my life here. I just said it was

46

pretty."

"Yeah, well, you may get to see more of it than you think."

"What are you talkin' about, Wop?"

"Gunny Pickering wants to see you. The word is, they're gonna put everybody off the boat who isn't eighteen yet."

Jesse felt the heat rise to his face. He was the second youngest man in the outfit. Few in the platoon knew it, but Gunny Pickering would know. He would have the service record books - or would he? Jesse wasn't so sure the service record books had made it to San Diego in time. "Where is he?"

Wop jerked a thumb toward the stern of the ship. "He's on the fantail. Said for you to report there more skoshe."

"Thanks, Wop."

Wop patted him on the shoulder as Jesse stepped around him. "Lots of luck, man."

Jesse nodded and moved towards the rear of the ship, fighting back the tears. It didn't seem right that he should be put off the ship just because he wasn't eighteen. He had gone through the same training as every man aboard and had done as well or better than any of them.

Pickering tried to smile as Jesse approached but the attempt was not completely successful.

"You wanted to see me, Gunny?"

"Yes, Langley. Just trying to get our records straight. Take care of some routine matters. Thought I'd save the time of digging out the service records."

He doesn't have the records. They're probably sitting on a dock in San Diego.

"Sure, Guns. What d'you need to know?"

Pickering was casual, almost too casual. "Let's see. You get your yellow fever shot before we left Pendleton?"

I don't believe this. "Sure. That's the mother of a shot that hurt clear under the arm."

Pickering laughed. "Oh yeah, that's right. I remember you complaining about it. Let's see here. Oh yeah, what's your date of birth? Since you lost your I.D. card while you were on your little vacation, I'd have to dig out the service records to get it and I don't have the time."

"Nineteen February, forty-four."

Pickering jotted down the date and glanced up at him. "You sure?"

"What the hell kind of question is that, Gunny? If a man doesn't know anything else, he knows his own damn birthday."

Pickering smiled, "Yeah, I guess you're right there. Well, that'll be all. Send Manning back here."

"Sure thing, Guns." Jesse strolled forward in search of Bergie, wishing there was some way he could make the ship move through the Canal faster.

The Carribean

One day east of the Canal, shortly after dawn, Wop rattled Jesse's cot. Jesse was awake instantly. "What the hell you doin', Wop?"

Wop had him by the shoulders, still shaking. "You gotta go topside, man.

Stoney Livingston

You won't believe what you see. I saw it and I still don't believe it."

"Okay. Okay. Stop shakin' me or you'll rattle my teeth loose."

"Come on, man. Hurry."

Jesse slipped his combat boots on and stepped from his cot to the second step from the top of the ladder. In three steps he was through the hatch and staring into a rose and salmon sunrise. Silhouetted on the horizon as far as he could see, U.S. Navy warships blackened the dark ocean and the skyline.

"Jesus Christ! What year is this?" He turned to Wop. "Is this 1944, or is it 1962?"

Wop hunched up his shoulders. "You tell me. What the hell is going on?"

Jesse panned the horizon then turned back to Wop. "Wop, this has got to be the biggest armada since D-Day. I didn't know there were this many ships still in the navy."

"These can't be all from *our* navy."

"Maybe not. Hell, who knows? Whatever we're involved in, it's gotta be the biggest thing since World War Two. What the hell can it be?"

"You got me." Wop shrugged.

Corporal Warner stepped next to them. "0800. In D compartment. Class on Russian."

Wop turned to him. "Russian? Did you say Russian?"

"You heard me right. Pass the word to anyone else you see who might have got up early." Warner stepped back into the hatch and disappeared below deck.

Wop looked into Jesse's eyes. "We better get ol' Lucy oiled up and keep her that way. We're gonna go to war with Russia."

"There must be some other explanation," said Jesse hopefully.

The marines attended classes in Russian. They learned the table of organization of the Soviet Army, its weapons, armament, aircraft, support vessels and theory of combat. The days grew long with classes, inspections, gun drill, p.t. and weapons cleaning. The roll, pitch and yaw of the *Noble* became more exaggerated as the sea grew increasingly rougher. It seemed to mirror the mood of the men.

Jesse's greatest moment of glory came on the fantail of the ship during a live-fire exercise with the machine gun. He struck a target balloon at six hundred yards on his first six-round burst.

In late October, the battalion commander announced over the ship's p.a. system that their destination was Cuba. At dawn, the day after the announcement, the *Noble* lay within thirty miles of the island. That was as close as they got. A Soviet YAK bomber flew high overhead and was intercepted and escorted away from the armada by U.S. Navy and Air Force jets.

That evening, the *Noble* set a course to the east and south. The following afternoon, the 1st Battalion, 7th Marines sat offshore of Roosevelt Roads, Puerto Rico.

Jesse stood at the railing, staring down into the crystal-clear turquoise water lapping at the ship's hull. Wop, Bergie and Dave Boomer stood next to him.

Dave said, "I don't know what in the hell happened, but whatever it was is apparently over. I sure would like to go ashore. I bet I forgot how to walk on dry land."

"I hear these Puerto Rican women are as hot-blooded as Mexican chile peppers," said Wop.

"I got this awful feeling that if we get to go ashore, the Crotch is gonna make us wish we'd stayed aboard the *Noble*," said Jesse.

"Damnit, Jesse, you're such a damned pessimist, I can't stand it," said Bergie.

"Yeah, Bergie, Jesse may be a pessimist, but I'll bet he's right on this one," said Dave in his soft voice.

Vieques

They hit the beaches the following morning in full combat gear – an amphibious assault on a mock enemy. The first twenty-four hours ashore they participated in battlefield exercises, eating C-rations packaged in October of 1944. At the end of that period, the 81 mortar platoon fired live ammo on a designated firing range, using the ammo Jesse had helped load aboard the *Noble* in San Diego. Jesse prepared ammo and handed it to the assistant gunner and, along with the rest of the ammo carriers, watched, dumfounded, as round after round failed to explode on impact. With a "dud" rate of almost sixty- percent, Jesse was glad they had not landed in Cuba.

Gunny Pickering explained that the ammo was old, most of it left over from World War Two, and newer ammo would be supplied shortly, but that did little to alter the fact that they would have landed on enemy-held terrain with unreliable ammunition for the mortars. Jesse gave the matter more than a little thought. He began to see other things besides the men near him as important to the outcome of a battle.

The third day on the island was devoted to rest and recuperation. Jesse stretched himself out in the white sand on the beach, his boots off, feet barely in the water when the gentle waves rolled in.

"Hey, Jesse, you gotta see this."

He looked up and behind to see Dave Boomer strolling his way with a smile spread across his face. He sat up. "See what?"

"There's a grunt lieutenant on the other side of that hill." Dave pointed inland. "Got his whole damn platoon marching a column of files from the right to get in line near these two trees."

"What the hell for?"

Dave laughed. "He found two whores willing to set up shop out here under those trees and service his platoon at a buck-and- a-half a shot."

"You got to be kidding?"

"I swear, man. Come on, you gotta see it to believe it. He's got them damn grunts standing at semi attention in this heat for a shot at a two-bit whore – by rank, no less."

Jesse grabbed his boots and stuffed his feet into them. "I knew them grunts was lackin' a little bit of class but this is ridiculous. Where's this hill?"

They picked up Bergie, Wop, Padre, D. W. Savage, Grubby J., Stubby, Bill Monroe and several others on their way to the high ground. By the time they reached the hill from which they could view the infantry platoon lined up in the heat, there were no fewer than twenty men from the 81-mortar platoon in accompaniment.

Jesse sat in the tall grass on the hill and lit a cigarette. "See that guy at the

Stoney Livingston

far tree? The one second from the front of the line?"

Wop nodded.

"I've got a buck says he's not under that tree for more'n two-and-a-half minutes."

Wop shook his head. "No bet. He looks pretty green to me."

"Hell, I'll take that bet."

Jesse turned. "Get your buck out, Bergie. Wop, you hold the money. Dave, you got a watch?"

Dave nodded.

"You keep the time. If that guy is out from under that tree in less than one hundred fifty seconds, I get the money. Bergie gets it if the guy's a second longer."

As the man in question stepped out of formation briskly and moved up to the tree, Bergie said, "Start the time now."

"Bullshit, Bergie. Wait until the guy gets under the tree," said Jesse. "Okay. Now."

Dave put his eyes to his watch. "One of you guys tell me when you see him again."

Jesse lit another cigarette and took a deep, slow drag.

"Whatsamatter, Jesse? Gettin' nervous?" asked Bergie.

Jesse exhaled slowly and smiled. "You wanna double the bet?"

"Ninety seconds," said Dave, staring intently at his watch.

Bergie looked at Dave, then back to Jesse. "Hell yeah." He pulled another dollar from his utility blouse pocket. Jesse added another bill to Wop's hand.

Jesse took another drag from his smoke.

"Two minutes."

"Hell, I'll bet another two on this guy."

Jesse exhaled. "You're gettin' greedy, Bergie. But you're faded." He dropped two more dollars into Wop's hand.

"He's out," said Padre.

"Two minutes twenty-four seconds," announced Dave.

Jesse reached over and gently lifted the money from Wop's hand. "It's a real pleasure doin' business with you, Bergie."

"Goddamnit, that isn't even possible. How did you know that?"

"I didn't. I was just tryin' to learn something about this kind of a situation. I figured it was worth a few bucks to help me remember the outcome. I bet twenty years from now, you're gonna remember exactly how long it took that sergeant to get the job done."

Stubby laughed. "I don't believe you guys. You'd bet on anything."

"I'll bet I wouldn't," replied Bergie.

All twenty men on the hill roared with laughter at Bergie's remark. The infantry platoon lined up near the trees took the laughter as aimed at them. The platoon leader ordered his men to face left and charge the hill.

"Oh shit!" shouted Bergie. "The grunts think we're laughing at them."

Baby Huey stood. "Fuck them grunts."

The Mole stood next to Baby Huey. "Yeah. Fuck them grunts." He charged down the hill into the platoon of infantry.

Jesse stole a quick glance at Dave and shrugged. "What the hell?" He bounded to his feet and charged down the hill, a rebel yell on his lips as he cut through the tall grass, hot on Mole's heels. Behind him, Jesse heard the yells from

50

the throats of twenty men from the 81 platoon.

*****

They sat on the beach, Captain Eldridge and Gunny Pickering, and the Company First Sergeant in the center of the group. Eldridge moved his eyes from one man to the next. When he had completed the circle, he let a moment pass as he studied them, his peripheral vision taking in what it could of the battered twenty or so marines of the 81 platoon.

Mole massaged his jaw. Baby Huey held his hand over a tender nose. Wop stood to one side of his body, favoring his right leg. Stubby rubbed his jaw from time to time. Most of the others suffered some form of discomfort as a result of the fight but none of the injuries was serious.

"What in the hell were you thinking when you charged down that damn hill into a forty-man platoon of grunts?"

For a moment no one spoke, then Jesse said, "Personally, Sir, I was thinkin' it would be nice to have some reinforcements."

There was a nervous laugh, then Bergie said, "Hell, it didn't look to me like you needed any goddamn reinforcements. You was kicking ass from what I saw."

"What the hell were you doing watchin' me?"

"Christ, you threw two of 'em on top of me."

"Yeah, well I didn't do so bad myself," said Wop. "I had this one guy in a headlock and he.... "

Wop's voice trailed off. They fell silent, waiting for Captain Eldridge to speak. The First Sergeant and Gunny Pickering faced away from the captain, containing their smiles as best they could.

Eldridge cleared his throat. "You know, gentlemen, every once in a while there comes along an outfit that's like this one. I was in a squadron like this once. You're gonna be a tight outfit. You're gonna be a damn good combat unit."

The men held their silence.

"You're also going to end up in more shit than most of you deserve. But if most of you can stay out of the brig, you'll be one of the best fighting outfits in the Corps.

"Now, I'm only going to tell you this one time, so listen well. We don't fight other marines. If you feel an urge to fight, find somebody besides another marine. Your life may depend on that guy someday. Do I make myself clear?"

"Yessir." They answered in unison.

Eldridge looked them over again, slowly. He allowed a smile to pass his lips. "Did you whip their asses?"

"Yessir!"

Japan

Jesse sat in the snow, his back against an outcropping or rock. It was March but it felt more like January or February to him.

"Damn. It's colder'n hell out here," said Bergie as he munched on a C-ration cracker, his breath visible as a white cloud.

"No shit," said Stubby, rubbing his mittened hands together briskly.

"Just think, we got four more weeks of this cold weather training bullshit," said Mole.

"Trouble with you, Mole, is you never look at the positive side of things," said Wop.

Mole looked up at Wop from his canteen cup of lukewarm coffee. "I'll look at the positive side if you'll point-it-the-fuck out."

"If we kick ass as the guerrillas on the battalion tac test, we all get a ninety-six- hour pass our last week in Japan."

"Fat chance," said Worm. "We almost got our asses whipped by Fox Company last week."

"Yeah, almost. But not quite. We did pretty damn good under the circumstances," defended Wop.

"Under what circumstances?" asked Mac.

Jesse said, "Fox company got the highest score ever given on this test. And the Crotch has been doing it since forty-seven."

"So?" asked Baby Huey.

"So you guys are stupid," said Ish. "What Wop and Jesse are trying to say is that Fox got the highest score ever given and they didn't wipe out the guerrilla force. That means we didn't exactly sit on our asses."

The First Section, 81mm mortar platoon, H & S Company, former 1st Battalion, 7th Marines, re-designated 2nd Battalion, 3rd Marines, huddled on the lee side of a large hill on the north side of Mount Fuji. In their third week of cold weather training, the mortar platoon had been assigned to act as enemy guerrillas on a four-day tactical test taken by each rifle company in the battalion. Fox Company had been first. Golf Company was on the second day of its four-day stint.

"Third Section got killed or captured to the last man," said Bill Monroe.

Ish looked up at the oldest PFC in the first section. "Look who the hell they had in charge of the Third Section, Bill."

"Good point," agreed Bill with a nod.

"Damn. It's cold," said Jesse.

"Hey, here comes Shoe. He must have spotted something on the other side of the hill," said Baby Huey.

Shuebruk puffed into their position. "There's a couple of Jap kids coming this way."

Jeep, the First Squad leader, and always the serious one, said, "Kids? Are you sure?"

"Goddamnit, Jeep, I know what a kid looks like, even if he is a Jap. There's two kids on the other side of the hill, a boy and a girl – little fuckers – and they're coming this way."

"Could be a trap. Them damn grunts in Golf Company would stoop to anything to come out on top in this tac test," said Wop.

Jeep turned to the guerrilla teams. "Scatter out. We'll just hide from the little buggers and let 'em pass through our position. That way, if they are reporting to Golf, they'll say they didn't see anything in this area."

The marines disappeared into the dry and leafless timber, taking their rations with them.

Jesse watched silently from behind a fallen tree trunk as the two children walked casually down the hill. They stopped only ten yards from his position and sat in the snow. He glanced at Wop, only five yards away, and shrugged.

After resting a short time the two children stood and searched the area, picking up remnants of unwanted C-rations as the marines waited in their cold hiding places, shivering in the damp snow. For ten minutes none of the marines moved, nor did they breathe heavier than was necessary to sustain life, but after ten motionless minutes in the snow, Jeep stepped into the open.

"Ohio guzymas."

After an initial start, the two children smiled broadly. *"Ohio guzymas."*

The rest of the marines stepped into view. The little lips of the children broke into beaming smiles as they repeated the greeting to each and every man.

The marines communicated with the two youngsters using gestures and sounds, giving them rations and sharing their water. As the afternoon wore on and the sun began its retreat below the horizon, Jesse and Wop removed their field jackets and gave them to the two young Japanese.

"It's getting dark. They're gonna have to go home now," said Jeep.

Wop, who had appointed himself the official interpreter, gestured for the children to go home because of the approaching darkness. The little girl began to cry.

"Now look what the hell you've done. You scared her shitless," said Mole.

"Hey, man, I didn't do anything. Maybe she's cold."

"I don't know if she is or not but I know I am. If they don't go home I can't get my field jacket back. If I don't get my field jacket back, I'll freeze to death, and I'm not really into all of that, if you know what I mean," said Jesse.

The little girl ran to Jesse and hugged his leg. He looked down at her. "Where do you live? You know? Home? Mama-san?"

"Mama-san, Papa-san. Gotemba," said the boy.

"Gotemba?"

The boy nodded.

"Jesus Christ! Gotemba is fourteen or fifteen miles from here," said Wop.

Jesse turned to Jeep. "Now what do we do?"

"Shoo 'em off. We've gotta harass Golf Company tonight. They found their way up here. They can find their way back home."

Jesse looked around at the men for support. He looked back at Jeep. "We're the ones kept 'em here all day, talkin' and laughin' and eatin' C-rations. It's too dark and too cold, Jeep. We gotta take 'em home."

"What are we gonna do – ask Golf Company for a time-out? You know we can't take those kids home. Hell, they probably come up here all the time looking for brass cartridges. They'll be okay. Just tell 'em to go home."

"The little girl can't be much older'n five. The boy is probably about seven or eight. They'll never make it in the dark."

Jeep stared into Jesse's eyes. The two didn't especially like each other but each carried a grudging respect for the other. "All right, Jesse. If you wanna take 'em home – take 'em home."

"I'll go with him."

"No you won't, Wop. I'm only losing one man on this TAC test. Jesse won't get five hundred yards before he's captured by Golf Company."

"They'll let him go when they see he's got the kids," persisted Wop.

"No they won't. It's the rules of the game." Jeep turned to a staff sergeant wearing the white armband of a referee. "Isn't that right, Sergeant Mondale?"

"Them's the rules," replied the referee stoically.

Jesse picked up his M-14, propped against a tree. "To hell with the rules.

53

Stoney Livingston

I'm takin' these kids home." He picked up the little girl and placed her on his back. After the boy returned Wop's field jacket, the three moved into the heavy thicket of dead trees and began the long trek to Gotemba.

The trip to Gotemba was difficult in the darkness. Three times they altered their route to avoid Golf Company positions; once they hid from a squad-sized night patrol. The boy seemed to enjoy the game at first but he soon grew weary and cold. With three miles left in their journey the little girl began to cry. She was cold. Jesse and the boy had no heavy jacket but their brisk movement kept them warm. Jesse took the girl from his back and made her walk for almost a mile. She warmed up but stumbled and staggered from exhaustion and lack of sleep. Jesse put her on his back in "piggyback" fashion once again, the warm field jacket bundled about her. She fell instantly asleep.

They entered the streets of Gotemba near midnight. The boy let out a happy squeal as a man approached them in a stooped, brisk walk, shouting in Japanese. Jesse didn't have to be fluent in the language to know the man was their father and that he was overjoyed to see them. The boy rushed to the man's outstretched arms.

Jesse stood motionless, his rifle sling digging mercilessly into his left shoulder, arms numb from holding the girl in position on his back. He waited patiently for the peasant farmer to complete his greetings to his son. The little girl on his back awakened and called for her father. The man looked up from his kneeling position next to his son and seemed to notice Jesse for the first time.

"She's all yours, pardner." Jesse knew the man would speak no English. It didn't really matter what he said.

The farmer took his sleepy daughter into his arms and thanked Jesse profusely in Japanese – at least Jesse thought the man was thanking him.

The boy spoke rapidly and made gestures indicating a rifle and hiding. The father's eyes widened. When the boy finished speaking, the little man looked into Jesse's eyes. He took Jesse's hands in his and wept.

"Whoa. Whoa. I don't know what that little rascal said, but it wasn't all that bad."

The father stepped back and signaled Jesse to come with him. Jesse shook his head. "I've gotta get back to Mount Fuji." He pointed north.

The man motioned violently for Jesse to wait, then disappeared, leaving Jesse with the two children. It was almost ten minutes later when he returned. Jesse and the two children still stood in the middle of the deserted street. Jesse had taken his rifle from his shoulder and the blood had finally begun to flow freely into his arms.

The children's' father ran to him, excited and out of breath. He pushed some paper money into Jesse's hand and smiled. *"Arigato guzimas."*

Jesse looked at the crinkled paper bills. A thousand yen. Not quite three dollars. Not much money, even for a PFC. in the Marine Corps, but Jesse knew it was a fortune to the farmer. That was probably what had taken so long. He had to round up the money. *Probably borrowed it from several of his friends.*

Jesse grabbed the man's hands and held them tightly. He forced the money into a palm and folded the hand together. "No money. I didn't do this for money."

The man wept silently. Jesse stood, confused and embarrassed by the older man's tears. He couldn't let the man lose face. He'd heard of the Japanese committing suicide rather than face humiliation.

54

Forever Patriots

It was thirty minutes before daylight when Jesse arrived at his rally point with the guerrilla team. He found Wop in the darkness first, then the others. He called them together and gave them what intelligence he had been able to uncover on his trips through Golf Company's lines.

Jeep whispered in the darkness, "You mean, Golf's company headquarters is on that hill just south of us?"

"Yep,' answered Jesse. "And if we hurry we can move around the south side of the hill and be in position to hit 'em right at daybreak. There's a trail on this side of the hill with a steep ledge. If we leave four or five men there they can pick off the company headquarters when they try to go down the back side – away from our assault on the south side."

"Are you sure?" asked Jeep.

"Positive. I skirted the position on the way to Gotemba but I came right through it on the way back."

"Hot dog! We got their asses now," said Worm.

"Sh. Keep it down," ordered Jeep. "Okay, Jesse, Shoe, Worm, Stubby and Wop – take the trail on the north. Jesse knows where it is so he'll get you into position. The rest of us will assault the hill."

"Where does the referee go?" asked Wop.

"If you don't mind, Jeep, I'd kinda like to have him with us – just in case Golf doesn't have one with the lead elements when they come off the hill. There'll be plenty of refs in the company position."

"Makes sense to me."

"One more thing," said Jesse.

"What?" asked Jeep.

Jesse reached inside his utility blouse and extracted a bottle of *sake*. "If we each take a small shot, this thing will just make the rounds."

"Where'd you get that?" asked Stubby.

"It's a long story."

"So shorten it," said Mac.

"Those kids' father tried to give me money for bringing them home. When I wouldn't take it, he went and got me this bottle. I couldn't refuse that. He might have lost face or something."

"Hell, we can't have that." Jesse recognized Wop's voice in the darkness.

Golf Company's entire headquarters staff, including the company commander himself, was killed or captured in the mock battle that took place at dawn on that March day in 1963. The Golf Company TAC test was shortened by a day as the result of the ensuing confusion caused by the loss of all communications from the command post. The 81-mortar platoon received 96-hour passes upon the completion of all TAC tests, and for a short period of time, the First Section was the pride of the platoon.

Okinawa

Pineapple and Jesse sat in the small bar in Henoko, Okinawa. The *Dawn Bar*, like so many of the smaller bars in Okinawa, had been put off limits when the new rules requiring two separate restrooms went into effect in April. Neither Jesse

55

Stoney Livingston

nor Pineapple cared much for the new rules. They liked the small bar. Drinks were cheap and it was a quiet place. The old mama-san, who owned the bar, treated them like family and Margie, the bartender, was Pineapple's girlfriend. To top this off, both Pineapple's and Jesse's favorite songs were on the jukebox – six plays for a quarter.

Jesse reflected on all he had seen and done since enlisting in the Corps. It seemed like most of his eighteen years had been spent in the last fourteen months. During that period of time, he had seen the biggest armada of U.S. Navy ships since D-day during the Cuban Missile Crisis, a hurricane in the Carribean while on board the U.S.S. Noble, an ocean as smooth as a mirror, flying fish, dolphins, sharks, the shrine at Hiroshima, the Ginza in Tokyo, Tokyo Tower, The Panama Canal, a Shinto shrine, a huge Buddha temple, and a million other things he couldn't remember at the moment. He had just scratched the surface.

On this night, Pineapple was in one of his melancholy moods. When he was like that Jesse left him alone and drank silently, his own thoughts and the songs occupying his mind. He smiled and joked with Mama-San and Margie. Thoughts of Shannon overpowered him from time to time, especially when Elvis sang "Anything That's Part of You" at six plays for a quarter. Sometimes Mama-San and Margie interrupted his reverie by asking him to teach them English, which he did for a short while at each request, but soon his thoughts drifted back to Shannon, and Margie would smile and ask him for another English lesson.

Five marines from a tank battalion straggled into the bar. Pineapple and Jesse sat passively on their stools, glanced at them disinterestedly for a moment, then returned to their drinks.

One of the men walked to the jukebox and put in two quarters.

Pineapple turned on his barstool and spoke to him softly. "Hey, man, how about waiting until our songs have played out? They'll be done in a couple of minutes."

Without looking at the speaker, the half-drunk tanker said, "Fuck you. My money's as good as yours."

Pineapple stood six-feet-two-inches tall and weighed in at two hundred and ten pounds. He disregarded the man standing by the jukebox, having made his assessment of the man's ability prior to speaking to him, and turned his attention to the other tankers sitting at the small table only a few feet away. After a brief visual recon of his adversaries, he glanced at Jesse. Jesse met his gaze, shrugged, then nodded almost imperceptibly. He didn't want a fight but he knew one was coming.

Pineapple stood and picked the tanker at the jukebox up by the collar and the rear of the waistband on his trousers and calmly slammed his head into the wall. From that point it was difficult for Jesse to remember what happened in what order.

The remaining four tankers joined the fight instantly. Mama-San grabbed what bottles she could from the big mirror behind the bar and Margie screamed. Jesse and Pineapple were giving an excellent accounting of themselves and more likely than not would have carried the battle had it not been joined by an enemy of all marines on liberty.

"M.P.s coming! M.P.s coming!" shouted Mama-san.

Jesse and Pineapple both broke off the fight and headed for the only restroom in the small building, Jesse in the lead. Jesse dove head-first through the small bathroom window and landed on the ground outside in a combat roll, broken shards of glass spattering the ground around him. Pineapple was right behind him. The protestations of the tankers faded into the night as the two put distance between them and the *Dawn Bar* just as fast as their legs would permit.

Okinawa: Northern Training Area

"You got the cutters?" Wop whispered to Mac.

Mac looked around the barbed-wire compound of the Third Division Escape and Evasion School and nodded.

"Ten minutes after they change the guard, right?" asked Worm.

Again Mac nodded.

Worm turned to Jesse. "You got the K-Bar?"

"Not on me. It's in the corner – under my field jacket."

The Captain of the Guard's whistle sounded, notifying them of another role call. It had been the same every fifteen minutes around the clock for four days. The lack of sleep was beginning to manifest itself in short tempers.

"Fuck this shit. What if I don't get in formation – they gonna set me back two weeks?" complained Pup.

"C'mon, Pup. Shit, we're all in the same boat." Wop offered words of encouragement.

Pup reluctantly joined the ranks at stooped attention. The overhead barbed wire stood only five feet from the ground, making it impossible to stand erect.

The Marine sergeant playing the part of a Chinese communist prison commandant, complete with Chinese uniform, strolled into the compound with a sentry. He walked crouched to avoid the wire, passing down the first rank of men. The bright compound flood lights blinding Jesse's vision darkened as the commandant stopped in front of him.

"What is your name?" he asked in a voice complete with accent.

"PFC Jesse Langley."

"What is your unit?"

"PFC Jesse Langley, 2015213."

The commandant glared at him for a moment then turned to the sentry. "Take him."

Jesse glanced quickly at Wop. He was supposed to be in the escape in less than two hours. He felt despair at the thought of spending the next week-and-a half in the compound. Maybe they would end his torture session early. The sentry grabbed him by the arm and pulled him roughly from the ranks.

Jesse jerked his arm from the sentry's grasp. "Don't touch, slope-head. Man could get hurt that way."

The sentry struck him in the mid-section with the butt of his rifle. Jesse doubled up in pain but didn't lose his feet. The commandant shot the sentry a glance to let him know he had gone too far with the play-acting.

Jesse straightened himself until his head brushed the overhead wire and smiled at the sentry. "I'm glad you did that. You guys all look alike. Now I've got something to remember you by."

The sentry made a move at him but was cut off by a wave from the commandant. They marched him outside of the wire to begin his interrogation.

In the first four days, the men inside the wire had seen most of the tortures and, while not life-threatening if kept controlled, they were at the very least uncomfortable. Jesse, like all the others, had been given information to disclose in the event he was unable to endure the hardships of the school. He wondered which one of the tortures he would get tonight.

Thirty yards from the wire, near a granite hill, they stopped. The Commandant faced Jesse and said. "One more time. What is your unit?"

"PFC Jesse Langley. 2015213."

He pointed to the three iron doors in the rock. "These are quite uncomfortable. A man can neither sit nor stand the way we have carved out the rock. In ten minutes your muscles will cramp into balls the size of grapefruit. Let me ask you one more time – what is your unit?"

"PFC Jesse Langley. 2015213."

The commandant opened a door and motioned to the sentry who prodded Jesse into the dark space behind the door with his sheathed bayonet. Jesse's shoulders were wider than the cave dug into the rock and the sentry smashed his right arm when he slammed the door. Jesse stifled a cry of pain. He heard the iron bolt crash into place. He was alone in a dark space, sixteen inches deep by four feet tall by eighteen inches wide.

Jesse tried to find a comfortable position but there was none. The air was dank and suffocating. The odor of old vomit filled his nostrils. *Musta been that damn Frog. One of the guys told me he threw up in one of these holes.* He tried breathing through his mouth. It helped some but the stench was almost overpowering. The muscles in his right calf began to cramp. He tried to massage the leg but couldn't reach it. He let his mind drift. That didn't work. He thought of Shannon and forgot his pain.

He saw her walking down the hall in high school. She was crying. She was going to drop chemistry. He saw her washing a car. She splashed him with the hose. He smiled. They studied chemistry. She kissed him. There was a night in the park. A full moon. Then she was gone. She came back. They talked under an apricot tree. She graduated. A British sports car. California.

The door opened. The floodlights from the compound blinded him as he fell out of the cramped and putrid hole. The men inside the wire were gathered on the hole side of the compound. They growled menacingly at the sentries walking up and down the wire poking sheathed bayonets at them.

He heard Wop's voice above the rest. "Hey, man, this is bullshit. This is supposed to be a Division School."

Grumbles of assent followed Wop's remark. The whistle blew. The men remained against the wire, ignoring the order to form ranks. The commandant's voice blared over a loudspeaker.

"You choose disobedience in the face of hospitality but we understand it is the way you marines have been indoctrinated by your government. In order to impress upon you the need for obedience we will demonstrate the futility of disruptions and disorder. We will not tolerate lack of compliance with camp rules. This prisoner will suffer punishment for all of you. Guards, bring the prisoner to the pit." The speaker crackled and fell silent.

Jesse tried to regain his feet but his legs wouldn't support him. They felt like rubber stilts. He looked up at the two sentries standing over him. "What's cookin'?"

They grabbed him roughly under the arms and dragged him to the pit, fifteen yards south of the wire, where they threw him unceremoniously into the eighteen-inch-deep mud and doused him with two buckets of ice cold water.

He lay there, his face barely above the surface of the mud, smiling at them.

Forever Patriots

He shivered from the wet and cold.

A sentry approached with another bucket. Jesse braced himself for the cold water. Instead he was suddenly covered with salamanders and snakes. He knew the snakes were supposed to be of the non-poisonous variety but what if whoever caught them didn't know their snakes? A shiver made its way from his toes to his hairline. This time the cold had nothing to do with it.

"Whatsamatta, maline? You don't rook so happy now. You want more?"

Jesse looked up at the face of the commandant. He spit a salamander from his mouth and said, "You know what your problem is? You need to find yourself a woman."

A snake slithered across Jesse's face.

The commandant ordered another bucket and smiled wickedly as the sentry covered Jesse with more of the slimy creatures. "What is your unit?"

Jesse pushed several of the snakes and salamanders from his face and chest. "Third Salamander Battalion, Seventh Rattlesnake Regiment."

Laughter burst from within the confines of the wire.

More cold water. Several buckets of mud. They stopped long enough to let him clear his mouth and nostrils and draw a breath, then they repeated the process. They tired in twenty minutes and removed him from the pit.

Cheers rang out from inside the wire. He heard Bergie shout, "Fuck 'em, Jesse. They're fuckin' with the wrong guys this time."

"Fuck you!" It was Mac this time. The men picked up the chant. "Fuck you! Fuck you! Fuck you!" reverberated into the jungle that was the Northern Training Area on Okinawa.

The loudspeaker blared. "You malines are not as intelligent as your army brethren. The prisoner will continue to undergo indoctrination for all of you who insist on belligerency."

"Great," mumbled Jesse as two of the sentries pulled him out of the mud pit.

"Fuck You! Fuck you! Fuck you! Fuck you!" The chorus continued.

Jesse looked into the face of one of the sentries as his feet gained solid ground. "Yeah, fuck you." He pulled the sentry passed him and into the pit.

Raucous cheers from the prisoners.

A sentry fired a blank round into the air as two others rushed to the aid of their muddy comrade. A squad of sentries burst from the barracks, sheathed bayonets fixed.

"Fuck you! Fuck you! Fuck you! Fuck you!"

The muddied sentry pulled Jesse back into the pit.

"Fuck you! Fuck you!"

The squad of sentries dashed to the edge of the wire and probed it with sheathed bayonets.

"Ow! Goddamnit! You guys are gettin' too carried away with this shit." It sounded like Bergie

Three sentries dragged Jesse from the pit and shoved him violently toward the swinging cage. One of them opened the bamboo door and helped the others stuff Jesse inside. Jesse sat doubled over, his buttocks on the large bamboo shafts, his head mashed down into his knees which were forced up against his chest by the limited space in the small bamboo cage.

Jesse felt the large rope pull the cage into the night air. With sticks from the ground ten feet below, the sentries spun the cage. Dried and semi-fluid vomit covered almost every shaft of bamboo inside the cage, some of it peeling or dripping off into the night air as the cage increased rpm. Jesse staved off his body's urge to respond to the unpleasantness of his surroundings.

For more than twenty minutes Jesse endured the pain of his bent position, the bamboo pushing at him from above and below, and the stench of vomit mixed with mud and reptile fluids. The commandant ordered the spinning cage stopped. When the door was opened Jesse remained in his crouched position, unable to move his cramped muscles.

He smiled up at the face of the commandant. "You'll forgive me if I don't stand right away? I got real comfortable here and it's gonna take me a minute to get out of the mood."

The face of the commandant remained non-committal. He motioned to the two sentries. They removed him from the cage gingerly.

"Come with me," the commandant ordered.

Jesse followed on shaky legs, glancing at the men inside the wire. Bill Monroe gave him the thumbs up.

Jesse was herded into the commandant's quarters. In the small office were a desk and two chairs. Behind the desk was a curtained doorway.

"Have a seat." The commandant motioned to the chair opposite the desk. Jesse sat gingerly, waiting for them to spring their next trick. The commandant dismissed the sentries and sat behind the desk.

"Would you like a cigarette?" He offered a pack of Salem.

"Not my brand." Jesse wanted a smoke badly.

"No one will know. You did a pretty good job out there."

Do not accept favors from the enemy. Part of his training in the event he was ever taken as a prisoner of war. "If you got enough for all of us I'll be real proud to spread 'em around."

The commandant leaned across the desk. "Don't be stupid. I'm just offering you a smoke because you were left too long in the hole and things got carried away from there. You pissed off my men." The commandant had lost his accent.

Was this another trick? He wondered. "Good. I hope they stay pissed off."

The curtain behind the desk parted and First Sergeant Foreman of Fox Company stepped into the room. "What's your name, Marine?"

"PFC Langley. 2015213."

Foreman pointed to the first sergeant chevrons on his collar. "I'm not part of the school, Langley. I'm here to observe."

Jesse knew of Foreman. At age twenty-eight he was the youngest first sergeant in the Marine Corps. He was well liked by the men in Fox Company. Jesse smiled. "If you're not part of the school, Top, does that mean we can quit playin' the part for a minute?"

Foreman looked at the commandant. "Would you excuse us for a minute?"

After the other man disappeared behind the curtain, Foreman took the seat behind the desk. "Now, what did you want to say? Were you going to complain about them going too far? I saw what happened...."

"Hell no, Top. I was gonna ask you if you smoked something besides those damn menthol cigarettes. Maybe even give me a few extra for the guys in the compound."

Foreman's smile covered his face. He reached into his breast pocket and pulled out an unopened pack of Lucky Strikes. "You ever think about transferring to a line company, you call me. Keep the pack."

Jesse quickly tucked the smokes into his muddy map pocket on the inside of his utility blouse. "Thanks, Top. Now can we get back to work? I've got other business to take care of yet tonight."

Foreman's smile disappeared. He looked over his shoulder, then back to Jesse with a quick wink. "Commandant. You can have the prisoner back now."

Okinawa: Henoko

"Jesse-san number one GI. Good time all night. Alla time."

Jesse rolled over in the bed and reached for the bottle of *sake* on the stand next to him. Peggy fondled him and nibbled at his nipples as he poured a drink. "You want some, Peggy-San?"

"No. Peggy-San drink too much alla time club. Why you drink so much, Jesse-san? You no like Peggy-san?"

He put his free arm around her and drew her close. "Of course I like Peggy-San. Can't you tell?"

She felt him growing hard and smiled. "Jesse-San number one GI! Drink alla time and still give Peggy-san good time. How you do?"

Jesse smiled. "Practice."

Korea

The peter boat rocked rhythmically in the rough water, circling, waiting for the order to join the others in a line and hit the beach. They had been in the small boat for almost forty-five minutes. Despite a blistering summer sun that should have reddened them, faces were turning green.

"Goddamnit. Are we gonna spend the next ten years out here in this hollow cork or are we gonna hit the beach?" complained Mole.

"By the time we get the boats all loaded in this weather, the armistice will have been over for another ten years," offered Padre.

"Why the hell we gotta play soldier in Korea anyway?" asked Shoe.

"It's just a show of force. The ten year armistice is up and the brass is afraid the commies might invade the south again," answered Jeep. "Where were you at the briefing?"

"What the hell are we gonna do with blanks? Scare 'em to death?" asked Bergie.

"There's live ammo on the ship. I saw it," said Wop.

"That's a good place for it," said Mole. "That's just great. It's nice to know if we get hit, we got all the ammo we need out in the middle of the Godamned ocean.

Jesse looked over to Pappy. "Hey, Pap, you ain't lookin' so good. Look a little green around the gills."

Suddenly Pappy jumped up and tried to make it up the side far enough to vomit into the ocean. He almost made it but came up about four inches short. A putrid-smelling-pinkish-green fluid burst from his mouth.

"Oh shit!" shouted Mac.

The reaction was almost atomic. Men clamored for the sides. The long wait

61

Stoney Livingston

in the rough water and the foul odor and sight of Pappy's vomit set them off like a chain reaction in a nuclear bomb. The peter boat straightened and joined the line of other boats in the rough water. The flat-bottomed craft made for the Korean shore with the marines of the First Section spewing their breakfasts into the salty water splashing by the square bow.

CHAPTER FOUR: SHANNON

The main gate at Camp Pendleton diminished in the rear-view mirror of Jesse's '57 Oldsmobile as he put more distance between him and The Corps' largest base. It was over. His three years – plus a couple of week's bad time – were over.

He glanced over his shoulder at the seabag lying on the back seat of the big Ninety-Eight Olds. *What a trip.* There had been no war – not in Laos, Cuba, Korea, The Philippines, Formosa, nor at any of the other "trouble spots" he and his battalion had visited. They had become the most-traveled battalion in the history of The Corps. He had done his duty. He had served his time. He had even managed to get out of The Corps with his lance corporal stripes – probationary – but he had hung onto them.

The sun shone brightly through the early morning mist that hung over Oceanside as he hit the on-ramp to Highway 101 and headed north. With more than eight hundred dollars in his pocket and clear title to the Oldsmobile, Jesse felt good. He had his health, his sanity, and most importantly, his freedom.

He knew he would miss the guys in the outfit. He was already thinking of them. But right now the most important thing in the world to him was his freedom – his freedom and Shannon. She was less than ninety miles away; still living in Riverside.

Jesse patted Will's letter in his breast pocket. In it, Will had told him of Shannon's divorce filing. It wouldn't be final for a few months – sometime in July – but that was only a matter of time.

He hummed a happy tune as the heavy car rolled north. He wondered what she looked like; wondered if she had changed. His mind buzzed with questions. Would it be proper to tell her how he really felt before the divorce was final? He pondered long on that one. Finally, he decided it would not be proper to divulge his feelings during an interlockery period in a divorce. He'd play it cool. Just drop in to say hello, ask after her health and the kids – there were two now, a boy and a girl – and be on his way. The day after the divorce was final he'd blow into town and sweep her off her feet.

Jesse's spirits were high. After he left Riverside he'd go back to Tucson and take all the tests for special student admission to the University of Arizona. When he turned twenty-one in February he'd be eligible to enter the university as a full-fledged student. Life was beautiful.

As he drove through Weir Canyon his heart thumped in his temples. He couldn't believe he was going to get to see Shannon again. He thought briefly of all the women in all of those countries he had known. He shook his head and the thoughts disappeared. That was different. Shannon had been married then.

The sharp blast of a horn brought his attention to his driving. He looked in his rear-view mirror and saw traffic stacked up behind him for more than a mile. The man in the car behind him had his hand out of the window, fist clenched, shouting.

63

Stoney Livingston

Jesse smiled and pushed the accelerator to the floor. The rocket V-8 responded with a throaty roar and soon the line of cars looked like a long disjointed worm in his mirror.

In thirty-five minutes, Jesse sat in a phone booth at a Shell gas station in Riverside and dialed Shannon's number. He held his breath as the phone rang.

"Hello?"

It was her voice. God how he loved her voice.

"Hello?" she said again.

"Oh. Hello. Shannon?"

"Who's thi...Jesse? Is that you?"

Jesse swallowed hard. "Yeah. It's me. How are you? Everything okay?"

He heard the smile in her voice. "I'm fine, Jesse. Gee, it's good to hear from you. How are you?"

"I'm okay. Just got out of the service this morning. On my way to Arizona. Thought I'd give you a call and see if maybe I could stop in and say hello on my way through town."

"Are you in Riverside?"

"Yeah. I'm at a Shell gas station near Jefferson and Magnolia."

"You're only about six blocks from the house. Do you know the address?"

"Is it still the same as it was when you sent that card to me during the Cuban Crisis?"

"It hasn't changed."

"Is it okay for me to stop by? Just for a few minutes. I've got to get back to Arizona and get a job and apply for admission to the University," he blurted. He didn't want her to think he was planning more than a short visit.

"Is it okay? Are you kidding? You'd better. If my favorite person in the whole world can't come to my house then no one can. Are you really going to the university? Oh never mind. You can tell me all about it when you get here."

"I'll see you in a few minutes."

Jesse's hand trembled as he hung up the receiver. His heart beat wildly in his chest like a snare drum signaling a hanging. His knees felt weak. He sat for a moment in the phone booth, making a conscious effort to get his body under control.

Shannon stood in the yard as he stopped the Oldsmobile at the curb in front of her house, her white smile made more dazzling by her tanned complexion. She looked a little thinner than he remembered. She was only inches away as he stepped out of the car and closed the door. He looked into those yellow-brown eyes and stood speechless. He knew if he spoke, he would blurt out his undying love. This was not the time. He clamped his jaw tightly shut, lest a brash and foolish sound issue forth.

"You look great, Jesse. I guess the marines didn't change you all that much, huh?"

He wanted to at least give her a brotherly hug but fear held him back. "I hope not. You don't look so bad yourself for an old lady with two kids." That wasn't really what he wanted to say. What he wanted to say was, *Shannon, I love you with all my heart. I'd die for you. I _have_ died for you – a thousand times.*

She put her arms around him and hugged him quickly, almost as if she read his thoughts. Her touch unnerved him, brief as it had been.

"Come on, let's go in the house. You drink coffee?" She touched his arm. He flinched at the feel of her fingers.

64

"Only thing I like more than coffee is sour mash."

She raised an eyebrow.

"Only after the sun goes down of course – the sour mash I mean."

She laughed that beautiful laugh that made Jesse think of high school and the park and those nights of chemistry homework. She didn't look a day older now than she had then.

"Still the same old Jesse."

The lump in his throat made speech difficult. "Yeah."

She led him into the house where he waited patiently while she poured the coffee. It smelled fresh. She had probably brewed it after his call. In the livingroom they both sat on the sofa, Jesse on one end, Shannon almost in the center.

Shannon picked up a pack of Newports from the coffee table. Jesse reached into his pocket and pulled out his pack of Camels.

"God. Are you still smoking those things?" she asked.

Jesse smiled. "They suit me fine. Ain't found anything better or I'd be smokin' em." That wasn't what he had wanted to say either.

He lit her cigarette then his, with his Zippo, extinguishing the lighter between cigarettes. Shannon looked at him questioningly.

"Habit. Don't want to keep a match or a lighter lit too long. Gives the guy in the bush too much time to draw a bead if it's dark."

Shannon laughed and slapped him on the sleeve. "Jesse, you'll never change."

He almost came apart at her touch. "Is that good or bad?" he said.

Her face became serious. She looked into his eyes. "I don't know. In some ways, I wouldn't want you to change at all. In others ... I don't know. Maybe if you have to change one thing, you have to change everything, and in your case that would be awful."

"What in the world are you talking about?" he asked.

She smiled and patted him on the knee. "I don't know. It doesn't matter. So, tell me about the service."

He flinched again at her touch. "Not much to tell really. I went in to fight a war and we never had one. Now I'm out. Time to get on with things I guess. How you been? Are you doin' okay? How are the kids?"

"I'm okay and the kids are fine. They'll be awake in an hour. You came right in the middle of their nap time."

Jesse held in check his urge to put his arms around her. She was so close. He felt her without touching her. Her presence overwhelmed him. "Things didn't work out, huh?" he asked, forgetting what they had been talking about.

Shannon shook her head. "We never should have gotten married. Bill will never grow up. You were more grown up at sixteen than Bill will ever be."

"It never did me much good." He wanted to take the words back but he couldn't reach them in time. The speed of sound was too fast.

Jesse saw the hurt in her eyes. They moistened. She smiled and said, "You're better off for it."

Jesse didn't know what to say. He wanted to run. It had been a mistake to see her before the divorce was final. He could think of no appropriate response. He sipped his coffee and tried to think of something chic to say. It eluded him. Silence passed between them with the pressure of a nuclear bomb.

"How's Will?" Jesse finally said.

65

Stoney Livingston

"He's fine. I just got a letter from him the other day. He's the leader of a band and swears it's driving dad crazy. Mom is fine. She still talks about you in her letters."

"I guess I must have made an impression, huh?"

"Mom thinks you're one of a kind. Those are her exact words."

Jesse smiled. "Your mother always had a keen sense of perception."

"I agree with her. I wish things had turned out differently," said Shannon.

"You make it sound like the end of the road." Jesse smiled but his heart was crying.

"In some ways it is. Oh, life goes on, but that little bit of perfection is gone. Once it's gone, you don't ever get it back."

"So who cares about perfection? Comin' as close as you can is good enough. That's the most anyone can expect," said Jesse.

"Jesse, I've never met a guy with a more casual outlook on life than you have. I wish I could be that strong. But I can't live in a fantasyland. I see shades of grey."

Jesse wasn't sure what she meant. He cleared his throat nervously. "I don't think I live in a fantasyland, but then again, maybe I do. I kind of like it here though, no matter what it's called."

"Oh, Jesse, I remember those days in chemistry class and those nights at home. It seems like they only happened yesterday, and yet it seems like they never happened at all. Do you know what I mean?"

Jesse struggled to hide the emotions welling up inside. "Yeah, I know what you mean." He paused. "Do you have enough money to make it?" He needed the eight hundred dollars in his pocket badly but he would give it all to her if she needed it.

"We never have enough money to make it but we always make it. Don't worry about us. Mom and dad will help. We'll get by. You just get yourself in school and get a degree. What are you going to major in?"

"Aerospace engineering."

"Wow! But how can you do that without a high school diploma? Did you get a G.E.D.?"

Jesse shook his head. "Arizona doesn't accept a G.E.D. but they have a special student clause. If you're over twenty-one, pass the college entrance exam, show maturity, and pass an oral review board, they admit you as a special student. The only thing I'm not allowed to get a degree in as a special student is law and medicine. Who wants to be a lawyer anyway? Ugh."

Shannon laughed again, the whiteness of her teeth made more prominent by her tanned face. "You'll make it, Jesse. I know you will."

Jesse really didn't want to make it in college near as much as he wanted to put his arms around her and hold her for the rest of his life. His resolve to remain silent about his feelings was weakening. He glanced at his watch. "I better get going, Shannon. It's a long way to Tucson and I've got a lot of work to do once I get there."

He thought he sensed disappointment on her face but figured that was only because he wanted her to be disappointed. "But you haven't seen the kids yet," she said.

"I'll be back. I want to see them but I can't stay any longer right now." That part of his statement was true. He would become a blubbering idiot if he stayed much longer.

Forever Patriots

She stood with him and walked to the door. He turned and said, "I'll be seein' you, Shannon. If you need something, write me. I'll send you an address when I get settled."

"It's good to see you, Jesse." She put her arms around him and hugged him quickly. "You'll always be my big brother. I've always been able to count on you. Be careful. And write."

Jesse looked into her eyes and swallowed the lump in his throat. It almost choked him. "I will. I will." He turned and walked out the door to the Olds parked at the curb, Shannon's hug the only thing on his mind. He had to try the door handle three times before he was able to open the car door. He waved goodbye and watched Shannon grow smaller in the rear-view mirror until she disappeared when he turned the corner at Magnolia.

*****

Jesse exited the old grey school bus ahead of the rest of the men on the melon-picking crew and ran for the phone booth at the end of the bunkhouse. Today was the day he had decided to call Shannon. Twelve hours in the Coalinga sun, picking cantaloupe did nothing to rob his young body of energy. He felt refreshed and strong as he stepped into the booth.

The college crew from the University of Arizona had proven itself in Yuma at the beginning of the melon season. With the cancellation of the Braceros program, there had been doubt that the farmers could secure enough labor to harvest their crops. Across the southwest, Universities and college placement centers had recruited students or prospective students to fill the ranks left barren by the absence of the Mexicans. The pay was good, so Jesse had joined when contacted by the placement center at the University of Arizona. Rob, his old friend from high school, had come along, and the two were having a good time, despite the hard work.

"Hey, man," shouted Rob from the door of the bus. "Where's the fire?"

Jesse ignored him and lifted the receiver to the pay phone. He counted out the coins he had been saving and placed them carefully on the small ledge then dialed the operator and waited.

After giving his instructions to the operator and waiting some more, he listened intently as the phone rang. He couldn't believe it. His day had finally come. He had been so patient to avoid contact with Shannon until her interlockery period was over. Now he could tell her his true feelings and be done with all of his foolish, unfounded fears.

"Hello?"

"Shannon?"

"Jesse?"

"Yeah. How are you?"

"I'm fine, you rat. Why haven't you called or written before this?"

"I just thought it would be better to wait, and besides, I've been moving all over the place with a melon-picking crew. Is everything okay?"

"Everything is great. Except I haven't heard from you in months." There was playful chastisement in her voice.

Jesse paused to think how he should start his confession of love. He had planned it a hundred ways and rehearsed each way a hundred times but, now that he was at the phone, his mind went blank. Her voice captured his every thought.

67

Stoney Livingston

"I met this really neat guy, Jesse. You'd like him."

Jesse felt a hard thump in his chest. "What?"

"I met this really neat guy. His name is Chuck Hoffstedder. You'd really like him. He treats me right and he's great with the kids."

The pain in Jesse's chest became almost unbearable. "That's great, Shannon. I'm happy for you. It's about time you found a decent guy." He looked up from the phone to see Rob standing next to him, an anxious expression on his face. Jesse turned away to hide the tears he felt welling in his eyes and was vaguely aware of Rob's leaving.

"I knew you'd be happy for me. That's why you're so special, Jesse. You've always been there."

Jesse cleared his throat. "So, when's the big day?"

"December. On the tenth. I hope you can be there."

"I'll call you later and get the details. I'm out of change right now."

"Give me your number and I'll call you right back."

"No, that's okay. I'd better be going. I'll call you later and we can talk longer."

"You call me collect, Jesse Langley."

"We'll see. I gotta go now, Shannon. I wish you all the happiness in the world, Kiddo."

"Thanks, Jesse. Oh, by the way, Will wants you to get in touch with him."

"Later, Shannon. I'll call later and get his number. Right now I really gotta go." Jesse's ears vibrated with an unfamiliar ringing. He felt feint.

"Well, okay. But call this time."

"I will," he said, his own voice inaudible over the ringing in his ears.

"Bye, Jesse."

"So long, kid." He hung up the phone and walked slowly down the dirt road that led to the housing area, his mind somewhere else. He stopped under a large cottonwood, sat with his back to the trunk, and lit a cigarette. He had no notion of the passing of time.

"Where the hell you been?"

Jesse turned to the direction of Rob's voice as Rob walked toward the bunkhouse. He could barely discern him in the darkness. "Right here."

"You missed supper."

"I wasn't hungry."

"I take it things aren't going so well with Shannon?"

"I just want to be alone, Rob."

"We got an early day tomorrow. It's getting late."

Jesse lit a cigarette. "I don't really care about tomorrow right now, Rob."

Rob put his hand on Jesse's shoulder. "I'm sorry, man." He turned and walked back to the bunkhouse, leaving Jesse alone with his thoughts.

Jesse took a deep drag on his cigarette and tasted the salt from his tears.

*****

"You're leaving?" asked Rob around a mouthful of oatmeal.

"Gave the boss my notice this morning. Told him I'd be gone at the end of the week," said Jesse.

"What are you going to do?"

"Pass the salt and pepper, will you? I don't know. I'll go back to Tucson and look for a job there. I just can't stay in California anymore. I want as far from here as I can get."

"I understand how you feel but we're a long way from Riverside. Another month and the season will be over. You can make it."

"I don't want to make it, Rob," said Jesse around a mouthful of bread. "All I want is out of here. Beyond that, I don't really know, except that I want this week over and done with."

*****

Jesse listened to the radio for any late-breaking news of the conflict in Vietnam and let his mind drift back to the first day he had seen Shannon. He moved forward in time until he arrived at the present with an empty whiskey bottle in his hand. It had been almost a week since he had left the melon crew in Coalinga, California and he hadn't drawn a sober breath since. He wondered what it would be like to be twenty-one years old and not have to worry about under-age drinking laws.

He stood on unsteady feet and staggered from the apartment to his motorcycle parked outside. He mounted the Triumph uncertainly, nearly tipping it over. After two kicks at the starter, the 650 cc engine roared to life. He pulled onto Sixth Avenue and headed south, toward the city of Nogales, sixty-five miles from Tucson.

As the wind slapped his face at seventy-miles-per-hour, Jesse's emotions ran the gamut from anger to ecstasy to frustration. His thoughts bounced from Shannon to Viet Nam to the University of Arizona. He pushed south, increasing his speed.

Jesse disliked the Marine Corps. The often-misguided use of misplaced authority was more than he could tolerate at times, but things would surely be different in the wartime Marine Corps.

He had served three years in the infantry but had not seen combat – no real shooting war. All of the men in his family since the Revolutionary War had fought for their country. His mother and father had related stories of family history and told him that, during the Civil War, there had been family members on both sides of the conflict. He wondered if military service counted if you didn't fight a war.

He slowed and turned west from the highway and into the desert, giving little thought to the dangers of such carelessness – until he ran into a barbed wire fence.

He was thrown clear of the fence as his motorcycle came to a sudden stop, entangled in the prickly wire. He felt for broken bones and found none as he lay on his back on the soft desert floor. He put his head back onto the ground and studied the moon with a sigh. "You got any idea what the hell I'm doin' here?" he asked the moon. The moon answered with a bright but silent smile.

"C'mon, old friend, you got any suggestions? I'm in a helluva mess. What the hell should I do? Those are my buddies over there."

The moon's response did not change. He stood and moved to his fallen motorcycle, the effects of the liquor consumed earlier obliterating any pain.

"Even the moon thinks I'm losin' it," he said to his Triumph as he pulled a pair of side cutters from the small tool box mounted under the seat.

He cut the three-strand fence and disengaged his bike from the tangled mess of wires. Disgustedly, he threw the last strand away from his machine.

69

Stoney Livingston

"Damned barbed wire," he mumbled as he mounted his Triumph and restarted the engine.

He drove to San Xavier Mission, southwest of Tucson, and parked his bike on the small hill overlooking the mission from the east.

Jesse was not a person given to attending church. He wasn't so certain there was such a thing as a god, but he thought of the old mission as a friend, almost an animate object. He envisioned Father Kino and the Papago Indians toiling in the hot Arizona sun to construct this monument of man to the Christian God of Catholicism. It seemed like a strange way to pass the time to him but he was glad they had been so inclined. He stood next to the Triumph and admired the mission. He felt a kinship with the two-hundred-year-old structure and its builders. Ghosts whispered to him, but the message wasn't clear.

He wondered if the unfinished tower was really the result of one of the Indians falling to his death, as he had been taught in grade school, or if the Spanish Crown had simply run out of money with which to complete the project.

He lit a cigarette and took in the silence of the desert. Somewhere, not far away, a coyote howled into the night.

"I know just how you feel. That about sums it up for me too," he said softly to the unhearing coyote.

He took in the beauty of the old mission and tried to convince himself that his personal problems were trite when compared to the total scope of all that was man and his history and his future, but he was unsuccessful. He experienced self-pity and did not like what he experienced.

What the hell's wrong with me? Is it Shannon that's still driving me nuts, or is it my buddies over there in Viet Nam? Or is it simply the fact that I've gotta find out what I would really do under fire? What if I ran? How could I, with all the training I've had?

Shannon, help me. Do I have to go through my whole damn life without help from somebody? No, you won't have time to help me. You'll be getting married in a few months. That takes a lot of time, I guess.

Screw it. I don't need any help from anybody. I'll make it on my own, just like I always have.

CHAPTER FIVE: CAMP PENDLETON

Jesse sat in an armless chair facing the Marine recruiter in the downtown Tucson recruiting office. Thoughts of San Xavier Mission lingered in his mind, last night a fuzzy dream.

"I can't take you back in for just a year. You've been out more than thirty days," said the brightly polished staff sergeant.

"What's the minimum I can go?" asked Jesse.

The staff sergeant held his chin between the thumb and forefinger of his right hand. "I can get you in for two years but that carries no guarantees. That's the minimum."

"Two years? I don't wanna win the war all by myself. I just wanna fight my share of it."

The staff sergeant smiled. "That's the best I can do."

"Do I get Two-Three?" asked Jesse.

"I can't guarantee a specific outfit on a two-year enlistment, but if you want to go for three, I can give you whatever outfit you want."

Things were not going the way Jesse had anticipated. There was no way on this earth he would re-join the Marine Corps for three years. He had already done that and he wasn't up to another round. He studied the recruiter carefully, searching for any sign the man might be bluffing. He saw none.

"Will I at least be assigned to Vietnam in my primary M.O.S. on a two-year enlistment?"

The recruiter looked through a stack of papers. After several moments, he looked up at Jesse and smiled. "I don't see any problem with that at all. With an MOS of 0341, you won't have a problem. Mortarmen are in high demand."

"Okay, sign me up for two years – but I don't want to spend the rest of my life in California. I came to fight, not play war-games at Camp Pendleton."

Thirty-six hours later, Jesse left Tucson on a Greyhound Bus destined for Staging Battalion, Camp Pendleton, California. The trip was a grab bag of emotions for him. Even as the bus crossed the Colorado River into California he couldn't believe he had re-entered the Marine Corps. Never was a man happier to leave an institution than he had been the morning he had passed through the main gate at Camp Pendleton for what he had thought would be the last time. Now, as he looked at the river, he wanted to return to Arizona and, yet, he wanted to be in Vietnam. The thought of Camp Pendleton was unsettling. He hoped the staging would be over in a week or two and he would be on his way to Vietnam.

The bus arrived in Oceanside, California just in time to greet the pink wispy clouds that covered the early morning sky. Jesse began to have serious second thoughts as the Greyhound lumbered down Hill Street on its way to the depot. Oceanside was not his favorite spot in the world. He didn't really know why but he despised the town. Perhaps he associated Oceanside with the peacetime Marine

Corps, which, to his way of thinking, was the epitome of stupidity and boredom. He felt that Oceanside was simply a civilian extension of Camp Pendleton.

The air brakes on the bus shooshed loudly as the driver stopped at the rear of the depot. Jesse remained seated, wondering if he should just stay on the bus and continue his journey to wherever he might end up. The other passengers shuffled down the aisle, bumping into each other in their efforts to set foot on solid ground and stretch their cramped muscles.

Even after the last passenger dropped out of sight through the front door of the bus, Jesse sat, looking at what he could see of Oceanside through the windows, remembering his prior tour of duty in the Corps. His heartbeat quickened as the thought of running away flashed through his mind.

His desperate thoughts were interrupted by the bus driver. "This is the end of the line, Bub. You've gotta get off here."

Jesse looked up. "Yeah, it's the end of the line all right." He stood, retrieved his handbag, and walked to the exit.

As he stepped onto the asphalt he noticed two Marine MPs. One of them addressed a group of nine or ten men. Jesse recognized most of them as passengers on his bus. The MP explained they would be providing transportation to Mainside, Camp Pendleton for all those reporting to Staging Battalion.

Jesse smiled as he thought how different this was than reporting to boot camp in 1962. He fell in with the group and boarded a military bus for Camp Pendleton.

As the bus passed through the main gate, Jesse felt a thumping in his chest. His breathing was quick and shallow.

"You all right, man?"

He turned to the big man sitting next to him. "Yeah. I guess I was just thinking about my first tour. It all seems so unreal. I can't believe I'm back here."

"I know what you mean. I sure as hell never had any intention of coming back when I left."

"What made you come back?" asked Jesse.

"I don't know. I wasn't doing much in civilian life. Couldn't find a decent job. Times were hard. It just seemed like the right thing to do, I guess. How about you?"

Jesse stared blankly at the back of the man's head in front of him. "I don't know. I thought I knew, but I don't. Not really. Lots of reasons."

"Well, it's a place to live. And we can kick a little ass while we're at it. I've never been to Indo-China. How about you?"

"What? Oh." Jesse pulled himself out of his thoughts. "Yeah, I was there for about a month in '63."

"What's it like?"

" All I can remember is hot and humid," said Jesse.

The bus stopped at Staging Battalion Headquarters and emptied its cargo. Each man was assigned a staging company. After reporting to Alpha Company Headquarters, Jesse was assigned to the First Platoon. He strolled briskly to the platoon commander's office, his arms unaccustomed to the weight of the seabag he carried. The platoon commander, a young second lieutenant, looked him over as Jesse stood at attention in front of his desk, the seabag at his feet. After a much longer time than a first lieutenant would have taken, he said, "At ease, Lance Corporal. My name's Colson."

Jesse stood at ease in front of Colson's desk as the lieutenant read his orders. Colson looked up from the official papers and said, "So you re-enlisted to go to Vietnam?"

"Yes sir." Jesse wished this damned lieutenant would just give him a rifle and a plane ticket to Saigon and forget the formalities.

"Well, we hope to have the battalion formed in three or four weeks. In the meantime, you'll have to get your shots, draw your seven-eighty-two gear, get fitted for uniforms, go over your records at headquarters, take a physical and take classes in your primary MOS."

Jesse's eyes hardened. "Sir, I was told I'd be sent to Vietnam right away. I don't need to be fitted for uniforms. I brought my old gear with me."

Colson paused, seeming to enjoy Jesse's disappointment. "Marine, under the circumstances, three or four weeks *is* right away. And as far as your uniforms are concerned, you're entitled to a complete re-issue on your two-year enlistment. You probably don't have the new dress greens anyway – do you?"

"Begging the Lieutenant's pardon, Sir, but I think the new dress greens look like hell. If I wanted to look like a dogface, I would have joined the Army. Can I just skip the dress uniforms and pick up my combat gear so I can get to Vietnam?"

Lieutenant Colson's face reddened. "You're in the Marine Corps, Langley. You *will* act like a Marine. You *will* dress like a Marine. And you *will* show the proper respect for an officer. Is that clear?"

"Yessir, that's clear. It's also clear that while some tailor is fittin' me for dress uniforms, my friends are dying in Viet Nam. I apologize for any insubordination. I had just hoped that some things had changed with a war goin' on."

Colson looked unsure, his polished gold bars losing some of their luster. He glanced up at Jesse. "Report to Staff Sergeant Ribbon in First Platoon. He's in the next barracks to the west."

Jesse stood at attention. "Aye, Aye, Sir. Will that be all?"

Colson started to speak but didn't carry through. "That'll be all."

Jesse did an about-face and left the room.

Staff Sergeant Ribbon was a Marine of twenty-five years. He had survived the landing on Iwo Jima the day Jesse was born. He was a veteran of the Chosin Reservoir in Korea and numerous bar fights before and since. He had seen the Corps completely desegregated – much to his dismay at first – but when he found that blacks had the same ratio of good to bad Marines as did whites, he wholeheartedly supported a mixed Marine Corps. The only important fact to Ribbon was that the Marine Corps remain the best fighting unit in the world. He had no use for civilians or members of other armed forces but would risk all for another Marine: black, brown, yellow, red or white.

"So you came back in to go to Vietnam, huh?"

Jesse found himself staring at the battle ribbons on Sergeant Ribbon's uniform and wondering if the good sergeant had changed his name to match his uniform.

"Yeah. I guess I'm just a hard learner. Where did you get all those medals? I know it wasn't in a staging battalion," replied Jesse as he tried to identify each one.

"Some in the Pacific, some in Korea, some even in peacetime. Hell, they give medals out too easy nowadays."

"I ain't never been overly impressed by medals, but I gotta admit, I'm impressed by that collection."

"They're a pain in the ass to pin on every morning, but the old man wants me in full uniform every day. Says it's an inspiration to the rest of the men."

"A Navy Cross, a Silver Star, two Bronze Stars with Combat V, Commendation Medal, four Purple Hearts and more damn campaign medals than a six-term senator, and you say they're a pain in the ass to pin on?" Jesse studied the Navy Cross at close range.

Sergeant Ribbon studied Jesse. "Think about it a minute. You got any marksmanship badges?"

"Yeah."

"What?"

"Expert rifle and expert pistol."

"Do you like pinnin' them damn things on every morning?"

"No, but there's a helluva difference between an expert rifle badge and a Navy Cross," said Jesse.

"Not when you first get it there ain't. Hell, I remember gettin' a goddamn sharpshooter badge with the '03 in boot camp back in forty. I slept with that damn thing for a month. Then I was satisfied just to wear it. Then it became a pain in the ass whenever I had to change uniforms. I'd lose it and have to replace it or have my ass chewed out by some damn second lieutenant."

"Sorta like Colson?" asked Jesse.

Sergeant Ribbon chuckled softly. "I see you met the little rooster. I think he'll be okay when he gets a little time in. He's still wet behind the ears. He may be a little older'n you, but he's still younger, if you know what I mean?"

Jesse nodded. He liked this big, barrel-chested staff sergeant.

Ribbon continued, "He's a pretty tough little sonofabitch. He was some kind of middleweight boxing champion in one of those Ivy League colleges. That college is all that's wrong with that boy. Soon's he gets it outa his system, he's gonna make a damn good marine."

"Maybe so, but I hope I don't have to stay here and wait for him to make the grade. I want out of Camp Pendleton as soon as I can get out. I came to fight in Vietnam with my old outfit, not wet-nurse second lieutenants in the States."

Sergeant Ribbon looked at Jesse, his expression saddening, the sides of his mouth drooping slightly. "Don't be in such a hurry to die, son. Someday you're gonna find something to live for, instead of somethin' to die for. If you hurry too fast, you won't get in the living part."

"Maybe, but right now all I want to do is go to Vietnam and get it over with."

Sergeant Ribbon shook his head. "Well, find an empty rack and wall locker. You're one of the first ones to report in so you'll have a nice selection. Nothin' going on for a while. At 1300, report here for orientation by your favorite lieutenant."

Jesse smiled as he moved toward the far end of the barracks. "Thanks, I needed that."

At 1300 hours, Jesse reported to the west end of the barracks for orientation by Lieutenant Colson. Several other men had reported in since Jesse had last spoken to Sergeant Ribbon, and there were no less than twenty-five men in various modes of dress, ranging from military tropicals to T-shirts and Levis, all of them milling about nervously, waiting for Colson to speak.

Lieutenant Colson cleared his throat. "All right, Marines, form a semi-circle."

There was a short period of shuffling, moving footlockers and bunks, and settling down, then Colson spoke again. "Gentlemen, look around you. Every man in this room, with the exception of our staff, is fresh from civilian life." He paused. "That's right, everyone of you has returned to the Marine Corps from civilian life. Every one of you got out of the Corps to pursue a civilian lifestyle. But you're all back in. Why? Well, I can't say for certain, but I'll bet recent developments in Vietnam may have something to do with it."

The returning Marines cheered raucously. Jesse stood silently, waiting for the lieutenant to say something worth listening to.

Colson continued. "I know you're all anxious to get down to business, as was clearly pointed out to me this morning by one among you." His eyes rested momentarily on Jesse. "But there are a few things that have to be taken care of."

A chorus of groans emitted from the group.

Colson held his hands, palms forward, to quiet the men. "The Marine Corps now finds itself in a rather unique position. We have many well-trained men like you, re-enlisting from civilian life. This staging battalion is to be formed of 'seasoned civilians.' To my knowledge, it's the first time in the history of the Marine Corps that this has ever been done."

Cheers and smiles from the troops greeted this news.

"Of course, you're only forming a staging battalion. You will not be forming a new battalion. Once the staging battalion is formed, it will be sent to the far east and you will be individually assigned to existing units in Okinawa or Japan or, possibly, Vietnam. It all depends upon how things develop between now and then."

Someone in the rear said, "When do we go?"

Other voices echoed the question.

Colson answered, "You'll all be going as soon as the battalion is up to strength. In the event the battalion isn't T.O. within four weeks, graduating recruits from Parris Island and San Diego will fill us out and we're on our way to southeast Asia."

The men were divided on the issues of leaving and working with recruits. A mixture of cheers and groans greeted Colson's words.

"In the meantime, gentlemen, you will participate in close-order drill, inspections, field days, P.T., guard duty, and the various and sundry things that make up a marine's life in garrison duty."

A deep groan, almost a grunt, burst forth from the group.

"You will also attend classes in guerrilla warfare, jungle fighting, mines and booby traps – and you will be given an orientation on Vietnam."

The men fell silent.

Colson spoke for another fifteen minutes, outlining the schedule for the remainder of the week, giving only brief glimpses beyond that time.

That afternoon, Jesse received his inoculations. Since his old service record had not yet arrived, he was given every shot required as though he were a new recruit. When he arrived back at the barracks with arms that were stiff and sore from the inoculations, he noticed a new man placing his gear in the locker next to his own.

"Howdy," he greeted the newcomer.

"Same old shit," replied the man dryly. Jesse liked him immediately.

Jesse offered his hand. "Jesse Langley."

"Joe Fitzgerald. How long you been here?" Joe offered his hand.

"Since this morning."

Joe Fitzgerald was a small man by Marine Corps standards – a full inch

75

shorter than Jesse's five-feet-nine-and-one-half inches. His blond hair was cropped in a flattop, giving the appearance that he was even lighter than his one hundred fifty-five pounds.

"Is everybody here straight from civilian life or what?" asked Fitzgerald.

"As far as I know they are. How about you? When did you get out?" Fitzgerald replied. "Fifty-three. At the end of the Korean War."

"You don't look that old."

"My next birthday I'll be thirty-five."

"Okay, old man. My next birthday I'll be twenty-one, but it's the miles, not the years that's important, right?"

"Yer right. When's chow? I'm starvin'."

"Four o'clock is first call," answered Jesse.

"You mean sixteen hundred don't you?"

"Oh yeah, I forgot. I guess I've gotta be retrained. Chow is at sixteen hundred hours for you folks that can't tell time in civilian anymore."

The rest of the week was a busy one for the staging battalion. But the week following – uniforms drawn, inoculations completed, insurance forms filled out and the majority of the detail work performed – boredom set in. Boredom was soon followed by anxiety. As the ranks of the battalion began to grow, tension grew accordingly.

Lieutenant Colson organized two flag football teams and made arrangements with the battalion commander for two hours of practice in the afternoons. This seemed to help the morale problem, even among the men who didn't play. The non-players took sides and supported one team or the other. Colson didn't appear able to understand why there was so much non-player support, but Sergeant Ribbon had no problem identifying the reason for so much enthusiasm among the non-players. As coach of the "White" team, he was in the forefront of supporting non-players with a bet of $150 on Friday's game. Every man in the platoon made a bet of some size, ranging from $5 to $150. Failure to place a bet was tantamount to a slap in the face to Marine Corps tradition.

Friday morning of his second week at staging battalion, Jesse put on his football shorts, white shirt, sneakers, and flags, and reported to the area used by his team for practice. Even though he wanted to be in Vietnam, he was resigned to the fact that he must wait his turn. In the meantime, football was certainly preferable to close-order drill – even flag football. Jesse loved to play football. In high school he had played end as a freshman and halfback as a sophomore. Sergeant Ribbon had made him a quarterback on the white team and he enjoyed it even more than the other positions he had played. He threw a football hard and fast and possessed an uncanny accuracy.

"Hey, Jesse."

At the edge of the playing field, Jesse turned to the voice. It looked like Will Hunt striding in his direction. Jesse walked briskly toward him. PFC stripes were proudly displayed on Will's tropical uniform. The two men hugged and shook hands.

"Will, what the hell are you doing here?"

"I should ask you that question. Are you or are you not, the biggest hater of the Marine Corps on record?"

"I sure as hell hope so," replied Jesse. "But that still doesn't explain your

76

presence. Where the hell did you get that uniform? You steal it or something? You can get in a lot of trouble for that, you know."

"I'm a legal clerk at division legal," answered Will.

"In the Crotch? You're in the Crotch?"

"Made PFC out of boot camp," boasted Will.

"No kidding? It's sure good to see you. I only wish it wasn't in a Crotch uniform. Are you crazy? They could send you to Vietnam. I can't believe this."

"Not me. That kind of duty is for you grunts." Will displayed his ever-present smile.

They both laughed and Jesse felt relief. He didn't want Will going to Vietnam. "God, it's great to see you, Will. How's your folks?"

"Fine. Dad's getting a little crotchety, but mom's still the same. Jerrie and Jimmy are doing just fine."

"You know I'm not really interested, but how's Shannon?"

"She's doing great." Will looked away. "I guess you know about Chuck?"

Jesse swallowed the lump in his throat and nodded. "I'm happy for her, Will." He turned away and walked toward his team, not wanting Will to see the tears welling in his eyes. Will caught up with him and walked alongside.

"What're you doing this weekend?" Will asked.

"No plans, really. You got something in mind?"

"Hell, I don't know. I got some wheels and I thought if you wanted to, we could go up to Disneyland or Knotts Berry Farm, or whatever," replied Will. Then he added, "I know my folks would like to see you. They're living in Riverside now. We could have dinner on Saturday and kind of just lay back in the cuff – you know what I mean?"

"Sounds like a winner to me. When do you get liberty?" said Jesse.

"I'm off now. How about you?"

Jesse replied. "I gotta practice this morning for a football game; then, this afternoon we go out and play. As soon as we've won, I'm off till five o'clock Monday morning."

Will laughed. "You sound like you've got it all figured out."

"I do. Mostly. At least I hope I do. If we lose, I'll be mooching offa you all weekend."

Will said, "I'll go get my gear ready. I'll come back, watch the game, and we split when it's over."

"Sounds like a good plan. I'll see you after noon chow." Jesse trotted onto the practice field.

*****

Will laughed and recounted the game from a spectator's point of view as he drove north on Highway 101. "That was so damn funny when you hit that big guy in the nuts with the football and the fight started. Then when you guys made that touchdown on the next play, I thought for sure it was really going to hit the fan."

Jesse pulled $150 from his left breast pocket. "That wouldn't really have made much difference. We ended up with the money."

Will laughed again. He swerved to miss a construction barricade. "Think they'll ever get this freeway completed from Oceanside to LA?" he asked as he dodged more barricades.

"Yeah, probably about the time it's obsolete," said Jesse, sipping on a bottle

77

Stoney Livingston
of beer.

The two spent Friday night at Disneyland. When the park closed, they bought a case of beer, using Jesse's phony military I.D. card to establish his age, and returned to their motel room, where they drank beer and reminisced about high school until four in the morning. Jesse had many questions about Shannon but held them in check, asking only one or two casual ones as they talked of old times.

Both awoke at eight. They were checked out of the room and on their way to Knott's Berry Farm by nine. The day dragged for Jesse. He was anxious to visit Will's parents – and who could tell? Maybe Shannon would drop by. At noon he suggested they leave for Riverside. Will, who always seemed happy and agreeable, was all for the early departure.

As they searched for an exit from Knott's Berry Farm, Jesse joked with Will, looking over his left shoulder while he walked past the corner of a building in the old west exhibit. He didn't see the two young women approaching on his right. He walked into the one nearest him, sending her sprawling onto the plank sidewalk. Quickly he stooped to assist her to her feet. "I'm sorry. I didn't see you. You okay?"

The young woman stood and jerked her arm from Jesse's grasp. "Why don't you watch where you're going? I don't need your help. Take your hands offa me." The girl's voice was loud, indignant.

Jesse knew his face turned a shade of crimson. "Are you sure you're okay? I'm really sorry. I didn't see you, honest."

"That's real original."

Jesse's face went from crimson to purple. "You think I did that deliberately?"

"Guys have done worse," came the tart reply.

Jesse stared at her. He regained his composure rapidly as he became assured she wasn't injured. His embarrassment grew to anger. She was most definitely a pretty young brunette by any man's standards, but a little too young, thought Jesse, to be so certain that guys would go to such extremes to meet her. He looked her square in the eyes and said, "I told you I was sorry and I am. And I'll tell you something else: I've said 'no' to prettier girls than you, and my genius wouldn't allow me to pull the old 'bump-into-her-on-the-sidewalk' trick, just so I could speak to your pretty face."

"Oh? What's your style? A wolf whistle?" she replied tartly.

"These guys bothering you, sweet thing?"

Jesse turned to see three young men about his own age, standing five or six feet to his left. He made his assessment in less than a second. He left himself no time for fear. "Which one of you wants to know, and how many of you want to do something about it?"

The abruptness of his words and his total lack of fear seemed to momentarily confuse the three, and before any one of them could form a reply, a female voice said, "Everything is okay, guys. My sister and fiancé are always causing a scene. Thanks anyway."

As the three young men shrugged, shook their heads and walked away, Jesse turned to the voice. The voice had a Long Island accent, yet it was soft. He looked into the face of the most beautiful redhead he had ever seen. Her emerald green, almond-shaped eyes, set in a flawless complexion, framed by shining auburn hair, drew the breath from his body.

In his concern for the brunette, he had totally ignored her companion. She stood only inches from him, not moving. She was speaking. At least her lips were

78

moving. *Damn. Those are without a doubt the prettiest lips in the world,* he thought.

"... matter?" she asked.

"Pardon?" asked Jesse stupidly.

"I asked if something were the matter," she replied.

Jesse looked into deep green eyes. He wondered if they were really that color or if his own eyes were deceiving him. He shook his head. "No. I don't think so." He lost track of what he was saying. There was a short pause, then he continued, "But I think your sister has got me all wrong. I didn't mean to run her over. I didn't see her."

"I know," replied the redhead. "And she's not my sister. She's a friend of mine."

"But you said...."

"I know, but it was all I could think of on short notice that might easily explain the argument," interrupted the redhead pleasantly.

Jesse continued to look into the emerald seas of her eyes, oblivious to the rest of the world. "It worked pretty well. You had me convinced."

"From what I saw, it was probably a good thing for them." Her eyes seemed to sparkle when she said it.

"You don't know how right you are on that one," said Will, who had been standing quietly nearby. He moved forward, offering his hand. "Hi. I'm Will Hunt, and my partner here is Jesse Langley."

"My name is Barbara and my feisty friend is Cindy," offered the Long Island accent.

Will shook Barbara's hand, then Cindy's. Jesse nodded to Cindy silently and shook Barbara's hand. Her grasp was warm and firm. He didn't want to release her hand. He didn't want to release any part of her. Her touch caused a warm feeling to flow from his hand, up his arm and into his chest. Her eyes seemed to sparkle when they met his. He wondered if it was his imagination.

"Why do you keep staring at me?" she asked, the corners of her eyes squinting in a smile.

Jesse let go of her hand and looked quickly away. "I'm sorry. I don't know. I mean, am I?"

"Is my make-up mussed?"

"You're not wearing any."

Barbara smiled. "See, you *are* staring."

"Yeah, I guess you're right. I was staring. You got a steady boyfriend?"

Barbara turned to Will. "Your friend doesn't waste much time, does he?"

Will laughed. "He never did, but he'll be leaving California pretty quick and I guess he's kinda outdoing himself."

Barbara turned back to Jesse. "Are you in the service?"

"Yeah, for a while."

"No kidding? Me too. At least I will be next month."

"You? In the service?" asked Jesse.

Barbara nodded.

"What branch?" asked Will.

"The Marine Corps."

"The Marine Corps? We're both in the Marine Corps and neither one of us has ever seen a W.M. like you," said Jesse.

"No kidding? Where are you stationed?" asked Barbara.

79

Stoney Livingston

From that point, the conversation was smooth and relaxed, though Jesse didn't speak much to Cindy. The four had a late lunch and spent the rest of the afternoon together. They toured the amusement park for a short while, then hopped into Will's '56 Chevy and drove to Huntington Beach. They talked and laughed and generally had a good time. By the time they dropped the girls off in Buena Park, at Barbara's real sister's house, Jesse and Cindy were managing short sentences to each other.

After meeting Barbara's real sister, Nancy, the two young marines said their good-byes. As Jesse turned to leave, Barbara said, "Jesse."

He turned to face her and she kissed him lightly on the lips. "Thanks. I had a great time. And the answer to your question is no. There is no steady boyfriend."

*****

Jesse didn't speak for the first thirty minutes of the trip to Riverside. His lips still tingled from Barbara's kiss. As they drove through Weir Canyon, he looked absently at the rounded green hills. The color of Barbara's eyes was darker, deeper, richer. "She was sure one beautiful girl."

Will laughed. "No kidding."

"What bothers me is that she seemed like more than just a beautiful girl."

"I could be wrong, but it looked to me like she kinda went for you in a big way." Will was laughing again.

"Why?"

"Why?" repeated Will.

"Yeah. That's what I said – why?"

Still laughing, Will replied, "How the hell would I know? Maybe you've got some kind of message for the ladies or something. What's the matter, don't you think she liked you?"

"Yeah, I think so, but I wonder why. I even wonder why I liked her. Hell, I just met her. Sure, she's beautiful and sexy, and all that, but I actually liked her as a person. You know what I mean?"

"Yeah, I know what you mean." Will paused. He looked briefly at Jesse. "This is the first time I've heard you say anything like that about a gal since my sister."

"Oh, it's nothing like I feel about Shannon," defended Jesse, "but it *is* a feeling of some kind. Some kind besides sex that is. The thing that bothers me is that I don't know why. She's definitely a beauty, and fun to be around, and she's ..."

"Classy," offered Will.

"Maybe that's it. She has class." Jesse thought for a moment. "But someone that good-looking always seems to have a little more class than they might really have."

"I don't know about that. I realize, old buddy, that you didn't even remember Cindy after you saw Barbara, but she was a fox-and-a-half. Barbara has more class in her little finger than Cindy does in her entire, luscious little body."

"Maybe so. Maybe you're right. Hell, I don't know. Forget it. How much longer to your folks' place?"

*****

Jesse's reunion with the Hunts was a pleasant one. He had always liked Will's father. Jesse found him amusing, though the elder Hunt took some of his own

80

Forever Patriots

statements very seriously. Rarely did Jesse agree with him, but his disagreements were always lighthearted, from politics to football.

Mrs. Hunt was as pleasant as any person Jesse had ever known. Her disposition was enough to light a darkened room.

Will's younger brother and sister were both big surprises to Jesse, who had not seen them in four years. Jimmy was fourteen and Jerrie was nine. Both had grown considerably.

Mrs. Hunt made a big to-do over Jesse re-entering the Marine Corps to serve in Vietnam – to the point where he became a little embarrassed. He was grateful when Mr. Hunt joked about the whole situation and he was able to reply with a few funny remarks of his own. It was a happy reunion with old friends and Jesse found himself wishing it were some four-and-a-half years ago. He would do things much differently. At the very least he would tell Shannon he was in love with her. He missed her in this house. It felt like she should be here but she wasn't.

*****

Monday afternoon, Jesse called Will at the base legal office and made arrangements to borrow his car for the evening.

He had only one sports coat, which he wore for the occasion. He purchased a tie in Oceanside and drove to Barbara's sister's house in Buena Park, dressed for dinner. After being greeted by Nancy, he waited five nervous minutes, conversing with her, not sure of what he was saying, until Barbara walked into the room. Once again, he was speechless.

She walked up to him and took his arm. "Hi, Jesse. You look nice all dressed up."

He attempted to appear casual as he examined her countenance quickly. She wore a blue chiffon dress, with a modest cut to slightly above her breasts. "You don't look all that bad yourself."

Barbara turned to her sister. "Don't wait up, Nan. We may be late."

"That's okay, I like your guy. I'm not going to worry."

"Thank you. It was nice seeing you again, Nancy."

"You kids have a good time."

Once in the car, Barbara said, "You know, that's the first time in my experience that Nan ever said anything like that. Normally, she doesn't say much of anything. Normally, I don't go out much. I think she approves of you."

"The woman obviously has impeccable taste."

Barbara smiled. She sat in the center of the bench seat, not quite touching him but near enough for Jesse to feel her presence. He looked forward with anticipation to dinner. He wanted to know more about this girl who affected him in a way he could neither explain, nor understand.

He glanced at her. "Help me find this restaurant. I have no idea where it is."

*****

After several tense moments at the restaurant, the maitre de located Jesse's reservation, scribbled on a scratchpad by a disinterested employee who shouldn't have been answering the phone in the first place. He seated the young couple amid several apologies and sincere wishes for a pleasant meal. Jesse was embarrassed by the episode but Barbara lessened his self-consciousness by remaining at ease and assuring him that it didn't really matter.

81

Her tact and maturity began to erode his self-confidence. He should have been less flustered by the mix-up than he had been. He had wanted everything to be perfect, and when the reservation couldn't be located right away, he had nearly panicked.

"What are you thinking so hard about, Jesse?"

"Oh, nothing really. Do you go out often?"

She smiled and laughed softly. "You wouldn't believe me if I told you how rarely I go out."

"You're right. I'd find that hard to believe."

"It's true."

"But why? You've got to be one of the best-looking girls in the whole state of California. You shouldn't have any trouble finding a date."

She sipped from her water glass. "Dating is a two-way street. Both parties have to be interested. I just guess I haven't been very interested in most of the guys out here. I'm not into surfers, nor academicians."

"Why me?" he asked.

"For a variety of reasons."

Jesse began to feel a little uncomfortable and wasn't really sure he wanted the answer, but he pressed on. "Give me an idea. I can't think of any special reason, except maybe that I'm in the Corps, just like you."

"That was my initial reason. I really just wanted to talk to you and Will and find out what I could about the Marine Corps from someone who was part of it, but when we went out to lunch and down to Huntington Beach, I began to like you. You and Will both. I had a great time and we really didn't do anything all that exciting. It was just good clean fun. To tell you the truth, that was the most honest fun I've had in years."

"You're kidding?" he said.

"No, I mean it. You were a lot of fun in a group of four but I wasn't sure what it would be like to be out with you alone."

"Besides almost not getting us into this place, how am I doing?" he smiled nervously.

"You're the same person. I think that's why I was attracted to you. I may be wrong, but I don't think there's a phony bone in your body."

"You've never played poker with me." He smiled broadly.

The waiter placed the wine list before Jesse. "Would you like to order some wine, sir?"

Jesse glanced apprehensively at Barbara, who quickly answered, "We'd like a little time to look over the wine list."

"As you wish." He moved stiffly from their table.

"I've got good I.D. if you want wine," offered Jesse.

"I don't think they'll even bother to ask in this place." She hesitated. "I'm not really a big drinker, Jesse, but if you'd like some wine, I'll have a glass with you."

Jesse beamed. "I prefer sourmash whiskey myself but I think I would like some wine tonight. That's what they drink in the movies when the hero is out with the pretty girl, isn't it?"

"You're a funny guy, Jesse. What kind of wine do you like?"

She had him there. "To tell you the truth, I don't know the first thing about wine. I've tasted Ripple and Thunderbird and I know I don't like those."

She smiled as she picked up the wine list and leaned close to him so he could read it with her.

The Chevy was the last car in the parking lot when they finally found their way outside. Barbara sat close to him. He felt her hip against his as he leaned forward to turn on the ignition switch.

"Jesse?"

He looked into her eyes. Even in the dim lights of the parking lot they sparkled. She leaned into him and kissed him full on the lips. Her soft lips parted slightly and the warmth of her mouth found his. He felt his body grow weak, as though all of the energy within him was suddenly and electrically sucked into the atmosphere. Barbara's body began to tremble almost imperceptibly. Slowly she pulled her lips from his, keeping her face only inches away.

She spoke first. "I thought it would be that way." She touched his hand. "You're a very, very special guy, Jesse Langley."

Jesse replied softly, "I was kinda thinkin' the same thing about you. I feel like I'm dreamin'. This doesn't really happen in real life. Are you for real, Barbara?"

"I don't know what's wrong with me. I normally don't attack a guy like this. You probably think I'm crazy, or cheap, or who knows what, but something happened to me the very first minute I saw you. You seemed so different. I saw you were actually concerned about Cindy, then you were embarrassed and humiliated, then you became angry at Cindy over the way she was acting. And in the very next breath, you stood up to those three guys by yourself. When you finally noticed me, you looked at me strangely. It wasn't the way most guys look at me. It was.... well, it was nice. It was gentle. It was really neat. I didn't sleep an hour last night, wondering if you would ever call. I felt something missing when you left."

A myriad of thoughts rushed through Jesse's mind, none of them intelligible. This didn't happen, even in the movies. He turned away and started the car. "Now I know I'm dreamin'." He put the transmission into reverse, looked over his shoulder and released the brakes.

Barbara covered her face with her hands and began to cry quietly. Jesse stopped the car, shut off the engine and set the parking brake.

He touched her shoulder. "Wait a second, Barbara. Don't cry. Why are you crying? Don't do that. Are you okay? What did I do?"

She lifted her face from her hands. Tears streamed down her cheeks. Between sobs, she replied, "What did you do? Nothing. I poured my heart out to you. I talked to you like I've known you all my life. I almost begged you to hold me. I threw myself at you and you suddenly lost interest. Well, I'm sorry. I really am. I've never, ever been affected like this by anybody. I don't know what's going on. I'm confused. I think I love you. You're going away soon. I can't love you. I just met you. But what if I do love you and I never kissed you or told you, and you never came back?"

Jesse brushed a lock of hair from her forehead. "Whoa. Slow down. I thought I could handle anything but I need a minute to regroup here. Let me think about all this for a second."

They sat for a moment, Jesse stroking her hair gently as his mind raced for explanations and logic. He found neither.

"Barbara, I'm flattered. I don't know what I've done to earn this kind of feeling from you but I'm honored and humbled by it. And if I were truthful about my feelings for you, I'd have to admit that something has happened to me that I can't really explain. I can't tell you I love you, but I definitely feel something very ... very ...

83

Stoney Livingston

I don't know what it is, but it's strong and it's real. I guess I just need a little time to go over a few things in my mind."

Barbara looked at him. "I'm not asking you to love me. I was just explaining how *I* feel. You don't have to feel the same way I do. I just don't want you to leave me and never know. You are a different kind of person, Jesse Langley. And you are what this girl has always wanted but never really believed existed. I feel so close to you that I can't believe it myself – how can I expect you to believe it?"

Jesse saw the flash of a movement behind him, outside his door. Involuntarily he ducked. Something struck him a glancing blow behind his left ear, the force throwing his head forward and into the steering wheel. His recovery was swift.

With the windows rolled down for the warm California evening, Jesse knew he had no time to start the car and get away. He quickly opened the door, striking his assailant and knocking him to the ground. He sprang from the car, hoping to press his newfound advantage, only to see the man jump to his feet.

"Jesse!" shouted Barbara.

Jesse turned to see a second man with his arms through the open passenger window, holding Barbara by the throat, a nickel-plated knife blade under her left ear. He glanced at the man on his own side of the car, who, he suddenly realized, was also holding a switchblade knife.

He held his hands out, palms forward. "Okay, okay. You win." He looked at the man holding the blade on Barbara. "Let her be."

The man facing Jesse laughed. In a heavy Mexican accent he said, "We don' take jore orders. We geeve the orders. We take what we wan'. We have thee car, jore money, an' for chure we take the woman." He waved his knife menacingly.

Jesse tensed. "Listen, man, leave her alone. Take whatever you want but *leave her alone.*"

The man holding Barbara said, "You don't listen so good, man. We got it all." He opened the door and pulled Barbara out of the car. "Whewee! We hit the jackpot this time! Take a look at what I found." He pushed Barbara around the car, holding onto her left arm.

Jesse's assailant gave a low wolf whistle. "Jesus! I get thees wan first."

Barbara's captor shouted. "Bullshit. You can have seconds on this one. I'm gonna try her out first." He looked Barbara up and down. "You're gonna love it, baby. You'll be beggin' me for more before we're done. Get in the back seat, you good-lookin', redheaded bitch."

"You might as well use that knife. I'm not getting in the back seat with you or anybody else." Her voice cracked a little.

The big man hit her in the stomach with his fist, then slapped her viciously in the face. Jesse lost all fear and self-control in the same instant.

As Barbara fell, Jesse jumped her assailant, kicking him in the lower rib cage with such force that he heard ribs crack. The man screamed in agony and dropped his knife. Jesse moved in for the kill, ignoring the Mexican accent behind him. As he delivered blow after blow to the injured man's face and body in a wild flurry, he felt a burning pain at the base of his neck, turned to face his attacker, and found himself staring at an empty-handed and frightened man. Jesse's movement had been so quick that the embedded knife had been wrenched from the man's hand. Inertia dislodged it from the base of Jesse's neck when he had stopped his turn. He heard the switchblade hit the Chevy and bounce to the paved parking lot.

84

He ignored the larger man, who lay on the ground incapacitated, and attacked the disarmed man with the fury of a demon. In short order, the man was down and Jesse was kicking him in the ribs, the groin, the face, the throat.

"Jesse!" Barbara had struggled to her feet. She picked up a fallen knife and clung to it.

"Barbara! Get in the car and get out of here!"

She moved an unsteady step in his direction. "Not without you! Let's go!"

"Barbara. Don't waste time." He kicked the Mexican accent in the face again. "One of 'em might get up." Another kick to the groin.

Neither assailant moved, but Jesse wouldn't stop. He moved to the larger man, the one with the broken ribs. He bent down, and grabbed the man's ears. Using them as handles, he smashed the man's head into the asphalt repeatedly.

"Jesse, stop it! You'll kill him!"

"I hope so." He continued slamming the man's head into the parking lot. Suddenly, he felt dizziness. He released his grip on the ears, stood and staggered to the Chevy. He felt warm blood running down his back.

"Jesse. What's wrong? Please, let's go."

Jesse gritted his teeth and quietly said, "Okay. I was gettin' tired of this anyway."

Barbara jumped into the passenger side of the car and slammed her door. Jesse kicked broken ribs one more time, shook his head to clear his vision, and sat behind the steering wheel. He hurriedly started the engine, put the transmission into reverse and backed the car out of the parking space. He felt a slight bump as he ran over the arm of the larger man.

Once out of the parking lot, Jesse turned to Barbara. "You okay?"

She nodded. "I'm okay, but I think you're hurt. Are you okay?" She put her arm around his neck and recoiled at the touch of his blood.

"Jesse! Oh my God! You're bleeding."

Jesse smiled weakly. "You found me out. I hate to admit it, but I've gotta get to a hospital. I need two things: first, I need you to stop the bleeding; second, I need to know where the nearest hospital is."

Tears flowed down Barbara's cheeks. Her breathing was rapid and uneven.

Jesse spoke firmly. "Barbara, I need your help. Where is the hospital?"

She looked for landmarks. "Turn left up there at that first traffic light. About a mile on your right there's a big hospital."

He touched her hand. "You'll do all right. Now, about the bleeding – I think the wound is near the spine – low on my neck – maybe in line with my shoulders. Help me get this jacket off so you can see it."

With trembling hands, she assisted in the removal of his sports jacket as he made the left turn. She looked at the wound. "Oh no! Oh no!" She began to cry again.

Jesse said, "I'm sure it's not as bad as it looks, and I hate to ask you to do it, but please place your hand over the wound and apply as much pressure as you can."

Barbara nodded and placed her hand on the purple gash. "Please, God let him be all right," she said.

"I'm okay." He glanced at her. "How are you doin'?"

She buried her face in his shoulder. "Jesse, I'm so sorry."

"Me too, but not because it's anyone's fault. I'm sorry 'cause one of the most beautiful evenings I've ever known has been temporarily interrupted. And I'm sorry that I didn't do something before that guy hit you."

Still applying pressure to the wound, she took her head from his shoulder and stared at him. She shook her head. "You're an unbelievable human being, Jesse Langley."

He squinted as he looked at her in the semi-darkness of the car's interior. "You're not so bad yourself."

On the verge of unconsciousness, Jesse stopped the Chevy at the emergency room door.

Jesse opened his eyes slowly. They hurt. Everything seemed to hurt. He was in a darkened room but knew he wasn't in a hospital. He knew also that he wasn't alone. He tried to remember how he got wherever he was. He recalled arriving at the hospital. There was a vague image of an x-ray room. His memory clouded at that point. There was a doctor, Barbara, and a man and another woman. *That must have been Nancy and her husband. I must be at their house.* He winced at a stinging pain near the base of his neck.

A voice whispered softly, "Jesse? Are you awake?" He could feel her warm breath on his ear.

"I'm not real sure. Where are we?"

"At my sister's. You're in my bed."

He tried to sit up, but grew immediately dizzy and dropped his head back onto the pillow.

"Don't move. The doctor said you lost a lot of blood. He gave me some medicine for pain if you need it, but he said you should stay in bed for a few days and get plenty of rest."

Jesse felt the stinging pain again. He also felt the soreness in his muscles and the burning in his knuckles where he had bloodied them in his assault on the two men. "What does your sister and brother-in-law think of me being here?"

"I told them everything that happened. I don't think Ed believed me at first, but when the police arrived, he became a believer in a hurry. He said you could stay forever if you wanted to."

"The police?"

"An ambulance brought both of those guys to the same hospital. They were in pretty bad shape. I told the police the whole story. They took the knife I had as evidence. It was just like the one they found in the parking lot at the restaurant. One of the officers asked me how you did it and, you know, I couldn't tell him."

Jesse smiled in the darkness. "I couldn't either. I just know that when that big guy hit you, it was all over."

"Nan thinks you're about the biggest real-life hero she's ever known."

"What time is it?" asked Jesse.

"It must be about three-thirty in the morning."

"Have you slept yet?" he asked.

"No, but I honestly haven't been sleepy. I was worried about you. If something were to happen to you, I couldn't stand it."

"Are you okay?" he asked.

"I am now," she answered.

There was a short silence.

"Barbara?"

"Yes?"

"May I have another kiss?"

She moved over him, careful not to irritate his injuries. Her hair brushed his cheek as she kissed him softly on the mouth. He smelled her body. It wasn't perfume. It was just the way she smelled – clean.

He returned her kiss, his pain and injuries completely forgotten. She gently lowered her body onto his. He put his arms around her, feeling only a silken gown covering her firm flesh. He felt her young, strong body beneath the gown, her buttocks, her back, the curve of her waist.

She gently broke the kiss and gracefully crawled under the fresh sheets. Jesse felt her body touch his, the only barrier between them the silken gown and the pajama bottoms he wore. She snuggled carefully close to him, kissing his neck and throat. With her lips less than half an inch from his, she whispered, "I'm so in love with you, Jesse Langley, that I just know I'm going to explode. This is a storybook love and you are my brave knight. Can you feel my love? You must."

Jesse replied, "I feel something that I've never felt before, but I don't know what it is. I want to touch and kiss you and hold you and make love to you, but I'm afraid."

She placed a forefinger gently upon his lips, then kissed his lips and her finger as one.

They made love, slowly and gently, discovering each other's bodies, reveling at each new sensation caused by each new touch, each new kiss. When it was over, it wasn't over. Jesse touched her gently from her toes to her head, taking in the sensation of each touch. Nor could she let a moment of their time together slip by without touching him. They made love again and yet again.

Shortly after daybreak, Jesse spoke for the first time since their lovemaking had begun. "I keep waiting to wake up. It feels so real and yet I know it can't be."

With her face buried in his neck, she said, "Jesse, this is the most real thing that has ever happened to me."

They fell asleep, he on his back with his arms tightly wrapped around her, she with her face buried in his neck.

When he awoke, Barbara was still in his arms. She was awake, but unmoving. He kissed her forehead as he gently stroked her back. Judging by the dim light in the room he guessed it to be early evening.

Barbara kissed his breast. She pressed her cheek against his chest. "Hold me."

He held her tightly, so tightly he felt her heart racing against his chest. They made love slowly, savoring the passion and tenderness. When it was over the room was in total darkness. They fell asleep, their bodies entangled.

At dawn, Jesse awakened to find Barbara still wrapped in his arms. He felt rested and alive. He kissed her gently on the lips, hoping not to wake her, but her response was immediate. Her tongue found his and their bodies became one.

Afterward, he lay with his cheek on her breast, stroking her body. "If this is as good for you as it is for me, I'm happy for you," he said.

She smiled. "I was only just hoping that you were one-half as happy about it as I am. That would be enough."

"I've never experienced anything like you. It makes it kinda tough to go off to some little banana war."

He felt her body stiffen momentarily. She said, "Jesse, don't go."

Stoney Livingston

"Believe me, I don't want to go anymore, but I haven't got a choice. I signed up."

"So did I, but we always have a choice. We can leave the country."

"You mean desert?"

She sat up in the bed and looked into his eyes. "Yes, I mean desert. Run away. I'm in love with you, Jesse. I don't want you killed in some jungle, ten thousand miles away, in a war nobody even knows why we're fighting. Maybe that's selfish but that's how I feel, and I've been raised a patriotic American just like you. I've found something I know I'll never find again. I don't want to take even the smallest chance that I might lose it. Please, Jesse. Let's go to Canada or Mexico."

Jesse looked at her, wide-eyed. The most beautiful woman he had ever seen, with or without clothes, professed a boundless love and asked him to desert his country in time of war. He couldn't comprehend it.

Jesse pushed the sheets from his body and stood on shaky legs. "I've gotta leave."

He walked into the bathroom adjoining her room and took a shower, careful to keep his bandaged neck dry. Ten minutes later he entered the bedroom, a towel wrapped around his waist. Barbara sat on the edge of the bed in a red silken gown with tears in her eyes but she fought them back and none rolled onto her cheeks.

There was a stack of clothes, neatly folded, at the foot of bed.

"These are Ed's. Yours were ruined." She nodded at the clothing then looked into his eyes.

Neither spoke for a moment, then Jesse said, "I'll send them right back."

"Ed said you could keep them."

"Tell Ed I said thanks."

She nodded.

The silence was deafening as he quickly and painfully dressed. After tying his shoes with his swollen hands, he stood. "I don't understand life too well sometimes, Barbara. But I know I'm not going to leave my outfit in time of war. I'm not sorry for the time we've had together. I *am* sorry that it was so short."

Tears flowed down her cheeks. "I love you, Jesse Langley, and I don't want to lose you to a war. I won't even try to stop you now, because I know better. But I'm always going to love you, just remember that. Always."

Shannon had said those exact words. "Goodbye, Barbara."

He turned and left the bedroom, tears filling his eyes. He didn't know why he was crying. Maybe it was because he was angry at the world. Maybe it was because not much around him seemed to make any sense. Maybe it was because he was lost. He let himself out, found the Chevy parked in the driveway, and drove slowly from Buena Park.

*****

"Jesus Christ. What happened to you? What happened to my car? Where the hell have you been?" Will fired the questions as he glanced from Jesse to the car then back to Jesse.

"It's a long story."

Will looked intently at the front seat of his car. "Is that blood or what?"

"Yeah."

"The other guy's, I hope."

"Not exactly."

88

"All right, goddamnit, Mr. Langley. What the hell is going on?"

"Will, really, I've gotta report back to my company."

"Is that a bandage on the back of your neck?"

"Yeah, but everything's okay now. Sorry about your car. A corpsman told me that hydrogen peroxide will clean blood out. It works good on clothes anyway."

"Hop in. I'll run you over to staging and you can fill me in," said Will.

The ride to staging battalion was short and Jesse avoided Will's questions, promising to tell him all if the Marine Corps didn't lock him up and throw away the key for his two-day unauthorized absence.

*****

Sergeant Ribbon studied Jesse's face. Jesse had just finished telling him about the fight in the parking lot, and the hospital, and about the "friends" he had stayed with for a day and a half.

"I'm tempted to say, 'bullshit', but for some stupid reason known only to the inhabitants of Valhalla, I believe you."

"It's true, Sarge," Jesse defended.

"Get into your tropicals and let's go see the lieutenant."

Jesse waited outside Lieutenant Colson's office as Sergeant Ribbon presented his story. The big staff sergeant stepped out of the office and motioned for Jesse to follow as he continued to walk out of the building and onto the company street.

As they walked to the barracks, Jesse said, "I don't get it. No court-martial? No Office Hours? No fine? No penalty?"

"He told me to take care of it. Now unless you want some kind of punishment, the goddamn matter is taken care of."

"That's fine by me, Sarge. Thanks."

"Don't thank me. Thank the lieutenant. He says he thinks you're a good marine. Made me promise to keep you out of trouble till we leave next week."

"Did you say 'next week'?"

"Shhh. He'll probably make it official tomorrow. Just keep it quiet until then."

"No problem. Thanks for the scoop."

As they opened the barracks door, Ribbon said, "Why don't you take it easy the next couple of days? Let sick bay have a look at those stitches and stay the hell outa trouble."

"Appreciate it, Sarge."

An hour later, Jesse lay on his bunk, reflecting on the events of the past several days. His thoughts were interrupted when Joe Fitzgerald stepped up to his bunk. "How in the hell are you, stranger?" asked Joe.

"Oh, Hi, Joe. I was just layin' here thinkin' how good a shot of sourmash whiskey would go."

"You gonna eat first?" asked Joe.

"Not today. I'm in a mood. I'll be at the club when you're done eating." Jesse stood and walked out of the barracks.

By the time Joe arrived at the E.M. Club, Jesse had finished five or six rounds of Jack Daniels.

Placing two more drinks on the table and sitting beside Jesse, Joe said, "So where the hell you been?"

"I went to see a friend in the LA area and we were jumped by a couple of punks."

"What's the bandage doing on your neck? Knife?"

"Yeah, how'd you know?"

"Seems logical. How bad is it?"

"It's not so bad. Worse thing is my knuckles and my muscles. Basically I'm sore all over."

"I take it you got in a few licks before you got stuck?"

Jesse paused. He really didn't want to go over the whole thing again. "Yeah. I did pretty good. You'd a' been proud." He smiled. "So what did I miss?"

"Not much really. Hell, the most exciting thing that happened was your disappearance. We had a pool on when or if you'd come back. You cost me four bucks. I had fifteen hundred hours on Thursday."

Jesse downed his shot-and-a-half of Jack Daniels. "Sorry about that. You want another?" he said.

"Goddamn, I just got here. You worried about prohibition or sumpthin?"

Jesse smiled and leaned across the table. Joe leaned toward him until their faces were only inches apart. "You ain't too damned smart, Joe."

"I'll bite. Why am I not too smart?"

"If you think I'm going to sit and sip one drink all night when you're buying, you're crazy. I've got the bread. You might as well let your damn flattop down and let 'er rip. I'll carry you back to the barracks if you can't handle it."

"Shit. You ain't got enough money to get me high, much less fall-down drunk." He gulped down his bourbon & water.

"That's more like it. Hell, let's save so many trips to the bar. We'll buy three rounds at a time," said Jesse as he stood and headed for the bar.

An hour later, Jesse stiffened in his chair as he sensed someone's presence behind him. "Don't say it, Will. I know you're bent but I figured it'd wait till tomorrow."

"How'd you know It was me?"

"I saw someone come through the door and walk straight up behind me, like he knew where he was going. Who the hell else would it be? Have a seat. You know Joe? Joe, this is a good friend. Name's Will Hunt."

"Howdy," said Will.

Joe barely managed a faint wave. His lips moved slightly but no sound accompanied the lip movement.

"Joe's a little under the weather, Will. Sit and hang tight. I'm gonna finish him off this time. You wanna drink?"

"A beer. Then I want to talk."

"Are you bent out of shape about the car? Didn't the hydrogen peroxide work?"

"It's not about the car."

Jesse turned to face Will. His expression grew sober. "Is it about Shannon?"

"No, goddamnit!"

Jesse relaxed. A grin worked its way across his face. "Then sit down and have a drink. I'll be right back with another round."

That next round was too much for Joe. He passed out. Jesse, seeing the end was near, had seated himself next to his drinking partner and was in position to prevent Joe's fall. After two attempts, he was able to prop Joe up in his chair, using the wall as partial support. He turned to Will and smiled. "Can you believe he thought he could actually drink me under the table?"

Despite his apparent anger, Will laughed.

"So what's on your mind, my friend?" asked Jesse.

"Plenty. Let's get Joe back to the Barracks, and then we can talk."

Jesse looked at Joe, then back to Will. "Nope. Joe's okay. I ain't ready to go to the barracks, and we can talk right here."

Will sat close enough to Jesse so that he would not have to raise his voice. "C.I.D. will be lookin' to talk to you in the next few days."

"What the hell for?" Jesse asked, carelessly.

"I saw the police report of what happened in L.A. Is it true?"

"Hell, I don't know. I never saw the report. What did it say?"

"Basically, it said you were jumped by two guys with knives and you kicked both their asses and caused them to suffer grievous bodily injuries."

"Tha's basic'lly what happened." Jesse finished another shot-and-a-half of Jack Daniels. He was having trouble with his speech. He knew he should slow his drinking down but since he was this far gone, why bother?

Will laughed. "How in the hell did you do it?"

"Well, i's like this. This one son-a-bitch had a hold of Barbara. They had knives. Hell they probably would a' had us if that big guy hadn't ..."

Will waited a moment. When it became apparent that Jesse was going to say no more, he asked, "You okay? You need some air?"

Jesse shook his head. "No goddamnit, I'm not okay, and no goddamnit, I don't need no air. Le's get Joe back t' the barracks. C'n you gimme me a hand?"

In the barracks, they removed Joe's shoes and shirt, put him between the sheets, and covered him with a blanket. He appeared peaceful and serene lying on his back, covers pulled up to his neck.

"Tha's a real pisser," said Jesse as he stared blankly at Joe's unmoving figure.

"What's a real pisser?" asked Will.

"That damned Joe passin' out like that."

"Why? You won the drinkin' contest, didn't you?"

"Yeah, I won the battle but he won the damn war. He's in my rack, and by the time I'm ready t' hit the hay, I won' be able t' reach his high altitude model. You wouldn't wanna try gettin' him up to the top rack would you?"

"Hell No."

Jesse licked his lips. "I didn't figure so. Oh well, to hell with it." He sat on the edge of the bunk and scooted his footlocker out between his legs. From within, he produced an unopened bottle of Jack Daniels and offered it to Will. "Drink?"

"Yeah, what the hell," replied Will as he took the cap from the bottle and belted one away. He coughed violently as he returned the bottle to Jesse.

"Good stuff, huh?" asked Jesse.

Will, unable to answer between coughs, simply nodded.

"I thought you'd feel tha' way."

Will finally recovered enough to speak. "You were telling me what happened in that parking lot?"

"Yeah, I was. Now I ain't. You wan' 'nother drink?"

"What 'dya' mean, you ain't?"

Jesse took another long pull from the bottle then looked at Will. "Will, ol' partner, I got sort of a problem. If you keep askin' me all these questions, how in the hell 'm I gonna have time ta think things through?"

"What things?"

"See? There you go again, askin' questions."

A marine in a bunk not far away said, "Hey, keep the noise down!"

"Hey, screw you," said Jesse. He paused for a moment. "No, that ain't right. Yer right. Sorry 'bout that." He turned to Will. "Let's take a walk."

The cool September air was refreshing as they strolled between the barracks. Jesse passed Will the bottle. Will took a short swig and handed it back to Jesse, who promptly put down another large swallow.

"How do you drink that stuff like that?"

"Practice, Will. Practice. I got a lot of practice since Shannon up and got married."

"You sure as hell ain't gonna get her back with that stuff."

"I don't drink this stuff to get her back, you shithead. What 'r' you, crazy? I drink this stuff 'cause it's a good pastime. Y' know, like a hobby. Like model airplanes, or tennis or whatever-the-hell-a-hobby is."

"Sometimes I think you pursue your hobby too much."

"That has been duly noted. I'll take it up fer discussion at the next meetin' of the Hobby Board of Directors."

They walked away from the billeting area, into the woods just beyond the main road. Jesse sat upon a fallen tree trunk. He passed the bottle to Will who took another swallow. He didn't cough this time. Retrieving the bottle from Will, Jesse said, "So, how's yer love life, my friend?"

"Compared to your adventures, it's a blank page."

"Whatever happened to that little blonde you were so sweet on? What was her name?" Jesse thought for a moment. "Oh yeah, Sharon Fiedler. Whatever happened to good 'ol' Sharon?"

"Goddamnit, Jesse. This is serious. What the hell happened in LA?"

"What's so serious? It's over and done with. The whole damn thing is over and done with."

"I don't think so. If it was over and done with, C.I.D. wouldn't be getting involved."

"Screw C.I.D."

"Your attitude is the pits. Goddamnit, those guys hang people."

"So?"

"So? So shit. So what happened up there?"

"Goddamnit, Will. Are you some kind of Perry Mason or sumpthin?" He offered the bottle, which Will accepted without comment.

Will took a large swallow and returned the bottle to its owner. "Jesse, I think they're trying to hang you with vehicular assault."

"Wi' what?"

"Vehicular assault. A secondary report from the hospital stated that at least one of those guys had been run over by a car."

"They probably *both* thought they were run over by a *train*." Jesse giggled.

"I'm serious. One of 'em had been run over by a car – at least his arm had."

Jesse clucked. "Them guys weren't all that smart. They prob'bly tried

92

crossin' a busy street in those dark clothes and, wham!"

"They were still laying in the parking lot when the police found em."

Jesse took another pull from the bottle. "Now ain't that just like a civilian. Probably some local citizen saw 'em down and figured it was his chance to finish 'em off and get a medal."

"Jesse, goddamnit. You were driving *my* car."

"Jesus Christ. Don't get a twist in your skivvies. I beat those creeps by myself – without the help of the damn car. The only thing I used the car for was ta leave. I might've run over that big guy's arm when I backed out but I don't really give a damn. If I hadn't been so dizzy, I'd have cut his nuts off with his own knife. I needed a doctor of my own. I didn't have the time to stay an' complete my work."

"They're both still in pretty rough shape."

"So what? I hope they both croak. But I want 'em to suffer a long time before that happens. I'm done talkin' about tha' shit. I'll just tell you one more time: I did not use your car as a weapon. Period. You wann' 'nother drink?"

Will sighed. "Might as well. Can't dance, and it's too late to plow."

The following week, Jesse pondered life's questions in so far as they related to him. He spent every waking moment trying to resolve his inner conflict concerning Shannon and Barbara. He knew that once he left the continental U.S. there would be nothing he could do to change things. He would no longer have the freedom of choice. He would be physically committed to combat with no chance of returning to the States for at least thirteen months.

Every night he religiously drank a fifth of Jack Daniels, usually out in the woods by himself. He smoked his cigarettes and drank his sour mash and pondered how he had arrived where he was. If he could really fall in love with Barbara then that must mean he could find another and yet another. If that were true, what was so special about falling in love? Why had he waited four-and-a-half years?

Wait a minute. Who said I was in love with Barbara? Maybe it's a new kind of feeling, sort of like being in love, but not exactly. Baloney. That's like being sort of pregnant. You either are or you aren't, Langley. Which is it? You're not pregnant, therefore you must not be in love. Whoa, old boy. Too much sour mash. Let's try this again tomorrow night.

Variations of these thoughts presented themselves every night. His questions were never satisfactorily answered. When he finished his bottle, he walked unsteadily back to his barracks and crawled into his bunk. He was grateful for the whiskey for it allowed him to sleep.

On the weekend before the battalion's scheduled departure, he started drinking Friday night and didn't stop until about midnight Sunday, with only a few hours sleep in the interim. Will had asked him to go to Riverside for the weekend but Jesse had refused. Joe had suggested a trip to the beaches and Jesse had shrugged it off. Late Sunday night, Jesse found the answer he had been searching for but he couldn't accept it. When he passed out in his bunk the answer left his conscious mind and when he awakened early Monday morning he couldn't retrieve it.

Later that morning, two C.I.D. investigators questioned him for three hours. He repeated the story of the two muggers until he finally tired of it to the point where he informed the two investigators he would "... no longer talk to people who don't listen." They left, advising him not to leave the base until they had completed their

Stoney Livingston
investigation.

Monday evening, as he sat in the wooded area, drinking his Tennessee Whiskey, trying to recapture the knowledge he had lost, Will found him.

"Howdy, Will. You lost?" asked Jesse.

"I saw Shannon this weekend. She said to say hello," replied Will as he sat on the fallen tree trunk next to Jesse.

Jesse's heart raced but it didn't show in his voice. "How is she?"

"You gonna offer me a drink?"

"You know you don't like this stuff."

"Tonight I do."

"Well, 'scuse me. Here." Jesse offered the bottle.

Will took a large swallow and coughed violently. "She's fine."

"You always did start out coughing. It's nice to know you can count on some things." Jesse smiled. "You must have one helluva serious problem to ask for a drink of whiskey. What's the matter? Sharon Fiedler give you the cold shoulder? Hell, don't worry about it. There's more fish in the sea."

Will's move was such a total surprise to Jesse that he was taken completely off guard as his friend struck him in the cheekbone with his fist. Jesse rolled from the tree trunk, still hanging on to the bottle. He gained his feet, dusted his trousers, stood straight, and looked at Will.

"I don't believe you just did that," he said as he rubbed his cheekbone with his unencumbered hand.

"I don't either," said Will.

"Well then, goddamnit what the hell am I supposed to do? I didn't mean any disrespect towards Sharon for Chrisake. If you took it that way I'm sorry, but goddamnit don't do that again." He sat next to Will as though nothing had happened.

He offered Will the bottle. Will accepted the offering. "That's it? You don't wanna fight or kick my ass or something?"

Jesse looked at him. "Yeah, I do, but I figure you must have had one helluva reason to do that. As soon as I figure out what it was, I'll let you know."

"You're a real shithead, you know that?" Will returned the bottle.

"*I'm* a real shithead? Who's the one threw the sucker punch to an old friend? Did I do that?"

"You're a shithead."

"All right, goddamnit, I'm a shithead. How's Shannon?" asked Jesse nonchalantly.

"What the hell's wrong with you?"

"Hell, you seem to be the only one here who knows and you won't tell me," replied Jesse as he took a long pull on the bottle.

Jesse was in the process of lowering the bottle from his lips when Will slapped it from his grasp. As the bottle struck the ground, Jesse turned on him. "All right, Will, you got my attention. Now what the hell is wrong with you? You tryin' to commit suicide?"

"You stupid son-of-a-bitch!"

"Is that a promotion from shithead? Jesus Christ. I've never seen you act this way. What the hell got stuck in your craw?"

"You're the stupidest son-of-a-bitch I've ever known."

Jesse studied him in the partial moonlight for a moment. "You know, Will, if I didn't know better, I'd say you were bent out of shape about sumpthin. But I'm tellin' you right now, that's the last stupid son-of-a-bitch or shithead or anything else I'm gonna be tonight. Now you either tell me what the hell is buggin' you, or leave me alone – or we're goin' to knuckle junction more skoshe."

"Is there anything left in that bottle?" asked Will.

Jesse picked the whiskey bottle from the dirt and held it to the moonlight. "'Bout a third. Here."

Will accepted the bottle and took two big swallows. He looked up at Jesse. "You been actin' really stupid this past week. I mean even stupider than you normally do. Here, you want a drink?"

Jesse accepted the bottle. "So?"

"So I tried to tell you about C.I.D. You didn't give a damn."

"So?"

"So. You wouldn't tell me about what happened."

"So?"

"So. I looked up Barbara this weekend to get the story from her."

Jesse grabbed Will by the front of his shirt. "Goddamnit, Will, you leave her out of this. It's none of your goddamn business. She just happens to be who I was with when all this happened."

Will stood his ground. "You hit me if you want but that won't change things, will it?"

Jesse released his grip. "Change what?"

"The fact that she loves you. I mean really loves you -- the way you love my sister."

Jesse turned his back to Will. He walked a few steps and drained the bottle.

Will continued, "You know Jesse, I remember what you said when Shannon got married to Bill. You know, about nothing any woman ever said was true. About how you'd never tie up emotionally with another broad. And how you'd love 'em and leave 'em and all that shit. Well, I'm tellin' ya, you're makin' a big mistake with Barbara." He paused, waiting for Jesse to respond. After a moment with no response, he continued, "I never thought I'd see any person act or feel the way you did about Shannon, but I saw it in Barbara. I'm tellin' ya. That girl is so in love with you, I just can't believe it. What's your story? You really *do* have some kind of message for the ladies, don't you?"

Slowly, Jesse turned to face him. "Will, let it lie. Just leave it alone. This is none of your business. Barbara is just infatuated. I'm the departing hero going off to war. That's all. Nothing more. For Chrisakes, any girl who would join the Marine Corps is a bubble off anyway."

"If you were a little closer, I'd knock your fucking head off."

"You know Will, drinkin' ain't good for you. Gives you delusions of grandeur."

"She's not your average BAM," replied Will.

"That I'll grant you. But goddamnit, she *did* join the Corps."

"Is that all that's bothering you, mister bad-ass? You afraid she's going to turn into a goddamn grunt?"

"Will, you s'pose we could start this conversation over? I really don't want to talk about this. It doesn't make any difference. I'm leavin' day after tomorrow and she'll be married before I get back, so why the hell are we fightin'? We been friends too long to let a woman cause this kind of problem."

95

Stoney Livingston

"You're wrong this time, Jesse. I know you are."

"To hell with it. I'm goin' to bed. G'night, Will. I know your intentions are good, but your advice is bad." Jesse walked away and left Will standing in the darkness.

The following night, Jesse felt trapped and helpless. First Staging Battalion was scheduled to leave the next day. He should contact Barbara but he knew, in his heart, he wanted to see Shannon. It seemed unfair that he should feel that way and he wrestled to rationalize. He fought his desire to leave the base and won. He opted for his tree trunk in the wooded area, where he started drinking shortly after dark. He found it refreshing to have a place where he could go and be with his own thoughts without interference from the rest of the world.

The staging battalion had made all preparations. All of the last minute details had been taken care of. They would depart from Long Beach the following night on the U.S.S. Breckinridge. Jesse had been disappointed they weren't flying. Eighteen days at sea with only a short respite in Hawaii seemed like the long way to him. He wanted to get over there, win the war, and get back to the States. The war might be over by the time he got there at this rate.

He sipped his whiskey and tried to think of Barbara but her vision was dim. An image of Shannon appeared clearly in his mind. A lot could happen in thirteen months.

Jesse had about three fingers left in his bottle when he heard the rustle of clothing and the muffled sounds of booted feet striking soft ground. Aided by the moonlight, Jesse recognized the two men as they drew near.

"What're you two guys doin' out here?" he asked.

"We could ask you the same thing. Seems like kind of a funny way to spend your last night in the States," replied Joe.

"It pleases me, goddamnit."

"When were you gonna say goodbye?" asked Will.

"I'm not into a whole bunch of that goodbye stuff. Hell, Will, I'll see you when I get back, and if I don't get back, one goddamn little goodbye ain't gonna change things none."

"You gonna offer us a drink?" asked Joe, sitting down on the tree trunk.

"You got me there. Sorry about my manners. I was thinkin' about something else." He offered the bottle.

Joe took a healthy pull and passed it to Will who took a swig, coughed violently, and returned it to Jesse.

"First drink t'night, Will?" asked Jesse.

"Yeah," replied Will hoarsely, still coughing.

Jesse took a small sip and handed the bottle to Joe. "I got this funny feelin', fellers, that I'm gonna get ripped tonight. As a matter of fact, I've got a real good start."

Joe said, "It's a damn good thing you got a good start, 'cause I just finished your bottle." He handed it back to Jesse.

"The hell you say?" Jesse shook the bottle and gave a short laugh. He handed it back to Joe. "Here, hold this a minute."

Jesse walked to one end of the tree trunk, reached his arm inside and withdrew another bottle, this one unopened.

"Oh shit," said Will.

"Whatsamatter wi' you, Will? Dontcha wanna drink?" asked Jesse.

"I can take it or leave it, but I was just thinking about the last time I saw you go on a two-bottle binge."

"Hell, Will, that was tequila, not sour mash, and I was only sixteen."

"Yeah, I know. And I didn't think you were going to live to see seventeen." He turned to Joe. "You know what this crazy shithead did? He got on his damned Triumph and rode over the roof of this rounded church they got down in Tucson. When he hit the bottom on the other side he damn near killed himself."

"I was okay. It was my bike took the worst a' that beatin'."

"That's only because you were too damned drunk to feel any pain."

"I won ten bucks."

"It cost you twenty-nine-fifty to fix the bike."

"What the hell, I'd never rode my bike over a church before." Jesse paused. "I ain't done it since either."

All three laughed.

Jesse opened the fresh bottle. He carefully poured half of it into the bottle Joe held.

"Now, Joe, damnit, I don't want you to think I'm stingy with my booze, but I wasn't expecting guests this evening. Will won't drink too much. I figure half the bottle for you two, and half for me. I intend to get totally snockered tonight and that's the minimum amount I need to do it right."

Joe smiled. "Can't say all that much for your hospitality but I appreciate your honesty."

For the next hour, the three sat smoking their cigarettes and drinking the whiskey. They talked about sex, football, the upcoming world series, the Marine Corps, Vietnam, college, civilian life, and just about anything else that came to mind.

Joe was telling a story about the Korean War when he suddenly stopped mid-sentence and passed out. Jesse clumsily knelt beside him. Joe was already snoring.

"Well, I'll be damned." He laughed. "The little sucker is out colder 'n a mackerel. He was gettin' awful hard to unnerstan' anyway."

"Yeah he was," agreed Will. Luckily, the bottle had been in his hand when Joe had passed out.

"I like 'm. Whad'ya think?" asked Jesse.

"Yeah, he seems like an all right guy. Hope he makes it back."

"Hell, Will, we're all gonna make it back one way or the other. Joe'll do okay. He lived through Korea, didn't he?"

Will answered, "Yeah, I guess you're right. He's a pretty tough little guy."

"You damn right he is. And I respect him for comin' back into this chickenshit outfit to fight another war. I don't know that I'd do it twice."

"You got that right."

There was a short silence.

"Jesse?"

"Yeah?"

"I told Shannon you were leavin' tomorrow."

Jesse's heart pounded in his eardrums as it always did when he heard her name spoken. "How is she?"

"She's fine. She said to tell you hello and to be careful."

"No shit? Be careful? Was she kiddin'?"

97

Stoney Livingston

"I don't think so. She said she couldn't imagine anything ever happening to you unless you wanted it to happen. She was really strange-sounding when she said it."

Jesse felt her presence next to him. He could see her face and those beautiful golden-brown eyes. He took a long pull from his bottle. "I'm gettin' drunk, Will."

"I'm gettin' high just smellin' this shit."

Jesse raised his bottle in toast. "To smellin' this shit." He finished what was left of his bottle. Will took a small sip from his.

"Jesse, you gonna call Barbara?"

"Jesus Christ. We were takin' about Shannon. How the hell did Barbara get involved in this conversation?"

"I'm tellin' ya', damnit, she feels the real thing for you. I'm not shittin'. It was like lookin' into your face back when you were sixteen and you first fell for my sister. It was that same look."

"Will, I been tryin' to keep my cool. I'm drunk. I mean, toxon stinko. I leave tomorrow and that's the end of it. To hell with it. Okay? Leave me alone. I mean, goddamnit, I love you like a brother, but let me have one or two faults, okay?"

Will shouted, "What a fucking waste!" He brought his face close to Jesse's and continued to shout, "Now you listen to me, you shithead! I want you to get my sister offa that goddamn pedestal. She's human. She's not perfect. She's also married. You had your chance. You never even told her you loved her. What the hell was she supposed to do? Wait the rest of her life for her old friend to confess his undying love?"

Jesse said softly, "Will, there's a whole lot to that story you don't know, so ..."

"I'm not done talkin', goddamnit!"

"*'Scuse me!*" said Jesse indignantly as he pulled at his empty bottle.

Will continued, "You let it happen. You could have stopped her romance by just opening your goddamned mouth."

"Maybe."

"Maybe, hell. We both know it. You threw it away. Now, you're throwin' the rest of your life away and I'm gettin' tired of it. You met Barbara and now you're throwin' her away. You plan on goin' to Vietnam and never comin' back. Don't try to bullshit me. I know it. Well, fuck you! If you don't care enough about your friends to want to come back, then fuck you. That's all I got to say. I'm goin' back to my barracks now and I better see your sorry ass in November of sixty-six. So long, pal." He stood unsteadily and walked away, tears streaming down his face.

Jesse watched him disappear in the darkness. He looked down at Joe, sleeping peacefully on the ground. "You know Joe, there went a good friend. And you know something else? He's right."

Jesse wept silently in the darkness, thankful that none could see, wanting Shannon and his life back, wishing he had just one more shot of whiskey to end his pain.

CHAPTER SIX: THE LANDING

The USS Breckinridge was a converted passenger liner, luxurious compared to the APA troop transports and LSDs with which Jesse was familiar. The sleeping area was roomy and clean and the heads were almost civilian in appearance. There was even room to walk about above decks without tripping over some form of rigging. The promenade deck was a novelty that Jesse especially enjoyed. He stood on the promenade and imagined he and Shannon were on a sea cruise to some far-off and exotic paradise. As soon as he was able, he slipped away from his assigned sleeping quarters and explored the ship until well after lights out, marveling at the size and utilization of space. If men could build ships like this, he wondered why they had to fight wars.

Jesse spent most of the first forty-eight hours at sea playing poker when not engaged in assigned duties. Two days out, he was a winner by more than two hundred dollars.

The sun glowed brightly but with faint warmth as Jesse leaned against the railing of the bow, peering down into the ocean. They were less than a day from Hawaii and he was looking forward to seeing the islands once again. The slice of water pushed by the bow grew closer to the ship, indicating forward movement was slowing. Suddenly the wake closed in on the sides of the ship and disappeared. They were dead in the water.

Joe, standing next to Jesse, looked up at the stacks. Jesse followed his gaze. Not a puff of smoke was to be seen. Joe glanced at Jesse. "You ever get the feeling we're not supposed to go to Vietnam?"

"Be the pits if a storm blew over, huh?" offered Jesse.

"No shit. We could bob around out here like a cork in a bath tub. You come up with some of the weirdest thoughts." Joe shook his head.

An announcement over the ship's p.a. system advised all aboard that difficulties in the engine room necessitated a four-hour shutdown.

"Let's start a game on deck," suggested Jesse.

"I'm outa the mood. I think I'll write a letter or sumpthin."

"Who the hell do you know who can read?"

Joe replied indignantly, "This little number don't have to read. I'll draw pictures."

"You got a steady girl back home?" He hadn't seen Joe with a woman since their meeting and had given the matter little thought until now.

"A dozen of 'em."

"Any of 'em special?"

"Hell, they're all special, at least when they're with me." Joe smiled.

"You ever been married, Joe?"

"Yeah. Worst ten years of my life. Got married right after Korea. Whew! Was that ever a mistake."

Stoney Livingston

"Then why'd you do it?"

"Hell, you don't know it's a mistake till you've done it. I mean, you know, before we got married she always had her hair just so, and her make-up was perfect, and she dressed to the nines. She waited on me hand and foot till I was almost embarrassed. She cuddled and cooed and she couldn't get enough sex. Everything I did was perfect – I could do no wrong."

"That sounds pretty good to me. So when did all that change?"

"About four hours after we got married."

"Four hours? What happened?"

"She wanted her mother to go with us on our honeymoon."

"You serious? What for?"

"Mummy had never seen Niagara Falls."

"So buy her a bus ticket," said Jesse.

Joe smiled. "That's what I suggested. From that point on, my life was miserable. My old lady never bothered even puttin' on a little lipstick. Ninety percent of the time she had her hair in rollers. Sunday was the only day she dressed up – she wore her fancy bathrobe. She wouldn't even put toast in the toaster. I don't think I screwed her four times in ten years and I was so drunk every time, I'm not sure if I was ever successful. And to top it all off, I don't think I did a single thing right in the ten years we were married. She bitched about everything I did, from the way I fried my own eggs, to the kind of car I bought."

"Jesus. How can a guy make that big a mistake about a woman?" asked Jesse.

"I was young and stupid and horny. And I believed everything she told me. I mean, she was convincing."

"How long did you know her before you got married?"

"'Bout six months. Not long enough; that's for damn sure. I'd have bet my last nickel she was the only one in the world for me. And believe me, I tried, but after ten years of that shit I'd had enough. I called it quits and she got almost everything: the house, the car, the furniture, the boat."

"Damn. Did you get anything?"

"Yeah, the payments on all the stuff *she* got," replied Joe with a wry smile.

Jesse kept searching. "So you never got serious with another girl?"

"Of course. I'm serious about all of 'em – serious about having a good time. If they start giving me all that crap about love and all that shit, I just say *sayonara*. I gotta make up for ten years of that love and marriage bullshit."

Jesse fell silent. He had hoped for a more clear understanding of marriage and love but Joe's story only confused him. He looked at Joe and chuckled. "Well, you better get to drawing your pictures. I think I'll walk to the fantail and look for Russian subs."

"Let me know if you find anything."

Jesse leaned on a lifeboat cable, staring out to sea, seeing nothing, not even the ocean. He imagined himself and Shannon married but couldn't imagine that she would ask to take her mother on the honeymoon so he was unable to get to the next step of Joe's story to see how he and Shannon would resolve those other problems.

He looked up at a soft wisp of a cloud, the only one in the sky.

Jesse's thoughts continued to ramble for more than two hours. He finally gave it up when another marine asked him to join a poker game. The game was good for him. It took his thoughts from Shannon and provided him with an additional $310. He could do no wrong. The cards seemed to fall perfectly for him that day. When the game folded as the ship's repairs were completed and the large vessel got underway, Jesse counted his money and stuffed it into his pocket.

With his day's winnings, Jesse promised Joe a night on the town in Hawaii, Joe choosing the location.

When the ship docked at Pearl Harbor, Joe seemed to search the deep recesses of his memory for a place to go. Finally, he made a decision and the two ended up in the "alley bars" of Honolulu on their first night in town. Joe called them "alley bars" because they sat on the smaller streets and alleys, just off Hotel Street, one of Honolulu's main thoroughfares.

They walked into a small bar called Niki's at around nine p.m. The sound of *Only Sixteen*, sung by Sam Cooke, drifted to Jesse's ears as they entered. He agreed to stay for one drink at Joe's insistence, providing he could play the jukebox. Once they located a table, Jesse handed Joe a ten-dollar bill and asked him to order a shot of sour mash whiskey while he played some music.

When Jesse returned to the table after punching up six songs, Joe was gone. There were two glasses at the table but no Joe. Jesse sat and swallowed his whiskey. He ordered another from the plump Hawaiian waitress, whose kimono was split up to about the center of her thigh. Before she returned with his drink, a young, dark-haired girl sat next to him at his table, rubbing his leg with hers as she seated herself. It looked to be an accident but Jesse wasn't so certain.

"Buy a girl a drink?" she asked.

With a little less eye make-up, Jesse thought she would be quite attractive. He guessed her to be in her mid-twenties but couldn't be certain in the dim light. He shrugged. "I guess I could do that, but I think the guy you really might want to talk to is Joe, my partner. I think he went to the restroom. He'll be back any second now."

The young woman giggled. "I don't think he's coming back right away."

Jesse didn't know why but he tensed. "You know something I don't know?"

She giggled again. "He met an old friend. They left in a hurry. I saw him write you a note." She pointed to a napkin on the table.

Jesse picked up the napkin and turned it to receive the maximum light. He could barely discern the words but finally managed to put it together: *Met old friend. Am okay. Will explain later. Joe.*

"He could've introduced me before they left. He must have been in one big hurry."

His new companion looked at him. "You *are* Jesse, right?"

"Yeah, who told you that?"

"My friend, who is also the friend of your friend," she replied.

"This is a real friendly place around here. Now would you mind telling me what's going on?"

The waitress returned. Jesse paid for his drink and ordered another for himself and one for his new friend. As the waitress walked away to fill their order, the girl said, "You shouldn't drink so fast. You'll pass out before the night gets started."

"What're you – my mother? What's your name? You do have a name, don't you?"

"My name is Claudia, and no, I'm not your mother, but I don't like a guy passing out on me."

Stoney Livingston

Jesse looked at her. "And just who put you in charge of babysitting me? Is that included in the price of one drink or two or three, or what else? I think you're nice-looking and sexy and all that, but I'm really not out chasing women tonight so don't worry about me passing out. If I pass out it'll be because I want to and it won't have any effect on your evening."

The waitress returned with their drinks. Jesse ordered another sour mash even as she placed their glasses on the table. He turned to Claudia as the waitress left. "Is Joe okay? What's the big secret?"

"I think you better drink your drink and let's get out of here," she replied.

"*Let's* get out of here? What's this 'lets' business? I didn't take you to raise. I told you, I'm not out lookin' for a woman. I'm stayin' here till Joe gets back."

"He's not coming back here."

"How do you know?"

"Drink your drink. I'll tell you what I know once we're outside."

"You're awful eager to get me outside. You got a couple of friends waiting for me out there?"

She laughed. "You *are* a suspicious one, aren't you?"

"Well, you gotta admit, this whole situation is a little strange. Where's Joe? Who's this 'friend' he left with? And who are you?"

The waitress returned with Jesse's drink. He ordered one more. Claudia grasped his forearm and squeezed hard. She looked up at the waitress. "Forget it, Tillie. I think we're going to the Beach House to check out the action."

"Okay, Hon. Just let me know if you change your mind," replied the waitress as she moved to another table.

Jesse slowly looked down at his arm. Claudia released her grip. He looked up at her face. "I don't believe you just did that." He paused a moment. "Look, if you need money that bad, I'll just give you some. How much do you usually charge? I'll just give it to you and you can pretend we did it and you can go find someone else. The only thing I ask is that you tell me what happened to Joe. Did he leave with a working girl?"

Claudia smiled. "You're a funny guy. I'm not exactly sure what you think I am but I don't have time to explain here, nor can I. There are too many people around. I *will* tell you that if you don't leave, you could be in real trouble. Please, let's just leave and I'll explain as we walk."

"You got a compact mirror?" he asked.

"Yes, why?"

"I just wanna look at a mirror and see if I suddenly turned into Clark Gable or something."

She laughed.

Claudia's laugh stopped suddenly. Jesse read fear on her face. He followed her gaze toward the door to see a large man approaching their table, anger evident in his eyes, even in the dim light. He stopped at the edge of their table and stared down at them. Jesse found his vision centered on the largest man he had ever seen. The big Samoan weighed near three hundred pounds and stood over six-and-a-half-feet tall.

The newcomer grabbed the edge of the table and flipped it across the room like a poker chip, sending customers scurrying to get out of harm's way.

Jesse stood. "Hey! I had an unfinished drink on that table."

The big man glanced briefly at him. "I don't give a shit about your goddamn

102

drink." He turned to Claudia. "All right you little bitch, where is the two-bit whore?"

Jesse looked at Claudia then to the big man. "Forget the drink. I didn't know you two knew each other." He moved away from where the table had been, out of the big man's reach.

The big man moved toward Claudia, kicking Jesse's chair out of his way. She stood and stared at him defiantly. Only inches away, he stopped and looked down at her. Jesse was mesmerized. The man's size and power were both obvious and awesome.

The big man said, "I asked you a question, bitch! Where is your whore of a mother?" Claudia said nothing, but continued to look at him defiantly with her dark eyes, half-hidden by too much make-up. He slapped her across the face, knocking her to the floor.

Jesse knelt at her side and assisted her to her feet, speaking to the big man as they stood, "Hey, Guy, take it easy. You ought'a be able to settle this without breakin' her jaw." He turned to Claudia. "You okay?"

She nodded. A small rivulet of blood ran from the corner of her mouth. Jesse turned back to the big man. "You're a big man, mister, and I ain't sure you know your own strength. You could 'a killed her. I don't know what you're mad about but I'm sure you don't have to beat her to death. That won't solve anything." He supported Claudia with his right arm.

"Get away from my daughter, you little asshole."

"Daughter?"

"You heard me, asshole. Get away from my daughter and get outa here before I tear your fuckin' head off."

Jesse looked around the bar for support. No one moved. All watched silently. He was tough, and he was brave, but he wasn't stupid. "Okay. Sorry. I didn't know she was your daughter."

As he walked toward the door, he heard the big man curse at his daughter. He flinched as he heard the slap of an open hand on her face. He couldn't look back. He was ashamed. He didn't know what he expected of himself but he felt he should have done something. He stopped just outside the open door.

"I'll ask you one more time, you no-good little bitch. Where's your mother? Who's she whoring around with now?"

Jesse recognized Tillie's voice, "Dammit, Jerry, leave the kid alone. She was just having a drink with that young fella when you walked in. There's no harm in that."

"Shut-up, Tillie. You know damn good and well this little bitch knows where her old lady is." He turned to Claudia. "Dontcha, bitch?"

Claudia maintained her silence. Jerry slapped her again, knocking her up against the long bar. As she reeled against the bar, he moved in to inflict more punishment. So intent was he on his victim, he never saw the origin of the blow that put him out. He fell to the barroom floor unmoving.

Jesse stood near the bar, a three-foot-long four-by-four in his hands. He faced the crowd menacingly. No one moved.

Tillie said nervously, "Don't worry about anyone in here, kid. They'd have done what you just did if they had the guts." She bent over the big man. "You better get outa here. He's okay, but he'll be coming around soon."

Jesse dropped the four-by-four outside the door and walked briskly to the corner, hoping to see a taxicab or bus, or anything else that would move his body from the immediate vicinity. He spotted a cab moving toward him and waved and whistled until the driver finally realized he might have a fare and pulled quickly to the curb.

"Where to?" asked the driver as Jesse stepped inside.

"Pearl."

"Waikiki," said a female voice. Claudia slipped though the door and sat beside him in the back seat.

"Which is it?" asked the driver.

"I don't care. Take the young lady wherever she wants to go first. Seems like she's adopted me or something."

The driver put his cab into gear. "Waikiki it is."

Jesse glanced at Claudia. "You okay?"

She nodded. "Yeah. I'm okay. Why'd you come back?"

"He didn't apologize for spilling my whiskey."

She laughed. "You're really a barrel of fun. At least I'm glad to know it wasn't an act of chivalry ."

"Well, you *did* try to get me out of there sooner. Maybe if we'd'a left a few minutes sooner, you wouldn't have been there for your father to use as a punching bag."

"Stepfather. My real father died when I was ten."

"Sorry."

"Me too. He was a great guy."

"So your mother is the one who left with Joe?"

"Yes. It's a long story, and I didn't want to go into it in the bar. My stepfather has friends everywhere. He knows Joe. I didn't want him to find out who it was mom left with, and I didn't want him to find out you were a friend of Joe's. He'd have beaten you to death."

Jesse shuddered. "That's a pleasant thought."

"You know, no one else has ever even knocked my stepfather down before, much less put him out cold."

"I had a little help."

"I don't even know anyone who would face him with a shotgun, much less a piece of wood."

"He wasn't looking. It don't take a brave man to hit a guy from behind," lied Jesse, remembering his fear as he had re-entered the bar.

"Have it your way. Thanks all the same."

"I can't say it was my pleasure but you're welcome." He stared out the window of the cab.

They rode in silence for two or three minutes. Finally the driver said, "Whereabouts in Waikiki you wanna go?"

Claudia looked out the window. "Let us out at the next corner."

The driver stopped the cab. Claudia opened the door and stepped outside. She turned back to Jesse who remained seated. "C'mon. I want you to meet my mother."

"I just had a meeting with one family member and I'd really rather not see him again this evening."

"He doesn't live here, silly. Do you think my mother would take Joe to his house?"

"I'm not sure about much of anything tonight. It appears to me that just about anything can happen around here."

"C'mon, relax. You're safe here," she said, leaning into the cab.

"From who?"

"From everyone but me," she answered with a coquettish smile, white in the darkness.

He paid and tipped the driver. As the cab pulled away, Claudia said, "You mean to tell me that Joe never told you about my mother?"

"Not a word."

"They both had it planned to meet at Niki's as soon as your ship docked at Pearl. The only thing that went wrong was my stepfather. Even though they've been separated for more than a year, he follows mom everywhere. He beats up every man she speaks to. He's crazy with jealousy. Wait'll you meet my mom. She's forty-three and looks younger than me. I'm glad she doesn't compete with me for boyfriends."

"I imagine you'd win your share."

Claudia laughed. "Wait'll you meet her, then tell me that."

"Your only problem is too much eye make-up. I think you'd look better without it."

She glanced at him as they turned from the sidewalk toward a modest home, set back from the street. "You do, huh?"

"Yeah, I do."

She laughed again. "I should have known that if Joe liked you, you'd have to be a little different than your normal gyrene. How old are you?"

"Old enough to take care of myself better'n most."

"I'm twenty-four. I know you're somewhere around my age, but I don't know exactly, so tell me," she demanded.

"It's not the years, but the miles that count. I'm younger'n you in years and older in miles. Let's just leave it at that," answered Jesse, embarrassed by his youth.

"Okay. Well, here we are – home." She turned and unlocked the front door, opened it and motioned him inside. The house was nicely done in contemporary furniture of conservative taste, and immaculately clean. A man's, then a woman's voice drifted from the kitchen.

"Mom. I'm home. And I've got a straggler with me," said Claudia raising her voice.

Two figures appeared in the lighted kitchen doorway. "Mom, this is Jesse. Jesse, this is my mother, Katrina O'Leary Haliniak."

As Katrina hugged Jesse, then shook his hand, he knew without a doubt, he was looking at the prettiest woman in the Hawaiian islands. She was slim and petite and, if he had to guess, not a day over twenty-five years old. Her hair hung straight and long to her waist.

"You're kidding?" he said. He couldn't think of anything else to say.

They all laughed.

Joe answered, "It's true, old man. I've known her for twelve years and she hasn't aged a day. What took you so long to get here?"

Jesse tore his gaze from Katrina and looked at his friend. "Joe, I ought'a kill you. What's the big idea of splittin' like that without at least letting me know what was going on?"

"Relax for a minute. Hell, you took so long at that jukebox we couldn't wait any longer. I thought Claudia would be a nice surprise and she could explain everything to you on the way over here. It's a long story. You see, Katrina's ex is this big Samoan guy and...."

Jesse interrupted, "Yeah, I know. I met him. We weren't formally introduced but I feel like I got as close to him as I ever need to."

Katrina's face fell. "What happened?"

"Let's sit down. I want to hear this story," said Joe.

Claudia told the story, leaving nothing out, often quoting her stepfather and Jesse. When she finished, Katrina said, "Are you serious? You mean to tell me that Jesse here knocked that big monster out cold with a board?"

"It was a big board, Ma'am," Jesse answered.

She laughed a hearty laugh, "Don't call me Ma'am. Call me Katrina. And I think that's the funniest story I ever heard in my life. That no-good bully has whipped guys twice your size. One night, he went into Niki's on a drunk and beat up five men, then sat down and drank a case of beer. And you beat him up with a board?"

"It was a big board," he repeated.

The house reverberated with their laughter. Jesse found it contagious and joined in.

Grabbing Jesse's arm and pulling him toward the kitchen, Katrina said, "Come on, Jesse, sit down at the table and have a drink. Any man as serious about his whiskey as you, needn't go thirsty in this house." She turned to Claudia. "Hon, get Jesse a drink, will you please?"

Jesse thought he caught a fleeting glimpse of jealousy in Claudia's eyes as she stepped into the kitchen.

The four of them drank and told stories well into the night. Jesse learned how Joe had met Katrina on his way home from Korea. Jerry Haliniak, the big Samoan, had been courting her about a month when Joe had first met her. She had ignored Haliniak for Joe's company until one day when Haliniak had confronted the two of them outside of Niki's bar. The big man had easily bested Joe in a short but brutal fight. In order to save her lover's life, Katrina had promised never to see Joe again.

Mutual friends had helped to keep them in touch over the years and for the past four years, Claudia had corresponded directly with Joe on a casual basis. It was she who had helped to engineer the meeting at Niki's.

Shortly after two in the morning, Jesse said, "Well, this has been great but I've gotta get back to the ship and get some shut-eye."

"We have room here," offered Katrina. "You can't go staggering around at this hour. You'll never find a cab, and the buses quit running an hour ago."

"I'll be okay. A little walk won't do me any harm."

"You'll never get back to Pearl on foot before daylight. Just stay here," said Claudia.

"Oh? When did you become my commanding officer?"

Joe cleared his throat. He said to Katrina, "Let's turn in, babe. I think the two Spartans wanna talk."

Katrina smiled, "I thought you'd never ask." To Claudia and Jesse she said, "Good night, you two."

Jesse and Claudia both said goodnight as Joe and Katrina disappeared into the darkness of the small hallway. Claudia looked at Jesse shyly. "You want to sit in the living room?"

"For a minute, then I've really gotta go. I've had too much to drink and this is a situation where I'd like to be in full control." The thought of Jerry Haliniak suddenly

106

showing up at the front door was heavy on his mind.

Claudia sat next to him on the sofa. "Is there something wrong with me?"

"Not that I know of. Why?"

"You've been trying to get away from me since I first spoke to you. Is my make-up really that bad?"

Jesse was uncomfortable. He didn't really have an explanation. There probably wasn't a man in his battalion who wouldn't give a week's pay to be where he was, and yet here he was trying to make an exit. "No I just feel like being alone for a while. I have nothing against you. As a matter-of-fact, you're pretty cool for a girl. Didn't you ever feel like just being alone for a while?"

"I know you're not queer, so if it's not me, what is it? You married or got a steady girl?"

"No. And no steady girl. I don't want a steady girl."

"You're a strange guy, Jesse." There was a short silence then Claudia said, "I want to show you something. Excuse me a second." She stood and moved into the kitchen. Jesse heard water running in the sink. Shortly after it stopped, Claudia returned to the living room.

He studied her as she re-entered the room. Something was different but he wasn't sure what it was. She sat next to him on the sofa. "What do you think of my eye make-up now?"

She had none. Her eyebrows were perfectly shaped for her features and her lashes were long and thick. She really didn't need make-up on her eyes to enhance her beauty, rather to cover the dark bruise under her right eye.

"I like you better with the shiner. Who did that – your stepfather?"

She nodded. "Two days ago."

"What's to keep him from coming into this house right now?"

"Prison." Claudia paused. "We have a restraining order against him. He might get away with this at Niki's," she pointed to her eye, "but if he's ever caught here, I won't need a witness."

"That might be a real comfort to you, but me, I'd rather have a rifle." He smiled. "You got pretty eyes – even the one with the shiner."

"Stay with me tonight, Jesse."

"I beg your pardon?"

"I asked you to stay with me tonight." Jesse felt doubt overcoming his resolve to leave and be done with this crazy family. He looked into her big ebony eyes and sensed loneliness. But maybe he was reading her wrong.

"I want you to just stay with me tonight, Jesse. I'm not asking for anything more, nor do I expect anything more. I like you, and I just want someone to talk to and be with – without having to worry about putting on a bunch of airs and worrying that all you're interested in is sex. I know I'll probably never see you again, but that doesn't have to mean that you can't stay here, does it? I don't have to have sex. I just want you to hold me."

*****

Jesse stood on the fantail of the Breckinridge and watched Pearl Harbor fade into the distance. He was confused about life in general and women in particular. He could still feel Claudia as she lay curled up with her back to him. The scent of her perfumed hair wafted into his nostrils despite the twenty-two-knot wind around him. They had not indulged in anything physical other than the act of

107

pressing partially-clothed bodies against one another, but it had been a comfortable feeling. Somehow, the loneliness within both of them had abated, almost like magic, and the two had slept comfortably through the night. He shook his head.

"You okay, old man?"

He turned to Joe. "Yeah, I was just shakin' some strange thoughts outa my head." He paused for a moment, glancing absentmindedly out to sea. "Joe, what's the scoop on you and Katrina? You gonna marry her when you get back or what?"

Joe looked wistfully at the ocean. "No. I shoulda married her twelve years ago. She was the right one then. But it would never work now."

"What the hell are you talking about? If you still love her and she loves you, why'n the hell wouldn't it work out?"

A sad look spread across Joe's face. "I wish to hell I was as young and naive as to believe in that fairy tale. I'd marry ol' Katrina in a second. But it don't work that way."

"That's because you got a lousy attitude goin' in."

Joe appeared to think about Jesse's statement for a moment. "Maybe so." He shrugged and walked away, leaving Jesse once again to pursue his private thoughts.

After leaving Hawaii, the routine and boredom of a marine's life aboard a troop carrier set in: daily inspections, clean up details, mess duty, classes on Vietnam and soviet weapons. When the powers that be could find nothing more to occupy the time, recreational activities were allowed. Most of the men spent their time writing letters or playing cards, though many were unable to continue the latter after losing heavily the first three or four days at sea. These men became listless. The waiting was difficult for all, but for the card players who could no longer afford to play cards it was unbearable.

The marine commander, Colonel William Pool, organized a "smoker": Marines against sailors, by weight division. The first time Jesse had heard the term "smoker" he had no idea what was meant until it was explained that during boxing matches in boot camp, the recruit spectators were allowed to smoke cigarettes, as many as they wanted, while the matches were in progress. Since smoking was prohibited except at very specific times in boot camp, the marines began to call the boxing matches "smokers" to designate the freedom to smoke as being at least as important as the matches themselves.

With regard to Colonel Pool's smoker, the sailors had been together for quite some time and knew who their best boxers were in each division. They had no problem choosing who would represent the Navy. The Marines however were forced to ask for volunteers. There were none forthcoming until the pride of the Corps was challenged by a sailor over the ship's p.a. system. So angered were the marines by the insolence of the sailor that no less than ten men in each weight division volunteered.

Since there was no time to hold elimination bouts, the men decided among themselves who would defend the honor of the Corps. Jesse was chosen as the marine middleweight. He had mentioned his experience as an amateur but said he would gladly defer to anyone who felt confident they could whip the middleweight swabbie, whoever that might be.

On fight day, flyweight, the smallest division, began the festivities. Both sides had boasted total annihilation of their opponents and, among those who had money, the betting was heavy. The earlier fights were fun to watch, mostly as slapstick comedy. The smaller men were lightning fast but there were no knockouts. Lack of boxing experience often made for awkward moves which both sides found hilarious.

The welterweight division was the first weight class that provided the spectators with a sample of real boxing. The Marine representative had been golden gloves champion in the state of Alabama in 1961 and there was no doubt he outclassed his Navy opponent. Though he didn't score a knockout, he did drop his opponent in the third and final round for the count of eight. He won a unanimous decision.

By division the marines were one victory ahead of the Navy when Jesse took his turn in the ring. Both middleweights were experienced boxers and the first round was a sparring match. Onlookers were disappointed because neither side could claim the first round as a decisive victory.

Midway through the second round Jesse's opponent made an error and Jesse took advantage. Seeing that he had shaken his adversary with a series of counterpunches, Jesse quickly moved in for the kill, throwing rapid, well-placed punches in a flurry. The sailor fell to the deck, unconscious. Jesse had scored the first knockout of the day.

The light heavyweight division proved to be a disaster for the combat-bound marines. The sailor, named Lewis, a black man who had the appearance of a professional boxer, devastated his marine opponent in the latter stages of the first round. The marine was saved by the bell, only to be finished off in the first fifteen seconds of the second round.

The heavyweight match went into the latter part of the third round when the marine finally landed a solid punch. He had just enough strength left to finish off his opponent before the bell rang. The marines had carried the day and defended their honor to the satisfaction of most.

Jesse was given light duty for two days to recuperate from the effects of the bout. He used the time to catch up on his correspondence and to wager almost every penny he had on the World Series.

Jesse listened daily to his money disappear as the Twins lost the Series in five games. As the final out of the fifth game made it official, Jesse shook his head and covered his bets.

"That's all you got left?" asked Joe as Jesse held two one-dollar bills in the air and waved them as if drying them out.

"Yep."

"Wasn't a real smart bet, was it?"

"Nope."

"That ain't very much bread."

"Nope."

"You need a loan?"

"Nope. What the hell do I need money for? We'll be in Vietnam in a few days."

"Yeah, that's true. But have you noticed that not a word has been mentioned about seven-eighty-two gear and weapons yet?"

"You know the Crotch. They're gonna wait until the last possible minute then they'll probably hand them to us on our way down the nets."

"Maybe. But Lewis says he doesn't think there's any small arms on board,

109

except for the navy stuff." Jesse and Joe had become friends with Seaman Lewis, the Navy light-heavyweight boxer.

Jesse looked at Joe, a serious expression on his face.. "You don't think even the Marine Corps would send guys to combat without weapons do you?"

"It's beginning to look that way."

Jesse shrugged. "What the hell. Think of the taxpayer dollars we'll be savin'."

Early the next morning Jesse got his first look at Da Nang. He descended the debarkation net without a weapon and boarded the Mike boat gently bobbing up and down in the soft swells.

As the Mike boat pulled away from the *Breckinridge* with its cargo of unarmed marines, Jesse imagined what he would do if they were attacked. He tried to conjure up a viable scenario but couldn't muster much. *Jump overboard and swim like hell. It ain't much of a plan, but that's it.*

As they motored up the inlet to Da Nang, Jesse was struck by the beauty of the buildings. He hadn't expected to see the European influence this far from Saigon, but it was very definitely European – and yet there was something oriental mixed in that gave Da Nang a flavor of its own.

The grey masonry and concrete walls of the buildings fronting the channel were unkempt and partially overgrown with vegetation but they were closer to western civilization than Jesse had expected to see. From his high school reading of Dickens, Jesse could almost imagine he was in old England, and yet the architecture was not English. He wished he knew more about buildings. He had expected bamboo huts everywhere north of Saigon.

"It's beautiful," said Jesse.

"Who woulda believed this shit in Chicago?" was Joe's response.

Several small clumps of Vietnamese stood on the shore next to the buildings and waved to the marines as they passed. The hot morning air carried with it a humidity that made the ninety-degree heat far more difficult to bear than a hundred-and-ten degrees in the dry desert southwest. Jesse wondered why the Vietnamese wasted their energy waving. It had to be a major effort.

As they approached the small beach they were alerted to prepare for landing, which simply meant bracing one's self for the slight bump as the front of the Mike boat touched bottom. Shortly the front ramp of the boat fell to the sand and the marines stepped ashore.

Amid the stares of the curious Vietnamese, the marines were loaded into olive drab semi-trailers with barred windows and transported to the airstrip. A misty rain began to fall.

The modern streets and European buildings gave way to a simpler environment as they approached the airstrip. Thatched huts or simple buildings of cheap wood construction became the rule. The roads in the area were mostly dirt, though construction equipment was plainly visible everywhere. After passing one final checkpoint, the newly arrived marines found themselves stepping onto a fresh concrete staging area, complete with a gentle rain and no overhead cover.

Joe said, "Ain't that just like the Air Force? Spend a million dollars on a goddamn cement slab and forget to cover it in a country where it rains every damn day."

"They operate a lot like the Crotch, I see," replied Jesse.

The Marines were separated into groups by assigned units.

"Langley, Jesse, Lance Corporal," shouted a voice.

"Yo."

"1st Battalion, 4th Marines," said the staff sergeant on the other end of the voice.

Jesse looked at Joe. "The brigade? I thought they were in Hawaii." He picked up his seabag and stood with two other men already assigned to the 1st Battalion, 4th Marines.

Joe's name was called for the 2nd Battalion, 4th Marines and the two thought they would be going to the same physical location until they learned that 1st Battalion, 4th Marines was located by the airstrip near Chu Lai, in the southern part of the I Corps, while the second battalion was stationed much closer to Da Nang.

Jesse and the men assigned to the 1st Battalion, 4th Marines had to wait for a KC-130 aircraft to transport them and their gear to Chu Lai but Joe and his group were ordered mounted up in trucks within fifteen minutes of final assignment.

Jesse and Joe shook hands.

"Keep your head down, Joe."

"Don't spend any wooden nickels, you crazy cowboy."

Then he was gone. Jesse watched the trucks disappear into the steady drizzle and wondered if they would ever meet again. He shivered and pulled his raincoat tightly about his neck. Vietnam was suddenly a sad and lonely place.

It rained off and on the remainder of the day. C-Rations were issued at about 1530 hours for the men who still awaited transportation. Though Jesse was hungry, he was cold and wet from the steady drizzle that somehow managed to ignore the raincoat, and apprehensive about the approaching darkness. He managed to eat only the cookies and drink the coffee in his rations.

At 1700 hours, the twelve men assigned to the 1st Battalion, 4th Marines boarded a KC-130. In less than twenty minutes, the big plane touched down on the steel-matte runway at Chu Lai.

When he stepped down the ramp and exited the aircraft, Jesse was struck by the feeling that he was not a part of what he saw, but merely an invisible observer. The steel-matte runway, the sand, the mud, the sandbag bunkers, the jeeps and trucks, a machine gun emplacement, and strands of concertina wire, were all part of a John Wayne movie. He didn't know the name of the picture but he knew he had seen it. It didn't seem right that he had somehow intruded into this celluloid world. He kept waiting to hear the director's voice. His mind searched for something real but went unrewarded. He wondered where the producer and director were. *This is one helluva movie set.*

A mighty-mite, the Marine Corps version of the jeep, manufactured by American Motors, pulled up to the row of men standing in the mud next to the aircraft. The driver, a tall, lanky man, said, "Anybody going to H & S Company, 1st Battalion, 4th Marines?"

"I am," answered Jesse.

"Hop in. I'll give you a lift." The driver looked at the others. "There's a six-by on its way here for the rest of you."

"They send you here to pick me up?" asked Jesse.

"Nope. I came down to pick up mail but I always check for replacement troops," answered the driver.

"You got a rifle?"

111

Stoney Livingston

"Sure." The driver picked up his rifle, lying next to his seat.

"I'm with you," said Jesse, throwing his seabag into the back of the mighty-mite.

As the mighty mite pulled away from the airstrip, Jesse asked, "Where's One-Four?"

Pointing to their front and making a sweeping gesture, the driver said, "All over. We got the northern and eastern perimeter of the air strip."

The mighty-mite spun its tires and slid a short distance sideways as the lanky driver took a turn too fast for the available traction.

"Sorry, just tryin' to get to battalion before dark."

"I'm with you, friend. Don't hold back on my account," said Jesse.

The ride to battalion headquarters seemed to take forever to Jesse but in reality was little more than five minutes. It was almost dark when the driver stopped the mighty mite in the battalion compound.

"This is the battalion H.Q. tent." The driver nodded to a tent on the right. "I guess you better report here first."

"Thanks." Jesse hopped out of the vehicle and retrieved his seabag. The driver waved and drove away, leaving him standing alone in the mud.

Jesse looked around the compound in the growing darkness and saw no activity. No movement of any kind. He waited to awaken from his unreal dream at any moment. He closed his eyes then slowly reopened them. Nothing had changed. He seemed stuck in a John Wayne movie.

He turned to the H.Q. tent, pulled back the flap and entered quickly. There was no light inside and it was difficult for him to see at first, but as his eyes grew accustomed to the darkness, he found he was standing next to a field desk with a man seated behind it.

"Lance Corporal Langley reporting for duty to the 81 platoon."

The man behind the desk looked up at him and said, "Hang on." He turned his head. "Hey, Sergeant Major. New man for 81's. Anybody going out there tonight?"

The sergeant major stepped from out of a darkened corner.

"What's your name, Marine?"

"Langley, Lance Corporal, Sergeant Major. Reporting in."

"Welcome aboard, Langley." He offered his hand.

Still shaking the sergeant major's hand, Jesse said, "Sergeant Major, I hate to be a pain in the butt, but can I draw a rifle and some ammo?"

"Not till after chow in the morning."

"What happens if the VC hit the compound tonight?" asked Jesse unable to comprehend the fact that he was expected to spend a night in the combat zone without a weapon.

"There's a case of grenades over there in the corner. Help yourself. You got a poncho?"

"I don't have *any* seven-eighty-two gear."

"That's too bad. We don't have any extra around here. You'll have to rough it tonight. There's a fly tent we use to cover the mess area. The ground is fairly dry. You'll be okay there for one night. Grab your gear and I'll show you."

Jesse picked four grenades from the case and walked outside, following the sergeant major, stuffing the grenades into his raincoat pockets. He picked up his seabag and walked carefully to the rear of his escort. The sergeant major stopped at a large tarp directly across the cleared area facing the H.Q. tent.

"This is it. It's not much, but it'll keep the rain from hitting you in the face. You might wanna put your seabag on a piece of high ground just in case it rains real hard. Don't pull the pins on those grenades unless we're totally overrun. We're stretched pretty thin but we've been here long enough to know the turf. You should be okay until tomorrow when we can get you to 81s. Any questions?"

"A million but they'll wait. Thanks."

"Sleep tight. Reveille at 0500. See you after chow." The sergeant major disappeared into the darkness.

Jesse placed his seabag on a small mound almost in the center of the tarp. He lay on his back, fully dressed, and propped his head against the seabag. The drizzling rain had penetrated the collar of his raincoat and his upper torso was wet. His trousers from his knees to his bloused boots were wet and muddy. He was tired and cold from the dampness, and he was afraid of the unknown.

He slept listlessly off and on through the night. Twice he heard the rattle of small arms. Periodically he heard artillery barrages. He hoped they were friendly. He awakened from one of his brief periods of sleep just as the sky began to turn grey in the east. He sat up against his seabag and waited for the light to illuminate the compound. Slowly the camp came awake. When he felt it was safe, he pulled out his crumpled pack of cigarettes only to find the first four too soggy to light. He decided the fifth one would burn and deftly used his Zippo lighter to ignite the driest end, cupping his hands to hide the flame even though it was almost full daylight.

He left his seabag and strolled to the H.Q. tent. The sergeant major was just finishing a cup of coffee as Jesse entered.

"Morning, Langley. How'd your first night in Vietnam go?"

"I'm not crazy about the sleeping arrangements but I've seen worse."

Sergeant Major Howell looked at him and smiled. "You just might make it over here, Langley." He pointed to a small coffeepot, sitting on a tiny stand atop two burning heat tablets. "Have some coffee. There's a canteen cup next to the pot."

Jesse rubbed his hands. The smell of the coffee, mixed with that of the heat tabs, brought a rush of memories of his first tour. "Thanks." Pouring the coffee, he asked, "How the hell do you keep your cigarettes dry?"

The sergeant major laughed. "Already found out about that little problem, huh?"

Jesse nodded as he sipped the bitter coffee.

"You gotta get one of these. They run about fifteen piasters in the villages," answered Howell.

Jesse looked at the soft plastic, two-piece cigarette pack holder. "How much is fifteen plasters?"

"'Bout twelve cents."

Jesse smiled. That was about all he had left after the World Series. "Thanks."

As Jesse drank his coffee, Sergeant Major Howell asked him about his background. When he finished his coffee, the sergeant major said, "Let's get some chow. Take that mess kit over there. Goddamn clerk never gets up till 0730."

He followed the sergeant major through the chow line, taking whatever was put into his kit. They ate, squatting, near the fly tent, neither man speaking much. It was as though they both wanted done with the unpleasantness of the food so they could get on with other things. After washing their mess gear and returning to the

113

Stoney Livingston

H.Q. tent, Jesse was tired of waiting.

"Sergeant Major, where's the armory? I want a rifle."

"Turn right out the door. Second tent on your right."

"Is it okay to draw one?" asked Jesse.

"Yeah, go ahead. Maybe by the time you get back with your gear we'll have transportation to 81s for you. Here, take these papers. You'll need 'em to draw your gear." He handed Jesse a set of papers in triplicate.

Papers in hand, Jesse left the H.Q. tent in search of the armory. Inside the armory tent he handed the papers to the surly blond lance corporal seated on a campstool behind the makeshift counter. "I'd like to draw a rifle and some seven-eighty-two gear."

The lance corporal looked at Jesse as though bothered by his appearance. "People in hell want ice water, so what?"

Jesse wasn't sure whether the man was joking or not. He smiled and said, "Yeah, but I'm authorized." He pointed to the papers.

The lance corporal slowly stood and looked at a row of M-14s. "Another fucking John Wayne. Come over here to win the fucking war single-handed."

Jesse became a bit uncomfortable, still not sure if the man was joking, and not finding the joke funny, if that's what it was. "Just my share," he replied.

The lance corporal picked up an M-14. He slammed it down on the wooden counter top. "Here, boot."

"Hey, take it easy. I may have to use that thing," said Jesse as he picked up the rifle and examined it for damage.

The lance corporal ignored him as he dug out seven-eighty-two gear. Jesse watched silently as the man placed a cartridge belt, two canteens, a first aid pouch, a bayonet, four M-14 magazines, a poncho, helmet and liner, shelter-half, entrenching tool, and a pack on the counter.

When he finished dropping the items on the counter, the lance corporal said, "There it is, boot. Now sign for it and get the fuck outa here."

Jesse studied the big blond man for a moment. "Let's get somethin' straight. First, I'm no boot. I've probably got more time in grade than you have in the Corps. Second, I'm on your team, so there ain't no sense you and me fightin'. Third, there's no sling for the rifle, no pouches for the canteens, no pouches for the magazines, no scabbard for the bayonet; the first aid pouch is empty and you're one magazine short."

The lance corporal looked threateningly at Jesse. "You want a sling?" He handed Jesse a three-foot length of cotton rope.

"What about the magazine pouches?" asked Jesse.

"Tuck 'em inside your fucking cartridge belt, John Wayne."

"What about a pressure bandage for the first aid kit?" asked Jesse, working to hold himself in check.

"Pretend, big shot."

Jesse made one last attempt at civility. "Look, I don't know what you got against me. All I want is the basic equipment. I'm not askin' for new gear."

The lance corporal lifted the pack from the counter and threw it into Jesse's chest. "Listen, you fucking new guy, I told you to sign and get the fuck outa here. If you don't wanna sign, leave this shit and get outa my armory. You fucking new guys think your shit don't stink. I don't have to kiss your ass."

Jesse vaulted the counter, striking the lance corporal in the chest with his booted feet, throwing him into the neatly stacked rows of M-14s. The rifles came crashing down, Jesse and the lance corporal among them.

Both men were half-buried in rifles and seven-eighty-two gear, and Jesse was attempting to remove the larger man's trachea manually when the sergeant major and two other men rushed into the tent.

Jesse refused to release his death grip on his opponent's throat when ordered to do so by the sergeant major. The three new arrivals finally tore them apart but the blood running from the lance corporal's mouth and throat were mute testimony to Jesse's intention.

"What the hell is going on here?" shouted the sergeant major.

The lance corporal attempted to speak. His lips moved, but the only sound that issued forth was that of bubbling blood.

"Jesus Christ. You two men get him to sick bay!" shouted the Sergeant Major.

The two marines holding Jesse hesitated, looking at the sergeant major. "Let him go, goddamnit! And get this man to sick bay." The sergeant major repeated his order.

The two released Jesse and rushed to the lance corporal. When they exited the tent, assisting the injured armorer, the sergeant major looked at Jesse. "What the hell happened in here, Langley?"

Jesse was still breathing heavily, his adrenaline not yet reduced to normal levels. He looked at the sergeant major, fearful he was about to be court-martialed for attacking an American Marine in a combat zone. "Sergeant Major, I'm sorry. I tried to take that guy's shit but I just couldn't. He's supposed to be on my side but he thinks he's Gods' gift to the world. When he slammed me in the chest with a pack, that was the end of it. That guy needs a shrink."

"Looked to me like you were trying to kill him."

"I was, Sergeant Major. Another fifteen or twenty seconds and you'd be arrestin' me for his murder. He's bigger'n me and I didn't aim to give him a second shot."

"You better hope he's all right," said the sergeant major calmly.

"He'll never be all right, Sergeant Major. He's an asshole."

Howell eyed Jesse. "You got a real way with words, son." He looked around the tent. "Let's get this mess cleaned up. Maybe I can get your gear drawn and have you out of here before there's anymore goddamn trouble. We need experienced mortar men in the field, not in the brig."

Jesse helped the sergeant major re-stack the rifles and put things in an orderly array. When he left the armory he was equipped with pouches for his canteens and magazines. He had a pressure bandage in the first aid kit and a scabbard for his bayonet. There were no slings for the rifles – at least they hadn't been able to find any. Jesse tied the cotton rope to the sling swivels and slung the rifle over his shoulder. He neatly made his pack, complete with shelter half. After placing his poncho neatly inside the pack, he signed the papers and stepped outside the tent.

The sergeant major stationed a corporal in the armory and led Jesse back to the H.Q. tent. Once inside the tent, the company clerk said, "Sergeant Major, Samuels is on light duty for a few days." He looked at Jesse and said, "Who helped you work Samuels over?"

Jesse studied the man. He didn't look like Jesse's idea of a clerk. He was a big man, about a year Jesse's senior, broad in the shoulders and tanned as brown as leather. Jesse answered softly, "His attitude."

The clerk smiled. "He's needed it for a long time. He was in on one firefight, and ever since then he thinks the world has to kiss his ass. Only trouble is, you damn near overdid it. Doc says a few more seconds of that shit and ol' Sam woulda been colder'n a slab of marble."

Jesse smiled. "I'll try to do a better job next time."

A marine stuck his head into the tent. "Someone in here going to 81's?"

Jesse looked at the marine. "I hope so." He turned to Sergeant Major Howell.

"Get outa here, Langley. And save all that damn fightin' for the gooks."

"Thanks, Sergeant Major." He picked up his gear and stepped outside.

"Where you from?" asked the driver.

"Arizona."

"No shit? I'm from Texas. How are things back in the States?"

"Same as always I guess."

He followed the driver to his vehicle, a mechanical mule. Referred to as a mule by the infantry, the vehicle was little more than a platform on wheels with four-wheel drive and four-wheel steering. This one was loaded with containers of hot food destined for the 81-mortar platoon.

"There ain't a whole lot of room but you can squeeze your stuff on," offered the driver.

Jesse carefully placed his seabag and pack onto the deck of the vehicle. Once he was seated, the driver said, "Hang on."

The drive to the mortar position took about five minutes on the muddy roads. Jesse was watchful and alert, wishing the driver wouldn't talk so much.

A stand of small pine trees signaled their destination. Jesse hadn't expected pines. As they entered the trees, there was a sign nailed to one of them. It simply said, "Sherwood Forest." He searched the trees nervously as the small vehicle sloshed down the muddy road cutting through the center of the forest.

Exiting the pines, the driver said, "Well, yer here. The Marines have landed." He stopped the mule in front of a dirty brown tent.

"You might as well take your gear off here. I gotta go to that next tent over there." He pointed to another dirty brown tent.

Jesse jumped off the vehicle and picked up his seabag and pack. The driver sped off to the next tent, slinging mud from the tires of his mule.

The South Pacific Ocean splashed against a near vertical cliff a mere three or four hundred yards from where he stood. The landmass appeared to abruptly drop off into the blue water a hundred feet below. The pine forest through which he had just passed seemed a sharp contrast to the mud and ocean. Several sandbag bunkers and mortar gunpits only added to the fantasy of the scene. Jesse became certain as he studied his environment that he would awaken in Tucson, Arizona in a matter of moments. He was just as certain that when he did, he wasn't going to re-enlist in the Marine Corps.

CHAPTER SEVEN: SHERWOOD FOREST

A gunnery sergeant stood just outside the tent. He was dark-skinned, six-feet tall and sported a thin mustache. He reminded Jesse of an older Mexican friend he had known as a boy. He thought of Pablo and drifted back to the Bar-X ranch for a moment.

"Jesse Langley, Lance Corporal, reporting to 81's, First Battalion, Fourth Marines. Am I in the right place?" he said after a moment.

The gunnery sergeant gave him a neutral look. "You've got the right place. Set your gear down inside the tent, out of the mud, and we'll go over your assignment."

Jesse was a little disappointed. He had expected a handshake or, at least, a welcome of some sort. He stepped inside the tent and placed his seabag upon dry soil.

The gunnery sergeant followed him inside. "I'm Gunnery Sergeant Reyes, Platoon Gunnery Sergeant."

The two shook hands and Jesse felt better. Reyes looked at his orders and said, "You got any experience on an 81 mortar?"

"About two and a half years."

"How much time you got in grade?"

"I don't know. If they count from my re-enlistment day, a little over two months. If they count from when I was promoted, about a year and a half or two."

"Well, at least we didn't get a boot."

The remark irritated Jesse. He wanted to say, *You sure as hell didn't. I can gun a mortar as fast as any man you've got, including you, you pompous ass*. But he said nothing. He'd had a pretty rough start in this outfit already; no sense making things worse by irritating his platoon gunnery sergeant.

Reyes continued, "Well, this makes it tough on me, Langley. We don't have much rank over here and most of our squad leaders are lance corporals. You may have more time in grade and experience than our squad leaders and gunners but you're new to combat."

He paused, apparently waiting for Jesse to speak. When there was no response, he continued, "The best I can do is make you an assistant gunner on Gun One. The gunner is a PFC but he's one of the best in the platoon."

"Let me make sure I've got this right, Gunny. I'm going to be an A-gunner to a PFC who has less rank, less time in, and less experience than I do?"

"For now, yes."

"I guess you've got your reasons, but I'd just as soon be an ammo carrier. Gunner and a-gunner both carry pistols. I went through a lot of work to get this rifle this morning and I'd hate to have to return it to that guy at Battalion Armory."

"Don't worry about the rifle. I'll just have you and Salsbury trade weapons. He's the man you'll be replacing as A-gunner."

117

"If Salsbury likes his pistol, I don't mind carrying the rifle," offered Jesse, almost in desperation.

"You'll change your mind in a few days. No more than we use our rifles, it's more trouble to keep clean than it's worth."

"Okay, Gunny, if you won't let me be an ammo carrier, I'm looking for a squad leader job. The sooner I'm T.O. with a rifle the better I'll feel. I know mortars, Gunny."

"I like confidence Langley, but don't overdo it."

"I think you'll see in time, Gunny."

"Maybe I will. I hope so. But for now let's go to the First Section tent and get you settled in." Reyes stood. Jesse picked up his seabag and pack and followed him outside.

The sun was shining brightly and the hot moist air was already uncomfortable. Perspiration darkened the back of Reyes' utility jacket. When they arrived at the First Section, the sides and ends of the tent were rolled up to allow for ventilation. Reyes pointed to a cot. "That one's unoccupied. Go ahead and drop your gear. I want you to meet the gunner on your gun."

The tent was deserted with the exception of two other marines. One of them, a young man in his early twenties with chestnut hair and an athletic build, was already moving toward Reyes and Jesse. As he approached, he reached out his right hand. "Hi. I'm Jim Hensley. You in First Section?"

Jesse shook Hensley's hand. He took an instant liking to the PFC. "Jesse Langley. Pleased to meet you."

Reyes said, "Hensley, Langley here is a Lance Corporal, but I'm making him your A-Gunner. He's got 81 training but since he's new to the Nam I'm putting him in a position lower than his rank calls for. I'm sure he'll work his way up but I had to start him somewhere. I'll talk it over with Cuz. Ultimately the final decision is his."

"Hell, Gunny, let him be the gunner. He's got the rank," said Hensley.

"Maybe after we see how things work out. For now, he's your A-gunner. Show him around. I'll brief Cuz in a few minutes," said Reyes.

"Okay, you got it," said Hensley.

Reyes left the tent.

"Asshole," said Hensley softly once Reyes was out of earshot. He turned to Jesse. "He's the biggest wimp in the Crotch. He's afraid to make a decision. Shit, you should be the gunner."

Jesse smiled. "Hell, the bipods are heavier than the tube. I don't mind bein' the A-gunner."

Hensley smiled. "I never thought of it that way. You had chow yet?"

"Yeah. At least I think that's what it was."

"Me too. By the way, where you from in the States?"

"Arizona. How about you?"

"Michigan. Near Detroit. Little place called Troy. Wish to hell I was there now."

"It's getting cold back there this time of year."

"I'd give a hundred bucks to see a snowflake. This damn rain, heat and humidity get old in a hurry."

"Maybe, but I'm not into snow. You can have it."

"Hell, you're a damn desert rat. A little snow would probably kill ya'."

"It wouldn't improve my disposition; that's for sure."

118

Hensley looked at Jesse's gear lying on the cot. "You don't want that rack. It's got a loose leg. There's one on the other side, by D.D. Scott's, that's in better shape."

"Thanks. Appreciate it."

"You might not. Wait'll you meet DD."

"Something wrong with him?" asked Jesse.

"He's just a little crazy is all. He was in a rifle company until about two weeks ago. They transferred him here after he got his third Purple Heart."

"You mean he's been wounded three times already?"

"First man to get three hearts in this war."

"No kiddin'?"

"He's okay. He just acts a little crazy once in a while."

"Why don't they send him home?" asked Jesse.

"They're going to. He's just waiting on orders. You know how the Crotch is. They're probably sitting on some damn general's desk, waiting for a signature."

"If I was him, I'd remind somebody."

"He has. Every day."

Jesse picked up his pack and seabag and moved them to the cot next to D.D. Scott's.

"Hey, Jim," said Jesse.

"Yeah?"

"They use your first or last name around here?"

"Mostly nicknames. If a guy doesn't have a nickname, he'll answer to whatever you call him."

"What's yours?"

"Dude."

"Dude? How'd you get a name like that?"

"I can't really remember. Maybe it's because I'm always combing my hair and getting ready for the girls back in the States."

Jesse smiled. "How much longer you got?"

"April '66."

"By then you may not have any hair left."

"They'll still love me; that you can count on."

"I got a million questions about this place. You got time to fill me in?"

Dude sat on D.D. Scott's cot. "Fire away."

In thirty minutes, Dude explained the daily duties, the rules, the do's and don'ts, who was cool and who wasn't. He explained that no one wore skivvy drawers because of the rash and chafing caused by the heat and humidity. He further advised Jesse of the sought-after duty and those assignments to avoid if at all possible. Each man in the First Section, which included guns one and two, was profiled.

He finished by saying, "And our section leader's name is Tuleano. He's okay, but he's a little crazy. He's a big Samoan dude. Broad at the shoulders and narrow at the waist. I saw him hit one of the guys in the jaw one time. Broke it in two places."

"Why didn't somebody report him?" asked Jesse.

Dude looked at Jesse, eyes open wide. "Tuleano's a damn good sergeant. He just had a bad day. Besides, the guy he hit was a shitbird anyway."

"What about the guy he hit? Didn't he report him?"

119

"Nope. We all saw him trip and fall into the gunpit."

"Oh, I see." Jesse raised an eyebrow.

"Hell, Tule is okay. You just gotta watch his moods."

"I'll try to remember that."

Other marines drifted into the tent, having completed the morning mess. Jesse was introduced to each man, including D.D. Scott. Scott was blond with blue eyes, an inch taller than Jesse, with broad shoulders that displayed strength. Scott had a disarming smile and Jesse liked him immediately, though he wasn't sure of Scott's mental stability. Something intangible about Scott bothered him. Jesse hoped he wouldn't become whatever it was Scott had become. He wondered if the man had always been a little odd or if he had been made that way by combat.

By 0900 hours, he had transferred his rifle to PFC Salsbury and was in possession of Salsbury's M-1911-a1 .45 caliber semi-automatic pistol and holster.

Salsbury, or Sal, as he was called, was a small man. At five-feet-eight and one hundred fifty pounds, he was the smallest man in the First Section. He apparently knew the 81 and took orders well, judging from what Dude had told him prior to the weapon exchange.

Jesse reversed the pistol holster and hooked it to his belt on the left hip, a move in total disregard of regulations. He hoped it would be overlooked in a combat zone.

D.D. Scott, sitting on his cot, looked at the holster on Jesse's left hip. "You some kinda crazy cowboy or what?"

"Nope. Just left-handed," answered Jesse.

"Looks to me like that'd take longer to drag out, twist, cock, and fire than just changing hands from the right side," said DD.

"It don't." Jesse felt the heat rising to his face. It really wasn't any of DD's business as far as he was concerned. And he had hoped the location of the holster would go unnoticed.

"Bullshit," said DD.

Jesse became aware of others in the tent watching silently. He turned his back to DD slowly and began to rummage through his seabag. "Trust me."

DD persisted, "Supposing I was a gook and I jumped out of the bush with this machete." He sprang to his feet, his machete held high in the air.

In one smooth series of movements, Jesse spun, lifted the holster flap, drew the pistol, cocked the hammer, and pointed it at DD's chest – all before DD's feet hit the ground. "I'd blow your gook head off."

DD, who had not fully gained his balance from the sudden lurch to his feet, smiled as he tottered. He looked at the muzzle of the .45 pointed at his chest. "Shit man, you just cocked the hammer. You didn't jack a round into the chamber with the slide."

Jesse looked straight into DD's blue eyes. "I carry one in the chamber for gooks jumping out of the bush with machetes."

DD searched Jesse's eyes. He smiled and dropped his machete onto his cot. "All right, goddamnit. Show me the chamber."

Jesse pointed the pistol to the ground and pulled the trigger. The firing pin clicked into an empty chamber.

Chuckles from around the tent greeted DD's sigh of relief. "Jesus Christ, man. I could've cut off your goddamn head."

"I could've had a round in the chamber. I'm on your side. I didn't figure you

Forever Patriots

to waste someone who had to take a turn at gun watch."

DD laughed. "You're right there." He paused. "How in the hell did you do that so fast?"

"I used to be in a quick draw club. We'd put on our colts and see who could draw and shoot the fastest without blowin' his foot off."

DD laughed again. "You play poker?"

"Some."

"Well, you ain't playin' with me."

The tent reverberated with laughter.

Corporal Cousins, the gun one squad leader, said, "Hey, Langley, you play softball?"

"Sure, but this is football season ain't it?"

Several eyes turned to DD, who dropped his chin to his chest and looked down at his cot, giving his best impression of a wounded basset hound.

"Yeah, but DD shot the damn football day-before-yesterday when he missed a pass," replied Cousins.

"It's too damn hot for football anyway," defended DD.

"Well, it don't matter now. The game starts at ten hundred. Second Section has the duty, so it looks like Third and Fourth," said Cousins.

"That damn Cannuck in Third section gonna be playing today?" asked Private Howard, the section wireman.

"No. He had FDC watch last night," answered Cousins.

"Good. I'm tired of hearing about Montreal's hockey team. Who gives a shit about hockey anyway?"

Jesse spent his first full day in Vietnam playing softball in a muddy field that had been cleared by the Seabees for some unknown purpose. When the game broke up in the late afternoon, the men returned to the tents to play poker, write letters, clean rifles, or engage in whatever other pursuits that might be available. Jesse soon learned the basic drink in Sherwood Forest was luke-warm Kool-Aid. There was no ice and no electricity with which to make any. Occasionally each man was issued two cans of warm beer, hardly a satisfying quantity if one was an avid beer drinker, and Jesse was grateful that beer was one drink he could take or leave.

The shower area was made up of two, fifty-five-gallon drums placed on high platforms. The water was not heated but by taking a shower in the late afternoon, one could be reasonably certain the water would be warm to the touch. Jesse discarded his skivvy shorts after his first shower, having already experienced a slight rash from the heat and humidity. He shaved, using his helmet as a basin and a double-edged blade in his Gillette razor that was overdue for burial. He borrowed a piece of broken mirror from DD so he could see what he was doing.

DD told Jesse of his adventures, giving special emphasis to his last Purple Heart.

His company had been ambushed and DD was struck in the leg by a bullet. As he lay in the rice paddy, his company commander, Captain Knowles, rushed to his aid. Throwing DD over his shoulder in the fireman's carry, the captain had sloshed through the muddy rice paddy, toward the friendly treeline with DD draped over his shoulder, firing his M-14 at the enemy behind them.

That same captain had been promoted to major and was the current executive officer for the First Battalion, Fourth Marines. He was due to rotate to the

121

U.S. shortly and DD wanted to be transferred wherever Major Knowles went. He spoke reverently whenever referring to the major.

About an hour before sunset, Sergeant Tuleano appeared in the First Section tent. Jesse saw him for the first time.

He spoke from the opposite end of the tent. "Hey, Cuz, we gotta supply two men for waterborne patrol tonight. Give me the new man and one more."

"Jesus, Tule," said Dude. "He just got here. He hasn't slept in his own rack yet. Give him a break."

"Okay, you go in his place."

Jesse stood. "That's okay, Sarge. I'm ready."

Tuleano looked at Jesse briefly. "You and Dude report to FDC in five minutes." He turned and left the tent.

"Goddamnit. I had that damn duty three nights ago," complained Dude.

"You know how Tule is. You shouldn't have said anything," said Cousins.

"Yeah, I know how he is. Sometimes he can be a real asshole." Dude turned to DD. "Can I borrow your rifle, DD?"

"You damn straight. Better you than me," replied DD. Dude accepted the rifle and cartridge belt.

Jesse looked at Sal. "How about it, Sal? Can I borrow my rifle back?"

"My pleasure, especially for waterborne patrol. Anytime you want it for that gravy job, just take it. Don't even ask."

"Real prime duty, huh?" asked Jesse.

"You'll find out just how prime tonight," replied Sal.

"I can hardly wait." Jesse picked up the rifle and cartridge belt.

Dude said, "We'd better haul ass. Tule said five minutes and he don't wait for anybody."

Jesse followed Dude to the Fire Direction Center. Both men stepped into the FDC tent. "Tule, this is Lance Corporal Langley. We're both ready for this bullshit duty," said Dude, not without bitterness in his voice.

"Where you from, Langley?" asked Tuleano.

"Arizona."

"They still got cowboys and Indians out there?"

"Some, but it ain't like the movies."

"I'll talk to you about that in the morning. Right now, I gotta get you guys to the river. You'll feel like a goddamn sailor by tomorrow. It's really a shitty detail, but we gotta do it. I'll cut you some slack tomorrow."

"Thanks, Sarge."

"Okay, get going. Dude, you know the drill. There should be a mule pulling up right about now."

The words were barely out of Tule's mouth when Jesse heard the mechanical mule's engine. It idled down and stopped in front of the FDC tent. Jesse and Dude left the tent and jumped onto the platform. Silently the driver put the vehicle into gear and proceeded to his next stop. They stopped at three different locations and picked up four more marines. When they finally arrived at the river it was almost dark. A gentle drizzle softly drummed on their helmets as they put on their ponchos.

A marine wearing a tanker's helmet approached the assembled newcomers. "I'm Corporal Hartley. I'll be your guide for tonight's tour. We've got to get aboard before dark and get into the water, so follow me."

122

Forever Patriots

They followed Corporal Hartley to the river's edge where they joined ten other marines.

Jesse looked at the two Amtrack vehicles standing silently in the dim light at the river's edge. "You gotta be kiddin' me. We're gonna patrol a river in one of those floatin' coffins?"

"Didn't take you long to figure that one out. Pretty soon you're gonna make general," answered Dude.

"What do we do in one of those damn things?"

"Well, if you're lucky, you get to sit on top in the rain and get sniped at. If not, you ride inside and hope the damn thing stays afloat until daylight," answered Dude.

"Not even the Marine Corps is that stupid."

"Take a look at the uniforms. There ain't a swabby in sight. It's too much like work for the Air Force, and no dogface would be dumb enough to set foot on one of those damn things."

"What's the purpose?"

"I've never been real sure. All we do is ride up and down the river in that noisy bastard, looking for gooks."

"They'll hear us two miles away."

"Exactly. And that gives 'em plenty of time to set up ambushes, booby traps and snipers."

Jesse shivered, partly from the rain and partly at the thought of being a target in a shooting gallery. "Have we ever killed any gooks doing this kind of stupid shit?"

"Not that I know of, but we've lost a few guys on our side. Last week a guy from Charlie Company was shot right through the ear by a sniper. Two weeks ago one of these damn things sank and we lost ten men. Three weeks ago a gook recoilless rifle hit one and it damn near sank. They got to shore but three or four guys went back to the States in ponchos."

"Does the Commandant know about this?" asked Jesse.

"You gonna tell him?"

"If I have to do this shit again, I'll at least give it a try. This is stupid."

"Tell me about it."

Corporal Hartley said, "You first eight marines, board that far track. You second eight are with me in the near track."

Jesse and Dude boarded Hartley's Amtrack amid the grumblings of all present. The interior of the steel box was dimly lit in red. It wasn't intended to read by but it was better than remaining in total darkness.

"I still don't believe this shit," said a marine from Bravo Company as he sat down awkwardly on the steel floor.

"I don't either but this is my tenth trip up and down the river," said another.

"Jesus. Who'd you piss off?" asked a third.

"I haven't found out yet. I've been kissin' everyone's ass, starting with my fireteam leader. I've worked my way up to platoon commander and I'm still goin' on these little pleasure cruises. I guess I'll have to work my way up to the company commander."

Most of the men chuckled.

Corporal Hartley stepped into the troop compartment.

"I need two men to ride up top for the first watch."

123

Stoney Livingston

No one spoke.

"I can see you're all experienced marines. That's good," said Hartley. He turned to Dude. "You got the first watch."

As he moved to pick another volunteer, Jesse said, "I'll go."

Dude looked at him. "Are you crazy? I thought you had some time in."

Jesse smiled. "I'm just stupid I guess."

"All right, men, let's go," said Hartley.

Jesse and Dude exited the gaping front ramp and climbed the external ladder to the exposed top of the large amphibious vehicle. Hartley started the engine and closed the ramp. The vehicle lurched forward then moved slowly down a gentle slope and into the river. The top of the amtrack was awash momentarily as it plunged into the water. Both Dude and Jesse were familiar with amtracks and stood quickly, but the water rose to four inches above the tops of their combat boots. Once steadily plodding upstream, the two sat on the wet steel top.

Dude spoke closely into Jesse's ear to be heard above the rumble of the engine and pelting rain, "If anything is going to happen it's most likely on the first or second watch."

Jesse leaned into Dude's ear. "Why?"

"If you were a VC, why would you stay up half the night to kill a few stupid marines if they're gonna make it easy for you to do it just after dinner?"

"Good point."

They fell silent, each searching his side of the river in the darkness. Jesse couldn't remember when he had last felt so stupid or embarrassed. It was almost pitch dark, and even without the rain to muffle sound, the constant loud rumble of the amtrack engine would have obliterated any noise from the surrounding jungle. A Viet Cong soldier with an infrared scope could pick them off unnoticed from the nearby shore. In all likelihood, the sound of the amtrack would cover the report of the sniper rifle and, unless one was looking at or talking to the victim, one wouldn't know the other had been shot until he was discovered missing.

In the darkness Jesse couldn't distinguish the shoreline. After ten minutes of straining his eyes and ears, he lost interest in this futile task. His mind began to wander and he found himself among his friends back home. Next, he was on his Triumph motorcycle. Soon, his thoughts drifted to Shannon. He relived every moment he had ever spent in her presence from the day he had first met her. It was a good time to reflect. The incessant roar of the engine had dulled his senses. He could be of no real use, except perhaps as a target for the Viet Cong and, if a guy was going to check out, he might as well do it with pleasant thoughts on his mind.

A voice above the din of the engine returned him to Vietnam.

"Okay, you guys. Second watch is coming up. You can go below."

Jesse shivered from the dampness. The rain was still falling but had turned misty. He stood and stretched his cramped muscles then climbed into the open hatch.

The floor of the amtrack was under an inch of water. Three of the marines paid it no heed and slept peacefully as the water sloshed about with the pitch and roll of the heavy vehicle. The fourth man sat with his back to a bulkhead, smoking a cigarette.

Once inside and the hatch screwed down, Dude said, "What time is it?"

Jesse held his watch close to one of the red lamps. "Hell, I don't know. My watch is all fogged up from the rain."

124

"What the hell you doin' with a dress watch in the Nam?"

Jesse shrugged. "It's all I have."

"That covers it, I guess. Shit. You need a diver's watch just to tell time in this damn place."

"If I run across one of 'em, I'd like to have one of those Zodiac Seawolfs," said Jesse.

"You and the rest of us. Don't hold your breath. The only one I know of in the platoon is owned by Collins, and he isn't about to let go of it."

The night passed slowly. Sleep was difficult at best; most of the men sat propped against a bulkhead with their eyes closed and thought private thoughts. A couple of them told brief war stories but, other than that, the night was long and boring. There was no enemy contact and the amtracks returned to their staging area shortly before dawn.

Standing beside the amtrack in the grey dawn, Jesse noticed his hands were white and wrinkled like prunes. They reminded him of his childhood days at the Hot Springs swimming pool when his hands turned white and wrinkled from too many hours in the water. He wondered if the rain ever stopped long enough to let the soil dry completely. He missed the desert.

Another mechanical mule appeared with a different driver than the one of the previous evening. Jesse and Dude jumped aboard and rode silently back to Sherwood Forest, Jesse making careful observations of the landscape as they went. He was especially on the alert when passing through a small village. He saw several children stop their play to observe the marines pass down the muddy road.

Jesse tensed as the driver slowed the vehicle and came to a stop near a group of four women. Two were older and dressed in the drab garb of rice paddy workers. The other two were young, in their late teens, and dressed in the silk pants and bright tunics, called Ao Dais, so popular in Vietnam.

"Why we stoppin'?" asked Jesse.

The driver replied, "Relax. I just want a bottle of panther piss."

"Panther piss?"

"You know. Beer. This stuff smells like piss and it's rough as a panther. But hell, there ain't much American beer to be had, so panther piss is where it's at."

Jesse nodded. He pulled out his cigarettes and attempted to light one but it was wet and limp and he was unsuccessful. A small boy of seven or eight approached the mule with a plastic cigarette pack cover. He jabbered rapidly in Vietnamese.

Jesse turned to Dude. "Hey, Dude, do they take American money here?"

"Hell no. Not yet anyway. How much you need?"

"I don't know but I need one of those plastic things to protect my smokes from all this damn water."

Dude handed the boy some paper money from his utility jacket pocket. The money was soaked but the boy gladly accepted it. Dude handed the plastic box to Jesse. "Here. Me souvenir you," he said, mocking a Vietnamese speaking English.

"Thanks."

The driver purchased one beer in a clear bottle. He opened the bottle using the side of the mule and continued the journey, drinking the warm beer as the mule sloshed down the muddy road.

Jesse looked over at Dude. "You drink that stuff?"

"Not me. I don't want any ground glass in my gut."

In between swallows the driver said, "Shit, I been drinkin' this crap for almost three months and it ain't killed me yet."

"Maybe it never will, but to me a hot beer isn't worth the risk," replied Dude. "Especially that bitter-tasting shit."

The driver shrugged and returned his attention to the muddy road. Four marines marched the same direction the mule traveled, two on each side of the road. As the mule drew nearer the men on foot, Jesse noticed that one man on each side of the road carried a flamethrower. The driver slowed as he passed between the two pairs of men.

"Hey, Brownie, you on shit detail again this morning?" shouted Dude as the mule passed the four.

A large black man answered, "Who me? Same old thing. Some guy at headquarters ran out of lighter fluid and I'm on my way to light his cigarette."

"See ya' at noon chow," said Dude.

Brownie waved.

"Where they going without a rifle squad?" asked Jesse.

"They don't need rifle support. They're just going to the dump to burn trash," replied Dude.

"Why don't they just put a little gasoline on it and light it with a match?"

"That'd be too damn easy. It's better to have four guys walk a mile or two each way in the heat and humidity and use up strikers and napalm, so if we need flames in a hurry, the guys will be too tired to carry the damn flame tanks. And just in case they're not too tired, the Crotch makes sure we get no flames by using all the napalm burning garbage."

Jesse nodded. "That makes sense."

They entered Sherwood Forest.

After morning chow, which consisted of oatmeal, powdered eggs, powdered milk and bread, Jesse shaved and showered then cleaned the rifle and cartridge belt before returning it to Sal. He seemed to have recovered from his drowsiness of only an hour earlier and was ready for a day's work.

Inside the First Section tent he asked Dude, "Now what happens?"

"Get some sleep. You'll probably have gun watch tonight."

"You mean there really are 81s in those gunpits? Hell, I thought they were just decoys to fool the gooks."

Dude lay on his back, his cot creaking from the body weight. Closing his eyes, he smiled and said, "For as screwed up as they are, you might as well call 'em decoys."

"I haven't touched a mortar for nine months."

Dude opened one eye. "Pay call is this afternoon. After the eagle shits, I'll go down to gun one with you for a few minutes."

"Thanks."

Using his helmet as a pillow, Jesse lay on his back, wondering what his friends back home were doing. He tried to figure out what time it was in Tucson, Arizona but he wasn't sure. He allowed his mind to drift. He smiled as he thought of Shannon. He realized the real reason he had come to Vietnam was to die. His smile was because he found nothing heroic to do in the act of dying. Softball and waterborne patrol were certainly not the answer. He fell asleep.

"Hey Langley, wake up. Pay call. The eagle shits today, man," said DD, shaking his cot.

Jesse sat up and pulled on his boots. He followed DD to the pay line and waited for his turn at the paymaster.

As he stood before the paymaster, the young second lieutenant said, "Name?"

"Langley, Jesse. Lance Corporal."

The lieutenant searched the pay roster. He looked up at Jesse. "You're not on the pay roster, Lance Corporal. What's your serial number?"

"2015213, Sir."

Again the lieutenant searched the pay roster. "You're not on the pay roster, Marine. You'll have to have your pay records checked and sent to the Battalion. Next."

Jesse stepped away from the field desk and walked to Gunny Reyes' tent.

He spied Sergeant Tuleano just inside the tent. "Sergeant Tuleano, have you seen the gunny?"

"Just call me, Tule. No, I haven't seen him for about an hour. Whatcha need man?"

"Pay. I need pay."

"Go get in the pay line," replied Tuleano.

"I've been in every pay line they've had since I've been back in and the Crotch hasn't found my pay records yet. It's startin' to piss me off."

Tuleano jumped from his cot. "Goddamn it, man, you come with me. I'll get you paid."

Tuleano marched to the front of the pay line. "Lieutenant, this man needs paid. The Marine Corps can't find his pay records but that isn't his fault. He's over here fighting for our country. The least the country can do is pay him."

The lieutenant looked up at Tuleano, whose reputation earned at Pork Chop Hill was well known. "I didn't realize he was a hardship case, Sergeant."

"That's okay, Sarge. I'm not a hardship case. I'll wait." Jesse felt self-conscious as he looked at the others in line.

"Bullshit." Tuleano turned to the lieutenant. "How much can you pay him?"

"How much time you got in?" The lieutenant asked Jesse.

"A little over three years, Sir," replied Jesse.

The lieutenant mumbled, "Let's see, ...a lance corporal over three with combat pay ..." He paused. Looking up at Tuleano he said, "Two hundred forty dollars is all I can do on emergency issue without pay records."

"He'll take it." Tuleano answered for Jesse.

The lieutenant counted out twenty-four brown ten-dollar bills in military payment certificates. Jesse re-counted the MPC for the lieutenant and signed the pay roster. He stepped away from the pay table.

"Thanks, Tule."

"Shit man. You fight, you should get paid."

"Thanks just the same. I appreciate it." Jesse walked away, looking at the strange, brown ten-dollar bills in his hand.

DD cleaned his rifle in the First Section tent. "Hell, I was hopin' you wouldn't get paid so I could buy some of those old-style utility uniforms from ya'. Where'd you get them things anyway?"

"They were issued to me a few years ago," answered Jesse.

"Them rough-out boots too?" asked Sal.

"Yeah."

"I like the old utilities better'n these new ones," said DD. "Hell, we look almost like the army in these damn things."

"Yeah but at least you guys got short sleeves," said Jesse.

"Hell, man, that's combat zone modifications. There's a gook down in the village cuts off the sleeves and hems 'em up for two bits a shirt," said DD.

"Is that authorized?" asked Jesse.

"Hell yes. If they didn't, we'd all die from the heat."

"Where's this village?"

"About a mile down the road. You wanna go?" asked DD.

"Can we?"

"All we need is a third man – that's the rule. And we gotta be back an hour before dark." DD was beginning to show more enthusiasm.

Jesse turned to Sal. "You wanna go, Sal?"

"Might as well. I can hardly wait to see those old mama-sans chewing their betel nut, and their teeth and gums gettin' a deeper purple by the second."

"You're weird, Sal," said DD.

Cousins broke into the conversation. "I've gotta go too, so that's it for this trip. Four is all we can send from each section at a time."

In thirty minutes they were in the small village where Dude had purchased the cigarette pack carrier earlier that same morning. DD was quite popular with everyone in the village. He always brought C-rations, as he did on this occasion, which he promptly gave to several of the small children. He hugged and kissed the women, old and young alike, and he waved or shook hands with the old men, often speaking to them in broken Vietnamese.

Jesse noticed the absence of military-age men in the village. "Where are the younger men?" he asked.

Cousins shrugged. "They're either in the Vietnamese army or with the Cong. Who knows?"

The uncertainty made Jesse shiver. "This is a strange place."

"No shit," agreed Sal.

DD introduced Jesse to the old man who sewed the clothes. After leaving five utility jackets with the old man, Jesse joined Cousins, who was looking at a bright silken blouse in a bamboo hootch.

Jesse picked up a heavy silk pajama set. "Cuz, how much is this in American money?"

"About two dollars. But they won't take MPC. Haven't you got any piasters?" said Cuz.

"To tell you the truth, I didn't even think about it."

Cuz pulled a roll of Vietnamese money from his shirt pocket. "Here. Give me ten bucks and I'll give you ten bucks worth of piasters."

Jesse made the exchange.

He purchased the pajama set and searched for other items peculiar to Vietnam. He would send them to his mother. She may not like them but at least he thought of her. He spent another fifteen minutes shopping, finding nothing of interest. He turned to Cuz. "Wonder where DD and Sal are?"

Cuz smiled. "Come on. I'll show you."

Three bamboo buildings away, Cuz and Jesse stepped through a stringed seashell door. "Welcome to Mama San's," said Cuz.

128

"Is this a cathouse?"

"Sort of. Actually it's more of a bar than it is a cathouse. Mama-San only has two girls, and they can't keep up with the demand."

Jesse looked at six marines standing in line next to the back wall. There were two doors on the wall, behind which the girls conducted business. Jesse laughed. "You gotta be kiddin'. Are they for real?"

"How long you been here, Langley?" asked Cuz.

Still laughing, Jesse replied, "Hell I can't remember. A day or two is all."

"Wait'll you been here a couple of months. You'll change your mind," said Cuz seriously.

Jesse looked at the anxious faces in the waiting line and laughed again. "No, Cuz. Something about standin' in line kinda takes the pizzazz out of it for me."

"Oh well, we might as well have a beer. Looks like DD and Sal are next."

Jesse said, "They wouldn't have any American beer here would they?"

"Almost." Cuz winked at him then spoke a few words of Vietnamese to Mama-San, who stood behind a roughly hewn wooden counter. As she sat two brown bottles of San Miguel beer on the counter, Jesse noticed her teeth, lips, and mouth. They were deep purple. He paid for the beers and walked outside to drink.

Cuz followed him through the door. "Thanks. Stuffier than hell in there, ain't it?"

"It ain't much better out here, but at least a breeze picks up now and then." Jesse paused. "Ol' Mama-San's teeth – what's wrong with them?"

"Nothing. Over here it's considered beautiful. That's what happens when you chew the betel nut."

"Give me a round-eye any day," said Jesse.

"Me too. But try to find one over here. Do you realize what a round-eyed whore could make in a month over here?"

Jesse smiled. "I don't believe the human body could take that kinda punishment for a solid month."

"Maybe not," agreed Cuz. "But what a way to go."

Jesse looked at his bottle of beer. "You ever get any cold beer around here?"

"Not unless you get down around the airstrip. The Air Force and Army have ice. They even have an enlisted man's club."

"Why couldn't we have one at Battalion Headquarters?"

"Hell man, we're the perimeter."

"Well then, why couldn't they let us go to the Army club in small groups?"

Cuz took a sip of his warm beer. "The doggies don't want the animals from the jungle in their goddamn club."

Jesse nodded. "Well, it was a thought. They don't seem very grateful for all the protection we're givin' 'em."

Cuz agreed. "We oughta open a hole in the perimeter some night and drop a flare right over their goddamn enlisted club so the gooks could see where to go."

They both laughed at the thought. Jesse looked at his empty beer bottle. "When do you suppose ol' papa-san will be done sewin' my utilities?"

"Hell, he's probably done by now."

"With that old manual sewing machine?"

"You should see that old man run that thing. I bet there aren't many people who can keep up with him on an electric sewing machine. I mean, that old man is

129

fast."

Jesse looked into the surrounding jungle. "You really gotta hand it to these people. They're resourceful as hell. Too bad a bunch of power-hungry politicians gotta bring a war to a country this beautiful. That beach just north of our gun positions is one of the prettiest I've seen in the world. A big fancy resort hotel and a bunch of tourists with money to burn would sure ease some of the poverty around here."

"Who knows? Maybe after we kick Ho-Chi-Minh's ass, somebody will build one."

"Yeah, maybe," replied Jesse absentmindedly.

DD and Sal exited Mama-San's, arms around each other's neck. DD spoke broken English. "DD Boom-Boom. Go back camp now."

"I'm for that," agreed Sal.

Cuz looked at the pair, then to Jesse. "Do those two look like the cat that ate the canary or what?"

Jesse smiled and shook his head.

The four stopped at the old man's hootch. Jesse's shirts were completed. He paid for the service and they returned to Sherwood Forest shortly before dark.

The First Section had the gun watch. Each man in the section took his sleeping gear to a position near the guns, which were located about one hundred yards from the section tents.

As Jesse strolled to his position near gun one, he thought of the organizational structure of the 81mm mortar platoon and, as badly as he hated to admit it, he felt the Marine Corps had at least done that right.

Each squad consisted of a squad leader, gunner, assistant gunner and three or four ammo carriers. A mortar section was made up of two squads plus two radio operators, an ammo corporal, a wireman, a driver, a section leader, and a forward observer. The latter, and one of the radio operators, was usually attached directly to a rifle company while on maneuvers. The four sections comprising a mortar platoon were often attached directly to one of the four rifle companies in the battalion by corresponding letter and number. First Section was attached to "A" company, Second Section to "B", Third to "C", and Fourth to "D". It all worked out well on paper.

During the nightly gun watch, one man remained awake on each gun at all times while a third stood radio watch. In the event mortar fire was needed, the sleeping squad members, at all times in full uniform, were quickly awakened and the mission fired.

Often during the night there were prearranged fire missions on pre-designated coordinates. These types of fire missions were called H & I. They were intended to harass and interrupt enemy movements by striking suspected gathering points or trails used by the Viet Cong during the hours of darkness.

Most H & I missions were fired by artillery but mortars were used in areas inaccessible to artillery such as the lee side of a hill or into canyons.

Jesse got his first real look at gun one after he placed his poncho to the rear of the gunpit.

"You wanna do a little gun drill to get the feel back?" asked Cuz.

"I could probably use the practice – at least until I get the hang of it again," answered Jesse.

Cuz turned to Dude. "Okay, Dude. Let Jesse take the gun. You A-gun. I'll

130

give a few small deflection and elevation changes to start."

Jesse and Dude took their positions by the mortar, Jesse on left side of the tube, hand ready to adjust the sight.

"Let me know when you're ready," said Cuz.

"We're ready," Jesse answered for both of them.

Cuz read a mock fire mission: "Fire mission. Deflection 2907..."

Jesse repeated the dope and began immediately to adjust the sight. He checked the cross level bubble and turned the traverse with his right hand, leveling the bubble as he moved by using his left hand on the bronze cross-level sleeve, lining the vertical crosshair in the sight on the left edge of the aiming stakes located to the front of the gun.

"...Troops in open. One round. Willie Peter. Will adjust. Elevation 1156. At my command."

"Gun one up," said Jesse. He stepped away from the gun.

Dude looked at him, then at the gun. "You sure?"

"Not really. It's been a long time, but it's kinda like ridin' a bicycle."

Dude stepped around the gun to the left side. He checked the elevation and deflection bubbles; both were dead center. He then checked the dope on the sight to see if the proper deflection and elevation had been placed on the scales. It was perfect. He looked through the eyepiece to see if the vertical cross hair was within two mills of touching the left side of the aiming stakes – less than one mill.

Dude turned toward Cuz. "Shit. It's almost perfect."

Cuz moved next to the gun. "Let me see." He made his examination, drawing the same conclusion as had Dude. "Was that luck or can you do it that fast all the time?"

"How fast was it?" asked Jesse.

"Six seconds," answered Cuz.

"Since it was my first try, I gotta say it was luck. But in a day or two, I should be down to two to six seconds on all small deflection and elevation changes."

The crew on gun one moved closer to Jesse. Cuz spoke softly. "How long does a large deflection and elevation take you?"

Jesse felt uneasy with the sudden attention as the squad eyed him anxiously. "I can't remember exactly, but I think somewhere between seven to twelve seconds."

DD said softly, "You're shittin'?"

"No, I'm serious."

Cuz asked, "How about to the rear?"

"That depends. Seventeen to twenty-two seconds, I think," answered Jesse.

"Are you crazy? No one in the whole goddamn division can gun a mortar that fast," said Rodriguez.

"Sssh," said Cuz. "Keep it down, Bean." He turned back to Jesse. "Are you serious?"

Jesse looked at Cuz, then to the rest of the men in the First Squad. "Say, Cuz, did I do something wrong or something? I mean, Christ. Everybody is looking at me like I just grew a third eye."

Cuz stared at Jesse, his expression serious. "If you can gun like that, we can all get rich tomorrow."

"What are you talkin' about?" asked Jesse.

131

Stoney Livingston

DD broke in with a whisper, "Calhoun in Second Section, that's who he's talkin' about. That crazy, bastard thinks his shit don't stink. His buddy, Windler, is a weight-lifting bastard of a wireman and backs Calhoun on everything. Calhoun's the fastest gunner in the platoon and he's won the money to prove it. But his times are nowhere near what you say you can do."

Jesse looked at the men in the squad. "Now, wait a minute. I need a little practice. Maybe I used to get those times but I don't know if I still can."

Dude smiled at Jesse, "Let's run a little more drill while we can still gun by daylight. I'd give a month's pay to see you beat that pompous bastard."

For the next twenty minutes Cuz read off practice fire missions of all types while Jesse ran the gun. When it became too dark to operate without the red and green lights on the aiming stakes, gun drill was halted and the men assembled around Cuz to compare the elapsed times of the various types of missions.

"I don't believe this shit," said Cuz. "Listen to this. On six small D & E changes, the times ranged from a high of nine seconds to a low of two seconds."

The men in the squad rubbed their hands together and hopped from one foot to the other.

"Five large D & E changes showed times of five seconds to sixteen seconds."

The hopping from foot to foot intensified.

"And deflection to the rear on four missions showed times of twenty-one to forty-two seconds."

Jesse said, "If Dude and I had time to work on those 'to the rear' missions we can really cut that time. You gotta work a while with the same a-gunner to get those times down."

Cuz laughed. "Shit. You don't need an a-gunner. Your worst time is damn near good enough to beat Calhoun on his best day."

"Let's go after Calhoun," Sal said.

"Hold on. Not so fast," said Cuz. "Jesse, you take the first watch. Dude, you take the second. In the morning, after chow, if we have free time, we'll meet out here for gun drill. I want you guys to get as much rest as possible."

"Okay by me," answered Dude.

"Me too, if that's what you want," agreed Jesse.

"Okay, let's hit the rack. Sal, you got third watch, Bean fourth. Malone fifth. Me and Collins and the radio operators will stand radio watch," said Cuz.

"Shit. My favorite watch," complained Rodriquez.

"Quit bitchin' and get some sleep, Bean," said Cuz.

"I just hope Langley beats the shit outa Calhoun tomorrow." Bean got in the last word as he stepped down into the sandbag bunker adjoining the gunpit.

Jesse's first night of gun watch was uneventful. He was grateful for the lack of rain and the partial moon to aid his senses. There were no H & I missions scheduled so he had nothing to do but sit by the gun and wait until his watch ended.

From time to time his mind drifted, but quickly returned to the present. He wondered how Joe Fitzgerald was doing. He thought of Shannon and wished he could turn the clock back but knew he could not. He tried to analyze what it was about her that made her so important to him. She was just who she was. That was his only answer. Thoughts of Will entered his mind and he hoped his friend would never have to suffer the discomfort of Vietnam. Too bad his old outfit of '63 wasn't in Vietnam as a battalion. He was certain they could win the war in thirty days. He

132

thought of Dave Boomer, his best buddy in the old outfit, now married and living in southern Utah. He wondered what Dave was doing as he sat in a muddy gunpit in Vietnam. He thought briefly of Barbara, but she was only a dim memory. It seemed as though a hundred years had passed since that day at Knott's Berry Farm.

He stood and walked around the mortar. Something about the whole war just didn't seem real. He didn't feel like a real person. He was just playing out a part in a badly done movie. At the end of the next reel things had to change.

A soft rain began to fall.

By daylight the rain had ceased but the ground oozed up mud and water with each footstep as the First Section left their guns and returned to the tent. Aside from the standard complaining, the men were in good spirits. The sun was shining; there were no U.S. casualties during the night and, later in the day, First Section would challenge Second Section to timed gun drills. And this time they were confident of a win.

Morning chow, shaving, police duty, and weapons cleaning completed, Jesse, Dude and Cuz began gun drill exercises, emphasizing deflection to the rear where the assistant gunner was an all-important cog in the machinery. In less than ten minutes, the rest of the squad was present. Soon the second squad joined the rest of the First Section and competed against Jesse and Dude. By ten hundred hours the First Section and, most importantly, Jesse, were confident.

Jesse noticed Tuleano conversing with Cuz as he watched Jesse operate the mortar on a large deflection change. From time to time Jesse caught glimpses of Tuleano gesturing at gun one. He had wanted a promotion to squad leader because of the rifle. Now he became concerned he was about to become the First Section's resident gunner.

"Okay." Cuz turned to the mortar. "Jesse, you and Dude knock off. Report back to the gun at 1300 hours."

Jesse and Dude stepped away from the gun and walked slowly toward the section tent, Jesse nodding at Tuleano as they passed.

As the two strolled up the slight incline to the tent, Jesse said, "Jesus, this humidity is a killer. Sweat keeps rollin' into my eyes and I can't see. Not to mention the fact that it burns like hell. God can't be too damn smart if he can't design eyebrows good enough to keep the sweat outa a man's eyes."

Dude jumped away from Jesse and glanced up at the sky, then back to Jesse. "Shit, man, be cool. I don't wanta be hit by a bolt of lightning."

Jesse smiled. "Well, think about it. How damn difficult would it have been to design the eyebrow with a little more finesse?"

Dude backed away another step, looking quickly at the sky, then back at Jesse. "Hey, I'm no religious fanatic but you really ought to lighten up. I mean, shit, you already got the damn VC, the heat, the insects, the snakes, the leeches, the rats, the food, the rain and a million other things, trying to kill you. There really ain't no sense pissing off the man upstairs."

"Bullshit. There ain't no man upstairs."

"Well, just in case – you know what I mean?"

Jesse looked up at the clear blue sky. He shrugged. "Yeah, I guess you're right. No sense takin' an unnecessary chance." He continued toward the tents.

At 1300 hours all guns were manned for platoon gun drill. Dude acted as the gunner during the first hour. At 1430 hours, platoon gun drill ceased and a ten-minute break was ordered. Jesse took his helmet off as he sipped tepid water from his metal canteen.

"Hey Langley, what's that wrapped around your head? Some kind of Indian headband? You want a feather for it?" asked DD.

"Screw you, DD. Its a sweatband. I cut up one of my old utility sleeves. It helps keep the sweat outa my eyes."

"Well, I I sure as hell hope it works. I'd hate to see Calhoun win this bullshit."

Tuleano, who sat on a sandbag at the edge of the gunpit, rubbed his hands. "Shit. No sweat. Langley here is gonna win and I'm gonna have an extra $200 to take on R & R next week." He smiled and clapped his hands then turned to Jesse. "You ready, Mr. Gunner?"

"Anytime," answered Jesse.

From the start it was apparent the contest was no contest. Jesse bettered Calhoun's time on every type of mission by relatively large margins. As he saw his advantage grow by leaps with each drill, Jesse felt sorry for his opponent. It was not his intention to humiliate the man. He deliberately slowed his speed and was still able to have his mortar up before Calhoun's. At the end of the specified hour, Jesse had not lost a single mission.

The marines in the First Section congratulated Jesse as they collected their bets and returned to the tents to escape the afternoon sun. Jesse and Dude remained at the gun to wipe it down and oil the metal lightly. When the gun was satisfactorily cleaned, Dude said, "I guess I'll go up to the tent for a nice, piss-warm drink of Kool-Aid. How about you?"

Jesse looked over to gun three where Calhoun still cleaned his mortar. "In a few minutes. I think I wanna talk to Calhoun first."

"No you don't. Not really. Trust me. Windler's standin' right next to him and he's an asshole."

"Hell, he's on our side."

"Yeah, I know. I hope we win the war in spite of that fact."

Jesse smiled. "I just wanna talk to him for a minute. Save me a seat in the game will ya?"

"Okay. It's your funeral." Dude stepped out of the gunpit.

Calhoun and his assistant gunner had just finished swabbing the bore of their mortar when Jesse stepped into the gun-three pit.

"Howdy," offered Jesse.

The assistant gunner looked at Jesse and said, "Hullo."

"Name's Langley. Jesse Langley." He offered his hand to the a-gunner.

"Peako," returned the a-gunner.

"Calhoun," said the gunner quietly. "You're damn good with the mortar."

Windler, who stood in the gun pit, had yet to acknowledge Jesse's presence.

Jesse turned to Calhoun. "You're pretty good yourself. I just had a lucky day."

Windler stared coldly at Jesse with his small eyes. He was about an inch taller than Jesse, but a full fifteen pounds heavier. His arms were muscular and well developed and his neck and chest size were testimonials to time spent lifting weights and working out. His thin dark mustache and his dark hair contributed to an Hispanic look. Except for the hate displayed in his small green eyes, he appeared to Jesse a real lady-killer.

A full thirty seconds passed without a spoken word. Jesse became uncomfortable, wishing he had listened to Dude.

Peako said, "Shit, Windmill. The guy won fair 'n' square. He's the fastest anybody around here has ever seen. There ain't any reason to be shitty about it."

Still Windler did not speak. He continued to stare coldly at Jesse.

Jesse turned to Peako. "That's okay, Peako." To Windler he said, "Sorry you feel that way. Just remember, I'm on your side." He turned and strode for the First Section tent.

"Deal me in," said Jesse as he sat on the edge of a cot.

Dude looked at him inquisitively. "You and ol' Windmill bosom buddies now?"

Jesse raised an eyebrow. "He's a rough one to get close to – that I gotta admit."

A chuckle made its way around the poker game.

"You got a way of understating a damn sure fact, Langley," said DD.

Again the card players laughed.

Jesse's eyes widened. "Goddamn, DD. Don't move."

DD froze. "What the hell is it, man?"

"The biggest damn mosquito I ever saw in my life is perched on the tent flap about two inches from your neck. If that sucker bites you, you'll need a blood transfusion."

Slowly, DD leaned away from the tent flap, turning to observe the reported intruder as he moved. His eyes grew large and round as he saw the mosquito, a full three inches in length. He slowly eased away from the large insect.

"Jesus. This is going to be one long war," complained Dude.

DD looked at Dude. "Dude, hand me your pistol."

"Shit, DD, you can't shoot a damn bug even if it is the size of a goddamn Mig-21," said Cuz.

"I'm damn sure not gonna arm wrestle the bastard."

The insect remained motionless, looking as deadly as any three-inch long mosquito should look.

"Hey, Doc. C'mere," Dude shouted to the platoon corpsman, who sat at the far end of the tent.

The corpsman approached the game. "Whatcha need, Dude?"

"Is that thing really a mosquito?" He pointed to the large insect.

The corpsman looked at the object of everyone's attention and laughed. "That's not a damn mosquito. I can't believe you guys haven't seen these things before."

DD was doubtful. "If it ain't a mosquito, what the hell is it?"

The corpsman replied, "I can't remember what the hell they're called but they eat mosquitoes. They're harmless to man."

DD, still not convinced, said, "How come it looks so much like a mosquito? It don't have to look like a mosquito just because it eats 'em. Hell, I eat grapes but I don't look like a grape."

Jesse moved closer and studied the odd creature carefully. "Doc," he said. "This thing looks like a mosquito down to the last detail."

"I'm telling you, he's not a goddamn mosquito. Look." He gently picked up the large insect.

135

Stoney Livingston

DD was convinced. "Okay, okay. Just let him go. It gives me the willies to see you playin' with that damn thing."

The corpsman threw the large insect out the open side of the tent.

"Hey, not so hard. No sense pissin' 'im off. I'd hate to see 'im change sides," said Dude.

"No shit," agreed Bean.

The players returned their attention to the cards, the strange insect already forgotten. There were many things strange to them in Vietnam.

A runner entered the tent. "Hey, Dude, platoon commander wants to see you."

"Damn. Okay. I'll be right there." He finished out the hand. "Deal me out. I'll be back in a few minutes."

In less than fifteen minutes Dude walked back into the tent, tears flowing freely down his face. He walked past the game, directly to his cot. He opened his seabag and began roughly throwing his gear inside.

No one at the poker game, nor anyone else in the tent, moved. Dude continued to throw his personal effects into the seabag in jerky movements. The tears continued to flow but he uttered no sound.

Bean spoke first. "Hey Dude, you all right, man?"

Dude stopped his frenzied packing and slowly turned to the marines playing poker, his face contorted with sorrow and grief. "It's my little brother, man. He's dead!" Dude sobbed. "I'm over here in this mother-fucking, stupid-ass war and my baby brother gets killed in a fucking car wreck in Detroit, Michigan, U.S.A."

Jesse felt a pang in his chest. Not much seemed to make sense anymore. "I'm sorry, Dude." He stood, patted Dude on the shoulder and walked outside the tent.

The rest of the section moved towards Dude's cot.

"Anything we can do, Dude?" asked Cuz.

Still sobbing, Dude replied, "Yeah, Cuz, bring my baby brother back. You're my squad leader, goddamnit. Do something."

The corpsman moved in. "Take it easy, Dude. Sit down on your rack."

"Fuck that rack, Doc. You're a corpsman, and a damn good one. You can bring him back, Doc." He looked at the corpsman, then at the men in his section. He reached out his arms. "You guys – you're my buddies. I need your help."

DD said, "You fuck-an-A-straight, Dude. You need our help, you got it."

Others joined DD's lead.

"Yeah."

"You bet yore ass."

"Anything you need."

Dude sat on his cot, put his face into his hands and sobbed. His body jerked and quivered with each wave of sorrow and grief.

Jesse stood outside under a small pine tree. He listened and he felt Dude's pain and sorrow as if it were his own. None of this made any sense. He felt one of Dude's tears flowing down his own cheek.

That afternoon Dude was gone. As the sole surviving son in his family, he was removed from the combat zone. He was given orders for emergency leave and further ordered to report to Camp Lejune, North Carolina upon completion of his leave. Due to the reason for his departure, there was no fanfare or hoopla. The men

136

in the platoon shook his hand, one by one, then he was gone.

Jesse was officially promoted to gunner and Salsbury was once again an assistant gunner. Sal got his pistol back and Jesse was officially signed out with Dude's pistol. He also got Sal's rifle.

The week following Dude's departure was a time of concentrated learning for Jesse. He learned each man's peculiarities; studied words and phrases in Vietnamese, attended gun drill, played poker, went on two daylight recon patrols, stood two nights of gun watch, one more night of waterborne patrol, one night ambush, wrote a few letters, sighted in his rifle, and made one trip to the airstrip at Chu Lai to help Cuz pick up a new sight for gun one.

During this period, Jesse had no contact with the enemy, though he volunteered for every ambush and patrol he could, with the exception of waterborne patrol. He began to wonder if there were any such things as Viet Congs. He was bored. Even the nights began to hold no fear. Nothing seemed to happen, day or night.

Eight days after Dude's departure, Tuleano stormed into First Section's tent at reveille. Every man in the section could see he was in a foul mood. Tuleano made no effort to hide his moods and the simplest among them knew how to react.

He shouted, "Get your asses outa the rack and get to chow. After chow we're gonna police this fucking tent. Then we're gonna do gun drill."

Not a man complained. They bounced from the cots, dressed quickly, and went to the tasteless hot chow on the mule sent from battalion headquarters. The morning mess completed, they reported to guns one and two. Jesse and Bean had been on a night ambush until dawn and, under normal circumstances, would have been allowed to sleep in. Not so when Tuleano was in a bad mood. He pushed them relentlessly. At 1100 hours he secured gun drill and ordered the men to fill new sandbags for additional fortifications.

As the men dispersed to get their entrenching tools, Bean stopped next to Tuleano. "Goddamn, Tule. Take a break, man. Shit. We been here a couple of months. What's the fuckin' hurry to build another bunker?"

Tuleano charged the thinly built man, slamming his open hands into the smaller man's chest hard enough to knock him violently to the ground. Tuleano knelt over him, grabbing him by the throat with one hand and raising his other for a blow to the face.

Jesse, who had been standing nearby, grasped Tuleano's free arm and held it tightly. "Take it easy Tule. Hell, he didn't mean anything. He's tired. We had a long night."

Tuleano released his grasp on Bean's neck and, twisting his torso for maximum effect, smashed Jesse in the side of his face with a huge fist. The blow connected so solidly that Jesse's feet left the ground and he fell over the sandbag wall of the gunpit onto the base plate of the mortar, his helmet flying from his head and bouncing against the tube.. He scrambled to his feet just as Tuleano jumped into the gunpit after him.

Tuleano's feet hit the ground and he was able to stop his momentum only inches away from the muzzle of Jesse's cocked pistol. He stood in a wavering crouch, his flat nostrils flaring.

"Shoot me, you chickenshit bastard!" he shouted.

Jesse spoke softly, through tightly pursed lips. "I don't want to, Tule, but if you ever come at me again, now or any other time, I'll kill you so fast you won't even

137

have time to wonder why." Lowering his voice further, Jesse continued, "Now back away from me or I'll blow your kneecaps off. I'll take your orders and do my job, but don't ever hit me again. Ever."

The soft quiet tone of Jesse's voice, the tightly drawn lips, the cold calculating stare, and the cocked pistol pointed at his face, jarred Tuleano back to reality. His tense muscles relaxed as he backed away to the edge of the gunpit and sat on a sandbag. "Shit, man. I'm sorry. You okay?"

Jesse held his position, pistol still pointed at Tuleano only a few feet away. With his unencumbered hand, he rubbed his jaw.

"Fuck it, Tule." Bean had recovered his composure. "That's okay man. Forget it. This place just gets to a guy after a while. Shit."

DD said, "Hell yeah, man, besides, ol' Jesse wouldn't have really shot you. Hell, he don't carry a round in the chamber. He pulled that shit on me once."

Jesse remained immobile, the pistol still pointed at Tule.

DD turned to Jesse. "Shit, Jesse, show Tule you was just bull shittin'. We don't go around shootin' each other. We save that shit for the gooks. Go on, show 'im."

Jesse relaxed his left arm and let it fall to his waist. With his right hand he jerked the slide to the rear. A live round extracted from the chamber and was ejected into the gunpit. He released the slide, chambering another round. He held the hammer back while he pulled the trigger and slowly let the hammer fall to the pin, put the safety on and holstered the pistol. None of the seven or eight men in the section, who watched, spoke. Jesse stooped and picked up the unfired round and his helmet. He walked out of the gunpit, dropping the bullet at Tuleano's feet as he passed.

"Jeez," said Bean softly.

"Shit. That crazy fuckin' cowboy mighta done it," said DD.

Houston Barnett, the section radio operator, said, "You gotta admit, Tule, you hit 'im pretty damned hard. I thought you were gonna kill 'im when you jumped into the gunpit."

Tuleano turned to Rodriquez. "That fucking Preacher pulled time in grade on me and bumped me from R & R in Hong Kong this week. Hell, I had..."

Jesse continued to the First Section tent. His body trembled with excess adrenaline as he dug his entrenching tool from his neatly stored seven-eighty-two gear. His reaction to Tuleano's attack had frightened him. He wondered if he was turning into an animal like the battalion armorer he had encountered on his first morning in the combat zone. He couldn't let that happen.

He was returning to the gunpit with his entrenching tool when he met the section walking toward him. Cuz explained Tuleano's change of heart regarding the sandbags and the reason for his foul mood. Jesse joined the others as they returned to the First Section tent.

Bean spoke to Jesse quietly as they entered the tent, "Hey, thanks for steppin' in out there."

"You'd have done the same for me."

"Shit man, I don't know. My *huevos* aren't as big as yours. Tule goes crazy from time to time. Most of us just stay out of his way when that happens."

"I'll try to remember that the next time he tries to kill somebody in our section."

"Screw it, let's play cards," suggested DD.

Just like the large mosquito-like insect, the incident with Tuleano was forgotten.

At DD's insistence, a raid was planned on the army and air force supply dump at Chu Lai. The mission was simple: steal as much as possible in the way of tubing and equipment to set up a still. Jesse felt fairly certain he could make whiskey if he had the equipment and the right ingredients. That had been one portion of his high school chemistry class that had remained with him, that and those wonderful nights at Shannon's side while she studied chemistry and he studied her.

Two days later, with the help of a PFC at battalion motor pool, most of the First Section drove down to the airstrip and "requisitioned" the needed equipment from the army supply depot.

Jesse wore captain's bars, while DD acted as his driver. The PFC from battalion motor pool drove a deuce-and-a-half, commonly called a six-by. It was a large, two-and-a-half-ton truck, the bed of which was covered with a tarp, giving it the appearance of a covered wagon from the rear. Barnett rode in "Captain" Langley's mighty mite as his radioman, while Sal, Cuz, Bean and several others rode in the six-by.

"Captain Langley" presented the forged requisition forms to the sentry at the depot and was allowed to pass.

The six-by was loaded with the required equipment in less than twenty minutes, Jesse shouting orders at the men during the entire time period. They were not stopped, nor questioned as they methodically stole whatever they wanted. The young marine captain must have sounded very hurried and businesslike as he barked orders to his men.

Afterwards, on the muddy road back to Sherwood Forest, Jesse removed the captain bars amid the laughter and congratulations of DD and Barnett.

DD said, "Can you believe how easy that was? Shit, we oughta go back tomorrow and take a damn Phantom."

Jesse said, "Then we'd have to steal fuel and bombs and all that other stuff. Let's just set up our still and forget about another raid for a while."

"Aye, Aye, Captain," laughed DD.

The raiding party unloaded their booty deep in Sherwood Forest, about four hundred yards from the section tents. At that location, the trees were tallest and the undergrowth the heaviest. They labored in groups of three or four over the next several days to complete assembly and make changes in their design as work progressed. As a sideline to the still, several five-gallon gasoline cans were filled with yeast, sugar, and various juices obtained from Battalion mess. Jesse expressed concern that they had no way to contain the expanding gases but Bean assured him the lids were strong enough to withstand the expansion.

The afternoon of the fourth day after completion of the still, the first small amount of alcohol dripped into a canteen cup. Sitting in the brush, DD took the first taste. Several men in the section watched him anxiously, waiting for a reaction.

Suddenly, DD gagged and coughed; his eyes watered and his face reddened. When he was finally able to speak, he croaked, "Goddamn, Langley, you tryin' to kill me?"

Jesse raised an eyebrow. "A little stout is it?"

"Stout? Stout? No shit it's stout! My damn tongue feels like all the moisture was just sucked right out of it. Goddamn, I need water!" DD reached for one of his canteens.

139

Jesse put a drop on the end of his tongue. It burned like what he imagined was the hottest fire in hell. He winced and placed the canteen cup carefully onto the soft soil, then dug his Zippo lighter from his pocket and carefully filled it with the clear liquid in the canteen cup. He pulled out a cigarette and struck the flint wheel on his lighter. It ignited with an almost invisible flame. The cigarette lit, he closed his Zippo and put it back into his pocket.

"Great," said Bean. "We got us a goddamn lighter fluid factory."

Jesse took a drag from his cigarette. "Maybe we could dilute it with something?"

DD looked at him with both eyebrows raised, his face still beet-red, eyes watering, breathing heavy and irregular. "There ain't enough water in that ocean out there for that half-canteen cup of whatever-in-the-hell-it-is."

Jesse said, "I musta done something wrong."

"No shit," agreed DD, his breathing slowing a bit.

"Well, we could try a little of the wine. It's probably drinkable by now," said Jesse, hoping to take the attention away from his failure as a distiller of fine spirits.

They opened one of the gasoline cans hidden in the brush. Opening was difficult due to gas pressure, but once the task was accomplished, they drank the immature wine.

"Too much yeast," said Jesse.

"Yeah," said Bean, smacking his lips. "This stuff is lousy. You just leave your share and I'll take care of it."

"I couldn't let you do that for us, Bean. It wouldn't be fair," said DD, smiling, apparently having forgotten his near-death experience with the unknown substance in the canteen cup of a few minutes earlier.

"Let's grab the open can and transfer it to a water can and get it back down to the tent. We don't wanna stay out here too long. I'll take the jet fuel in case someone needs his lighter filled," said Jesse, nodding at the partially filled canteen cup containing the potentially deadly fluid.

After evening chow, the men in the First Section tent wrote letters, played poker or cleaned weapons. It was one of those rare nights when not a single man had any night duty and they all took advantage of the situation by drinking the "jungle wine" as Bean had christened the sweet drink introduced by Jesse.

Well after dark, most were still awake, sitting in groups of three or four, quietly talking and drinking from their canteen cups. They were loose and relaxed.

Tuleano walked into the tent. He found his way to Cuz, who sipped from a canteen cup and talked quietly to Jesse and Bean.

"What's the scoop?" whispered Tuleano. "Why the hell is everybody still up?"

The wine had relaxed Cuz completely. "Sit down, Tule. Here." He offered Tuleano his half-full canteen cup.

Tuleano smelled the cup, then took a cautious swallow, then several swallows. He handed the cup back to Cuz. "Shit, man, I needed that. Where the hell did you get it?"

"You wouldn't believe it, Tule. It's a long story," said Bean, his eyes drooping in the darkness.

"You got any more, man?" Tule was smacking his lips.

Jesse reached to his right and dragged the half-empty five-gallon wine can close to him. "Get a cup, Tule. We got plenty."

140

Forever Patriots

Jesse listened to war stories as Tule and Cuz swapped tales of woe and glory. At 0100 hours, Sergeant Bekin stepped into the tent. He had just been relieved at FDC watch. Tule offered him what little wine was left but it did little more than whet Bekin's appetite. He pleaded for more but there was no more to be had.

"Wait a minute. We do have some booze left – but I wouldn't recommend it for human consumption," offered Jesse.

Bekin insisted, so Jesse produced his "jet fuel" brew. After topping off his Zippo lighter, he handed it to Bekin with several warnings. Bekin thanked him, transferred the clear liquid from Jesse's canteen cup to his own and left for his own tent with the brew held carefully near his midsection.

The next morning dawned bright and clear. No rain. No clouds. Only hangovers. It was noon before the majority of the First Section was able to function without extreme pain. Sergeant Bekin of Fourth Section slept for a day and a half. The platoon commander thought Bekin had a strange illness and let his Fourth Section leader sleep undisturbed. Jesse was quietly concerned about Bekin's condition and breathed easier only when the man returned to duty status.

They heard about the plane crash the day Sergeant Bekin awakened. An Air Force KC 130 crashed into Hong Kong harbor, killing all one hundred fifty-eight aboard. They were all U.S. servicemen returning to Vietnam from R & R. Sergeant Dove of the 81 platoon, First Battalion, Fourth Marines was among the passengers.

Tuleano sat on the sandbag parapet surrounding gun one during a break from gun drill. The rest of the first squad sat nearby. "Hah! That bastard got what he deserved. If he hadn't been such a prick, he wouldn't have been on that plane," said Tule.

"I guess it was just meant to be. I mean, look at the way it happened. Who would have ever guessed that he would pull rank? I never saw him do anything like that before," said Cuz.

Tuleano agreed. "Yeah, you're right. I guess God needed him upstairs." He laughed at his own joke.

*****

The afternoon sun beat down mercilessly as Tuleano sat behind the gunpit with Cuz. Platoon gun drill was proceeding as usual – gun one was up well before any of the others. Jesse knelt on the left side of the gun with the sight eyepiece in the horizontal position, waiting for the other guns to come up on the last mission.

Gun two was next up. Wilson wasn't a bad gunner. Only time and a lot of practice stood between him and Jesse. On a platoon fire mission, one could predict with a fair amount of certainty the order of ready guns: Jesse on gun one, Calhoun on gun three, then Wilson on gun two. Guns four through eight usually mixed up their times, coming up a little later. Tule knew he had the best section in the platoon.

Jesse had never mentioned the incident with the pistol, and Tule must have figured it was just as well left alone. Jesse watched Tule reach into his pocket and pull out the bullet Jesse had dropped at his feet. Tule looked at it carefully. It looked like any other .45 caliber bullet, but this one was special. Tule believed it had his name on it and, as long as he kept it in his pocket, he was safe.

A muffled, popping explosion, three or four hundred yards from the gun ripped through the still afternoon air. It was followed quickly by a second explosion of equal magnitude. Instantly every man had his personal weapon at the ready and was

141

in the prone or kneeling position, protected by a trench, bunker or gunpit. Hearts pounded wildly and helmets were pulled tightly onto heads.

Several seconds of silence followed the second explosion.

Cuz shouted, "Anybody hear the incoming rounds?"

Tuleano replied, "Shit man, I didn't hear squat except the damn blast!"

"There must be a gook in the Forest with satchel charges," suggested Cuz.

"What the hell would he be blowin' up in the Forest? Shit, man, there ain't nothin' in there but a panther or two," said Tuleano.

Jesse looked at Cuz, then to DD, then to Bean. "Shit!" Suddenly he jumped from the gunpit and charged at full speed into Sherwood Forest.

"Hey, Langley, where the fuck you goin?" shouted Tuleano. But it was too late. Jesse was running flat out, his pistol dangling at his side.

DD looked at Cuz. "Goddamnit, me the shortest mother's son in the whole damn platoon. Now I gotta get back into this shit." He bolted from the gunpit in pursuit of Jesse, Bean on his heels. The remainder of the first squad instantly took up the chase.

Perplexed, Tuleano joined in. Behind him, the second squad was in full pursuit.

Jesse encountered the edge of Sherwood Forest at a dead run. Inside the treeline, he moved away from the trail and proceeded as rapidly as he could with reasonable caution, toward the still. He tried to control the loud heartbeat in his ears as he moved through the brush but he still heard the frantic drumbeat in his head and felt it in his temples.

As he neared the still, he saw what appeared to be soap suds dripping from the trees. He ran this right index finger into the suds and licked his finger. *Jungle Wine!*

When the First Section, using a little more caution in their approach, arrived at the still two minutes later, they found Jesse sitting against a tree, smoking a cigarette.

"What the fuck? Over," said Barnett, the section radio operator.

Jesse replied, "It seems that Bean was incorrect about the expanding gases in the wine cans." He laughed. "I wouldn't go any closer. Those damn Jerry cans are bulging so bad, they could explode at any minute."

Those who had stepped past Jesse retreated to his position.

"What the hell is this shit?" asked Tuleano puffing from exertion.

Cuz quickly explained about the still and the wine. Tuleano said, "Well, at least we still have the still." He laughed at his own play on words.

A rustling in the trees behind them sent the marines scattering. The platoon commander, accompanied by the Second Section, marched into view. First Section moved out of hiding.

"Shit." Tuleano muttered softly as he stepped into the open.

"What do you have here, Tule?" asked the platoon commander stoically.

"Not much, Lieutenant. Looks like somebody was makin' wine out here. I guess it got too hot or something and some of the cans exploded."

The lieutenant's eyes widened as he spotted the still about twenty-five yards away, under a large tree. "What the hell is that contraption?"

"I don't know, Sir. The danger of explosion is high, so I stopped the men here," replied Tuleano nervously.

"It looks like a crude distillery to me, Sergeant. Do you know anything about this?"

"No Sir. The first thing I knew of this was about five minutes ago," replied Tuleano honestly.

"You know damned good and well that someone in our outfit was involved in this." The lieutenant paused then shook his head. "No, I don't want to know any more about it. Just get combat engineers up here to blow those Jerry cans. When that's done, dismantle the still."

Jesse couldn't stand it any longer. "Begging your pardon, sir, but someone might have done us a favor."

"How's that, Langley?" asked the lieutenant.

"Well, Sir," Jesse paused. "Well Sir, under your strict supervision, we might learn how to operate that thing over there and maybe we could turn out enough brew to give each man a shot or two a day. And it would be interesting and help take our minds off this chickenshit war for awhile."

The lieutenant ignored Jesse's suggestion and the sounds of assent from the two sections present. He turned to Tuleano and said, "Get the engineers up here and blow this shit."

"Aye, Aye, Sir."

The lieutenant turned and strode angrily back to camp.

When the lieutenant was out of earshot, DD threw his helmet to the ground. "Goddamnit, Tule, that shave-tail sonofabitch needs an ass kickin'. We went to a lot of trouble to set up this operation. Can't we just move the still somewhere else and tell the lieutenant the engineers took care of it?"

Tuleano looked at DD, then to the rest of the men in his section. It was plain he didn't want to destroy the still. Few men in the outfit enjoyed a drink more than Tule. "Sorry, men, I got my orders." He paused. "Barnett, you and Sal stand guard till the engineers get here. The rest of you report back to the guns."

There were mumbles and groans of dissent, but each man quickly made his way to the gunpits.

Later that afternoon, Jesse received a letter from Will. He stepped away from the noise of mail call and opened the letter, reading it as he walked back to his tent.

Will wrote newsy letters and Jesse was grateful for news from the U.S. Will told of his adventures at division legal, then went on to write about Jane Fonda and her involvement in protests against the war. He asked if Jesse had heard from Barbara, then he put in a line or two about Shannon. The news from Riverside was the same: he still wasn't making progress with Sharon Fiedler. His father said the U.S. should win the war in six months, and his mother was worried for Jesse and wished him well. C.I.D. had apparently not looked further into his confrontation with the two civilians. He wished Jesse well.

"Not bad, Will," he said softly as he finished reading. His mention of Shannon, as brief as it had been, had made the entire letter for Jesse.

He looked around to see others reading their mail. Some, with happiness evident on their faces, already had writing material in hand to reply to their correspondence. Still others had the look of disappointment. Jesse felt sorry for these men who wanted such a little thing as a piece of paper with words on it, and yet, even this little thing was denied them. Maybe the pen *is* mightier than the sword, he thought.

143

Stoney Livingston

Cuz sat next to him. "Girl friend?" He gestured to the letter in Jesse's hand.

"Naw, a good buddy of mine. Known him since about the ninth grade of school."

"Well, here's one from Jim Hensley to all of us. Read it and pass it around."

Jesse accepted the letter and read silently:

Dear Friends and Buddies,

It was sure a shock to me the way things happened my last day in the Nam, and I don't remember it very well. All I could think of was my little brother being dead. Well I'm at home now, and I can't do my brother any good. He's gone. I should have told each and every one of you guys how great I think you all are. I guess I was just in shock or something.

Things here in the world are so different than they were in Viet Nam. I can take a hot shower anytime I want. I can have any kind of food I want, twenty-four hours a day. The round-eye women are all over the place. I have a roof over my head when it rains and I'm not always shivering from the wetness at night and roasting in the sun by day. If it's too hot, I can go inside an air-conditioned building. If its too cold, I can turn up the heater. If I need to go a long way, I drive a car, I don't walk with sixty pounds of crap on my back. I don't have to carry my rifle to the bar, and would you believe I haven't stood guard duty or been on a night ambush once since I've been home? No more halazone tablets in my water, no more lukewarm Kool-Aid from a canteen cup, no more mosquito repellent all over my body, no more leeches, no more rice paddies, no more hootches, no more C-rations, no more rashes, no more dysentery, no more incoming, no more killing, no more sleeping in the mud. Listen, you guys, life is good here in the Real World.

Just since I started writing this letter, I realized how shitty you guys have it over there. I had almost forgotten. Even if you never fire a shot, or get shot at, you guys have got the short end of the stick. There are a bunch of hippies in this country who are protesting the war. There are several famous people involved too, like Jane Fonda and Joan Baez and a bunch of others. They should be shot as traitors. They're over here protesting and in some cases actually aiding the enemy, while you guys put up with the real bullshit, and some may even die. It doesn't seem right to me. I don't think they would have allowed that kind of bullshit in WWII.

Of course, not everybody is protesting. Most of the people are on our side. They just want us to win and get the hell out of there. I'm glad I'm home, but I wish every one of you guys could be here with me. I'd find you three girls each and all the beer you could drink.

Well, I guess I'll sign off. This is kind of a long letter for me. If any of you guys feel like it, drop me a line. Every damn one of you had better make it home.

Your Buddy,

Dude

Jesse folded the letter, placed it into the envelope and handed it to DD. "DD, here's a letter from Dude. Read it and pass it on."

The letter had almost made its round when Bean sat on the edge of Jesse's cot. "Dude's an all right guy, huh? I wish we had some beer or jungle wine or something. Dude's letter was like a kick in the nuts. You know what I mean?"

Jesse looked up at Bean. "Yeah I know what you mean. It kinda hit me a little bit too." He paused. "I wonder if the rest of the guys could use a drink?"

"You don't have to wonder about that shit, man."

A slow smile crossed Jesse's face.

"Hey, man. You holdin' out on us?" asked Bean, smiling and knowing, almost for certain, the answer.

Still smiling, Jesse said, "You guys took your time followin' me to the still."

Bean laughed and slapped his knee. "You crazy cowboy. I should'a' known you gave up the fight too easy. How much did you get?"

"I took the two best-looking cans an carried 'em south about thirty yards. They're covered with brush."

"Oowie! Lets go get one."

Jesse looked around the tent and spotted Cuz at the far end. "Hey, Cuz. Bean and I are gonna walk up to the buffalo and draw some water. We'll be back in a few minutes."

"Okay." Cuz picked up a five-gallon water can at his end of the tent. "Here this one's about empty. I think the one down by Sal's rack is dry too."

"Good enough," said Jesse as he accepted the can. "Back in about a splecond, which, as you know, is pretty damned quick."

Fifteen minutes later, Jesse and Bean returned to the tent, each carrying a five-gallon water can.

"What took you guys so long?" asked Cuz as they walked into the tent.

Jesse placed the water can he was carrying at Cuz's feet. Quietly he said, "We had a helluva time gettin' that second gas can open."

Cuz looked Jesse in the face and Jesse saw the twinkle in his eyes. He reached down and un-snapped the metal cap on the water can. Kneeling, he sniffed the contents, then looked again at Jesse. "You should have been a goddamn general. We'd have stolen Hanoi by now." He reached for his canteen cup and carefully poured it half full.

Bean and Jesse watched as he gingerly sipped from the metal canteen cup. He sloshed the liquid about in his mouth and swallowed. "Hot damn! I believe you've outdone yourself, Mr. Langley. This is definitely vintage brew. Won't you two gentleman join me?"

They smiled and carefully poured the jungle wine into their canteen cups. Soon there was a line formed at the water can.

"All right, guys. One – I say again – one canteen cup. We've got the gun watch tonight and I don't want any fuck-ups," ordered Cuz.

There were complaints, but the section followed his order. Cuz was respected. He was fair. He was experienced.

Jesse disengaged from the conversation about Dude's letter so he could finish his own letter to Will before dark. After he had completed, addressed and sealed the envelope, and written "Free" where the stamp normally went, he walked to the mail drop in front of the section leaders' tent.

He returned to his tent and picked up his helmet, poncho and cartridge belt, and walked slowly to gun one. He was early for the gun watch as it was not yet dark, but piece and solitude were what he sought.

As he smoked a cigarette, he listened to the ocean crashing onto the white sands north, and the steep cliffs below the gun position. He couldn't help but think what a beautiful place this was. War is such a waste, he thought.

He fieldstripped his cigarette, then stepped into the bunker located by gun one. In the dimly lit bunker a large rat scurried for cover. The rat wasn't quite fast

145

enough. Jesse grabbed an entrenching tool leaning against the sandbag wall and chased it into a corner where he used the edge of the "E tool" as an axe, almost cutting the large rodent in two. Blood spurted onto his face, the feel of it causing a sudden fear to well up inside him. He struck the large rat briskly several more times. The body quivered and jerked, then lay still. He picked up the furry body with the small shovel, carried it from the bunker to the edge of the cliff and tossed it into the ocean below.

He cleaned the E-tool by sticking it in the soil, then returned it to the bunker. After washing the blood from his face with water from his canteen, he lit another cigarette in the waning light and thought of Arizona and his friends. Then he reflected on the war in Vietnam – what little he knew of it – then Shannon. Always there was Shannon.

First Section began to drift down to guns one and two. It was almost time for gun watch.

That night, Jesse fired his first night support mission. It was about midnight when the call came.

"Fire mission!" said Cuz.

Sal was on the gun and he quickly awakened the other members of the first squad.

"Go ahead," said Cuz to Tuleano, who by then was manning the landline from FDC.

"Fire mission. Deflection 3150. Troops in open. One round Willie Peter, charge four, will adjust. Elevation 1075. At my command," said Cuz, repeating the information given to him over the field telephone.

In less than fifteen seconds, Jesse said, "Gun one up." Sal stood-by with the large white phosphorus round near the mouth of the tube.

"Fire gun one," said Cuz.

Sal dropped the round into the tube. *Thump-pow!* Jesse quickly re-leveled the deflection and elevation bubbles and re-aligned on the red and green lights on the aiming stakes.

"Gun one up," he said.

"Roger. Stand by," said Cuz.

In less than one minute, Cuz said, "Stand by for correctional deflection. 3120. Eight rounds H.E. light. Charge six. Elevation 1010. At my command."

Four seconds elapsed. "Gun one up."

"Stand by gun one," said Cuz.

A full minute passed. Cuz shouted, "Goddamnit, Jesse. Find out what the hell is taking gun two so damn long!"

Jesse jumped out of his gunpit and ran to gun two, twenty-five yards away. As he jumped into the gunpit, he noticed the bipods were at an odd angle and the cross-level bubble was buried in one end of the vial. Without speaking to Wilson, he picked up the bipod legs and set them perpendicular to the tube. He adjusted the gun onto the aiming stakes. In twenty seconds, he shouted, "Gun two up." He returned to gun one on the run.

"Fire the barrage," shouted Cuz. The ammo carriers readied the rounds and handed them to Sal, who carefully but rapidly dropped them down the tube. Jesse leveled the bubbles and re-aligned between each round. On the last round of the eight round barrage for gun one, there was a sickening clunk as the round struck the bottom of the tube and failed to fire.

"Misfire, gun one!" shouted Jesse. He immediately removed the sight and handed it to Cuz who left the gunpit. The ammo-carriers also made a rapid departure, leaving only Jesse and Sal at the gun.

Jesse lay prone, in front of the mortar, holding onto the bipod legs as Sal kicked the tube sharply several times. Still the round did not fire.

"Shit! Okay, Sal lets dump this sucker." Jesse stood and moved to the left side and rear of the tube. He stooped and twisted the barrel and removed it from the base plate. Slowly he lifted the base of the tube. Once the tube was parallel to the ground, Sal placed his hands near the open end, positioning his thumbs to stop the round as Jesse tipped the rear of the tube upward. The round began to slide.

"She's movin'," said Jesse.

"Okay," replied Sal nervously.

Jesse held the tube steady as the round slid forward. "Got it," said Sal. He pulled the projectile completely free of the tube and left the gunpit with the misfired round.

Jesse replaced the rear of the tube into the inner ring of the baseplate. Cuz jumped into the pit and handed him the sight. Jesse mounted the sight and checked the dope. He leveled the bubbles and realigned on the aiming stakes. Without waiting for his assistant gunner to return to the gunpit, he dropped another round down the tube.

"Cease fire. End of mission," said Cuz. "Courtney, you stay on the land line. Everyone else, report to the bunker."

Inside the bunker, most of the men lit up cigarettes. It was true the bunker was packed with mortar ammunition, but that seemed of no consequence. It was safer than lighting up outside in the darkness, where you could be a sniper target.

Cuz started speaking only after Sal returned. "That was damn good night gunning, Jesse."

Jesse felt self-conscious. "Thanks, Cuz."

"You were perfect until the misfire." Cuz paused.

Jesse knew what was coming.

"Where the fuck did you learn to clear a misfire without waiting for a cook-off?"

Jesse was ready with his answer. "Hell, Cuz, our guys out there needed the support now, not one or two minutes later. Besides, the tube wasn't that hot."

"Seven rounds fired, one right after the other with a charge six, and you tell me the tube wasn't hot?"

"Well, it wasn't that bad," Jesse replied timidly.

"Bullshit. You trying to get yourself blown to shit – along with Sal – or what?"

Jesse was silent.

"Let me see your hands."

Jesse held out his hands, palms down.

"Now, turn 'em over."

Reluctantly, Jesse turned the palms upward. Even in the dim light afforded by the two candles in the bunker, the blisters were plainly visible.

"Shit man. You crazy cowboy," said Bean. "It ain't worth that kind of crap."

"No it isn't," agreed Cuz. "And it damn sure isn't worth risking your life and Sal's, and the gun. Next time wait for the cook-off."

"Okay, Cuz. Next time I wait for the cook-off."

Cuz arched an eyebrow. "That's good enough for me – for now at least."

The following morning, they heard about PFC Brown from the flame platoon. It was about an hour after morning chow when one of the men from the flame platoon stopped at the mortar position and spoke with Cuz. Soon Cuz advised the men who knew Brown of that morning's occurrence.

Brown and his flame team had gone to the dump to burn trash, as was the normal routine but, on this morning, things went sour. Brown had pulled the trigger to strike the match and fire the flamethrower at a large mound of trash. He was shooting Napalm and it had ignited the trash immediately. While he was shooting, the old hose from the tank to the gun ruptured, covering Brown with the jelly-like Napalm. Brown released his trigger and tried to dump his flame tank but the spraying Napalm was ignited by the still burning gun tip. The flame leapt from the gun tip to Brown's saturated clothing and the PFC became a ball of fire. His tank continued to spray Napalm randomly about, making rescue impossible.

Brown finally rid himself of the flame tank and his men were able to extinguish the flames at some considerable risk to themselves.

PFC Brown was lifted out by helicopter within fifteen minutes of the occurrence. He died aboard the old CH-34 Choctaw.

Jesse remembered Brown. He had seen him on the way back to Sherwood Forest after his first waterborne patrol. The manner of the man's dying seemed such a waste to Jesse. Burning trash!

That afternoon a new man joined the first squad. PFC Jim Cusick was his name. Once again Jesse parted with his rifle. Cusick was fresh out of boot camp and infantry training regiment. He was assigned the position of last ammo carrier in the first squad.

The mortar platoon carried on its daily routine.

The war seemed far away.

CHAPTER EIGHT: NIGHT AMBUSH

The day following Brown's death, PFC Dwight David Scott received his long awaited orders for Camp Lejuene and the Continental United States. He stood in the First Section tent and read the orders aloud, making special note at the end of his reading that the battalion executive officer, Major Knowles, was shipping out the same day and had also been re-assigned to Camp Lejuene. Most of the men congratulated him for two reasons: first, he was getting the hell out of Viet Nam; second, he was being assigned to the same base as Major Knowles.

Later, in the early afternoon, DD rushed into the First Section tent, his face an ashen white, his lips tightly set.

Howard, 1st Section wireman, looked up at him from his cot. "What the hell's the matter with you, DD?"

DD picked up his helmet, cartridge belt and rifle and left the tent without speaking. DD was barely out of sight when Tule stuck his head through the opened tent flap. "Okay, everyone on your feet. Helmets and weapons. Outside in one minute."

"What's up, Tule?" asked Howard.

"I'll tell you all at the same time. Just get it outside."

Jesse stepped outside and waited patiently, smoking a cigarette. Once the section was formed, Tule said, "Okay, men, we're goin' on a search and rescue."

"Search and rescue? We ain't the damn Navy," said Bean.

Tule glared at him and moved a step in his direction.

Jesse said, "What kind of search and rescue mission, Tule?"

Tule stopped and looked at Jesse. He glared at Bean again. "Major Knowles was showing the new Battalion Exec our perimeter. They were standing by the cliffs just south of our position when a gust of wind caught Major Knowles off balance and he fell over the side. The new exec looked for him but couldn't find anything."

"What's the time element?" asked Cuz.

"About three hours."

"Great," said Barnett.

"Where's DD?" asked Cuz.

"He said screw it, he was gonna find the major on his own. I let him go."

"I hope to hell the major's okay," said Howard.

"How the hell can he be okay? He fell off a goddamn cliff fer chrisake," said Bean.

"All right, quit the grab-assin' and let's get to looking. We start at the 81 position and move south along the coast until we get to Seventh Mess Battalion. If he's not found by then, we work our way back north to our position again," ordered Tule.

The marines searched doggedly south discovering no sign of Major

Knowles. At the mess battalion, the men took a break for chow and, though they ate in the shade of the mess battalion's tents, they consumed C-rations. During the break, Jesse was surprised by a voice from the past.

"You crazy sonofabitch. What the hell are you doing back here?"

Jesse recognized D.W. Savage from the old 2nd Battalion 3rd Marines, approaching at a slow walk. "Came to fight a war. Got boring as hell in the States," answered Jesse, smiling broadly. They shook hands warmly.

DW laughed. "Of everybody I ever knew, you're the last person in the world I woulda thought woulda come back into this chickenshit outfit."

"Just had to fight my war, I guess. So what the hell is a mortarman doing cooking? Why aren't you in 81's?" asked Jesse.

"Screw that shit," answered DW. "I told 'em I was goin' nuts and I was gonna shell battalion headquarters if they didn't get me out of the infantry. So they made me a cook."

Jesse said, "Have you heard from any of the other old guys?"

"Yeah, some of 'em. The Crotch started doin' funny things a few months ago and most of the old outfit was split up. Stubby's in Two-Nine. Little Luke, Hymie, Monroe and the Beast are in Three-Three. Wink, Doo, Guy, Sanchez and a bunch of the others went to One-Seven. Lucy got him a cushy job at division. JD bought it in the DMZ." DW paused.

Jesse felt a twinge of sadness. He and JD had been close. They had all been close in that outfit. "Are you sure?"

"I got it from Onee. He was there. A gook mortar hit their position at night. JD never knew what happened."

"How about Pineapple, Pup, Smitty, and the rest of 'em?"

"Don't know. Haven't heard a thing. Oh yeah, Bergie got a Big Chicken Dinner. He tried to shoot a second lieutenant on our side."

"Seriously?"

"Yeah, but I heard the lieutenant had it coming. He had 'em doing p.t. in the heat, and standing inspections like they were at Camp Pendleton or somethin'."

"So did Bergie smoke 'im?" asked Jesse.

"No. Norm Rapp spotted him headed for the lieutenant with a pistol. He tried to talk Bergie out of it but Bergie wasn't havin' any a' that shit. Norm finally had to wrestle the damn pistol away from 'im."

"So how did the lieutenant find out about it? Did Norm turn him in?"

DW laughed. "Hell no. He almost got court-martialed himself. The lieutenant heard the scuffle but when he got there, Norm had the pistol away from Bergie and tucked behind his back. He asked what the hell was goin on and Norm said, 'Nothing'. Bergie was so damned mad at that lieutenant that he stood right there in front of him and said, 'I was on my way to blow your fuckin' brains out, but Sergeant Rapp here took my pistol.' Can you believe that shit?"

Jesse smiled. "Yeah, that's Bergie. So they gave him a B.C.D.,huh?"

"Yep. Six-six-and-a-kick," replied Savage, referring to six months in the brig, six months loss of pay and a Bad Conduct Discharge from the Marine Corps.

"That's too bad. Bergie was a good man," said Jesse.

"Yeah. As long as you were his squad leader. You were about the only guy he ever took an order from without tellin' you to stick it."

Jesse smiled, "I wasn't exempt from his famous 'stick it' phrase either, but he was a good field marine. I'd like to have him with me now."

"Shee-it, he's better off in The World, with all the round eyes and cold beer."

"Yeah, I guess you're right." Jesse noticed his section forming to retrace their steps to the north and moved to join them. "You take care, DW. If you get a chance, stop in and see me. I'm with One-Four, just north of here."

"Keep yer ass low," said DW.

"See ya," said Jesse with a parting wave.

The return trip was as uneventful as their sweep to the south had been. There was no sign of Major Knowles.

That evening the First Section stood the gun watch. It was about 0100 hours when Jesse was awakened by the sound of an M-14 from inside the gunpit, firing into the forest. The noise was deafening. Adrenaline pounding in his veins, he stuffed his helmet onto his head and rolled next to Sal who knelt only five feet away, rifle in his shoulder, pointed into the depths of the forest.

"What the hell you shootin' at?" Jesse asked in a loud whisper. Other First Section members began to spill out of the bunker. The whole camp was coming awake.

"There's something out there in the brush!" shouted Sal.

"Did you challenge?" asked Jesse.

"Yeah, but they didn't answer."

Jesse had heard no challenge and he was a light sleeper.

The crackling sound of a breaking twig in the tree line to their direct front startled Jesse. He turned to Sal. "You got the gun, Sal. Give me some illumination." He turned to Cuz, who had just arrived at his side. "Pass the word down the line that I'm out front. I don't want shot by our own guys."

Jesse charged into the darkness with his .45 pistol, a K-bar knife and two hand grenades.

"Hey! Where the hell you goin'?" shouted Cuz. Jesse disappeared into the darkness.

Jesse slowed at the edge of the forest and assumed the prone position. He quietly crawled under some overhanging brush and waited for the first illumination round. When the canister popped on the illumination round overhead, Jesse tensed. He held a grenade in his left hand, pin pulled, spoon held tightly in place with his fingers.

He waited to see if a friendly patrol had accidentally entered Sherwood Forest. If such was the case they would surely identify themselves with the illumination above them. He waited, eyes straining at the dancing shadows in the forest. Nothing happened. No sound. No visual contact.

A second illumination round popped above the forest, followed quickly by a third. It was brighter, but now there were three sets of shadows intermingling, caused by the bright light emitting from three different locations. He heard a movement about twenty yards from his position. His guts knotted. Too many trees to throw the grenade that distance safely. He could wait for them to move again or he could move toward the sound. Choosing the latter option, he slowly crawled towards the spot where he had heard movement, careful not to make a sound. He could hear his own breathing over the hissing-sizzle of the illumination rounds as they floated to earth. He held his breath to silence the pounding in his head but his heartbeat continued to thump incessantly in his eardrums, almost drowning out the fizzling sound of the descending illumination rounds. He wondered what the hell he was doing out here.

Jesse stopped behind a large pine trunk. He breathed through his mouth as slowly and as quietly as he could. He estimated his position at less than ten yards from where he had last heard the movement. He could easily toss his grenade and be protected by the large tree trunk. *What if the noise had been made by friendlies, and for some unknown reason, they had failed to identify themselves?* He decided to wait a little longer. He held his breath and listened. He could hear only his own heartbeat.

A fourth and fifth illumination round burst into the air. The popping of the canisters startled Jesse even though he had heard the rounds fired only seconds earlier.

He heard a movement less than ten yards away but was unable to ascertain exactly what it was – perhaps a man brushing against a bush. Still holding his grenade carefully, he cupped his hands and spoke to the rear to throw his voice location. "*De sung xuong*! Drop your weapons!" He shouted in both Vietnamese and English.

The brush crackled loudly of breaking twigs and wrenched leaves. The sound moved rapidly from directly in front of Jesse to his right front. He released the spoon on the grenade and leaned around the tree to his left to keep the trunk between him and the sounds. As his left arm moved forward to throw the grenade, he saw the quickly fleeing enemy: *a black panther!* He held short his throw and released the grenade to his left. His short throw and brief hesitation barely left him time to fall prone and gain cover before the grenade exploded. Fragments whizzed in all directions overhead. Small branches fell as they were severed from the trees above.

With his ears still ringing from the explosion, he shouted, "Cease fire! Cease fire! It's only a panther. I say again. Cease fire! Cease fire!"

A voice came to him over the ringing in his ears. "You okay, you crazy goddamn cowboy?" It was Tule.

"Yeah, I'm okay. Don't let anybody shoot. I'm comin' in."

There was a short pause. Tule said, "Okay, man. Come on in."

Jesse picked up his helmet, which had fallen off during the explosion, and placed it on his head. He walked out of the forest and back to the gun position. Illumination fire was ceased and Jesse reported to the platoon commander's tent for debriefing.

In addition to the platoon commander, Gunnery Sergeant Reyes and Sergeant Tuleano sat on folding stools. When Jesse finished his report, the lieutenant asked, "Who gave you permission to leave your post?"

Jesse looked at the lieutenant. "Sir, I didn't leave my post. I went after what we all thought were gooks inside our position. We can't mortar our own position. Except for illumination – which we had covered."

Tule looked quizzically from Jesse to the lieutenant.

The platoon commander said, "And what makes you think you're qualified to attack an unknown force of unknown size without orders to do so?"

Jesse paused a moment. "Sir, I'm as qualified as anybody in the platoon."

Tule looked from Reyes to the platoon commander to Jesse.

"Very well then, Lance Corporal. Exactly *why* did you do what you did?" asked the lieutenant.

Jesse looked into the lieutenant's eyes. "Well, Sir, if I'm gonna be shot, I want it to be by a gook, not an American. If I waited for the formation of a patrol, by the time we got to the woods, the guys would be trigger-happy and shootin' at every sound. Second: I give the enemy credit for having a brain. I try to think like he would think and I plan my moves on what I think would surprise him. And third, and most importantly: I want to win this war. I haven't even seen a live VC since I've been here. What the hell are we fightin'? I wanted to see one of these guys. I can't help win the war sittin' on my ass, waitin' for an order from somebody."

The lieutenant stared at Jesse. Silence filled the tent as a full minute elapsed. He turned to Reyes. "Gunny, you or Tule got anything you want to add?"

Reyes answered, "Not me, sir. I think it best if we let Sergeant Tuleano handle it from here."

The lieutenant looked back to Jesse. It appeared he could not yet muster a response of sufficient substance. "You're dismissed, Langley. I'll think about what you said."

"Thank you, sir." Jesse stood and stepped into the darkness.

The following afternoon, Jesse played poker in the First Section tent. He was a little more than eight hundred dollars ahead since his arrival in Vietnam, and poker was one of the few leisure activities he could both enjoy and profit from.

Since ten o'clock that morning rain had fallen in a steady stream. The sides of the tent were dropped to keep the water outside and the door flaps at the ends were folded open to allow light and fresh air to enter.

Jesse read his hand casually, holding his poker face. Someone stepped into the doorway near his end of the tent, momentarily blocking the light. Jesse waited for the man to move but it remained dark on his side of the poker game. Without looking behind him, he said, "Hey, how about steppin' out of the light back there?"

"How about kissin' my ass?"

Jesse knew the voice instantly. It had been a long time, but he knew it just the same. He turned to see David Stubbs from his old outfit, rifle slung at his shoulder, standing just inside the tent, water dripping from his helmet and poncho. Jesse was up instantly, hugging and shaking hands with him. "Stubby, you rotten sonofagun. What the hell are you doing here?"

"What the hell am *I* doin' here? What the hell are *you* doin' here? Mad Dog said he heard you were back in and over here and I called him a damn liar. Told him I'd blow his ass away if he ever told another lie like that. I thought you were the smartest guy in our old outfit. I can't believe this shit. You were my hero, man. What the hell happened?"

"It's a long story," replied Jesse.

"I just walked nine miles to hear it, so it better be a good long story, you dumb shit," said Stubby.

"Hey, Jesse, You gonna play?" asked Bean.

"Deal me out for awhile."

"What about this hand?" asked Collins.

Jesse glanced quickly at Stubby. "Just let me finish this hand, Stubby. You mind?"

"Shit, go ahead. I wouldn't want to take you away from business." He smiled.

Jesse reclaimed his seat. The game was seven-card stud and Jesse had just seen his sixth card when Stubby had arrived. He held a nine-high straight, but the five, six, seven and eight were all hearts. There were still four players in the hand

153

though betting had been heavy. Collins was one of those still in and his money was low. Jesse wanted his wristwatch.

"How much to me?" asked Jesse.

"Fifteen bucks," replied Bean, obviously proud of what he held.

Jesse looked at his hand, then to the money in front of Collins. "Your fifteen and ten more."

Sal to his left, folded. "Shit. You three guys must have fifteen aces the way you're betting."

Collins looked at Bean, then to Jesse. "Here's twenty-five." He counted his remaining money. "And fifty-two more."

Cuz, who had folded his cards early in the hand, whistled. "Whew. The man said he thinks he's got a winner."

"Yeah, or he's bluffing," said Bean as he tried to read Collins' face.

Bean studied his hole cards, then the up cards on the blanket, then the money in the pot. Jesse's cards looked like a straight. Collins showed two queens. He threw his cards face down onto the blanket. "Shit. I'm out. It's too rich for me."

Jesse smiled. "Your fifty-two and fifty more."

Silence around the game.

"I'm all in. If you'll take my IOU, I'll call. Hell I'll even raise you," said Collins.

"You're not all in as long as you're wearing that Zodiac Seawolf," replied Jesse, nodding to the black-dialed diver's watch on Collins' wrist.

"What'll you credit me for it?" asked Collins with no hesitation.

"A hundred and ten bucks, same as a new one in civilian life."

"Shit, you're on!" He took the watch from his arm and placed it into the pot. "Your fifty and sixty more."

"Call," replied Jesse, counting his m.p.c. into the pot.

Stubby shook his head. "Yer crazy. You know he's got a boat."

"Stubby, I was meant to have that watch. I can feel it."

Cuz cleared his throat. "Here they come. Last card."

Jesse slowly read his card – a four of hearts.

Collins didn't even glance at his last card. "Anything else you wanna buy? I'd like to make another bet."

Jesse looked at him. "Hal, I just want your watch. I've got you beat. Don't waste your money."

Collins laughed. "No way you got me beat."

Without continuing the discussion, Jesse placed his hole cards face up on the cot. "If you can beat a straight flush, bet it."

He picked up the watch and placed it on his wrist, then scooped the m.p.c. to his position at the game. "Deal me out. I'm gonna visit with an old buddy of mine. Collins, if you wanna borrow some money, help yourself, but keep track of it. Bean, watch my dough, will ya?"

"No sweat," replied Bean.

"Son-of-a-bitch. I can't believe you had a straight flush. How much can I borrow?" said Collins.

"Whatever you need," said Jesse as he and Stubby moved away from the game. Stubby said, "Do you even know what he had?"

"Didn't matter. His highest possible was four queens."

"That's what he had."

"That's a helluva hand to lose with, but you'll notice I'm wearing the watch."

154

Stubby smiled and shook his head. "It reminds me of old times. The Cuban crisis, Hong Kong, the Philippines, and all those other places."

"Yeah, but the pots are bigger now," said Jesse.

Stubby laughed.

The two reminisced throughout the afternoon. They drank jungle wine and recalled every story they could about each man in their old battalion. As the hour grew late, Stubby said, "I guess I'm gonna have to haul ass."

They looked at each other, the lightheartedness of only a few moments earlier forgotten. It was replaced with a feeling of sadness and camaraderie – a feeling not totally unfamiliar to these two.

"Thanks for coming to see me, Stubby."

Stubby grinned. "It was worth it. It was good to see you again, man, even though you really blew the image." His grin grew into a smile.

Jesse wanted to hug him and tell him how close he felt to him. How much all of the guys in their old outfit meant. How he wished they could all get together again, like in 1963. He couldn't. He didn't know how to talk to a man like that, not even Stubby.

"Take care, Stubby. Say hello if you run across any of the old guys."

"Stop in and see me if you ever get up my way," said Stubby.

"I will."

"Keep yer ass low, Jesse."

"You too, Stubby."

They shook hands. It was an hour before sunset when Stubby jumped aboard the mechanical mule ordered up by Tuleano to aid him in his late return to his unit.

Jesse felt a deep loss at Stubby's departure. The wine had loosened his feelings and brought them too close to the surface. He wished the war would disappear and he would wake up in an engineering class at the University of Arizona. He knew he would never again find the camaraderie he had known in the 2nd Battalion, 3rd Marines of 1963. True, he didn't care for the Marine Corps, but that was the best bunch of guys he had ever known. And now some of them were in this war that could go on for months. And some were being killed.

Shannon came into his mind. He'd give a month's pay just to see her smile. Hell, he'd give a month's pay just to see her from a distance.

"Hey, Langley." Cuz's voice returned him to the present. "Gunny wants to see you."

"Okay, Cuz. I'll be right there." He put on his helmet and reported to the Gunny's tent.

"You sent for me, Gunny?"

"Yes, Langley. You're going to be in charge of a night ambush tonight."

"Me?"

"Yes, you. You'll have command of Barnett, who'll be your radio operator, and McCreery and Rodriquez."

"A four-man ambush? Sounds like a good size for a raidin' party, but that's a bit small for an ambush, ain't it, Guns?"

"You'll have a PF Lieutenant and twenty of his men. He normally has thirty but ten of them are at the rifle range this week."

"Uh, Gunny? What the hell is a PF?"

"Popular Forces. We call 'em PFs. They're volunteers – part-time soldiers."

"Can they be trusted?" asked Jesse warily.

"So far we haven't had any problems in that area. They're not much for fighting though. They need a lot more training."

"Why me? I can't speak twenty words of Vietnamese. How will I communicate with these guys?" The effects of his home brew were rapidly disappearing.

"They've set up this same ambush ten or fifteen times and have never had any contact. It's mainly a routine night watch. But this way, we can report 'joint operations' with the Vietnamese to the folks back home."

"Oh," said Jesse resignedly.

"Take a look at the map here," said Reyes, pointing to a map spread across his field desk. "See where these two trails meet at a point on the shore near the river? Basically, you set up in a triangle. Ten men cover this trail. Ten men cover this trail, and ten men cover the river. You position yourself and your men where you want."

"Wait a minute, Gunny, you said that ten of this lieutenant's men were at rifle training. How do I get thirty PF's?"

"Just spread them a little thinner. Six or seven per side of the triangle."

Jesse nodded.

Reyes pointed to the map again. "This is your rally point in the event you make contact." He moved his finger to another set of coordinates. "This is your secondary. You got it?"

Jesse studied the map and nodded.

"Your call sign is Pied Piper Poppa Foxtrot."

"You're shittin' me? With a call sign that long, if we ran into anything, we'd be wiped out before we could identify ourselves."

"It works. You'll be all right. Get your men and your gear together and we'll get you to the new chapel at battalion H.Q. That's where you'll stage. You jump off at 2100 and move into position. You hold the ambush until 0230. If you have no contact, you move to your second rally point until daylight. Maintain radio silence until in position, then check-in every fifteen minutes with your call sign and the word 'blue' and nothing else. Is that clear?"

"Yeah, it's clear. Is it okay for me to borrow a rifle?"

"Be my guest. But there's no moon tonight so your distance shooting may be a little shortened." Reyes smiled as Jesse left the tent.

He borrowed Cusick's rifle, with which he was quite familiar, having traded it back and forth several times since his arrival in Viet Nam, and two extra magazines. His mind was on his small command, not the rifle, as he mustered his three men and briefed them thoroughly, expressing doubts about "PFs".

Two six-bys rolled into camp and a small Vietnamese officer exited one of them. He was dressed in green fatigues and wore gold lieutenant Bars. Jesse approached him, Mac, Bean and Hou close behind.

Jesse said, "Howdy. You Lieutenant Xuan?"

The smaller man nodded and Jesse offered his hand. The lieutenant shook his hand limply and Jesse introduced his men to the lieutenant. They shook hands briefly. There was no saluting. Marines do not often salute in a combat zone. Some, like Jesse, did not wear any rank or insignia whatsoever. Amenities completed, Jesse nodded to the PFs in the near six-by.

"Where do you want us to ride?" Jesse asked Xuan.

156

The little lieutenant looked at him blankly.

"Do you speak any English?" asked Jesse.

Still no response from Xuan.

Jesse felt frustration creeping up. "Ong noi tieng Anh khong?"

Lieutenant Xuan smiled and shook his head.

"Shit," said Jesse. He turned to his three marines. "Any of you guys speak Vietnamese?"

Bean replied, "Hell, you already spoke more than I know."

"All I know is boom-boom," said Mac.

"My eyes are round. I can't understand it, much less speak it," replied Barnett.

"This is gonna be a long night," said Jesse disgustedly as he turned back to the small lieutenant. He pointed to his men, then to himself. "Xe cam-nhong Mot? Xe cam-nhong Hai?"

Xuan smiled. "Mot." He seemed pleased the American marine was trying to communicate in Vietnamese.

"Into the first truck," Jesse ordered his men.

As the trucks bounced and slid down the muddy road in the steady mist, Barnett said, "Where'd you learn to speak Vietnamese?"

Jesse smiled at him in the growing darkness. "Hell, I don't speak it. I memorized the words and phrases in that pamphlet they gave me after I landed."

"I remember those things," said McCreery. "I used mine for shit paper the same day I got it."

The marines laughed. There were ten PF's in the truck with them and though they didn't understand what was being said, they laughed with the marines. Soon they were all laughing at each other, and no one knew why.

At battalion H.Q. the men debarked the six-bys. Jesse studied the unfinished chapel/recreation facility, the only structure in the compound not a tent. He didn't remember seeing it on his first night in Viet Nam but there were probably many things he didn't see. It was constructed of Bamboo, a large structure by Vietnamese peasant and combat marine standards. The straw roof and walls seemed fragile and "movie-like" to Jesse. At one end of the long building a room had been added to the north, giving the chapel an L-shape. The floor was dirt and there were several large bamboo poles evenly spaced down the center supporting the peaked roof. The interior was barren.

"Home sweet home," said Houston Barnett as he sat his PRC-10 radio onto the dirt floor.

Jesse glanced at his newly acquired Seawolf wristwatch. He had put his gold Wittnauer dress watch away in his willie peter bag. The heavier diver's watch felt good on his wrist, and it wasn't all fogged up from the humidity and perspiration. It was 1905 hours. "Okay, you guys, you might as well get some sleep. We jump off in about two hours."

Barnett was already on his back, using his radio for a pillow.

Jesse reached into his map pocket and pulled out his area map. He motioned to Xuan and shined his flashlight, with its red lens cover, onto the map. Painstakingly, he went over the plan with Lieutenant Xuan, communicating mainly with hand signals, and occasionally speaking a word or two of Vietnamese. In twenty minutes Jesse took off his helmet, sat it on the dirt floor and lay on his back, using the helmet as his pillow.

157

Stoney Livingston

It was pitch dark. All activity in the camp had long ago ceased. There was no moon. A man couldn't see his hand two inches in front of his face. What a stupid night for an ambush, Jesse thought. He would have to be dependent upon the PFs to get them into position by the river. He had never been over the trail, and to try to find his way in such darkness would require an infra-red night scope. He had asked for one but had been informed that none was yet available for infantry companies. He had wondered who in the hell needed them worse than infantry companies, but didn't ask.

Someone rolled over in his sleep and Jesse wondered if it was one of his men or the PFs. His mind began to wander. What if one of those PFs was a Viet Cong? He quietly pulled the .45 from its holster and placed it softly under his helmet. He held his breath and listened for movement. There seemed nothing out of the ordinary, but the thought of waking up with his throat cut did not ease his mind into sleep.

He shook his head to clear those thoughts away and dozed off, wondering how his old cat, Fuzzy, was doing.

Jesse opened his eyes abruptly. He didn't move another muscle in his body, only his eyelids. Something had awakened him, some strange movement or sound. He didn't know what it was but felt it was close. He held his breath and listened. It was too dark to see without light so he waited, body tense, ready to spring into action. He quietly caught his breath then held it again. Barely moving the fingers on his right hand, he groped for the flashlight he knew was lying by his side. The tips of his fingers found the L-shaped, plastic flashlight and he positioned it quietly so that he could turn it on and point it in any direction.

Still flat on his back he turned his head slowly to the left. There was a soft, almost imperceptible noise only inches from his left ear. Slowly and quietly he brought the flashlight across his body and pointed it next to his face then tensed his body for a leap to his feet and turned the red-lensed flashlight on.

Less than six inches from his face was the largest spider Jesse had ever seen. He reached under his helmet, grabbed his pistol and jumped to his feet. The helmet went rolling across the dirt floor, making a dull clanking sound as it rolled.

Instantly the men inside the chapel were moving. Jesse searched the floor with his flashlight but the large spider had disappeared.

"Hey, Jesse, what the fuck's goin on?" asked Bean in a loud whisper.

Lieutenant Xuan spoke rapidly in Vietnamese, trying to keep his voice at a low level. Other voices spoke Vietnamese.

Jesse replied to Bean as he swept the floor with his flashlight. "We got an eight-legged visitor. I'm not shittin' you, Hou, I just saw the biggest goddamn spider in the world. He was bigger than one of Tule's hands."

The marines could all relate to that comparison.

"I don't need this shit," said Bean, quickly standing.

Soon everyone in the chapel was on their feet. Still there was no sign of the spider. Lieutenant Xuan, the only other man with a flashlight, watched Jesse as he moved his hand about like a spider, then spread his arms wide to indicate large. Xuan nodded, indicating that he understood, and commenced a search with his flashlight, no doubt wondering what that crazy marine was going to do with that pistol in his hand.

"Shit, man, get over here with that damn flashlight and check out my area," said Bean.

158

The search continued for almost five minutes without a sign.

McCreery said, "You sure you weren't just dreamin?"

"Screw you, Mac. I saw this damn thing. I didn't dream it."

"Well, goddamnit, he musta got tired of all the noise and bullshit, and hauled-ass," said McCreery.

Jesse stood up straight. He was weary of the stooped position he had maintained during his search. "Yeah, I guess you're right. You guys get some rest." He looked at his watch. "We've still got thirty minutes before we..."

On a bamboo pole, at eye level, only inches from Jesse's face, was the spider. He shined his flashlight full on the large arachnid's body. A large phosphorescent blue diamond or hourglass on the top of the furry spider's abdomen appeared and disappeared as the abdomen expanded and contracted.

"Jesus. Would you look at that!" said McCreery.

The PFs gathered around the bamboo pole.

"You guys stand back. I'm gonna put this guy in spider heaven," said Jesse as he held his pistol by the barrel and aimed the bottom of the handgrips at the large spider.

The PF lieutenant put his arm in front of Jesse's chest and spoke in Vietnamese. A PF with corporal stripes stepped up to the bamboo pole. He reached up and carelessly picked up the spider then placed it on his shoulder and released his grip.

Jesse's skin crawled as he watched the large spider move around the man's neck.

The little corporal spoke: "USA, numba Ten. Vietnam, numba one."

Jesse shook his head. "They may be number one in Vietnam, but if it's all the same to you, I'd like to see him removed from our humble Chapel."

The little PF corporal smiled unknowingly at Jesse.

Jesse pointed to the spider. "Di di!"

Frowning, the corporal removed the spider from behind his collar and put him safely outside. The other PFs laughed nervously.

Jesse turned off his flashlight.

The next thirty minutes passed slowly for Jesse. Though he had seen the PF corporal handle the large spider like a pet parrot, he wasn't overly enthusiastic about another visit from him or any of his relatives.

At 2100 hours, Jesse stepped to Barnett's side and whispered, "Okay, saddle up. It's time to move out."

Lieutenant Xuan mustered his men. Shortly, the ambush party was on the move. They were challenged at the perimeter then allowed to pass. In the almost total darkness they were less than one pace apart as they moved down the trail and, even at that distance, the man to the front was invisible. They remained a cohesive unit only by following the sounds of movement made by the man to the front. Jesse wondered if the point man really knew where he was going.

After almost thirty minutes of blindly following the quiet sounds of the man to the front, they arrived at the ambush site.

Jesse strained his eyes as he watched Lieutenant Xuan dispatch ten of his men to cover the river from the point of the two trails. He thought it strange that Xuan would send half of his force to one location but perhaps the PFs had information indicating a greater probability of contact from that direction.

Xuan then dispatched his remaining ten men to cover the trail to the

Stoney Livingston

southwest, leaving only him and his radio operator with Jesse and Barnett. McCreery had been sent with the riverside ambush and Bean had gone to the southwest trail.

Jesse whispered to Barnett, "Is this little shithead really that stupid? Can't he see if we don't protect the southeast trail, and we get hit from that side, we'll be ripped up from the inside by our own crossfire?"

Hou whispered his reply, "Hell, they've probably done this ambush so many times that each guy has his assigned spot. The ten guys that are on the rifle range this week normally cover the southeast trail. They ain't here tonight, so the trail don't get covered."

"That's crazy. I guess a second lieutenant is a second lieutenant, no matter which army he's in," whispered Jesse.

"No shit. He probably figures that nothing is going to happen anyway, so why split up his girls?" whispered Hou.

"Well, damnit, you and I'll cover the third side, and the good lieutenant and his radio operator can join us."

Xuan was already moving to a center position on the third side. Jesse and Barnett followed closely, so as not to become lost in the darkness. There was an old French pillbox, or what was left of it, standing just north of the trail. Lieutenant Xuan carefully stepped over the remaining wall on the east side. Once inside the roofless, almost wall-less structure, he sat down. His radio operator followed suit.

Jesse entered and moved to his left, taking up his position in the corner nearest the trail. Hou sat down quietly behind him.

"Jesus Christ," said Jesse in a whisper. "He acts like he's on a stroll in the park. With two pistols, my M-14 and the PF lieutenant's carbine, we couldn't stop two good men in this inkwell if they knew our position."

"No wonder they need some help. The VC'd whip their asses in a week if we weren't here," whispered Hou.

"To hell with it. Report blue," said Jesse.

Hou keyed his handset and spoke softly into the mouthpiece. "Pied Piper, Pied Piper. Pied Piper Poppa Foxtrot. Blue. Over."

There was low volume squelch for a split-second as Hou unkeyed his mike. A quiet voice from within the radio said, "Roger Blue." Then silence.

At 2145 hours Hou checked in again on the radio. Jesse strained his eyes in the darkness but without a moon and, with the heavy overcast to hide the stars, he could see nothing. The soft, misty rain deadened sound and he could barely hear Hou reporting-in only three feet behind him.

At 2200 hours, Hou again reported "Blue." Jesse was becoming bored. His eyes hurt from trying to see where nothing could be seen. He closed them. They felt better. Things even seemed brighter than they were when his eyes were open. He wondered what Shannon was doing. She probably has no idea of what war is really like, he thought. Hell, who does until they try it? The movies sure play it up. Heroes and medals. Pretty girls. Nice weather. Good food. Great morale. A close outfit. Bullshit.

Jesse opened his eyes. He thought he heard a rustling to his front. He turned to Hou. "Pssst. Hou. Did you hear anything?"

Hou leaned into his ear. "No, I didn't hear a thing. You gettin' jumpy?"

Jesse shrugged, a gesture wasted in the darkness. "Maybe. I thought I heard something up the trail but I guess not."

At 2215 hours, Hou reported "Blue." At 2217 hours, Jesse heard another

160

rustling sound. This time, he felt certain.

"Hou, did you hear that?" he asked in a whisper.

"Yeah, I heard it. Could have been a water buffalo though," replied Hou in an unconvincing whisper.

"Yeah, or a panther, or a herd of VC."

"Now what the hell do we do? Over."

"Well, we could just sit here and wait, like we're supposed to do."

"How come I got this funny feeling you're gonna take option two – whatever-the-hell that is?" asked Hou in an anxious whisper.

"Goddamnit, Hou. Look how this stupid little PF lieutenant stationed his men. We're dead meat if we stay here and that noise is gooks. I'm goin' out there and have a look."

"A look?" whispered Hou incredulously. "A look with what? You got infrared vision? You can't see your hand in front of your face tonight."

"Neither can they if they're out there."

"Unless they've got a night scope."

Jesse hadn't even considered the possibility. The thought set him back. Finally, he said, "Then we're dead anyway. If I get picked off as soon as I hit the trail, you get the rest of the guys and get the hell outa here. If I'm able to get up the trail a ways, its either gooks without night scopes or some kind of animal."

"Why not just call in illumination?" asked Hou.

"We can't compromise the ambush just because we heard a noise."

"That doesn't mean you gotta be a damn hero. We can wait it out."

"If it's gooks, and we wait, we're dead, with or without scopes. Tell the PF Lieutenant I'm out front." Jesse stood and took off his poncho and helmet. "Tell 'em I'm the one with the headband if the lights come on." He quietly stepped over the low wall, rifle in hand.

The trail was sandy and bounded on both sides by heavy brush. Jesse tried to stay in the center of the trail by stooping low and feeling the sand. He sensed, rather than saw, the bushes when he got too close to the edge of the trail. He paused and looked skyward for a sign that the heavy clouds might part long enough to allow the twinkling of a few stars. He saw nothing but blackness. He shook his head as a raindrop struck him directly in the eye.

He moved forward slowly, stooped low, making almost no sound in the soft sand. He drifted right and almost encountered the brush. An unknown sense told him to move left just before he made contact with the vegetation. The early stages of vertigo gripped him. But for the ground beneath his feet, he couldn't tell up from down, nor left from right. He held his breath a moment then continued slowly on his way, checking carefully for trip-wires as he moved. He ignored the thought of land mines as best he could.

His mouth was dry. Despite the steady rain he wanted a drink of water but knew it would have to wait. In ten minutes he had gone almost fifty yards. Not a very long distance by some measures but it seemed miles in the blackness. Jesse had not heard a sound since leaving his position save the pounding of his own heart.

At seventy-five yards he stopped, maintaining his low crouch. With the soft rain falling he felt certain he couldn't have heard any movement at this distance from the ambush site, save perhaps a herd of stampeding elephants. What if he had walked right by the VC? As dark as it was, the possibility definitely existed. His mind began to race. Fear welled up inside him like a volcanic eruption. The almost total darkness placed him right at the edge of panic.

He had not moved a muscle since he had stopped. He gripped his borrowed M-I4 and struggled to regain control over his fear. The rifle reassured him. It was solid and real, the only real thing in a dark void. His muscles loosened. Hell, if he had actually walked past the VC once, he could do it again.

Jesse slowly stood erect to turn around for his return to the ambush site. A soft, almost imperceptible noise only inches from his face, alerted him.

The VC stepped onto the trail, striking Jesse full in the chest with his own body, apparently unaware of Jesse's presence. He swung his rifle to bear on Jesse, but was too close, and the barrel struck Jesse on the right biceps. The VC rifle fired twice in rapid succession. The VC then turned and retreated down the trail at a dead run, crashing into the bushes in the darkness.

Jesse felt pain in his right upper arm at almost the same instant he heard the crack of the rifle. His instantaneous thought was that he had lost his arm. He couldn't feel the M-I4 with his right hand. He had squeezed the trigger on his rifle and when it hadn't fired, he became almost certain his arm had been blown off. Then he realized the safety was on. He moved his trigger finger forward and released the safety. The first proof he had that his arm was still attached to his body was when his own rifle fired. At the time, he was falling backward, onto the sandy trail. The muzzle flash from his M-I4 pierced the darkness.

Jesse rolled onto his chest and, from the prone position, fired down the trail in the direction of the fleeing enemy. The M-I4 fired twice and stopped. With his left hand he reached up and checked the receiver. His magazine was empty.

He withdrew the magazine and tucked it under his belt, replacing it with a fresh one. He heard several sounds from several locations to his front. The sounds seemed to be moving away from him at a rapid rate. He fired twice then rolled to the opposite side of the trail. The sounds became faint.

He turned and shouted over his shoulder as loud as he could. "Hou! Give me illumination!"

"It's already on the way," came Hou's faint reply.

As he waited for the illumination round to make the trip, he flexed his right hand. It seemed to be working but there was very little feeling in his biceps. With his left hand he reached over and touched his right upper arm. He felt warm blood, though he didn't seem to be bleeding badly. He continued his examination and discerned two short, shallow and distinct grooves in his muscle, spaced less than one-half an inch apart. There was a small piece of skin hanging below the lower groove but the wound didn't appear serious. He wondered why his arm was so numb.

The illumination burst overhead. He looked down the trail but saw nothing. Instantly, he was on his feet and running as fast as he could in the direction of the retreating VC.

As the first illumination round began to fizzle and lose candlepower, a second illumination burst overhead. Still Jesse continued his mad dash, pursuing the little man who had shot him. Jesse wanted him and all of his comrades. Gone was his fear, replaced by anger and humiliation.

At almost four hundred yards from Hou's position, Jesse stopped to catch his breath. He searched the area but saw nothing. He listened but there was no sound save that of his labored breathing. Only then did fear and common sense overcome his other emotions.

He turned about and trotted back down the trail. As he approached his ambush position, he slowed and shouted, "Hou, I'm comin' in. Don't let anyone start shootin'."

Hou replied, "Okay, come on in."

The entire ambush party was gathered around the dilapidated French pillbox, casting dancing shadows in the artificial light of the illumination rounds.

"Goddamn, you've been hit!" said Hou.

"I'm aware of that fact, Mr. Barnett."

"Shit man, with that goddamn sweat band on your head, you look more like some kinda crazy Indian than a Cowboy," said McCreery.

"Indio," said Bean. "No shit! You do."

Jesse ignored them. "What the hell is everybody doing all bunched up over here?"

"It's where the action is, you crazy Indio. Hey, man, you better get a bandage on that arm," said Bean.

"Later. Right now, we go after the VC."

"What the hell for? You musta chased 'em halfway to the DMZ," said Bean.

"Goddamnit, Bean. Take five of the PF's and get back to your position. Mac, take another five and get back to your position." He turned to Hou. "Hou, I'm taking seven of the PF's with me. The rest of you hold this position, including the good lieutenant and his radio operator."

Hou nodded.

Jesse looked at the PF corporal who had earlier handled the large spider. He pointed to him and six of the PF's and motioned them to follow him. The corporal shook his head. Jesse looked at the little man in disbelief. He was in a hurry and he didn't feel like wasting any time on discussion. He grabbed the little corporal by his shoulder and shoved him down the trail, then smacked the forearm stock on his M-I4 with his left hand and motioned to his six other "volunteers" to follow the corporal.

Jesse and the seven PFs moved quickly down the trail, Jesse shouting to Hou as they left, "Keep the illumination comin'. Give us ten minutes. If we don't find anything, we'll be back."

"Roger."

Jesse and his PFs arrived at the spot where the initial contact had taken place. The marks in the sand told the story if one knew how to read them, and Jesse knew only too well. He noticed one of the PFs picking up the spent brass cartridges and smiled. The Vietnamese were a poor people and, combat or no combat, they left nothing of value lying around – and brass was worth something.

They moved further down the trail, the corporal at the point, Jesse in the rear, reliving his almost fatal encounter.

The tracks indicated nine men. Fear began to well inside of Jesse. He was certain of only two possibilities: the VC were planning a raid in complete ignorance of the ambush, or one or more of the PFs were infiltrators.

The tracks left the trail and entered the jungle. Jesse wanted to follow but knew he could not. It would be risky business with a platoon of marines, but with only seven PFs, any one of whom could be a VC, it was suicide. He called a halt to the search and motioned the men back to the ambush site. The little corporal breathed a sigh of relief, glad to be done with point duty.

Once back at the ambush site, the men assembled quickly and departed for their rally point for the remainder of the night. The illumination ceased, and once

163

again they were in wet darkness. Jesse put on his helmet and poncho and followed the procession as it wound its way to a large thatch house.

An old man greeted them at the door. He had been waiting. He knew they would come, for he had heard the shooting and had seen the illumination. He didn't like the intrusion but he liked the communists even less.

The PFs took up positions around the house. Only the marines and Lieutenant Xuan entered the old man's home. The interior of the house consisted of one large room. On one side of the room was a bed with a straw mat next to it, on the other, several poorly made cabinets. Jesse wondered what was inside the cabinets.

The marines and Lieutenant Xuan seated themselves on the dirt floor in the center of the room. Shades over the two windows in the house kept the dim candlelight confined to the inside.

Hou removed his poncho and examined Jesse's wound. "Jesus Christ! There's enough gunpowder impregnated under your skin to blow a battleship out of the water. How close were you to this guy?"

Jesse looked from his arm into Hou's eyes. "Hou, you wouldn't believe me if I told you."

"Shit, man. It looks like he was close enough to give you a tonsillectomy," said Bean.

"If his rifle barrel hadn't hit me in the arm, that's probably what it would have been."

"*Madre de Dios!* You are *un Indio Loco*," said Bean. "How did he get off the first shot – you didn't see him?"

Jesse looked away and mumbled, "I had my rifle on safe."

Hou smiled as he tied a pressure bandage over Jesse's wound. "Might as well give the other guy an even break, huh? I gotta admit, that name 'Indio' sure as hell describes what I saw coming back down the trail, drippin' blood and breathin' fire."

"Yeah, I guess I musta looked a little ragged," admitted Jesse.

"A little? Shit, man, you scared the hell outa the PFs. They were more afraid of you than they were the VC," said Bean.

"Well, goddamnit, we might'a' got a few of 'em if they'd've reacted the right way," said Jesse.

"Shit. According to you, the right way is a one-man-goddamn-frontal assault. Where the hell did you learn that trick?" asked McCreery.

"You know, Mac, you're probably right. I don't regret going out to reconnoiter but once our ambush was compromised I should have let it go." He paused. "I guess I just thought I could whip their asses by myself. I just took the PFs along for company. I don't know what the hell happened. All I know is that some sneaky little sonofabitch who was trying to kill us all, shot me by accident and I never wanted him to have a second chance."

"Screw it, Indio. You did good, man." Bean turned to McCreery. "Hey, what's your problem, Mac? The man probably just saved your useless ass and you sit over there and bitch about it."

"That's okay, Bean. Let it go. Mac's right. I never shoulda been playin' John Wayne in the first place," said Jesse. He stood and looked at Hou. "Thanks for the patch job, Hou." He turned to the old Vietnamese in whose home they took shelter and nodded to him. He placed his pack of cigarettes on the floor and left the house.

Forever Patriots

Outside, Jesse sat under a large tree for protection from the rain. He knew he would have some tall explaining to do in the morning. He had broken the cardinal rule of the ambush by leaving his position and moving toward a suspected enemy. If only he had been able to kill or capture one of the Cong, perhaps things wouldn't look so bleak. Not only had he failed at that, but he had managed to receive a bullet wound or two while the enemy escaped unscathed.

He felt depression and shame as he sat under the tree, water dripping from his helmet onto his poncho. He wondered if they put things like this into a man's service record book. He had never cared about his service record before. The numerous disciplinary actions against him brought with them no shame as far as he was concerned. They were peacetime infractions.

After a while, he smiled. The shame lifted. Hell, he'd do it all over again, except this time he'd remember to set the safety off his rifle before starting down the trail. Now, *that* he felt stupid about. If his rifle safety hadn't been on, he would have responded with the first shot, and there would have been more than three rounds in the magazine. Jesse had been so concerned about his first small command in Vietnam, he had failed to check his rifle magazines. The one in the rifle had not been fully loaded.

He hoped someday he and Will Hunt could laugh about this story. After all, the whole thing *was* kinda funny. No one was seriously injured, unless he counted his pride. Everyone was scared half to death and the VC got to taste a new marine tactic. Maybe they would surrender sooner. He chuckled quietly as he imagined Will's response to such a tale.

He shivered involuntarily from the cold wet clothing under his poncho. A nice hot shower, then a warm, dry place to sleep would be okay, he thought. How come in the movies the guys got to sleep in a bed – most of the time with a blonde or brunette – eat good food, wear dry clothes, and never stand guard duty? Must've been a different war.

His wounded arm began to itch and sting. He stood and walked back to the old man's house. There was no light inside.

"That you, Indio?" asked Bean.

"Name's Jesse Langley, goddamnit."

"Used to be. It's Indio now, man."

"Screw you."

"You're not my type," replied Bean. "Get some rest, man. I got it covered."

Too tired to resist, Jesse said, "Wake me when you feel like it." He lay down near the door. In the darkness, he felt for his cigarettes. They were gone. He smiled. The night hadn't been a total waste after all.

At first grey light, the ambush party saddled up and walked back to battalion headquarters. The night before seemed unreal as Jesse observed his surroundings – nothing ominous. It was a pretty place, even in the softly falling rain, which continued to make him miserable. It was strange to even consider that a man could die in the middle of so much beauty.

Jesse looked at his arm. The large pressure bandage did not cover all of the powder burns. He was self-conscious. *This is my battle trophy? A point-blank wound? Dumb.*

Hou, Mac and Bean were all feeling much better and joked with one another as they walked down the trail.

165

Stoney Livingston

Bean said, "Yeah, that's right, Mac. Ol' Indio here figures we got an unfair advantage over the gooks so, to even things out, he puts his rifle on safe, walks into one of the little fuckers, and lets him squeeze off two quick ones before he takes his turn."

"You think he gave the gook a big enough handicap or do you think maybe one more free shot would have been more sporting?" said Mac.

"Screw you guys. I never should have told you about that."

"Hell," Bean ignored Jesse, "as fired up as ol' Indio was, he coulda let that gook squeeze off a magazine. Wouldn't a' made no difference."

The teasing continued until they entered the compound at battalion headquarters. Once inside the compound, they fell silent.

The marines and the PFs reported to the debriefing tent as a unit. A corpsman and doctor were summoned to attend to Jesse's wound as he addressed the new battalion executive officer, Major Kipper, and the Battalion Sergeant Major. The doctor examined the wound as Jesse told of his ill-fated ambush. Jesse stopped once, mid-sentence, and looked up at the doctor who was cleansing his wound. "Doc, it didn't hurt all that much when I walked in here." Without waiting for a reply, he faced the major and finished his story.

The major shook his head. "You broke a cardinal rule of the ambush, Marine. You moved once you were in position."

"Yes Sir, I know that, but we were totally exposed on that side. The PF lieutenant had placed all of his men on the other two sides of the ambush," explained Jesse again.

"The time to correct that was when you initially set up, not half an hour later," replied the Major.

"Yes, Sir. But I don't speak Vietnamese, and it was so damn dark that communication by hand signal was impossible. I was given to understand that this ambush was not much more than a night watch so we could report to the politicians that we were on combined maneuvers with the Vietnamese. When we heard the noise forward of our position, I felt compelled to investigate for the safety of my unit."

Major Kipper looked at Jesse through squinted eyes and spoke through tight lips. "Do you know what 'cardinal rule' means?"

Jesse sighed. "Yes Sir."

"What does it mean, Marine?" asked the major.

Jesse waited only long enough to get his wording just right. "It means, Sir, that it's a rule that is never, under any circumstances, deviated from." He paused for only an instant, then quickly added, "Unless you figure that maybe the guy who made the rule wasn't aware of this possible set of circumstances."

Hou turned away to hide his stifled laugh. Even the sergeant major turned his head

Major Kipper looked at Jesse critically.

The sergeant major, who had quickly composed his appearance, said, "Could you tell what kind of weapon the VC had?"

Jesse was grateful the line of questioning was changing. "No, Sergeant Major. It was too dark. But judging from the way things happened, I'd say it was longer than a carbine. Otherwise he'd have probably drilled me dead center."

"Did you recover any brass?" asked the sergeant major.

"Not personally, Sergeant Major, but one of the PFs picked up some brass."

The sergeant major turned and spoke to Lieutenant Xuan in what appeared to Jesse to be perfectly fluent Vietnamese. When he finished speaking, Lieutenant Xuan turned and queried his men. There were some verbal replies and some shaking of heads, then the lieutenant turned and addressed the sergeant major. At the end of Xuan's short discourse, the sergeant major looked at Jesse.

"The good lieutenant here says his men claim they saw no brass."

"It was there, Sergeant Major. I checked the point of initial contact. I saw the brass, but I was more interested in the tracks. I saw one of the PFs pick up the brass, then we moved on."

"Can you identify the man who picked up the brass?" asked Major Kipper.

Jesse sighed. "No Sir. I was paying more attention to goin' after the VC."

"We might have gained valuable information from the brass," said Kipper.

"Yes Sir. I didn't think about that at the time, Sir. If you'll give me a few minutes alone with this PF lieutenant and his twenty-man shit-detail, I'll produce the brass, Sir."

"These people are our allies, Marine. Give them their due respect," said Kipper. "Watch how you refer to these men."

"I'll give'm the respect they're due, Sir, just as soon as I find out which one of 'em picked up the brass," replied Jesse, his face flushed.

"I can understand your anger but we don't need an international incident, Langley. For now, we'll disregard the brass question," said the major.

Kipper looked at the sergeant major. "Anything else, Sergeant Major?"

The sergeant major looked at Jesse, then back to Major Kipper. "Not at this time, Sir. I think if the good doctor is finished with his work, Langley and his men should report back to their unit." He looked at the doctor. "What's the prognosis, Sir?"

The doctor replied in his best clinical voice. "We've got two superficial bullet wounds to the right biceps. The wounds were inflicted at a very close range as evidenced by the powder burns on the biceps. I would estimate the size of the projectile to have been about .30 caliber. I've administered tetanus and penicillin, cleansed the wound and administered a dressing with bacitracin ointment. This type of wound does not lend itself to suturing as flesh was actually removed from the body in a small furrow. Cleaning and dressing the afflicted area daily will minimize the chances of infection. There will be scarring, but if the wound is properly cared for, and allowed to heal from the bottom upwards, it will be minimal." He turned to Jesse.

"Take this tube of bacitracin and these bandages. Clean the wound twice daily for a week then return to sick bay so I can have a look. You may experience some pain. If you do, take a couple of A.P.C. If the pain persists, come and see me and I'll get you something stronger."

Jesse nodded. "Thanks, Doc."

"One more thing," said the doctor as he scribbled on a piece of paper, "Light duty for a week until I've had a chance to check your progress." He handed Jesse the paper.

Jesse turned to Major Kipper. "Will that be all, Sir?"

"That'll be all, Marine. Report to your platoon."

"Aye aye, Sir." Jesse turned to his men. "You heard the man. Saddle up and move it out." He shot a parting glance at the twenty PF's as he exited the tent.

*****

The week following the ambush was a long one for Jesse. He

recommended Hou receive a commendation medal for his reaction to the enemy fire by calling in illumination immediately. Gunny Reyes denied the recommendation.

The story of the night ambush quickly circulated through the platoon, and within two or three days, everyone, including Tule, was calling Jesse "Indio". He removed his headband, but it was to no avail. The name stuck. He had finally earned a nickname.

His right arm stiffened up a bit and throbbed from time to time but the pain was far less than he had expected. He used his light-duty time to catch up on letter writing and even wrote a love letter for Bean to his girlfriend. Once Bean had copied the letter in his own handwriting and shown it to the other men in the First Section, Jesse was flooded with requests to write love letters to other girlfriends and sweethearts. He enjoyed writing the letters. The words he wrote were the words he wanted to write to Shannon.

Jesse wasn't sure he wanted to be known as the resident writer of the 8l platoon but since he was not in top physical condition, he reluctantly became the ghostwriter for several of the men in the First Section. He played poker and drank lukewarm Kool-Aid and dressed his wound twice daily.

The marines in the 81 platoon treated him differently for a day or two after the incident but within forty-eight hours, everything was as it had been before the ambush.

Jesse caught up on his correspondence to friends and relatives. As he wrote to each one, he drew a mental picture and wondered what each was doing. He wrote of the beautiful white beach at Chu Lai, or the magnificent jungles, or even the engineering masterpieces of tiered rice paddies. He did allow himself to complain of the humidity in one or two of his letters, but made it clear he was proud to be an American and felt privileged to serve his country, even if it was only a "banana war." He tried to make his letters lighthearted and humorous except to those very close to him, but even those close to him were not told everything.

He felt a kinship to the United States that he supposed men like Washington and Jefferson must have felt. In letters to his close friends he revealed these thoughts and he revealed too his confusion about their mission. Were they really expecting to win the war this way? At the rate things were going, he estimated it would take over a year – maybe two – to win the war. To Jesse, it didn't make any sense to suffer for more than thirty days.

He queried his friends on opposition to the war in the U.S.

One day, at ten in the morning, Major Knowles' body was found, floating face down in the shallow water near the 7th Mess Battalion. When DD heard the news, he ran the distance to the 7th Mess Battalion to observe the bloated body of his old company commander. Upon his return to the 8l platoon a short time later, he walked into the First Section tent with a blank, faraway look in his eyes, eyes bloodshot from lack of sleep and recent tears. His normally square shoulders and straight back sagged. Silence greeted him as each man looked up from whatever he was doing. Eyes turned quickly away when they saw the forlorn figure of D.D. Scott slowly walking through the tent towards his cot. No one spoke, not even the normally loquacious Bean.

DD sat on the edge of his cot, reached for his rifle and chambered a round. He was in the process of bringing the barrel to bear upon his face when Jesse tackled him. The cot split into two pieces with the sudden increased force placed upon it, and the two men fell to the dirt floor, DD trying to push Jesse away and at the same time, bring his rifle into position to blow his own brains out. Jesse struggled desperately to twist the M-I4 from DD's grip. Others quickly joined the struggle, and after much shouting and wrestling about, DD succumbed to superior numbers. The rifle was wrenched from his hands by Cuz, who quickly removed the magazine and ejected the live round from the chamber.

Breathing heavily, Jesse removed himself from the pile of sweating bodies and returned to his cot. He lay on his back and stared at the tent ceiling.

The others slowly released their holds on DD and gave him room to compose his thoughts and gather in some air.

Bean spoke first. "What the fuck you doin', DD? You think the Major would approve of this kind of shit or what, man?"

DD slowly stood. The marines parted as he moved to Jesse's cot. He stopped and looked down at Jesse, who continued to stare at the ceiling of the tent. His wound had broken open and a small amount of blood oozed to the surface of the bandage.

Jesse kept his gaze on the ceiling. "You done, DD?"

DD nodded. "Thanks, man. I was just fucked up." Tears slid down his cheeks.

Jesse continued to look straight up. "Yeah. I know, man."

"Your arm is bleedin'," said DD.

"Yeah, I know that too. It ain't the blood so much as the pain when the rear sight of your rifle dug into it."

"I'm sorry, man."

Jesse replied, "Not yet you ain't. When I get my breath back, that's when you're gonna be sorry, cause I'm gonna whip your ass all the way to the airstrip." He turned his head and looked at DD, a broad grin covering his face.

DD smiled back through his tears. "I guess you're not such a bad-ass after all."

"I'll do in a pinch. So will the rest of these guys who didn't want your raggedy-ass blown all over the tent."

DD suddenly became aware of the others. He looked at each man in turn. "You guys are all right."

Bean smiled. "Get your shit together, DD. I'll go to battalion with you to turn in your gear. If it's all the same to you, I'll carry your rifle."

The marines laughed. DD laughed with them.

CHAPTER NINE: THE CHASE

After DD's departure, the routine of the war returned. There were night ambushes, waterborne patrols, recon patrols, combat patrols, gun watches, gun drills, clean-up details, letter-writing, poker games, gravity showers, bugs & insects, snakes, heat, humidity, mud, dirt, laundry details, weapons cleaning, working parties, lukewarm Kool-Aid, an occasional softball or volleyball game, and the inevitable rain.

It was about three or four days after DD left that Jesse received a bone-handled Bowie knife at mail call. He laughed aloud as he read the opening line in Dave Boomer's accompanying letter: "They wouldn't let me send you a Colt or a Winchester so I sent the next best thing. I figure with this knife, you'll have an unfair advantage over the VC, but war is hell and that's the way it goes."

He studied the heavy-bladed knife with its bone handle and recalled the many experiences he and Dave had shared. A wild charge down a grassy hill on the island of Vieques flew through his mind. They had given those grunts a good fight but superior numbers had taken a toll on the eighty-one platoon that day. Later, Dave had sat quietly while the company commander chewed them out for fighting other marines. Dave was almost always quiet. With him at his side, Jesse believed the U.S. could send the rest of the troops home but he was glad Dave was in Utah. He was married now and things were different for a married man. Jesse considered the profound changes Dave had undergone since his marriage: no whiskey; no cigarettes; no raising hell. For a moment Jesse envied Dave the serene life he led. Only for a moment. He smiled, warmed inside by their friendship and experiences together.

He wrote Dave a long letter and thanked him profusely for the knife.

At mail call the following afternoon, several letters simply addressed to "an American G.I." were received at the 8l platoon. One of the letters had a return address of Phoenix, Arizona. Jesse was given the letter as a result of his home state of record.

The envelope and letter were lightly perfumed and smelled out of place in the steamy bunker where Jesse read it. It was written by a nineteen-year-old girl, named Charlotte Bobbins, who was working her way through college. She espoused patriotism and freedom and said she was proud of "...all of our young men in uniform." Though Jesse enjoyed the letter, his first inclination was to discard it and remember only that he had received a letter written to "an American G.I." He changed his mind as the afternoon wore on and wrote a brief letter, thanking her for her support.

A week later, First Section conducted gun drill on a rainy, misty morning. Less than twenty minutes into the drill Tuleano called the two squads to the pit at gun one. As the marines shuffled around the gunpit lighting cigarettes and looking for

Forever Patriots

a place to sit or stand, Tuleano said, "Okay, marines, quit grab-assin' and listen-up."

There was another brief moment of milling about. "First Section is movin' out this morning on a temporary assignment to another outfit up north."

Without knowing why, several of the men groaned.

"What outfit?" asked Bean.

Tuleano looked at him. "Goddamnit, Bean. Why does it always have to be you?"

Bean shuffled his feet and glanced at the ground. "Shit, Tule, I'm curious is all."

Tuleano beamed. "Well, this time, I don't give a damn. We're gonna bail out the U.S. by-god-army."

"How the hell can we bail out the army by going north? I thought the Crotch was responsible for I Corps and the army had the three Corps to the south," said Cuz.

Tuleano said, "Well, that's the way it mainly is but the army's got a few special forces units operating in I Corps."

"Screw the army. Let the gooks run 'em down to II Corps – or all the way to Saigon for that matter," said Bean.

Tuleano glared at him. "They're on our side, you stupid shitbird."

"Where we going?" asked Hou.

"Just south of the DMZ – about three clicks west and a little south of some big agricultural development center – a place called Hill 174. Seems like these Special Forces guys bit off a little more than they can chew," answered Tule.

"Why are they sending us? Aren't there any units closer?" asked Jesse.

"Sure there are closer units, but I guess the brass considers our area pretty secure and we won't be missed here as much as some of the units north of us might be. Hell, I don't know. Do I look like a goddamn general?"

Tuleano turned to the others. "We'll draw two days rations; full packs; combat load for the guns; extra socks and whatever shaving gear you've got. Put everything else in your willie peter bags until we get back. We gotta be at the LZ in thirty-five minutes. Squad leaders; Ammo Corporal, stay here. The rest of you get movin'. Let's go."

The marines quickly left the gunpit while Tule continued to brief the squad leaders and ammo corporal.

Twenty-five minutes later, as they boarded the Choctaw helicopters, Jesse glanced at Bean, "I wonder when the army is gonna give the Crotch a few Hueys so we can get somewhere before we're supposed to be coming back?"

"Shit, man, don't hold your breath," Bean replied with his bright toothy smile as he lifted the inner ring of the mortar baseplate into the old Choctaw.

Donaldson was the last man to board the First Squad helicopter. He had been issued an M-60 machine gun and three hundred eighty rounds of ammunition for this trip and even though the ammunition had been distributed among the squad, he was obviously unhappy he had been selected to carry the machine gun. He pouted as he placed the gun on the deck of the helicopter.

Both squads and section headquarters were airborne in two minutes. The three CH-34s grumbled and vibrated north.

The flight to Hill 174 was long and tense. They sat huddled in a box in the sky – ducks over a hunting pond – waiting for the hunters below to blast the slow moving, unarmed helicopters out of the air. Jesse sat next to the open door and

171

Stoney Livingston

studied the crew chief who crouched on the other side of the door, M-I4 held tightly.

After a moment, Jesse turned to Cuz on his left and raised his voice to be heard above the engine noise. "I wonder why these fly-boys don't mount an M-60 in the door? Hell, it'd be simple."

"They'll get around to it one of these days," replied Cuz dryly.

Jesse smiled. He looked idly out the open door at the lush green landscape five hundred feet below.

Suddenly Donaldson began writhing about the deck, clutching at his right thigh.

Sal said, "What the hell's wrong with you, Don? You tryin' to get out as a nut case?"

"Oh shit, man! He's been shot!" shouted Bean.

Blood flowed in a stream from the back of Donaldson's thigh. There was a moment of panic and confusion as Cuz moved to his aid.

"We're receiving ground fire!" shouted the crew chief as he pointed his M-I4 to the ground below and fired at nothing in particular.

The helicopter jerked violently left, then right, in an evasive maneuver. The crew chief continued firing at the trees below. The squad was evenly divided between assisting Donaldson and securing the mortar and ammo against the violent movements of the helicopter.

Jesse picked the M-60 from the deck and moved next to the crew chief, closing the cover on an eighty-round belt. The gun was ready for action. He shouted into the crew chief's ear. "Can you see anything?"

The crew chief nodded and pointed at a small hill. "Three o'clock – the top of that hill."

"I'll be damned," said Jesse as he spotted three figures dressed in black, standing in full view of the unarmed helicopters. "They got a lot of balls." He turned to the crew chief. "Hang onto my waist."

The crew chief nodded and grabbed Jesse's cartridge belt as the latter braced himself in the open doorway. Jesse pulled the operating rod handle to the rear and squeezed the trigger, advancing the ammo belt. He cocked the gun again and fired a short burst, watching the tracers as they fell short of their target and a little to the right. He made a quick adjustment and squeezed off a long burst, using the tracers to zero in on the targets. The bullets chopped up the turf around one of the small figures. The figure turned, took a few steps, and fell limply to earth. The other VC disappeared into the trees.

Jesse backed into the interior of the helicopter. He put his face close to the crew chief's and said, "Can you get the pilot to make another pass?"

The crew chief grinned and shook his head. "You grunts are all crazy." He nodded at the ground. "They've had enough for today. That was damn good shootin'."

"Thanks." Jesse moved from the door. Bean and Sal held Donaldson on his stomach as Cuz put a pressure bandage on the back of his thigh. The bleeding appeared to have been stopped but Donaldson had lost a lot of blood in a short period of time. The deck of the helicopter was slippery and dark red.

When Cuz finished tying off the pressure bandage he shouted to the crew chief. "This man's lost a lot of blood. We've gotta get him to a hospital."

The crew chief nodded and spoke into the mouthpiece attached to his flight helmet. The First Squad helicopter broke formation and flew east, leaving the other two Choctaws to continue their journey north. As the single helicopter flew at maximum speed, the marines comforted their wounded comrade as best they could.

"Don, you chickenshit, you got a million-dollar wound. It's round-eyes and cold beer for you from now on," said Hou.

Donaldson lay on his back, his leg elevated by the mortar base plate and several packs. He smiled weakly. "It sure as hell doesn't feel like a million bucks. It feels like shit. As matter of fact, *I* feel like shit." He turned his head to view Cuz. "Don't bullshit me, Cuz. How bad is it?"

Cuz looked at Donaldson's pale face. "Shit, man, you're gonna be okay. It's just enough to get you a plane ride back to the World. They'll be calling you 'Jody' in a month."

Donaldson smiled weakly. "I feel weak and sleepy."

"Yeah, well don't plan on goin' to sleep, Don. You lost a lot of blood. Just hang in there until we get to a doctor," said Cuz.

"It won't be much longer. I see a bunch of tents now," said Sal as the helicopter began its descent.

Stretcher-bearers and a corpsman stood by as the Choctaw landed. Donaldson and his personal gear were placed on the stretcher. The marines were still bidding farewell as the helicopter left the ground to resume the journey to Hill 174.

Sal looked at Cuz. "You think Don's gonna make it?"

"Can't tell for sure but I think so. It's mainly a matter of blood loss. They'll pump a little juice into him, patch him up, and send him home."

Sal looked at the darkening blood on the deck of the helicopter and shuddered.

"Indio here got one of the gooks," said Hou.

Cuz looked up at Jesse. "No shit?"

"No shit. I saw him fall like a rag doll," answered Hou.

"Where'n the hell did you learn to handle an M-60 like that?" asked Cuz.

"Cuban Crisis. They gave me one and said it was our new machine gun to replace the A-4. Said I'd better learn it good because I might be usin' it against Russkis." He paused. "Man can learn real good, shootin' off the fantail of an APA."

Hou said, "No shit. You should'a seen this nut, Cuz. He looked like John Wayne holding a machine gun on his hip, wiping out the whole damn Jap army."

"You been here too long, Hou," said Jesse.

"You actually hit a gook from up here?" asked Bean.

"I think so. Can't be positive though."

"He hit 'em all right. I saw 'im crumple up and fall. Hell, I'll bet he was dead before he hit the ground," said Hou.

"Shit, man, I don't know of anybody in the platoon who's seen a VC long enough to shoot one. We should have stopped and got the body. Everybody is screaming for body count. Shit, that would have been one for 8I's," said Bean. He appeared as proud as if he had pulled the trigger himself.

The Choctaw sat down atop Hill 174, deposited its payload, and left as clumsily and as slowly as it had arrived.

Section FDC and gun two were both up and running as the First Squad prepared its gunpit. In fifteen minutes gun one was nestled in its own hastily dug pit. While Tule conferred with the squad leaders, the gun crews mingled. The stories of Donaldson and Jesse were told and re-told. The marines ignored the Special Forces troops. It was as though the mortar section occupied the hill alone.

Bean extracted a canteen from his cartridge belt and took a drink of the tepid water. "Shit, man, we don't even get warm Kool-Aid up here. This is the shits."

"Write your congressman," said Jesse.

"My congressman don't read Mexican, Amigo."

Cuz shouted, "Fire mission!"

They scrambled into the gunpit as Cuz began reading the dope.

"Up," said Jesse.

"Gun one up," said Cuz into the field phone.

There was a short pause.

"Fire one," said Cuz.

Sal dropped the round down the tube. *Thump-pow!*

"On the way," reported Cuz.

After a minute Cuz gave corrections, "Deflection 2952."

"Deflection 2952," repeated Jesse.

"Elevation 1055."

"Elevation 1055."

There was a short pause.

"Up."

"Roger, gun one up."

Another short pause.

"Fire," shouted Cuz.

Thump-Pow!

"On the way," Cuz reported into the field phone.

Another correction followed. "Deflection 2940."

Jesse repeated the commands. "Deflection 2940."

"Six rounds. Fire for effect."

"Six rounds. Fire for effect."

"Elevation 1068. At my command."

"Elevation 1068. At your command."

Almost no pause: "Up."

"Roger. Fire for effect."

Thump-Pow! Jesse rechecked the sight and re-leveled the elevation and deflection bubbles before Sal could turn around and grab another round from Bean.

Thump-Pow! The process was repeated until all six rounds were fired.

The target was in a draw behind a ridgeline and, as is most often the case with mortars, the gun crew could not observe the impacting rounds. They could only hope the shells had found their marks.

"Cease fire. End of mission," said Cuz.

Sal swabbed the bore. Jesse reset the gun to 2800 deflection and 1100 elevation and the gun crews broke for chow. The afternoon sun glowed brightly through the humid air as the sweaty, dirty marines heated their C-rations and made light of the day's activities.

"Hey, Indio," shouted Cuz from above the gunpit.

"Yo?"

"Tule wants to see you up at FDC."

"Be right there, Cuz."

The FDC was set up inside a sandbag bunker. The light inside was dim and, as Jesse stood in the entrance waiting for his eyes to become accustomed to the semi-darkness, Tule said, "Over here, Indio."

"Yeah, Tule. What's up?"

"Captain Patterson, this is Lance Corporal Langley. We all call him Indio. Indio, Captain Patterson here wants to talk to you."

Jesse looked at the Special Forces Captain. "Yes Sir?"

Patterson was a big, solid man with a square jaw and a crooked nose. His dark hair was almost shaven. He looked mean and tough and intimidating.

"That was some mighty good shooting, Marine."

Jesse felt his face warm up. Praise from a stranger came hard to him. "I just put the dope on the gun, Sir. Your FO should get the credit if we hit the target."

"It's a team effort, son, and to be honest, I was leery of bringing marines into a Special Forces operation. Not only was I worried about inter-service rivalry, but our methods of operation are quite different than standard army infantry. The more I talk with Sergeant Tuleano here, the more I find you marines are trained to operate like we do."

"Yessir." Jesse wondered where the captain was headed with his conversation.

"About five clicks west and a little south of here is a large VC base camp. Charlie knows how we operate and he knows we don't carry anything bigger than a sixty mortar."

"What's a 'click', sir?" asked Jesse.

The Special Forces captain paused and looked at Tule then back to Jesse. "A kilometer. A grid square on the map."

"Oh. We still use yards and feet," said Jesse by way of explaining his ignorance.

Captain Patterson nodded and continued, "In the early morning hours we can move two clicks west and south of here and be in range to blast the hell out of 'em before they know what's going on. Our FO and his radio operator should be in position in a few hours. If he's successful, we move off the hill at 0400. By daylight, if the Cong are watching our position here, they'll see one real 81 and one dummy. Gun One and Sergeant Tuleano will be with our patrol in the valley. We blast hell out of their base camp and return to the hill. Any questions?"

"Can I take our machine-gun?"

Patterson smiled. "You bet your ass, Marine. Anything else?"

"We used some of our ammo on the way up here. You got any to spare?"

"Take what you need. Anything else?"

"No, sir."

"Good. Sergeant Tuleano has given all of the briefing to Corporal Cousins. Get the details from him." He paused for a moment. "Sergeant Tuleano and corporal Cousins both said your gun was the one for this job and did so with no hesitation. I'm counting on their judgement in your ability."

Jesse glanced at Tule and smiled, then looked at the Captain. "Will that be all, Sir?"

"That'll be all."

At 0400 hours, Cuz's Squad, with Sergeant Tuleano, Hou and Courtney, accompanied by ten Special Forces troops, moved down Hill 174. Bean, in addition to the inner section of the mortar base plate, three rounds of HE medium and all of his normal combat gear, carried two one-hundred-round belts of 7.62 ammo for the

175

Stoney Livingston

M-60 machine-gun.

Jesse carried the mortar bipods, the M-60 with an eighty-round belt in place and two more hundred-round belts hooked over his shoulder, his normal combat gear and two rounds of heavy Willie Peter.

The Special Forces troops each carried two rounds of HE medium in addition to their normal combat gear.

Despite its heavy burden, the patrol moved quickly and quietly, neither branch of the service willing to complain in the presence of the other. The silent pride of the two friendly factions was almost deafening. Even Bean, who loved to complain, said nothing as the patrol moved quietly southwest. He put on his best smile in the grey dawn when Captain Patterson signaled they had arrived at their destination.

Precisely at 0630 hours the first mortar round was fired. It was one of the Willie Peter carried by Jesse. As Sal dropped the round down the tube and it quickly sped on its way to the target, Jesse said, "That's one I won't have to carry back."

Sal pouted. "I hope to hell we fire some of this HE."

Cuz shouted a deflection change, requested the second Willie Peter round and indicated a slight elevation increase. As the second round sailed away from gun one, Jesse smiled broadly. "That felt good."

After a pause Cuz shouted, "Expend all ammo! Search up one turn, traverse right one. Repeat elevation. Fire when ready."

The first round left the tube even as Cuz finished his command. Jesse elevated the tube one turn of the crank and traversed right one turn. He then leveled the deflection bubble, looked at Sal and said, "Fire." The process was repeated almost as fast as Sal could turn around and accept another round from Bean until all mortar ammunition had been fired.

The last round had barely left the tube when Sergeant Tuleano shouted, "Okay men, mount up. Break it down and let's get the hell outa here."

Sal quickly swabbed the bore as Jesse poured one of his canteens of tepid, halazone-tainted water over the hot tube. The water bubbled and fizzed as it struck the hot metal, sending up a cloud of steam.

The aiming stakes were down, the gun disassembled and the squad ready to march when Captain Patterson approached at a rapid walk.

"That was some good shooting, Marines. Our FO reports direct hits. Estimates 90% of the munitions and structures destroyed and casualties of no less than 80%. I'd say it was a good day's work." He paused briefly. "You men will take the lead back to camp and Special Forces will provide the rear guard." He turned to Tuleano. "Sergeant, pick your point and let's move out. My men will remain about five hundred yards behind you."

"Aye Aye, Sir," replied Tuleano as Patterson moved quickly to the rear.

"Hey, Tule, I'll take the point with the M-60 if you get someone to carry the inner ring," offered Bean.

"Are you crazy, Bean?" Sal looked at him with raised eyebrows.

"Shit, man, we already been over the ground. The dogfaces are the one's gonna catch the shit if anyone does."

"Hell, I'll carry your goddamned inner ring. You can have all that point shit you want," offered Cue.

"All right. It's done. Cusick, grab the inner ring. Bean, you know the way back?" asked Tule.

"I always know the way back," smiled Bean.

"Okay, lead off. Indio, you next. You got the rest of the ammo for the M-60," ordered Tule.

"Took the words right outa my mouth, Tule," said Jesse, falling in behind Bean who was already twenty-five yards gone.

Bean moved quickly through the brush, retracing his steps of earlier that morning. The closer they got to camp, the more slowly he moved. Jesse was glad to see him slow a bit. He knew the others were struggling to keep up under the weight of the guns, and had been about to say something to Bean when he had slowed his pace. Jesse's eyes darted to the hills left of the trail. This would be a damn good place for an ambush, he thought.

"VC! Ten o'clock!" Shouted Jesse as he saw the muzzle flashes and dove wildly for the protection of the ground, From twenty yards away, he saw Bean's head snap back as the rifle fire struck him square in the face. Blood, flesh, bone and brain entered the atmosphere in pieces and mist. Bean's body fell silently to the soft earth.

Breathing heavily, Jesse crawled the distance to Bean. The VC continued to fire but the undergrowth provided protection from visual contact. He reached Bean and stared at the body. Bean's left eye hung from a gaping hole. A bullet had struck the cheekbone and shattered it like powder then angled slightly upward and, in its flattened state, had forced the eyeball and part of the brain to the path of least resistance.

Jesse wretched. He vomited violently.

The sound of Hou's voice from fifty yards away settled him. "Indio! Bean! You guys all right?"

The firing from the ridgeline continued.

Jesse wiped the vomit from his mouth and shouted. "They got Bean, Hou. He's dead! Half his face is blown off!"

"Hang in there. We've got radio contact with the dogfaces. They'll be up in a few minutes."

"The dogfaces? Bean was in *our* outfit, not *theirs*. Let's take the gooks now!" His voice broke.

"Take it easy, Indio. They got us pinned down. Help's on the way."

Jesse turned to Bean's body and unhooked the two ammo belts, his breath coming in short, fast gulps. He put them on his own body, bandoleer-style, linking two ends together, picked up the M-60 and moved toward the ridgeline, running in a half crouch.

He paused near the edge of his cover and checked the empty c-ration can clipped to the left side of the gun. It acted as a stationary roller to aid in feeding the ammo belt into the chamber. No assistant gunner was needed, even while shooting from the standing position. He pulled the operating rod handle to the rear and snapped the trigger. The belt fed forward one link. *Damn! Bean didn't even have one in the chamber.* He cocked the weapon again. The VC continued to hammer away at the marines behind him.

Jesse moved to a clear field of fire and squeezed the trigger. Round after round struck the hillside in the trees where the enemy took refuge. The VC firing stopped but Jesse was unaware. Still he pressed the trigger.

The bolt clanked forward on an empty chamber as the eighty-round belt exhausted itself. Jesse quickly took cover and reloaded with a hundred-round belt. He stepped into the open, firing at the hillside in five or six round bursts, holding the

177

long ammo belt draped over his left elbow to reduce drag and aid chambering. At a half-run he advanced, spraying the trees as he moved forward.

Among the trees he began to gain control of his logical thought processes. He released the trigger of the M-60 and stood silently, leaning against the trunk of a large tree.

Jesse listened intently but the only sounds he heard were the beating of his own heart and the crackling of the hot M-60 barrel as it steamed and fizzled from the moisture of the tree leaves brushed in his assault on the hill. The smell of the hot metal reminded him of an overheated flathead Ford V-8.

A twig cracked to his left. He turned and fired a ten-round burst into the thick trees. Something fell. He charged the noise, firing into the trees as he advanced. An arm and shoulder became visible as the wounded VC tried to regain the upright position. He fired again and saw the man fall. Jesse continued his charge until he stood over his fallen enemy. Only a glance was necessary to tell him there was no more fight left in his foe. Intestines lay strewn about the ground. Blood ran freely from the body to the earth, drawn there by gravity, without the aid of a pumping heart to speed the process. Jesse stared at the lifeless form and shuddered.

He found a blood trail leading north and moved forward stealthily, careful now. The reality of death had settled into him. He wondered how many VC had been involved in the ambush, and how many had been injured. He moved further north, forgetting his squad, remembering only that these VC had killed Bean. His fear was gone. He had killed one of the enemy. His confidence in himself and the M-60 made him invincible, if only for a moment.

Home and America seemed far away. His high school friends were not real. There had never been a peaceful life – a life where people were civilized – where a person could be reasonably assured that his neighbor was not going to kill him with a booby trap or a machine-gun – where even the land was serene and hospitable. That had all been a dream – a sweet and wonderful dream. Vietnam was reality.

About a mile north of Bean's lifeless body, Jesse found the wounded VC who had left such a clear trail of blood. The man had apparently been left behind by his comrades to guard their retreat.

The wounded VC soldier was in no condition to provide an adequate rear cover. His heavy blood loss had made him weak and blurred his vision. He fired his rifle aimlessly into the heavy brush as he heard Jesse's soft footsteps only twenty yards from his position. His initial burst of rifle fire failed to find the target and proved his undoing. Jesse performed a simple flanking movement and came upon the wounded man undetected. He wanted to take the man prisoner if possible.

Standing only ten yards from the unsuspecting Viet Cong soldier, Jesse said, "Drop the rifle, Bub."

The VC rolled over to bring his weapon into the firing position and Jesse fired a ten-round burst, killing the wounded man instantly. He studied the mutilated body of his dead foe and shivered involuntarily. "You should have dropped the rifle."

He lit a cigarette with hands that trembled and considered returning to his unit but something that he could not control would not let him return until he had done what he started out to do. He fieldstripped his cigarette and pushed north, leaving the fallen VC and his weapons behind.

As he moved north, he tried not to think of the little man he had just killed, but in attempting to keep the thoughts buried, they became foremost in his mind. Perhaps the dead man had fired the shot that had killed Bean. Perhaps not. *I wonder if he has a family or a girlfriend? Hell, even VC probably have girlfriends. Well, that's the way it goes. Let her grieve for him.* His ending thought sounded tough and final but it was not his true feeling. He grieved for the dead VC and wondered if he was going crazy.

Fear began to slow his progress and make him cautious. He approached a large river and found his fear almost uncontrollable. He had neither maps nor any knowledge of the area, except to know that he was somewhere in the DMZ, but some unknown sense told him the river was the point of no return – the dividing line between North and South Vietnam. He was fearful because he knew without doubt that he was going to cross the river. Never mind that there would be no shame in turning back. Never mind that he was not authorized to be in North Vietnam. Forget everything. He had made a promise to himself and he had no choice but to continue his pursuit. The thought of being one of the first Americans in North Viet Nam added to his adrenaline flow.

He wasn't certain the VC had crossed the river for he had lost their trail two hundred yards south of the rolling green water. The north bank of the river beckoned. He was sure he would find some sign there. He had to be sure. He couldn't go back until he had exhausted every possibility.

He hid in the tree line on the south side of the river, watching the opposing hillsides for some sign of life. He saw none. The growth was so dense a regiment could easily be concealed. Three men could hide forever. He thought of only three men because he felt fairly comfortable with that number. He had learned to track and read sign long before he had ever heard of the U.S. Marine Corps. An old Apache Indian cowboy named Elmer Greyrock, a friend of his father, had taught him many things about the wild before Jesse had reached his teens. Most of young Jesse's close friends before the family had moved to Tucson had been Apaches.

As he looked at the steep hills north of the river, Jesse wished he could remember more of Elmer's teachings. Better yet, he wished to hell Elmer was at his side to guide him across the river.

He found a narrow place upstream where he thought crossing would be quickest. As he scanned the jungle prior to making his final decision, his heart almost stopped beating as he spotted a steel cable. It was a mere twenty-five yards east of the crossing he had picked as ideal. The cable was scarcely above the water, almost unnoticeable at first glance.

He stepped back into the cover of the dense jungle growth and moved slowly in the direction of the cable. He slowed his movement, searching for booby traps. He stopped and extracted the Bowie knife Dave had given him from its scabbard and probed the ground before him, searching carefully for land mines, thinking he would have to sharpen the knife as soon as he had time. Probing in the ground ruined the edge of the blade.

A fine wire stretched before him, only inches from his nose. His stomach knotted. *This is the real thing. This is not guerilla warfare school. There's no red powder attached to this wire – more like a Malaysian Gate or high explosives; no training sergeant to tell you how dead you were or how good you were.*

His skin crawled and he wanted to run – get the hell out of there – go back to his outfit – return to Sherwood Forest. He fought the welling panic. He sheathed his Bowie knife and sat, clinging to his M-60 machine-gun. He felt stupid and small and alone. His eyes searched in vain for signs of a living enemy he could challenge. He listened intently but heard only his own heartbeat.

Several minutes passed as he sat on the jungle floor, clutching the machine-gun, wishing he had never heard of Vietnam, or Bean, or the First Battalion, Fourth Marines. Soon it became apparent his wishes were not diminishing his problems. He retreated to his former vantage point to reconsider his options.

He crouched in the brush and stared at the river. The cable was gone. At least it was no longer visible. Maybe he had imagined it. Did they know he was still following them?

Jesse moved west, searching for an ideal spot to cross the river. He found none. He found instead a large log, lying not far from the river's edge. He decided to wait for darkness and cross at a wide section of the river. The chances of encountering booby traps and trip wires were greatly reduced by crossing the river at an unlikely point.

He sat in the shade of the jungle canopy and unrolled the poncho from his cartridge belt. He opened the small can of peaches and saved his can of crackers and his spaghetti and meatballs for a later time. The peaches were gone in a few short seconds. He drank the juice, careful not to spill a drop. Quickly, he re-rolled his poncho and buried the empty can, using his knife to dig the shallow hole; covering the evidence carefully and depositing leaves to hide its existence.

Jesse reached into his left breast pocket for his pack of cigarettes but removed his hand empty. If there were VC nearby, the cigarette might give him away. *Damn. After such a sumptuous meal, a cigarette would sure be great.* He smiled. He was glad to know his sense of humor hadn't deserted him. For reasons he didn't understand, his confidence returned. His spot was picked. He waited for darkness.

At one point in the afternoon, Jesse was certain he heard the sound of humans just south of his position. He prepared his one-man ambush and lay in wait, fear pounding through his body but naught came of the unidentified noises. He heard nothing for almost an hour, then he heard the sounds again. It sounded like several humans carefully moving through the brush, but he couldn't be certain. The foliage made it difficult to judge distance but he guessed some of the sounds were less than fifty yards away. He held in check his desire to empty his machine-gun into the endless jungle and run south.

The sounds moved south until he could no longer hear them. Still he waited. If the VC were looking for him they'd be back and he'd be ready. Time dragged on but the sounds did not return.

If the VC were still south of the river, what had happened to the steel cable?

He quietly scratched his head under his helmet. *Damn. I must have dandruff or jungle-rot of the scalp. I wonder if there is such a thing? A hot shower would be nice right about now. Oh brother, what about a tube of "store-bought" toothpaste and a toothbrush?*

He smiled. *Yeah, war is great fun.* He shook his head. *I don't even have to die to smell like I'm dead. I should've joined the goddamn Air Force. At least I could die in relative comfort. Who would believe this shit? Hell, I'm the dummy doing it and I don't even believe it. Barbara wasn't so wrong after all. I am gonna die in this place. And it is a waste. My apologies to you, Barbara. You ain't so damn dumb. I'm the dummy.*

He looked at his watch. The date showed "22." *What day of the week is*

180

this? Hell, what month is it? Jesus, I don't even know what month it is. Wait a minute. It must be November. Yeah, it's November. I know it's not that close to Christmas, and I'm sure I dated the last letter I wrote sometime in November.

A movement on the ground, five feet to his right front caused Jesse to tense. It was a snake of some kind but he had no notion of its exact species. It didn't appear to be a constrictor so he assumed it to be poisonous. He couldn't fire his weapon for fear of alerting the VC to his presence. The snake continued its slow searching movement, tongue flicking in and out as it moved slowly across the jungle floor, heading almost directly at him.

Slowly and deliberately Jesse touched his bone-handled Bowie knife with his right hand. *This is stupid. I oughta blast hell outa that damn snake and haul ass for the south.*

The sheath remained motionless as Jesse ripped the big knife upward and slashed at the snake, striking it about four or five inches behind the head. Suddenly the snake was in two completely disassociated pieces. The rear portion bounced and writhed harmlessly about while the front showed a gaping mouth and fangs dripping with venom.

The quiet of the jungle was interrupted by the dull thud of Jesse's helmet striking the ground as he crushed the snake's head three or four times, then twisted and ground it into the soft soil. When his work was completed he stepped back to be certain there was no more movement. He looked at the blood on his camouflage helmet cover and shuddered, then turned to see the rear portion of the six foot snake quivering and jerking almost calmly, only inches from his booted feet.

The sudden flow of adrenaline and fear he had just experienced left him weak and shaky. He sat on the soft ground and watched the jerky movements of his latest foe. *To hell with the VC. I'm smokin' a cigarette.* He lit the Camel with hands that were so weak it seemed an effort to lift his Zippo to his face. They shook and trembled as he chased the flame with the end of his cigarette.

By the time he finished smoking the short cigarette he had regained his composure and his determination. *Goddamn, I'm tired of this Shit. Fear, fear, fear! In my entire life I've never known this much fear. A hundred times a day my damn heart jumps into my throat and my stomach lands in my testicles. This is bullshit – not to mention the fact that it can't be too damned healthy.* He wondered if he was a coward.

He looked through the trees at the gently rolling river, then to the land north, then back to the lifeless body of the snake.

Screw the whole damn world. Nothing on this earth is gonna change who I am – and right now I'm the baddest-ass in the DMZ. He pulled his Bowie knife and slit the snake's belly.

It was almost dark by the time Jesse finished eating what he wanted of the snake meat. In total disregard of the rules of guerrilla warfare he had cooked the meat over a small fire. The snakeskin was wrapped around his waist and tied. Quickly, he doused the fire and moved closer to the water's edge.

He wondered if the VC were aware of his presence. He doubted it. The smell of the roasting snake meat would probably not have been suspected of an American GI. It was the Vietnamese who built fires, not Americans. The Americans used the little blue heat tablets. He smiled at his own brazenness.

The shadows finally blended into the night and the faint sounds of the nocturnal creatures came to Jesse's senses. Some sounded familiar, others not so familiar, and some were totally foreign to any sound he had ever heard. The world held so many secrets, and a man could only scratch the surface of his environment if he lived a long, natural life. Who needed wars to shorten things?

Jesse was grateful for the partial moon. Even though it wasn't much help under the canopy of trees, it would at least be enough to help him find the north side of river. It seemed so peaceful to see the light of the moon dancing on the rolling water he almost forgot he was in a combat zone. He imagined his high school friends – and Shannon – sailing down the river in the soft moonlight, taking time out for an occasional swim.

He jumped as something disturbed the surface of the water about thirty feet from his position. Fish? Snake? He shivered involuntarily as the thought of snakes in the water passed through his mind. His eyes searched the rippling water but he saw no further sign. *The snakes will be looking for me now that I've killed one of 'em.*

Slowly and quietly he dragged the large log to the water's edge, then returned for his M-60 Machine gun. With his combat boots, helmet, cartridge belt, and machine-gun ammunition, Jesse knew he could not swim if he lost his grip on the log, but figured he could discard the gear in time to save himself if the need should arise.

He eased into the water, creating almost no sound. Soon he was unable to touch the river bottom with his booted feet. Using his left arm and his feet, he moved slowly across the river. Even though he had chosen a wide, relatively slow section of the river, his eastward drift was much greater than anticipated. He struggled almost frantically to increase his northward progress, still striving to keep his left hand and his boots underwater so as not to make a sound that might be heard on the northern side of the river.

When his feet found the river bottom near the north bank, Jesse quietly lifted the machine-gun from the log and stood, holding the gun above his head as the log drifted slowly downstream. With the loose end of the loaded ammo belt dragging through the water, he waded the remaining thirty feet to relatively dry land and collapsed near the water's edge.

As he lay breathing heavily upon the moist ground, he experienced a stinging sensation on his left upper arm behind the biceps. It felt like something was attaching itself to his body. He reached quickly with his right hand and grabbed his left upper arm, ripping the leech from his flesh. He held onto the slimy creature only long enough to dislodge it from his arm then flung it to the ground. In the soft darkness, Jesse searched until he spotted it. His skin crawled as he watched the slimy, grey-green leech wriggle upon a small rock. It was about three inches long and as repulsive as anything Jesse ever wanted to see. He was glad for the darkness. He really didn't want a clear look at it in broad daylight. With his wet boot, he slowly mashed it against the rock.

He turned his attention to his left arm. A small trickle of blood oozed from an uneven circle of marks. He opened his first aid kit and applied bacitracin ointment, which he had carried since his wounding, even though it was not standard issue. He decided to save his only pressure bandage in case he might need it to dress a serious injury. He knew infection was an ever-present danger and made a mental note to apply bacitracin regularly.

When he finished dressing the marks he sat upon a rock near the water's edge. *Why am I doing this? This is stupid.* He had no answer. It was as though some unseen force drove him. *Hell, by now those guys are sacked out in Hanoi or*

182

where-ever-in-the-hell VC go at night. What the hell am I gonna do with a machine-gun and a couple hundred rounds of ammo if I run into fifty or sixty VC? This whole damn idea was stupid. The Crotch has probably written me off as a deserter. Damn.

His thoughts drifted to Bean. He saw the face, the eye hanging limply from its socket. *Goddamnit. How can any of those guys go back to camp without gettin' even? We can't let the VC kick our ass and kill our guys and fade off into the sunset. That's bullshit. We oughta chase the little bastards to China. That'll make it a long-ass commute and maybe they'll get tired of makin' the trip only to have their butts kicked back to China again.*

Jesse didn't understand how grown men could draw a line on a map in a real war and say, "It's not fair to cross this line. That's your side and this is mine." *What the hell kind of idiot thought up that idea? I wonder if he plays with his cap gun before he goes to bed at night?*

He looked at the river and tried to pretend it was the Salt River in Arizona. It didn't work. Not enough high cliffs. Too much vegetation. He wondered about his friends. None of them had any idea where he was or what he was doing. They probably wouldn't believe it if he ever told them. He was lonely. He wanted out of Vietnam. He wanted his motorcycle, a coke, a hamburger, and a new start in life. Life had suddenly become very precious. He no longer had a desire to die, as a hero, or any other way.

He moved north, following the sides of the hills, knowing neither where he was going nor why, hoping only that he would find some VC to kill on their own turf. That might make them think a little bit, he thought.

About 0300 hours, Jesse found a place to rest and bedded down for the remainder of the night. The moon had disappeared and further travel was impossible.

At daybreak he ate his cold can of spaghetti and meatballs. He covered all evidence of his passing and continued his journey, remaining away from established trails and traveling on the slopes of hills, protected by the trees. He saw farmers working in small fields but passed them unnoticed. In the late afternoon he finished his rations. He had water but knew he would have to find food the following day or return to the south.

He rested after his meal of crackers, scratching his head and wishing for a shower. He used a small portion of his water and a finger to brush his teeth. The results were unsatisfactory but better than nothing. He applied bacitracin to his left arm, which had become slightly swollen and bruised around the area of the bite. He dried his socks and cigarettes in the late afternoon sun. A bowel movement would have been in order but he had no physical urge.

He smoked a limp cigarette, yellowed by water stains, as he cleaned and checked the machine-gun and his pistol. A water buffalo stood silently in a clearing below him. Jesse looked at the large animal and spoke softly. "You better hope I find some chow, bub."

His invasion of North Vietnam was an adventure. Everything he saw was new and exciting. Booby traps were not as great a concern in the daylight as they were in the darkness and most of his precautionary measures involved remaining hidden from view. The natural beauty of the terrain was inspiring. At times he pretended he was Tom Sawyer or Huck Finn exploring new country. It was difficult to imagine living in such a beautiful place and ever having the stomach to kill another man. It was contrary to the feeling given off by the land.

He continued his trek north, slowing considerably after dark, but moving forward, searching for signs of enemy troop movements. By 0230 hours the moon was of no use to him. He sat with his back against a tree and fell asleep. He was bone tired and hungry.

A few hours passing brought with them a grey dawn and a gnawing hunger. He decided that if he made no enemy contact by dark he would return south. He hoped that Bean would understand.

Jesse followed the ridgelines, all senses reaching for information that might warn him of danger. In the late afternoon the hunger pangs went away. His body seemed to have resigned itself to making do without food. He was tired and weak but every bit as alert as when he had started his journey.

The sound of metal against metal caused him to take cover. Distance was difficult to judge but he reckoned the direction to be to his left front. With the sun low on the horizon and at his back, Jesse moved cautiously toward the strange sounds.

As he moved around the slope of a hill, a village came into view. He squatted in the dense foliage and made mental notes. The slope he was traversing rose another eighty feet to a relatively flat top. From the southeast, the climb to the top of the hill was gradual, but the west and north sides from the top through the first sixty-foot-drop in elevation were sheer cliffs. Five hundred yards northwest of the hill stood the village. It was rather large considering its apparent isolation. Jesse counted no less than twenty bamboo hootches. A stream ran through the village, no doubt supplying drinking water and perhaps providing power.

Again Jesse heard the metallic sound. It appeared to emit from a small hilltop about three hundred yards due east of the Village. The long barrels pointing skyward from beneath the camouflage nets gave Jesse a start. *Anti-Aircraft guns!* Quickly in the gathering darkness, Jesse pulled his field notebook from his pocket and marked relative locations on pages yellowed by water stains. He discovered bunkers and more guns. Troop strength was difficult for him to estimate, as he was totally unfamiliar with anti-aircraft installations and their T.O. strength. There appeared to be SAM sites under construction but Jesse could not be certain at his distance.

It became too dark to distinguish features before Jesse satisfied himself he had all the information but he could do no more. As he placed his notebook into his breast pocket he smiled. *The guys in First Force Recon would'a' been proud of me on this trip.*

Determined to return to Hill 174 with his newly discovered intelligence information, he picked up his machine-gun and retraced his steps south.

His urgency created haste, and in his haste he became careless. He had spotted a trail earlier in the day – on his way north – that wound in the same general direction he wanted to go. If he took the trail he could probably save a full day of travel. With the moon to aid his progress, Jesse made good time. Shortly before 2200 hours he encountered a party of VC.

The sound of gunfire started his heart racing. The fire was not directed at him but appeared aimed in the opposite direction.

He moved cautiously toward the sounds of gunfire. He knew he was close to the river and the sounds seemed to be coming from the area where he had seen the cable on his trip north.

An illumination flare brightened the sky. Jesse took cover momentarily to observe his surroundings then moved quickly forward using the vegetation to guard his passage and the sounds of the automatic rifles to cover his movement. The flare died out only to be followed by another. Jesse heard no return fire from south of the river – only two automatic rifles on the north side. He moved swiftly with the aid of the artificial light.

His vantagepoint allowed him to view the two VC shooting at a large log in the river. The nearest man was a mere thirty feet from where Jesse hid. The second was only ten or fifteen feet beyond the first. The two were having a grand time, splintering the log with their automatic rifles. They laughed, and gestured and spoke light-heartedly.

Jesus. You talk about confidence. They know the U.S. won't send troops up here so they send up flares and shoot logs and try to fabricate invasion stories. He wondered if there were more troops in the area and how far from the river they were billeted. He considered moving up or downstream for a safer place to cross but, in the moving, chances were even that he would run into more of the enemy in the darkness. This was his safest route. There were only two men here.

He lay down behind the M-60 and sighted in on the farthest man. He waited for the man nearest his machine-gun to commence firing on the log. *Guess what, guys? I didn't read the rulebook.* As the little man nearer opened fire on the log, Jesse fired a short burst, killing his comrade. Instantly the remaining VC ceased his fire and turned in Jesse's direction, taking cover as he searched for the source of the machine gun fire.

Jesse's grenade exploded only inches from the hiding VC. The illumination flare had just burned out, and the explosion of the grenade was bright and blinding but Jesse was not watching, and the VC was unconcerned about his night vision. His body was slammed against a sandbag wall and dismembered.

Jesse waited, adrenaline flowing to the flash point, eyes straining in the darkness. He heard no sounds save his own heartbeat. The smell of burned gunpowder wafted into his nostrils, increasing his anxiety. *What if there are more? If this is an outpost, where is the camp?* He moved cautiously through the brush, down the small hill to the rear of the outpost. He quickly examined the results of his work, threw weapons into the river and destroyed what he couldn't carry to the water. He took evidence of the passing of the two VC and moved into the river.

The two men he had just killed were about the same age as he. *What the hell were they doing, playing with guns after dark? Don't they have parents? Why the hell do all the parents start the wars and send their kids off to fight 'em?*

On the south side of the river he moved into the heavy growth and collapsed to the ground, unconcerned about snakes or VC or the cold wetness of his body. He was aware of shivering but it seemed almost as if he were watching his pitiful form from somewhere outside his body. He didn't feel the cold but he was shivering. His teeth clattered a bit too. He tried to analyze what he was experiencing but was unsuccessful. His breathing slowed and became less strained and he drifted into a restless sleep.

*****

As the ten Special Forces troops approached him, Jesse continued his slow walk, dragging his feet slightly. He saw the stretcher and wished he could accept the offer but knew he wouldn't. He wasn't wounded. He stood a little taller and lifted his feet a little higher as the soldiers drew nearer.

185

The first man in the column waved, "Need a ride, Gyrene?"

Jesse shook his head politely and continued his slow walk.

He walked through the column of soldiers, drawing stares as he passed each man. He nodded to each of them in turn until he was in the lead of the column, returning to the hill. Silently the patrol fell in behind him.

"Jesus Christ, man. Let us carry some of your gear. You don't need the M-60 now, and it's for damn sure those two AK-47's won't do you any good with your arms fulla shit," offered a sergeant.

Jesse stopped. He smiled, his lips cracking and bleeding with the stretching of his skin. "Yer right. Take the gook stuff, but I've still got some ammo left in the gun. I'll carry it home."

The sergeant relieved Jesse of his battle trophies.

Jesse continued his walk, stumbled slightly, and then regained his balance.

"You okay, man?" asked the sergeant.

"Yup. Just had to get used to not havin' those Russian burp guns to balance me out."

"I gotta be honest. You look like shit," said the sergeant.

Still walking with the M-60 draped over his shoulder, Jesse replied, "I feel like shit."

"Who hit you in the face?" asked the sergeant.

"Tree."

"Is that a snakeskin?" he asked, referring to Jesse's waistband.

"Yeah."

"How did that happen?"

"He tried to eat me. I ate him instead."

"No shit. What kind of snake was it?"

"Mean one."

"What the hell happened to your left arm?"

"Leech."

The sergeant nodded. He apparently finally realized that speech was difficult for Jesse and he stifled his natural inquisitiveness.

Jesse and the soldiers entered the compound.

Captain Patterson approached and nodded. "Report to my bunker, Marine, while you're still able to walk. Lie down on my cot."

Still walking, Jesse replied, "Thank you, Sir. If you've got any chow, I could sure use some."

He entered Captain Patterson's bunker, placed the M-60 on the cot and sat next to it. Captain Patterson was right behind him, followed by the sergeant and the two AK-47 automatic rifles. The sergeant deposited the weapons on the earthen floor. He looked up at Patterson and said, "He wouldn't accept the stretcher, Captain. Hell, it was all I could do to get the AK's away from him."

Patterson nodded. "I know, Sergeant Coscone. Thank you. That'll be all for now." Coscone left the bunker.

Patterson opened a can of Spam and offered it to Jesse who accepted the food timidly. "Is this Government Issue?"

Patterson shook his head. "CARE package. I figure you could use something with a little more flavor than C-rations."

Jesse nodded in agreement. "Appreciate it, Sir."

"You look like shit."

Jesse smiled, causing his lips to start bleeding again. "Yes Sir, I know. Your sergeant pointed that out to me."

"When you're done eating, I'll need a complete report." Patterson paused. "You feel up to it?"

Around a mouthful of Spam, Jesse replied, "Sir, I need a map. I gotta show you something that's pretty damned important."

As the Captain pulled a contour map from his field desk, Jesse asked, "81's gone?"

"They went back south. I'll get you out in the morning."

Jesse nodded, still eating the Spam carefully. It hurt his blistered and swollen lips to chew. His stomach growled.

Patterson spread the map. "How long since you've eaten?"

"Couple of days I think. Couldn't afford to fire a shot to kill anything to eat."

Jesse stood weakly, placing the half-eaten can of Spam onto the cot next to the M-60. He leaned over the map and studied it carefully. Slowly and deliberately he told his story, using the map to assist his memory. When he was finished he looked up at Captain Patterson.

"Are you sure of those coordinates on the anti-aircraft guns?" asked Patterson.

"School trained, Sir. Division Schools. Map and Aerial Photography. Those emplacements are located smack-smooth on top of Hill 193 at coordinates 758965 on this map."

"You've got weapons, intelligence information... what else?"

"Oh yeah, I almost forgot." Jesse unhooked his poncho from his cartridge belt. He rolled it out on the map. "Two confirmed kills. I was kinda in a hurry to leave."

Patterson stared at the poncho. "Are those what I think they are?"

"If you think they're ears, yes."

Patterson didn't speak. He appeared to be deciding upon the appropriate response.

"Goddamnit, Sir. The only thing I've heard from my outfit since I've been in this goddamn country is 'Body Count. We've got to have body count.' Well Goddamnit, there's your body count. I couldn't bring the whole body, so I brought a piece of it. They're both left ears so I can't be accused of paddin' the score by taking one left and one right and calling it two bodies. Those guys didn't need them ears anymore and I did."

"Take it easy, Indio. It obviously works. I believe you. I guess I just wasn't expecting it." Patterson sat on his folding stool and stared at the ears lying on the poncho. He looked up at Jesse and said, "Sit down, son. I want to explain something to you, something you're not going to like, but Goddamnit, I didn't make the rules."

Jesse sat on the edge of Patterson's cot and listened to the captain's explanation of the "rules of the Vietnam War", as he understood them. When he was finished, Jesse stared at the soldier sitting before him. A full minute passed.

Jesse slowly shook his head, holding back tears. He said softly, "You mean, if I hadn't gone into North Vietnam, I'd have gotten a Silver Star just for killing two gooks?"

"It's not how many gooks you kill, it's the bravery exhibited in your actions."

Jesse continued, "And for chasin' the gooks where they belong, and killing

187

some more, and discovering an anti-aircraft emplacement, and bringing back captured weapons, I'm gonna be court-martialed?"

"I can't be certain of the court martial but, the way I understand it, according to my orders, that's what would happen to me or any of my men if we crossed into the North."

Jesse stared at the earthen floor of the bunker. "I don't believe this shit." He brought his gaze up to meet Patterson's. "Sir, my country would not pull this kinda shit on me. I volunteered to come over here and fight for my country. Now you tell me the first real chance I have to get in my licks, my country is going to court-martial me? That's stupid. What the hell are we over here for – fun in the sun?"

"Maybe your commanding officer can persuade the brass to forget the whole damn thing."

"Forget the whole damn thing? Not on your life, Sir. They can all go to hell in a basket. They can forget what they want. Me, I'm never gonna forget one goddamn second."

"Take it easy, Son. We don't really know what's going to happen. Don't go off half-cocked and ruin the rest of your life."

"Well, Sir, I guess if what I did was wrong by government standards, then me and the government don't agree. And I'm not fightin' for no goddamn government I disagree with." He drew his pistol and tossed it onto the cot next to the M-60.

Patterson shook his head. "You don't mean that. You're a better soldier than that. Don't fuck yourself up by losing control. It isn't worth it. Just think of this whole incident as a turd. It'll pass someday."

Jesse smiled. His lips cracked and he winced.

"That's a little better, son. Now get your goddamn artillery off my bunk and find a place to bed down. I've got intelligence to encode and send. I'll have you out of here in the morning."

Jesse picked up his pistol and placed it into his holster. He rolled up his poncho, ears and all, and re-attached it to his cartridge belt. Picking up his M-60 and the Spam, he said, "You keep the AK-47's. Call it a trade for the Spam."

"You're easy," smiled Patterson.

Jesse picked a spot as far from the nearest soldier as possible and spread his poncho on the moist ground. Several of the men tried to make conversation but Jesse politely turned them all away. Captain Patterson sent a medic to see to his medical requirements and the man did what little he could but Jesse wanted no more attention.

The coming of darkness brought with it a privacy of its own. In the darkness Jesse could think his own thoughts freely, without fear that an unconscious facial expression might divulge what he was thinking. He relived the past several days over and over in his mind. It all seemed unreal.

He felt betrayed by his own country. They had betrayed the Bean too. How could they let an American die in defense of his country and not demand the ultimate retribution? Where in the hell were the Patrick Henrys and the George Washingtons and the John Hancocks of years gone by? Were there no real Americans in the government anymore? *What the hell am I doing here? I gave up my motorcycle for this? My freedom? My girl? What girl? Not Shannon. She's married. I must be going nuts.*

Of course there's always Claudia, good ol' Claudia. I wonder how Joe's doing? That sneaky little bastard had an 0141 MOS. A goddamn office clerk. Well,

188

that's good. At least he won't have to be court-martialed for invading North Vietnam. Shit. What a life.

Exhaustion finally won the battle and he fell into a restless sleep. Dreams of snakes with huge fangs dripping with poison fluids, and explosions in the dark, and hidden cables in a river and little men with no left ears, made his sleep difficult.

He awakened at dawn almost as tired as he had been the evening before.

Shortly after his C-ration breakfast, Jesse boarded an army Huey helicopter and flew south. He was amazed at the speed and smoothness of the Huey compared to the slow vibrating movements of the lumbering Choctaws used by the marines. *I wonder when the army's gonna declare these things obsolete so the Crotch can get a few?*

His flight to Chu Lai was much quicker and more comfortable than the ride from Chu Lai to Hill 174 had been. It passed without incident. Jesse was quick to notice the Landing Zone: it was battalion headquarters', not the 81 platoon's.

The battalion sergeant major met him personally with his mighty-mite and driver. As the Army Huey lifted from the ground and sped away, Jesse said, "Mornin', Sergeant Major."

"Mornin', son. How you feel?"

"Not great, but I've been worse."

"Throw your gear in the mighty-mite. We've got to debrief at Battalion."

Jesse placed his M-60 into the vehicle and climbed in behind the driver. The sergeant major said, "Heard you showed the army a few things about guerrilla warfare and reconnaissance."

"I didn't know the rules, Sergeant Major."

"Would it have made a difference?"

Jesse studied the kindly expression of his battalion sergeant major. "No, Sergeant Major, I don't guess it would have. I'm not into that turning-the-other-cheek shit."

The driver stopped the mighty-mite in front of the Battalion Headquarters tent. Jesse retrieved the M-60 and waited for the sergeant major, who promptly led him into the large tent.

Jesse stood at attention before Lieutenant Colonel Wilson's desk. "Lance Corporal Langley reporting as ordered, Sir."

"Sit down, Langley. You look like shit."

"Yessir." He sat in a folding chair.

The colonel spoke again. "I know you made a report to a Special Forces Captain but I want you to go over every detail from morning chow on the day this whole thing started, until your return last night."

Jesse looked at the colonel, then the sergeant major, then to two other officers who were present. He hesitated.

The colonel said, "These gentlemen are from Division G-2. Captain Hosmer and Major Baxa."

Jesse started to stand but Major Baxa said, "Stay seated, Marine. Just relax and take it easy. We understand you've been through hell for the last several days. We want you to feel at ease and try to remember every detail. Don't leave out anything."

"Meaning no disrespect, Sir, but I'm not real sure I wanna help you burn me."

"We're from G-2, not CID. Our job is gathering intelligence. I give you my

189

word that nothing you say in this tent during this debriefing will be used to burn you," offered Baxa.

"I'm glad to hear that, Sir, because I was gonna tell you anyway."

The sergeant major smiled. "We were counting on that."

Jesse recounted his story, leaving out no details, referring to the map when requested to do so by Major Baxa or Captain Hosmer. At the conclusion of his report there was a short silence.

Jesse spoke first. He looked at Colonel Wilson and said, "If I'm under arrest, Sir, I'd like to see to it that my M-60 gets back to the 81 platoon. It's a damn good gun and I wouldn't want to be accused of losin' or stealin' it on top of everything else."

Softly, Colonel Wilson said, "You're not under arrest, Marine. You did one helluva job as far as I'm concerned. I don't go with the politicians either. Report back to your outfit and take that damn M-60 with you." He turned to the sergeant major. "Have my driver take this marine to his unit."

"Aye Aye, Sir," beamed the sergeant major.

Jesse stood at attention. "There is one more thing, Sir. I lost my dog tags. I don't know when or where."

"I'll see to it you get a re-issue," said Colonel Wilson.

"Will that be all, Sir?"

"No, not exactly. I understand you took the ears with you when you left the Special Forces camp," replied the Colonel.

"Yes, Sir, I did." He reached behind him and un-strapped his rolled poncho. He unrolled it carefully, revealing the human ears. He picked them from the poncho and placed them gingerly upon the Colonel's desk, wondering, as he looked at them, if he was turning into some kind of ruthless animal. No, he thought. He would never do such a thing again. The deed had sickened him at the time but he had been determined to prove body count. *To hell with their body count.* He quickly re-rolled and re-strapped his poncho to his cartridge belt.

"Will that be all, Sir?"

"That'll be all. Dismissed."

"Aye Aye, Sir." He did an about-face and left the tent, M-60 in hand.

CHAPTER TEN: WINTER

Jesse's reunion with the first section of the 81 platoon was a jubilant one. It would have been perfect but for the empty cot once occupied by Bean. True, Donaldson's cot was empty but Jesse soon learned he had survived his wound and was at a hospital in Japan.

The men in the platoon insisted on an hour-by-hour description of his adventures but Jesse made light of what little he told of his one-man invasion of North Vietnam. He grew weary of the story rapidly and shortened it with each re-telling.

Sal was fascinated with the snakeskin so Jesse gave it to him. He wasn't sure why he had kept it in the first place. It had seemed like the thing to do at the time but now he felt foolish for having brought it back to camp.

In the days following his return, Jesse healed quickly and once again it was business as usual in Sherwood Forest. He had replaced DD as the platoon celebrity but Jesse wasn't certain he liked his new position of reverence. Bean was missed by all, including Tuleano, who often remarked on his absence. Jesse caught up on his correspondence and taught gun drill. Except for the primitive living conditions, the war seemed far away and unreal.

Cuz and Jesse shared the First Squad workload and their working relationship grew closer. Jesse wrote love letters for those who requested the service and he played a lot of poker. Hou, whose normal function was that of field radio operator, expressed a desire to learn the operation of the mortar. Courtney, the First Section wireman, received a "Dear John" letter from his girl in the States and lapsed into a state of depression. All the sympathy and words of wisdom from each man in the First Section did little to assuage his determination to suffer and wallow in sorrow. P.F.C. Jim Cusick, the newest man in the First Section, showed promise as a gunner, improving his gunnery skills daily under Jesse's tutelage. His name was officially changed to "Cue" by no less a personage than Cuz. Tuleano, a man who loved a good fight and a good fighter, openly exhibited respect for Jesse, and Gunnery Sergeant Reyes seemed to greet Jesse more warmly and more often than he had before the "invasion" of North Viet Nam. Windler had no change of heart.

At one mail call Jesse received nineteen letters. His junior-year-high-school English teacher had ordered one of his classes to write Jesse as an English project. Though Jesse appreciated the thought from his former teacher, he found it difficult to answer some of the letters. In two days he managed to complete short replies to each but was painfully aware how superficial some of his letters were. He tore them all to pieces and started over. The second time around he answered each letter carefully, devoting time and thought to each reply. He told of the beauty of Vietnam and the horrors of war. He told of the lack of creature comforts for his fellow marines and of the hunger and poverty of the hard-working peasants. He admitted in every one of his letters that his old teacher had been correct about the importance of schooling and asked that each one of them carry their education to the highest level possible.

Between letters, Jesse and the platoon continued the routine chores of perimeter duty. On nights when there was enough moonlight, Jesse would leave the camp at just about dark, often not returning until the early hours of morning. Everyone in the First Section tent was aware of Jesse's excursions but no one knew for sure where he went, though each had his own theory, usually centered around the nearby village.

Less than two weeks after Jesse's nightly trips began, most of the platoon was still eating morning chow when a single shot broke the stillness of the hot damp air.

When Jesse strolled into the platoon area, whistling *Limbo Rock* slightly off-key, he met Tuleano leading a patrol from the first squad's area.

Tuleano stood with his hands on his hips, eyes widened, nostrils flaring and lips quivering. Jesse waved to him as he approached. "Hey, Tule, I need a little help." He grinned as he stopped only two steps from his section leader.

Tule didn't need to be told that Jesse had fired the shot. "What the hell are you talking about, Indio? Goddamnit, don't you know we were getting ready to blow your ass away? Are you crazy, man?" he stammered.

Jesse's grin broadened as he looked at the expectant faces within his field of vision. "Damnit, Tule, that's a helluva way to talk to a guy that just brought home the biggest package of bacon you ever saw in your life."

"What the hell are you talking about?" asked Tule, his anger appearing to subside a bit.

Jesse casually pulled out his pack of cigarettes. "Well, to tell you the truth, Tule, I'm not really sure it's bacon. I thought it was bacon when I caught a brief glimpse of him a while back – but now I ain't so sure." He lit the cigarette.

"Spit it out, Goddamnit! What are you talking about?"

"I built a pit and covered it up to catch a wild boar I saw early last week. Well, I caught him but he's the ugliest damn wild boar I ever saw. As a matter-of-fact – I think he's a warthog. But he's got to be better eatin' than those damn C-rations. Anyway – I had to shoot him 'cause he was too big for my pit. He was fixin' to escape and vent his frustration on my puny ass."

Behind Tuleano, Cuz stifled a laugh.

The platoon commander walked rapidly toward the gathering of men. "Tule, what the hell's going on here? Who fired that shot?"

As if he had prepared his speech for weeks, Tuleano turned to the lieutenant and glibly said, "Sir, we were going to surprise you with roast pig but the trap we dug was a little too small for the animal we captured. When I sent Indio out to check the trap this morning he had to shoot the warthog to keep him from getting away."

"Warthog?" The lieutenant paused. "Are they good eating?"

Tuleano smacked his lips. "Sir, you haven't lived till you've eaten warthog roasted in a pit."

"No kidding? What do you eat with it?" He asked.

"Out here, Sir, anything we can get. But pineapples and yams are great," replied Tuleano knowingly.

192

The lieutenant looked at the marines standing nearby, somber looks on every face. "Well, since you men went to so much trouble – I've got a buddy in the airwing. I'll contact him and see if he can't get us some fixin's to go with this thing." He turned to Tuleano. "You should have notified me as soon as the shot was fired."

"Yes, Sir, I'm sorry. I guess I was still hoping we could keep it a surprise."

The young lieutenant looked at his men. "Well, you might as well carry on. I'll get to FDC and see what I can do. Thank you, men." He turned and walked toward the FDC tent.

Once the lieutenant was out of earshot Cuz said, "Damn, Tule, I didn't know you were the master of ad-lib."

Most of the men laughed softly. Tuleano said, "Lieutenants are the easiest people in the world to bullshit. Why do you think I'm a sergeant and he's just a second lieutenant?"

The laughter was uproarious and unanimous.

Tuleano turned to Jesse. "All right, Indio, you crazy shit, let's see this damn warthog of yours."

Jesse led them to his kill and waved his arm graciously. "I give you fresh chow."

Tuleano studied the large warthog on the ground beside the pit for a moment, then turned to Jesse. "Goddamn, man. You waited long enough to shoot him."

Jesse replied, "Well, this way we don't have to lift him out."

Tuleano organized working parties to haul rocks, wood and sand. Jesse taught Cuz and Cue the art of skinning and dressing game. By the time the animal was properly prepared, all three men were covered with blood.

With Tuleano's permission, they went to Chu Lai's white beach for a swim and a laundering. In keeping with regulations, three others accompanied them to stand guard duty. Sal, Hou, and Courtney drew the guard. They were grateful to be relieved from the rock-hauling detail, as no rocks were located near their position, and thanked Tuleano profusely for his wise choice of sentries.

Once the hog was covered and cooking, the lieutenant informed them he was declaring the day a holiday in honor of the warthog. He promised yams, pineapples, corn, fresh bread, real coffee and fresh produce by late afternoon. Their lives seemed uplifted by the news. True, it was still just as hot and humid as it always was, and the mosquitoes took no holiday, and the Kool-Aid was just as warm, and night would bring back reality, but the day was theirs.

The volleyball net was set up and the competition began. Poker games, letter writing, and all the things that normally comprised a day's activities were carried on, but for some reason this day held the atmosphere of a fiesta.

At 1500 hours, a marine Choctaw helicopter lumbered its way to the 81 platoon LZ. Anxious marines picked the contents of the helicopter clean in seconds. The platoon commander spoke briefly to the pilot who then lifted off amid cheers of gratitude.

The meat was not properly cooked when the warthog was uncovered and the fiesta was carried over to the following day. Re-calculations by Tuleano and a modification of the cooking pit ensured that the warthog would be ready about noon the following day. The fresh produce flown in by the helicopter was used to supplement the hot field rations served at evening chow. The pineapples, yams and other canned goods were stored for consumption with the warthog.

193

Stoney Livingston

On gun watch that night, First Section fired only routine H & I missions. At morning chow the gun watch was relieved and, shortly after eating, the men enjoyed leisure time. Jesse, who could almost always be found in a poker game, on this day, chose to write letters. He wrote first to his aunt and uncle in Phoenix, telling them of his successful capture of the warthog and of high expectations for the day's noon meal. He expressed concern for Tuleano's experience in the cooking department but told his aunt and uncle it didn't matter to him. He was going to enjoy it no matter what.

He wrote to Will and spoke of the war in general, advising him to remain in the States. He asked for news, especially concerning Shannon, and expressed concern over the U.S. strategy in Southeast Asia. He asked that Will give best regards to his folks and signed off.

It was shortly after noon when Jesse got the first taste of his kill. The meat had cooked so slowly and so long that it fairly fell away from the bone. It was perfect. He congratulated the chef, the disappointment of the previous day forgotten. Lines formed and soon the men ate fresh meat, yams, pineapples and corn.

In the late afternoon a patrol moved through Sherwood Forest while returning to their unit. Christmas was nearing and the spirit of sharing worked in the patrol's favor. As they shared the fresh meat, several of the men, including Jesse, expressed curiosity over the three German Shepherd dogs accompanying the patrol

As the dogs gnawed bones nearby, the sergeant in charge of the patrol explained that they were part of a new program to sniff out booby traps, tunnels, spider traps and assorted other forms of hidden death. Jesse tried to buy one of the dogs to operate as "point man" on combat patrol but the dog's handler, a sad-looking PFC with a long face, wouldn't part with his animal at any price. He explained the training involved and the fact that the dog was government property.

"What's his rank?" asked Jesse.

"He don't have no rank. He's just a dog," replied the handler with a heavy West Virginia drawl.

"Hell, if he's a marine, he's got to have a rank, even if he's just a private."

"I told you. He's just a dog. He ain't no marine."

"He takes orders don't he?" Jesse insisted.

"Yeah, but that don't mean he's a goddamn marine."

"He eats government chow, don't he?"

The handler paused a moment. "Yeah, so what?"

"He gets water rations, right?"

"Sure."

"If he's wounded, a corpsman would attend to him wouldn't he?"

"Yeah, but that's because there's no veterinarians over here."

Jesse smiled. "Obviously you've never had one of our doctors work on you."

The men standing nearby laughed. Jesse continued, "I'll bet he's got a serial number, right?"

"Yeah, so what?"

"Well, think about it." Jesse paused. "He eats government chow, gets a water ration, gets attended to by a corpsman if he's wounded; he takes orders, and he has a serial number and a name." He looked into the eyes of the long-faced PFC. "I think the only reason you won't tell us his rank is that you're afraid we'll request him assigned to our unit and you won't have a company commander anymore."

The men of the 81 platoon guffawed loudly at the serious expression on the

194

young PFC's face. Jesse smiled and said, "There's more meat for you and the company commander if you're still hungry."

The handler laughed good-naturedly and offered his thanks.

The enjoyment of the leisurely day ended with the setting of the sun. The reality of who they were and where they were returned with the disappearance of the shadows. To add to the feeling of gloom, a light rain began to fall.

*****

As Christmas neared, packages from home containing cookies, candy and other gifts were received by many of the men. Regardless of the contents, if it was from home and not Government Issue, the welcomed boxes of goodies were invariably referred to as "care packages."

If a man received a care package, he shared its contents without hesitation. Though they didn't have much in the way of material things compared to those back in the States, they seemed to have an ample amount of everything but the closeness of sharing Christmas with family; yet, in a strange kind of way, they seemed almost as close as family.

Jesse continued to dominate the guns, though the gunning ability of every man in the First Section improved dramatically under his tutelage. He held nothing back. He wanted each and every man to know as much about the 81 mortar as possible.

Though Jesse professed to be an agnostic, he seemed to have more Christmas spirit than any man in the platoon. When questioned about the subject by Hou, Jesse replied, "Hell, Hou. You Christians are kinda tied down. I enjoy Hanukah almost as much as Christmas."

Three days before Christmas, in the late afternoon, Tuleano stepped into the First Section tent. The rain had kept most of the men inside on this day.

"Hey, Cuz. You got a real badman in your squad," smiled Tuleano.

Cuz looked up, almost disinterestedly, from his letter-writing gear. "Yeah, who's that?"

Tuleano swelled his chest and began to read from the wet piece of paper he held before him. "Wanted for the slaughter of innocent victims of the People's Republic and other vicious crimes against the State. Reward 100,000 piasters. For Lance Corporal Jesse Langley 2015213 no pref. This reward shall be paid in lawful currency to any citizen of the Peoples Republic or any member of any invading army who will turn in the body or any identifiable part thereof of this heinous criminal to any representative of the People's Army."

Jesse, looked up from his cards. "I guess they found my dogtags, huh?"

"Hot damn," exclaimed Hou. "You must have really pissed 'em off. DD Scott was only worth 25,000 piasters and he was the first guy in the war to get three purple hearts."

"I really do wish they'd left my religion out of it." Jesse referred to the "No pref." in the reward poster.

"No shit," said Sal. "How much money is that in American?"

Jesse looked up from his cards, eyebrows arched. "You thinking about collecting it, Sal?"

Uproarious laughter from the section ensued.

Sal was beat red. "Goddamnit, Indio, I was just curious is all."

"It's about ten years wages for a gook, but a thousand bucks don't go far in the States," said Cuz.

"Hell, Jesse James was worth more than that. Indio was robbed! He oughta be worth more than that. Let me see that thing," said Hou.

The rest of the afternoon and into the evening, the men in the First Section discussed the reward poster; some even wrote letters, describing the infamous Jesse's popularity with the Viet Cong and North Vietnamese.

The following night at dusk, Jesse disappeared into Sherwood Forest in search of game. His success with the warthog encouraged him to forage as often as possible. He had no luck near his platoon's position so he wandered beyond the normal limits he had mentally set for his foraging. At 0130, he abandoned his hunt.

His nightly excursions had become almost routine and, as a result, his level of caution was well below what it should have been. He was careful enough during his hunt but, when it came time to return to camp, he let his defenses down, often taking portions of trails to speed his progress, trails that could be mined or watched by an ambush party.

He walked almost casually in the fading moonlight, utilizing a well-traveled trail. In another two hundred yards, he would be in familiar territory and at that time he planned to slip into the brush and work his way back to camp.

As he walked, he noticed what appeared to be another trail coming in from his right, joining with his path a scant fifty yards to his front. Seeing the other trail set off a warning in his mind. He remembered the ambush the night he was wounded. There were two trails.

He stopped abruptly and assumed a crouched position, listening intently for any strange sound. The distant click of a rifle safety ran his fear to the limit. He left the trail in a desperate dive to his left flank, striking the ground in a thudding belly flop. The move was far from graceful but it served the purpose of saving his life.

The night erupted with small arms fire, including the staccato burst of a light machine gun. But for a small rise between Jesse and the ambush party, he would have been killed many times over. Bullets ploughed into the small mound protecting him. Some flew overhead within inches of his prone body.

"Shit!" he mumbled his own voice inaudible in the rattle of small-arms fire.

Above the racket, he heard screaming and shouting. A rifle grenade exploded only fifteen yards in front of him. Once again he owed his life to the small mound of dirt. Fragments whizzed all around him as a second rifle grenade exploded nearby. An illumination round burst in the sky overhead. *Jesus Christ! When did the gooks start using mortar illumination this close to our perimeter?*

The small arms fire slowly died down. He heard the command: "Cease fire! First squad, move it out. Bring back some bodies."

English! Now Jesse was angry. He shouted, "Hey, shitheads. Don't you issue a goddamn challenge before wastin' all that ammo? And by the way, you guys can't shoot worth a shit."

Movement from the ambush party ceased. A voice said, "Who the hell said that?"

Still prone, Jesse replied, "I did, Goddamnit! I'm the one you guys just spent ten thousand dollars worth of ordinance trying to kill. Was all that goddamn noise really necessary?"

The voice answered, "Step onto the trail and be recognized."

"Bullshit. You meet me halfway. I'm tired of being shot at tonight."

"Fuck you. If you don't step onto the trail in ten seconds, we open up again,"

Forever Patriots

replied the voice.

"Okay, since you put it that way. You guys can't hit your ass with both hands anyway – but I don't wanna see anymore taxpayer money wasted." Jesse's heart beat furiously. Fear of being shot by a nervous marine caused his throat to constrict. Breathing became difficult. Slowly he stood and stepped onto the trail.

"Advance to be recognized," ordered the voice.

Jesse moved slowly forward. Twenty yards from the hiding marine came the order, "Halt."

Jesse stopped and scanned the trees.

"Washington," whispered the voice.

"Apples," replied Jesse.

The voice stepped from behind a tree. A tall thin corporal approached him carefully. "What the hell are you doin' out here?" he asked.

"Huntin'."

"Huntin'? Huntin' what? VC?"

"Nope. Huntin' food."

"Food? That's the craziest damn thing I ever heard. You expect me to believe you're outside a perimeter after dark, by yourself, huntin' food?"

Jesse studied the corporal. He was angry, relieved, exhausted, and embarrassed. The anger showed, perhaps as a means of hiding his embarrassment. He said, "You know, you just tried your damndest to blow me away and I'm not so sure I really give a damn what you think."

"What's your name, marine?"

Jesse paused a moment. "Langley. 81 platoon, H & S Company, 1st battalion, 4th marines. What's yours?"

"Simpson. Bravo, One-Four. Does your platoon commander know where you are?"

"Not exactly. I ranged a little farther than I normally do."

A marine stepped from behind a tree ten yards from Jesse and Simpson. "Hey, Paul, remember that propaganda reward poster we saw yesterday?" He turned to Jesse. "You the guy in the poster?"

"Yeah, but don't get any crazy ideas about collecting the reward. I shoot straighter'n you guys."

The new arrival laughed. He turned to Simpson and said, "Okay, Paul, secure the illumination and let's rally to two. We're most definitely compromised."

"Okay, Sarge," replied Simpson, motioning to his radio operator to join him.

With sentries posted at the pre-arranged rally point, Jesse, Simpson, and the sergeant discussed the ambush from inside a hootch.

The Sergeant, whose name was Taylor, said, "I can't believe we didn't nail your ass. What caused you to jump the trail?"

"I heard one of your guys hit his safety latch."

"Hell, we opened fire almost immediately," said Simpson.

"Well, it didn't really take me very long to decide I didn't wanna be on that trail when I heard that safety latch click."

"I guess to hell it didn't," said Simpson.

Taylor looked at Simpson, "It was that goddamn boot."

"Thank him for me," offered Jesse.

Taylor laughed softly. "I'm going to have one hell of a debriefing. We expended enough ordinance to wipe out a company and come up with a live marine who's out waltzing through the jungle at 0200 hours." He looked at Jesse and paused a moment. "I'm going to have to report it. Shit, we didn't even kill a water buffalo."

"I know. Don't worry about it. I appreciate your concern. Hell, we're so short of qualified gunners, they probably won't do anything to me until the war's over, and by then maybe they'll forget about it."

"I'll tell it like it was."

"That's fair enough, Sarge. Now if you don't mind, I'd like to get back to my outfit," said Jesse with more confidence than he felt.

Taylor replied, "I'm gonna have to ask you to stay with us until we report back to battalion in the morning."

"I was kinda figuring something like that, but I had to give it a try." Jesse grinned.

Taylor smiled. "Well, you might as well hit the rack. Nothing else is on tap for tonight. I hope."

Jesse was exhausted and fell asleep quickly. His last conscious thought was of Shannon. *I hope to hell she never finds out about this stupid-ass maneuver.*

The Battalion Sergeant Major looked at Jesse, who sat opposite his field desk, his eyebrows arched quizzically. "Hunting? Did you say 'hunting'?"

Jesse looked the sergeant major square in the eyes. "Yes, Sergeant Major. Hunting."

"Hunting? As in VC or as in deer season?" asked the sergeant major.

"As in deer season, Sergeant Major. Except that I'm really not that particular. There's a lot of strange wildlife around here that I don't know much about, but most of it seems to be pretty good eatin'. Last week I got a...."

"Goddamnit, Langley! I've been in this man's Marine Corps for more years than you've been on this earth. Before you joined this battalion, I'd have sworn I'd seen it all. I've seen heroes, goofballs, weirdoes, assholes, belligerents, insubordinates, and plain-fucking-crazy people. But I'll swear to God, you're the biggest goddamn combination of 'em all that I've ever laid eyes on."

"Well, actually, Sergeant Major, I was..."

"Goddamnit, Langley, don't interrupt me again or I'll be successful where the VC, the North Vietnamese, and Bravo Company have failed! In other words, I'll shoot your fuckin' ass and use you for fertilizer! Do I make myself clear?"

Jesse winced. "Yes, Sergeant Major. Seems real clear to me."

The sergeant major continued, "Do you realize what the hell kind of problems you can create by being outside the perimeter on an unauthorized patrol?"

Jesse studied the tent floor. "Yes, Sergeant Major."

The sergeant major softened his voice and changed his tactics. "What would you have done in Sergeant Taylor's place?"

"Sergeant Taylor did the right thing. It's just a lucky thing for me his men can't shoot worth a shit, and he's got some new guy who signals the ambush with his rifle safety."

The sergeant major reddened. "Goddamnit, Langley. You're missing the whole point. You can't go around compromising our ambushes, costing us thousands of dollars in ordinance, alerting the whole damn I Corps – not to mention almost getting your hard head blown off. This is not Disneyland. This is not a John Wayne movie. This is the real thing, Langley. Men are dying a real death here every day."

Jesse said nothing.

The sergeant major continued, "I know you're a good marine, son. But you can't just be a good marine when you feel like it. We've got rules for reasons. A good marine follows proper procedure." He paused, waiting for Jesse to respond.

"Would it be permissible for me to speak, Sergeant Major?"

"Go ahead, Langley," sighed the Sergeant Major.

"Can you tell me why we're fighting the way we're fighting?"

"What do you mean by that, Son?"

"Sergeant Major, I consider you an intelligent man. Please give me a little credit in that area too."

The older man nodded.

"We can win this war in thirty days. I know it and you know it. Instead of fighting like we should, we do almost everything we can do to stall. We give the VC time to gather strength and supplies. We go on missions with PFs who aren't worth a shit in combat, just so we can tell the politicians that we're participating in joint operations. Our government sits idly by while a bunch of longhaired beatnik freaks destroy property and protest the war. The North Vietnamese cross the DMZ and shoot the hell out of us and we aren't allowed to pursue into the DMZ. We go on recon patrols and nobody acts on the intelligence we provide. We go on combat patrols to act as decoys. We roar up rivers in amtracks at night like the biggest bunch of idiots in the world. No useful purpose is served. We live like rats, except the rats eat better. We roast in the heat and shiver in the rain. And every day, Americans are dyin' over here." He paused. "I just want you to tell me why?"

"I can't answer that one, son. I honestly can't. Nevertheless I don't want to see you in my tent again for another hair-brained stunt. Jesus Christ, you've been in the Nam less than three months and you've raised more hell than every man in the battalion combined."

"I'll try to stay out of your tent, Sergeant Major. I really do want to win this war and go home with an honorable discharge."

"Good, then stay behind the perimeter line."

"I'll do that, Sergeant Major."

The sergeant major winked at Jesse. "I'm glad to hear that. I'm more worried about the rest of the battalion than I am you."

"Am I arrested this time, Sergeant Major?"

"Not yet, but so help me God, if you pull one more stunt, your ass is mine. Now get out of here and get back to your platoon."

Jesse stood. "Thanks, Sergeant Major."

The sergeant major shook his head and smiled.

The 81 platoon had fired the illumination mission for Taylor's ambush. Tuleano had briefed his section on Jesse's involvement and, by the time Jesse returned, the rest of the platoon was aware of his latest adventure.

"Jesus. I swear they're gonna make a movie about your ass," said Hou as Jesse cleaned his pistol.

"Does that mean I get some kind of royalty or something?" asked Jesse.

"Shit, I don't know how that works." Hou turned to Cuz. "Hey, Cuz, if they make a movie about you, do you get royalties?"

Cuz replied, "Not in Indio's case. It'll go to his next of kin. Hell, he's pissed off every outfit in the country on both sides. Sooner or later, one of 'em will get even."

Sal said, "Hey, Indio, what's happening tomorrow?"

"Nothing, I hope."

"There's a cease fire for two weeks, starting at midnight tonight," said Courtney.

"You believe that and you'll eat shit and howl at the moon," said Hou.

"No, seriously. They announced it on the armed forces radio this morning. It's official."

"That's just two weeks more for 'em to stockpile their supplies," said Jesse.

Cuz said, "Well, I know one thing that *is* for certain. The Lieutenant said we get three cans of beer tomorrow, except for Fourth Section. They got the gun watch."

"On Christmas Eve? Shit. What about the cease fire?" asked Sal.

"Cease fire don't mean we go to sleep. And I wouldn't feel too sorry for Fourth Section. We got the watch on Christmas Day," answered Cuz.

That afternoon at mail call, Jesse received three letters: A newsy one from Charlotte, a funny one from Will, and a serious one from his mother, expressing her concern about the war and his part in it.

More important than all of his letters was a Christmas card. His hands trembled as he saw Shannon's name on the envelope. He opened it, careful not to damage the card inside. It was a cheery card with a picture of a Christmas tree surrounded by presents; four stockings were hung on a fireplace mantel. Inside, Shannon had written two paragraphs. She wished him a merry Christmas and told him to be careful.

It was the first time since he had been in Vietnam he had received any correspondence from her. True, it read like a card from a sister to a brother, but at least she had thought of him. He read and re-read the handwritten note twenty times before replacing it in the envelope. He put the card into his map pocket, next to his chest.

With his treasure tucked neatly inside his utility jacket, he felt as rich as any man who had ever lived. He cheerfully answered his three letters. He then wrote Shannon a long letter, read it, tore it up, and wrote a two-paragraph reply to her card. He thanked her for her thoughtfulness, wished her happiness and a Merry Christmas, and signed the card: "Your Big Brother". That wouldn't sound so bad if her husband read it.

The following day, there were no assigned duties other than gun watch. The warm beer was distributed at 1600 hours and was gone by 1700 hours.

Jesse called the 7th Mess Battalion on the EE-8 field phone. He arranged for ten cases of beer from D.W. Savage. Savage was happy to supply Jesse the beer free of charge. On the field phone he said, "I'm tired of these rear-echelon poges suckin' up as much cold suds as they can stomach while you guys get shit. Get a mule down here and I'll overload the damn thing."

After securing permission from Lieutenant Chadsworth with a promise that he would be personally responsible to see to it that things didn't get out of hand, Jesse drove the section mule to the Seventh Mess Battalion. He shared a cold beer with Savage, wished him a merry Christmas, and returned to Sherwood Forest at dusk.

The gun watch was posted but, due to the cease-fire, lights were allowed inside the tents so long as the flaps were all pulled down and secured. The cease-fire brought hope to many that the war would soon be over. Lights in the tents after dark were certainly an indication of an imminent peace.

Early in the evening, several of the men gathered in the Third Section tent. One of the men from Fourth Section had a guitar and another an harmonica. They played together as best they could and the men sang Christmas Carols until they had attempted every song remotely related to Christmas known to man. At one point, somewhere around 2030 hours, Lieutenant Chadsworth stepped into the Third Section tent and wished his men a Merry Christmas. He cautioned against too much noise and spoke quietly to Jesse, advising him not to allow anyone to consume too much beer. He then walked back to his tent on unsteady feet.

Jesse could refuse no man a beer. If a man appeared to have reached his limit, Jesse handed him another beer and told him to be careful.

Most of the men would have rather been home but, taking into consideration all things, their spirits were high.

After the caroling, they broke into small groups, some returning to their own tents, leaving Third Section's tent, which had been chosen to house the beer. As the evening wore on, Jesse became relaxed. He held no animosity for anyone. He thought the cease-fire was a damned good idea and suggested they could even share some of their promised Christmas dinner with the VC.

The others were evenly divided on that proposal.

By ten thirty, the beer was almost gone. Jesse decided he would return to his tent since there wasn't enough beer left to guard and, besides, he had gun watch in the morning. As he sat on a cot in the Third Section tent, wishing those near him goodnight and a Merry Christmas, he noticed Windler staring at him from two cots away.

What the hell. It's Christmas. He looked at Windler and held up his can of Carling Black Label. "Merry Christmas, Windler."

Without warning, Windler jumped the cot between them, breaking the one upon which Jesse sat as he crashed into him. So sudden and unexpected was Windler's attack that Jesse was taken completely by surprise. His half-empty can of beer went flying as he and Windler folded into the cot and struck the ground.

Windler had him in a bear hug and Jesse became painfully aware of the weightlifter's strength. He felt his back crack a couple of times, under the pressure. Fear gripped him as he realized that Windler was trying to kill him.

He could smell the beer on Windler's breath, even over his own, as his attacker cursed him violently while trying to extract the life from his body.

They rolled on the earthen floor, turning over cots and equipment in their path. Jesse heard shouting but could not understand what was being said.

He knew Windler would kill him unless his death grip could be broken. The position Windler enjoyed allowed Jesse just enough freedom to move his left hand to his holster. His oxygen almost gone, he lifted the flap on the holster. He felt the reassuring touch of the handgrip on his pistol as he twisted his wrist and jerked it from its resting-place. With what strength he had left, he tried to swing the forty-five into Windler's temple. He had neither the strength nor the reach, but he did hit his opponent on the right lower jaw, causing him to loosen his grip just enough to allow Jesse to strike several more short, quick blows.

In an attempt to protect his face, Windler loosened his hold to go for Jesse's pistol. Jesse quickly took advantage of the freedom of movement and, by kicking and flailing his arms, was able to escape from Windler's advantage. He jumped to his feet and back-peddled three paces.

201

Stoney Livingston

Windler was only a half-second behind him in getting to his feet but Jesse used that time to cock the loaded pistol.

Windler stared into the muzzle of the pistol, only inches from the bridge of his nose. The tent had fallen still, except for those standing behind Windler, who rapidly moved off to the sides.

"You're crazy, Windler! What the hell's the matter with you? It's Christmas for chrisake," shouted Jesse, his hand shaking as he held the pistol pointed at Windler's head.

Windler looked at Jesse through slits of hate. No one in the tent spoke. Suddenly Windler shouted, "Go ahead, you chickenshit fucker! Pull the trigger! Go ahead, you wimpy cocksucker! What's-a-matter? No guts? Big, bad-ass hero, phony fucker!" Windler screamed at the top of his lungs.

Jesse looked at the screaming man before him. He uncocked the pistol. "Fuck you, Windler. You ain't worth the cost of the bullet."

As he spun the pistol around and attempted to re-holster, Windler lunged forward, bellowing loudly. He struck Jesse in the throat with his fist, causing the pistol to fall from his grasp. The two men were carried to the ground by Windler's momentum.

This time Jesse's arms were free and his reaction instantaneous. He put both hands around his opponent's throat, placing his thumbs just below the Adam's apple. As Windler pummeled his ribcage, Jesse squeezed the throat, ignoring the punishment he was receiving. While still squeezing, he jerked Windler's head back and forth, sometimes striking the ground, sometimes the leg of a cot or a helmet or canteen laying on the floor, with his opponent's head.

The strength of Windler's blows decreased rapidly. Arms reached for them both, some pulling Jesse upward, trying to separate him from Windler. There was shouting. *Who the hell is hollerin' so loud?*

Strong hands pried his own from Windler's throat. As his left hand was pulled away, he wrenched it free and struck Windler hard on his right cheekbone and quickly resumed his stranglehold but it was a short-lived victory. There were too many hands. He was pulled from Windler and dragged several paces away.

He breathed heavily, panting. His adrenaline flowed with the force of a volcano. Through the maze of arms restraining him he watched Windler, fearful the man might get up, and suddenly even more afraid he wouldn't. Several men knelt close to Windler. Jesse saw Windler's hand move to massage his throat.

"Let go of me, Goddamnit," said a voice. Jesse recognized it as his own.

"Take it easy, Indio. This battle's over, man. You won. Take it easy." It was Tuleano.

Lieutenant Chadsworth burst into the tent. "What the hell is going on in here?"

"Oh, shit," said a voice in the rear of the tent.

The lieutenant looked at Tuleano, then Jesse, and then Windler, who was in the process of being placed onto a cot. "Indio, you and Tule report to my tent immediately."

"Yes, Sir."

Ten minutes later, Lieutenant Chadsworth stepped into his tent. Jesse and Tuleano stood. "Sit down, Goddamnit." He turned to Jesse. "I authorize you to have some extra beer and you show your gratitude by getting involved in a goddamn brawl."

202

Forever Patriots

Jesse's eyes misted but held the lieutenant's gaze. "I'm sorry, Sir. Honest to God, I don't know what set him off. All I said was 'Merry Christmas', and he went nuts. That's all that was said between him and me all night. He needs a rubber room, Lieutenant. There's no way in hell I could've been provoked into a fight. I gave you my word."

"You all in one piece?" asked Chadsworth.

"Yessir." His ribs and throat hurt but he wasn't about to admit it. "What about that crazy bastard, Windler? Where is he? I'm not shittin' you, Sir, he'll be trying to finish the job. He's out of his head."

"He's under guard, Indio. He went off the deep end right after you left the tent. It took ten men to hold him down. I'll address that issue tomorrow."

Jesse breathed a sigh of relief. "Well, Sir, I don't know what to say, except that I'm sorry."

"It's over and done." He turned to Tuleano. "Well, Tule, what do you think of this whole situation?" Jesse thought the Lieutenant slurred his words a little.

"Shit, Lieutenant, when I walked into the tent, I thought my man Indio here was in deep shit. As it turns out, he's got the edge. I don't know what started it but I believe Indio's story."

"Very well then, let's forget the whole incident ever took place. Reach into that ammo box and let's toast Christmas. I've got a half a bottle of Old Crow in there. That should just about do it."

Shortly after dawn they brought in the bodies – eight marines killed in the early morning hours of Christmas. Some had no boots on, indicating they had no time for creature comforts before dying.

The small outpost had apparently relaxed security measures for Christmas and the reported cease-fire. The invading VC were driven off but the eight marines paid the ultimate price for laxity in a combat zone.

Jesse stared at the bodies as they were lifted from the six-by. Dead men always made him sad but dead Americans made him feel a sadness so deep he could barely hold back his tears. On this Christmas morning, as two marines placed a young man at the end of the row of bodies, Jesse wept silently. The young man had one boot on. He looked about Jesse's age, as did most of the marines in Vietnam.

A second lieutenant spoke to Gunny Reyes. "Gunny, Battalion ordered us to place the bodies here, near your LZ. A couple of choppers should be here at 0800. If you could cover them until then, I'd be grateful."

"What happened, Sir?" asked Reyes.

"The bastards hit us a little after midnight. They took us totally by surprise. We got two VC bodies and took twelve casualties of our own, eight of 'em dead. It was a hit and run operation and they did it right."

Jesse stood near the infantry lieutenant, staring at the dead marine with one boot. He spoke softly as a tear trickled down his cheek. "So much for their fuckin' cease fire."

He turned and walked to the First Section tent, the infantry lieutenant watching his back as he walked away.

As the empty six-by and the mighty-mite left the 81 position, Jesse returned with his poncho and placed it over the young man at whom he had been staring. He spoke quietly, "Merry Christmas, pal."

203

Others soon followed with ponchos and shelter halves, until the eight bodies were completely covered and safe from the flies and other flying vermin.

The day after Christmas, almost one-half of the men in the 81 platoon were transferred to other units in Vietnam. Men from the 1st battalion 3rd marines on a position-by-position basis replaced them. Jesse, Cue, and Sal were all that remained of the original first squad. Courtney, the First Section wireman, remained, but Hou was transferred.

There was little time to say goodbye. Cuz and Hou were a little choked at the brief farewell and, since no one could justify such a transfer, they merely cursed the Corps and wished those remaining well.

Corporal Bailey replaced Cuz as first squad leader and Lance Corporal Cummings moved in as Jesse's assistant gunner, moving Sal back down to first ammo carrier. Cue moved to second ammo carrier. Private Tully became third ammo carrier. Hou's radio was taken over by PFC Robert Whitman. Corporal Armstrong, the First Section forward observer, got a new radio operator, PFC Benjamin Franks. The other replacements took time to learn and remember, except for Lance Corporal Casimer Rolandowski.

Ski, as he was called, seemed to be at home in Sherwood Forest almost immediately. He had a dry sense of humor and a caustic way of speaking that most of the men found difficult to understand clearly when he really laid his Chicago accent on.

Ski stood 6'0" tall and weighed about 195 pounds. With his blond hair and hooked nose, he looked the part of the Polock he played. He loved being of Polish descent. He told more Polish jokes than the rest of the section combined and seemed to enjoy them all, even the ones that made no sense to anyone else.

Ski was the new gunner on gun two and, at the end of his second day in Sherwood Forest, after an exhausting gun drill, he strolled to gun one. He stepped into the gunpit and looked down at Jesse, who was wiping the bipods with a clean rag.

Jesse glanced up. "You slummin', Ski?"

"Who da' fuck taught youse how ta gun da mortar?"

Jesse grinned and continued wiping down his bipods. "Rest easy. It wasn't a Polock."

"Where da' fuck did youse say youse wuz frum?" He was really laying on the accent.

"Arizona."

Ski slapped his thigh. "Well, dat explains it. Out dere in Arizona, you fuckin' cowboys got all dem wide open spaces. Youse probably had da first fi'teen years a yer life ta practice wid da' 81. When we tried dat chit in Chitown, da' cops didn't go fer it. Blew up too many fuckin' bidnesses."

Jesse chuckled. "You don't do too bad for a city boy."

"You play poker?" Ski relaxed his accent.

"Some."

"I'll teach youse what ya need ta know dis afta'noon."

Sal, who stood behind Ski, smiled a knowing smile. Jesse winked at him. Jesse had lot of Sal's money as the result of various poker games.

The week following the arrival of the transfers was a period of adjustment

Forever Patriots

for both factions. The men from the First Battalion, Third Marines had been stationed near Da Nang, and were used to operating quite differently than the units on the Chu Lai perimeter. Like most marines, they were quick to adapt to their new environment with its new set of rules and, within a matter of days, they acted out their daily routines as though born into their new way of life.

Corporal Bailey was not similar to Cuz in any way except for the rank. Bailey was about Jesse's size with curly brown hair, dark brown eyes, and freckles set in a tan complexion. His dissimilarities to Cuz did not end with mere physical features. Where Cuz had been firm and confident, Bailey was bossy and strutting. Cuz wanted the mission accomplished in the most efficient manner. Bailey insisted that everything be done by the book. Cuz commanded respect. Bailey demanded it.

Bailey's first official act as squad leader was to inform Jesse that he would become PFC Cummings' assistant gunner. Jesse said nothing. Five minutes into his first gun drill, Tuleano called Bailey to the FDC tent. When Bailey returned to the First Section guns ten minutes later, Cummings was Jesse's assistant gunner again.

Bailey held three inspections his first three days at Sherwood Forest. He was satisfied with none of them. As the first squad stood at attention in the morning sun, Bailey made his fourth inspection. He stepped in front of Jesse as the latter drew his pistol and assumed the position of inspection arms.

Bailey's heels clicked smartly together as he turned and looked into Jesse's eyes. He carefully removed the pistol from Jesse's hand and gave the weapon a thorough inspection.

"This weapon has no lubriplate on the moving parts," said Bailey.

"It's been my experience that the .45 performs well with a light coat of oil. Lubriplate allows sand and dirt to adhere to the slide and can sometimes cause the weapon to jam, Corporal," replied Jesse, standing at rigid attention.

"The book says you will use lubriplate."

"The fella that wrote that information into the book obviously didn't have to use the .45 to protect his life or he'd use a light coat of oil."

Cummings, standing next to Jesse, stifled a chuckle. Bailey shot him a glance then returned his attention to his disrespectful gunner. "Until the Marine Corps changes the book, you *will* use lubriplate. Is that clear?"

"I hear you."

"Your boots aren't shined, Marine."

"They have a fresh coat of saddle soap, but they're the old-style rough-out boot and I don't shine my boots in a combat zone," replied Jesse smartly. "I only put saddle soap on them to preserve the leather."

"Now you can shine them to preserve your ass."

Jesse stifled an impulse to break ranks and kill the pompous corporal standing before him.

Bailey continued, "And while you're at it, shine that buckle. It looks like it's never seen any Brasso."

That was too much for Jesse. "I don't know where you came from, but polishing brass in this part of the Nam is plain fuckin' stupid."

"What did you say, Marine?"

"I said polishing brass in this part of the Nam is plain fuckin' stupid. I don't know any other way to say it."

Bailey returned the pistol to its rightful owner. "You're on report, Langley." He faced right and briskly completed his inspection.

Stoney Livingston

As the first squad returned to their tent following Bailey's inspection, Cummings walked slowly next to Jesse who was obviously angry. "Don't sweat it, man. He's always been an asshole. He likes to move in and let everybody know who's in charge. He thinks he's another damn Napoleon."

"Thanks, Rich, but it's not him I'm sweatin'. It's what he can do that bothers me. The Crotch makes him a corporal and he thinks they made him a senior God."

"How do you think the rest of us feel? We've been with him for about four or five months – since before we left Pendleton."

"Has he always been this way?"

"Sometimes he's even worse."

"Oh, shit. Don't say that. I don't need that kind of aggravation."

"I'm serious."

"Why the hell didn't you guys do something about it a long time ago?"

"What the hell could we do? Hell, he'd throw the book at you if you gave him any shit."

Jesse shrugged. "I guess you're right. He ain't worth it."

That afternoon, Tuleano ordered Jesse to his tent.

"You sent for me, Tule?" asked Jesse as he peeked inside the section leaders' tent.

"Yeah, Indio, Goddamnit. Come in. Sit down."

Jesse complied with the request, sitting on the edge of a cot. "What's up?"

"What the hell happened between you and Bailey?"

"Oh, so that's it. Well, I'll tell you what, Tule. The man is a stone-cold asshole. That's it in a nutshell."

"Goddamnit, man, He wants to write you up for insubordination."

"Tule, a mosquito has more brains in the end of his dick than that pompous bastard has in his whole body. He wanted me to shine my brass. Where in the hell does he think we are – embassy duty in Bonn fer chrisake?"

"You humiliated him in front of his men."

"Anybody that stupid needs to be humiliated in front of the whole damn world."

"Now listen, Goddamnit, I've talked him out of this shit this time, but next time I don't think I'll be so successful. I want you to get with him and work these chickenshit problems out. We don't need this kinda crap over here. We gotta work together. He's got a spotless record and he's spoken of highly by his old platoon commander, so he must know what he's doing."

"Okay, Tule. I'll give it a try."

"That's all I ask, man. Give it a try."

The following morning provided Jesse with his first opportunity to discuss another difference of opinion with his new squad leader subsequent to his meeting with Tuleano.

At the start of gun drill, Bailey relayed the dope to his gun crew. Jesse's gun was up and ready well before Ski on gun two.

Bailey stepped into the gun one pit. "Why is the eyepiece in the horizontal position?"

Jesse shrugged. "I kinda got used to gunning that way. It gives me a lower profile and makes me a smaller target for snipers, and the way it rains over here, that's the way we end up using it most of the time anyway."

Bailey looked up at the clear sky. "The book says that the horizontal position is for use in inclement weather only," barked Bailey. "It gives you a longer reach to the traverse crank and makes accurate gunning more difficult."

Jesse struggled within his soul, recalling his promise to Tule. "But, Corporal Bailey, I'm fast and I'm accurate. I don't think it's too much to ask to let me use the sight in the position I'm most comfortable with. This is a combat zone."

"This is a combat zone," mimicked Bailey. "You fucking guys all use that excuse to ignore the rules and regulations when you think it's to your benefit. Well, I'm telling you right now, the sight goes back to the vertical and I don't want anymore shit out of you."

"I wasn't trying to give you any shit. I was just trying to explain my rationale."

"Rationale? Did you learn a new word in school today? I'm impressed. Fuck your rationale! Put the sight to the vertical and let's do this drill by the book."

Jesse stepped away from the mortar. "Put it to the vertical yourself."

"What did you say?" screeched Bailey.

"I said put it to the vertical yourself. Corporal."

"You're on report this time, you wise-ass, and Sergeant Tuleano won't talk me out of it like he did before. Your ass is grass! Disobeying a direct order in a combat zone will get you twenty years at Portsmouth."

Jesse looked at him, eyes narrowing. "You're right. I'm in deep shit." He said softly.

"You damn right you are."

"So are you, Bailey, 'cause I don't think you can whip my ass and I got nothing to lose by finding out. If you got the balls, step out from behind your stripes long enough to find out just how tough you really are."

"You'd love to get me into a fight so you could have me busted," replied Bailey, obviously wanting to hit Jesse so badly he could almost taste it.

"Don't let that thought enter your head. I don't play that way. I wouldn't utter a word against you if you stomped my ass into the ground. What's your excuse now, Corporal?"

The men on guns one and two had been silent from the very beginning of the verbal exchange. They remained so, waiting for Bailey to make the next move. When he did, he surprised everyone but Jesse.

Though he was unable to stop Bailey from tackling him at such close range, the squad leader was already bleeding from the nose as both men hit the ground. The First Section watched silently as the two tore at each other, each spectator holding a silence for his own private reasons.

Jesse lost his helmet in the initial attack. Bailey, whose chin strap was buckled, did not lose his helmet, but instead was able to use it as a battering ram until Jesse grabbed it and pulled it up and to the rear, causing the corporal a great deal of difficulty in breathing. Bailey managed to struggle free just short of passing out. The two mixed it up again in an old-fashioned brawl that lasted almost five minutes.

Jesse was putting the finishing touches on his work when Tuleano appeared suddenly in the gunpit. Jesse was supporting Bailey against the sandbag bunker with one hand and raining blow after blow upon his face and body with the other. Tule grabbed Jesse by the shoulders and threw him across the gunpit. Bailey collapsed onto the packed earth.

Stoney Livingston

Tule turned to Jesse, who was already struggling to his feet, breathing heavily. "What the fuck's going on here?" he said.

Jesse panted, "I was ...just...givin... Corporal Bailey there...an education. It's from...one of the chapters...in the goddamn book...he hasn't read yet."

"What the hell were you tryin' to do – kill him or educate him?"

"Hell, I don't...know. Whatever came first, I guess."

"I think you might've fucked up this time, Indio."

"I figured as much. But that's okay, 'cause it was worth it."

Tuleano turned to Bailey. "You okay, Corporal?"

Bailey nodded without speaking. He was sitting now, his head between his knees, breathing deeply.

"Both of you report to my tent."

"Hell, Tule, There ain't no need for both of us to go. Bailey didn't do anything. I was insubordinate, that's all."

"Insubordinate? Beating the shit out of somebody is what you call insubordinate?"

"I don't have any idea of what in the hell you're talking about. The good corporal and I never laid a hand on one another. I was talking about some bad-mouthin' I did about fifteen minutes ago. I'm sure Corporal Bailey will supply you with a complete report."

Tuleano looked at Bailey who still sat on the edge of the gunpit with his head lowered to his knees. "Is that the way you want it, Corporal Bailey?"

Bailey looked up at Tuleano through swollen eyes. "I can't remember any bad-mouthing. I think I must have tripped over the bi-pod leg on the gun. It was damn clumsy of me, but that's what I get for trying to show off a certain way to operate the sight."

Jesse was caught off guard. He looked at Bailey for a moment. "Now that you mention it, Corporal, you may have a good idea on that sight problem. I might even give it a try."

"You might give it a try?" Bailey raised his right eyebrow slightly, wincing from the pain the facial contortion caused.

"Why not? I'm willing to give a *suggestion* a try." Jesse put heavy emphasis on "suggestion".

Tuleano glanced at Jesse then Bailey. "Okay, Okay. Knock off the shit. I don't know what in the hell's goin' on here, but it had better cease right now. Knock off the bullshit and let's get back to gun drill unless Corporal Bailey here tells me different."

Bailey stood on shaky legs. "You heard the section leader. Get your asses in gear."

Bailey earned more respect from his men that morning than in his previous three years in the Corps.

Later, as Cummings cleaned his pistol, he spoke quietly to Jesse who sat next to him writing a letter. "I still can't believe that shit. He's burned a hundred guys for almost nothing, and he lets you disobey an order and kick the shit out of him and he doesn't do anything."

Jesse looked up from the letter he was writing to Will Hunt. "That's okay by me."

"Hell, it's okay by all of us. But I just can't figure out why."

"Maybe he's got combat fatigue or something," said Jesse.

208

"He must have something."

"To tell you the truth, Rich, I'm real surprised myself. I imagine there'll be a payback somewhere down the line."

A voice shouted, "Mail Call."

Rich and Jesse moved over to join the others gathered at the mechanical mule.

Among the mail received by Jesse that day was a care package from his aunt and uncle in Phoenix, which he promptly shared with his section, and letters from Will and Charlotte. He tore up the letter he had been writing to Will and started over in a direct reply to his friend's correspondence.

The letter from Charlotte was cheery and full of good humor. Jesse decided he liked her, and when he opened the flat cardboard container that accompanied her letter, he found an eight-by-ten portrait of his new pen pal.

Rich whistled softly, "That your girl?"

"Hell, I've never met her. We just kind of correspond."

"Well, if you don't want her, let me know and I'll look her up for you back in the States."

"You're all heart, Rich."

"Jesus. She's a mighty good-lookin' pen pal. I always did like blondes."

"You know, Rich, she doesn't look anything like I had her pictured."

"You had her better-looking than this?"

"No, not exactly. I'm not even sure how I had her pictured. I just know she didn't look like this in my mind."

"Well, you keep what you got in your mind and I'll take what you got in the mail."

"I appreciate the thought, Rich. I really do. But I'm going to have to decline your generous offer for the present." Despite his confrontation with Bailey earlier in the day, Jesse's spirits were high.

Tuleano walked briskly into the First Section tent. "Bailey, I need two men from you for night ambush."

"Langley, Cummings, report to Sergeant Tuleano for night ambush," said Bailey, almost before Tule finished speaking.

Jesse looked over to Rich. "This is the start of the payback I guess. It could be a long winter."

The following morning, the 81 platoon was abuzz with excitement, as word of Bob Hope's arrival at Chu Lai was announced. Bone-tired, but determined, Jesse and Rich Cummings made the trek to the airstrip to see the traveling Christmas show. Carol Baker and Anita Bryant were among the show's stars and, while Carol Baker wore her silken dress that clung to her every physical feature, Jesse found Anita Bryant, in her orange cowgirl costume, to be more attractive. Bob Hope was his usual magnificent self and the show was a smashing success. Jesse left the show with a longing for his country deep within his soul.

1966 started for Jesse and the First Section atop Hill 76, on the outer perimeter of Chu Lai. New Year's Eve, the section had been lifted in by helicopter to support the rifle platoon already in position. Jesse didn't mind the change of scenory but was disappointed that the armed forces radio network did not reach the outpost. He had been looking forward to hearing the Rose Bowl football game on the radio in

209

Stoney Livingston

Sherwood Forest.

As he studied the terrain in the grey light of early dawn, he reflected on his experiences since his last ride up the back side of Mount Lemon on his Triumph motorcycle and wondered if he would ever see Tucson again. The war seemed to drag on forever with no important gains. It was almost as if someone who had a lot of power was holding back the infantry. He shrugged. His mind focused on the ridgeline before him.

A light misty rain cut visibility by fifty percent, but he could make out the hills only a thousand yards to the west. They were higher than hill 76, and more defensible. Their proximity to hill 76 made the marines a prime target for recoilless rifles and mortars. Jesse shivered at the thought of being mortared.

New Year's Eve had been a sober affair. The hill had remained on fifty-percent alert all night in anticipation of another holiday attack by the VC. With the coming of daylight, the security had been relaxed to allow the men to rest for the next night.

Rich stirred in his poncho next to the M-60 machine gun. He opened one eye slowly. Jesse smiled at him from behind the gun. "Good morning, Glory. Happy New Year," said Jesse.

"It is? Oh, man, is this ever a lousy dream. I'm going back to sleep and when I wake up, I want to be in a nice dry bed with a New Year's blonde to start the New Year off for me the way it should be started."

Jesse lit a cigarette. "You wish in one hand and shit in the other, and see which one fills up first."

Rich sat up, throwing his wet poncho to the side. "Goddamnit, Indio. You got a way with words that just pisses me off. Twenty years from now this will probably be the only New Years morning I'll ever remember, 'cause I'm stone-cold sober, and you gotta start me out with that shit."

"It's gonna get even better. Here comes Mister Personality."

Rich looked over his shoulder. "Oh, Christ, what a way to start the year."

Bailey stopped at the machine-gun just as Rich lit a cigarette. "You can secure the watch. The grunts get it all now. We've got guns to clean right after chow."

The days turned into weeks. Every day it was the same: C-rations three times a day, clean the guns, fill sandbags, build bunkers and hootches, play cards or shoot craps, H & I missions and sentry duty at night; an occasional support mission, and lots of boredom.

Jesse was disappointed when the newer C-rations were supplied. Camel cigarettes were harder to come by. He traded his cigarettes or food with those who drew his brand of smokes with their rations. He began to lose weight. He wanted off the hill. He volunteered for every patrol and ambush that left the hill but the mortarmen were considered too valuable by the rifle platoon leader, and each request was denied.

Jesse's opportunity to leave the hill came unexpectedly in the middle of a bright sunny afternoon.

He was inside the comm hootch, playing poker, when he heard the sentry shout, "Two gooks just grabbed a round from the dud pit! They're in the brush at the base of the hill!"

Jesse quickly placed his cards face down in front of him and ran for the trail, which flowed like a blood vein down the side of the hill. Cue grabbed his M-14 and was only four or five paces behind Jesse as he started down the trail.

The rifle company quickly organized a squad to pursue but before they were mobilized, Jesse and Cue were at the base of the hill, the sentry shouting instructions: "About fifty yards on down and to the east fifty."

Jesse waved, indicating he had heard the instructions, and continued down the hill, his pistol still on his hip, a grenade in his left hand, pin pulled and spoon held back by the first three fingers. Cue was six or seven steps behind.

As he encountered a thick stand of brush, Jesse shouted over his shoulder, "Cue, you go left. We'll circle. Don't shoot me, Goddamnit."

"Got it." Adrenaline flowed through Cue's voice. He had never been this close to the enemy and Jesse knew it.

Forty-five seconds passed. Jesse heard the rustle of brush and fell prone. "They're over here, Cue! I heard 'em. Don't shoot. Come around to this side. We'll push 'em into the rifle squad with a grenade or two."

"On the way," shouted Cue as he moved around the thick stand of trees and brush.

When he came into Jesse's view, Jesse put his right hand out, palm down, indicating to Cue that he should get low and hold his position. Cue knelt and sighted his M-14 into the heavy brush where Jesse pointed.

Jesse drew back his arm to throw the grenade, shook his head and lowered his arm. He spoke loudly enough for Cue to hear. "I'm probably gonna regret this but I'm gonna give 'em a chance to surrender." He faced the area where he suspected the enemy to be hiding. "De sung xuong! Gio tay len! Lai day! Mau len!"

The brush moved. Jesse cocked his arm. Cue nervously took up the slack in his trigger. Two Vietnamese children, a boy and a girl, each about eight years old, stepped out of the trees. Both were crying. Neither carried a mortar round.

Jesse said, "Cue, keep your eye on the brush behind 'em." To the children he said, "Lai tay!" He watched carefully as the two approached his position of cover with their little hands held high over their heads. "Dung lai!" he shouted.

The children froze in their tracks.

"Quay lai, " ordered Jesse.

They slowly turned around, allowing the marines to check for weapons and booby traps visually.

"Lai day," Jesse said gruffly.

The children approached him gingerly, fear clearly written on their faces. He motioned for them to sit down. To Cue, who still held his position, he said, "Let's just hold what we got till the grunts get here." Jesse stuffed the pin back into the grenade spoon, rendering it safe.

"Roger."

It wasn't thirty seconds later when the third squad arrived. They swept the tree line and returned to Jesse's position to find the two mortarmen entertaining the two dirty little Vietnamese children. Jesse had been saving a jelly bar for his evening chow but gave it instead to the two frightened children, who seemed very hungry.

The corporal leading the squad said, "You gonna make mascots out of 'em or what?"

"They're hungry and scared shitless," replied Jesse, looking up at the corporal, who looked at the children and shrugged.

"They're cute enough all right, but in ten or fifteen years, they'll probably be

211

Stoney Livingston

lookin' to blow your head off," said the corporal dryly.

Jesse looked at the two Vietnamese waifs. "Maybe. But I'm not gonna give 'em a reason today."

"We found the round," offered the corporal.

"You bring it here?" asked Jesse.

"Hell no, man. I ain't over here to get blown to shit by no misfired mortar round. The Crotch don't pay me enough to touch one of those things."

"Damn. Where is it?"

The corporal turned to one of the men in his squad. "Smitty, show this crazy mortar man where that live round is, then get the hell outa the way before it blows up."

Smitty nodded nervously and motioned for Jesse to follow. A minute later, Jesse strolled out of the tree line carrying the live round.

"That's close enough, Goddamnit," ordered the corporal as Jesse approached the children.

Jesse stopped. "We gotta take the kids home and find out who owns 'em. You speak any Vietnamese?"

"Yeah, di di and boom-boom," replied the corporal sarcastically.

"Great. Well, if you'll back off and let me get close enough to talk to the kids, I'll try to find out where they came from."

"You gonna carry that damn round with you?" asked the corporal.

"I want to show it to their village chief and tell him to advise the kids to knock it off or we'll have to shoot 'em."

"Fine. Just give my men time to disperse. We'll follow on your flanks." He turned to his men. "First team, left flank, skirmishers, left. Second and third teams, right flank, skirmishers right."

The riflemen took their positions immediately.

"Name's Jesse Langley, but everyone calls me Indio. This is Cue," said Jesse as the corporal moved away. "Thanks for the help."

"I'm Faye. Third platoon. You're welcome." He moved to the flank.

Jesse walked up to the children and knelt next to them. In his softest Vietnamese voice he asked, "Lang cua ong o dau?"

Both pointed southeast in unison. Jesse smiled, "Xin chi duong den cho do."

The little girl smiled and placed her hand in Jesse's. He felt a lump in his throat as the softness of her little hand and her toothy smile from a dirty face impacted his emotions. The little girl tugged on his hand and they moved southeast, Jesse, Cue and the children taking the trail; the riflemen wearing themselves out, trying to keep pace on the flanks.

As they walked almost casually, Cue said, "Hey, Indio. How come you didn't just toss that grenade of yours into the bush back there?"

"Hell, I don't know, just a feeling, I guess. Why?"

"Just curious." Cue paused. "I just don't know anyone else would've done that. I sure as hell wouldn't have. Hell, I just wanted to blast the hell outa the tree line and not take any chances."

"I was scared too, Cue. But it just didn't feel right – hell, I don't know."

Cue shrugged. "Well, it all turned out okay, but I don't mind telling you, you scared the shit outa me back there."

Jesse laughed, "Hell, I scared the shit outa *me* back there."

212

Forever Patriots

They approached the village cautiously, Cue holding the boy's hand and Jesse the little girl's, the rifle squad still struggling on the flanks.

At the edge of the village, Jesse stooped and spoke to the little girl. "Dan xa tru'ong."

While Jesse, Cue, and the boy remained in position, the little girl skipped into the village. The rifle squad took up positions on the flanks. They were well within range of the mortars on hill 76, and the corporal's PRC-6 radio was still within range of the base camp, but the uneasiness remained. This village was off limits. It was reputed to be sympathetic to the VC and could easily be harboring the enemy.

They didn't have long to wait. The little girl came into view, two or three steps in front of a grey-bearded, stout, little Vietnamese.

"I'll bet he ain't livin' on C-rations," remarked Jesse.

Cue nervously searched the village behind the approaching chief, half expecting to see a platoon of VC at his heels.

The village chief raised his hand in greeting as he approached. "Chao."

"Chao," Jesse repeated the greeting.

The chief began to speak in Vietnamese.

Jesse interrupted. "Whoa. No Savvy." He turned to Cue. "Goddamnit. How do you say...Oh, yeah." He turned to the old man, "Xin loi ong toi khong hieu. Ong noi tieng anh khong?"

The old man shook his head. No, he did not understand English.

Jesse held the mortar round so the chief could easily see it. "Sung coi. Thuac no." He ran out of Vietnamese. He turned and pointed to Hill 76. He then pointed to the mortar round, then the children. He drew the index finger of his right hand across his throat and said, "Chet."

The old man understood the word clearly. Death was an all too common experience in Vietnam. He motioned for Jesse and Cue to follow him. As he turned and walked back into the village, Cue looked at Jesse.

"What the hell, Cue, you're only gonna die one time." Jesse fell in behind the old man.

Inside the small village, a tall, thin man, with bony shoulders and a thin goatee approached.

"How do you do? My name is Chin Li. I am cousin to Duc To Bai. He has asked me to thank you. The children have spoken of the wrong thing they have done."

"Howdy, Chin Li, my name is ..." He paused, the reward poster flashing through his mind. "...Indio." He pointed to Cue. "This is PFC Cusick. We call him Cue." The four adults shook hands.

As if the shaking of hands had been a signal, the women, children and older men left the thatch houses and appeared on the street.

Chin Li explained, "Our people are afraid of the American Marines. The propaganda from our cousins to the north tells us you are baby killers and you would rape our women."

Jesse looked at the ragged and dirty women, gums purple from chewing betel nut. He turned back to Chin Li. "Believe me, your women are safe, even from the Marines."

Chin Li nodded. "We know that not all we hear is true."

"Where did you learn to speak English?"

"In Saigon, many years ago, where I also learned Chinese, French and

213

Stoney Livingston

Portuguese."

Jesse smelled the aroma of cooking food. His stomach growled. "Well, Chin Li, we're going back to our hill, but please remember to keep the people of your village away from our wire. We do not want to kill innocent civilians." He enunciated his words carefully so as to not be misunderstood.

"I will tell our people of your warning. Perhaps you may come and visit our village. Our people will treat you with kindness. You have been good to our children."

Jesse looked at the little girl who stood very near. He winked and smiled at her and was rewarded by a toothy grin. He looked up at Chin Li. "I will suggest that our commanding officer visit with you to arrange trade if you desire."

"I look forward to such a meeting. Please tell your officer that we humbly request Indio and Cue be present."

"Thanks, Chin Li, I'll do that. Tell the chief we must go, and we hope to visit later."

Chin Li spoke to Duc To Bai. The old man nodded and showed the two marines a toothless smile, his gums a deep purple from the betel nut.

In the platoon commanders' bunker, the young lieutenant's face was obviously flushed, even in the shadows. "Marine, you are a mortar man. You risked your life and the life of another man in your squad! You went in pursuit without orders, and you disregarded the use of proper tactics! You assaulted a suspected enemy position with a hand grenade and a pistol! Who the hell do you think you are?"

"I just figured that ..." started Jesse.

"Keep your mouth shut, Marine. I'll ask you a question when I want you to speak."

"But you ..." Jesse thought better and held his silence.

The lieutenant glared at him. "You then went to an unfriendly village and parlayed with the leaders of said unfriendly village."

"They seemed friendly enough to me, Sir."

The lieutenant glared at Jesse once again. He lowered his voice. "Just what was it you had in your mind when you charged down the hill?"

"Well, Sir, the first thought was to retrieve the mortar round so it couldn't be used against us as a booby trap. The next thing was to neutralize the enemy."

The lieutenant turned to the squad leader. "Corporal Faye, in your judgement, were things handled properly down there?" He jerked his head in the direction of the trail leading down the hill.

Faye looked at Jesse and Cue then back to the lieutenant. "Yes, Sir, I think they were. These two had everything under control when my squad arrived on the scene."

"Whose idea was it to enter the village?"

"Well, Sir, Indio ...er, Langley there suggested it, but I agreed."

The lieutenant looked at Jesse, then Cue. "In the future, Marines, you will not leave this hill without permission. Is that clear?"

"Yessir," mumbled Cue and Jesse, almost in unison.

"That'll be all."

Once outside the bunker, in the hot afternoon sun, Cue said, "What the hell was wrong with that stupid dick head?"

"He's a second lieutenant," answered Jesse casually, as if Cue should have

214

already known the answer to the question.

"Well, if we'd waited, the kids would have got away or the grunts woulda blown 'em to hell. This way, we got the round back and we didn't piss off the whole ville by killing their kids. As a matter of fact, they asked us to come back."

"Yeah, Cue, that's the way you see it, but if you had on a set of gold bars, you'd probably be just as pissed off as he was. There's just something about gold bars that turn a man's mind to shit."

Cue said, "Speaking of shit, here comes Bailey."

Bailey smiled and shook his head as he approached. "I guess I'm getting used to your crazy antics, Indio. I'd a busted you a month ago for something like this."

Jesse smiled. "Well, now that you've become wiser and more mature, why don't you go tell the platoon commander that it's okay for me to be a little crazy? He's having a goddamn kitten over us leaving the hill. Thinks the grunts should handle everything but the mortars."

Bailey smiled, "I'll go talk to him. You two get back to your bunker."

Later that day, shortly after mail call, as Jesse wrote a letter to Dave Boomer, Ski said, "Hey Indio, listen ta dis shit." He waved a Newsweek Magazine in the air. "Listen." He quoted: "Our troops in Vietnam are bein' well fed. Accordin' ta Defense Secretary MacNamara, da U.S. is sendin' 2.2 pounds a' fresh meat per man, per day ta da combat zone."

Jesse moved next to Ski and read the article. When he finished, he looked over at Rich who sat idly nearby. "Rich, this outfit owes us a whole bunch of fresh meat. Two-point-two pounds per day per man. Who really believes that?"

Ski said, "Yeah, an' ya c'n bet yer ass some fuckin' bleedin' heart is gonna tell us how good we had it over here. Shit. Two pounds a day is more dan I ate in peacetime fer chrisake."

Jesse pointed to the magazine. "Well, you must be mistaken. I know it's true 'cause I read it in Newsweek."

Ski laughed. "Fuck you. Is dat why yer so overweight – too much fresh meat?"

"Who's getting it all?" asked Sal.

"Da fuckin' rear echelon assholes, who d'youse tink?" answered Ski, "Da guys dat need it least, get it most. De're prob'bly sellin' it on da black market and gettin' rich while we eat C-rations t'ree times a day, and sleep in a mudhole when we don't have da watch."

The conversation continued, but Jesse moved away to read a letter from his Aunt Lacy, who lived in Phoenix. Included in the letter was a newspaper clipping of his grandfather's obituary. His Aunt Lacy knew he had been close to his grandfather, but so did his mother. Maybe he would get a letter from her at the next mail call.

He read the drab words of the obituary and withdrew to private thoughts. He walked to the side of the hill and sat down, remembering his grandfather, wishing he could bring him back. He looked at the valley below, with its orderly sections of rice paddies. His grandfather had been one tough old bird. He missed the older man's strength. It was gone forever from this world and yet the world carried on as though he had never existed.

He sat until just before sunset, when he slowly stood, stretched his cramped muscles, and returned to his bunker.

215

Tuleano went on R & R, returning six days later with a bottle of Australian whiskey for Jesse. The whiskey was so bad Jesse gave it away after only two swallows.

A new man, PFC Tursack, arrived on the hill and became the last ammo carrier, behind Tully.

The platoon commander in charge of the hill opened a line of communications with the village and the men were allowed to have laundry done and clothing mended by the villagers. On those occasions when Jesse went into the village, he visited Chin Li and became interested in the history of Indo China. The visits by the marines were good for the local economy, and guarded friendships developed.

On a night radio watch, Jesse heard a radio operator on his net reporting the rape of a Vietnamese woman by two marines. The incident had occurred near Da Nang. Jesse felt shame for the Marine Corps and the United States and outrage at the two unknown marines.

The boredom that is war without combat dragged on. Jesse turned twenty-one and mentioned not a word to any of his fellow marines. He thought how ironic it was that he should turn twenty-one in a combat zone. Like most young Americans, he had big plans for his twenty-first birthday – the day he became a full-fledged adult. Like many plans made too far ahead, his big birthday plan came to naught. He stood his machine-gun watch in silence, wondering if Shannon even remembered he was alive.

In late February, on a cool morning, Tuleano advised the 81 section to pack their gear. They were going back to Sherwood Forest. Jesse didn't have time to say goodbye to Chin Li. He regretted the urgency of the move and detested the decisions made by those in positions to play with lives.

The platoon was reunited at Sherwood Forest for only a little over twenty-four hours. Lieutenant Smith, the new 81 platoon commander, advised his men that the 1st Battalion, 4th Marines had been reassigned to Phu Bai and its surrounding area. They were further instructed they would be traveling light for a period of time and would not have need of their seabags until a permanent position was selected for the battalion.

Seabags were staged for shipment to Da Nang where they would be stored until needed.

CHAPTER ELEVEN: PHU BAI

It was mid-morning when the First Battalion, Fourth Marines arrived at Phu Bai. The camp wasn't much to look at that February of 1966. Most of the fortifications were new and far from completed but Jesse could see that Phu Bai was destined to become a large base. The distance from the hills put it out of range of all but the heaviest artillery pieces. The sandy soil was a welcome change from the clay mud on Hill 76 and, even in the light rain, the march from the landing pad to the center of the compound had been relatively easy.

The glimpse of hardback tents under construction by the Seabees was a welcome sight to Jesse but his elation was short-lived. Gunnery Sergeant Reyes informed them their tents were not ready for habitation and they would make camp on the perimeter for two or three days. Groaning and complaining, as marines often do when contented, they moved to the perimeter and made hasty preparations for defense.

After the noon meal of powdered potatoes, canned meat and green beans, they lined up for pay call. Jesse left his money on the books. Since his emergency pay in Sherwood Forest he had not drawn any money.

Later, as Jesse sat cross-legged in the sand at a poker game, a runner from company headquarters approached. "Hey, Indio, the Old Man wants to see you."

"The Company Commander?"

"Who else?"

"I've never even met the man. I didn't know the rest of H & S Company was already here at Phu Bai."

The runner shuffled his feet. "Well, I don't know about the rest of the company, but I do know the Old Man is here and he wants to see you."

Jesse placed his cards face down on the poncho. "Deal me out. I've gotta find out what the skipper wants."

Jesse saw his company commander for the first time as he entered the small CP tent. "Lance Corporal Langley reporting as ordered, Sir." He saluted smartly, his rifle slung on his left shoulder.

"At ease, Langley." The captain pushed a document across his field desk. "Do you recognize this?"

Jesse studied the document casually. "Yessir. It looks like a photocopy of a postal money order."

The Captain nodded. "And whose name is on the money order?"

"Mine, Sir."

"And what is the amount?"

"Five hundred dollars, Sir."

217

Stoney Livingston

The Captain handed Jesse several more copies of five hundred-dollar postal money orders. "Do you recognize these?"

Jesse glanced at the documents. "Yessir. More of the same."

The Captain shuffled a sheaf of papers and handed them across the desk. "These are your payroll records since your arrival in Vietnam. With only one exception, sometime in October, you haven't drawn any money. Now, C.I.D. wants to know how you can send five hundred dollars home every pay call without ever drawing a cent. And frankly, I'm a bit curious myself."

Jesse stood silently, watching his company commander.

"Look, Langley, I really don't give a damn where you got the money, as long as you didn't steal it, but I'm supposed to ask you if you got it in the black market."

Jesse felt a wave of relief spread though his body. "The black market, Sir? I wouldn't know where to find it."

The Captain smiled. "I didn't think so, Lance Corporal." He paused briefly. "Off the record, did you get that money playing poker?"

Jesse grinned. "Off the record, Sir, I do play a little poker."

Both men were smiling. The Captain said. "That's what I was hoping. Wish to hell some of these officers would get up a decent game – can't play with the enlisted men you know."

Jesse nodded.

"Well, to hell with C.I.D. That'll be all. Report back to Eighty-Ones."

Jesse snapped to attention and saluted briskly. "Thank you, Sir." He did an about-face and left the tent.

Jesse drew two cards.

"Five bucks," said Tuleano as he threw his MPC into the pot.

"Call," said Jesse. "Say, Tule, exactly what the hell is the black market?"

"It's when you buy or sell illegal stuff." Tuleano laid his cards out on the poncho, "King-high straight," he said proudly.

"Oh, so that's all there is to that black market business. I thought it might be some big ol' black building hidden in an alley somewhere." Jesse spread his cards on the poncho next to Tuleano's. "Club flush."

Tuleano watched silently as Jesse raked in the pot.

Corporal Bailey approached at a brisk walk, canteens clanking against his bayonet scabbard on one side and a magazine pouch on the other. "Hey, Tule, the skipper wants the First Section to mount up and move to a heli-pad. We're going to look over CAC-7."

Tuleano stood and shook his head. He turned to the rest of the section, spread over a two-hundred-square-yard area. "All right, you guys, saddle up. We're gonna visit a CAC-7 – whatever-in-the-hell that is."

That afternoon the First Section was given the tour of a small village, west and slightly south of the main camp of Phu Bai. They learned that CAC stood for Combined Action Company. A Combined Action Company was a unit, usually of company size, but they could be larger or smaller, that lived in a village and provided perimeter defense and performed many civilian tasks, such as building houses, farming, or making repairs to bicycles or some other mechanical device. Other tasks included teaching economics and business and a fundamental explanation of democracy.

As Jesse saw it, the theory behind a CAC unit was at the same time simple

218

and complex. No doubt, it would be good business to help the struggling Vietnamese villagers and to protect them from harm, thereby strengthening the uncertain alliance between the two factions, but the nature of man, with its infinite frailties, was overlooked in the planning stages of the CAC program the way he saw it.

The plan would work well if the leader of the CAC unit was at the same time a leader of combat troops, a statesman, a linguist, a farmer, a mechanic, an engineer, a teacher, a politician, an historian, and most importantly, a fair but firm disciplinarian. Few men possessed all of the required attributes from Jesse's point of view. There might be some successful CACs – even the most poorly led would achieve some degree of success. But the simple fact-of-the-matter was that months of hard work would be wiped out instantly if one lone marine abused his power.

CAC-7 was the paragon of the CACs in early 1966. The unit commander, Captain Robert Carlson, from Providence, Rhode Island, served his country and his Corps well. He had the confidence of the villagers and the respect of the men in his command. The marines in CAC-7 felt almost as if they were part of Vietnam's heritage. Most considered the people of "their" village as citizens of the United States and accorded them the rights any U.S. citizen has the privilege to expect which, as Jesse knew, was a better shake than the villagers got from the communists or their own government.

Jesse found the interaction between the marines and the Vietnamese gratifying. It restored some of his faith in his country to see Americans working side by side with the Vietnamese in the course of their daily activities. If he could find one shortfall, it was in the area of military preparedness and, even in that area, he wasn't certain there was room for much criticism, except for the lack of artillery.

The tour of the village lasted about an hour. The men were all introduced to the village chief and anyone else who turned out to greet them. At the end of the hour came the real reason for the hasty flight to the village – the mortars.

CAC-7 had received two 81mm mortars on the day prior and not a man in the company knew even the basic fundamentals concerning their operation. The remainder of the day was spent training selected members of CAC-7 how to operate the mortar, adjust fire, run a fire direction center, charge the rounds, clean the gun, clear a misfire and various other elements involved in the proper use of mortar support. That night was spent at CAC-7 as guests of the village chief and his family. Jesse was thankful for the fresh food despite its foreign taste.

The following morning the First Section returned to Phu Bai and moved into a brand new hardback tent, complete with wooden floors and wood frames to support the canvas. It was like moving into a Park Avenue apartment to Jesse. He thought he had died and gone to heaven. The rumor of hot showers only added to the certainty that they were indeed in heaven. The rumor about the hot showers turned out to be one of the rarest things in the military service concerning rumors – it was true. Not only were there hot showers but there was also hot food and some of it was not canned. There was a PX tent in the compound and, while quite small, it contained many of the items longed for by every man in the platoon: things such as razor blades, shampoo, toothpaste, soap, Kool-Aid, cigarettes, after shave lotion, shaving cream and other sundry items. Life at Phu Bai was even more comfortable than it had been in Sherwood Forest.

During the first week at Phu Bai, Corporal Bailey, Sal, Corpsman Gwyn and Rich Cummings all went on R & R to various countries in the Far East. All returned in seven days with tales of decadence and passion, vowing they would return to those lands of paradise at their first opportunities.

At Phu Bai there were no waterborne patrols. For the 81 platoon there was only gunwatch. The days were spent playing cards or volleyball or writing letters when not on gunwatch or running gun drill. There was always that ever-present working party or police (spelled `clean-up') detail, but life in the growing camp was far preferable to anything yet encountered by Jesse since his arrival in Vietnam. It was still just as hot and humid and the body constantly perspired but, under the circumstances, the quality of life was much improved.

In a tent constructed especially for the purpose of showing movies, most of the men were able to see two films their first week in camp. Never mind that one of them was of such poor quality that almost half of it was without audio, nor was the second much better, but they were part of things from home and home was important.

Jesse sat in a six-man card game at the far end of the third section tent. He said, "Damn, Doc. Don't you have a different record? It's great to hear some music for a change, but I believe I've heard enough of that James Brown and *It's a Man's World* to last me the rest of my life."

"I like James Brown and this is my tent not yours, Indio."

"Yeah, I know but these guys asked me to play cards in this tent. Hell, all I'm asking is a break from that one song where the guy screams all the time – like somebody just gut-shot `im."

"Shit, man, you don't even know what good sounds is all about," Gwyn shot back.

"Maybe not but I know that after fifteen or twenty times in a row, that James Brown guy is makin' it harder than hell to pay attention to the game. Why don't you take it to my tent and piss off somebody over there?"

Gwyn picked up the arm to his record player and carefully reset it on the first groove of the James Brown record in question.

"Jesus Christ, Doc. Give us a break with that song," said another voice.

"It's not your tent either, Cue," replied Gwyn.

"Well, Goddamnit, it *is* my tent and I'm gettin' tired of that shit too. And I used to like James Brown until about twenty minutes ago," said Ramirez.

Gwyn ignored him. The record continued to play. When the song finished, he started it over again.

Jesse stood and walked to Gwyn. He looked the big black man in the eye and said, "Doc, I know it's your tent, and I know you like the song. But for cryin' out loud, give us a break will ya? I'm askin' ya – *please*."

"It's my tent, my phonograph, my record, and my business what I play."

Jesse stared at him. "What's the matter with you, Doc? You never been this way before. I always thought you were pretty damned considerate of other people until you brought that damn portable record player back from R & R."

The corpsman glared at Jesse. "You don't like this music because it's not that honky shit. If it was Hank Williams or some other shit kicker, you'd listen to it all day without sayin' a fuckin' word."

Jesse tensed, then relaxed. "No, Doc, that ain't true. I'd get tired of a choir of angels if I had to hear `em sing the same song over and over as many times as I've heard this one today."

"That's bullshit. You just ain't got the rhythm, man, and you're jealous of the

220

man's talents."

"I'll tell you what, Doc. I don't know what your problem is today, but if you play that goddamn song one more time, it'll be the last time you play it on *that* record player." Jesse turned and walked back to the card game.

"Jesus. I don't know what the hell is wrong with the guy. Ever since he got back from R & R he's been an asshole," said Ramirez as Jesse resumed his place at the card game.

"I don't know either and, at this point, I don't really give a damn. Is it my deal?"

"Nope. Cue's got the deal."

Midway through Cue's game of seven-card stud, Gwyn restarted the James Brown record. Jesse stood and walked toward him, drawing his pistol from its holster.

"Oh, my God! Don't shoot him, Indio!" Shouted Cue as Jesse's forty-five fired once.

The only portable phonograph in the 81 platoon became a piece of history as it shattered with the impact of the heavy slug.

Gwyn looked at Jesse, a mixture of fear and hate clearly visible on his face. "You gonna shoot me now, you crazy honky bastard?"

Jesse stared down at Gwyn. No one in the tent moved as he held the loaded pistol in his hand.

"Stop the racial crap, Doc. I don't see a black asshole. All I see is an asshole." He holstered the pistol. "There it stays, Doc. I'll pay for your phonograph but if you want more satisfaction, come and get it. You're about as aggravatin' as a cornfield crow lately and I'm gettin' damn tired of it."

Straightaway the big corpsman charged, tackling Jesse at the mid-section. A cot broke with a snap under the weight of both men as they fell heavily downward on it. Instantly the others in the tent moved in and separated them. It took eight men to hold them apart.

Tuleano burst into the tent. "What the hell's going on in here? Who fired that shot?"

No one spoke. Gwyn and Jesse were still being restrained by a full squad, neither man willing to quit before a solid blow had been struck.

"I fired the shot," said Jesse, still struggling.

"Who the hell did you shoot?" asked Tuleano calmly.

"Gwyn's portable phonograph."

"A goddamn phonograph? You shot a goddamn phonograph? Was it in the goddamn assault at the time?"

Cue chuckled softly. Ramirez picked it up and turned the chuckle into a subdued laugh. Suddenly the tent reverberated with laughter.

"I saw it, Tule. The goddamn phonograph was in full assault. It probably would'a' taken all of us out if ol' Indio hadn't counter-attacked," said Ramirez, tears of laughter streaming down his cheeks as he pantomimed the imaginary assault.

"It was pretty damned close," agreed Cue, half chuckling and trying to hold a straight face. Jesse and Gwyn were no longer restrained.

That's enough of this shit." Tuleano turned to Gwyn. "Was it your new phonograph that was in the assault?"

Gwyn looked at Jesse and smiled. "Yeah, it sure as hell was. And it damn near took the position."

221

Cue pointed to Jesse's stack of m.p.c. at the poker cot. "The phonograph may have lost the war but, if you sue for reparations, you might get a better one out of the deal"

Gwyn eyed the stack of money and his smile broadened. "You know, Indio, that *was* a damned grievous injury sustained by my client."

Jesse walked to his stack of money and picked it up then returned to stand in front of the corpsman. He placed his hand in front of Gwyn's face and let the multi-colored bills fall to the floor of the tent. "I ain't all that sure I want to win too many damned wars." The laughter was re-newed.

"All right, quit the grab-assin'. You can finish this little conversation when you get off Hill 280." He turned to Jesse. "Get your gear ready. First Section is moving out in thirty minutes." As an afterthought he added, "And next time you clean that pistol, be damn sure it's empty."

Jesse looked at Gwyn. "That the way you want it, Doc?"

Gwyn fanned the bills, which he had just retrieved from the floor. "I can't imagine havin' it any other way." White teeth exposed in a broad smile flashed his victory sign. Jesse walked slowly from the tent.

Hill 280 sat at the mouth of a large draw with high, emerald-green ridge lines on each side, running away to the northeast in almost parallel fingers. It was a steep hill by Vietnamese standards and one that would be very difficult to attack successfully. The trade-off was that escape would be all but impossible in the event a strong enemy force decided to make the hill a strategical issue. It was the trade-off that bothered Jesse.

The first several days on Hill 280 were spent building fortifications and laying concertina wire. That first day on the hill was filled with sunshine and high spirits despite the lack of creature comforts. The high spirits vanished on the second day with the coming of the rain. It lasted five days, a steady downpour, turning the clay to greased earth, slowing progress and allowing pent frustrations to be displayed in the form of short tempers, threats and voiced negative opinions of various congressmen and senators currently conducting business in the Capital of the United States.

On the evening of the fourth day, Jesse received a letter in a light blue envelope. At first, he thought it was from Charlotte, but he didn't recognize the handwriting as hers. He studied the postmark. *South Carolina? I don't know anyone from South Carolina.* The name on the return address had been written with a fountain pen and the rain had obliterated it.

He opened the letter carefully, shielding it from the leaks in the roof of his bunker. Without looking at the signature at the end of the letter, he began to read. He wanted to see if he could guess who the writer was without reading the signature. It was almost like Christmas.

My Dearest Jesse,

I have written this letter so many times that I know it by heart. I just haven't had the nerve to send it. Not until now that is. It has been almost five months since I have seen you, since that day you left me at my sister's house in Buena Park. Many things have happened to me in the period of time that has passed. I have learned a lot about people and life, and the more I learn, the less I understand about my feelings for you.

Forever Patriots

Please don't tear this letter up until you have read it through. Listen to me long enough to know that I have feelings of my own, and while they are sometimes selfish, they are never intended to be that way.

That day you left me was the saddest day of my life. In such a short period of time I saw you in so many different lights that I felt as if I had known you all of my life. I saw your bravery and your toughness, but I saw also a tender, caring person with compassion for others. And despite your toughness, you could be as easily embarrassed as a little boy. While we were together for those few short days while you were hurt, I dreamed of a life with you forever. Yes, forever!

Well, those dreams were shattered when you walked away from me, but I have held onto the pieces in the hopes that someday I could put them back together. It was only pride that kept me from going down to Camp Pendleton to see you – pride and a hope that you would call before you left. I didn't sleep five hours that entire week while I waited for your call.

Why am I writing after all this time? There are too many reasons, but the most important one is that I want you to know that you have ruined my chances of ever being happy with another man. It's you or no one, Jesse. If it must be that way (and it has to be), then I want you to know. It is so important to me that you know and believe that everything I said and everything I felt with you was real. I do love you, Jesse Langley. Despite what you may think. I do.

I want to be with you right this very minute. I don't care where it is, even Vietnam. We hear things in the news about the war and I'm afraid for you. If something were to happen to you I don't think I could stand up to it. I know you, Jesse, and I know you will do more than you should. You are brave, and without a doubt the most patriotic man I have ever met, but you are also foolish enough to be a hero without even thinking about it. PLEASE! Do think about it. They bury heroes, Jesse. Please, don't take any risks you don't have to take. Even if I must go to my grave an old maid, I want to beat you there. I mean that.

I'm not given to crying, but I cry a lot now, sometimes in the middle of the day for no apparent reason. My friends think I'm losing it. They don't know I lost it a long time ago when you left. I've never experienced anything even remotely close to you, Jesse Langley. May God forgive me, but I would gladly give up the rest of my life to spend those days in California with you again.

I will close now, not because I want to, but because I'm crying again. I love you.

Barbara

Jesse studied the light blue pages, with dried splotches of ink on the last page where her tears had fallen. His mind wandered back in time and space. He felt a quiver run up his spine. He searched his conscience and found Shannon, not Barbara. Barbara had asked him to desert his country and his comrades. He felt shaky inside. Shannon's image began to disappear. Her golden-brown eyes began to sparkle and turn a deep green. Her brown hair turned a deep auburn.

He felt sadness and pity for Barbara. She described his feelings for Shannon. It seemed odd she could mirror the feelings he had for someone else. He felt her pain and emptiness and, for the feeling, was closer to her.

He left his bunker and stepped into the rain, which had momentarily become a heavy mist. He walked to gun one and sat on the edge of the gunpit, deep

Stoney Livingston

in thought, unaware his poncho was still in the bunker, insensitive to the water as it ran down the back of his neck.

"Bad news from home?"

He looked up to see Rich Cummings standing the gunwatch. "Oh, hi, Rich. I didn't see you. No, not bad news, just strange feelings about good news. Hell, I don't know what's real and what isn't anymore. You got a girl back home?"

Rich smiled. "I sure as hell do. She's something else. Of course if she's not there when I get back, I guess I'll understand. It's a long war."

"That's baloney, Rich. If she's the right one, she'll be there."

"Maybe, but you can never tell."

Jesse stood. He wanted help and assurance but Rich wasn't helping. "You're wrong on that one, Rich. If it's real, you can tell. Somehow, you can tell." He walked back to his bunker, still unaware he was soaked through his uniform.

*****

The bright sun was a welcome change as Jesse sat next to Cue in the machine-gun pit. Cue said, "I know you're doing all right at poker, but I'm tellin' you, we can make a killing if we play pinochle against Courtney and Willis."

"Hell, I don't even know how to play pinochle."

"I can teach you in twenty minutes to be a champ."

"I don't know, I'm kinda suspicious of a card game where they don't use anything but the big cards."

"Trust me. It's a great game. After you..."

"Cue! Up the valley! I saw something!" Jesse was behind the M-60 and sighting down the barrel.

Cue searched the valley. "What? I don't see ...Shit, it's a plane! He's coming right at us!"

Jesse cocked the gun. "Is it a Mig?"

"Shit! I can't tell."

Jesse's finger tightened on the trigger. "It's a Hun." He let his finger fall from the trigger as he straightened.

"A what?"

"An F-100. One of ours."

The single-seat fighter passed within one hundred feet of the machine-gun position, at an elevation almost even with them. They clearly saw the pilot give them the thumbs up with his right hand. The marines on the hill responded in kind, shouting and cheering.

Jesse studied the markings on the vertical stabilizer. "What the hell is the New Mexico Air Guard doing here?"

"I don't know but he's sure a crazy bastard. You got a brother in the New Mexico Air Guard?" asked Cue.

"Nope."

"Well, he's probably a cousin or something. Man, that's creepy to see a plane coming at you like that. I hope to hell the gooks don't bring their air force down here."

"I can't figure out why they haven't yet. They're bringin' everything else down here except tanks and planes. I guess they know if they went conventional they'd lose in a New York minute. All they gotta do is bide their time and see what the hell we're gonna do before they have to commit."

224

"Well, that's enough playing general. How about the pinochle idea?" asked Cue.

"Okay, okay. What the hell do I have to lose?"

Jesse had that question answered for him about a week later. He and Cue practiced and played penny games for six days between various routine duties. When Cue thought Jesse was ready, he suggested the game to Courtney and Willis. It was only natural that the undisputed pinochle champions of hill 280 scoffed at the idea of playing a rookie like Jesse but financial considerations made the challenge more interesting and they graciously accepted.

Had he not been a party to the game, Jesse would never have believed that it was possible to lose a game of pinochle so badly. In one short game of double-deck pinochle, lasting no more than fifteen minutes, he and Cue lost $150 apiece.

He watched quietly as his opponents counted their winnings then turned to Cue. "You got any more good ideas, Cue?"

Cue looked dejectedly at the lost money. "Nope. I'm fresh out of good ideas. What the hell, we didn't have anyplace to spend it anyway."

"Now why didn't I think of that?"

Willis, a short, light-complected, stocky black man from the streets of Philadelphia, said, "Listen, guys, anytime you want a pinochle lesson, you just ask Uncle Willie."

"Screw you, Willie. It was just luck," challenged Cue.

Courtney raised an eyebrow. "Oh? Wanna try again?"

Jesse said, "If he does, it's with a different partner. I've had all the fun I can stand for one day."

Willis and Courtney laughed. Cue's face turned crimson.

PFC Larry Cannon squatted next to Jesse. "If Cue had a decent partner he might have a chance of breakin' even."

Cannon was a soft-spoken Texan from Grand Prairie. He was easy-going and well liked by everyone. Jesse smiled. "I know. Don't tell me. Down in Texas you learn how to play pinochle when you're two years old."

"Three," corrected Cannon.

Jesse stood. "Then sit yourself down and teach these mean old men a lesson, 'cause I'll guarantee you, they taught me one. They treated me like an unwanted stepchild and all I said was, 'could one of you nice men teach me how to play pinochle'?"

Cannon squatted, rubbing his hands. "How about it, Cue, you feel up to getting your money back?"

Cue, who would rather play pinochle than eat, turned to Willis. "Deal 'em, Uncle Willie."

Jesse watched the game, as the undefeated champions of the hill remained that way. Granted it was a much closer game than the one in which he had participated but the end result was the same: another victory for Courtney and Willis.

After the game, Jesse consoled the losers. "Look at it this way, guys. It was a close game. You put up one helluva fight."

"You call eighty-two bucks a close game?" asked Cannon.

"Trust me, Larry. That's a close game compared to the one I lost just before you strolled up."

"Somehow the eighty-two bucks I lost still feels like eighty-two bucks."

Willis smiled. "Think of it this way – it's goin' to a good cause."

Cannon took the bait. "What good cause?"

"It's good, 'cause you a shitty pinochle player." They all chuckled, more at the way Willis said the words than for the words themselves

*****

Jesse sat on the side of Hill 280, staring at the horizon, unsure of what to do about the letter he had received from Barbara. She deserved an answer but what should he say? He had lived like an animal for so long he wasn't sure he had human feelings anymore. He wasn't sure what was real and what wasn't. He felt Barbara's touch and feared saying something stupid or something he didn't want to say. He felt vulnerable. It was the vulnerability of emotion – the worst kind.

He fought the fear, determined to overcome it, took his pen in hand and wrote rapidly, putting the words on the paper as quickly as they came to his mind, vowing he would not change a single comma.

Barbara,

Long has been the time since last I saw your beauty and it is I who am to blame, not you. Not in truth. Maybe what I had with you was too good for me to believe or accept and maybe I was just looking for a quick way out before someone busted my bubble. I don't know anything for certain except that I too was not pretending. Whatever I had with you was very real.

Life has taken us on different roads for whatever reasons life has to do things, and if the roads should someday cross again, then maybe we will learn the lessons about each other that we really didn't have time to study on our first trip. I don't think it will happen, but if so, then it will be.

You are young and pretty and you should have no trouble finding a really decent guy who will worship the ground you walk upon. Look around; search for the right guy. If you don't find him, and we should meet again someday, then perhaps we may find ourselves together again.

Maybe this letter isn't making much sense, but I'm not really sure of how I feel about anything anymore, so how can I explain something I'm not sure of myself? I can't give my heart to you when I don't even know where it is. I thought I knew once, then you came along and, for a while, I wasn't certain. Now I'm not sure I even care, or if matters of the heart are of any import in this world at all.

I wish you a long and happy life, no matter where it leads you. I really mean that. I can offer you no more.

Jesse

He re-read the letter and almost tore it up. Then he recalled the promise he had made to himself. He found an envelope, addressed it and wrote "free" where the stamp should have gone. He walked briskly to the mail drop, before he had time to change his mind.

*****

Life on Hill 280 was boring for Jesse. The confines of the hill provided no change in the daily routine. He utilized time to catch up on his correspondence and further hone his literary skills by writing letters and poems for the men who requested his services, but he yearned to do something to help win the war – if there was still one going on out there somewhere.

*****

Two days after reporting to the 81mm section stationed on the hill, PFC Robert Lawrence, recently of Detroit, Michigan, approached Jesse. "Hey, Indio."

Jesse sharpened his Bowie knife as the new man advanced. "Yeah?"

"You planning on some action in the near future?" Lawrence nodded at the knife.

"Never can tell. Hell, even if there isn't any, a dull knife is kind of a dumb thing to carry around. It defeats the purpose of the blade," Jesse grinned.

"They told me about you down in Phu Bai."

"I'm flattered but I'm sure most of it was bullshit."

"I don't know, you've got a lot of friends down there."

"That's nice to know. Didn't think that kind of thing happened over here."

Lawrence continued, "Say, listen, I've seen some of this stuff you're writing for these guys and it's not bad."

Jesse squinted into the sun. "You some kind of a critic?"

"Well, I *am* the manager of 'The Shades of Black'," answered Lawrence proudly.

"What's that, some new kind of Kool-Aid?"

Lawrence's face fell. "That's a singing group, man. Where have you been?"

"Well, I'm sorry. I've never heard of 'em. Course, I don't listen to rock 'n' roll much since the Beatles. They ruined popular music as far as I'm concerned."

"We're doing great. We had a top ten song last year." Lawrence paused. "But we need new material."

Jesse looked at the new man. It was easy to tell he hadn't been in Vietnam very long. His skin was not yet blistered by the sun. He looked rested. And the biggest giveaway of all – he was about ten pounds overweight for his six-foot-two inch frame. "I don't know the first thing about writin' music."

"You don't have to write the music, just the lyrics. I'll do the music."

"I don't know the rules."

"There aren't any. You just write what sounds good to you and if it's useable stuff we can work out a deal. You know, a flat rate or a percentage of the take, or whatever you like."

Jesse smiled. "Let me see if I've got this right. I spend a few minutes writing a bunch of lyrics and, if it becomes a song, I can get rich?"

Lawrence nodded. "Basically that's it."

"It sure seems funny to get rich so easy." Jesse waved his knife at the hill in an encompassing gesture. "These guys are bustin' their asses every hour of every day, and some of 'em are dyin' as dead as hell and, as far as I know, none of 'em are gettin' rich."

"That's because they can't sell their product. I'm telling you, there's big money in music."

Jesse smiled. "Okay, I'll give it a try. Give me a few minutes to finish my cheap labor and then I'll start my high-payin' job."

Lawrence rubbed his hands together. "Great. I'll be in my hootch when you've got the material ready."

Twenty minutes later, after humming "Love Me Tender" over and over until he completed his lyrics, Jesse handed ten scribbled verses to Lawrence.

227

Lawrence's eyes widened as he read the words. "Wow! This is great. You're a natural born songwriter."

Jesse began counting his money mentally as Lawrence moved articles within his reach. He positioned his rifle, canteen, canteen cup, helmet, empty mortar canister, wooden ammo box, mess kit, and rifle magazine in a semi-circle before him. Jesse watched curiously as Lawrence picked up a mess knife and fork and began to tap the articles laid out before him.

"How does this sound?" asked Lawrence as he bobbed his head back and forth to the upbeat rhythm he created by tapping the various objects with knife and fork. He began to sing Jesse's lyrics to the fast beat of his improvised instruments.

Jesse was totally amazed at the creation that flowed forth but it sounded nothing like he had envisioned it would. Lawrence went through the entire song. When he finished, he looked up at his writer, perspiration flowing from every pore in his body. "Well, what do you think?"

Jesse raised an eyebrow. "That was supposed to be a love song. I mean, it sounded catchy and all of that, but the tune didn't fit the words."

"Sure it did. It was perfect. That's what the public wants."

"They want that? I don't think I was cut out to be a songwriter. If you like it, you can have that one, but don't tell anybody who wrote it. I think I'll retire from this job. Lottsa luck with your song." He turned and walked to the gunpit.

Two days after Jesse's short stint as a songwriter, the Fourth Section replaced the First Section on Hill 280. Phu Bai, with its showers, hardback tents and hot food, was a welcome sight. PFC Emanuel Lopez from Mesa, Arizona, a new man in the Third Section, introduced himself to Jesse, and the two talked about the few places they knew in common. Jesse liked Lopez right away. He talked of home and his high school days and his mother's cooking. It made Jesse's mouth salivate to hear of machaca burros and green corn tamales.

Jesse's first night back at Phu Bai, Lopez reported to the guns as Jesse fired a night mission. He was impressed with Jesse's skill and said as much.

"Hell, Manny, all it takes is a lot of practice. You'll get there one of these days. There ain't a guy here can't do it with enough practice."

"You mind giving me a little night gun drill?"

"You serious? It's 0200."

"If you don't mind. I could sure use the night drill. The only time I ever gunned at night was once at Pendleton, on the range, and that isn't anything like out here."

"Okay, why not?"

Manny was serious about learning to operate a mortar in the darkness. To the gratification of the others scheduled for gunwatch the remainder of the night, Jesse and Manny stayed on the gun until dawn, leaving the others free to sleep.

When the two finally retired shortly after daybreak, Jesse shook his head. "Maybe I was wrong. You're never gonna learn to run that gun at night."

Manny's face fell. "What the hell you mean by that?"

"I mean I'm tired, and the next time you want night gun drill, tell your squad leader. I'm in for some sleep. We still got an hour before reveille. See ya later."

Manny smiled. "Later."

That afternoon the First Section mingled with the Second and Third

Sections, saying hello to old friends and meeting several of the new replacements. Among the new men were Manny, Private Hill from Cincinnati, Ohio, Lance Corporal Ruddleston from Pittsburgh, Pennsylvania, PFC Markowics from Franklin, Tennessee, and PFC Brubaker from San Diego, California.

Ruddleston and Hill were both black men, about as diverse in their outlooks as they were in appearance. Hill was five feet nine inches tall, heavy-set at two hundred twenty pounds, with skin the color of dark ebony. His reputation for trouble was verified by the lack of stripes on his collar. After almost three years in the Corps, he was still a private, having attained the rank of PFC. twice, only to be busted back to private after some minor infraction. He ate anything he could get his hands on and was boisterous and pushy. He didn't give the impression he would really hurt anyone, though there were some who weren't so sure, Jesse among them.

Ruddleston, who for reasons known only to him, associated with Hill often, was light skinned and freckled. His six-foot frame was powerful and sinewy at one hundred and ninety pounds. He was a quiet and confident man, not given to the loud displays often exhibited by his friend, Hill. His plans for the future included a civilian life and a career as an electrician, just as soon as the war was over. He had learned the trade from his father, who he said was considered by many to be the best electrician in Pittsburgh, or so he told Jesse.

A platoon meeting in the late afternoon lasted only long enough for the men to meet each other officially as a unit, then the sections were shuffled. Jesse, Bailey, Courtney, Salsbury, Cue, Whitman, Tuleano, Rich, and eight others remained in the First Section. Five men were transferred to other sections in return for Townsend, Frazer, Markowics, Manny, and Brubaker. The First Section remained at full strength, which was a rare thing for an infantry outfit. Tuleano was rightfully grateful he could operate his section without doubling up on the duties.

Jesse was promoted to squad leader. The change in status did not carry a corresponding increase in rank but it did give him the freedom to officially lead a squad, free from Bailey's direct influence. As the First Section ammo corporal, Bailey could still be bothersome but his duties included both the first and second squad so, at the very least, the second squad would occupy half of his time. For this Jesse was thankful.

Rich Cummings, though not as fast as Jesse on the gun, was an exceptional gunner. He was fast, accurate and careful and, like Jesse, he shared his abilities and knowledge with others. With Rich as his gunner, Jesse's job was almost too easy.

The daily routine at Phu Bai was similar to that while out in the field at Camp Pendleton, California, with the exception that the enemy was real and not imagined. The club, a large tent where beer was sold on a limited basis, provided the most in the way of entertainment in the compound. But even the club became boring after a few days.

Bailey talked to Jesse on more even terms once the latter was appointed a squad leader. Bailey explained to Jesse that he should change his behavioral patterns to reflect his new status. Jesse smiled and told Bailey that he liked the way he was and he'd rather be Jesse than a squad leader. Bailey shook his head and returned the smile. The two maintained a fragile alliance of cooperation, neither completely trusting the other.

Markowics, who owned a guitar, bought another one from one of the men at base headquarters and entertained in the late afternoons in one of the gunpits. He used his second guitar to teach others. Several of the men in the First Section gave it a try, but few were successful.

Manny, after one too many beers from the club, talked Markowics into playing Mexican music so that he could sing along, and the party was on. Jesse and several others joined in and the party turned into a full-blown fiesta when Cue managed to obtain four cases of warm beer. Even Tuleano joined the festivities. At dark the noise was curtailed, but many stayed near the gunpit, sipped warm beer and talked quietly of home. New friendships developed.

Larry Cannon and Jesse were discussing pinochle quietly in the darkness near gun one as Bailey approached. "Listen up."

There was a shuffling in the darkness and groans and complaints as the men complied with the request by cutting short their conversations.

Bailey spoke again. "CAC-7 is under heavy attack and we've gotta send some mortar ammo and someone who can gun in the dark. Any volunteers?"

The words were barely out of his mouth when Jesse said, "I'll go."

Bailey couldn't see him in the darkness. He spoke to the direction from which Jesse's voice had originated. "You're a squad leader. The lieutenant wants a gunner."

"Who's a better gunner?" asked Jesse. "If those guys are under attack, I'll bet they really don't care what my t.o. title is."

Bailey hesitated briefly. "Okay, you got it. Report to the lieutenant's tent. I need a driver. Anyone else want to volunteer?"

Cannon said, "Yeah, I'll go."

Bailey said, "That you, Cannon?"

"Yeah."

"Go with Indio."

"I'm on the way," replied Cannon.

Inside the lieutenant's tent, Jesse and Cannon were quickly briefed on the situation at CAC-7. An enemy force of unknown size began an advance about twenty minutes prior to the briefing. CAC-7 was low on mortar ammunition and had no one in camp who could effectively operate the gun at night. Jesse and Cannon were ordered to take the lieutenant's mighty-mite and a trailer with ammunition to the besieged company where Jesse would operate one of the two guns until the enemy was repulsed.

Pointing to a contour map, the platoon commander, Lieutenant Smith, said, "The enemy is known to have infiltrated these areas. You'll have to leave the road about here and travel eastward through these fields. They're fairly dry right now and you should be able to make it without any trouble. In the event your vehicle is disabled, destroy the ammo immediately." He handed Jesse two incendiary grenades. "This will help you get the job done should it become necessary."

Jesse accepted the grenades silently.

Smith continued. "The mite trailer should be loaded by now. If you don't have any questions, let's get moving."

Jesse and Cannon conversed quietly as the mighty-mite moved through the darkness. Without the aid of the moon to guide them, progress was slow. It was all Cannon could do to keep the vehicle on the road. On more than one occasion he was aided in his task by the trees and bushes lining each side of the small dirt path.

230

After what seemed an eternity, Jesse ordered a halt. He pulled out his compass and looked left. "I think this is as good a place as any to go boondockin'."

"It's dark as hell out here. You couldn't see a gook if he was two feet in front of you," said Cannon nervously.

"Well, let's hope they're still on the southeast side."

"What the hell do we do if they're not?"

"We fake it."

"Somehow I'm gettin' a feeling that I should have stayed in Phu Bai."

"Hell, ain't neither one of us got any brains or we wouldn't be here. We might as well get it over with. Make a half-left and don't run over any mines or fall in any bomb craters."

"You're a barrel of fun," said Cannon dryly as he put the mighty-mite into low gear.

The purr of the engine sounded to Jesse like the roar of Niagara Falls as it pierced the silence of the night like a sharp knife. Cannon drove by feel rather than by sight.

After five minutes of driving in the open field Jesse turned to the prc-10 radio between the seats. "I'm gonna advise CAC-7 that we're comin' in. We should be pretty close by now." The sound of distant small arms fire drifted to them.

"Yeah, goddamn. We don't need our asses shot off by our own guys."

As he keyed up the handset on the radio, Jesse sensed, rather than saw, that something was not as it should be. He didn't know what it was but something brought fear to his throat in a constricting wave. He squinted his eyes, peering into the darkness, trying to make out any form that might be distinguishable. The mighty-mite continued to move forward at a steady twenty miles per hour in the blackness.

"Shit. Larry. We got gooks all around us. Step on it!"

The barely visible forms of men on the move became evident as Cannon mashed the accelerator pedal to the floor. "Oh, shit! We're right in the middle of'em!" said Cannon.

The little jeep lurched forward, jerking the heavy trailer behind it. Jesse keyed the radio handset. "CAC-7, this is Pied Piper Whiskey. We're comin' in from your northwest. And be advised, we're comin' in fast. We're in the middle of an unknown number of enemy troops. Don't shoot us. Out."

Without waiting for a reply, Jesse threw the handset down and picked up his M-14. The mighty-mite bounced wildly over the terrain as Cannon frantically hung onto the steering wheel. More and more of the human forms became discernible. Still no shots were fired.

Jesse held his fire as they drove within ten yards of one of the men, wondering if the unidentified man might be ARVIN.

The unexplainable silence from the contingent of men was suddenly shattered as a man on the mighty-mite's right flank opened up with his rifle. Even at the close range of twenty-five yards, the fast moving vehicle was a difficult target to strike in the darkness as it bounced over the uneven ground.

The first shot was followed by several more, then the night seemed to come alive with gunfire from every direction. The bullets whizzed by the mighty mite at every conceivable attitude and angle. Occasionally there was the heavy plunk of metal on metal as the mighty-mite took a hit.

Jesse moved the selector switch on his M-14 to the full automatic position

231

and sprayed the area to his right front, unable to confirm in the darkness whether or not his bullets found a mark. He reloaded with a fresh twenty-round magazine and fired several short bursts into the night. Bullets continued to fly at the speeding mighty mite. The little vehicle endured the punishment and sped through the cluster of troops.

There was a sudden jolt as the vehicle struck one of the VC head-on. The stricken man's body flew up over the hood and landed on Jesse's chest. Using his rifle as a lever, Jesse pushed the dead VC from the vehicle. The body fell to the ground with a sickening thud.

The mighty-mite seemed to disappear from under them as it fell into a bomb crater at forty-five miles per hour. The sensation of floating lasted only a brief instant as the tires struck bottom almost immediately, nearly unseating Jesse with the impact.

Their speed was such that the loaded vehicle continued through the crater, easily jumping out on the other side. For a moment the heavy trailer appeared certain to capsize, but it righted as it jerked the mighty-mite violently from side to side.

"Where the hell did you learn to drive?"

"Fuck you," screamed Cannon. It was all he could do to maintain control of the vehicle.

The soft popping sound of an illumination canister was almost lost in the rattle of small arms fire that continued in a steady stream, but the light of one-half-million candle power made all aware that the soft popping sound had indeed been an illumination round.

"We're too far left. Bear right. About one o'clock," ordered Jesse.

The fortifications of the CAC unit were to the right front at about seven hundred yards. Frantically Cannon mashed his accelerator foot harder to the floorboard. "C'mon, baby. You can do it," he said to the mighty mite.

With the aid of the artificial light, the size and strength of the enemy unit became apparent. The light also afforded the VC ample opportunity to clearly see their fast-moving target.

They had safely negotiated their way through the entire advancing enemy unit and were a full four hundred yards in front of the point. Jesse inserted a fresh magazine into his rifle and twisted to the rear, spraying as much as he could of the area behind him. He thought he saw at least one of the enemy fall but could not be certain. The mighty-mite roared into the CAC compound.

Jesse jumped from the still-moving vehicle and ran for the nearest mortar, about twenty yards on his right. The marine standing beside the gun moved away as Jesse knelt next to it and picked up the bi-pods. He quickly swung the gun to face in the direction from which he had so recently arrived, set elevation dope on the sight and leveled the cross level and elevation bubbles.

"Give me about ten HE light with a charge three," he ordered.

One of the marines standing in the gunpit handed Larry a round. He dropped it down the tube unceremoniously.

"Grab that other gun, Larry, and keep the lights on. They've got the fuses set wrong. The light is still burning when it hits the ground," said Jesse.

"Roger," replied Cannon.

One of the marines from CAC-7 stepped into the A-gunner's position on Jesse's gun and dropped the rounds down the tube on Jesse's command as the latter performed a search-and-traverse on the advancing VC.

Small arms fire from within the compound was deafening as the V.C. continued to advance. The enemy was assaulting from three directions simultaneously.

Captain Carlson approached Jesse at the double in a half crouch. Jesse looked up from his gun. "Ev'nin', Captain. Two men from 81's reportin' as ordered."

"I'm damned glad to see you two here. Welcome aboard. What have we got out there?"

"Looked like about two rifle companies. They may have recoilless with 'em. I couldn't be sure. Can't tell you what you've got coming at you from the other sides." He returned his attention to the gun and spoke as he worked. "Sorry about firing the barrage without clearance, sir, but Larry and I know what's out there on that side and, I'll guarantee you, they needed thinning out. We brought a shit pot full of ammo, sir, and I'd like to expend most of the HE right now if I have your permission."

The captain perspired heavily. "It's for damn sure we won't need it if they get inside the wire."

Jesse felt the pressure on Carlson. "We could save about twenty rounds for the FPL, if it comes to that, Sir," he offered.

Carlson glanced at the mighty mite and the heavily loaded trailer. He nodded. "Okay. Go ahead. Give me a minute to find out where the hell we're going to need the greatest concentration of fire. In the meantime get your rounds charged up. Everything will be close in."

"Aye aye, Sir."

CAC personnel assigned to the operation of the mortar went to work unloading the trailer and breaking open the wooden ammo boxes. Jesse used the time to inspect the mortar and determine the fitness of the weapon. On the second gun, Cannon continued to fire illumination rounds in timed sequences, moving the mortar left and right to cover all sides of their position with light.

Thoughts of Shannon danced through Jesse's head as he considered the unenviable position of the CAC unit. *This could be it, Langley. You wanted out didn't you? Well, big shot, you just might get your wish. A miniature Dien Bien Phu all your own. How's that for glory? Too late to change your mind now, stupid. There are at least three hundred VC out there who might take exception to a change of heart. What a goddamn mess. Poor Larry, he never would have volunteered for this if I hadn't done it first.*

Carlson's voice brought him back to the present. "It looks like the barrage you fired to the northwest thinned 'em out a little." He spread a contour map on the ground and motioned Jesse to squat down.

With the aid of a red-lensed flashlight, Carlson pointed to the map and instructed Jesse how much ammo to expend in each area. When he finished his instructions, he said, "Give me a minute or two to plot the first mission and then give 'em hell."

"That won't be necessary, Sir," said Jesse as the captain stood to leave.

"What won't be necessary?"

"Plotting the missions, Sir. Just leave the map. I have a compass and know the elevation and charges for the range. I'll be firing in about half a minute, with your permission."

Carlson hesitated. Time was short. He handed Jesse the map. "Have at it, Marine."

233

Quickly Jesse accepted the map and placed it on the ground. He lined it up on magnetic north, and glanced at the areas circled by Carlson. After a ten or fifteen second study, he turned to his mortar and lifted the bipods, moving the tube almost 180 degrees. He looked at the rifleman acting as his assistant gunner who stood silently nearby not knowing what was expected of him.

"Give me a charge zero on every HE light we've got. I'm gonna be movin' this thing around. Keep one round ready at all times. Drop it every time I say 'fire'. You got it?"

The rifleman nodded. "You're the fuckin' boss, man. If you tell me to, I'll throw the damn things at 'em."

Three other men in the gunpit began frantically pulling the six cheese-like charges from each round. Jesse leveled the sight bubbles. "Fire."

The rifleman dropped the round down the tube. He was taken off guard when Jesse repeated his command within two seconds. That was the only time he was late firing a round. From that point in time he had a round poised in the mouth of the tube as quickly as he could retrieve it from one of the other men.

As the small arms fire from within and outside the camp intensified, Jesse continued his search-and-traverse of the area outlined by Captain Carlson. When he finished his work in the first sector he moved the bipods and reset the gun. For twelve minutes he moved about on the gun with a single-mindedness of purpose. Even with a zero external charge, the base of the tube glowed a cherry red, much like an old fashioned tent stove on a cold night.

Jesse looked up at his a-gunner. "Get somebody to pour some water on the tube. It's gettin' too hot."

One of the men passing the ammunition stepped forward and emptied his canteen onto the tube as Jesse continued to run the gun, unaffected by the distraction of the steam. A stray bullet struck the sight, only inches from Jesse's face as he moved the bipods.

"Goddamnit." He looked at the mutilated sight.

With no more time spent than it took to utter those words, Jesse traversed one turn to his right then turned the bronze cross-level sleeve to even the pitch of the tube. "Fire."

Without hesitation the rifleman dropped the round down the tube. Jesse continued to operate the mortar without the sight until advised by his assistant gunner that there were only twenty rounds left.

He smiled up at the man. "Cease fire. End of mission." He straightened up, his muscles cramped from the stooped position he had held for so long.

"I guess we grab our rifles and protect the gun until we get orders to fire the Final Protective Line," he said, as he looked at the sweating men in the artificial light. Larry continued to fire one or two illumination rounds every minute from the other gun.

The three men from CAC-7 exhaustedly assumed positions around the gunpit to wait for the VC to penetrate the perimeter, or the order to expend all ammo, whichever came first.

Carlson came running into the gunpit. He looked directly at Jesse. "We're inflicting a lot of casualties but they keep coming. Still can't tell how many there are. Battalion says we'll have help in twenty minutes." He breathed heavily, knelt and pointed to the map lying on the ground. "See this area here?"

Jesse nodded.

Carlson made an oblong circle on the map with his ink pen. "This is where their strength seems to be. They're almost inside the wire. If we don't stop 'em at the wire, we won't be here in twenty minutes. Can you drop 'em in that close without killing half of the company?"

"Yes, Sir. I think so," answered Jesse.

"Fire the FPL!"

"Aye aye, Sir." Instantly, Jesse removed the damaged sight from his gun and rushed to the other gunpit.

"Larry, I need your sight. We're gonna fire the FPL. All the HE is charged and ready to go on my gun. If you just hold it where you've got it for the illumination, you should be okay," He removed the sight from Cannon's gun and replaced it with the damaged one.

"The FPL?" said Cannon.

The mere mention of the term in a real situation was enough to send chills through the entire body. On training exercises it was always a lot of fun to fire the Final Protective Line and watch the beautiful interweaving patterns carved out by the machine gun tracers in the darkness as explosive mortar rounds burst among the orange streaks of light. It also meant that one would not have to carry any ammunition back to camp. But the FPL was only a term for training. It didn't appear to be as much fun in real life.

"Yeah. Looks like we may have bitten off a little more than we can chew this time. Skipper says that battalion has help on the way but we've gotta hold out another twenty minutes."

"Shit, man. Hey, if we don't make it, Indio ... well ... you know."

"We'll make it, Larry. We'll make it."

They both heard the Captain's voice. "Fire the FPL!"

Jesse ran for his gun, almost falling as he jumped into the gunpit. Quickly and mechanically he replaced the sight and placed elevation dope on the scale. He shot a magnetic azimuth with his compass to the southeast side of the defense perimeter and lined the tube up to correspond with his compass reading. He turned the elevation hand crank until the elevation bubble in the sight was centered.

"Jesus fucking Christ! You aren't gonna fire that goddamn thing in that position are you?" exclaimed his assistant gunner above the din of the intense small arms fire.

"It's either that or you're gonna get that chance to throw 'em at the gooks at spittin' range," replied Jesse.

"Shit, they're gonna land right on top of us!" Even in the flickering light, fear was plainly written on the man's face.

"Where the hell do you think the gooks are – Seattle?" Jesse paused briefly. "Now, drop a round or get out of the way so I can do it."

Reluctantly, the man placed a round into the tube. Before dropping it, he said, "I hope you know what the fuck you're doin'."

"So do I," replied Jesse as the round slid down the tube.

With a *thump-pow*, the round was on its way. "You just keep droppin' 'em until we're out of ammo. I'll be doin' a search-and-traverse but just ignore me. Expend all ammo." Jesse ordered.

"You got it."

Jesse moved the gun left and right, up and down, as the rounds were dropped down the tube. So intent was he on maximizing the effect of the barrage that he was unaware when the ammo was gone until he heard his assistant gunner's voice. "That's it, man. We're out of ammo."

Drenched in perspiration, Jesse glanced at him. "Do your thing. I'll take care of the mortar."

"We're gone," said his A-gunner. He turned to the other members of the mortar crew. "You heard what the man said. Report to the platoon." Jesse watched as they disappeared into the confusion that was all around him.

The sound of small arms was almost deafening. Tracers pierced the night like so many red-hot arrows of death. The mortar barrage landed on the southeastern edge of the perimeter, a scant one hundred-fifty yards from where Jesse knelt, adding its explosive sound to the concert of death. Jesse could only hope he had been on target and the impacting rounds hit none of the marines.

With his body in a low crouch Jesse ran to Cannon's gun. He handed Larry one of the two incendiary grenades given to him by Lieutenant Smith. "Just pull the pin and drop it down the tube if they breach our perimeter. I'll take a few illumination rounds to the other gun and spell you for a while."

Cannon accepted the grenade. "This is it, ain't it?"

Jesse answered as he balanced four of the large illumination rounds in his arms. "Not without the biggest damn fight these little shitheads have ever seen. Take a break. Send one of these guys over to my gun with some more illumination and I'll light up the area for a while. Keep yer ass low. We got a lotta drinkin' to do yet." He left without waiting for a response.

A minute later, Cannon stepped into Jesse's gunpit loaded down with illumination rounds. Jesse helped relieve him of his burden. "What the hell you doin' here? I thought you were gonna stay on the other gun."

"What the hell for? The grunts got more experience pullin' pins on grenades than I do. I'd just as soon die with you as anybody."

"You sound like we're already dead for chrisake. I don't know about you but I've still got a lot of fight in me."

Casually Cannon dropped a round down the tube. "Yeah, me too, but if it's just the same to you, I'd rather be here."

Jesse reached into his left breast pocket and pulled out a pack of cigarettes. He offered one to Cannon. As he lit his cigarette, Cannon said, "What the hell we gonna do, give away our position?"

They both chuckled. "Hey, Larry, you got a bayonet?" asked Jesse.

"Yeah, but I think my M-14 bounced out of the Mite in that field. You might as well use it." He took the bayonet from its scabbard and handed it to Jesse who quickly affixed it to the barrel of his M-14.

"Thanks, Larry. Here. I won't need this with the bayonet." He drew his pistol from its holster and casually handed it to Cannon.

Cannon accepted the pistol. "I guess it's better than throwin' rocks." He picked up another illumination round and dropped it down the tube. "Y'know, this is the shits. We coulda been sacked out at Phu Bai, in a dry tent, with the prospect of hot chow in the mornin'," he said.

"Yeah but we're too smart for that. I guess we showed them a thing or two about intelligence, didn't we?" said Jesse.

"Yeah we sure as hell did. Oh well – to hell with it. By the way, did I ever tell you that a rifle with a bayonet on the end of it is about the scariest damn thing in the world? Next to the sound of incomin' mortars, that is."

"I hope the gooks feel the same way. Listen, Larry, I think I'll go to the wire. You can handle illumination if you get one of the grunts to help you. Besides, the wire is where we want to stop 'em, not in the gunpit."

Cannon shook his head. "One more ain't gonna make any difference."

"It might."

"I never seen anybody in my life so damn anxious to stick his head into a fire. Yeah, go ahead, but you better damn well get a few for me."

Jesse fieldstripped his cigarette butt. He looked at Larry, expecting it would be the last time he would ever see him or anyone else. "Keep your ass low, Larry."

"You too, Indio."

Jesse ran for the perimeter.

As Cannon fired another illumination round, Jesse heard shouting and cheering to his front. Small arms fire from the marines slowed, almost imperceptibly, for a brief moment. He heard a voice shout, "They're retreating! We've got 'em on the run! Pour it on!"

Jesse didn't know the voice but it didn't really matter. The VC had been stopped at the wire. He could see the forms of men scurrying over each other, like so many ants, as they broke and ran toward the trees to the southeast. He put his rifle to his shoulder and fired several rounds, not knowing and not really caring, if he found a live target.

It was over as quickly as it had begun. Jesse heard the shouts for corpsmen as he walked back to the gunpit. The smell of gunpowder and cordite hung in the air like a heavy fog. It burned the lungs to breathe. Stepping into the gunpit, Jesse said, "Here's your bayonet. Turns out the VC heard I was on my way to the line and hauled-ass."

Cannon smiled and accepted the bayonet. "I was wonderin' if you'd remember where you got it. You know how some people are. They never return a damn thing." Cannon paused for a moment. "What the hell happened out there?"

"I don't really know. The gooks broke and ran about the time I got to the perimeter. I don't think they were able to penetrate the wire – at least not enough of 'em to get the job done. Basically, it looks to me like our side just beat the hell out of their side – plain and simple."

Captain Carlson approached the gunpit. Jesse stood.

"Sit down, men. Sit down. Relax. You earned it. By the way, what are your names?"

Still standing, Jesse answered, "Lance Corporal Jesse Langley here, sir." He nodded at Cannon. "PFC Lawrence Cannon is the one, sittin' down on the job."

"Langley, Cannon, you men did one hell of a job. But for your quick action and professionalism we'd have lost the compound to a far superior force."

Jesse paused for a moment, unsure of how to respond to words of praise from a superior officer. "Oh, I don't know about all that, Sir. It looked to me like your guys weren't exactly ready to roll over and let the gooks walk in," he finally said.

"The simple fact of the matter is that you advised us of the approaching enemy force from the northwest. You blasted the hell out of them with the mortar before they were within accurate rifle range. You provided accurate and timely illumination. You fired HE missions accurately without the aid of FDC, and you dropped that last twenty rounds right on the edge of the wire. That was the clincher. I can honestly say that you two men have done more to contribute to the enemy's defeat than the rest of us combined. I know it's your job but we're all damned proud to call you marines. I've got to attend to several matters but I'll be speaking to you later on. I just wanted to express my appreciation and thank you both."

"Thank you, Sir." Jesse and Cannon spoke in unison as the captain moved out to continue his rounds.

Jesse looked at Cannon quizzically. "Am I dead and dreamin' or did that marine officer just address us as human beings? And further, said officer thanked us for doing something?"

Larry said, "Hell, I'm not sure of anything anymore. I never heard nothin' like that before from any officer. This has been one helluva strange night. I'm so damn tired and sleepy I could pass out sittin' up."

"Yeah, I know what you mean. I'm about give out myself. We'll probably have a hundred-percent alert until the reinforcements get here – if they get here."

No sooner were the words out of Jesse's mouth when the distant sound of helicopter blades broke the silence. Someone shouted, "Fire illumination. We've got choppers coming in."

Without standing, Cannon leaned over and picked up an illumination round. He stretched his arm up to the tube and dropped the round. It left the tube with a *thump-pow.* "How's that for service?" He smiled.

"Not bad for a worn-out Texan."

"You damn desert rat. What the hell do you know about Texas?"

"Enough to know that when things got real boring down in Tucson, I used to drive to El Paso and whip three or four Texans for breakfast just to start my day out with a little exercise. And I do mean a *little.*"

"If I didn't like your sorry ass, I'd get up and kick it up around your shoulders."

"I'm too damned tired for this. Let's see if the grasshoppers brought us any ammo," said Jesse.

The two walked to the LZ.

Jesse sat up in the grey light that was dawn. He rubbed his eyes and stretched his cramped muscles. He had fallen asleep easily enough when the fresh troops took up the perimeter but neither he nor Cannon carried anything but a poncho to protect them from the weather, and a poncho does little to soften rocky ground. He probed his ribcage to discover fresh bruises, which he quickly attributed to his less than satisfactory sleeping arrangements.

He watched Cannon sleeping peacefully on the other side of the gun and smiled at the fetal position his friend had assumed to save body heat. "Wake up, Larry. Reveille. Reveille."

Cannon bolted upright. "Wha ... wha ...?"

Jesse laughed. "You're a helluva sight this morning. You look like you been shot at and missed and shit at and hit."

Cannon rubbed his tongue around his teeth and smacked his lips. "If you want to know the truth, I feel just that way." He looked at Jesse. "Jesus. You don't look like Mr. Clean yourself. When's the last time you took a shower?"

"Yesterday. Or was it last month? Hell, I don't remember."

"Where's our C's?" asked Cannon, referring to their C-rations.

"Apparently they bounced out of the mighty-mite during that little driving exhibition you put on last night. You might say we lack provisions of any kind right at the moment."

Cannon stood and stretched his muscles. "Well I guess that means we're gonna have to mooch from the grunts, huh?"

"Kinda looks that way." Jesse reached into his breast pocket. "I've got a couple of packs of coffee here. That oughta give us the strength we're gonna need to hit up the grunts."

"Sounds like a damn good idea to me." Cannon rubbed his hands together in anticipation of hot coffee.

Jesse begged a blue heat tab from one of the reinforcement troops and prepared the powdered coffee in his canteen cup. As they drank the hot coffee, Jesse surveyed the compound. During the night, the replacement troops from Phu Bai had done their work well. Fortifications were rebuilt, ammunition re-supplied, rations restocked, and the perimeter scoured. Work on some of the nearby houses in the village was already underway. Jesse stared at the neat rows of ponchos in the center of the compound. Each poncho was tightly wrapped around a human body.

Cannon counted aloud, "...forty-one, forty-two, forty-three, forty-goddamned-four. Holy hell!" He turned to a corpsman standing nearby and said, "How many did we lose?"

The corpsman nodded to the ponchos. "That's the other side. Our team is over there." He pointed to five ponchos in a neat row near Cannon's mighty-mite. "We lost five KIA and twelve WIA. Two of them probably won't make it. We've got forty-four confirmed dead VC and maybe more. Three wounded prisoners. Anything else I can tell you?" He looked at Cannon, half expecting more questions, but none were forthcoming.

"No. No, thanks." Cannon watched as the corpsman went about his business. He turned to Jesse. "All of that noise last night and we only lost five men?"

"That's enough, ain't it? How the hell would you feel if you were one of those 'onlies'?"

"You know what the hell I mean, Goddamnit."

"Yeah I know what you mean. I thought we lost a lot more too. Just goes to show you how much we know."

Captain Carlson approached briskly. "Good morning, men."

"'Mornin', Sir," replied Jesse.

"G'mornin', Sir," echoed Cannon.

"How do you feel this morning, gentlemen?"

"Like hell, Sir. Stayin' up half the night gettin' shot at and killin' people always makes me feel like hell in the morning," answered Jesse dryly.

Cannon winced. "I guess I'm a little tired myself, Sir." He shot Jesse a warning glance.

"It was a long night for all of us. I know. If it hadn't been for you two, those ponchos might be filled with marines instead of VC."

Jesse felt uncomfortable with the direction the conversation was headed. "I guess your men have got things under control now, huh?"

Carlson looked at Jesse questioningly. "We were reinforced by two companies, with attachments. By tonight I think it will be business as usual. Most of the reinforcements will be returning to Phu Bai but some will remain with us for a few days. That brings me to my next question. How would you two men like to be attached to CAC-7?"

"We're from a different battalion, Sir," said Jesse quickly.

"We can get around that. Let me tell you where I'm coming from." He

239

Stoney Livingston

paused. "When I filed my detailed report of the assault on our position this morning, the importance of trained 0341's operating the mortars was quite apparent. The importance of our mission here is such that Division has authorized a T.O. section of mortars be attached to our company. I would be proud to have both of you serve with me."

Jesse looked at Cannon then at the Captain. "Sir, I'd be proud to serve with you but I don't want to be in a stationary position when we finally go after the gooks. I want to be there when my outfit marches into Hanoi." Jesse paused. "I got nothin' against what you're doin' here. As a matter-of-fact, I think it's great. It's just not for me."

Carlson turned to Cannon who shuffled his feet as he looked at the ground and said, "I guess I feel about the same as Indio. I mean, it would be great duty and all of that, but sittin' around the same place everyday would get to me."

"The mortar section will need a section leader." Carlson was looking directly at Jesse.

"We appreciate the offer, Sir. We really do, but we'd like to remain with our outfit if it's just the same to you," said Jesse.

Carlson studied both men. He shook his head and said, "I'll respect your wishes, but if you ever change your mind, drop me a line and I'll have you here in twenty-four hours."

"Thank you, Sir," said Jesse.

"No. *Thank you,* gentlemen. It's been a privilege to meet you both." He smiled at Cannon and said, "If you can stand it around here for a few more hours, I'll see to it that you get an escort back to Phu Bai."

"That won't be necessary, Sir, but we'll be glad to stay and help if you need us," offered Jesse.

Carlson paused for a moment. "No, go ahead, men. I can see you've had about all of this luxury you can stand. Report back to your outfit – and thanks again. I'll see to it that your commanding officer is made aware of your actions last night."

"Thank you, Sir," said Cannon.

"We just did our job, sir" said Jesse.

"Yes, you did – and damned well too. Now get the hell outa here before I change my mind."

Jesse moved toward the mighty-mite. "You heard the man, Larry. Let's get the hell outa here."

Cannon moved out at the double. When he arrived at the front of the mighty-mite, he stopped abruptly. "Oh, damn. Look what them gooks did to the lieutenant's mite. He's gonna have our asses for this one."

Jesse said, "*Our* asses? Hell, I was just along for the ride. You were drivin' it. I didn't run into the gook and mash the right front all to hell. And I damn sure didn't shoot all those holes in it."

"What about that blood? It's on your side."

Jesse shrugged. "Hell with it. Let's take the lieutenant's mite back to him and tell 'im we want one in better condition."

Cannon smiled as he sat behind the wheel. "Let's haul ass."

The following day found the First Section back up on Hill 280. Once again the daily routine of life on the hill set in and Jesse became bored.

The sight on gun two was found to be defective during one of the gun drills

240

and the weapon was deadlined until a replacement sight could be located. Gun one suffered a cracked inner ring during a firing exercise at maximum charge with HE-medium. The inner ring from gun two was used as a replacement part. One of the bi-pod legs on gun one was slightly bent so Jesse borrowed the better set of bi-pods from the rapidly deteriorating gun two.

"I'll take three cards," said Cue, throwing four dollars into the pot. As he picked up his cards, he said, "Hey, Indio, you hear about the Seabees down inside the perimeter?"

"No. What about 'em?" asked Jesse as he studied his cards.

"One of the grunts was telling me this morning that the Seabees got eight brand new mortars last week, sights and all."

"What the hell does a Seabee need with a mortar?" asked Cannon, who had folded his cards on the previous bet.

"Hell, I don't know. They're inside the perimeter, surrounded by a full regiment, and they get brand new mortars. We can't even get a sight," answered Cue.

"Maybe we could work some sort of trade with 'em," offered Jesse, looking up from his cards.

Cue laughed. "Look around. What the hell have we got? Hell, them guys have got everything. They live like a bunch of kings. Their baseplates are even painted battleship grey instead of olive drab, fer cryin' out loud."

Jesse raised an eyebrow. "Grey?"

"No shit, that's what this grunt told me. Grey."

"Who the hell ever heard of a grey baseplate?" asked Cannon.

"A Seabee, who da fuck else?" said Hill, who was on temporary assignment with the First Section.

"I can't believe even the navy would use grey paint in Vietnam," said Courtney.

"Me neither," agreed Jesse.

"There ain't but one way find out for sure and that's to see 'em for yourself," said Cue with a smile.

With a smile even bigger than Cue's, Jesse looked at him and said, "I believe you're right, Cue. We're just gonna have to get a close-up look at those guns in person."

"Shit, you can't get near da Seabee compound if dey even think you in da Crotch," said Hill with the voice of some experience.

"You're right, Hill," Jesse paused. "in the daylight."

"Whatchoo mean, 'in da daylight'? You sho as fuck ain't sneakin' up on dem trigger-happy muthas in da dark."

Jesse looked at Cue, his eyes smiling, then to Hill. "Yeah, I guess you're right, Hill. It was just a crazy, fleeting thought. I'll get over it."

"No shit. Dem crazy mo'fuckas almost shot me in broad daylight, and all I wuz doin' wuz tryin' t' trade 'em outa a few scraps o' chow," said Hill with a sad look.

Two mornings later, Jesse, Cue, Cannon, and Manny sat in the gun one pit as Hill approached, a puzzled yet determined look on his face. "Awright, Goddamnit, how'd you mo'fucka's get dem Seabees apart from dem fuckin' guns?"

Jesse exhaled a puff of smoke. "What the hell are you talkin' about, Hill? I

Stoney Livingston

swear, it's gettin' so you're beginnin' to worry me the way you talk in riddles all the time."

"Don'choo gimme no shit, Indio. You know zackly what da hell I'm talkin' 'bout. Now, all I wanna know is, how da fuck youse did it," sputtered Hill.

Cue laughed. "Hell, it was easy. All we did was walk down to the Seabee compound and explain our situation to 'em. We told 'em we needed a sight, an inner ring and a set of bi-pods. They felt so sorry for us that they gave us an outer ring and a tube extra."

Hill looked at Cue with a serious expression. "You really think I'm dat fuckin' stupid, don'choo? Where da hell is gun two?"

Slowly and deliberately, Jesse pointed down the hill in the direction of Phu Bai.

"You shittin' me - right?" asked Hill.

"Wrong," answered Cue.

"You mean dem dumb fuckin' swabbies traded guns?"

"They didn't have much choice. They were asleep. We left our gun so they couldn't bust us for stealin'. More like just tradin' up. You know, sorta like tradin' in an old car for a new one," explained Jesse.

"You crazy mo'fuckas sneaked into da middle o' da whole fuckin' regimental compound, carryin' a mortar, right?"

"You got it," said Cue.

"Booshit."

"Well, we *did* have a little help. A friend of mine in Bravo Company just happened to have the sentry duty where we crossed into the compound," said Cannon.

"You had ta have more help dan dat."

Manny said, "They're not shittin' you, Hill. I was with 'em. We got the sentry's position marked on the map and Indio walked us right up to it in the dark like he was going to Sunday morning church call."

Hill looked at the four smug marines. "I hope ta hell I nevva have ta be in your fuckin' squad." He was looking at Jesse. "You're about da craziest mo'fucka I ever seen, man. One a dese days you gonna get yo' fuckin' head blown inta da fuckin' atmosphere."

"Probably," agreed Jesse.

"Now we'll have t' shoot da damn thing. Dat's more work for me." He shook his head. "Thanks a bunch, you crazy fuckas." He turned and walked back to gun two, mumbling under his breath all the way. The men at gun one chuckled as they watched Hill's broad back move away from their position.

Two days later, First Section was advised they would be leaving the hill to rejoin the battalion. The 1st battalion, 3rd Marines would assume responsibility for Hill 280. The arrangement called for a swap of the respective units' guns. The First Section simply left their guns in place and took the relieving unit's guns.

Jesse reported the sight to gun one defective so the new unit kept one of its own sights.

"Why'd you report our sight as busted?" asked Cue as they walked down the winding trail from the top of Hill 280.

Jesse grinned as he carried the sight, safely tucked away in the olive drab

242

sight case. "How long do you think it would take them guys to figure out that this sight isn't exactly Crotch issue? When's the last time you saw a grey sight?"

"But what about the baseplate on gun two? Don'tcha think we should have taken that too?"

"Naw. Hill did a bang up job on the baseplate. It almost looked like the real thing. Besides, by the time they take it out of the ground we'll be long gone."

"Yeah, I guess you're right."

The relief mortar section came into view, trudging up the hill. "Keep a straight face, guys, and keep walking as soon as you get your piece," ordered Jesse.

The two sections met about halfway down the hill. As the men from the 1st Battalion, 4th Marines accepted the exchange mortars from their counterparts in the relieving unit, a voice said, "Jesse?"

It had been a long time since last he had heard his given name used and Jesse was slow to respond.

"Jesse Langley?" said the voice again.

This time Jesse looked in the direction of the voice. He recognized Bill Monroe from his outfit of 1963. He moved the short distance to him and shook his hand. "Bill! What the hell are you doin' here? It's good to see ya."

"What the hell am *I* doin' here? What the hell are *you* doing here? I heard you were over here. Somebody said Stubby saw you last monsoon but I didn't really believe it. I still don't believe it. I thought you were going back to Arizona and punch cows or something. Sure as hell never thought you'd ever re-up."

Jesse motioned to his squad. "Go ahead. I'll catch up." He turned to Monroe. "It's a long story, Bill. Have you heard anything from any of the old hands?"

Monroe dropped his eyes for an instant then returned his gaze to Jesse. "Yeah, and a lot of it's bad. Not the guys from old Two-Three. Most of them got out before this shit started, but the guys from One-Five were still pretty green when they got here. Hymie got it as he boarded a chopper about two months ago – a gook fifty caliber machine-gun."

"Dead?"

"Blew half his head off."

Jesse looked back up the hill. He turned his face back to Monroe. "Anybody else?"

Monroe nodded. "Yagel bought it big time outside of Da Nang. A gook recoilless blasted him to pieces."

Jesse felt a loss he couldn't explain, but he didn't have to. He looked into Monroe's eyes. "How about Guy, Wink, Doo, Little Luke, Frog and the rest?"

"I don't know about Frog, but Little Luke didn't like the idea of killing people so they let him transfer to the corpsmen. I don't know how they do that, but he's in the same outfit – the only difference is that he carries a medical kit instead of an M-14."

"How about the others? You hear anything?"

Monroe hesitated. "Yeah I heard all right. Doo stepped into a booby trap and got blown up pretty bad. He survived it but I hear he lost both legs."

"Goddamn, Bill. What the hell happened to that outfit?"

"You ain't heard the worst. Burp and Itch were on a patrol in a relatively secure area near Da Nang. Itch decided to mess around with Burp's mind. He yelled, 'Gooks' real loud behind Burp and Burp turned around and shot him with his pistol."

Jesse's chest heaved. "How is he?"

243

Stoney Livingston

"Dead. The bullet hit him in the throat. Burp tried to save him but Itch was probably dead before he hit the ground. The corpsmen couldn't get Burp off of Itch's body. He fought 'em off until they finally overpowered 'im. They took Itch away in a poncho and Burp in a straightjacket. I heard he was in a rubber room somewhere in California."

Jesse sat weakly down upon a rock near the edge of the trail. With trembling hands he lit a cigarette. Tears flowed unashamedly down his cheeks. He took a deep drag from his smoke.

Monroe tried to hold back his tears but he too was unsuccessful. As the salty droplets overflowed his eyes he reached out and hugged Jesse. "It was fucked. The whole situation was fucked. But there isn't anything you or I could have done, Jesse. The Crotch would have probably transferred you like they did me last Christmas, even if you had been in the outfit."

Monroe's words tended only to sadden Jesse further as he realized the man was probably right. There was most likely nothing he could have done. Nothing to help keep his friends alive. He said, "I gotta go, Bill." He stood shakily.

"I'm sorry, Jesse. I'd have thought you'd have heard some of the news."

"Nothing." He started down the hill, his squad long since out of sight. He turned briefly to face Monroe. "See ya, Bill. Keep yer ass low."

Monroe clenched his fist and extended his thumb upward. "You too, Jesse."

Jesse's heart weighed a ton as he walked slowly down the hill.

CHAPTER TWELVE: OREGON

The morning of March 20th, 1966 dawned overcast and windy as Alpha and Bravo companies, with mortar and machine-gun support, sat by their gear at the Phu Bai airstrip. The march from the tents at Phu Bai just before dawn had been brisk, windy and cool. They were prepared to embark on a two-company sweep near the village of Ap Chin An, a known VC stronghold. They waited in the chilling wind, frustrated and uncomfortable.

"Dey're sure makin' a big t'ing outa dis reinforced VC platoon," Ski said as he opened a can of c-ration cookies. "Christ, if dat's all it is, dey oughta just send a platoon a' our guys in ta kick some ass and get it over wit'. Dis bullshit a' sittin' aroun' da airstrip all day is fer da birds."

"They just wanta make sure we're wide-awake before they pick us up," said Rich Cummings, who sat on his pack next to Ski.

"You know the drill. Shit, we been through it a thousand times – hurry up and wait," said Cue as he cleaned up the last peach in his can of C-ration peaches.

"Yeah, but dis is gettin' ridicullus. Dis is da second day in a row. Hell, da wedder's worse today dan it wuz yesta'di. If we couldn't go yesta'di because a' da wedder, it don't take no genius ta figger out dat we can't go today."

"All the more reason we'll probably go today." Jesse exhaled a drag on his cigarette.

"We're not going any-damn-where today," said Sal. "We been here almost four hours already,"

"Well, if we don't go in the next hour or so, it'll be too late for today," Jesse said.

"Hey, Indio. Tell me something," Cue said.

"What?"

"This is the airstrip, right?"

"Yeah. So?"

"So why are the choppers never at the airstrip? Where the hell do they stay? Out in the jungle?"

"That's a real good question, Cue. I'll bring it up at the next meeting of the Joint Chiefs of Staff."

"Well, think about it. I don't ever remember us going to an LZ or an airstrip that we didn't have to wait for the choppers."

"Dat's because da LZ's and airstrips we frequent are in lower-class neighborhoods. Dose airwing guys don't mind dropping in fer a visit, but dey're not da kinds a places dey'd wanna stay," Ski explained.

A voice down the line shouted, "Grab your gear. Saddle up. Here come the Taxis."

"I'll be damned," Ski said softly as he stared up at the approaching Choctaw helicopters. "Maybe we *will* make dis sweep taday."

Alpha and Bravo Companies boarded the first wave of helicopters. Within fifteen minutes of the first wave departure, a second group of helicopters arrived to load the First and Second Sections of the 81 mortar platoon and all headquarters personnel.

Once their helicopter was airborne, the 1st squad, First Section, 81 mortar platoon fell into an uneasy silence. They had all been in helicopters many times before and the feeling of helplessness was always the same. Inside the slow-moving Choctaw, they felt like ducks in a shooting gallery. The one thing foremost in everyone's mind was getting out of the helicopter alive. The battle would take care of itself later.

Jesse, who knelt by the open door of the helicopter, noticed the crew chief-gunner nod as he responded to a message in his headset and wondered why he had nodded. The pilot sure as hell couldn't see him. The gunner tugged on Jesse's shirtsleeve and leaned close to be heard above the sound of the engine. "We've got a hot LZ. About two minutes to target."

Jesse nodded. He turned to face the men inside the vibrating, old helicopter and shouted, "We've got a hot LZ. When we hit the ground let's get out on the double. Debark clockwise. Less than two minutes to target."

The men shuffled about, shifting their gear and weapons so all that need be done at landing was to step off the airship and be rid of their exposed confinement.

A stray small arms round penetrated the helicopter, striking the base plate of the mortar. The round ricocheted from the base plate and out the side of the Choctaw, tearing an oblong hole in the sheet metal.

"Get this goddamn thing on the ground! We're like sittin' ducks." Sal's voice cracked.

"Take it easy Sal. We'll be down in less than a minute," Rich said.

"I'm not waiting a goddamn minute!" He grabbed the outer ring of the base plate and moved for the open door.

Jesse met him halfway. In a crouch, his M-14 at port arms, he shoved Sal back to his previous position. "Sal, I said we're debarking clockwise. Since no one else seems inclined to step out at five hundred feet, you're just gonna have to wait your turn."

"We're sitting ducks up here!"

"What the hell you gonna use for a parachute?" asked Jesse.

Rich put his hand on Sal's shoulder. "Take it easy, Sal. We'll be down in a few seconds."

Sal shrugged Rich's hand from his shoulder and pouted silently.

When the Choctaw landed, they exited the helicopter quickly, moving to the nearest favorable position to locate a mortar. The gun was set up, stakes out and ready to fire in less than two minutes. The crew then went feverishly to work, digging a more permanent gun position. Small arms fire was intense but it appeared to be six or seven hundred yards to the northeast of the gun. Stray rounds buzzed overhead, doing much more mental than physical harm.

"Land line to FDC is up," Whitman reported to Jesse.

Jesse picked up the field phone and rang FDC. "Gun one is up."

"Roger gun one. Fire mission."

"Standby," Jesse said into the phone. He turned to his gun crew. "Fire mission." Back into the phone he said, "Go ahead."

FDC replied, "Fire mission. Troops in fortified tree line. One round Willie Peter. Will adjust. Charge three. Deflection 2917. Elevation 1110. At my command."

Jesse repeated the mission as he was given the commands. In twenty-five seconds, Rich shouted, "Gun one up."

"Gun one up," Jesse repeated into the phone.

"Roger gun one. Standby."

The seconds ticked by, then the minutes. Still FDC did not give the command to fire. When five minutes had elapsed, Jesse said, "Stand easy on the gun. Let me find out what's going on." He rang the field phone.

"FDC. Go ahead."

"Bailey, this is Indio. What the hell is going on? Do we fire the mission or not?"

After a short pause, Bailey replied, "Mark that mission as number 101. Keep the dope ready. We have another fire mission."

"Stand by," said Jesse into the phone as he marked the settings in his pocket notebook with the numbers 101.

Once again FDC gave deflection, elevation, round and charge. When Jesse advised that gun one was up, FDC advised him to mark the new dope as mission 102 and then proceeded with a third mission. This process continued until pre-selected mission 105 dope was recorded.

"Gun one, fire mission."

"Standby," said Jesse into the field phone. He turned to Rich Cummings. "Hey, Rich, take over the land line. I'm goin' up to FDC to find out why'n the hell they've got us running gun drill when we oughta be shootin'."

"Gotcha," replied Rich, taking the phone from Jesse's hand.

As he followed the comm-wire towards FDC, Jesse heard Rich repeating the new commands to his gun crew.

The FDC tent was a bustle of activity. Radios crackled and squelched. He could hear the voices of the forward observers for Alpha and Bravo Companies calling in fire missions. He did not hear either FO request any mission to be marked as a pre-selected, on-call mission. From what he could ascertain, these were desperate requests for mortar fire – right now.

"Hey, Gunny, why aren't we shootin'? Sounds to me like they need some help out there."

Gunny Reyes looked up at Jesse from his field table, taking his attention from the map he had been studying.

"Indio. What the hell are you doing here? You're supposed to be with your squad."

"Hell, they're just runnin' gun drill. They don't need me for that. Why ain't we shootin'?"

Reyes studied Jesse for a moment then addressed him in the clear, crisp, military manner he reserved for speaking to someone of lesser rank who dared to question what he was doing. "It looks like we've stepped into a little bit of shit. The VC strength is a lot greater than estimated. The colonel wants us to hold off on the mortars until we're re-supplied with ammo. Now get back to your squad. I've got enough to worry about here without you stirring up a bucket of shit."

"But, Gunny. It sounds to me like Pat with Alpha could use the help now."

"Let me worry about that. You get back to your gun."

Stoney Livingston

"Okay, Gunny. I'm gone."

Only three strides from the FDC tent he noticed several groups of marines approaching from the direction of the Alpha Company line. There were five groups of three or four men each. As they drew closer Jesse could see that each cluster of marines carried a wounded man in a poncho.

Puffing from exertion, a man in the leading group shouted, "How about a hand?"

Several marines, including Jesse, ran to their aid. As he relieved a man holding the corner of a bloody poncho, the man said, "We got a whole lot more casualties. We need some help gettin' em back here." Without further ceremony, the man left to return to the Alpha Company line.

From FDC, it was approximately one hundred yards to battalion headquarters, which had been hastily arranged in an old Pagoda. Outside the Pagoda corpsmen were already attending to the earliest casualties. The corpsmen instructed them where to place the latest batch of wounded. After depositing the wounded man he had helped carry, Jesse returned to the FDC tent.

He stepped into the tent and up to Gunny Reyes' field desk. "Hey, Guns. The guys in Alpha need some help gettin' their wounded back here. Since we ain't shootin', I'd like to give 'em a hand."

Reyes looked up at him. "I should have known. All right, Indio, but, remember, you're in 81's not a rifle company. When that work's done, report back to your section."

"Aye, Aye, Guns. Would you notify my squad?"

"I'll take care of it."

The smell of cordite hung in the air like a California fog. The blast of an occasional enemy mortar round was accented by the steady reports of 30 cal. machine-guns from within the enemy tree line just three hundred yards from where Jesse crouched. He cursed his battalion commander for getting them into this mess. Voices on his right caused him to looked in that direction and see another marine motioning to him, waving frantically. Jesse left his position and moved to the other man at the double. "What's up?" he asked as he approached within earshot..

The marine, who he now recognized as a corporal from the first platoon, answered, "We've got dead and wounded about fifty yards up the trail. How about some help?"

Jesse bolted in the direction indicated, at a dead run, leaving the corporal to guide the next man who might venture up the trail. He was aware of the crack of rifle bullets as they passed within inches of his head from what seemed to be every direction. He wondered about that.

A mud-smeared marine on his knees about twenty yards in front of him, protected from the enemy tree line by a small rice paddy dike, waved his arms and shouted frantically.

Wish I could hear what the hell he's saying. Jesse became aware of a ringing in his ears he hadn't noticed earlier.

In order to get to the marine who was waving to him, he would have to expose himself to the enemy as he crossed an intersecting trail that led directly to the enemy tree line. He hit the trail at full gallop and dove across it, sliding in the mud like he was attempting to steal third base. His skid stopped only inches from the man who had been waving at him. Even before he hit the mud on the other side of the

248

trail, he felt the wind churn at his back. When he struck the ground he then heard the report of the 50 cal. machine-gun.

He craned his head back and looked up at the muddy marine before him. "Jesus Christ! Why didn't you tell me they had a fifty set up on the trail?"

"What the hell did you think I was waving my arms for? The exercise?"

"You're Sergeant Wilkes, aren't you?"

"Yeah. Where the hell you from?"

"81's. I figured you guys could use some help out here so here I am – for whatever-the-hell that's worth."

"We've got four dead and seven wounded on this side of the trail. And we've got to get 'em back to the battalion CP fast or some of the wounded won't make it."

"Gotta get rid of that fifty first." Jesse nodded at the enemy-held tree line.

"That's how we got three of the wounded and two of the dead."

Jesse peered over the top of the dike, in the direction of the tree line, for a second or two before dropping back down into the mud. "Where the hell is it?"

Sergeant Wilkes took his bayonet from its scabbard and began to draw in the mud, explaining his diagram as he went.

When Wilkes completed his diagram, Jesse said, "Give me a rocket launcher and an a-gunner and I'll take a shot at it." Jesse couldn't believe he had said it but it was too late now. It was out of his mouth.

Wilkes considered a moment. "We got no rocket launchers but we've got a whole shit-pot full of LAWS."

"You mean that plastic toy?" Jesse had seen the Light Anti-tank Weapon but was unfamiliar with its operation.

"That's right."

Jesse shrugged. "Give me one and show me how to use it and I'll give it a try."

Wilkes pulled a LAW from a pile of rubbage – at least it looked like a pile of rubbage – until Jesse examined it more closely. He shuddered involuntarily when he recognized the body of a marine. "What the hell hit him?"

"The fifty," said Wilkes gruffly.

Jesse stared for a moment at the crushed skull; the bloody arm dangling from the torso at the shoulder by a thread of skin, the internal organs scattered about the front of the blood-soaked utility jacket. "Jesus," was all he could think to say.

For the next three or four minutes Wilkes explained the operation of the LAW while Jesse tried to pay attention and keep the mangled marine's body from his thoughts. Shortly, with his newfound knowledge, Jesse tucked the LAW under his right arm and surveyed the ground between where he knelt and the tree line. "There's sure one big reinforced platoon in there."

"You sure as hell don't have to go out there. We could always pack the wounded south and into the trees."

Jesse shook his head. "I'll give it a whirl. Just let me eyeball the situation and work up my nerve." The two men fell silent.

For the first time since leaving the helicopter, Jesse's heartbeat made itself felt in his temples. He wondered if he could go through with this insane gesture but, even while he doubted, he knew he was going. *Why the hell am I like that? Is everybody that way or am I the only person in the world who forces himself to do something by first saying that I'm gonna do it, then having to do it just to save face?*

249

Stoney Livingston

His mind wandered for a moment or two. Fear clutched at his throat and his heartbeat was a base drum gone wild.

He would have to cover about a hundred-and-fifty yards in that open rice paddy with nothing for cover but a few dirt trails, ten to eighteen inches above the level of the rice paddies. He scanned the paddies for a route, picked what he thought was his best bet, then chose an alternate. He was ready.

With his M-14 rifle in his left hand and the LAW tucked under his right arm, still in the folded position, he dashed into the rice paddy, running in a zig-zag pattern, his boots making sucking noises each time he pulled them from the muck. He covered more than fifty yards before he made his first stop. He fell to the thin mud of the paddy and lay prone, his helmet pressed against the foot of ground that rose from the paddy to protect his body from the bullets. He breathed heavily, gathering strength for the next rush. *Why wasn't I hit? Jesus! With all the lead in the air, I shouldn't have gotten fifty feet, much less fifty yards!* His first rush had gone almost unnoticed in all of the confusion. They would be waiting for him now.

He crawled laterally for twenty yards, took a deep breath and stood for his next rush. He zig-zagged until he figured the odds were that his time in the erect position was ticking way past the allowable limit and that any second a bullet from that fifty would slam into his body. He wanted to fall but was nowhere near a dike. He gritted his teeth and continued to slosh through the muck. Only when his chest caught fire and his legs failed did he fall into the soft, sticky mud of the rice paddy. As he struck the mud, he realized he was short of the dirt dike by almost fifteen yards.

Frantically he crawled for the protection afforded by that precious foot of earth. He crawled until his chest seemed to burn with the hottest fires in hell. The muck and goo in his mouth and nostrils were constricting the flow of oxygen to his lungs at a time when he needed it most. Bullets thudded into the muck around him, splattering him with more of the slime that was called earth. His helmet struck the dike. He lay there for several moments, gasping for breath, his chest heaving then caving in as his lungs clutched oxygen from the air. He rolled onto his back, surveying the ground already covered.

He smiled. He had covered more than seventy yards on his last rush. How? He had only planned to cover about forty-five or fifty. He wondered if he had gone to sleep or passed out. Maybe he was dead or dreaming. For almost five minutes he lay there, not knowing if he had the nerve to go those last few yards to get into position. *What the hell. I've come this far, I might as well go the rest of the way. Damn this LAW is gettin' heavy!*

He crawled left for quite some distance then stopped for a short rest. Suddenly a volley of small arms fire broke out from the Alpha Company line. Jesse jumped from his protective barrier and made his next rush. After gaining several yards, he dove headlong into the paddy, burying his face in the mud. The machine-gun fire was deafening. *Jesus! Don't they have any respect for machine-gun barrels?*

His left wrist exploded in pain as his M-14 was wrenched from his grasp. He searched his wrist and hand but found no blood, then pulled the M-14 from the mucky water of the paddy and examined it closely . It had been struck on the bolt by a rifle bullet. The bolt had been smashed and, as the bullet ricocheted, it had ripped the rear sight from the rifle. Quickly he discarded the M-14 in the mud and continued to crawl through the paddy.

250

The rice paddy mud churned for fifteen or twenty yards in every direction from his crawling, muddy, sweat-soaked body. The thud of the 50 cal. machine-gun as the heavy slugs ripped the air inches above his head was deafening. *Just like advanced infantry training.* His lungs felt like they would burst into flames at any moment but he knew that, without oxygen, combustion wasn't possible. His throat was dry and swallowing was difficult.

Abruptly he could go no further. He was there. A dike rose eighteen inches above the paddy to protect him from the onslaught of lead.

He sucked much needed oxygen into his lungs, the thick air cascading into his body with an eerie, wheezing sound. After a short rest he carefully opened the LAW. He didn't trust anything made of plastic. It didn't seem right that a weapon made of plastic – no matter what kind of plastic – was suitable for a man to carry into combat. Despite its supposed destructive powers, it looked and felt like a toy.

He raised his head above the cover of the trail and quickly sighted in on what he thought to be the machine-gun position. Small splotches of mud began to lift from the trail and the surrounding rice paddy as the enemy gunners zeroed in on his helmet. He squeezed the trigger. Nothing happened. Jesse dropped behind the cover of the trail and rolled onto his back, cradling the LAW on his chest to keep it out of the mud, flinching as round after round of small-arms fire struck the dike and the paddy nearby.

Jesse remembered Wilkes had told him he could re-cock the weapon one time. If it didn't fire after a second cocking, he was to destroy it. He re-cocked the LAW, careful not to place his hands directly fore or aft of the hollow tube.

"Well, this is it, you miserable son-of-a-bitch. You'd better do your thing this time." He mumbled as he rolled onto his stomach, placed the LAW into the firing position and stuck his head above the cover of the trail. This time he was oblivious to the hail of bullets. He didn't even hear the heavy report of the 50 cal. machine-gun he knew was belching at him from within the tree line. Slowly he squeezed the trigger, careful not to waver from his target a mere hundred and fifty yards in front of him.

The LAW misfired again. With the weapon still resting atop his shoulder, Jesse closed his eyes and slowly let his tired body slip behind the dike. He lay there for several moments, his mind unable to accept what had just transpired. He took the LAW from his shoulder and stared at it for a moment. He said softly, "Why?" The LAW didn't respond.

He tried to remember if he had done everything exactly as he had been instructed. After a full minute of deliberation and inspection of the unfamiliar weapon, he concluded he had followed procedure to the letter. He wished he knew more about the LAW but wishing wasn't going to make anything better. Nothing was going to make anything better. He grasped the LAW by one end of the tube, stood in full view of the enemy, and tossed it in the direction of the 50 cal. machine-gun. He fell behind the cover of the small dike, after prominently displaying the middle finger of his right hand, untouched amid the hail of lead.

When the LAW struck the ground fifteen yards in front of his position, it fired, sending its 66mm rocket in an unknown direction for an unknown distance, the backblast splaying mud for twenty-five yards in all directions.

"That figures," he said, spitting mud and hoping the round had not gone south, towards Alpha Company's position.

Now what, hero? You sure screwed that scene up. What would John

Stoney Livingston

Wayne do now? Hell, the damn LAW wouldn't have misfired a second time for John Wayne.

Suddenly, Jesse's blood turned cold as he heard the faint whish-whish of falling mortar rounds. The sounds grew louder and louder until Jesse thought it would deafen him. Fear constricted his throat muscles. The only way a man could hide from a mortar round was to be underground – far underground.

The rice paddy erupted into geysers of muddy water and chunks of earth as the mortar rounds impacted. Jesse put his arms over his helmet and buried his face in the muck, waiting for the end to come. After what seemed an eternity, he lifted his face from the mud long enough to draw a deep breath, then buried it again. Shrapnel whizzed overhead and the ground trembled and turned liquid as more rounds exploded.

It was gone as quickly as it had come. The barrage left only the scarred rice paddies as proof that mortars had made their presence felt. Even those scars were disappearing as the filthy water of the paddies oozed into the pockmarks, filling them and making them invisible.

Jesse slowly and almost imperceptibly lifted his face from the slimy mud, breathing as softly and as quietly as his tortured body would allow. He felt his heart beating wildly from somewhere within his body. The beat felt as though it were coming from his throat and at the same time from low in his intestinal tract, not from where he knew damn well his heart should be. His ears rang so loudly he could hear nothing else, though he was sure the battle raged all around him. He was unaware of any sound save the ringing in his ears. He was also unaware that his once green uniform was a solid dirty brown, or that his eyes were completely closed with mud or that his mouth was full of the filth that was called soil. It took several moments for Jesse to become aware of any of these things.

That goddamn ringing. Why in the hell doesn't it stop?

Jesse's chest constricted with a deep inner pain caused by fear as he realized he couldn't see. He wiped his eyes, but his muddy hands only worsened his predicament. The uniform was no help either. He teetered on the cliff of panic.

He opened his pistol magazine pouch, extracted a magazine, pushed all seven rounds into the mud with his thumb, and scraped around his eyes with the lip of the magazine. Shortly he could see well enough to satisfy himself the enemy was not advancing through the paddy. He placed the empty magazine back into the pouch, rolled onto his back and lay there, staring into the cloudy sky.

Where is the artillery? Where is the air support? Where are the naval guns? Why haven't our own 81 mm mortars opened up? That poge-ass colonel really screwed this operation up. No prep fires. No support. No resupply. No nothin'. His heart rate began to subside. Breathing became less difficult.

He stared at the clouds, recalling the briefing that all squad leaders had attended at 1800 hours only the day before. He could still hear Reyes:

"We jump off at dawn. It's about a twenty minute flight by helicopter, then we debark the choppers about seven hundred yards south of this tree line." He pointed to a contour map. "We set up the First Section here and the Second Section here, about 900 yards from the enemy positions.

"Ammo corporals have the amount and type of ammo we'll be taking in with us. After we break up here, they'll get with you squad leaders for distribution." He paused. "Any questions?"

"How big did you say dis gook position is?" asked Ski.

252

"A reinforced platoon."

"Not dat I'm doubtin' anybody's word, but where did dis information come from?"

"I don't know where they got it, but it came from S-2."

Ski let out a groan that was echoed by several others.

"Gunny?" said Jesse.

"You have a question, Indio?"

"Yeah. I see a simple plan where two line companies and two sections of 81's are going to beat up a platoon of gooks, but I don't see any support. Where's arty, or how about air or naval guns?'

Reyes appeared a little put out but answered in his usual crisp manner. "We'll be out of arty's range but there'll be a cruiser sitting off the coast and we should be just in range of her 8-inchers. As for air support, I'm not sure. As of an hour ago, we haven't got any definite answer from division. These things are put on a priority basis and, at this point, a reinforced platoon doesn't rate very high on the priority list. Besides, we should have more than enough support with our 81s."

"Is dis new battalion commander stupid or what? How long has he been in a line outfit?" Ski asked.

Sergeant Tuleano, who was also a bit dissatisfied with the battle plan, said, "This is his first command. He's been in G-3 for eighteen years."

This set up a chorus of complaints from the squad leaders.

Reyes held up his hands. "If we run into some shit out there, we'll get the support. Colonel Soliman is a marine and a damn good one. He's going to be right there with us. If we need it, you can bet your ass we'll get the whole damn airwing."

Jesse felt the mud drying on his face as he furrowed his brow. *I'd just like to see one little Skyhawk. I'm not greedy. I don't want the whole airwing, just one little Skyhawk with a belly full of napalm to fry that tree line so I can get out of this goddamn rice paddy. Where is that cruiser with her eight-inch guns?*

If that's a reinforced platoon in there, I'll kiss the battalion commander's ass in Times Square and give him a month to draw a crowd. We could use a whole damn bunch of reinforced platoons on our side. I wonder just how big that outfit really is?

Slowly, awareness crept back to him. The sounds of battle continued to rage around him. His ears still had a constant ringing in them but at least it had settled down to a less bothersome level. His mind left Viet Nam again.

As he lay on his back in the putrid mud, Jesse was confused by a myriad of thoughts, all seemingly flowing through his semi-consciousness simultaneously. He caught visions of his Triumph motorcycle as he drove recklessly down a canyon in eastern Arizona, a boxing opponent in an amateur fight when he was fourteen years old. His old high school loomed clearly in the visions of his mind. He saw a football flying towards him in a perfect spiral. What a catch! And the open field running. Touchdown. Sixty-five yards! Then there was Shannon. There was always Shannon. This was another stupid stunt he hoped she would never hear about. Who would tell her? There was comfort in that thought at least.

The staccato bursts of AK47's from the enemy tree line, mixed with the intermittent sound of semi-automatic rifles, jerked Jesse back into the rice paddy. The AK47s were bad but the sound most adrenaline inspiring to him was the heavy thud of the .50 cal. machine-gun.

He looked south, where what was left of Alpha Company continued to hold the road. Small arms fire from the marines was all but non-existent, a testimonial to Jesse that ammunition was almost gone.

The dead and wounded in the rice paddy entered his consciousness and he tried to count those within his range of vision. From where he lay, he counted six but knew there were more in other sections of the paddy, obscured from his vision by the small dikes. Of the casualties he counted, he could not be sure how many were alive. There was almost no movement from any of them.

The mud protecting Jesse from the tree line exploded inches above his head. The heavy crack of the .50 cal. followed. Jesse rolled to his right ten yards, expecting the fifty to end his life with each movement. He stopped to catch his breath and clear his vision. The fifty again began to chop away his mud barrier and he rolled further right, keeping his helmet as close as possible to the small dike. After ten yards he stopped to clear his head and draw in much needed oxygen. The fifty gave him no rest. He continued to roll and squirm rapidly to his right, toward the tree line. Suddenly his body slammed into something solid.

It felt like a brick wall, whatever it was. All breath was forced from his lungs and for a few seconds he couldn't move. When he was again able to breathe, he searched his body for a wound but could find none. Through the muddy film covering his eyes the blurry image of a small dike formed. He reached out and touched the earth, which rose about a foot above the paddy. He had rolled into the dike with such force that the wind had been knocked out of him.

"Damn," he mumbled. He would have to go over the small footpath to continue his roll. He looked south towards Alpha Company's defensive line, then east at the tree line running diagonally from his lower right to the enemy position located to his direct front. *I wonder if they've got anybody in there?* He was exhausted, thirsty, half blinded, ears ringing, and generally fed-up. He was about as close as a man can get to not caring one way or the other what the hell happened to him. He took one more quick look in the direction of Alpha Company, shook his head, took a deep breath, and made his move, vaulting the dike and sloshing through the paddy in the direction of the tree line.

He broke into the trees on his right at a dead run, bullets whizzing all about him, tree branches slapping him in the face. He moved deeper into the untested tree line, his most important objective now the defensive line of Alpha Company.

As he moved stealthily through the thick growth of trees and vines he was aware of the small arms fire from the enemy tree line but realized he heard nothing coming from what he hoped was Alpha Company's direction. *Wouldn't that be a laugh if I went the wrong way? Hell, that small arms fire could be Alpha Company. Maybe they were re-supplied with ammo.*

Jesse paused in a half crouch as he pondered the possibility of an error in his dead reckoning. The jungle growth was so thick as to prohibit a view of the sky except for a patch now and then. Even without the trees, the overcast was so heavy and so low he couldn't make south from north without a compass. How could he be sure he was going in the proper direction? He put aside any thought of returning to the rice paddy for a quick look. If he didn't know whether the small arms fire was friend or foe, he also didn't know whether to go left or right to find the paddy. His instincts told him he was properly directed, yet he became less and less sure of his instinct as he considered the possibility of walking into the enemy fortifications.

His doubts about his instincts were suddenly and completely eradicated when he heard the crack-thud of the .50 cal. machine-gun. He knew only too well that Alpha Company had no fifty caliber machine-gun on this operation.

He turned and looked in the direction from which the sound of the heavy machine-gun had originated. "Thanks, asshole," he muttered softly, then turned and continued southeast in the heavily wooded tree line.

Jesse's stealth and circuitous movement made it extremely difficult for him to know with any certainty how far he had traveled in the proper direction but he knew the tree line did not extend to the road, rather, it curled back to the north.

As he moved to his right flank, the trees began to thin. He could see almost thirty yards to his front. Quite suddenly he was at the edge of the tree line, reconnoitering the terrain before him. A rice paddy adjoined the tree line, moving to his left at least to a bend in the tree line where it turned due east then northeast. The elevated road and the Alpha Company tree line was a little more than one hundred yards south of his position. Jesse knew he was not in view of the enemy position but he wasn't certain about the marines.

If he ran straight south the hundred or so yards to the road and into the tree line behind it, made a ninety degree right turn and proceeded another two hundred yards, he estimated he would be on Alpha Company's extreme right flank. He knew the men on the flank were watching for movement right where he stood. The enemy may have missed him a thousand times at a much closer range but when it came to long-distance shooting, Jesse had confidence in the marines. There was no doubt in his mind some sharpshooter would dust him if he ventured into the open from his current position – providing the marines had any ammo left. He wasn't willing to take the chance.

Jesse re-entered the cover provided by the trees and moved east for almost one-half mile. As the tree line veered northeast, he left its cover and moved south, across the rice paddy and the road, quickly and without incident. It seemed for a short time that the war didn't exist, even though he could still hear the small arms fire in the distance.

He moved west in the tree line, parallel to and south of the elevated road. He moved almost casually at first but as he approached what he hoped was Alpha Company's position, he became increasingly cautious. He heard the crack of an M-14 a hundred yards to his front. He stopped and quietly assumed the prone position. The M-14 had not been firing in his direction, but toward the enemy tree line. Jesse knew that particular M-14 did not belong to the flank guard who would be silently waiting. If the M-14 was only one hundred yards from his current position, he knew he was considerably closer than that to a listening post on the flank.

How do I manage to get their attention without getting my head blown off? It was a reasonable question to be sure but Jesse could not come up with a sure-fire way of introducing himself without risking his life in the process. He tried to put himself in their position. After several minutes of intense deliberation and even more intense listening, he came to the conclusion that no way in hell would the guy outside the lines live longer than it took to throw a grenade.

He heard movement to his right front less than twenty yards from where he lay. *Damn!* His reaction was spontaneous. "One of you shitheads got a smoke? Mine are all wet."

There was a loud rustling movement. "Who the fuck said that?"

Still in the prone position, Jesse replied, "Me, goddamnit. And don't be shootin' and throwin' things at me. I'm Langley from 81's and I'm tired and thirsty,

255

and my goddamn cigarettes are wet. We gonna bullshit all day, or you gonna lighten up and let me walk in?"

A second voice replied, "Brooklyn."

Jesse's throat became instantly dry. "Goddamnit, don't throw that password shit at me. We didn't have a password for this chickenshit operation when we started, and we wouldn't need one now if that poge-ass, office clerk of a colonel hadn't been so goddamn stupid."

The first voice said, "What are you, some kind of fucking general?"

"It don't take a general to recognize the obvious," replied Jesse.

"Who the hell did you say you were?" asked the first voice.

"Langley, 1st squad, 1st section, 81's, 1st Battalion, 4th Marines. You may know me as Indio."

The second voice expressed recognition. "You that crazy bastard that hunts food at night?"

The first voice whispered, "No shit?"

"Yeah, that's me. Now, you gonna let me in, or do I have to whip all three of yore asses?"

The first voice again. "Three?"

"Yeah, three. Tell leadfoot over there on my left flank to back off or I'll pretend he's VC and shoot his nuts off."

The first voice answered. "All right, goddamnit, but put both your hands high in the air and move real slow."

Jesse complied with the request. One of the marines was twenty yards directly in front of him, a second about four yards to the left of the first. The third was about twenty yards to Jesse's left.

The second voice said, "Put your hands down. You look like shit. C'mon in."

Jesse dropped his hands and approached the nearest marine. "I feel like it. You got a dry cigarette?"

The three marines gathered around Jesse. One offered a cigarette. Jesse looked disgustingly at the offering. "I may be beggin', but I don't have to smoke a damn menthol cigarette." He looked at the other two. "One of you guys got a Camel?"

The tallest of the two replied, "Yeah, I got a pack a' them horse turds in my C's this morning." He dug into his pack, found the cigarettes and tossed them to Jesse.

"Thanks."

"You can have the whole pack. Them damn things'll kill ya."

Jesse nodded in appreciation as he lit a cigarette with his Zippo lighter. *Damn thing still works. I gotta remember to write to them about that.*

"Where the hell did you come from? What were you doing outside our perimeter?" asked the smallest of the three men, glancing first at Jesse, then lifting his head to peer out at the flank.

Jesse took a deep drag on his cigarette and pondered the question. He exhaled, watching the smoke as it dissipated into the air. He shook his head slowly and said, "You wouldn't believe me if I told you."

"Wait a minute. You're not that crazy who ran into the rice paddy with that LAW are you?" It was the smaller man again, still watching the flank.

Jesse nodded slowly, exhaled another puff of smoke and said, "Yeah, but I won't tell anybody if you don't."

256

There was a pause, then all four laughed softly.

The smallest of the three said, "Well, hell, it was a damn good try. I'm proud to know ya. My name's Jacoby. Mike Jacoby. The tall one there is Maxwell, but we call him Max, and the one with the baby fat still on his face is Stillwater. He's been in the Nam about a week."

Maxwell and Stillwater nodded in unison.

"Nice to meet you guys. Appreciate the hell outa you not blowin' my head off without a parlay."

"Least we could do for an almost-hero," said Jacoby.

Jesse field-stripped his cigarette, gave them what intelligence he had been able to gather, shook hands with each of them, and continued his trek westward, using the elevated road as cover.

As he passed to the rear of the men laying on the embankment on the south side of the road, Jesse looked for Sergeant Wilkes but was unable to pick him out. Even though the company had very little ammunition, each man constantly changed his position and fired an occasional round toward the enemy tree line. The reasoning behind this type of tactic was to present a larger force to the enemy. Jesse wasn't convinced that it would completely dupe the VC, but thought it wasn't such a bad idea under the circumstances.

He crossed the trail covered by the .50 cal. machine-gun but this time he was low on the south bank of the slightly elevated road and his passing went unnoticed by the enemy gunner. He felt the heat rise to his face as he contemplated the comical figure he must have presented to both sides as he made his wild charge into the rice paddy. He paused for a moment then continued west toward the 81 mortar section.

The din of battle, though still quite perceptible, faded somewhat as he approached ten PF troops. In order for this mission to be called a joint operation, the Vietnamese militiamen had been attached to Alpha Company. *Three hundred fifty marines and ten PF's. Some joint operation.* As he walked through the group, he noticed they appeared to be on a rest break, smoking or talking. One read a pocket novel.

Jesse stopped and concentrated on where he was, as opposed to where he was going. Anger swelled inside him as he realized that each and every uniform was clean. *These guys have probably never gotten any closer to the fighting than right here. One of 'em is even readin' a goddamn pocket book while the marines are on the line, almost out of ammunition.* He quickly checked out the weapons: one Browning Automatic Rifle (BAR), five .30 cal. carbines and four M-I Garands.

"Anybody here speak English?"

Almost no response, though the man reading the book did look up momentarily.

Frustration was about to overcome common sense but Jesse waited it out. After a few seconds passed, he spoke again. "The defensive line is a little low on ammo. They could use your help."

Still no response.

Frustration won out. Jesse walked up to one of the PFs sitting next to an M-1 Garand, which leaned against a tree. He picked up the rifle and quickly pulled back the operating rod handle. *There's not even a round in the chamber!* He sniffed the receiver, then released the bolt, chambering a round. He looked at the little Vietnamese militiamen. "This goddamn rifle hasn't even been fired today."

257

The smaller man, still sitting, looked up at Jesse and smiled.

Stupid Son-of-a-bitch. Jesse pointed to the rifle then to the PF, then to the direction of the Alpha Company line.

The PF shook his head in the negative.

Jesse then pointed to the rifle, the man's cartridge belt, then to himself, then the defensive line.

The PF shook his head again.

"That does it." He pointed the rifle at the little man's chest. "All right, shithead, take off that cartridge belt." He touched the cartridge belt with the barrel of the loaded M-I. The other PFs realized something out of the ordinary was taking place and began to move in Jesse's direction. He stepped behind the disarmed PF.

One of the approaching PFs chambered a round into his carbine. Jesse swung his Garand to bear on the man with the chambered round. He slapped the Garand with his open hand on the forearm stock, pointed to the approaching man's carbine, then to the ground. "De sung xuong!"

The man stopped but did not discard his weapon. Jesse once again slapped his rifle. The man refused to drop his weapon.

Jesse fired the Garand. The bullet struck the ground only inches from the man's leading foot, splaying mud onto his clean uniform. The little man dropped the carbine.

Jesse slapped his rifle stock three times in rapid succession, panning the remaining eight PF's with his M-1. He pointed to the ground. They complied with his request. Once the weapons were safely out of reach of the militiamen, he waved them back several paces. Soon he was again on his way to the 81 section with four M-1 Garand cartridge belts, full of eight-round clips, and one M-1 Garand rifle. He had taken what appeared to him the best of the four rifles.

"Cam on ong," he said to the bewildered PF troops as he left.

"Where the hell you been?" asked Rich, as Jesse approached gun one.

"You wouldn't believe me if I told you. Have they let you fire a mission yet?"

"Hell no. We keep changing the dope on the gun every three or four minutes, but they don't give us the order to fire. Jesus. You look like hell. What the hell are you doin' with that M-1 and all those cartridge belts?"

"I took 'em from somebody who wasn't using 'em. Rich, you wouldn't believe it. Alpha is almost out of ammo. There must be a million gooks in that tree line. They've got AK-47's, machine-guns, mortars, recoilless rifles, and at least one heavy machine-gun. There's dead and wounded strung out all over the rice paddies, and every last one I saw was a marine. No Gooks. They need mortar support now."

"Jesus! We knew it was bad by the number of ponchos coming by us with dead and wounded, but we didn't know it was that bad."

"Trust me. It ain't lookin' too good. If Alpha doesn't get some ammo quick, they'll be throwin' rocks. Any resupply come in yet?"

Rich shook his head. "Nothing. We haven't seen a chopper since they dropped us here."

A voice said. "You men there – lend a hand. We got wounded coming in."

Several of the men in the 81 section ran forward to meet the tired clusters of marines moving toward their position. Each cluster consisted of three or four men carrying a poncho, hammock style, with a wounded marine suspended inside. Keeping all four corners of the poncho taut and moving in unison was a difficult task,

Forever Patriots

and the men were exhausted as a result of their labors.

Jesse approached one of the ponchos and relieved a grateful marine on one of the corners. Without speaking, the relieved man immediately departed for Alpha Company's line. The man lying in the makeshift hammock said, "Indio, you wouldn't believe it out there."

Jesse looked into the face of Corporal Patterson, the forward observer for 81's, attached to Alpha Company. Still moving toward the command post, Jesse said, "What happened, Pat?"

"I don't know. I was calling in fire missions. They wouldn't fire the missions. Fuck, I don't know."

"How bad you hit?"

"I don't know. I don't know shit. What happened?" Patterson's voice began to waver.

Jesse noticed the leg wound in the upper right calf. He couldn't tell with any certainty but it appeared to be a shrapnel wound. "I don't know, Pat."

They arrived at the Pagoda temporarily being used as a command center. Two rows of ponchos stretched southward from the Pagoda entrance, one row contained the wounded, the other, with ponchos completely wrapped around contents, were the dead. As the marines gently lowered Patterson to the ground in the former row, Jesse asked, "Where's Franks?"

PFC Franks was Patterson's radio operator, a tall thin kid with blond hair. His dry sense of humor had always been a pleasant change of pace to Jesse on those rare occasions when the FO and his radio operator were with the section instead of attached to a line company.

"I don't know. I just don't know." Patterson's voice cracked as tears rolled from his eyes.

"Take it easy, Pat. Let's get you taken care of, then I'll go look for Franks."

The other marines moved away, returning to the Alpha Company line or the 81 mortar position. Jesse placed his M-1 on the ground and took his large bone-handled Bowie knife from its sheath then cut Patterson's right trouser leg from the bottom to the knee. He winced as the gaping wound on the calf was fully exposed by the parting material.

"You definitely got a piece of shrapnel, Pat. It's gonna look like hell forever, but you just bought a ticket home. You'll be okay. Roll over a little bit and let me get your battle dressing."

He removed the battle dressing from Patterson's first-aid pouch and applied it to the wound. "I gotta go, Pat. Say hello to the folks back home."

Patterson had regained some of his composure. "Thanks, Indio. Keep your ass low."

"Lower'n a snake's belly." Jesse smiled.

As the two shook hands, Jesse noticed the pool of coagulating blood on the Poncho below Patterson's leg. A pang of unknown origin sent a shudder through him as he picked up his M-1 and returned to Rich Cummings on gun one.

"Pat got hit in the calf with a piece of shrapnel. He won't ever run a ten-flat hundred but I think he'll be okay," said Jesse as he stepped into the gun pit.

"What about Franks?" asked Robert Whitman, the First Section radio operator. Radio operators stuck together as men often do who have something in common. Whitman and Franks had known each other well.

"I don't know, Mud," replied Jesse. "Pat didn't even know what the hell

259

happened to *him*."

Corporal Simmons approached the gun pit. He studied the men standing near the gun and said, "Alpha Company needs an FO. Anybody want to volunteer?"

"How about you, Simmons? You know damn good'n well that you and I are the only two qualified, 'cept for Tule," replied Jesse, staring hard into Simmons' face.

"They need me in FDC."

"What the hell for? They won't let us fire the guns. As a matter-of-fact, why the hell do they need an FO? If they don't let us fire the missions, why the hell send somebody out there to be a damn target?"

"Look, all I know is that Alpha has no FO's. No 81's. No Arty. No Air. No Naval guns. They want an FO, and I'm asking for a volunteer." He looked long at Jesse, waiting for a response. Jesse returned his stare, pulling out his pack of cigarettes and lighting up as he gazed into Simmons' eyes. He inhaled deeply and slowly, letting the smoke drift from his nostrils.

"I'll tell you what, Simmons – you tell the gunny and the poge-ass colonel that I'll go out there if they fire my missions. If they won't fire the missions, I ain't goin'."

Simmons continued his stare at Jesse. "I'll tell 'em." He turned and walked in the direction of the Fire Direction Center.

When Simmons was out of ear-shot, Rich said, "Are you crazy? Fuck that Cannuck son-of-a-bitch. Let *him* go out there."

"I thought it over pretty good, Rich. There's a .50 cal. machine-gun in that tree line that's tearing Alpha apart. Just give me two rounds and we'll blow it to gook heaven."

Jesse related some of his earlier experience, leaving out the part about his charge through the rice paddy.

After a short period, Mud said, "Here comes our favorite Cannuck, and he's carrying a map pouch and a set of binoculars,"

Simmons approached the gun-pit. "Okay, Indio. The old man says we'll fire your missions. Just remember, we've only got a basic combat load until resupply." He offered Jesse the map pouch and 7 x 50 binoculars in a contoured rubber-plastic case.

Jesse checked the map pouch and found it contained a compass and an area map. He put the map pouch and binoculars around his neck, and looked hard at Simmons. "Remember what I said. My first mission will be fired. That's all I want clear."

"You heard what I said," replied Simmons.

"Yeah, I heard. So did these guys." He nodded to the gun crew.

Simmons ignored the statement. "Nobody knows where Franks is, so you'll need a radio operator."

"Shit. I'll go. I guess if Indio's going to get his ass blown away, the least I can do is take notes," offered Whitman.

Jesse glanced over his shoulder, one eyebrow raised. "Thanks, Mud."

"What the hell," replied Mud casually.

"Let's saddle up and get out there. Rich, stand by, okay?" said Jesse.

"Give'em hell, Indio. We'll be there," said Rich.

Loaded down with his binoculars, map-pouch, M-1 Garand, four M-1 cartridge belts, .45 pistol, Bowie knife, first-aid pouch, poncho, and his canteens, Jesse once again began the all-too-familiar trek toward Alpha Company's line.

Trudging behind him, his PRC-10 radio on his back, PFC Robert Whitman mumbled about insanity, ignorance, and piss-poor working conditions.

As the two moved through the area occupied by the PFs, Jesse's muscles tensed and his heart pounded louder than he would like to have had it known but, aside from hostile stares and lack of chatter, the PFs made no move to retrieve the M-1 or any of the cartridge belts from Jesse.

Once safely out of sight of their allies, Mud said, "Them guys back there looked a little pissed-off about something. You don't suppose it was because they didn't have any Garand cartridge belts do you?"

"Screw 'em if they can't take a joke. What do they need cartridge belts for? They aren't doin' any shootin'."

Mud chuckled. "I'd still like to have seen it."

They approached a corporal on the west end of Alpha Company's line. Jesse said, "Where's the Captain?"

"We ain't got a captain. Lieutenant Malcolm is the company commander."

"Where can I find him?"

"'Bout the center of our line. Couple a' hundred yards and a bit to the rear."

"Thanks."

Staying well behind the elevated road, Jesse and Mud continued their search. In a few minutes they were at the command post, which consisted of a clump of trees. Lieutenant Malcolm, his first sergeant, a gunnery sergeant, four radio operators, and two riflemen, knelt in the center of the clump.

Jesse addressed Malcolm. "Sir, my name is Langley. I'm your new FO from 81's." He pointed to his radio operator and said, "This here is PFC Whitman. We call him Mud. He's my radio operator."

Lieutenant Malcolm was an athletic man, about five-feet-eleven-inches tall and weighing one hundred eighty pounds. With his short, dark hair, piercing blue eyes and smooth face, Jesse thought the company commander looked more like Rock Hudson, the movie star, than the commanding officer of a marine rifle company in Vietnam.

Malcolm inspected Jesse carefully. Jesse suddenly became aware of his appearance. Malcolm said, "Looks like you've had a rough day."

"I've had better, Sir.

"Can you read a map?" asked Malcolm.

"Better than most."

"Get me some mortars into that damn tree line."

Jesse smiled. "Aye, Aye, Sir." He turned to Mud. "C'mon, Mud. Let's go."

They left the relatively safe clump of trees and moved to the top of the elevated road. Ordering Mud to remain on the protected south side of the road, Jesse took a position behind a large tree on the northern edge. Small arms fire had slowed from within the enemy position but sporadic bursts kept Alpha Company honest. Even the VC had to conserve ammo. Jesse pulled his binoculars from the case and intently studied the tree line. He couldn't determine with certainty the location of the .50 cal. gun, but by using his experience and training, he felt confident he could guess, within fifty yards, the gun's exact location. He carefully put the field glasses away and pulled out his map. By shooting a magnetic azimuth with his compass, which he'd found in the map case, he double-checked the map's accuracy. He had heard rumors of maps in Viet Nam being off by as much as three hundred meters. This map appeared to be quite accurate.

Stoney Livingston

He raised his voice enough to be heard by Mud. "Fire mission."

There was a slight pause as Mud readied his pocket notebook. "Go," he said.

"Fire mission. Enemy machine gun dug in. One round Willie Peter. Will adjust. 564430. Azimuth three four fiive. Fire when ready."

Mud repeated the fire mission into his radio.

The voice on the other end replied, "Roger, Whiskey-Alpha. Stand by."

Jesse put the field glasses to his eyes and waited. He looked at his Zodiac Seawolf diver's watch and continued to wait a few moments longer. "Goddamnit," he said after a while.

He left his position and darted across the road to sit beside Mud, who was already holding out the handset. Jesse took the handset, keyed up and spoke. "Whiskey Six, Whiskey-Alpha. Over."

"Whiskey-six. Over."

"Whiskey-Alpha. Where's my fire mission? Over."

"Stand by."

Jesse lit a cigarette and smoked impatiently. When he finished his smoke, he field-stripped the butt and again keyed up the radio. "Whisky Six, Whiskey-Alpha. Over."

"Stand by, Whiskey-Alpha," came the reply.

Jesse glanced at his radio operator. "Mud, stay here. I'm gonna stand-the-hell-by down in the gunpits. I'll be back in about fifteen minutes. If I'm not, you can finish this damn police action without me."

He jumped up and jogged back to the 81 section, ignoring the PFs as he passed through their position. After what he had been through today, ten angry PFs were no cause for fear.

He stepped into gun one's pit. "Rich, is this gun set up to fire the mission I just called in?"

"Yeah, but they haven't given us the order to fire."

"You got a Willie-Peter set to go?"

"Hell yes."

Jesse turned to Sal, snatched the mortar round from his hands, deftly placed it in the tube, and released it in one smooth movement.

Thump-pow! The round was on its way.

Rich beamed.

"Who fired that round?"

"Oh shit! It's the goddamned battalion commander," whispered Rich.

Colonel Soliman approached the gunpit with long jerky strides.

"I did, Sir," said Jesse.

"And just who in the hell are you, Marine?"

"Lance Corporal Langley. Forward Observer for Alpha Company. They're out of ammo and they've had their ass kicked by one helluva reinforced platoon. I'm just trying to let the fuckin' gooks know we're still here, Sir."

"Come with me, Marine." Soliman turned his back to Jesse and strode toward the Pagoda. Jesse followed.

Jesse entered the Pagoda two strides behind the battalion commander. He had been in Pagoda's before but didn't believe they should be used as command posts for military operations.

Once again, upon entering the Pagoda, he was struck by the make-believe

262

feeling imparted by the environment. He was certain he had observed this scene in a WWII movie. The plaster was in various states of disrepair on all visible portions of the wall. The ceiling seemed to emit a fine dust wherever a projectile exploded within a few hundred yards of the building. To thicken the air, one needed only the stench of perspiring human flesh and a fog of cigarette smoke, both of which were present.

The colonel spun about on the heel of his right foot. He moved a step in Jesse's direction, looked him straight in the eyes and said, "Who in the hell do you think you are?"

The busy movements of the communication personnel in the room ceased.

Jesse looked into the soft-jowled, perspiring face of his battalion commander. He felt sorry for the figure before him. Perhaps he should feel sorry for his own well being but he couldn't. Mixed with his emotion of sorrow was the strong feeling of hate. *This guy doesn't have the moxie or the guts to command a line outfit. The son-of-a-bitch isn't qualified to lead a Cub Scout pack on an overnight bivouac.* Jesse felt suddenly superior to the man standing before him.

When he spoke, he chose his words carefully. He knew, without a doubt, his outfit needed him more than he had previously thought. His concern for returning to the line became paramount.

"Sir, I was only keeping a promise that I was given to understand came from my battalion commander."

Colonel Soliman glared at Jesse for a moment then, suddenly, his expression softened. "You look like you've had a rough time, Marine, so instead of having your ass locked up, I'm going to explain our situation to you, then I want you to report back to Lieutenant Malcolm in Alpha Company."

Jesse's expression didn't change.

The colonel continued. "S-2 seriously underestimated the strength of our enemy. We are in the assault. They are in a fortified position, with greater firepower, more ammunition, and at least twice our strength."

"More like four or five times our strength, Sir."

Colonel Soliman's face hardened for a moment then relaxed. "We have with us only a basic combat load of ammunition. If the enemy can determine our strength, he will almost certainly counter-attack. Until we're re-supplied I need every round of mortar ammunition I have held in reserve to lay a barrage in the rice paddy if the enemy should choose to assault our position. Now get your ass back out to Alpha Company and plot fire missions. Is that understood?"

Jesse felt tears well up in his eyes. He wanted to kill Soliman even more than he wanted to silence the .50 cal. machine-gun. He fought both the tears and the desire to kill his battalion commander. "Yes sir. Will that be all?"

"That had better be all, Marine."

"Yes sir." Jesse turned and left the pagoda. As he passed the ponchos filled with dead and wounded, tears streamed down his cheeks, making little rivers of tan on his muddy face. He fought against an urge to turn around and return to the Pagoda. He wanted to kill the colonel with his bare hands, to see his eyes bulging and his tongue hanging to one side of a purple face.

Jesse ducked into a row of bushes only twenty-five yards from the entrance to the Pagoda. He unslung his M-1 and ran the rear sight down for close-range work. Through the open doorway of the Pagoda, he could see the colonel moving about inside. He placed the rifle to his shoulder and took careful aim. The colonel must have been speaking to someone near the doorway, for Jesse clearly saw his lips moving, even in the shadows. The front sight blade of his rifle was centered in the rear sight aperture, the top of the front blade barely covering the bottom of the colonel's nose. Jesse carefully took up the slack in his trigger.

He pulled his cheek from the stock of his rifle and looked carefully in all directions. *What if somebody sees me? That would be great. Court martialed and executed for killing an American officer – even if he is a chickenshit, stupid, cowardly, son-of-a-bitch – isn't the way I want to go out. Besides, what if Shannon ever found out?.*

He relaxed his finger on the trigger, placed the safety on, slung the M-1 over his shoulder and returned to the Alpha Company line.

"Jesus Christ. Where you been?" asked Mud as Jesse approached.

"I had a talk with Colonel Dumbshit," came Jesse's tart reply.

"Is he going to let 81s fire the missions?"

Jesse shook his head. He felt the tears of frustration beginning to surface but suppressed them.

"I'll tell you what, that damn Willie Peter was right on target. Can't tell for sure if we got the fifty, but I'll bet we fried a few. Haven't heard a peep outa that heavy bastard since the round hit. Just two or three rounds of H.E. and I know damn good'n well it'd be out of action."

Jesse smiled. He explained what had transpired inside the Pagoda. When he finished, Mud said, "Hell, let's just go back to 81's. No sense staying out here and getting our asses blown off."

"I told the colonel I'd report back to Alpha and re-plot a bunch of fire missions." He stood. "Let's find the skipper and tell him the good news."

Mud stood and reluctantly followed Jesse, mumbling half under his breath all about Colonel Soliman's greatest attributes, none-the-least of which was his brain size compared to the testicles of a butterfly.

They found Lieutenant Malcolm in the center of Alpha's line, on the road, behind a group of large trees. As Jesse, Mud, Malcolm and his radio operator knelt behind one of the larger trees in the group, Jesse explained what had transpired from the time he had called in his first mission until he was summarily dismissed from the Pagoda.

Malcolm looked at Jesse closely and Jesse again became aware of how he must appear. His utility shirt was untucked. The bottoms of his bloused trousers seemed to blend into one smooth line with the tops of his boots, so thickly were they covered with mud. He carried a WWII M-1 Garand with four cartridge belts overlapping at his mid-section. His .45 pistol holster was mounted backwards on his left hip, and the large, bone-handled Bowie knife on his right hip was certainly not government issue.

"Well, I guess we wait for resupply," said Malcolm. "Why the M-1?"

"It's tough and accurate. Besides, it's the only thing around with any ammo left."

Malcolm smiled. "Take ten. About forty yards to the rear there's a large mound of dirt. I believe there might even be some c- ration coffee. I'll join you in..."

Suddenly Malcolm's radio operator slammed into Jesse's body, bowling him over from his kneeling position. Malcolm's head jerked sharply and his helmet sailed crisply from its resting position atop his head, careening off the trunk of a nearby tree. Almost instantly, Jesse heard the heavy report of the 50 cal. machine-gun. He grabbed the radio operator's arm and dragged him to a position of relative safety. A quick visual check of the radio operator's condition made him aware the gesture had been unnecessary. The fifty caliber slug had entered the center of the man's back, removing the breastbone as it continued through the front of the body.

Jesse stared, horrified, at the portion of the dead man's beating heart which hung outside the chest cavity. He fought hard to hold the bile rising to his mouth. The beating heart slowed to a stop. He pushed the body aside and gagged, some of the acid from his stomach forcing its way into his nostrils and burning them as he clamped his mouth tightly shut. He crawled towards Lieutenant Malcolm who lay on his back, arms and legs moving in twitching motions. Jesse searched for a wound. He put his hand behind Malcolm's neck to gently turn him over as he was unable to locate a wound on any portion of the front of the body. A small amount of blood on the upper portion of the back of the neck stopped his search.

"Corpsman! Corpsman up," he shouted.

He heard other marines passing the word down the line.

Mud crawled up next to Jesse, his radio still on his back. "How bad's he hit?"

"Don't know, but there's a little blood on the back of his neck. I'm afraid to move 'im. Let's wait for a corpsman. You okay?"

Mud replied, "Hell yes. I always do back flips on a prick-10 radio. It's good for your posture. But I'm not hit if that's what you mean."

"So much for us gettin' that fifty with one round of Willie-Peter."

"Well, it was damn close. It may be the same gun, but I'll bet it's a new crew," defended Mud.

"Didn't make a helluva difference to that guy." Jesse nodded toward the body of Malcolm's radio operator.

Mud looked at the radio operator, lying face up, the gaping wound in his chest clearly visible. He turned his face away, gagging. "Jesus!"

A corpsman arrived at the double, falling to his knees at Malcolm's side. Jesse said, "Can't be sure what kind of wound it is, Doc, but there's a little blood on the back of his neck." He turned to Mud. "Give 'im a hand will you, Mud? I wanna check somethin' out."

Mud nodded and moved in to assist the corpsman as Jesse moved away in search of Malcolm's helmet. He found it a few yards away, sitting on its top, a large hole in the rear, but no sign of any other hole evident. A more careful examination of the helmet revealed it had been struck at a slight angle from the rear. The bullet had penetrated the steel outer section and the ballistics liner, traveling slightly downward with the curve of the helmet and exiting out the bottom, somewhere near Malcolm's right ear.

"I'll be damned," he said. Malcolm was trying to sit up while Mud and the corpsman attempted to restrict his movements. Jesse moved the short distance to his company commander. He held out the helmet, "You may want to turn this in for salvage first chance you get, Skipper."

The corpsman whistled softly at the hole in the helmet. Mud's eyes widened but he said nothing.

"How you feel, Sir?" asked Jesse.

"I've had my bell rung, but I'm okay," he answered as he accepted his deformed helmet. "How about you all?"

"Mud and I are okay, but your radio operator bought it."

Stoney Livingston

Malcolm propped his torso up with his elbows and stared at the body of his radio operator. Perhaps full a minute elapsed, then he shouted, "Cover him, damnit!"

"Aye, aye, Sir," replied Jesse as he and Mud moved to comply with the order. Mud found a poncho nearby but could not bring himself to cover the body. He vomited in the brush while Jesse covered the dead man gagging and fighting back bile the whole time.

The corpsman addressed Malcolm. "It's just a very slight flesh wound on the right side of your neck, Sir, similar to one caused by a fingernail scratch. I've dressed it with bacitracin ointment, but you ought to check in at battalion aid for a tetanus shot and a little rest. I can't be sure about concussion."

"Hell, Sandy. I'm okay. Thanks. Let's get a detail to get Brian back to headquarters."

"Yessir but, just the same, you ought to take it real easy for a while."

"I'll watch after him for a spell – see that he don't work too hard and all a that stuff," offered Jesse.

Malcolm looked up at Jesse, arching an eyebrow.

By way of explanation, Jesse continued, "I mean, after all, Skipper, you've got two of 81's finest right here with you."

Jesse turned to the corpsman. "Glad to meet you, Sandy. They call me Indio, and this here is my radio operator. When we don't call him something else, we call 'im Mud. If you'll take care of the skipper's radio operator, we'll take care of the skipper."

Corpsman Sanderson looked from Malcolm to Jesse then back to Malcolm. "Okay, but don't let him move around too much, and especially not too quickly."

"You got it," said Jesse.

As Sandy moved into the bushes towards the rear in search of assistance, Jesse turned to Malcolm. "You okay, Skipper?"

Malcolm nodded. "Let's go back to that mound and have that cup of coffee," he said as he rose to the crouching position unassisted.

Sandy returned with three marines. They carried the radio operator's body toward the Pagoda as Mud and Jesse followed the company commander into the bushes south of the road. Soon, they were quietly drinking coffee, each man filled with his own thoughts, no one speaking. Jesse lit a cigarette.

"Indio, let me see your map," said Malcolm, sitting only a few paces away.

Jesse moved to Malcolm's side, pulling his map from the map pouch as he walked. "These little x's on the map are missions I've plotted, but obviously none of 'em have been fired," he said as he handed the map to Malcolm.

As Malcolm studied the map, Jesse continued, "Sir, without ammo we're dead meat here. If we don't get re-supplied real quick, I think it would be to our benefit to get the hell outa this position."

Malcolm looked up from the map. "Which direction did you have in mind?"

"Either way. At this point it really doesn't make a tinker's damn to me. I'd rather be mobile if I was out of ammo, than to try to hold an unfortified position with clubs and rocks. We could attack by moving across the road to our right flank and into the tree line on the enemy left front. Those trees are thick enough to hide our movement until we're on top of 'em. With bayonets and what little ammo we have left, we have a chance of breaking their perimeter if the colonel will let us fire the 81's."

"I put their strength at over a thousand. Those odds are a little stiff."

266

"I figured about twice that strength, and the more I think about it, the less I like the plan, but I still prefer it ten to one over stayin' here."

"What about the other direction?" asked Malcolm, grinning.

"Well, Sir, if I was gonna pull out, I'd move the 81's south and west about a mile. Once they were in position, I'd give almost every round of 7.62 ammo we've got to two M-60's and a rifle squad. I'd spread 'em out on the line and evacuate the rest of the company. When the rest of the company was in position at the new location, I'd move the rear guard out at the double under cover of the 81's. By the time it all comes off, it's dark, and since they don't know our position for certain, we're safe till daylight. By then if we don't get help, we'll just secede from the Union and declare ourselves neutral."

Malcolm's lips curled into a smile at Jesse's closing sentence. "They don't teach those kind of tactics at West Point or Annapolis. Did you just snatch that out of the air or what?"

"Either way you choose is better than staying here, Sir. Even if we hold out until dark, we're dead. They know our position. If their commanding officer had any balls he would have counter-attacked two or three hours ago. With their numbers and firepower they're going to get around to it eventually. Why the hell should we stay here where they can take us blindfolded with their firepower and numbers?"

"It'll be getting dark in an hour or so." Malcolm looked at his watch then up at the heavy overcast. "Let's go talk to the old man and see what he says."

"Begging your pardon, Sir, but I'd rather not talk to the old man. He's a stupid, blundering, inexperienced, chickenshit, cowardly son-of-a-bitch, and he ain't gonna listen to any plan that might take him away from the false safety of his Pagoda."

Malcolm furrowed his brows. "That's your battalion commander you're talking about, Marine."

Jesse gave Malcolm a hard look. "Sir, if I'm wrong, I'll kiss the battalion commander's ass. But before you pass judgement on me, talk to 'im. If you don't agree with me when you get back to the company, court martial me and I'll plead guilty to whatever charge you level at me. In the meantime, if you trust me to remain under house arrest, I'd like to get out on our right flank and check things out."

Malcolm glanced at his watch again. "Report back here in twenty-five minutes."

"Aye, aye, Sir," replied Jesse as he checked his watch, picked up his map, nodded to Mud, and set out for the right flank.

As they moved through the brush, Mud jovially said, "I knew there was a real reason I volunteered for this shit. It's worth it just to see you talk to officers. One of these days there's gonna be a big explosion and I want to be there to see it."

Jesse said nothing as he continued toward the flank.

Once on the flank, Jesse enjoyed a short reunion with Maxwell, Jacoby and Stillwater. After introducing Mud, he asked Jacoby, "You guys seen any movement in that tree line?"

"Not yet, but I don't know what the hell is keepin' 'em. What's goin' on at headquarters?"

"Nothin'. Absolutely nothin'," answered Jesse.

Jesse moved forward and to his right to gain a better viewpoint, pulled out his field glasses and studied the terrain. After a few moments he spoke quietly and calmly over his shoulder. "Jacoby, how many rounds of ammo you got left?"

Stoney Livingston

"About forty rounds per man. We haven't fired a shot in an hour but we passed some of our ammo down the line."

"The gooks are movin' through the brush. They're probably gonna hit the open rice paddy in three or four minutes. Can't tell how many for sure yet, but I'd say a least a platoon. Probably a big scouting party."

He raised his glasses again. "I don't see any VC. Every one of 'em looks like NVR."

"No kiddin? North Vietnamese Regulars?" asked Jacoby

"Can't be for sure but I've never seen the VC dressed in NVR uniforms before," replied Jesse.

Jesse moved back to Jacoby's position and picked up the EE-8 field phone connected to Alpha Company headquarters. He turned the crank on the side of its base to ring the phone at the other end of the wire. A voice answered, "Jacoby?"

"Negative. This is Indio, your FO. Is the skipper there?"

"Stand by."

"Indio?" It was Malcolm's voice.

"Yes, Sir. What did the old man say?"

"Don't worry about a court martial. How are things out there?"

"The gooks are sending a probe down the tree line. Looks like about platoon strength. You may want to send an M-60 and a case of grenades out here. Oh yeah, I almost forgot. Send a T-bone steak and a bottle of sour mash, but make it quick. We've only got a couple of minutes before they hit the paddy. I'm goin' back to work. Keep you posted. Out."

He turned to Jacoby. "I'm gonna call in a fire mission but I doubt if Colonel Chickenshit will let it be fired. With no more ammo than we've got here, I suggest we wait until they're about halfway across the paddy before we fire."

"Agreed. All right, you guys, you heard the plan. Grab your best position and make every round count. Fire on my command," ordered Jacoby.

Mud called in the fire mission from the information supplied him by Jesse as the latter adjusted the rear sight on his M-1.

"Stand by, Whiskey-Alpha," crackled Mud's radio.

Jesse grabbed the handset. "Whiskey-Six, Whiskey-Alpha Actual. Standby bullshit! Copy new coordinates. New coordinates 627376. Now get out your map and re-evaluate! Troops in open. One round HE. Will adjust. Over."

"Roger, Whiskey-Alpha. Standby."

He handed the handset back to Mud.

Jacoby said, "It's almost time. Jesus! There must be forty or fifty of 'em! They look like swarmin' ants!"

Jesse took his firing position. When the nearest enemy soldier was approximately one-hundred-fifty yards to the right front of their position, Jacoby gave the command. "Fire at will!"

Jesse squeezed the trigger and saw his target collapse into the muddy rice paddy. After that first round, confusion took charge. The enemy troops moved forward at a dead run, approaching the road almost a hundred yards to the right of Alpha Company's flank.

Jesse fired round after round, replacing a spent clip at the end of each eight rounds. Enemy troops fell but Jesse didn't know how many, if any, were falling as a result of his marksmanship. His rifle barrel was hot and smoking, and he had expended one entire cartridge belt of ammunition. He unbuckled the empty belt and discarded it. Rifle and automatic weapons fire struck all about their position. Tree branches fell. Dirt flew. The enemy troops gained the road and were in Alpha Company's tree line on the right flank, less than one hundred yards away.

The metallic sound of an M-14 butt plate slamming into the ground caused Jesse to turn. Private Stillwater was trying to clear a jammed round by forcing the operating rod handle on his rifle open by stomping the lever with his foot. Jesse jumped up to offer assistance. On his second stride in Stillwater's direction, the rifle fired, the bullet striking Stillwater in the abdomen. He fell onto his back, writhing and clutching at his mid-section.

Jesse fell to his knees next to him. "Mud, gimme a hand! Max, get on the landline! Get us a corpsman and tell the skipper we need help!"

PFC Maxwell grabbed the field phone and made contact with headquarters while Jesse and Mud worked feverishly on Stillwater.

Jesse ripped the front of Stillwater's utility jacket open, unsheathed his bone-handled Bowie knife and cut the bloody T-shirt, exposing the wound. "Shit!"

Mud gagged, and turned his head. The bullet had entered Stillwater's body two inches below the belly button, traveling upward, ripping the flesh open to expose his organs, which poured through broken skin as Stillwater writhed on the muddy ground. Neither Jesse nor Mud could guess where the bullet had come to rest.

"Shit," Jesse repeated. He opened his first aid pouch. He injected Stillwater with a hypodermic needle.

"What the hell is that?" asked Mud.

"Morphine. A corpsman friend of mine gave it to me."

Stillwater's lips quivered.

"Help me hold his skin together," said Jesse.

"You gotta be shittin' me?"

"You got any better ideas?"

"No, but, shit! Damn!"

The morphine began to have an effect on Stillwater.

"Now! C'mon. Let's get it done."

Mud grabbed the ragged edges of both sides of the wound and held them together, turning his face from the ghastly sight and gagging.

Three marines, one of them carrying an M-60 machine-gun, rushed by to report to Jacoby. He stationed them strategically around their position.

Corpsman Sanderson approached.

"Boy, am I glad to see you," said Mud, as Sanderson knelt beside Stillwater.

Jesse said, "I gave him morphine. I didn't know what else to do. He took a bullet down here." Jesse pointed. "And it traveled upward. I don't know where it is, but he's yours now, Sandy." He picked up his M-1 and moved toward his old position.

He picked up four of the grenades from a case recently dropped by the fresh troops. They were the old mark II of Korean War vintage. He wondered briefly how old they were and where they came from and if they were as reliable as the old mortar ammunition supplied on the Cuban Missile Crisis.

"Mud, stay here. I'm going forward for a quick look." He turned to Jacoby. "Hey, Jacoby, don't let these guys shoot me when I come back in. I'm going forward and toss a few of these eggs – make 'em think we're on the counter-offensive."

"Sounds like fun. I'll stay back here and watch."

"I won't be long."

Stoney Livingston

"Blessed are the foolish." Jacoby made the sign of the cross with his right hand.

"I'll holler real loud on my way back in. Just don't shoot me." He stepped into the trees in an easterly direction.

Jesse moved east cautiously, his rifle at sling arms, an M26A1 grenade in his left hand. He pulled the pin and held the spoon against the grenade with three fingers of his throwing hand. Approximately fifty yards out from Alpha's flank, he heard the enemy soldiers. Judging from the sounds, the enemy was about thirty yards to his direct front. He hid behind a tree, released the spoon, held the grenade one second and tossed it toward the sound of the advancing troops.

When the grenade exploded, Jesse was on one knee, pulling pins and throwing the rest of his grenades as far as he was able, spreading them on a line across the enemy front. Of the five grenades he threw after his initial toss, only one exploded.

He un-slung his rifle, and quickly returned to Alpha Company's right flank. As he approached the flank, he shouted, "Don't shoot. It's Indio and I'm comin' in." He burst into the flank guard's position at a dead run, stopping only when he reached the case of grenades. Dropping to a knee, he picked up one of the grenades and began unscrewing the top.

"Hey! What the fuck are you doin'?" asked the machine-gunner.

"Checkin' out these grenades. What the does it look like I'm doin'?" replied Jesse as he continued unscrewing the detonating mechanism.

Marines scattered in all directions.

Jesse extracted the detonating mechanism from the grenade. "Jacoby."

A voice in the brush answered timidly. "Yo?"

"You better get on the land line and tell the skipper we need grenades with blasting caps inside of 'em. And we need 'em quick."

The marines assumed their previous positions. Jacoby approached Jesse nervously.

"See?" Jesse displayed the grenade body in one hand and the detonating mechanism in the other. "No goddamn caps. Somebody has removed every damn one of 'em. You better tell the skipper that if he's got any more of the old Mark II's around, he better not count on 'em. Without these grenades we're in a hurt."

Jacoby turned to the other marines. "Fix bayonets!" he shouted while he frantically cranked the field phone.

Mud motioned to Jesse. "Indio, c'mere." He held out the handset of his PRC-10 radio. "It's Whiskey-Six. They want to talk to Whiskey-Alpha Actual."

Jesse accepted the handset. "This is Whiskey Alpha Actual. Over."

"This is Whiskey-Six actual. Can you mark your position with smoke? Over."

"Roger. Over."

"Throw your smoke. Coordinate air support. Over."

"Roger, Whiskey-Six. Whiskey-Alpha. Out." He looked at Mud. "You know the FAC frequency?"

"Yeah. And we can't get it on this radio."

"Don't they know that at company level?" asked Jesse.

Mud's radio crackled. "Whiskey Alpha. Whiskey six. Mark your position. The birds will make a pass, directed by Bravo's Forward Air Controller. He can't see your position and requires you to advise him of any corrections via the landline. We will

270

relay corrections for you. Do you copy? Over.

Jesse answered. "Roger. Moving to the landline. Standby."

Someone threw a red smoke grenade.

Jesse turned the hand crank on the field phone. An unfamiliar voice answered. Jesse said, "Advise air to look for red smoke."

"Roger red smoke," said the voice.

Almost simultaneous with the unknown marine's words came the loud report of Gattling cannon from about three hundred feet directly over Jesse's head. Mud dove for cover as Jesse instinctively fell prone next to the field phone. It took but a second or two for Jesse to realize the cannons were being fired by the U.S. Navy Crusader that had just passed overhead. The rumble of the powerful engine created tremors in his throat and momentarily deafened him.

Jesus Christ! That was scary as hell," said Jacoby, crawling from the underbrush.

A second crusader passed overhead, with the same instinctive results from the Marines. Jesse picked himself from the ground and moved toward the edge of the perimeter to get a better view of the enemy position. Another Crusader passed overhead, guns blazing. He was used to it already and did little more than flinch at the sounds.

Jesse thought the Gattling gun was a 20mm but wasn't sure, but the damage inflicted upon the enemy position was more than satisfactory. Trees fell. Earth exploded in chunks. He was certain anyone in that village was looking for a quick way out.

"Holy hell! I want one of those for Christmas," said Mud, who had moved next to him.

Jesse smiled as a fourth F-8 passed overhead, guns blazing. "I'm beginning to like the navy a little bit. Love them swabbies."

"Stay here a second, Mud. I'm gonna get on the phone and see if they can hit the target a bit to the east."

"Roj," came Mud's reply.

Jesse ran the short distance to the field phone and wound the crank.

"FDC," said a voice.

"This is Whiskey Alpha. Can you get those swabbies to hit the target again, about a hundred yards east of the last strike?"

"Roger. There is a flight of A-4s right behind the navy. Will advise."

Jesse looked up to see the underbelly of a Marine Corps A-4 Skyhawk, machine-guns blazing, less than one hundred fifty feet above his head.

The flight leader pulled his plane abruptly skyward at a steep angle, releasing some sort of bomb as the Skyhawk arched upward. It looked like a large barrel from Jesse's viewpoint as it arched upward gracefully, then tumbled to earth in slow motion.

The barrel disappeared into the trees. Suddenly there was a wall of deep orange flame, fifty yards long, appearing above the tree tops. Heavy black smoke drifted skyward in clouds so thick they appeared unable to stay aloft. Jesse smiled. *Napalm!*

The three remaining Skyhawks followed in rapid succession with similar results. The firing on the flank was more sporadic but Jesse paid little attention to anything other than the enemy's fortified position to his front. Dark black smoke now covered the enemy tree line.

Stoney Livingston

The voice on the field phone said, "Hey there, Whiskey. The navy's got time for one more pass. They're runnin' low on fuel and daylight."

"Roger. Tell them to hit the same position."

"No sooner said than done," came the reply.

The Gattling cannon chattered loudly as the first of the Navy Crusaders bore down on its target. The Navy jet was at about one hundred fifty feet above the ground. Jesse smiled. They must have seen the marines come in at that altitude and they weren't about to be upstaged.

Lush growth disappeared and trees fell as the 20mm projectiles struck the target area. As the last Crusader made its pass, a large explosion issued from the enemy position. The Navy jet banked sharply to the right and nosed upward, passing through a cloud of smoke and debris. Jesse watched as the Crusader appeared on the other side of the smoke.

"Whiskey," said the field phone. The A-4s report troops on your right flank, about 100 yards, moving north across the road. Are they friendly?"

"Standby." He turned from the phone. "Hey, Jacoby."

"Yo?" came the response from somewhere in the trees.

"Are we chasing the gooks on our flank across the road?"

"With what? Bayonets and mud clods?"

Jesse spoke into the phone, "The troops in question are enemy. Do you read me?"

"Like the Bible. You want one of the A-4s to mop up?"

"Affirmative, but one only. I'd like to see as much of that tree line disappear as possible. And be advised – do *not* target anything south of the road. Over."

"Ask and ye shall receive," came the reply.

Once again the Skyhawks hit the enemy tree line, this time using only their machine-guns. Jesse had wanted more Napalm but, apparently, there was none left. A lone Skyhawk strafed the enemy troops crossing the rice paddy. Several fell, but Jesse couldn't tell if they fell wounded or in fear. Others continued to run.

A few moments more and it was over. The Marine Skyhawks headed home and all small arms fire ceased. Two marines on the flank had been wounded, one in the left thigh, the other in the right shoulder. Corpsman Sanderson took charge of the wounded and moved them to the Pagoda. The sounds of helicopters became audible. Jesse couldn't see them through the trees, but the sound told him they were landing at the LZ near the Pagoda. Hopefully they would leave food and ammo before lifting the dead and wounded out.

Dusk was rapidly approaching. He scanned the enemy tree line with his field glasses. The only movements within the tree line were clouds of black smoke, drifting slowly upward in the heavy air. All firing by both sides had ceased.

Jesse turned to Jacoby. "Hey, Jake, if you got everything under control, me and Mud are gonna report to the skipper."

"Keep your ass low, Indio. You too, Mud," said Jacoby.

"Let's go, Mud," said Jesse as he stepped west, toward the center of the line.

They approached the company commander briskly, Jesse speaking as he neared Malcolm. "Sir, if it's okay with you, I'd like to get back to the LZ and see if we got any ammo."

"Go ahead. Let me know the status ASAP and I'll send a working party if we got anything."

272

Without slowing their stride, Jesse and Mud continued west. The light was fading rapidly.

As they approached gun one in the semi-darkness, Rich challenged, "That you, Indio?"

"Yeah. Did we get any ammo for the guns?"

"Hell no. They didn't even bring any small arms ammo. Said they didn't have time to take any on if they were going to get here before dark to take out the wounded," replied Rich.

"Damn." Jesse turned to Mud. "Mud, you stay here. Rich, how about you and Cue come with me?"

The three quickly covered the hundred or so yards to the several helicopters, still taking on wounded and dead. Rich and Cue waited outside the first helicopter while Jesse jumped inside and moved forward to speak to the pilot. About one minute later he jumped out of the helicopter with four one-hundred-round belts of M-60 ammunition.

Speaking above the sound of slowly turning helicopter rotors, Jesse said, "The pilot has authorized each chopper to give us four hundred rounds. All we gotta do is go get it." They split up, scurrying from helicopter to helicopter until they had collected four hundred rounds each from all eight helicopters on the LZ.

As Cue dropped his last hundred-round ammo belt onto the large stockpile near the edge of the LZ, he said, "I never realized how heavy this shit is."

"Rich, if I can borrow Cue and one other man, Mud and I'll get this ammo to Alpha," said Jesse.

"Sure. Take Sal. In the meantime, let's see if the three of us can drag this stuff back to gun one," replied Rich.

Staggering under the weight of their booty, the three returned to the First Section position. Darkness had set in and though there was a half-moon, the overcast negated most of the moon's glowing effect.

After a short rest, Jesse, Mud, Cue and Sal set out in the darkness for Alpha Company, carrying eight one-hundred-round belts of ammunition apiece. Jesse led the way, slowly and deliberately. They were challenged several times along the way, but allowed to pass without incident until they finally arrived at the large mound of dirt that served as Alpha Company's headquarters.

As the men dropped the ammo belts into a pile, Jesse said, "Skipper, you here?"

"On your right, about fifteen feet away, Indio."

He turned toward the sound of the voice. "Gotcha about Thirty-two hundred rounds of 7.62 ammo, courtesy of the air wing gunners. You might want to have your squad leaders divvy it up, Sir."

Though he couldn't see clearly enough in the darkness to be absolutely certain, Jesse was pretty sure there was a smile on Malcolm's face as he spoke. "Couldn't you do better than thirty-two hundred rounds?"

"Didn't have the time to talk 'em out of what they had in their guns, Sir," came Jesse's quick answer.

Malcolm raised his voice. "Sergeant Wilkes, distribute the ammo. Indio, c'mere. You missed your briefing."

Mud sat down, exhausted, as Cue and Sal stood idly by. Jesse joined Malcolm who sat on a tree stump.

"Yes, Sir?"

273

Stoney Livingston

"How much did you hear back at the LZ?" There was an edge to Malcolm's tone.

"Nothing, Sir. I barely had time to get the ammo."

"Then I guess you don't know that we've been reinforced by three battalions?"

"That's nice to know. Where are they? We could sure use the help."

"Well, one of 'em – Two-Seven – is on the north side of the gooks' position. Three-Nine and Two-Four are behind us about a thousand yards."

"A thousand yards?" Jesse whispered loudly. "Can't they read a map? Can't they see the smoke? What the hell are they gonna do a thousand yards behind us – give us moral support? They've got all the ammo. They're fresh. Why aren't they up here? By the time they get here and get organized for the assault, they'll be worn to a frazzle, and we'll fall asleep waitin' for 'em."

There was a long pause. Finally, Lieutenant Malcolm spoke very softly. "There isn't going to be an assault until after daybreak. We're to hold our position until relieved in the morning."

A longer pause ensued. At length, Jesse spoke: "Beggin' the skipper's pardon, Sir, but my mind isn't yet ready to believe that anyone – even in the Marine Corps – is stupid enough to believe that those gooks are gonna sit there all night so we can come swoopin' down on 'em at daybreak with three fresh battalions and stomp their asses. We have fresh troops, illumination from our mortars, ammunition – hammer and anvil! We've got 'em!"

"We've got 'em all right. Sometime after dawn," replied Malcolm tiredly.

Jesse stood in disbelief. "But, Sir, what the hell are we here for? Why did all of those guys die today? So we could sit on our asses and wait for the gooks to move out under the cover of darkness? Goddamnit, we owe those guys more than that! It's all for nothin' – a total damn waste."

Silence followed Jesse's remark. He caught the sparkle of a tear on Malcolm's cheek in a brief flash of moonlight.

"Those are the orders, Indio. Whether we like 'em or not. Those are the orders."

"Whose orders? What supreme asshole is in charge now?"

"It's still Colonel Soliman's show."

After a long moment's silence, Jesse said, "If you don't mind, Sir, I'd like to rejoin 81's. I can't look these guys in the face at daybreak. I'm really tired of the way Colonel Chickenshit wastes lives. It ought to mean something when a man dies. He ought to die for a reason."

Tears rolled down Malcolm's face. "Permission granted, Indio."

"Thank you, Sir. I'll have 'em send you a good FO at daybreak."

Jesse walked the short distance to Mud, Cue and Sal. "Okay, guys, let's go back to the 'toon."

The walk back to the First Section's position seemed to take forever. If someone had asked him his thoughts, Jesse could not have answered accurately. They were jumbled. He wanted Colonel Soliman removed from command. He wanted to assault the enemy position and avenge the dead and wounded. He wanted to go back to Arizona and pretend this war didn't exist. But most of all, he wanted the dead and wounded to miraculously reappear unhurt. He wondered what purpose had been served in their dying and suffering but couldn't find an answer. His body and his mind had had enough for one day. He was too exhausted to assault the damned enemy position anyway.

As they entered the gun pit, Rich greeted them. "You hear we're gonna hold this position till daylight?"

"Yeah," answered Jesse, a mixture of fatigue and disgust in his voice.

"There's supposed to be two battalions to our rear. They're gonna come through our position just after daybreak. In the meantime, we've got a hundred-percent alert," continued Rich.

"I don't think so, Rich. Screw their hundred-percent alert. I'll take the first watch. You take the second, Sal the third, Cue the fourth, Roberts the fifth, Tully the sixth, Mulleneaux the seventh, and Piroge the eighth. Whoever has the watch at 0500, wake me up. Got it? Now sack out. If somethin' happens, we need to be fresh."

The marines hastily arranged their respective sleeping areas and turned in, wasting neither time nor movement. In a matter of moments all, save Rich and Jesse, were sound asleep.

"You know, Indio, you'll be court-martialed if someone finds us all asleep," said Rich.

Jesse replied tiredly, "Yeah, I know, but I don't really give a damn. Those gooks probably aren't comin' at us tonight, and even if they do, there's no reason for 81's to be on hundred percent. It ain't like we're on the line. We'll have time. You better get some sleep yerself. Who knows what in the hell tomorrow will bring with this office clerk of a battalion commander in charge?"

"Hell, I don't need the rest as bad as you do. It's only an extra hour. Let me take your watch too. You look worse than I've ever seen you look and, man, that's bad."

"It shows that much, huh?"

"You bet your ass it does. You look like death warmed over. I carried ponchos with body parts in 'em that looked better than you do."

"Can you handle it? I could use the rest."

"No sweat."

"I appreciate it, Rich. Wake me if you get tired. I owe you one."

"You don't owe me squat."

Jesse smiled and leaned back into the side of the gunpit. "Thanks, Rich." In the sitting position, with his helmet tipped over his eyes, sleep overcame him.

Jesse awakened suddenly and checked his watch. *Five-fifteen! Where the hell is Piroge?*

Even in the darkness he was aware of a fog. He searched until he found Piroge asleep at the edge of the gunpit, his rifle lying next to him. Jesse pulled his bone-handled knife from its sheath, placed the dull top of the blade against Piroge's throat, and pressed hard. Piroge awoke suddenly, gasping for breath, bewildered.

Jesse, his face only inches from Piroge's ear, whispered, "Piroge, you shitbird. I oughta slit your goddamn throat. If you ever pull this shit again, I will. Do you hear me?"

Piroge, unable to speak due to the pressure at his throat, nodded. Jesse released the pressure and sheathed his knife. "Wake up Rich at 0530. Tell 'im I'm back out with Alpha."

"Okay," whispered Piroge hoarsely. "Jesus. You didn't have to do that."

"Yes I did." He turned to search for Mud, ignoring Piroge until he recognized the pungent odor of urine and realized that Piroge had wet his pants. He stopped for a moment and considered apologizing to Piroge for the rude awakening but the words came out differently than he had intended. "Next time I'll use the sharp edge of the knife."

Mud was never one to awaken quickly and on this morning he remained true to form. After much jostling, Jesse managed to elicit a response from him.

"Wha ...Wha ...Who ...Uh, what?"

"Let's go, Mud."

"Okay." He rolled over and was immediately asleep again.

Jesse reached out and twisted his available ear.

"Ow!"

"Shhh! You'll wake the whole battalion. Let's go."

"Go where?"

"Back to Alpha."

"Shit." Mud sat upright and pulled his boots on.

In a few moments, they were walking in the direction of the Alpha Company line, making quiet, muffled sounds in the dense fog.

Jesse was almost face-to-face with Lieutenant Malcolm before he realized they had arrived at the company headquarters' position. Perception was distorted in the fog. At times, Jesse wasn't certain he was standing perpendicular to the ground.

"You lost, Indio?" asked Malcolm.

"No, Sir. I promised you a good FO by daylight and, after thinking it over, I'm the only good one left, 'cept fer Sergeant Tuleano, and without him to run FDC, you wouldn't need an FO."

"Thanks for coming back out. I thought you might've had enough yesterday to last you awhile."

"Actually, what I wanted was a cup of that famous Alpha Company C-ration coffee. You got any to spare?"

"You bet. Over there by the big tree. Help yourself."

Though still quite dark, the first hint of grey was beginning to appear from somewhere outside the blanket of fog.

On this morning, Jesse found being attached to headquarters beneficial in that the morning coffee was prepared in a large urn. It even smelled like real coffee. As he sloshed the dark liquid around in his canteen cup, he studied Lieutenant Malcolm whose facial features became discernible with the first grey light.

"How's the head, Sir?" he asked.

"I'm better off than a lot of other guys in this outfit," Malcolm said. "How're you feelin'?"

"Tolerable well. I feel pretty good physically. It's the noggin' that ain't workin' quite proper yet. I still can't convince my brain that I'm going to sit here while a bunch of replacements are gonna take our objective."

"They're all marines," said Malcolm without much conviction.

"So're the guys in Alpha Company, Sir, and they did most of the bleedin'. You know as well as I do, they earned the right."

"Maybe, but we're marines, and our orders are to stay in position."

"Can't we just say 'screw the order' this one time and take the position ourselves? There ain't much left in there. The gooks are probably five or six hours gone by now. It'll be a cakewalk."

"Then it's not worth a court-martial, is it?"

Jesse paused for a moment. "No, I guess it ain't. Just another wasted gesture, like this whole damn sweep."

"VC! VC!" a voice on the elevated road shouted.

Jesse dropped his canteen cup and ran for the voice, thirty yards from where he stood. Arriving at a machine-gun position, he asked the gunner, "Where's the VC?"

The gunner pointed to his front. Jesse peered through his field glasses. He observed an elderly woman stooped over in the rice paddy, working what was left of her crop in that area. Even in the faint light and patchy ground fog, with the aid of his field glasses, Jesse was certain the old woman was no VC. With the glasses still to his eyes, he said, "Hell, that's just an old mama-san, workin' her rice."

"She's a fuckin' VC!" The gunner fired his weapon.

The machine-gun was still firing when Jesse lifted the quick-release latch and grabbed the hot barrel, jerking it away from the gun. Only then did it stop its deadly chatter. Jesse held the heavy barrel like a baseball bat and swung it similarly, striking the gunner first on the helmet, then the ribs, then the back, then the legs and back toward the head. He made two or three trips up and down the gunner's body with the heavy barrel before Mud, Malcolm and several others reacted and overcame him, restraining him and prying the barrel from his hands.

Corporal Sanderson, the corpsman, immediately attended to the injured gunner while Jesse continued to struggle against his restraint. After a while, he stopped struggling and lay panting.

Lieutenant Malcolm and the others restraining him slowly released their grasps. Jesse sat upright and watched the corpsman working over the bruised and bloody gunner. Jesse glanced into Malcolm's eyes. "I told him she was no VC, Skipper."

Sandy said, "Skipper, we gotta get him outa here. He's got a broken jaw, broken ribs, a broken leg and I don't know what else."

Jesse ignored the commotion, retrieved his field glasses and studied the rice paddy where he had last seen the old woman. She was still there, but she was no longer standing. The hump of her back was all he could see protruding from the rice paddy mud. He turned to the corpsman attending the moaning gunner. "Doc, we got an old lady layin' in the paddy out there. I'm goin' out there and see if she's still alive."

Sandy said, "If you wait a minute, I'll go with you." He looked at Malcolm. The skipper nodded his assent.

A second corpsman relieved Sandy. Jesse took off his utility blouse, removed his muddied white t-shirt, and put his utility blouse on . He tied the T-shirt to the barrel of his M-1 and stepped into the rice paddy, Sandy right behind him. Malcolm's new radio operator informed the line of the mercy mission in progress in the paddy north of their position.

Sandy, sloshing through the paddy five yards behind Jesse, said, "I know what the gunner did was wrong, but why did you have to beat him half to death?"

Moving slowly through the mud, rifle held prominently high to display the muddy white t-shirt, Jesse answered. "Two reasons. First: I didn't have time to beat him all the way to death; second: he earned it."

"Earned it? For what? Shooting that mama-san? A court-martial would have taken care that. We all heard you identify his target before he fired."

Jesse, still trudging forward, sighed. "I guess you just don't understand, do

277

you, Doc?"

"So explain."

"I'll make it real simple, Doc. He disgraced everyone in our outfit. He disgraced our country and, most important of all, he disgraced me. It wouldn't bother me a bit if he croaked."

"If he does, the Crotch will hang you."

"That would be one court-martial where I could look 'em all in the eye and tell 'em to get laid. I'd do it again in a second. We don't shoot unarmed old women where I come from. How about your hometown, Doc – they condone that kinda stuff there?"

"Nobody condones that kind of stuff."

"Maybe not, but they put up with it. Me, I don't put up with it."

"So I noticed."

"By the way, Doc. You realize by now the gooks are gone, right?"

"How do you figure?"

"They'd have blown our asses away by now if they were still in that tree line."

"But what about the white flag?"

"That's for our side. The gooks don't give a damn about white flags."

Sandy's voice wavered. "Don't you give a shit about anything, man?"

"Yeah, I give a shit about punks shootin' old ladies."

"Forget it. Can you see her yet?"

"Yeah. Up here on the left." They sloshed the remaining distance to the prostrate form and knelt next to it. Sandy turned her face to the grey sky. She was dead. At least seven rounds had entered her body, the deep purple puncture marks made by the bullets displayed in mute testimony the machine-gunner's marksmanship ability.

"What a waste," muttered Jesse. "The old lady's life was wasted for nothin', and the guy who killed her wasted his ability on a harmless old lady." He turned to the corpsman. "Here, Doc. You carry my rifle. I'm takin' her back with us."

With Sandy leading the way, they returned to the elevated road. Breathing heavily, his legs quivering, Jesse placed the old woman's body gently on the ground at Malcolm's feet.

"There's his VC, Skipper," he said, making no attempt to conceal the bitterness in his voice.

"I'd like a word with you, Indio," said Malcolm as he stepped away from the group of marines staring at the old woman's body.

Jesse retrieved his rifle from Sanderson and followed.

Once out of earshot of the others, Malcolm turned to Jesse. "Do you have any damned regard for what happens to you – any at all?"

"Some, but my principles come first."

"Your damned principles may have killed a marine this morning."

"He may have been wearin' the uniform but he was no marine."

"Who are you to make those kinds of judgements? Are you God?"

"I'm more important than God to me. If all the other Gods are so damn powerful and omnipotent, why do they allow war?"

"Not so you can kill those on your own side, that's for damn sure."

"He wasn't on my side, Sir. He quit bein' on my side when he murdered that old mama-san. I judged him then, now you stand there judging me." Jesse's voice almost cracked and it made him angry at himself. "I passed sentence on him and carried it out. You do the same. I don't have a machine-gun barrel but you can use my M-1 if you think I was so wrong." He was on the verge of tears and he knew his voice gave him away. He offered the M-1 to Malcolm.

Malcolm accepted the M-1 and stared at Jesse who stood defiantly before him.

"Sir, if yer gonna beat me with my own rifle, at least have the decency to be done with it," said Jesse.

"I should have your ass in front of the old man," he said, returning the rifle to Jesse. "Byler is seriously injured. There is a chance he won't make it."

"So that was his name. Well, as far as I'm concerned, I hope he doesn't."

"That's enough of that talk." Malcolm's voice carried a harsh tone.

"Yessir."

"This matter isn't over yet but, for now, we've got other work to do. Get Mud and report to my CP."

"Aye aye, Sir." As he turned to locate Mud, Jesse said, "By the way, Sir, if you find my canteen cup, hang onto it for me, will you?" He was back in control of his emotions. It felt good to know he hadn't misjudged his company commander.

Malcolm shook his head and suppressed a smile as Jesse disappeared into the trees. Patches of light began to pierce the ground fog.

The point man from the Second Battalion, Fourth Marines passed through Alpha Company's line as Jesse and Mud sipped on lukewarm coffee. The fresh troops took careful note of the remnants of Alpha Company as they passed.

Jesse thought he recognized one of the men passing through. Stepping in the smaller man's direction, he said, "Joe?"

The small man stopped and turned to face him. "Jesse?" He paused. They shook hands. "Boy, do you look like shit."

Jesse smiled. "I feel even worse'n I look. How things been with you?"

"I thought pretty shitty until I saw you. Now I don't feel so bad. What the hell happened out here?"

"With the help of our battalion commander, we almost bought the farm."

"I know what you mean. I thought Korea was bad, but I believe this one is worse when it comes to tactics," said Fitzgerald.

"I wasn't in Korea but if it was anywhere near as screwed up as this one, you can have it. Have you heard from Katrina?"

"Yeah, we write once in a while. She says to tell you hello if I see you. Claudia too. Don't you ever write to Claudia?"

Jesse shrugged. "I guess I just never got around to it. I didn't know her long enough to have that much in common with her."

"Jesus Christ. Not even a line?"

Jesse shook his head. "Maybe in the next couple of days. You want some coffee?"

"No time. Gotta get goin'. I'll be runnin' into ya again."

Jesse shook his hand again. "You take care, Joe. Keep yer ass low."

Fitzgerald hurried into the rice paddy.

"Friend of yours?" asked Malcolm as Jesse returned to his coffee.

"Yessir. We came over on the *Breckinridge* together. He got out at the end of the Korean war and signed up again right after *Starlite*. Things must be rough in

279

Stoney Livingston

Two-Four. He's supposed to be an office clerk. Crazy little guy from Chicago."

Malcolm arched his right eyebrow. Jesse smiled. He knew what Malcolm was thinking.

When the main body of fresh troops entered the enemy tree line, Alpha Company moved into the paddies to search for those still unaccounted for.

The newly arrived marines encountered no active resistance as they swept through the enemy position. One man was killed and two seriously wounded by booby-traps left behind by the retreating enemy. Ten charred bodies were found inside the enemy position, in addition to some miscellaneous body parts. No functional weapons were recovered, though some destroyed or badly damaged pieces were found. The fifty caliber machine-gun was not on the list of damaged weapons captured. Some intelligence information was discovered and was dispatched to S-2 for immediate action.

Bravo Company recovered two of its dead and one wounded from the rice paddy on the west. Alpha found three dead and four wounded in the paddy they had fought so hard to cross. By eleven A.M. the mop-up operation was completed and the position declared secure.

Jesse and Mud were requested to identify a body. Jesse thought that a bit unusual since neither he nor Mud knew anyone in Alpha Company. They both stood over the body of the dead marine. The left side of his face and part of his left shoulder had been blown away. His radio had been removed from his body and lay on the ground at his side.

Jesse said, "I think it's Franks." He turned to his radio operator. "What do you think, Mud?"

Jesse knew by the expression on Mud's face that the body was that of Franks. "Yeah. That's Franks." Mud paused for a few seconds, then said, "Damnit!"

"What a waste," said Jesse. "No wonder Pat didn't know what happened. It looks like a sixty mortar landed almost on top of them."

Mud looked at the radio. "It looks like his radio is still serviceable. I'll change pack boards and give this radio back to the 'toon."

Changing out the bloody pack board was not a job Jesse wanted. He didn't know what to say. He turned and walked slowly from the body.

The men of Alpha Company ate noon chow as the two fresh battalions moved about the former enemy position. Jesse ate the cheese and crackers from his rations and gave the rest of the contents to others. The morning fog had lifted and the day was bright and sunny. Only an hour prior, Jesse and Mud had identified Franks' body. Both he and Mud had shed quiet tears.

Jesse thought it ironic that Franks should be killed by an enemy mortar while attempting to get friendly mortars to fire upon the enemy position.

Mud looked up from his can of beefsteak and potatoes and said, "Hey, Indio, did you hear that we suffered *moderate* casualties yesterday?"

"What the hell are you talking about, Mud?"

"Well, you know how they started reporting this 'light, moderate and heavy, bullshit to the public?"

"Yeah. I heard about that. So what's that got to do with yesterday? Hell, even an out-and-out liar couldn't call our casualties 'moderate'. Christ, Alpha lost almost a third of the company."

"That's the way you and me figure it, but the way they're doing it is, they're

280

taking all of the rest of the units that reinforced us and counting them in on the numbers. I guess they figure sixty or seventy casualties out of about three or four thousand guys is *moderate*."

Jesse shook his head. "That sure makes me feel better. I'm glad to know we weren't really hurt as bad as I thought we were at first. What a relief." Jesse stood and scattered the last few drops of coffee in his canteen cup. He looked back at Mud. "This is bullshit, Mud. Nobody in the States has any idea of what's going on over here."

"Who's gonna tell 'em? It sure as hell isn't the news people."

The soft, mournful sound of a harmonica wafted across the battlefield. Jesse stood and moved toward the sound emanating from a point within fifty yards of where he ate his rations. He recognized Sandy, the corpsman, as the musician. He stood ten yards away and listened while Sandy played the mournful tune to its completion. When he finished, Jesse applauded.

"Thank you," smiled Sandy, bowing slightly.

"Doc, that was great. You wouldn't happen to know *Stranger on the Shore*, would you?"

"I think so. Let me give it a try." He placed the harmonica to his lips and began to play. After one false start, he found himself on track and the music flowed forth, surrounding all those within hearing with the most beautiful rendering of the song Jesse had ever heard.

Jesse lit a cigarette and strolled back toward the rice paddy. As he exhaled the smoke, he listened to the harmonica, looked at the beauty that was Vietnam, and felt a deep sorrow that so many were no longer around to share this moment. *When life is so fragile and so damned important, why the hell are men always trying to kill each other?* He missed Shannon. He wished she could share this depth of emotion with him.

"Pretty, huh?"

Mud's voice jerked him from his reverie.

"Yeah. It sure as hell is."

"Franks would have enjoyed that music."

"Damn, Mud. I was just thinkin' the same thing. We been together too long already."

They both smiled, but the tears in their eyes belied the story told by the shape of their lips.

CHAPTER THIRTEEN: THE BRIG

Jesse and Mud squatted in the shade of a large tree, sipping hot C-ration coffee as the mid-morning sun reached through the thick leaves to wrench whatever energy they had left from their bodies.

"What are we gonna do now, Indio? Are they gonna send us a relief, or are we gonna stay out here with Alpha?"

"I don't really know. I kinda like it out here with the line company. We're pretty independent."

"Yeah, but who needs it? This is only the morning of my third day as an FO operator and I'm beginning to feel like a grunt already."

"You could probably get transferred back to the 'toon if you wanted to, Mud. I'd just as soon stay out here, away from Bailey and Simmons. They're worse than the gooks sometimes."

"Yeah, I know what you mean. Back at the 'toon, I've gotta take orders from everybody. Out here it's only you. And I don't listen to you anyway."

"Yeah, I've noticed that. Remind me to write you up first thing tomorrow."

"You want that reminder in triplicate?"

"What else?"

A lanky PFC. approached. "Hey, Indio, the skipper wants to see ya."

Jesse faced the newcomer. "Hi, Max. You got any idea what it's about?"

Maxwell looked at the ground as though it might be going somewhere without him. "I'm not sure but the scuttlebutt is that you've had the cock, Indio. That damn Byler put the word on you for beatin' him with the machine-gun barrel yesterday."

"So?"

"I overheard the company clerk tellin' the skipper that some chasers are comin' out here from division to take you to Okinawa for a court-martial."

"A court-martial?"

"I'm just telling you what I heard, Indio. Hell, we all know that Byler had no business shootin' that old mama-san."

Jesse stood. "Where's the skipper?"

"That big stand of trees behind the elevated road."

"Tell him I'll be right there."

Malcolm was inside the stuffy CP tent, sitting at his small field table, when Jesse entered.

"You wanted to see me, Sir?"

"Have a seat, Indio." Malcolm gestured to the only folding stool in the tent other than the one upon which he was seated.

"Thank you, Sir." Jesse sat on the stool and pulled it close to the small folding table.

Malcolm studied him for a moment. "Indio, Division has ordered me to place you under arrest for beating Byler."

Jesse sat silently.

Malcolm cleared his throat. "There'll be two chasers here in about half-an-hour. You're being transported to Okinawa for a General Court-Martial."

"A General, Sir?"

Malcolm nodded. "I'll do everything within my power to assist you and your counsel in your defense."

Jesse shook his head. A tear balanced in the corner of one eye. He made a visible effort to suppress it. "It doesn't make any sense, Sir. Couldn't they just wait until the war is over? We've both got more important things to do right now. It just seems to me that this could wait. Hell, I could get killed and they could save all that taxpayer money. Besides, things are just startin' to liven up. We lost a lot of men day-before-yesterday. You need everybody you can get. Don't they think of things like that?"

"They have to justify the existence of some of the rear echelon I guess." Malcolm paused. "I won't tell you not to worry, Indio. Any court-martial is serious business but I promise you all the help I can give you."

"What about my M-1 and seven-eighty-two gear?"

"If you want to turn it in to me, I'll take care of it until disposition of your case."

"I'd appreciate it, Sir." He couldn't hold it back any longer. One of those damned tears rolled down his cheek.

*****

"Sir! Prisoner 7737 requests permission to cross the red line. Sir!"

The big guard looked at Jesse contemptuously. "Get across."

Jesse quickly crossed the red line painted on the concrete and followed the lead chaser. A second marine was right on his heels, nightstick at the ready.

Camp Butler, Okinawa was the last of the red-line brigs in the Marine Corps. No prisoner was allowed to cross any red line, whether painted on a doorway or on the ground, without first obtaining permission from a guard or chaser. A violation of this regulation was dealt with severely. Jesse's freshly bruised face testified to the milder form of punishment inflicted by overzealous guards in response to such an infraction.

He was manacled and chained ankles to wrists, with just enough slack in the chain so that he could take short steps, making it difficult to keep up with the lead chaser as the man stepped out briskly with long strides. The chaser behind him prodded with his nightstick. "Move it out. We ain't got all day."

Jesse jerked with pain when the nightstick struck him in the ribs. He looked over his shoulder. "If I wasn't chained, you wouldn't do that."

"What did you say?" The chaser shrieked.

The lead chaser turned his head to observe the exchange.

Jesse wished he had a little less pride. But he didn't. "I said, if I wasn't chained, you wouldn't do that."

The chaser jabbed him sharply in the ribcage. Jesse doubled up with pain. The lead chaser grabbed his chains and jerked them forward, causing Jesse to lose his balance and fall to the concrete, the chaser falling with him as Jesse snagged him with a hand. The second chaser moved in with his nightstick, swinging it at Jesse's head and neck, then jabbing him in the ribs. Jesse struggled to his feet, bringing his arms up to protect his face, making no attempt to assault either chaser.

"You out there! What the hell is going on?"

The two chasers regained their postures and stood stiffly, both keeping an eye on Jesse as they considered the question. The man behind Jesse said, "The prisoner was acting up, Sir. He attempted to strike PFC Watson."

Jesse said nothing. He lowered his hands slowly. He didn't recognize the Marine captain standing by the doorway ahead of them.

"Bring that man over here."

"We have orders to take him directly to defense counsel, Captain."

"I *am* his defense counsel, Lance Corporal."

The lance corporal appeared unsure of himself. "But, Sir, we have orders to take him to the visiting rooms."

The captain stepped from the open doorway in which he stood. "If you don't mind, I'll accompany you – just to make sure he doesn't try any more funny stuff."

"Yessir," replied the lance corporal reluctantly. He gave Jesse a hateful glance, a warning that more would come of this. Jesse smiled back at the hateful warning, and winked quickly.

The captain fell in behind and the four marched the short distance to the visiting rooms.

Jesse studied the grey walls and the heavy grey metal table bolted to the floor in the center of the room. The chasers removed his manacles at the request of the captain and left the room to stand outside while Jesse met with his counsel.

"I'm Captain Talbot. I've been assigned as defense counsel in your case." He offered his hand.

Jesse stared dumbly at his outstretched arm.

"We've got to work together, Indio. I don't hold with formality during our relationship for the course of your trial."

Jesse shook his hand. "How did you know to call me by that name?"

Talbot smiled. He opened his briefcase and extracted a letter. "I got this letter from a personal friend of mine." He passed the letter across the desk.

Jesse read quickly, fearful his time would be cut short and the letter would be snatched from him before he finished. But no guard came running to take the letter from him. When he finished reading, he paused thoughtfully for a long moment, then looked up at Lieutenant Talbot. "I think Lieutenant Malcolm is a helluva guy too, Sir."

"We went to OCS together. He's top drawer. I never met a man with more integrity. He says there were mitigating circumstances and that he will forward a detailed report in the next day or two."

Jesse sighed. "You know, Captain, I think this whole thing is a bunch of bullshit. Lieutenant Malcolm has got a line company that's about two-thirds t.o. strength, and they take me out of it, making him one man shorter. Then on top of that he's gotta take his time making out reports and writing letters to defend me. It's bullshit, Sir."

284

Talbot's gaze met Jesse's. "They given you a rough time this last day or two?"

Jesse shrugged. "I'm not real crazy about this haircut, and some of the chasers need an ass-kickin', but the food's better'n it was in The Nam."

"You don't have to play the tough guy with me, Indio. I know it isn't easy in here."

"So, what do you want me to do, Captain – kiss somebody's ass and tell 'em how sorry I am? That it won't ever happen again? Well, that's not gonna happen while I'm breathin'. Byler killed an old lady who wasn't doin' a damn thing but workin' what was left of her rice crop after we blew it all to hell. And *I'm* the one getting the court-martial. To hell with the Uniform Code of Military Justice."

Talbot shook his head. "That isn't going to get the job done, Indio. I'm going to do my best to get you out of this mess but I could use your help. You're not making it any easier with that attitude."

Jesse wiped his eyes with the back of his hand. "I'm sorry, Captain, but my folks didn't raise me to kiss anybody's ass. And they didn't raise me to look the other way when things were wrong. If you wanna do the right thing, tell 'em to let me out of here so I can get back to my outfit."

"You still don't understand, do you? This is a serious situation. You've been charged..."

"I'll tell you a serious situation, Captain. My outfit bein' short one of the best men they've got; that's a serious situation. And I'm not referring to Byler, though I gotta admit he can handle an M-60.

"Lieutenant Malcolm needs my help, and the help of anybody else he can get. This is stupid. There's a war going on in Vietnam, Sir – a real war, where people get shot and killed and all that good stuff. Why in the hell are the guys in the line outfits the only ones who know about it?"

"What if the only way you could get back to Vietnam was to admit you did wrong, and claim temporary insanity brought on by the events of the day prior?"

Jesse considered Mud and Malcolm and the rest of the men he knew in the First Battalion, Fourth Marines. He wanted to be there, not here. He stared into the blue eyes of Captain Talbot. "That's not what I'm fightin' for, Captain. I'm fightin' for truth and freedom and honesty and integrity, and all the things lawyers don't know a damn thing about. I'm not gonna lie in order to fight for truth. I'll rot in this hole first."

"Okay, Indio, tell me in your own words what happened. Start with the beginning of *Operation Oregon.*

"What the hell is *Operation Oregon?*"

"That's what they've named the sweep you were on when all this happened."

"Do the people in Portland know about this?"

Captain Talbot smiled, "I doubt it."

"That's too bad."

*****

Jesse sat in his cell and stared blankly at the freshly scrubbed grey wall opposite his bunk. He shared the eight-by-ten room with three other misfits. Two were charged with desertion, the third with attempted murder. They had not tried to intimidate Jesse when he had been thrown into the cell. His bruised body and torn clothes and his defiance of the chasers, even as they beat him and shoved him into

285

the cell, elicited only respect and admiration from these men who thought defiance of authority was the measure of a man. They had come to his aid when the chasers closed the cell door but Jesse had shrugged them off. They left him alone. And he felt alone – as alone as any human could feel. As he stared unseeing at the wall, his mind fought its battle. He couldn't let himself give in to the guards, the chasers, the lies, nor the system. Where was his support? Was there no one left in The United States who could support a man who defended his beliefs with honor?

He imagined how Nathan Hale must have felt as he went to the gallows – alone and forsaken by his countrymen. *Hell, you're no Nathan Hale. You're giving yourself too much status there, Langley.*

"Prisoner 7737." The sharp voice jarred him from his thoughts.

Jesse stood. "Sir! Prisoner 7737. Sir!"

"Step to the hatch."

"Sir! Aye aye, Sir!" He jumped to the cell door.

The crooked smile of the lance corporal met him at the bars. The man spoke softly. "You're dead meat, 7737. Your ass is mine if you fuck up just one more time. Do you understand me?"

"Sir! Yes, Sir!"

"It's time for your exercise. Move away from the hatch."

"Sir! Yes, Sir!" He stepped back two paces.

The lance corporal opened the bars, clanking his heavy key ring carelessly. "Move out, 7737!"

"Sir! Yes, Sir!"

Jesse moved toward the door at the double, stopping near the jamb and continuing to run in place. "Sir! 7737 requests permission to cross the red line. Sir!"

"Get across!"

At the next door he came to another red line and ran at stationary double-time as he requested permission to cross the line. "Sir! 7737 requests permission to cross the red line. Sir!"

The lance corporal stood, smiling as Jesse continued to run in place.

"Sir! Prisoner 7737 requests permission to cross the red line. Sir!"

"I heard you, 7737! What's the matter, don't you think I can hear?"

Jesse continued to run in place.

"I asked you a question, 7737!"

Jesse knew it was a no-win question. *So this is how he's gonna set me up.* "Sir! 7737 apologizes. He thought that perhaps he didn't speak clearly enough. Sir!"

The lance corporal smiled. "Well, 7737, maybe you *are* smarter than you look. Cross!"

Jesse jumped across the line.

"Too slow, 7737! Get back!

He jumped back behind the line. "Sir! 7737 requests permission to cross the red line. Sir!"

The lance corporal brought his face close to the bouncing face of Jesse as the latter continued to run in place. "Are you being a smart-ass, 7737?"

"Sir! No, Sir!"

"Now you're calling me a liar. Is that right, 7737?"

"Sir! No, Sir!"

The lance corporal moved a little closer. Deftly, he jabbed Jesse in the ribs with the end of his nightstick. Jesse doubled slightly then straightened and continued to run in place. "What are you doing if you're not calling me a liar, 7737?"

Jesse ignored him. "Sir! 7737 requests permission to cross the red line. Sir!"

"Answer my question, 7737!"

Jesse stopped his stationary double-time and looked at the chaser. He cocked his head. "Hell, I forgot. What was the question?"

"Are you talking to me, 7737?" Screeched the lance corporal. "You did it this time, maggot! You screwed up big-time. You better double-time it, 7737!"

Jesse broke into stationary double-time, a smile as long and as crooked as the Colorado river on his face. "Sir! 7737 requests permission to cross the red line. Sir!"

The lance corporal jabbed him in the kidney with his stick. Jesse spun and snatched the nightstick from the unsuspecting chaser's hand. "Guard!" shouted the lance corporal.

Two guards at the near end of the corridor came rushing to the chaser's aid. Jesse smiled and handed the nightstick to the surprised lance corporal. "I believe you dropped your stick, Sir."

The advancing guards grabbed Jesse from behind just as the chaser seized his black nightstick. While his arms were pinned behind him by the two guards, the lance corporal poked Jesse in the ribs and stomach with the stick. He felt pain clear into his throat as the bigger man struck him in the testicles. He went down on one knee.

"Get up, 7737, you smart-ass sonofabitch!"

Jesse's pain was so intense, drawing a breath was difficult. The chaser struck him in the temple with the stick, sending him to the prone position on the concrete, the guards releasing their holds on him, letting him fall. He crawled through the door and staggered to a stooped position, the chaser standing over him with his stick poised. Jesse tasted the blood in his mouth and rolled his tongue around the inside of his teeth. "Sir! 7737 has by-god-crossed-the-fucking-red-line," he smiled.

He ducked just in time to avert a blow to his head. He crouched low and faced the big lance corporal. The two guards tackled him.

Jesse squinted at the bright sunlight as a guard opened the narrow slot in his solitary confinement cell.

"7737?"

Through his scabbed lips, Jesse replied, "Come back tomorrow. The house is a mess."

The guard peeked into the slot. Jesse, squinted into the light and shaded his eyes with his left hand. "Listen, 7737, don't make it any worse than it already is. I don't have anything against you and I'm not into this power thing. I'm just doing my time here until I get out. You don't have to fight me, man."

Jesse moved closer to the slot. He had seen this marine every morning of the three days he had been confined to solitary and a diet of bread and water. He had thought it was his imagination but he had sensed empathy in the man's eyes.

"This is your third day of piss and punk. You get a full meal this evening. I figured you might be able to use something before then." His fingers came through the slot. Clamped between two of them was a Hershey candy bar.

Jesse peered into the slot, trying to see if it might be a trick of some sort. He could see very little. Gently he removed the candy bar from the fingers. "Thanks.

287

I could use a little nourishment. Why are you helping me? Is this thing poisoned or something?"

"I'll take the first bite."

"I'm sorry, man. It's just a little strange, that's all. Try to look at it from my point of view."

"I'm going to open the door now. Watch your eyes."

"Okay, go ahead."

Bright sunlight flooded into the drab cell with its four concrete walls, a bunk and toilet. The guard stood outside the door. "I can't come in. Hurry up and eat that candy bar and let's get moving."

Jesse stuffed the chocolate bar into his mouth.

"Slip the wrapper into my hand as you get in the hatch," ordered the guard. Jesse nodded and passed him the wrapper deftly as he entered the doorway.

"I still don't get it. I mean, don't misunderstand me, I appreciate the huss, but I don't understand it. You could be busted for this."

"Don't talk, just move it out."

"Sir! 7737 requests permission to cross the red line. Sir!"

"Get across."

Captain Talbot stared at Jesse's bruised and battered figure as he sat across the table from him in the visiting room. "What the hell happened to you?"

"I guess it's just another case of me stealing more chain than I could swim with."

"Don't you ever take that chip off your shoulder?"

"Why, Captain? So someone can have the pleasure of saying I'm beaten? I don't need it – not around here anyway. It would give pleasure to too many assholes."

"What happened?"

Jesse pointed to the stack of papers on the table in front of Talbot. "Didn't you have time to read up, Captain? I'm sure everything is documented. That's the way assholes protect themselves you know – they document everything."

"I've read the reports. They say you attacked your chaser and attempted to beat him with his own baton."

"Oh, they call 'em batons now, huh? I always called 'em nightsticks. Well, did you see the chaser's name on the roster at the hospital?"

"I didn't check."

"Don't bother, you won't find it there."

"So what does that prove?" There was irritation in Talbot's voice.

"That proves I didn't take his damn nightstick away from him and try to beat him to death. If I had, I would have at least put him in the hospital." Jesse smiled. His lips cracked and he winced.

Despite himself, Talbot smiled. "Lieutenant Malcolm must have an extraordinary perception. And you're right; he needs guys like you. I haven't been in to see you for this past three days because I've been to Vietnam."

"You saw Lieutenant Malcolm?"

"In the flesh."

"How's he doing?"

"They've just been sitting since *Oregon*, but something is in the wind. I don't know what but Malcolm seems to think that a new strategy is being developed at

288

Division."

Jesse leaned across the table. "Get me out of here, Captain. I'll come back to this damn court-martial thing after we win the war. I promise."

"I believe you would, but I can't do anything about that. It's my job to see that you get a fair hearing. I think we can get a reduction to a Special Court-Martial and, if we agree to a plea, maybe even a Summary."

"Plea? Plea to what? All I'm guilty of is trying to stop one of our guys from killing an old lady."

"Yes, that's true to a point, but you went beyond that when you beat him with the machine-gun barrel."

Jesse shrugged.

"We have mitigating circumstances. If we can arrange for a Summary Court-Martial, the worst you could get would be thirty days in the brig."

"No thanks. I've spent almost a week here now and I don't believe I'm into thirty days of this shit. Goddamnit, Captain, where the hell is honor?" Jesse shrugged. "What the hell am I askin' *you* for? You're an attorney."

"Don't give up on me just yet, Indio. I've been to Japan and seen Byler."

"Damn. You mean he's gonna survive?" The sarcasm was not lost on Talbot.

"Fortunately." Talbot glanced at his wristwatch. "I've got to go. I have an appointment with the Camp Commandant in about ten minutes. I'll be back to see you tomorrow."

"Do you smoke, Captain?"

"No, why?"

"I could sure use a Camel cigarette."

Talbot shook his head. "I'll bring you a pack tomorrow."

"Don't bother with a whole pack. As long as I'm in solitary they won't let me have 'em anyway."

"Psst. 7737."

Jesse came awake. The slot on his solitary cell was open and it was dark outside. "Who is it?"

"It's me, Clem, the guy who gave you the candy bar."

Jesse moved to the door. "What do you want? Am I bustin' out of here or what?"

Clem chuckled. "No, nothing that grand. Here. Here's a couple of cigarettes. I hear you like these horse turds."

The fingers came through the slot. Jesse took the two short cigarettes. "How did you know I smoked this brand? Who the hell are you, anyway? Why are you doing this?"

Jesse put one of the smokes between his lips. Clem put his fingers through the slot and passed him a Zippo. Jesse lit the cigarette and returned the lighter.

"Will you testify in court that McDonald beat you with his baton?"

"Who the hell is McDonald? Is he the big blond lance corporal with a pimple for a brain?"

"That's the one."

"Has he got something on you?"

"No," whispered Clem. "There's a few of us who'd like to see him put on the other side of the wire. He's beat the hell out of more guys than you would ever

289

believe, but not a single man will testify against him. They're all afraid that their word against his won't wash and he'll be in a position to murder 'em later."

"What's in it for you?"

"You may not believe me, man, but it's real simple: justice. It's bad enough that a guy has to follow the regs in this place but that's the law. It isn't the law that he has to be beaten."

Jesse couldn't believe what he was hearing. He wept silently in the darkness.

"Psst. 7737, you still there?"

"Yeah, man. I'm still here."

"Can I count on you if it comes to it?"

"I wouldn't miss it for the world."

"I gotta go, 7737. Say, what the hell is your real name anyway?"

Tears streamed down his face. "I don't know anymore. They call me Indio. That'll do."

"Proud to meet you, Indio. I'll be by later with some chow."

"Proud to meet you, Clem. Is that your first name or your last?"

"Last. And my nickname too I guess. I gotta go."

Jesse smiled in the darkness as the tears streamed down his face. *Only in the goddamned Crotch.*

The slot opened abruptly. "7737. Heave to. Time for P.T."

It wasn't Clem's voice. "Sir! 7737 is ready for P.T. Sir!"

The iron door swung wide. Lance Corporal McDonald stood framed by the bright light. Jesse hesitated.

"What's the matter, 7737? Were you expecting someone else?"

"Sir! No, Sir!"

"Well, 7737, you'll be glad to hear that I volunteered to take you on Physical Training when one of our men had to report to sick bay with stomach flu."

Jesse's eyes had not yet adjusted to the light. McDonald reached into the cell with his baton and struck him on the side of the head. Jesse fell to the concrete floor. McDonald stood in the hatch and laughed.

"Get up, 7737."

Jesse stood slowly and faced the big lance corporal.

"I said get out here, 7737."

"Fuck you."

"What did you say?"

"What's the matter, stupid? You got shit in your ears? I said fuck you."

McDonald smiled. "So you finally lost it, huh? I'll be glad to whip your ass, punk, but you know the rules. I can't enter without another man present." He turned and shouted over his shoulder. "Guard! I've got a bad-ass in here."

Jesse heard the puffing of another man rushing to the cell. His heart leapt into his throat. *It's too late to go back now.*

Boldly, McDonald stepped into the small cell, the other man close behind. It was the same man who had helped beat Jesse several days before – Watson. Jesse felt despair. He crouched and waited.

The two advanced into his cell slowly, confidently. A smile spread across McDonald's lips.

*****

"Jesus Christ, man! What the hell were you trying to prove?"

Jesse looked up at Captain Talbot from the examination table in the sick bay. "I don't know, Captain. It just seemed like the thing to do at the time."

"We had it set up to follow you to the P.T. field," said Clem, who stood at the Captain's side. "We weren't ready for anything to happen in the cell. They could have killed you before we got there."

"I didn't know you were gonna get there at all. I was doin' pretty good, considerin'."

Clem smiled. "I don't think they can sew that piece of McDonald's left ear back to his head. That was a pretty jagged bite. How do you feel?"

"Alive, and that's good. My ribs are a little sore. I've got all my teeth but I almost lost one when McDonald tried to jerk his head away. That's why his ear ripped. If he'd 'a' just held still, I could have bitten it off clean. Jeez can that guy scream. It sounded great."

Talbot made a visible effort to control his urge to laugh. "It isn't really funny when you think about it."

"I guess it depends on your perspective, Captain. I thought it was funny as hell." Jesse sat up on the table. "By the way, Clem, how in the hell did you get promoted to captain so fast? What's your real name and rank?"

Clem offered his hand. "Captain Ronald Clem, C.I.D. It's a pleasure."

"Likewise, Captain. Thanks for the candy bar and cigarettes too by the way."

"You're welcome." Clem turned to Talbot. "If you'll excuse me, gentlemen, I've got to follow up on McDonald and Company."

Jesse waited until Clem had left the room. "Well, what now, Sir? Back to the same old thing?"

"You're a free man, Indio."

"What?"

"Byler is going on trial for murder. The charges against you were reduced to an Article 134, and Captain Clem had those charges dropped in exchange for your cooperation against McDonald."

"Are you serious? They changed the charge to the 'Catch-all Article', then they dropped the whole damned thing?"

"Of course I'm serious. It's hardly something I would joke about."

Jesse smiled. "Ow. That hurts. Don't make me laugh."

"After a few days in the hospital I'll make arrangements for your transportation back to One-Four."

"I don't need any time in the hospital. I feel fine. Just get me out of here. I'm ready to go back today."

Talbot smiled. "It's too late to catch a flight out today. The best I can do is tomorrow afternoon."

"You mean I can just get right up and walk out of here?"

"They're processing your paperwork now. I'd say in about thirty minutes you can walk out the door."

"Damn, I don't know what to say. Thanks seems a bit trite, but it's the best I can do, Captain."

"Call me Phil."

"Phil?"

291

Stoney Livingston

"I can't have you calling me 'Captain' all night if we're going to pull liberty together."

"Me an' you? No kidding? What will the brass think?"

"I'll ask next time I see a brass. Where do you want to go tonight?"

Jesse looked at his reflection in the mirror opposite the exam table. "I look like death warmed over. It wasn't bad enough they had to bruise me all to hell. They had to shave my head too."

"It doesn't matter what you look like here. Two dollars will get you a short-time almost anyplace; five bucks will get you an all-nighter."

"You mean inflation hasn't caught up with us yet?"

"No but I see it coming." Talbot smiled.

"To tell you the truth, Cap...Phil – are you sure it's all right to call you that?" Phil nodded.

"Well, Phil, to tell you the truth, I was stationed here a few years ago and I'd like to visit some of my old friends up in Henoko."

"Henoko? Hell, that's clear up by Camp Schwab. Were you in the Third Marines?"

"Two-Three. 1963. Best damn outfit I was ever in. I made some friends in Henoko and, if you don't mind, I'd really like to see them again."

"Are you sure you feel up to it?"

Jesse looked at Phil out of the corner of his eyes.

"Sorry. Silly of me to ask. Let's get you processed out of here," he said.

"That sounds like the best idea I've heard in a long time."

The village of Henoko sprawled in two layers. Lower Henoko sat in a canyon, separated from upper Henoko by a cliff, though the slope of the cliff was gentle enough to be negotiated by a man on foot in most places, if he was careful. Upper Henoko was the commercialized area, where the shops and bars catered to the U.S. Marines from nearby Camp Schwab. Lower Henoko was affectionately called "combat town" by the marines. The natives there wanted nothing to do with the marines or the American dollar and, for the most part, the marines had no interest in Combat Town.

Jesse caught the familiar smell of a benjo ditch as he stepped from the small cab in Upper Henoko. It was not a pleasant smell but it brought back pleasant memories. He watched Phil Talbot pay the driver but his mind was elsewhere. There were so many people he wanted to see and not enough time to see them all. He had promised Masako, Pineapple's old girlfriend, that he would see her if he ever came back. He would try to find her later. His first thought was for Juneko. She was one of the most experienced women he had ever known, and that was what he needed; that and a bottle of American sourmash whiskey.

"Where do you want to start?" Phil's voice snapped him out of his reverie.

"The sun isn't down yet. Why don't we just stroll the streets? I'd just like to look at things. It doesn't look like much has changed in the last two or three years."

Phil smiled. "That's fine by me. You lead, I'll follow."

"You're the captain."

"Not tonight I'm not."

They walked casually through the dirt streets of Henoko, Jesse painfully self-conscious of his newly purchased civilian clothes and his closely cut hair. His lower lip was swollen and cracked, making even a small smile a difficult achievement.

They stood on the wooden sidewalk under an awning. Jesse smoked a cigarette as Phil watched a neisan walking to work at a nearby bar.

"That sure looks good, doesn't it?" asked Phil.

"That, my friend, is an understatement. She looks like heaven."

The neisan looked up disinterestedly at the two Americans. Her nondescript facial expression suddenly changed to one of recognition. She moved quickly in their direction, a white smile spread across her face. "Jesse-san. You come back Okinawa!"

Jesse struggled for recognition. Her face was familiar but he couldn't place her.

She stopped only inches away from them "You no remember Peggy-san?"

A smile covered his face, a trickle of blood sliding slowly down his chin. "Peggy-san! I can't believe it. You look great! I'm sorry I didn't recognize you at first. I guess I just wasn't expecting to see you."

She stepped into his arms and gave him a warm hug. When they separated, she touched his lower lip softly. Jesse-san hurt?"

He shrugged. "It's not so bad." He turned to Phil. "Phil, this is Peggy. Peggy, this is a good friend of mine, Phil."

"How do you do?" She held out her hand.

"Wow, your English has sure improved." He looked at Phil. "When I first met Peggy, she hardly spoke a word of english."

Peggy winked at him. "Not necessary speak English all the time."

Jesse choked on his cigarette smoke. "I didn't say that. You did. I was gonna keep it our secret."

She grabbed Jesse's hand. "You two come with me. I buy you drink. No work in Dumbo's no more. Work in new club called Conga. Good club. Good drinks. You come with me. I buy you drink." She looked at Jesse and smiled. "After work, we have good time. I never charge Jesse-san. You be patient."

Jesse felt a stirring in his loins as he remembered her touch.

The three of them walked the block to the Conga Bar. Peggy introduced them to the mama-san who ran the bar and set them up with the best booth in the house. When mama-san learned that Jesse was an old friend of Peggy's she bought the first round of drinks. Peggy bought the second.

Shortly after sundown marines from nearby Camp Schwab began to enter the bar. Jesse watched as Peggy and the other neisans hustled them for drinks and jukebox money. He thought of Peggy, doing this same thing six or seven nights a week; hustling marines and going into one of the back rooms once or twice a night for a "short-time" at two dollars a shot. He sighed.

"Something bothering you, old man?" asked Phil.

"No...well, yeah...kinda. I was just thinking of Peggy. She's sexier than hell, and she's smart as a whip, and she's got one of the greatest personalities you'll ever meet. And she's hustling drinks and screwin' G.I.s at two bucks a pop. How long do you suppose a hooker's career lasts before she's plumb wore out?"

"I'd say that depends on the woman. Not very long, even with the best, I would imagine. Probably about the same as a pro football player."

"They get paid more."

"You're right there. And I'll bet the retirement benefits are better too."

Jesse smiled a sad-looking smile. He was getting used to the cracked lips.

293

Stoney Livingston

If he smiled a bit crookedly they didn't hurt as much. "I guess I should talk. Hell, when I first met her she was brand new to this business. I took advantage of the American dollar and sampled her wares, and I kept coming back for more. As a matter-of-fact, I don't think I ever did get enough of her. I don't think any man can. She's about as perfect as a woman can be in bed."

"Stop it, you're killing me."

"What's the matter, Phil? Aren't officers allowed to mingle with the locals?"

Phil glanced nervously about the bar. "I could tell you stories about officers and women that you wouldn't believe. Hell yes, we fraternize."

Jesse raised his glass. "To fraternization."

They drank the toast.

In between customers, Peggy sat next to Jesse in the booth, pressing her thigh against his as hard as she could. She was thoughtful of Phil and saw to it he was occupied with another neisan at all times. When she was away from the table she signaled to the other girls to stay away from Jesse.

Jesse was torn between leaving to visit with others and staying to be near Peggy and feel her touch. He sipped his bourbon and water slowly. It was too early to start any serious drinking.

Jesse looked at the girl sitting on Phil's lap. "Hey, Phil, why don't you just go out back with her? You don't have to baby-sit me." He nodded to a nearby table. "I've got Peggy, remember?"

Phil smiled. "How could I forget?"

"Go ahead; let your hair down, and hers too. You afraid I'm gonna say somethin' to somebody?"

"No. The thought hadn't crossed my mind. Now that I've discovered this place, I can always come back. You, you're leaving tomorrow – unless you want me to change the orders."

"I'd love to but I can't. If I stayed an extra day, it'd turn into a week, then a month, then a year."

Phil ignored the girl on his lap momentarily and leaned into the table. "Why do you have this burning desire to go back to Vietnam? I can't figure it out."

Jesse studied his whiskey glass. "To tell you the truth, I ain't real sure myself. I like to think of myself as a patriot, you know, like Nathan Hale and Patrick Henry, and John Hancock and the boys, but there's more to it than that. It's a combination of a bunch of things."

"Like what?"

"Like when this war is over, I want to be able to tell my kid – if I ever have one – that I fought in the war... I mean really fought, not sat on my ass at division, makin' up war stories – no offense intended. I want to be able to look my kid in the eye and tell him or her that I did it all – and I haven't just yet.

"I don't want to skate out on the guys that are over there. Not just the guys in my outfit, but all of 'em, even the army. They're all Americans. And while they suffer like rats in a sewer, some long-haired hippie is carryin' a sign and bitchin' about the war back home. I wanna be able to hold my head up and say that I protected that bastard's right to protest the war, then I wanna go home and break his nose all over his face.

"I came over here to help win a war. We haven't won yet, so my job isn't done. I don't wanna go home a loser. I don't want anybody to ever be able to say that I didn't do everything possible to help win the war, and if that means gettin' back

Forever Patriots

to my poncho and C-rations tomorrow, that's what it means. Anymore questions?"

Phil looked into Jesse's eyes. "You'd make one helluva case study at some university, my friend."

Jesse shrugged. "You want another drink?"

"Hell yes, might as well." He glanced at his watch. "Say, it's already twenty-one hundred. Are you going to look up anyone else or is Peggy gonna fill the bill for the night?"

Jesse studied his Zodiac SeaWolf watch. "You know, there's plenty of time to look around and still get back before closing. You wanna stay here with sweet thing there or do you wanna reconnoiter?"

"You take the point. I'll follow."

Phil bought his neisan a parting drink and the two left the Conga for new adventures after explaining to Peggy that they would return.

Jesse smoked in silence as they walked in the semi-darkness of the dirt streets, lighted only by the flashing neon of the open businesses. He looked into the window of a small bar as they strolled past its narrow front. He stopped and gazed at the steadily burning green neon light.

"You see a ghost?" asked Phil.

Jesse answered wistfully, "Sort of. I was just thinkin' of a buddy of mine in our old outfit. We used to come into this little place and drink and play the jukebox all night long – six plays for a quarter. There weren't any girls working here, except for Pineapple's girlfriend Masako. But the drinks were good and they were cheap, and Masako was cute and fun. She reminded me of the oriental version of the girl next door." He looked up at Phil. "You mind if we stop in for a minute?"

"What are we waiting for?" Phil opened the narrow door and stepped inside; Jesse followed.

The place was empty. There were two small tables in the Dawn Bar. What little floor space existed was taken up by a jukebox and a pinball machine on one side of the room, and by the bar with seven stools, on the other. Jesse walked straight to the jukebox while Phil ordered drinks.

I'll be damned. Still six plays for a quarter. And there's Pineapple's favorite song. Holy hell, there's mine. He dropped a quarter into the machine and punched up each song three times. His song played first. As Elvis Presley's soothing voice offered its rendition of *Anything That's Part of You*, Jesse turned to join Phil at the bar and looked into shiny, moist, almond-shaped eyes that smiled at their upturned outer edges. He stared at the girl, feeling a closeness of which he had no understanding.

"Jesse-san? It is you, isn't it? You come back. You look hurt."

Jesse's voice failed him. He didn't know what to say. He was happier to see her than he would have been to see his old girlfriend, Juneko.

"Are you okay, Jesse-san? Why you don't speak?"

"I'm okay, Masako. How are you? You look great."

"Oh, Jesse-san, it so good to see you." She put her arms around him and held him tightly. He held her close, not moving, recalling the old outfit and Pineapple and her, and the good times they had shared together. She was all those things that could never be again. He felt a closeness to her that ripped at his heart.

She sobbed on his chest as he held her to him. "Jesse-san, Masako so lonely since you and Pineapple go away Okinawa. New boy-sans not same. Masako miss you and Pineapple very much. Please to forgive me my cry. I so happy you

295

come see Masako."

He kissed her cheek. "I didn't think you'd still be here. I was going to ask mama-san where you were."

"Masako stay here. Mama-san treat good. Masako love mama-san. No place better to go."

He dropped a hand to her waist. "Come to the bar and meet my friend, Masako. He's a good man. He helped me get out of *toxon* trouble."

Masako's eyes grew big and round. "Jesse-san in *toxon* trouble?"

"No more."

She smiled and took the two steps to reach the bar.

"Phil, I want you to meet the darling of Okinawa. Masako Yonishiro, Phil Talbot. Phil, Masako."

Masako held out her hand. "So please meet you, Phil."

"I'm pleased to meet you. So you knew ol' Indio...er Jesse here when he was stationed at Camp Schwab, huh?"

"Oh yes. We very good friends. Jesse-san number-one marine – number-one friend." She looked at Jesse in the brighter light of the bar. "You *are* hurt!" She stepped around the end of the bar and grabbed a bar towel, rinsing it quickly and wringing it out.

"I'm fine, Masako. Let's have a drink together."

She ignored his words and moved around the end of the bar, towel held high. He protested weakly as she patted his cracked lips and bruised cheekbones. Masako chatted to Phil as she doctored.

"One time Pineapple run away – go UA. Take Masako with him. We hide on small island just offshore. Jesse-san find and bring us food and water for almost three weeks. He have to wade long way at low tide or swim at high tide to get to us, but he always bring food, water, saki and candles. Masako never forget."

Phil smiled as he watched her work quickly but gently on Jesse's face while he sipped at his beer.

Masako continued. "One time, marines put Dawn Bar off limits when make new rules. Must have two *benjo*...bathrooms. Mama-san poor. Take long time to get money to make new bathroom. Jesse-san and Pineapple no care, come see mama-san and Masako anyway."

She continued to pat and wipe as she spoke. "One more time, five marines from tanks come into bar, takeover jukebox, give Masako and mama-san bad time. Jesse-san and Pineapple fight with tankers. MP's come, Jesse-san and Pineapple jump through window, no get caught. Tankers all get caught.

"One more time...."

"Whoa, Masako. That's enough already," said Jesse around the towel. He pulled her hands from his face and held them gently in his own.

Masako cried. "So sorry, Jesse-san. Masako so nervous to see you. Please to hold Masako." She stepped into his arms and hugged him again.

Jesse patted her on the back. "I'm happy to see you too, Masako – happier than you'll ever know."

Phil cleared his throat. "Say, Indio, I think I'll go back to the Conga. If I don't see you before daylight, you know where to find me."

"No, Phil, it ain't like that. Masako and I are just real good friends. Hang around."

"I know how it is. I think it's the prettiest damn reunion I've ever seen. I can't believe there was a marine involved in it. Semper Fi." He stood.

"Aw, c'mon, Phil, hang around."

"Not on your life. This is getting too damned emotional for me. Hell, I had the strength zapped out of me just watching the feelings between you two."

"Yeah, but it's friendship, real friendship."

"Yeah, I know. That's what makes it even worse. See you later."

Masako looked at the closing door. "You are unhappy I make friend want to leave? Masako sorry."

Jesse smelt of her jet-black hair and could smell none of the perfume worn by the other neisans. It smelled clean but there lingered a feint odor of the sea. It made him feel closer to her.

A hand patted him on the shoulder. He turned to see mama-san's smiling face. Apparently she had been in the back room or, in his delight to see Masako, he had not noticed her had she been in the bar. He withdrew from Masako's embrace and leaned across the small bar. "Mama-san, you old rascal! How have you been?"

She hugged him and patted him on the back. "Long time no see, Jesse-san. Mama-san think maybe you never come back. How long you stay Okinawa?"

"I can only stay tonight, Mama-san. I've gotta leave tomorrow."

He felt Masako stiffen at his side.

"You go to Vietnam? Kill VC?" asked mama-san.

"I'm gonna try."

"You go tomorrow?" asked Masako.

He looked back to Masako. "I'm afraid so, Masako. My friends are over there. They need my help."

She pulled away from him. "Your friends. Always you give to your friends. Is Masako your friend?"

"One of my very best friends."

"Then you stay with mama-san and Masako few days. We go to beach, see movies, go bowling. Have fun like before."

"I can't."

"Jesse-san, it is good you give to your friends but you must also give to yourself. You are only G.I. from old Two-Three that not try to take Masako bed, because you are Pineapple's friend. I understand. This makes you my friend too. Masako very lonely for old friend. You are only American friend I ever have. You have friends in Okinawa, same as Vietnam. You stay."

"My friends in Okinawa are not being killed by the VC."

"Many things kill besides bullets."

"I think I liked it better when you didn't speak English."

That drew a smile from her pouting lips. "You make me so angry. Masako not stay mad with Jesse-san very long. You too happy-go-lucky."

"Let's drink to that."

Mama-san poured another Jack Daniels for Jesse and mixed a sloe gin fizz for herself and Masako. She said, "Mama-san and Masako happy you come see us." They all touched glasses.

Masako turned to mama-san and spoke rapidly in Japanese. The old woman smiled a cupid smile and nodded. Masako rushed behind the bar and picked up one bottle of Jack Daniels and one bottle of sloe gin. She exited the bar and grabbed Jesse's hand as she walked past him.

"Mama-san say okay Masako go now. Not much busy tonight. We go beach where we swim altogether with old Two-Three long time ago. We drink and watch ocean and talk of old friends."

Jesse looked helplessly at mama-san and lifted his shoulders. Mama-san repeated the gesture, smiling. "You go. Masako so happy you come back."

They sat on the beach, under a half moon, watching the white caps of the surf as they crashed onto themselves, hearing the sounds unique to the ocean. Masako drank from her bottle of sloe gin.

"You remember Baby Huey and Mac?" she asked.

Jesse nodded as he tipped his bottle of sourmash to his lips.

"One time they find sea snake right over there." She pointed to an outcropping of rock. "Baby Huey not know sea snake poisonous. He pick up snake and chase Mac all over beach. When he find out sea snake poisonous, he throw snake and ...how you say... 'go to sleep'?"

"You mean pass out or feint?"

"That right... pass out. Get bloody nose when he fall."

They laughed in a moonlight that belonged only to them. Jesse put his arm around her and she snuggled close.

"That long time ago, Jesse-san, but Masako never forget."

Jesse took another pull on his bottle. "Yeah, that was a crazy group of guys, that's for sure."

"What happened to them?" she asked.

Jesse's eye's filled with tears as the whiskey and the thought of J.D. and some of the others flooded his mind. Masako put her face next to his and stared at his moist eyes, shimmering in the moonlight.

"Masako say something make Jesse-san sad?"

Jesse sniffed. "Some of them are dead, Masako. Some of them are dead." He swallowed hard.

Masako fell silent. She put her arm around him and held onto his torso without speaking or moving. She cried with him silently in the solitude that was theirs. She didn't ask their names. She didn't want to know. They were as one to her and Jesse knew it. For ten minutes they sat together, sharing a sadness they both understood, neither speaking, each grateful to have the other.

"You have seen Juneko?" asked Masako quietly after a while.

"No." He took another swig of whiskey.

She drank from her sloe gin bottle. "She is very pretty."

"Yes, she is. But you know what, Masako? You're the most beautiful woman on this island. You're as pretty as Juneko on the outside and, on the inside, you're beautiful. You're just a beautiful person – period."

"You just say that to make Masako feel good. Juneko is too pretty." She took another drink from her bottle.

"Hey, when did you turn into a lush? You didn't even drink when I last saw you."

"Many things change. Masako change too."

"Baloney." He took a deep pull from his bottle.

"Kiss me please, Jesse-san."

He reached out and pecked her gently on the nose.

"No, Jesse-san, you kiss Masako, real kiss."

He looked at her in the heat-less glow of the moon. The gentle breeze

298

Forever Patriots

coming from the coral reefs offshore whipped her hair about her eyes. "Masako, you've had too much to drink. I'm takin' you home." He wondered what his reaction to her request would have been had he not seen Peggy. Masako was the oriental apple pie – the girl next door – but Peggy oozed raw sex appeal. That's what he needed. He wanted no emotional attachment.

She stood in the sandy soil of the beach, the split dress and the moonlight accenting her femininity. "Why you say that? You tell me how beautiful I am, then you don't want kiss me." She staggered forward, losing her balance. She righted herself with a monumental effort but not before the split on the side of her skirt ripped almost to her waist as the result of her move.

Jesse felt a stirring in his loins. He took a quick sip of his whiskey. "Please, Masako, sit down. Let me get regrouped here."

She stood over him, her thighs only inches from his face. "Jesse-san, you always so polite and so much fun at same time. You like Masako very much in old Two-Three, but you never ask Masako go bed because Pineapple your friend. Masako like you very much, but you Pineapple's friend."

She knelt next to him, exposing her leg to her buttocks. "Don't you see? Pineapple gone, never come back. You here. Masako here. You like woman. I hear talk from Juneko and Peggy. Masako love you very much, Jesse-san. Masako want you love her. I need you love me, Jesse-san. I want sleep with man who care for me. Not like other G.I., who just want any woman. Masako no can do that. Not like some other neisan."

Jesse smelled the sloe gin on her breath. It was sweet but not sickening sweet. It was like her – just right. He dropped his bottle into the sand and placed his hands on her face. Gently he pulled her lips to his.

He had never kissed Masako except for a brotherly peck now and then. When their lips touched, he couldn't imagine how he could have been so stupid. At first touch, the kiss was gentle and soft. Her lips moved slightly to fit closer into his. The taste of Masako mixed with the taste of the whiskey and sloe gin and the blood from his cracked lips. The pressure increased and her mouth opened partially. Her tongue found his and unleashed a slow burning passion that increased with every twitch in their bodies. It was tender yet it was strong, the strength of need and want, the strength of finding something lost and wanting to hold onto it forever, the strength of a mutual and honest caring for one another.

Jesse put his hands on her back and ran them up and down her spine from her neck to below her buttocks. He felt of her long hair and her firm body and he felt too, the need she had for him, just as he knew she felt the need he had for her. A need born of mutual compassion and fond memories and honest sharing of thought – an understanding of being, and of being together.

He touched her thigh, the one exposed by the torn dress. She quivered and a soft throaty moan passed her lips. Jesse pulled away from her and stood. His breathing was heavy as he spoke. "Masako, I never would have believed what you can do to me with your kiss, but I'm also tellin' you it ain't gonna happen. Not with you."

"Masako no understand." Her breathing too was labored.

Jesse shook his head and picked up his bottle of whiskey. There was still about a quarter of a bottle left. He took a sip. "I don't either. I swear to God I don't. It doesn't make any sense to me, but I just can't. Not with you."

Masako stood and stepped next to him. Even in the moonlight, Jesse could

Stoney Livingston

see the hurt look on her face. "I so sorry, Jesse-san. You want go find Peggy or Juneko. Not want Masako. I feel so foolish."

"That's not it, Margie. I mean, yes, that *is* it. But not for the reasons you think."

She beamed at him.

"What are you smiling about?"

"You remember. Call me Margie. You call me Margie alla time before – in old Two-Three."

"Well, yeah, but..."

She hugged him. "Make Masako so happy hear Jesse-san say 'Margie' again."

"Damnit, Margie, aren't we gettin' a little off the subject here?"

"You will stay with Masako tonight?"

"I guess you haven't learned how to speak English all that well after all."

"Oh, I understand. No make love. Just stay with Masako. Sleep with clothes if you like. Make Masako very happy."

Jesse glanced at his watch. The move didn't go unnoticed by Masako. "You want neisan. You no want Masako but you want neisan. Peggy work at Conga. Juneko work at new club called Leatherneck. If it make you feel better, go see them. Then you come back Masako."

Jesse felt his chest muscles constrict with a deep sadness. His stomach knotted. He couldn't do that to her. He put his arm around her waist. "I must be crazy. C'mon, where do you live?"

Masako let out a small squeal and hugged his neck. He kissed her cheek. "I'm not that great a catch," he said.

"Masako think Jesse-san number one American Marine. Number one guy." They walked hand-in-hand down the beach to Lower Henoko.

Masako lived alone in a small two-room wooden structure, crowded on both sides by clones of her house. Jesse removed his shoes before entering the small but immaculately clean house. It was sparsely but amply furnished. There was no television but there was a record player.

Masako was excited and it was apparent in her voice. "I have special records. Would you like to hear?"

Jesse nodded, his mind wandering to Peggy then to Juneko. He thought of Masako as more of a sister than a woman. He watched her as she knelt to place a forty-five RPM record onto the turntable. The split dress revealed a firm and perfectly shaped leg, all the way to her waist.

The sound of the record sent him back in time. Ray Charles sang *Born To Lose*. Margie was smiling. "You remember song? Pineapple play alla time."

Jesse smiled sadly. "Yeah, I remember."

"You want drink? No have Jack Daniel but have Saki or sloe gin."

"What kind of sake, Japanese or Okinawan?"

"Both."

"I'll have some Japanese, thanks."

Masako smiled as she poured two sakes.

"What are you smilin' so pretty about?"

"You all polite, just like old times." She handed him his drink.

"To old friends," he said. They touched glasses and downed the clear liquid. Masako refilled the glasses and they sat on the mat at the edge of the room.

300

Forever Patriots

The record player clicked as it dropped another record. At the clicking sound, Jesse dropped his glass and rolled to the prone position. The noise was not so loud as it was sharp. He felt foolish as his heart beat in his throat and his sake spread over the wooden floor. Masako quickly knelt next to him.

"You okay, Jesse-san?"

"Yeah, I'm okay. The noise surprised me. I don't know what happened, I guess I just reacted without thinking."

She looked into his eyes. "You have suffer much. You are older now. I am so sorry. If I could, I make war go away."

"I know you would, Margie." He patted her hand.

The next record caught his attention. He looked at the player, then back to Masako. "Hey, how come Pineapple's song isn't as scratchy as my song? You aren't takin' care of my record as well as his, huh?" He smiled.

Her eyes bore into his. "Masako take care of both same way. Only listen to this one too much."

"It is a pretty song, isn't it?"

"Make Masako think of Jesse-san smiling face. Alla time smile and be happy, except sometimes when listen to this song. Pineapple not as happy as Jesse-san. No one as happy as Jesse-san."

"Margie, I really shouldn't stay here tonight. I'm not so happy as you think."

She wiped the floor as she answered him. Her smile had returned. "Maybe you shouldn't, but you stay. You love Masako. Maybe not much as Stateside girlfriend, but Masako not as pretty as American girl. Maybe not want others to know how you feel about oriental woman. Not so pretty as American girl."

Jesse got to his knees and scooted next to her as she sponged up the last of the spilled drink. "You don't believe that baloney for a second."

On her hands and knees, she turned to face him, her eyes only inches from his. The smile had disappeared from her lips. "Oh, Jesse-san, I hope that true."

"It is."

"Masako understand," she said.

"Jesse-san no understand. You listen to me, Margie, and you listen good. You're pretty by any standards. I'm not ashamed of you, and I love you like a best friend, not like a lover. You understand?"

She shook her head.

"Damnit, Margie, what do I have to do to make you understand?"

"You explain to Masako."

"That's what I'm tryin' to do."

"You love Masako like best friend?"

"Yes."

"You think Masako pretty as American girl?"

"Prettier than American girl."

"You been in jungle long time. Have neisan in jungle?"

"No, I didn't have a neisan in the jungle."

"You like neisan?"

"Of course I do."

"You love Masako, and you think Masako pretty, but you no want make love?"

"The way you're sayin' it, it doesn't make any sense."

"Same way you say it. It no make any sense."

She stood and walked to the sink where she wrung out the sponge and placed it neatly near the faucet.

"I can't believe this. If anyone would have told me this was ever gonna happen to me, I'd have told him he was nuts. If this don't beat anything I ever heard of in my life. Here I am, in the middle of...."

"Wait." She put an index finger to his lips. "Masako fix drink. Then we talk."

"I've had too much to drink already. And I'm not so sure I wanna talk – at least not about what we been talkin' about."

Masako smiled. "I fix for you a sloe gin fizz."

"That stuff tastes like sweet soda pop, and it leaves the world's worst hangover."

She ignored him and began to mix the drinks.

"Margie, how come I got this feeling that you think you're in command here?"

"Masako not in command. Masako know Jesse-san heart."

"How many times did I tell you to say *I* instead of using your name all the time when you talk English?"

She handed him the brightly colored drink. Her smile was back. "You go away too long time. I forget much you teach me. Maybe you could teach me more English tonight."

Jesse gulped down the drink. "Did you put any booze in this thing?"

Masako giggled. "Not taste like whiskey, but plenty sloe gin in drink. I make another." She took his glass.

When she returned his full glass, he said, "Why don't you do something about that split in your dress. Maybe you could pin it together or something."

"Jesse-san." She cooed. "You think Masako...I... have pretty leg?"

"I think you have pretty legs, plural. I think you have wonderful legs. They've gotta be the sexiest legs in the world, and that one definitely goes all the way up to...heaven, but since there isn't anybody here for you to show it off to, you might as well cover it." He sipped his drink.

"Jesse-san want Masako more now?"

He was in the process of swallowing when she said it and almost choked on his drink. "Margie, I don't think it's possible to want you more than I already do. I just don't want to get involved and, with you, I don't think there's any other way. Hell, I already am involved, I just don't want to take it any further."

She opened the torn dress, revealing her leg and buttocks. "Why you not want Masako? Lotsa G.I. alla time ask Masako go short-time or long-time. Masako never go. Never!"

"Quit it, Margie. Cover yourself."

She released the dress and moved closer to him. "Masako sorry, Jesse-san. Masako never do this thing before. Masako no can even make man horny."

"Quit talking like that, Margie. I never heard you talk like that. You sound like..."

"Say it, Jesse-san. Masako sound like Peggy or Juneko? You want Peggy or Juneko. What can Masako do make you want Masako?"

"God, we've got an awful language barrier here. I do want you. I swear I do. I just can't make myself do it with you. I don't know why. I just can't."

"Masako no understand." She pouted and moved closer to him.

302

"Damnit." He sat his glass on the floor, close to the wall so it wouldn't spill. He reached for Masako and pulled her gently to him. Her body melted into his as he kissed her with all the pent-up passion six months in the jungle could provide. They wilted to the floor as a single entity. Masako laughed and cried and held him tight and touched him and kissed him. Jesse shared her feelings. He shared her tears, her laughter, her kisses and her touch.

*****

Jesse stared at the green landscape below but saw nothing. His mind was still in Okinawa. His parting with Masako had been even worse than he had imagined it would be. He should never have gone home with her. He should have looked up Juneko, or gone back to the Conga and spent the night with Peggy. No. Not really. Masako had been good for him. He had thought he wanted only passion but, in her arms, he had found passion and much more.

Masako had given all of herself to him and he had given all of himself to her. There had been passion and tenderness and a closeness. *Damn, that girl can kiss! She can do other things too.* They even squeezed in an English lesson before daybreak, then dismissed class by making love until they were both covered in perspiration and exhausted from their passions.

The parting had been difficult. He didn't want to leave but knew he must. Masako cried and begged him to stay alive and come back to see her. He said he would try to come to Okinawa for his R & R. He held her and felt her love and her firm body pressed into his.

He would not come back. He could not - not if he had to leave her again. He wanted her with him but knew it was not the same as it had been with Shannon. Masako was a wonderful person - if the truth were known, probably too damn wonderful for him - but he knew too that his perception of life had been sensitized. He felt more deeply than he had before. Not that he had been shallow, rather he hadn't fully realized how precious life and thoughts and feelings were until he had seen so many disappear into nothing with the crashing of a bullet or a mortar or a booby trap. Then came Masako to make him better understand.

The more death he saw, and the closer he came to it, the more precious were all things living. What would he do if he saw Shannon? Emotion welled up inside of him at the thought of her. He wore his feelings too close to the surface. A man shouldn't do that. Others, not so smart, might take it as a sign of weakness, and weakness and survival were not compatible in the jungle, perhaps not anywhere.

He saw Masako, tears streaming down her face as she smiled and waved goodbye and said, "Thank you, Jesse-san. Thank you so much."

"Thank you, Margie. Thank you for everything. Thank you for showing me life again. Thank you for being you. *Sayonara*, Margie."

"Sayonara, Jesse-san. Masako love you."

He had felt the lump in his throat when he had answered. "And I love you, Margie. Sayonara."

He did love her - differently than Shannon - but there was no denying it was love. The more he learned about life, the more confusing it seemed to be.

The *whack-whack* of the helicopter blades brought him back to the landscape below. He wiped a tear from his cheek. He had been unaware he was crying. He looked at the door gunner, who studied the terrain below, unaware of Jesse's emotional release.

303

Stoney Livingston

Jesse turned his back on the gunner and stared absentmindedly at the mail sacks aboard the helicopter. He wondered if he had any mail. While he had been in the brig at Camp Butler he had received none. It's funny how little things can become so important, he thought.

He thought of Rich Cummings and wondered how he was doing with the squad. Of course, that wasn't really as important as whether or not he still had his job as FO of Alpha Company. He shivered as the terrain near Ap Chin An appeared in his field of vision. *They haven't moved for a week?*

He saw the elevated road and, from the air, he could see too the pockmarks caused by the mortars in the rice paddies, covered only by a thin layer of muddy water, appearing darker than the planted areas. The helicopter started its slow descent. He checked his utilities. He felt naked without his rifle and seven-eighty-two gear. *I hope Lieutenant Malcolm has still got my M-1.*

The UH-34 Choctaw settled gently to the soft ground. There was no enemy gunfire, only two marines from Alpha Company, standing at the edge of the LZ, waiting to gather in the precious mail. Jesse jumped from the helicopter and carried a mailbag to the waiting marines.

"There's one more," he said. One of the marines went in search of the other bag.

He followed them silently to the company CP. Sergeant Wilkes spotted him first. "I'll be damned. If it ain't the crazy from the 81 platoon. Couldn't take the good life, huh?" He offered his hand. "I'd damn sure like to shake your hand."

Jesse felt good. He shook Sergeant Wilkes' hand and smiled. "Where's the skipper?"

Wilkes pointed behind him with his thumb. "Back there, about thirty yards into the trees. Good to have you back. You gonna stay attached?"

"Don't know yet. That's why I gotta see the skipper."

"Well, you'll find him back there sure enough. Keep yer ass low."

Jesse waved as he stepped in the skipper's direction.

Mud's voice startled him. "It's about damned time. What took you so long to bust outa that place? I was beginning to worry about...Geez! What the hell happened to you?"

Jesse smiled. "Lousy barber and a couple of punks for chasers."

Mud nodded as he shook Jesse's hand.

"Well, do we still have a job here?" asked Jesse.

"Hell yes. It's been great since you left. All we've done is sit around, waiting for something to happen. I think they forgot about me. I haven't stood a watch in a week. I imagine that'll change now that "Johnny Basilone" is back."

Jesse ignored Mud's reference to a World War Two Marine Corps hero. "You seen the skipper?"

"Right over there by that big tree. C'mon, I'll show you."

He followed Mud, anxious to get his hands on his rifle.

Malcolm stood, as Jesse approached.

"Sir, Lance Corporal Langley reporting for duty – and his rifle."

Malcolm smiled. "It's good to have you back, Indio." He shook Jesse's hand. "Your rifle is in the CP tent, along with your seven-eighty-two gear."

"Thank you, Sir. It's good to be back. And thanks for your help. Captain Talbot turned out to be a pretty good guy."

"I know you want your gear, especially that old M-1." said Malcolm.

304

"That's a fact, Sir."

"That old rifle is too heavy for only holding eight rounds."

"Yessir, but it shoots 'em all with no jamming. You can always count on eight. With that damn M-14, you can count on anything between zero to twenty."

Malcolm laughed. "It's good to have you back. Go get your gear. I want to hear all about the charges, and whatever news you have of Captain Talbot."

"You mean Phil, Sir?"

"Phil?" Malcolm arched an eyebrow.

"Let me get my gear, then I'll tell you a story about a no-good, back-stabbin' guy named Phil, and this neisan named Peggy.

Stoney Livingston

CHAPTER FOURTEEN: SPARROW HAWK

Jesse listened intently as Malcolm quietly addressed the headquarters section of Alpha Company. They were gathered on the elevated road, near what had been the center of Alpha Company's line on Operation *Oregon*. Jesse knelt under the shade of a tree and smoked a cigarette, watching the smoke drift slowly skyward. His mind wandered back to Okinawa for a moment and from there withdrew to the reason for his trip to that place. He studied the group of men gathered for the briefing and found no hostile glances. The incident involving the old lady in the rice paddy seemed forgotten. Byler apparently had few friends, at least none willing to pursue the matter of his beating.

"Gentlemen, as most of you know by now, the operation we participated in more than a week ago has been belatedly code named Oregon. I personally apologize to any of you from that part of the country." He paused and let his gaze drift among his men. "The purpose of this briefing is to keep you informed about what's going on in this outfit. Since we left Chu Lai, we've been designated a Sparrow-Hawk Battalion. Now, for those of you who were ignorant, like I was before someone told me what the hell that meant, I'm going to tell you everything I know about it."

Sergeant Wilkes said, "Whatever it is, if this *Oregon* business is what it's all about, I'd sooner march to Hanoi barefoot with a broom."

A nervous laugh worked its way among the men..

"I can appreciate your concern, Sergeant Wilkes, but I'm not for certain what Sparrow-Hawk means. When I get done tellin' you what I've been told, maybe you could explain it to me."

"Be glad to, Skipper."

The men relaxed a little. There was less nervousness in the laughter.

Malcolm continued. "Basically, the way I understand it, a Sparrow-Hawk Battalion is either going to kick some ass or take one hell of a beating; I'm not sure which.

"You see, men, what we do is stay out here in the bush for about a month. During that month we're on call for anything that happens in I Corps. We have to be ready to mount-out in less than five minutes at all times, which means we'll be traveling pretty light for the next thirty days. When we're not headed for some trouble spot, we'll be conducting sweeps and ambushes. We will not set up a permanent camp.

"When we get the word to move out, we'll be going in as the sparrow or the hawk. As the sparrow, our function will be to entice the enemy to engage our inferior force and thereby draw them into a fight; then hold that fight until superior forces can be mustered to our position. As the hawk, we will be part of the superior force, coming to the aid of another sparrow outfit. So you can see, gentlemen, why it is imperative that we be ready to move out at all times."

306

He turned to Wilkes. "You got that all figured out, Sergeant Wilkes?"

"Yessir, I believe I do. If we get to be the little bird, we gotta hope like hell that the other bird is ready to fly in less than five minutes – just like we're supposed to be."

Malcolm replied, "That's it in a nutshell, men. It's your basic boot camp training. We're a team and we depend upon one another. We know that the other designated Sparrow-Hawk Battalion will be ready because we know *we'll* be ready."

Sergeant Wilkes said, "When will the rest of the battalion be joining us?"

"We'll be joining in the morning. Seems like Charlie and Delta companies have been busy on another operation south of here called *Utah*. The reports indicate they had a better time of it than we did on *Oregon*."

A marine in the center of the group said, "Does that mean they had survivors?"

A second voice said, "Yeah, Skipper, what about it? Are they going to relieve the colonel for screwin' up this operation or what?"

"That's enough! We were given some bad S-2 and the Old Man just acted on the information he was given. He's been around a long time. He knows what he's doing."

Wilkes said, "Skipper, we heard he's spent his last eighteen years in G-3 and this is his first line outfit command."

Malcolm's voice clearly showed his annoyance. "I don't give a damn how many years he's been in G-3. He's your commanding officer and I don't want to hear anymore scuttlebutt about this being his first line command."

He looked the men over then returned his attention to Wilkes. "Do I make myself clear, Sergeant?"

"Yessir," replied Wilkes timidly.

"Platoon commanders, inform your men of our new status. If there are no further questions or comments, I'd like to see the 81 FO. Dismissed."

As the group of men dispersed, Jesse stepped up to Malcolm. "You wanted to see me, Sir?"

"I didn't get around to it when we talked earlier but I'm going to give you my standard lecture on life; then I want to be done with it."

Jesse stood silently.

Malcolm continued. "Everything in life is not black and white. There are varying shades of grey. Not many of us are as pure as the driven snow. I think you're a hell of a leader and I want you to temper your judgement a little bit. Think before you react."

"Skipper, I know not everything is as pure as the driven snow. Hell, I'm probably guilty of more things than most of the guys in this outfit combined, but the important thing to me is that whatever I did was all right by *my* standards. It's only *my* standards I have to uphold. If I can do that then I can look any man in the eye and to hell with the rules."

Malcolm looked into Jesse's eyes for a moment. He shrugged. "In a way I kind of envy you if you can stick to that philosophy and survive. What the hell? Forget I even mentioned it. You ready for tomorrow?"

"I'm ready for next week, Sir."

Malcolm smiled. "Why did I ask?"

*****

307

Stoney Livingston

Alpha and Bravo Companies joined the rest of the battalion near the village of Dong Lai, about nine miles southwest of Ap Chinh An, the scene of Operation *Oregon*. The march to Dong Lai was made arduous by the humidity and the terrain. Loaded down with full combat gear, the two companies crossed rice paddies, marshlands, sand, several villages and seven rivers and streams of varying sizes.

In the hills south of Dong Lai the battalion made defensive preparations for the night. About two hours before dark Lieutenant Malcolm gathered a squad from the weapons platoon to test fire four of the LAWs.

Jesse and Mud, along with the rest of the headquarters section of Alpha Company, stood on the left flank of the four marines standing side-by-side on a firing line. The men were ready, their rocket launchers pointed at the hillside to their front. Malcolm said, "It's all yours, Corporal Hooper. Fire when ready."

"Aye aye, Sir," replied the tall black man holding a LAW at the ready on the far right of the line.

Jesse watched with more than a little interest as the man on the left flank squeezed his trigger. Nothing happened. After his own experience with the LAW, Jesse wasn't surprised. The man who had attempted to fire held his stance and waited for the next man to fire. The second man squeezed his trigger a bit more rapidly than the first but the results were the same – another misfire. With two misfires standing next to him on the firing line, the third marine quickly snapped his trigger mechanism. The third LAW misfired.

Corporal Hooper, who stood fourth to fire his weapon, chose not to fire but instead placed his LAW carefully on the ground, the muzzle pointed downrange. He then cautiously stooped low and ducked under the tubes on his left, until he reached the marine on the left flank, who remained motionless with his LAW still in the aiming position. Hooper placed his left hand painstakingly on the tube in front of the gunner's face and his right hand behind the man's head, on the rear section of the tube.

No one in the group of viewing marines uttered a sound as Hooper slowly squeezed the fore and aft tube sections together in an attempt to re-cock the electrical mechanism. Though every man in the audience was tensed for an explosion, it took them one and all by surprise when the rocket inside the tube ignited.

During the re-cocking procedure the gunner had strayed slightly upward with the muzzle and it was enough to create a small concussion on the ground behind him as the force of the backblast ripped into the soil. Jesse turned his face to shield it as hundreds of small pebbles split the air around him. When he turned back to face the firing line, the gunner was staggering left, the empty LAW falling harmlessly to the ground; his face impregnated with powder burns.

Corporal Hooper's back was turned to the headquarters section when the LAW fired. As he turned to face the group, his eyes appeared the size of boiled eggs. They were open wide and bulging, the pupils insignificant dots by comparison to the white. In his left hand he gripped his right wrist tightly. Beyond the right wrist was only a piece of hand with a thumb and little finger attached to it.

Hooper looked dazedly at the bloody stub on the end of his arm. "Lordy! Oh my God! Lordy mercy! My hand! Lordy! Oh God! Lordy!"

Sandy was on him immediately with morphine. Jesse assisted with blood control and Mud held Hooper's head in his lap as Sandy, the corpsman, went about his work. The other company corpsman in attendance moved quickly to the injured

308

gunner. Malcolm's Forward Air Controller radio operator called for a med-evac even as the morphine took its expected effect on Hooper. In twenty minutes, the two injured men were on their way to the nearest medical unit.

Malcolm stared at Sandy and Jesse, both covered with Hooper's blood. He turned to his radio operator. "Get all of the platoon commanders on the net. Advise them I want every goddamn LAW in this company brought to headquarters and left here. Then raise combat engineers and tell them to get up here and blow every last damn one of 'em to hell!"

"Yessir," replied the radio operator with enthusiasm.

At sunset, with most of the company watching, the engineers detonated their charges, sending the LAWS into oblivion. Loud cheers followed the blast. It seemed to be Alpha Company's solo victory in the past two weeks. That one small act did almost as much to raise morale as would have a total victory over Ho Chi Minh.

That evening, as Mud wrapped himself in his poncho, he said, "Those damn LAWs didn't even make a decent blast."

In the dark, Jesse was immersed in his own thoughts but he took the time to reply to Mud's comment even though it wasn't necessary. "I never saw anything wrong with the three-point-five. Can't figure out why they'd go to a 66 millimeter plastic toy like those damn LAWs anyway. They aren't that much bigger than the M-79, and we aren't up against tanks yet, so why do we even carry the damn things?"

"Alpha Company doesn't anymore," said Mud.

"Malcolm is a good skipper. I hope he doesn't catch hell for blowin' all that ordinance."

"Hell, Regiment will think we used 'em all against the gooks," replied Mud.

"Well, I think he did the right thing. That was such a waste today when Hooper lost his hand. Jesus Christ, there just wasn't any reason for it to happen."

"You got that right. Why do you think there are so many malfunctions?" asked Mud.

"I don't really know if it's bad quality or sabotage but I do know that I did just like I was told with that LAW I carried out into the rice paddy on *Oregon*. I tried it twice and it didn't do a damn thing until I threw it, then it decided to go off."

"It's kinda like those old grenades we got with no blasting caps. It's like somebody is sabotaging our stuff."

"Hell, Mud, they probably are. Just check your gear the best you can before we step off in the morning and don't depend on anything. Always try to have an alternate plan in a pinch."

"My alternate plan consists of getting the hell out of here in August."

"Why in the hell did you volunteer to come out here with me as an FO operator in the first place?"

"Stupid, I guess. What's your excuse?"

"Same."

"See ya in the morning, stupid," said Mud as he shivered against the damp air.

"G'night, Mud."

*****

Jesse curiously studied the small Vietnamese soldier standing next to

309

Stoney Livingston

Lieutenant Malcolm. The little man wore brand new army fatigues and brand new boots, both U.S. Government Issue. The army fatigues had bright gold second lieutenant bars on the collar. The man appeared almost a boy. He couldn't be more than nineteen or twenty years old, and green to boot, if one could judge by the newness of his clothing, the shine on his boots and the softness of his hands.

Malcolm glanced at Jesse briefly. "Indio, I sent for you because I want you to meet Lieutenant Huy." He turned to Huy. "Lieutenant Huy, this is Indio. He's our forward observer for 81's, and just about anything else if we don't have any other FO's attached to us."

Huy appeared confused. Marines do not salute in the field and he obviously wasn't sure of Jesse's rank as a result of the casual introduction by Lieutenant Malcolm.

Jesse stepped forward and offered his hand. "'Morning, Lieutenant."

Huy accepted the handshake. "Please, just call me Huy," he said, pronouncing his name quickly.

The man's hand was even softer than it looked. "How do you say your name correctly? It sounded like 'Hooey'."

"That's correct," replied the little man.

"Okay, Huy. If that's the way you want it, that's the way you get it."

Malcolm said, "Battalion has attached Huy to our company for a while. He's actually the battalion interpreter but he asked for field duty and he got us."

Jesse smiled at Huy. "You'll get your bellyful of field duty in this outfit. By the way, how old are you?"

Malcolm said, "I don't really think that's an appropriate question, Indio."

Huy waved Malcolm off with a smile. "No, that's quite okay, Sir. I have been asked this question many times by my own people. I look young, even to them." He turned to Jesse. "I am twenty-five. I will be twenty-six next month."

"No kiddin'? Hell, you've got me by almost five years."

Huy looked puzzled. He didn't understand the American idiom. Malcolm explained. "Indio means that you're five years older than he is."

Huy smiled broadly. He looked at Jesse and said, "I hope we can still be friends. Your company commander tells me I can learn much from you, despite your manner of speech."

Jesse laughed. He already liked the little man from battalion headquarters.

Malcolm said, "I'd appreciate it if you'd take Huy along with you and Mud for the next few days. Keep him out of danger as much as possible but teach him what you can about your job and the maps."

"Sir, I had planned on a little foraging today – if possible."

"Go ahead. When you get back, pick up Huy and show him around the company. Don't forget to take along a prick-six." ordered Malcolm, referring to the small, short-range radio.

"But sir, I request permission to accompany Indio," said Huy.

"I'm not sure that would be a good idea, Huy. If something happened to you on a two man patrol, I'd have a lot of explaining to do at battalion," answered Malcolm

"Yeah. Nothing personal, Huy, but I really do better if I'm on my own. I don't want to have to worry about you and the VC, and try to find something to eat at the same time," agreed Jesse.

Huy set his lips tightly. "If I go with you, you will be certain to find food."

310

Forever Patriots

Jesse raised an eyebrow. "We can't just go around shootin' anything we want. Sometimes we have to let our game go if we're not certain of the VC situation."

Huy's jaw tightened. "I will say it again for you because your company commander speaks highly of you. If I go with you, you will most certainly bring back to camp fresh game."

Jesse looked at Malcolm questioningly. "Sir, I'd sure like to give Buffalo Bill here a try. That cup of c-ration coffee and those two cigarettes I had for breakfast are fast wearin' off. If Huy here says he knows where to find game, who the hell are we to doubt his word? It's his country."

Malcolm smiled. "All right, you two. Get the hell out of here. But remember, take the radio, get the passwords, stay in range, and check for the signal if we have to pull out."

Huy smiled a "thank you, Santa Claus" smile and followed Jesse, who was already moving toward his radio operator's position.

"What's up?" asked Mud as Jesse and Huy approached.

Jesse answered as he knelt and rolled his poncho tightly. "Mud, this is Lieutenant Huy but you can call him Huy. Huy, this is Mud. Mud is the FO radio operator. Huy is the battalion interpreter on loan to Alpha Company."

"G'morning, Huy."

"Good morning, Mister Mud."

Without looking up from his poncho, Jesse said, "No, it's not mister Mud. It's just Mud."

"Oh, thank you, Indio. I appreciate it very much for you to correct my English. I still have much to learn."

"Hell, you do better than most of us. I'll try not to get on your case too much."

"Get on my case? What is the meaning of that term?"

Jesse looked up from his tightly rolled poncho and smiled. "You know, Huy, this could be a real interesting relationship if we both live long enough. The next thing I know, you'll be having us all speakin' the Queen's English." He looked at the expression of doubt on Mud's face.

"You're right, Mud; that's not gonna happen around here." He glanced at his rolled poncho then strapped it securely to his Garand cartridge belt.

"Why are you not carrying an M-14?" asked Huy.

"The M-14 is a fine long-distance rifle – on the rifle range. But it malfunctions too much in combat. This M-1 Garand is the best semi-automatic rifle ever made."

"But it holds only eight bullets."

"Yeah and it shoots the damn things out the barrel too. A twenty round magazine ain't worth a tinker's damn if the bullets stay in the magazine. I'll take quality over quantity any day."

Huy nodded knowingly. "That means you have had much trouble with the M-14?"

"Yeah, Huy, but I don't have trouble anymore." He buckled the Garand cartridge belt around his waist, his untucked utility blouse extending well below the belt. "Mud, Huy is going huntin' with me. He guarantees results so if we come back empty handed, just shoot 'im."

"You got it," replied Mud in a deadpan voice.

"C'mon, Huy. Let's go get some grub," said Jesse as he stepped out. Huy

311

quickly fell in behind.

The two walked southeast, Jesse a full fifty feet in front of the little Vietnamese. They had been walking for fifteen minutes when Jesse suddenly went into a low crouch, motioning Huy to get low and be still. After a few tense seconds, Jesse motioned Huy to his position. The interpreter complied nervously. Armed with only a .45 caliber pistol, it was obvious the little man was not overly anxious to meet with the VC. He quietly assumed a position within nine or ten feet of Jesse.

"What is it?"

Jesse whispered around his smile. "The biggest, fattest, juiciest goose I ever saw in my life." He pointed to their left front.

Huy peered carefully ahead, searching first for VC, then for a look at the goose. He turned to face Jesse. "That is a farm animal."

Jesse looked at the goose, then back to Huy. "How the hell can you tell that at this range? It looks like a damn goose to me. Is it wearing dog tags or sumpthin?"

"Trust me when I tell you it is a farm animal. You see how the wings have been clipped?"

Jesse studied the goose carefully. "Yeah, I guess you're right." He shrugged. "What the hell – that would have been too much to ask for anyway. Oh well, let's look for something else."

Huy moved closer to Jesse and said quietly, "Why look for something else? You have an excellent goose right in front of your eyes."

Jesse shook his head. "I don't play that way. The poor farmer that owns that goose is probably as hungry as I am. And it's his damn goose, not mine."

"No, no. You don't understand."

"So if I don't understand, 'splain it to me."

Huy looked at Jesse disdainfully. "We find the house who owns the goose and we buy the goose. The owner is wealthier and we have a fresh goose."

Jesse smiled. "Where have you been all my life? I like that idea. And I don't have to catch hell for the unauthorized discharge of a weapon. Sounds good to me. Let's do it."

Thirty minutes later, after startling the goose into action, Jesse stood outside a thatch house with Huy as the latter spoke rapidly in Vietnamese to an old woman whose gums had long ago turned a deep purple from chewing the betel nut. Huy shook his head several times during the conversation. After a lengthy discourse, he turned to Jesse and said, "It is okay to buy the goose."

"What the hell did you do, threaten to kill her if she didn't sell?"

"No. No. She just wanted too much for the goose," replied Huy indignantly.

"How much does she want?"

"Forty-eight piasters."

"You gotta be kiddin'?"

"You see, I told you she was much too high. She sees the Americans and she tries to get rich all at once."

Jesse looked at the old woman, then back to Huy. "Goddamn, Huy, I swear you must be kin to this horse-tradin' cousin of mine. He'd steal the fillings right out of your teeth if you let him get close enough. I've gotta give her more than forty-eight piasters for that goose."

"Please, Indio. Do not do this. Her price is much too high at forty-eight. It is not good for our local economy if you pay too much. The local people will not be able to buy for themselves because the farmers will sell only to the Americans at very high prices."

Jesse hesitated. "Yeah, I guess you're right, but are you sure that forty-eight piasters is a fair price? I don't want this old lady to sell to me out of fear. I wish I could find a way to pay her more without screwin' up the local economy."

Huy smiled. "I have an idea." He turned to the old woman and spoke again at length. At the end of Huy's discourse, she nodded and spoke briefly. Huy turned back to Jesse. "It is done. You buy the goose for forty-eight piasters and she will cook it for you. We can come back later and pick up the goose and you can pay her a few more piasters for cooking the bird for you."

"You know, you ain't all that stupid. That's a damn good idea. Hell, I haven't had home-cooked goose for years. Are you sure she knows how to cook one of these things?"

Huy frowned. "She is a farmer's wife. She cooks animals every day. It will be very good. You will like it very much. She is a very good cook."

"Enough with the 'very's'. Okay, okay. Tell her I'll give her a hundred piasters if she gets the bird a golden brown."

"She will get the bird a golden brown very easily but I cannot allow you to pay so much money. You will get the goose and she will cook it for sixty-eight piasters."

"Sixty-eight piasters? Goddamn, Huy! In my country they'd send you to jail for robbery if that's all you paid somebody for a deal like that."

"Perhaps what you say is true but you are not in your country."

"Okay, okay. It's done at sixty-eight piasters. Jesus Christ. That's less than a buck."

"It is very much money in my country. The old lady will be very pleased at this price."

"You're the boss. Tell her to get to it. Find out when it'll be ready and let's continue the hunt."

Huy turned back to the old woman who stood patiently chewing her betel nut. She nodded her assent and smiled a purple smile at Jesse. He smiled in return and waved at her as he and Huy walked away and into the hills surrounding the thatch house.

For the next three hours Jesse could hardly contain his hunger. The thought of the big goose roasted to a golden brown was almost more than he could handle. His stomach growled in anticipation. His mouth watered at the thought of biting into a perfectly cooked, succulent breast of goose.

Before returning to the old lady's thatched house, Jesse discovered a half dozen eggs. Huy couldn't tell him what kind of eggs they were but Jesse decided to take them back to camp to share with some of the men anyway. It would be a nice compliment to the roast goose.

Out of habit and training, their approach to the house was cautious, with Jesse in the lead by more than fifty feet. A hundred yards from the house Jesse fell prone and lay motionless. Huy, who had been daydreaming, continued forward for several paces before he realized that Jesse had taken up the prone position, his Garand tucked into his shoulder, cheek on the stock, eyes peering through the peep sight. He quickly took cover.

There was a small rise in the ground between their position and the house. It wasn't much but it did offer visual protection from anyone at ground level standing near the house. Jesse crawled the few feet forward he needed to take optimum

313

advantage of the gentle slope. Huy followed suit, crawling on his belly until he was next to Jesse.

"What is it?"

"Three men standing outside by a big cooking pot, talking to the old mama-san," whispered Jesse softly.

Huy cautiously looked over the small rise. The three men appeared to be arguing with the old woman but he could not hear enough of what was being said to determine the nature of the disagreement. He strained his ears for more sound.

"They look VC age to me. Who the hell are they?" asked Jesse nervously.

"I don't know. I can't hear what is said."

Jesse watched as one of the men moved to a nearby tree and urinated. When the man returned to the cooking pot, Jesse plainly saw the weapon. He looked at Huy. "They've got weapons. And they sure as hell aren't ARVN." Jesse keyed up the small PRC-6 radio. "Pied Piper Alpha, this is Whiskey Alpha. Over."

There was a short pause then a crackly voice, barely audible on low volume, answered his call. "This is Alpha. Go ahead, Whiskey."

Jesse pulled his area map from the inside pocket of his utility jacket and spoke quietly into the radio. "Alpha, I am at 504354. I have observation of three armed and unidentified troops at the farmhouse located at those coordinates. Can you check friendly forces in the area for patrols? Be advised, the unidentified troops are not, I say again, *not,* in uniform. Over."

In less than a minute Malcolm was on the radio. "Whiskey Alpha, this is Alpha Actual. We are checking friendly forces. We have a patrol en route. Do you require Whiskey? Over."

Jesse thought of the goose then, belatedly, the old woman. "Negative at this time. Appreciate the help. Will advise. Over."

"Roger. Alpha out." The radio fell silent.

Jesse left the radio with Huy and crawled forward to get a better view. He watched intently the scene before him. The radio crackled. Huy answered. "This is Whiskey Alpha. Over."

"Negative friendly troops at your coordinates. Do you copy? Over."

Jesse looked at Huy and nodded.

Huy spoke into the radio. "Roger. We copy. Will advise. Out"

One of the men pushed the old woman, who seemed intent on protecting the large cooking pot. The other two men laughed when she fell over backwards. As she picked herself up indignantly, one of the men stuck a knife into the pot and pulled out a piece of the meat cooking inside.

Jesse had intended to wait for the arrival of the patrol before taking any action but the thought of losing his goose was overpowering. He sighted down the barrel of his M-1. Without taking his eyes from his target, he softly said, "That does it. They're messin' with my goose. Hang onto your pistol, Huy. We're gonna kick some ass and take some names."

The last word had barely left his mouth when the M-1 fired. Three more in rapid succession followed the first round. With the fourth round scarcely clear of the barrel, Jesse was on his feet and moving toward the house at a dead run. Huy joined the assault.

The three men fell as Jesse jumped to his feet but he could not be sure if they were injured or just taking cover. As he neared the cooking pot, there was no doubt they were not searching for cover. Two of them had fallen in the grotesque position of death. The third moved but was not searching for cover, rather a way to ease his pain and find a more comfortable way to die.

The old woman had begun screaming when the first bullet had struck its mark, and she didn't let up as the two men approached on the run. Jesse quickly moved to the man who obviously breathed. He pulled his bone handled knife quickly from its sheath, put his rifle down, and moved in to complete his work should the injured man make a hostile move, or to help keep him alive if he didn't. There was no fight left in this one. "Huy, check those other two," he shouted over the screams of the old woman. "And tell her to keep it down."

The confusion lasted only a matter of seconds, then all was calm. The old woman sobbed quietly. Huy convinced himself the two motionless men were quite dead, and Jesse went to work on the third, trying to stop the bleeding from two wounds, one near the left shoulder and one in the chest.

"Huy, check around for more VC. I'm gonna try and stop the bleeding here. Damn! I knew I pulled one."

Huy left and returned shortly. "No more VC, Indio. Just these three, I think."

"Thanks. Run back out there and get the radio, will you? I don't think this guy is gonna make it but we gotta get him a med-evac anyway. Give me your pressure bandage. Quick."

Huy quickly removed the pressure bandage from his first aid pouch and handed it to Jesse then turned and ran full-tilt for the radio.

Jesse needed a third hand. He looked up at the old woman who continued to sob. "I need some help."

She looked at him between sobs.

Jesse pointed to the torn flesh on the wounded man's shoulder. "Blood. We've gotta stop the bleeding."

The old woman continued to sob. "Shit," shouted Jesse as blood squirted into his eye. He worked feverishly to stem the flow, but couldn't release the pressure on the wound long enough to get the bandage into position to tie. When Huy returned with the radio, Jesse had his left thumb jammed into the hole in the wounded man's shoulder, his other hand covering the exit wound in the back.

"I have notified Alpha Company of our situation. They said the patrol should be here in five minutes. Med-evac is also on the way."

"Thanks, Huy. Now, how about some help with this guy? He's got more blood than somebody twice his size. I don't know where the hell he's gettin' it. Help me get this bandage in place on the front of his shoulder here."

Huy's eyes narrowed. Imminent danger gone, he was able to think more clearly and more carefully. "He is a fucking VC! Let him die!"

Jesse looked up from his kneeling position over the injured man. "Are you crazy? Give me some help."

Huy stood his ground. "Do you think he would help you? He would spit in your face as you begged for mercy."

"Probably. Now are you gonna give me some help or am I gonna have to let this guy bleed to death while I whip your ass?"

"Okay. Okay. Goddamn crazy Marine! Shoots people then tries to save them. You will never win the war this way, you know."

"Forget the political philosophy, Huy. Give me a hand here."

Huy reluctantly knelt next to Jesse and rendered assistance, mumbling all the while in his native tongue. Jesse didn't have to be fluent in Vietnamese to know that Huy did not approve of wasting time on wounded VC.

Corporal Faye arrived with the second squad, third platoon just as Huy and Jesse secured the last pressure bandage to the wounded man.

"Jesus Christ. For a mortar man, you get into more shit than anybody I ever heard of," Faye greeted him.

"Nice of you to stop by. How's the wife and kids?" smiled Jesse.

Faye looked callously at the two dead and one wounded VC. He returned Jesse's smile and said, "You kinda took advantage of these gooks, didn't you? Hell, there weren't but three of 'em."

"Sometimes a man likes to have the advantage." said Jesse.

"How come the one is still kickin'?"

"New rifle. Haven't really got my battle dope yet. I pulled one; that's why I fired the extra shot. Sorry about wasting that extra round."

Faye grunted. "Well, see to it that it don't happen again. Hate to have to put you on report for wastin' government property." He sniffed the air. "What the hell smells so bad?"

In the urgency of the previous ten minutes, Jesse hadn't noticed the smell but, at Faye's mention, he caught a whiff of the pungent odor. He wrinkled his nose. "Whew! Whatever it is, I'm sure it's against the law."

The smell seemed to originate from the large cooking pot where Huy stood speaking with the old woman, who by now had controlled her sobbing. As Jesse peered into the cooking pot, his stomach turned. Floating in a black fluid reminiscent of gear oil was the prize goose. It was all there. It had been plucked and cut into pieces to be sure, but the sight of the head and beak and claws floating in the foul-smelling black fluid was almost more than Jesse's American-bred stomach could handle. He turned his face away from the pot.

"What the hell has this woman done to my bird?"

Huy stopped talking to the old woman and looked at him quizzically. "Number one good stuff."

"Number one my ass! She ruined the bird! I shot the wrong people! Jesus Christ! How in the hell can you ruin a goose like that? That bird died for nothin'."

Huy looked into the pot and drew a deep smell of the contents. "This is number one! We feast like kings! This is a very special goose she has cooked for you."

"Bullshit. It's got the eyes and beak and head and claws and guts and every damn thing else that don't belong in there. And to top it off, she's cookin' it in some kinda gear oil."

"No. You try it. You see. It number one," said Huy.

Faye smiled. "Seems like they have a different way of fixin' southern fried chicken over here."

Jesse glared at him. "Screw you."

Faye winced, mockingly.

The PRC-6 carried by Faye and the one held by Huy both crackled. Faye responded. "Alpha-Two-Three-Actual. Go ahead."

The voice on the radio came back. "Med-evac approaching your position. Mark with yellow smoke. Over"

"Roger med-evac. Mark with yellow. Out." He shouted to a lanky rifleman. "Okay, Scoop, give 'em a yellow pill."

The rifleman complied and soon the yellow smoke drifted skyward.

Jesse worked up his nerve for another look at the cooking bird as the helicopter was loaded with the dead and wounded VC.

"It is ready, Indio," offered Huy.

"Ready for what?"

"To eat, of course."

"That's a lousy joke, Huy. I had my taste buds all set for a roast goose and this old woman gives me a secret weapon. To hell with it. Let's go back to camp. We've still got those eggs back by that little hill. Tell the old lady she can have the goose and I'll pay her for everything."

"I don't think you should do that to her. She will know that you do not like the way she cooked your food."

"Well, I don't."

"Her day has been very bad. This will not be good for her."

"You think *her* day's been bad? I can't even stand to look at the goose, much less smell it or eat it. Tell her it's a present from me to her."

"She will not understand. She will think you suspect her of being a VC sympathizer."

"Just because I won't take a goose that's so screwed up a starvin' hound wouldn't touch it?"

Huy paused. "Indio, one of the VC you killed was her son."

Huy's words slammed into Jesse's mind like a steam locomotive. He looked at the old woman with her purple teeth and gums. She waited expectantly; for what Jesse wasn't sure. He returned his gaze to Huy. "Her son?"

"She tells me he was a very bad boy. He and his friends steal food and clothing from the family and live in the hills. She says she hates communists and they are lazy. They don't work. They just steal from those who do."

"But ...her own son?"

"She said he would never change. His mind was poisoned by the communists. She says now that he is dead, maybe they will both have peace."

Jesse walked close to the old woman and looked into her bloodshot eyes. "Huy, translate, will you?" He was vaguely aware of Huy nodding. "Ma'am, I'm very sorry. If I could bring your son back to you, I would do it, but I can't." Huy's sing-song voice registered in Jesse's consciousness as the little man translated quietly in the background. "I ask you to try and understand, and I hope you are able to know that I mean you no harm. If I can help you in any way, please ask me now, before we leave, because once we leave, we may never come back."

The old woman looked at Jesse with so much sadness in her eyes that Jesse could no longer hold his gaze.. He turned away. "Huy, would you find something to carry the goose in and give her the claws, head, neck and intestines? I'm gonna take a smoke break." He reached into his utility map pocket and pulled out a roll of paper money. He handed the money to Huy. "It's about three thousand piasters. Give it to her."

Faye and Huy stood silently as Jesse picked up his M-1 and slung it over his right shoulder. He walked away, his Zippo lighter clanking as he tried to light his cigarette on the move.

Jesse spread the boiled goose out on the dirty poncho. He looked up at Malcolm and said, "There you have it, Sir – one totally screwed up goose."

Malcolm wrinkled his nose. "It does smell a little raunchy."

317

Stoney Livingston

"Well, there it is. Any man with the guts is welcome to try it. I had some eggs, but I busted one of 'em open in all the excitement and they turned out to be snake eggs. This hasn't been my best day as a big game hunter."

None of the men standing nearby made any attempt to taste the boiled goose. Malcolm said, "You okay, Indio?"

"Yeah, I'm okay. I guess it was just a little strange back there at that old mama san's place. What are the odds of killin' the son of someone who is cookin' you a goose? Aw, I'm just goin' through withdrawal or somethin'. Hell, I'll be over it in a minute. Of course, her wastin' that beautiful goose like that only made matters worse."

"I got some Camels in my rations today. They're sitting over there on my pack."

Jesse retrieved the cigarettes without thanking Malcolm.

"Corporal Faye tells me you're pretty good with that old M-1," said Malcolm.

"I get by."

"Huy was impressed. He said you had all four shots fired before the VC made a move."

"Rapid fire's easy, once you get the hang of it." Jesse looked up at his company commander. "Huy pisses me off. He told me this old gal was gonna fix that bird up as proper as you please. Hell, you can't get past the smell to even taste it."

"The Vietnamese eat a little differently than we do."

"Amen to that one, Sir."

Malcolm steered the conversation away from the goose. "We're going on a battalion sweep tomorrow – be sweeping the villages along the river a couple of miles south of here. We've been issued two shotguns. If you want to take one of 'em along for working in the villages, be my guest."

"I'd like to try one of 'em for the close-in work but I don't want to lose my M-1."

"I'll carry your rifle on the sweep. This pistol isn't really much consolation in a firefight. It'll be kinda nice to carry a real weapon for a change."

"If you get killed, don't lose my rifle, and it's a deal."

"I'll do my best to live up to your expectations."

Jesse smiled. "Let's get Huy up here and give him this number-damn-one goose and be done with this day."

*****

"Corpsman! Corpsman up!" shouted Sergeant Wilkes as he worked feverishly over a fallen marine.

The battalion sweep had netted more passive resistance than had been anticipated. Jesse had heard the booby trap explode, then Sergeant Wilkes' summons for a corpsman. He rushed to see if he could be of any assistance. It had been a long morning for Alpha Company. Though they had not come face to face with the enemy, two men had already been injured by booby traps and one by sniper.

Jesse approached Wilkes who was kneeling over the fourth casualty of the morning. "How bad is it?" he asked as he assumed a kneeling position next to the wounded marine.

"Shitty! Here, help me stop the bleeding in this leg. He's hit pretty bad."

Jesse put his shotgun on the ground and squeezed the wounded leg tightly

318

while Wilkes tied off a tourniquet. The injured man writhed about on the muddy ground. "Take it easy. Try to lay as still as you can stand it. You gotta help us stop the bleeding," Jesse coaxed.

Through clenched and chattering teet, the wounded marine replied, "I'm tryin', man! I'm tryin'! Honest to God I am!"

Sandy arrived and took over for Wilkes. Jesse continued to apply pressure to the injured leg as Wilkes left to rejoin his platoon. Sandy injected the man with morphine and finished his bandage work. He turned to Jesse. "Indio, check on a med-evac for me, will you?"

Jesse turned to Mud, standing nearby. "Mud, raise somebody and see if there's a med-evac on the way. Quick!"

"It's already done. It's on the way," replied Mud.

Jesse returned his attention to the wounded man whose pain was being eased by the merciful morphine. "Jesus, I'll never get over how fast that stuff works."

Sandy reached into his pouch and withdrew a few morphine syrettes. "Here. Keep these with you. You know what to do with 'em if they're needed, right?"

"Yeah, if I have to."

"You might have to, the way these guys are steppin' into the booby traps today."

"You got things under control here, Sandy?" asked Jesse.

"Yeah. Go on ahead. I'll catch up when somebody from headquarters comes by."

"See ya later." He looked over his shoulder. "C'mon, Mud. Let's get movin'."

As they moved cautiously forward, Mud said, "The best that can happen to that guy is losing his leg."

"Yeah, I think so too. I'm no doctor, but it looked to me like it was all but severed at the knee."

"Poor bastard," said Mud.

About twenty-five yards to their right front a short burst of rapid rifle reports shattered the air. A marine in front of them toppled, his scream choked off by his own blood. Mud and Jesse fell prone instantly. "Mud," Jesse whispered, "did you see where the hell that came from?"

"I didn't see shit," Mud quietly replied.

"Get on the horn and advise the skipper that we've got a sniper back here. I don't have any idea where the rest of the company is but see if he can send a fire team back here to give us a hand."

"Roger."

Jesse strained his eyes, trying to locate the enemy. He saw the downed marine's twisted body, one leg at an awkward angle, one arm trickling the last of his blood from a wound in the biceps, a dark gaping purple gash in his throat with strips of flesh dangling like banners from one side of the fatal wound. Jesse shuddered.

"Skipper says to hold our position. He's got a squad on the way," said Mud.

In the far distance, Jesse heard the rattle of an M-60 machine gun followed by the sharp staccato burst of an AK-47 Soviet automatic rifle. The M-60 spoke again, then there was silence.

For what seemed an eternity the two men lay motionless, both trying to see what could not be seen. The point man for the approaching squad came into view in the dense growth beyond the fallen marine. There was a quick movement in the brush and the still air was pierced by the sharp sound of an AK-47. The point man disappeared from sight.

"I saw him, Mud! It's a spider trap! See if that squad leader has a Prick-6. If he does, tell him I'm going to toss a grenade at the trap to mark it."

"Roger." A moment went by, then he said, "He's got a radio and he says to toss away."

Jesse pulled the pin, released the spoon, held the grenade about two seconds then threw it quickly at the spider trap. The explosion threw sod and bark in all directions.

"He's got a fix on it. He wants us to back outa here. They're gonna use an M-79 on it," reported Mud.

"That's fine by me. Let's get the hell back down the trail a little ways," said Jesse as he moved away from the hidden enemy position.

Thirty seconds went by then the 40-mm projectile launched by the M-79 exploded. The initial explosion was followed by an intense burst of small arms fire from the marines, then silence.

Jesse turned to Mud. "Advise that grunt squad leader that we're comin' through his position if he's cleared his target."

"Roger."

Jesse heard the squad leader answer in the affirmative. He said, "Let's go. We gotta catch up before the point gets too far up the river."

Mud nodded as Jesse stepped off.

At the site of the spider trap, Jesse glanced at the carefully concealed hole, dug under a log and covered with brush. It was difficult to spot even when you knew it was there. There was no escape tunnel. This one was intended to be used on isolated men so that the position could not be discovered by a second man. Once discovered, the man hiding inside the hole was sure to be captured or killed.

Jesse looked briefly at the dead VC. Part of his left arm had been blown away by the M-79. The riflemen had done the rest. He shuddered involuntarily at the sight and turned his attention to the dead marine.

He looked about nineteen or twenty years old, with a baby-face the girls back in the States would have fallen head-over-heals for. Not anymore. His dirty, short blond hair was soaked in a pool of his own blood. Jesse looked away. He turned to the squad leader. "You know him?"

The short corporal nodded. "Second platoon. Didn't know his name but he was an okay guy."

"How's your point? Did he get hit?"

The corporal replied, "About as hard as you can get hit. He's deader'n hell." He pointed to the body of the dead VC. "This little bastard could shoot."

Jesse said, "Probably trained by the Crotch. Sorry about these two men. We've gotta catch up with the point and see if we can't get in a few shots of our own. You got everything under control?"

"Yeah. Thanks for the help. We probably never woulda found this little chickenshit if you hadn't spotted him for us."

"My pleasure." Jesse turned and headed for the point, Mud close behind.

As they walked alertly through and around the string of villages lining the river, Jesse regretted giving up his M-1 for the shotgun. Though he carried both double ott buckshot and slugs, he felt naked without the old Garand in his hands. It's strange, he thought, what the feel of a dependable rifle will do for a man in combat.

Forever Patriots

Unless one has been there, and needed a dependable rifle, words can never impart the secure and comfortable sensation provided by ten pounds of wood and steel. Jesse wanted to find Malcolm and get his rifle back in the worst way.

He slowed his pace and began speaking to Mud in a low but casual tone of voice, "Say, Mud, old buddy, take a look at that hootch over there with the old lady standin' by the door. Do it kinda casual-like and pretend we're on a stroll in the park."

After a casual glance, Mud said, "I don't see anything unusual. Am I supposed to?"

"The mama-san hasn't moved an inch since we came into sight. Those three kids were near the door when I first saw 'em but now they're just standin' off to the side of the house, watchin' the old lady."

"So?" asked Mud, still failing to find anything unusual about the activity.

"Mud, you dummy. We're center stage, not the old lady. Kids don't stand around and look at their grandmother for excitement. I want you to – real casual-like – ease a grenade into your hand, just in case. Let's try a little deception. Follow my lead, okay?"

"Goddamnit, Indio, you're startin' to make me nervous."

"Be cool." He looked up at the old lady and smiled. She returned a deep purple smile as Jesse waved. He stopped and pulled his cigarettes from his pocket. He was only about fifteen yards from the door of the thatch house. He spoke softly to Mud as he lit his cigarette. "I"m going to give the old lady a cigarette, then I'm goin' into that hootch on the signal. If she takes the smoke, that's the signal. If she doesn't, when I get'em back in my pocket, that's the signal. You got it?"

"Jesus Christ. What the hell am I supposed to do?"

"Just meander over to that big tree and look cool. If I don't surprise whoever in the hell is in there, throw your grenade and holler for help," answered Jesse as he exhaled a deep drag on his cigarette.

"Have I ever told you that your tactical planning stinks?"

"Quit bitchin'. The best defense is a horrendous offense." He strolled towards the old lady, smiling, the pack of Camels held aloft, his twelve gauge pump shotgun carried casually, one handed.

The old lady smiled a nervous, purple smile as he approached her with his offering.

He greeted her in Vietnamese. "Chao."

She waved sheepishly and repeated the greeting.

Jesse stopped before her and nervously waited for her to accept or refuse the cigarette. She shyly took the one protruding the farthest up out of the pack. The instant she had the cigarette in her possession Jesse dropped the plastic cigarette holder to the ground and gripped the shotgun with both hands, firing into the door twice in rapid succession. He crashed through the bamboo door and assumed a crouched position slightly to the left of the doorway on the inside of the one-room house.

The old woman screamed and followed him inside. Two men and one woman huddled in a corner of the room. They neither spoke nor moved. The only sound in the room was the chattering of the old lady. She was too close. Jesse slapped the forearm stock on his shotgun and said, "Dung noi!"

The old woman stopped her chattering in the middle of a word and stood very still.

Jesse shouted over his shoulder, his breath coming in short gasps, "Mud, raise the skipper and see if we can get Huy down here."

"Roger. You okay?"

"Yeah but something weird is going on. I've got three military-age suspects in here: two male, one female. Stay outside and watch until we get some help. Get somebody from S-2 down here, too."

"Roger."

Jesse motioned to the three in the corner. "Gio tay len!" The woman and one of the men complied immediately, their hands held high. The second man appeared to make a feeble attempt but did not do as instructed. Jesse pointed the shotgun at him. "Gio tay len!"

Still squatting, the second man complied but seemed to be in pain. He held one arm a bit lower than the other. Jesse addressed the younger woman. "Nhung sung giau o dau?"

The woman shook her head and spoke rapidly in Vietnamese. Jesse silenced her by slapping the forearm stock of his shotgun. "I know you got weapons around here somewhere. Co bao nhieu Viet Cong?"

Again the woman shook her head and began speaking rapidly.

"Dung noi!" shouted Jesse as he waved his shotgun barrel at her menacingly. She shut up abruptly. "We'll find out how many VC are hangin' around when Huy gets here."

Jesse shouted over his shoulder, "Mud, get a fire team over here, and find out when Huy or S-2 are gonna show up."

"Huy and a squad from second platoon should be here in about one or two minutes. No word on S-2 yet. What the hell's going on in there?"

"Nothin' yet, but I'm losin' my patience. What are those kids doin'?"

"Don't sweat the kids. I've got 'em under control. I see the squad now, and Huy's with 'em."

"Tell the squad to surround the house, then send Huy in here."

Jesse waited nervously, watching his three prisoners closely, not moving to search them until Huy was there to assist him. After what seemed an eternity, Huy entered the house.

"What you got, Indio?" Despite his serious look, Jesse found the young-looking Huy humorous – almost funny. For a moment the whole damn war was funny. But only for a moment.

"A damned strange situation is all I can tell you. Three military age people and no explanation."

Huy looked at the old woman, then to the three huddled in the corner of the room. He spoke rapidly in Vietnamese, pointing first to one, then to another, shaking his finger at each as he spoke. The man who appeared to have an injury spoke haltingly. Huy spoke to the other two in an angry voice. They moved carefully away from the injured man in the rear. Huy shouted to the man in the rear and he slowly stood.

As the man reached his full height of six feet, four inches, Jesse said, "This guy's not Vietnamese. He's a Chink! What's he doing here? And where in the hell did he ever come up with that turquoise sport shirt?"

"He says he is visiting relatives from Saigon," answered Huy

"Saigon hell. He's from China. He doesn't even look Vietnamese."

Huy spoke to the tall man again. Whatever Huy said, the man denied it vehemently. He shook his head violently.

322

"Ask him where he's injured and how he got that way," said Jesse.

Huy spoke rapidly and with authority. The man replied hesitantly.

"Bullshit," said Huy. He turned to Jesse. "He says that he fell and injured his side only yesterday."

"Get your pistol out, Huy. I want to take a look under that cot he's standin' in front of."

As Huy pulled his pistol, Jesse moved the tall man into a location that would not place him in a position to attempt an escape. "If this guy even looks like he's thinkin' about escapin', smoke 'im."

"With pleasure," said Huy. Jesse knew he meant it.

Jesse searched around the cot for booby traps and found nothing. He looked painstakingly at the mat beneath the cot and stood slowly, speaking in a calm and almost nonchalant manner. "Well, Huy, let's get these people outside and on down to someone in S-2. No sense in wastin' anymore time around here. You get them out the door. I'll follow you."

Huy looked at him quizzically. "Okey-dokey, if that's what you want."

Jesse looked him in the eyes and very deliberately said, "That's definitely what I want."

Huy quickly ordered the mama-san and the three prisoners outside. As the last prisoner left the room, Jesse moved to the doorway and shouted, "Hey, grunt squad leader. I think you've got a tunnel in here, underneath a cot in the corner of the room. The cot is clean, but I think the mat under the cot is wired. I'll wait here until you come in and look things over, but it's your baby from here on out. I don't do windows or tunnels."

"Is that you, Indio?"

"Yeah. Who's that?"

"It's Faye, you crazy mortar man. I'm on my way in."

In a matter of seconds, Corporal Faye stood next to Jesse. "Why don't you just check that tunnel situation out for me?" asked Faye, smiling broadly.

"Why don't you get serious? That dangerous. I don't like takin' unnecessary risks."

Faye laughed. "Comin' from you, that's about the funniest thing I've heard this year. You got any more good ones?"

Jesse smiled. "If it was me, I'd blow that mat to hell. That should set off the charges below. Then I'd get the biggest flame thrower I could find and fill it with napalm. If nobody surrendered on the first offer, I'd fill that hole full of jelly and strike a match."

"Sounds like a damn good plan to me." Faye spoke into his PRC-6. When he completed his transmission, he turned to Jesse. "They'll have me a flame thrower here in about fifteen minutes. You wanna stay and watch some real pros at work?"

"If I don't catch up with the point, the skipper's gonna have my ass. Let me know how it turns out next time I see ya."

Faye held up one thumb. "You got it, Indio. Send my first team in here, will ya?"

"Roger. I'll see you later."

"Later. Keep yer ass low"

Jesse picked up his cigarettes as he stepped outside.

Fifteen minutes later, Jesse, Huy and Mud stood guarding their prisoners at a collection point. "What have you been able to find out, Huy?" asked Jesse.

323

Stoney Livingston

"Fucking VC. You're right about the tall one. He doesn't admit it, but he speaks with a slight accent. I think he's from China. When S-2 gets here they will find out everything we want to know."

A marine lieutenant and two ARVN officers arrived on the scene. The marine lieutenant took charge of the prisoners after a brief report from Jesse and Huy. He thanked them and ordered them to rejoin the sweep. As the three turned to leave, one of the ARVN officers began beating the tall man wearing the turquoise shirt, while the marine lieutenant and the other ARVN officer stood and watched.

Jesse turned back to the prisoners.

"Oh, shit," whispered Mud under his breath.

Jesse hailed the lieutenant. "Excuse me, Sir, but these men are American prisoners of war. And the man this ARVN officer is beatin' is injured."

"Report back to your unit, Marine. This is an S-2 matter at this time."

"I captured these people, Sir. If I had wanted to beat the shit out of 'em, I could have done that myself."

"What is your name, Marine?"

"What's yours, Lieutenant?"

The lieutenant glared at him. He moved in Jesse's direction, scowling. "I asked you a question, Marine!"

The twelve gauge pump shotgun was quickly leveled at the advancing lieutenant from Jesse's hip. "Don't do it, Sir. I'm not going to fight you and the VC too." Jesse's voice was calm.

"You're aiming a weapon at me, Marine!" The lieutenant stopped his advance, his voice almost a screech.

"Yessir, and I fully intend to use it if you take another step in my direction." One of the ARVN officers on Jesse's right reached for his pistol. With the muzzle of the shotgun still pointed at the marine lieutenant, Jesse spoke quickly, "I know you speak English, ARVN. You wanna be first? If you do, go ahead and touch your pistol." The man froze.

Huy stood motionless. He looked from Jesse to Mud. "What the hell you gonna do now?"

Mud shrugged. "Hell, I never know."

Huy's lower jaw dropped.

The prisoners were obviously confused about what was transpiring. The tall man had been helped to his feet and stood with the others in mute confusion of the tense actions being played out before them.

The marine lieutenant's voice cracked, "Marine, I'll have your ass for this!"

"For what, Sir? For saving prisoners that *I* captured from havin' the shit beat out of 'em by a couple of goons that wouldn't have the balls to go man-to-man with a cripple? For not lettin' you browbeat me into ignorin' a blatant violation of the Geneva Accord? For defendin' myself against a man who would shame me and my country by allowing this to go on? Bullshit, Sir. Don't threaten me with a court martial again, *Sir*, or I'll blow your head offa your shoulders. Now take these two ARVN with you and find somebody else's prisoners to beat the shit out of. I'll turn mine loose before I give 'em to you – only I'll arm 'em so they can meet you on even terms."

"Holy shit! Have you gone crazy?" shrieked the lieutenant.

"Maybe. Maybe not. But if I were you, I wouldn't want to take a chance on findin' out. Now if you'll kindly get the hell outa here, I'll forget this whole matter ever took place."

The lieutenant looked at Jesse's dirty face, a soiled headband showing from beneath his helmet. He looked at the knees, protruding from the torn trouser legs and, lastly, he looked at the twelve-gauge shotgun pointed at his belly. "You're making a big mistake...."

"That's startin' to sound like another damned threat, Sir. Please leave now before I change my mind and blow your head off just for general principles."

The lieutenant turned to the ARVN officers. "Let's go, gentlemen. We will attend to this matter at another time." The two ARVN followed the marine lieutenant as he departed toward the rear.

"Mud, move the prisoners forward. I'm gonna check our rear and make sure the good lieutenant doesn't have a change of heart."

"Roger," replied Mud dryly. "You heard the man, Huy. Tell 'em they're our prisoners again. No funny business and let's get moving."

Twenty minutes later the prisoners were turned over to Lieutenant Malcolm with a brief explanation as to why they were not left at the collection point.

"You did what?" exclaimed Malcolm, his voice almost cracking.

"I retook my prisoners, so to speak, Sir."

"Goddamn, Indio, you're gonna ruin my future in civilian life if you don't stop this shit. What the hell am I supposed to do? Ignore the fact that you drew down on an officer of the United States Marine Corps?"

"He provoked it, Sir."

"Jesus. You provoke too damn easy."

"Sir, the tall gook is already injured. It don't seem American to beat the hell out of 'im."

"There you go with that again. How many times do I have to tell you, you can't do whatever in the hell you want to do in life – whenever you want to do it? The man was an officer on our side for Christ sakes. Didn't you ever read the Uniform Code of Military Justice?"

"Yessir, but I was kinda hopin' that subject wouldn't come up right now."

"And just how do you propose I handle that little miracle?"

"Well, Sir, if that man killed earlier this morning were reported as the one who brought you these prisoners, they wouldn't court-martial a dead man, would they?"

Malcolm shook his head. "In the next war, would you please join the army?"

"I ain't fightin' in the next one if they fight it this way."

"Get out of here and get back up with the point. I'll speak with you later in the day."

"Yessir. Oh, one more thing, Sir?"

"I'm almost afraid to ask."

"My rifle. Can I have my rifle back? I feel unarmed with this shotgun."

They exchanged weapons and cartridge belts. Malcolm said, "Now get the hell out of here before division legal shows up right in the middle of this operation, looking for a piece of your ass."

Jesse turned to Mud, who stood twenty yards away. "The skipper says to get your lazy ass to the point. If you don't mind, I think I'll join you."

Malcolm looked at his interpreter. "Huy, come here a minute. I want to talk to you about three prisoners."

Late in the afternoon the point turned south. After a short search, the point

325

Stoney Livingston

man found a likely location to cross the large river before him. He held up his forward movement until the point team was fully assembled, then the squad leader radioed a halt to the units following.

The squad leader, a tall, lanky sergeant from Waco, Texas, named Williams and nicknamed Waco for his hometown, ordered his pickets out while he discussed the crossing with the rest of his squad.

The point man, a skinny kid from New Jersey, said, "Okay, Waco, who draws the short straw on this one?"

"You're out. You been the point longer than anybody today." He looked at the seven men huddled nearby. Jesse and Mud were part of the group. He studied his squad carefully. This was a job nobody wanted. First in the water, first to die if the VC were waiting on the other side. This was a big river. The risks were proportionately big. It was obvious he hated being the one to make the choice of who should take the greatest risks day after day.

He was saved the agony of choice. A voice said, "Hell, Waco. I'll go first. I was wantin' something important to do today anyways."

Waco looked gratefully at his second fire team leader, Lance corporal J.J. Washington, from Mobile, Alabama.

Washington had grown up a black man in a white man's part of the country. He had lived the "separate but equal" life mandated by Alabama law for most of his twenty-two years. He knew that times were changing for all blacks in America and he wanted to do his part to be as much a citizen as any white man – maybe even more. He was soft-spoken and well liked by almost everybody in the company.

"You don't have to do no volunteerin', JJ," said Williams.

"That's okay. The gooks are probably nowhere near this place. Would you be, with all these damn grunts snoopin' around?"

Waco looked again at the rest of his men, then back to Washington. "You got it, JJ."

Without another word, Washington grasped his M-14 and moved toward the river.

Waco addressed the rest of the point team. "When JJ gets the other side secured, third fire team follow, then the FO team, then the first team, then me and the second team. Any questions?"

There were none. These men had all been through the same drill many times.

With the squad hiding in the brush along the river's edge on a skirmish line, J.J.Washington slid into the water. Each man waited at the ready, glad it was not him out there. All eyes and ears strained to pick up a sound or a movement that might indicate the presence of VC.

Washington waded safely ashore on the far side of the river and moved out of sight into the brush as he searched for higher ground to get a better view.

The third fire team was safely on the south riverbank and Jesse a mere fifteen feet from the same shoreline when the firing began. Waco and the first fire team were about halfway across the thirty-yard-wide river. In the chest-high water, they were helpless.

The intense small arms fire was interrupted from time to time by the explosions of rifle grenades. Bullets whizzed all about Jesse's head. The plopping sound of a bullet striking the water was followed immediately by the report of the rifle or machine-gun firing the round.

326

Forever Patriots

Jesse ducked under the water and swam toward the enemy shore. Even underwater he could hear the bullets tear into the river as they impacted with a plopping sound. His hand struck a bullet as it dropped slowly and harmlessly to the bottom of the dirty water. He dragged his heavily soaked body onto the muddy clay shoreline and crawled to the relative safety of the trees. Looking back to the river, he saw Mud struggling to make it to the bank. The PRC-10 was too heavy for him to control as he moved forward in a near panic.

Quickly Jesse discarded his cartridge belt and helmet, threw down his rifle, and ran back into the river, screaming, "Hang on, Mud!"

Mud was about twenty feet from the river's edge when Jesse grabbed the radio. "Let me have the radio!"

Mud needed no repeat of Jesse's request. Quickly he slipped out of the radio back pack and swam for the brush. He swam so frantically, he continued to swim for about three or four feet after he hit the clay soil, Jesse, breathing heavily, right behind him.

"You okay, Mud?" panted Jesse.

Mud had regained some of his composure. "Oh hell yes. I'm ready to try it again."

"Don't pull that dumbshit again. Dump the radio. We can always steal another one from somebody."

"Thanks anyway."

"You're welcome anyway. Now let's get to some high ground and see if we can't hold out until we get some help. See if the radio will work. And raise Whiskey-Six."

While Mud worked over his radio, Jesse retrieved his helmet, rifle and cartridge belt. He squatted next to Mud and pulled a soaked contour map from his map pocket. "Is it gonna work?" he asked, nodding at the radio.

"Yeah, I think so. Hang on. Yep. There it is."

"Stand by. Stay behind me about ten yards. I'm gonna try and make the ridgeline and call one in."

"Roger."

As Jesse turned to move up the hill he saw Waco in the river. He was obviously hit, but he was just as obviously still alive. "Waco's still in the water. Shit! Goddamnit!" Jesse looked around him. He listened to the small arms fire. It seemed to have tapered off a bit.

"Don't even think about it! He's too far out! And he's drifting downstream," said Mud.

Jesse glanced at his soggy map. "Call in a fire mission, Mud. Ask for eight rounds of H.E. light, no adjust. Just fire the damn barrage."

"Oh shit! C'mon, man, be reasonable! Don't go out there and get your ass blown away," Mud begged.

"481324, Mud. Call it in!" ordered Jesse as he once again discarded his excess weight and ran into the river.

Mud shouted after him, "You crazy bastard! I hope you live to get the ass-kickin' you deserve for bein' so fuckin' stupid!" He quickly brought the radio handset to his mouth as he Jesse swam madly toward Waco. "Whiskey-Six. Whiskey-Alpha. Fire mission. Over."

Jesse was oblivious to the small arms fire when he reached Waco. He calmly asked the lanky sergeant, "Where you hit, Waco?"

327

"I don't know. It feels like my leg. It hurts like hell," replied Waco through clenched teeth.

"Hang on. We're going to drier places." Jesse carried Waco piggy-back to the shoreline, just below where Mud knelt. He fell to the muddy clay, exhausted, as the first 81 mm mortar round fell within a hundred yards of their position. The ground shuddered and vibrated as the mortar rounds exploded one after the other.

Still breathing heavily and laying face down, Jesse said, "Cease fire. End of mission. Tell 'em to stand by."

"Roger."

"Waco's hit in the leg. Go to work on it. I'm gonna take a look at the opposition." He moved into a low crouch and once again retrieved his rifle, helmet and cartridge belt. Mud ordered a cease fire and moved to assist Waco even as Jesse remained in sight.

Jesse returned shortly. He turned his attention to Waco's wound. "How in the hell did you manage that?"

"Manage what?" asked Waco.

"Manage to find a pungy stake in the middle of the damn river?"

"Pungy stake?" Waco paused. "No shit. That's what it had to be. Oh, Christ. They put poison and all kinds of shit on them things."

Jesse said, "Yeah, maybe, but the river probably washed anything out that may have been in the stake." He inspected the wound more closely. "It don't matter. We've gotta get you out. Looks like you'll be back out here in a while though."

"How come you're so damn full of good news?" asked Waco.

"That's all there is around here – good news." Jesse paused. "While Mud is patchin' you up, I'm gonna call in another fire mission. It looks like the gooks aren't gonna stay and fight. They're moving south, into the mountains." He turned and picked up the radio handset. "Whiskey-Six. Whiskey-Alpha. Over."

The voice at FDC answered, "This is Whiskey-Six. Go ahead, Alpha."

Jesse responded, "We need a med-evac at 481323. Unknown number of casualties at this time. Estimate a half-dozen."

"Roger the med-evac at 481323. What's the situation, Alpha? Over."

"Charlie is moving to the south. They ambushed the point and are falling back into the hills. What's left of the point has the south side of the river secured. Advise Pied Piper Alpha to advance as soon as possible."

"Roger, Alpha. WilCo."

"Stand by for fire mission, Whiskey-Six. Over."

"Go ahead, Alpha."

"Fire mission. Four rounds Willie Peter. If the guns are up in less than a minute, you will have troops in the open. Azimuth 3200. Coordinates 481319. Fire when ready."

There was a pause on the radio. It crackled once then the radio operator said, "Whiskey-Six Actual prefers adjusting fire. Do you copy? Over."

"I copy. Tell Whiskey-Six Actual that I know where the gooks are on my map. If FDC can read a map, they'll be on target. Fire the barrage when ready."

"Roger, Whiskey-Alpha."

Jesse climbed the short rise from the river to observe the terrain below, especially the dirt trail about four hundred yards to his front. He heard Mud shout, "On the way."

"Roger on the way. Wait." He put the 7 x 50 field glasses to his eyes and waited. Five or six of the enemy crossed the trail and disappeared into the heavy undergrowth to the south.

"Mud," He shouted over his shoulder.

"Yo?"

"Stand by." The first white phosphorus round exploded with a gentle *pop*. Jesse smiled. *Right on target.* The other rounds quickly followed. Jesse wasn't certain but, as the smoke from the exploding rounds covered the terrain, he thought he saw more troops attempting to cross the trail.

"Mud. Give 'em a search and traverse. Left fifty, add one-hundred. Eight rounds of H.E. light. Search down fifty, traverse right fifty. Fire when ready."

"Roger."

The smoke was clearing on the trail. A man was down and writhing near the tree line. Jesse peered through his glasses. The man was definitely a victim of the burning white phosphorus flakes. Smoke emanated from the area of the man's chest. Another VC emerged from the relative safety of the tree line to aid his injured comrade. Quickly Jesse ran the rear sight up about thirty clicks, brought his M-1 to his shoulder and sighted down the barrel. *Just like in boot camp. Breath. Relax. Aim. Take up the slack in the trigger. Squeeze.* The rifle bucked into his shoulder.

Even at four hundred yards, Jesse saw the pieces of bone and flesh fly as the bullet struck the unwary VC in the head. The head jerked quickly backward and the rest of the body fell, like a wet rag doll. "Damn!" he exclaimed.

"What's the matter with that shot?" The voice was about twenty yards to his right.

"Nothing, except I was aiming for his chest, goddamnit."

"That's gotta be Indio from 81's, right?"

"Yeah. Is that you, JJ?"

"Yeah. How bad is it behind us?"

"I don't really know yet. Waco took a pungy stake in his leg pretty bad. I think we must have lost two or three more that were in the river when the shooting started."

JJ said, "I didn't see a fuckin' thing, man. I swear to God. I never saw nothin' until just a minute ago when they ran across the trail down there. I never even saw 'em when they were blastin' the shit out of us. It was like the trees was doin' the shootin'!"

A voice from the riverbank interrupted JJ's confession. "On the way Whiskey."

Jesse shouted, "Roger on the way. Wait." He strolled to JJ's position and squatted next to the black man from Alabama. He fished in his left breast pocket for his plastic cigarette pack holder and opened it. "I'll be damned. There is a fairy godmother. I've still got two almost-dry smokes. You want one?"

"How the hell can you sit here and smoke at a time like this?"

The whooshing sound of descending mortar rounds grew louder as they fell toward their target. "Hold that thought," he said as he put his cigarette in his mouth and his field glasses to his eyes. He watched the rounds exploding in the trees. When the last round exploded, he turned and shouted to Mud. "Hey, Mud, cease fire. End of mission."

"Roger, cease fire. End of mission." Mud's voice carried up the hill.

Jesse turned to JJ. "Why in the hell shouldn't I smoke a cigarette?" He glanced through his glasses at the man who had been thrashing about on the

329

ground. All movement had ceased. He turned back to JJ. "I earned it and so did you. What the hell are we gonna do, assault the gooks by ourselves? Hell, I'm game if you are. If you're not going to smoke a cigarette with me, let's go chase us some gooks."

"You know, I seen you runnin' around the rice paddies with that damn LAW tucked under your arm on Oregon. I know you're a crazy motherfucker but that shit ain't gonna rub off on me. I'll take the fuckin' cigarette."

"It's a little wet on one end but it'll still smoke," apologized Jesse as he handed JJ the cigarette.

JJ's hand trembled as he accepted the offered smoke. "Oh shit, man! All those guys blasted and I led 'em into it. Oh shit! Sweet Jesus! I never wanted anything like this to happen while I was on the point."

"Would you rather be one of the guys floatin' down the river?"

"You damn right I would. It's my fault they walked into the shit."

Jesse looked at him and softly said, "Now you're alive and you've got more experience. You're a better man for it. It wouldn't have made any difference who the point man was. They had us by the short hairs from the start. *God* would have walked into this one for chrisakes. Nobody will say otherwise. If he does, we'll let him take the point and see how long he lasts."

JJ smiled. "You're okay for a crazy bastard. Thanks, man. I don't believe you but it's good to hear you say it."

"It's always a pleasure to tell a man a good thing. And *I* believe it whether you do or not. Where you from, JJ?"

"Alabama."

"No kidding? I'm from the south too."

"No shit? Where 'bouts?"

"Southern Arizona."

JJ laughed so suddenly he choked on his cigarette smoke. When his short fit of coughing subsided he said, "That's a good one. I'll try to remember that next time I want to piss someone off."

Jesse field-stripped his cigarette butt. "I'm gonna move back down to the river and see how things are progressing. Let us know if you see somethin' we ought to know about."

"You got it, Indio. And thanks again, man."

Jesse moved back down to Mud's position. Waco was shivering. "You want some happy juice, Waco?" Jesse asked, displaying a morphine syrette.

Through his chattering teeth, Waco answered, "Not yet, man. I think I can handle it until we get some help. Thanks anyway."

They covered him with his poncho to help keep him warm and waited for the rest of the company to arrive on their side of the river.

When the south side of the river was completely secured, the dead and wounded were accounted for. The point had suffered a total of five casualties, two of which were KIA. The first helicopter to arrive took the three wounded. The dead would have to wait until another helicopter was available.

Jesse stared at the two ponchos, tightly wrapped around the bodies of the men lost on the river crossing. As he smoked his cigarette and felt his sorrow at the loss of the two men, Mud came running to his side, PRC-10 radio bouncing from side to side as each foot struck the ground.

"Indio! We're in deep shit! I just saw that lieutenant from S-2, and he's got a squad of goons with him. He's looking for you."

Jesse looked at his puffing radio operator. "Just a squad?"

"Goddamnit, this is serious!"

Jesse furrowed his brow. "Where is he?"

"Just on the other side of the hill – back where we crossed the river."

Jesse looked at the two ponchos. "I hate to do this – but it's for a good cause. I need some help, Mud. Find Sandy and get him down here to these bodies as fast as you can. I want that lieutenant to observe my dead body before the chopper takes it out of here."

"How you gonna convince that lieutenant that it's you laying there?"

"I'm not. Sandy is. These guys were both shot in the head. I'm gonna' pick the closest one to my size and get him ready for inspection in about five minutes."

"Shit. That's crazy."

"You got any better ideas?"

"Hell, I don't have *any* ideas."

"Then go find Sandy and tell him the plan. We don't have a lot of time to waste."

Corpsman Sanderson unwrapped the second body. The lieutenant from S-2 looked at the bloody headband, on a head that was half blown away. He saw the torn trouser legs. Even in death the knees seemed to protrude. A twelve-gauge shotgun shell lay half out of one breast pocket.

"He really was a good man, Sir," explained Sandy. "He had just been out here too long without a break. He's got a good record with our company as can be verified by Lieutenant Malcolm. His parents were proud of the way he served his country. As a matter-of-fact, only last week he told me that his younger brother wanted to join the Corps when he turned seventeen later this year."

The lieutenant took one last look at the dead marine. He studied the corpsman. "I see no reason to blacken the man's name. He's paid the ultimate price. Nothing transpired this morning. Cover him up." He turned and left, followed by his squad of rear echelon troops.

After a few moments Jesse and Mud emerged from the nearby trees.

"Damn, that was a right nice thing you said about the dearly departed, Doc. Had me all choked up. That brother thing was a nice touch," said Jesse.

Sandy smiled. "I know where you got the trousers, but how did you shave him so fast?"

Jesse pulled the bone handled Bowie knife from its tape-encrusted sheath and smiled. "It's a little awkward but it works, and I only had to shave one side."

He carefully removed his headband from the dead man.

"You not going to use that headband again?" asked Mud.

Jesse nodded at the dead man. "It's *my* headband, and he sure as hell don't need it." He turned to Sandy. "Thanks, Sandy, I really appreciate it."

Sandy smiled. "Hell, Indio, life in Alpha Company wouldn't be the same without you here to stir things up. Besides, I didn't like that salty bastard anyway, the way he came strolling up to headquarters section like some damn general, throwing his weight around. Actually, it was a lot of fun."

"Thanks just the same." He glanced at the dead man. "Thanks, Bud."

On those occasions when Jesse heated his C-rations, his preparations

331

were usually elaborate. He glanced at the setting sun, concerned only for a moment that he might not get to use the C-3 to heat his canned bread before dark, then carefully poked one small hole in the top of the can and trickled a few drops of water into it from his canteen. He then placed the can over a piece of C-3 explosive about the size of a small marble. The can was supported above the C-3 on three sides by small rocks. He ignited the C-3 with his Zippo and watched the short, white, intense flame as it bore into the bottom of the can. Within seconds steam spewed from the small hole in the top. He removed the can from the flame and held it with the tail of his shirt while he opened it fully with his P-38 can opener. Out came a soft, fluffy cylinder of bread. But for the halizone in the water used to moisten it, it almost smelled fresh-baked.

"What kind of a heat tab is that?" asked Sandy, who had watched the preparations silently.

"That ain't no heat tab, Doc. That's C-3. It's ten times faster'n a heat tab."

"Why the hell doesn't it explode?"

"The heat isn't contained. Hell, you can burn the stuff all day and it won't explode. Just don't use anymore than you need, 'cause you gotta let whatever you light burn itself out." He reached into his map pouch and pulled out a chunk of the plastic explosive about the size of a tennis ball, broke off a small piece and handed it to the corpsman. "Here. Try it. Just be careful to use a teeny bit and don't try to put it out when you're done. If you use a little too much, that's the way it goes, let it burn itself out."

Sandy accepted the gift nervously. "Thanks."

As he ate his hot bread, Jesse watched the corpsman intently while the latter prepared his rations with the C-3. He wanted to be certain that Sandy did not violate the relatively stable nature of the explosive.

"Hey, Doc, what's the harm to the body if you don't have bowel movements for a relatively long period of time?" asked Jesse casually, eyes never straying from Sandy's C-3.

"How long?"

"Oh, 'bout a couple of weeks."

Sandy looked up from his boiling can of beefsteak and potatoes. "Two weeks? That's a helluva constipation problem."

"No. No constipation. Just no need to go. Don't seem to eat enough food to have any left over after my body uses it all for fuel. Huntin's been pretty lousy this past couple of weeks."

"What about the C's?" asked Sandy.

"I'd just as soon do without as eat most of 'em. I'm tired of 'em I guess. Hell, I don't know. I just know that I'd rather eat cooked grasshoppers than them damn C-rations."

"Well, if you haven't had a bowel movement in more than two weeks, and you're not constipated, it's my guess that you're starving to death. Your body is using everything you feed it just to stay alive."

Jesse chewed his bread thoughtfully. "Generally, how long does starvin' to death take, given that I do eat some of this garbage from time to time?"

"That's hard to say. It could take six months or it could take another six days. Too many factors involved. One thing's for certain though, it doesn't do your body any good, even if you don't starve to death. You can suffer permanent damage if you let it go too far." Sandy stirred his beefsteak and potatoes and tried to take a

332

bite, burning his mouth in the process. He jerked his head away from the hot food.

"Told you to be careful. That stuff gets food hot in a hurry."

"Thanks," said Sandy as he puckered his mouth and sucked through his lips to cool the fire inside.

Mail arrived too late for distribution before dark so it was held until the following afternoon, after the company fortified a position for the night. Jesse, who always carried a small tablet in his map pouch, was able to answer letters from Charlotte and Will before darkness set in.

They had crossed a little stream called Khe Trai earlier in the day and were high in the hills to the southeast of the prior day's action. Though the march up and down the hills was exhausting, Alpha Company had no enemy contact that day. Jesse reflected on the prior day's events in his mind, but he didn't report them on paper. He wondered how anyone at home could relate to what was going on around him. *Hell, it doesn't even seem real to me. I know they would never understand.*

He wrote of the beautiful river he had seen yesterday, and the lush, green hills that surrounded his current position. He told of clear skies and things of beauty. He made no mention of death in either of his letters.

Just before dark, Lieutenant Malcolm advised Jesse that Waco had put him in for a bronze star for his bravery at the river crossing. Malcolm also advised him that he tore up the commendation. Bronze stars attracted attention and, as long as the lieutenant from S-2 remained attached to the1st Battalion, 4th Marines, Malcolm wanted no attention drawn to his forward observer. Jesse had no problem with Malcolm's decision.

Shortly after midnight, the enemy struck Alpha's left flank. It was over very quickly as the VC had never intended to make a fight, but rather to harass the Americans, cause them to lose sleep and, maybe, to inflict casualties. They succeeded in all aspects. In the short rocket attack, Alpha had two riflemen from the third platoon wounded, one of them seriously. No one saw the enemy. They seemed to be gone with the last bursting rocket.

At daylight a patrol discovered the position from which the VC had launched their attack but nothing of any real value was ascertained. The company moved further into the hills. Shortly after two P.M. forward movement was halted in relatively flat terrain and preparations for the night commenced.

Mud removed the heavy radio from his sweaty back and laid it carefully on the ground with a sigh of relief. "This place is just like Pendleton. No matter where the hell we go, there's a hill."

"Zeus designed it that way, Mud, just to piss off marines so they'll be that much more thankful when they reach Valhalla," said Jesse as he put a cigarette to his sweating lips.

"Great. Ten thousand comedians out of work and you're tryin' to be funny."

"Little touchy today, aren't we?"

"I don't know. I guess I just don't see any point to all this shit. If the damn generals had to carry this prick-ten all over the jungle, I bet to hell this war would be fought a lot differently."

"Amen to that, brother."

Mud pulled a pocketbook from his pack and began to read. Seemed to Jesse that Mud read a lot more than most of the men in the outfit.

"Hey, Indio." JJ approached at a slow walk.

Jesse hadn't seen him since the ambush at the river. "Hey, JJ, how's it hangin'?"

"Okay, man. Good to see you weren't one of the guys that caught it last night."

"Thanks. Same for you. Where you settin' up?"

Before JJ could reply, the sound of small arms fire began to the right front of their position. It started slowly, with four or five rounds fired from an M-14, then the answering fire from the VC small arms, then more M-14s and an M-60, then more VC rifles and automatic rifles. Then Jesse heard the *whoosh-whoosh-whoosh* of falling mortar rounds.

"Incoming!" He shouted. Everyone dove for cover.

The barrage was short, only seven or eight rounds, and there were no casualties other than one pack of C-rations that was destroyed. But the mental damage had been done. Rockets were one thing but mortars was another. They could strike from the other side of a hill and never be seen.

The small arms fire continued to the right front. Jesse said, "Let's go, Mud. We gotta find out what's going on." He turned to JJ. "How about you, JJ? You comin' with us or stayin' here?"

"Hell, I'm goin' with *you*. If there's only one damn gook in the whole country, you'll be wherever he is. I wanna see one of 'em this time."

Mud slipped his radio onto his back and started in the direction of the small arms fire. Jesse quickly passed him and charged up the hill to his front, JJ close behind him.

At a good vantagepoint, Jesse surveyed the hills with his glasses.

"What the hell is everybody shootin' at?" asked JJ.

With the glasses still to his eyes, Jesse shook his head. "Damned if I know. I don't see anything yet." He caught a puff of smoke in the lower right portion of his field of vision. "Wait. I do see something but I can't tell what it is yet. It's too far forward to be our guys, but I don't know if it's one man or a dozen. All I saw was a puff of smoke."

"Where? Let me see!" said JJ.

Jesse handed him the field glasses and pointed halfway up a ridgeline to the right front. "Over there, beneath those trees near that outcropping of rock."

JJ put the glasses to his eyes and studied the trees. "I see it! I see it!"

"Don't get too comfortable with those glasses, JJ. I need 'em to do my job."

Reluctantly, JJ returned the field glasses to their rightful owner. Jesse scanned the hills, looking for friendly troop movements. He turned to Mud. "Mud, raise the skipper and see if he wants us to call in a mission."

"Roger," came the standard reply.

Jesse continued to study the terrain while Mud conversed with company headquarters. He pulled his map from his pouch and looked at it briefly.

"Fire the mission," said Mud. "We've got a patrol trying to flank 'em on the left, but they're gonna hold their position until we fire the mission."

Jesse moved his attention to the left. He saw the patrol, about five hundred yards left of his target. "Mud, tell the skipper to have the patrol find cover. They're pretty close to the target. When they're notified, stand by for the fire mission."

"Roger."

334

Even as the mortar barrage struck its target, the enemy struck Alpha's left flank. Jesse heard the firing begin as he peered through his glasses at the impacting barrage. He took his eyes from the target only after the last round exploded. "Cease fire. End of mission. Estimate seventy percent of target area destroyed."

"Roger."

JJ watched nervously as Jesse swung his glasses to his left. "You see anything, man?" He asked.

"Nope. That hill is in the way. We're gonna have to move our position." Jesse stood and advanced at a half run toward the left flank.

In position behind a tree and panting heavily, Jesse turned to Mud. "Ask the skipper if he wants a fire mission on this flank."

Small arms fire broke out to the direct front of Alpha Company's position. "Forget it, Mud. Tell the skipper I want to meet with him as soon as he can spare a second."

"Roger."

"Shit, man, they must be all around us!" said JJ.

"Maybe. And maybe that's what they want us to think. How many of 'em have you actually seen?" asked Jesse.

JJ shrugged. "Hell, I'm not for sure I've seen any."

"That's my whole point. If they really had enough manpower to surround a whole company position with any authority, they would also have enough manpower to overrun us before we dug in. There's probably not more'n a hundred of 'em out there and they're tryin' to make it look like a thousand. They've got a couple of sixty mortars, but that's about the limit of their support."

JJ looked at Jesse inquisitively. "Even if you're right, a hundred gooks with two mortars is not exactly my idea of a stroll in the park."

"Mine either, but...."

"Skipper says to meet him at the LZ, now if possible," said Mud, moving the radio handset from his ear.

Jesse moved out at a dead run.

Malcolm listened to Jesse's plan patiently. When Jesse finished with his plans and the reasons he believed in them, Malcolm said, "I think you've got something."

He turned to First Sergeant Webber squatting next to him. "Top, pull everybody in as tight as the terrain will allow. In ten minutes, we're going to lay down a mortar barrage to the south, east, and west of our position. It's going to be in close, so tighten 'em up. I don't want anyone on our side hit by our own stuff."

The First Sergeant nodded. "Aye aye, Skipper."

Jesse busied himself marking coordinates and azimuths. He wrote the information on a piece of his notepad paper and handed it to Mud. "There it is, Mud. Call 'em in for simultaneous firing if they have enough guns in range."

"Roger," came Mud's standard reply.

As Mud called in his missions, Jesse said, "Skipper, why don't we take a platoon to our front and circle left? If we move fast enough, we could probably surprise a bunch of 'em."

Malcolm raised an eyebrow and looked at Jesse. "Yeah, that's what worries me. It might be a helluva surprise if it was a real *big* bunch of 'em."

"Skipper, we've got a golden opportunity to finally nail a bunch of 'em.

335

Stoney Livingston

Battalion wants body count. Let's give 'em something to count for a few days."

Malcolm smiled. "I take it you don't have any special reason for wanting to go home someday?"

Jesse ignored him. "C'mon, Skipper, we've got 'em this time."

"You're putting a lot of faith in your theory that there's a small force out there."

"I can feel it, Sir."

"I think you're right, and I want to get 'em as much as you do, but as the commanding officer of this company, I can't risk lives on a hunch. We'll get another chance."

"What if I could get fifty volunteers?"

"Let it go, Indio. That's all I want to hear about it."

Jesse looked into the trees. "Yessir."

Mud's voice ended the discussion. "On the way, mission fourteen."

"Roger on the way. Wait," replied Jesse as he moved to a slightly higher point to observe the impacting rounds.

"On the way mission seventeen," shouted Mud.

Jesse shouted over his shoulder, "Roger on the way whiskey seventeen. Wait."

"On the way missions nineteen and twenty," shouted Mud.

"Roger on the way whiskey nineteen and twenty. Wait."

The first barrage struck the hills about 600 yards northeast of their position. The hills and ridgelines made observation difficult but Jesse could tell by the clouds of smoke and dust that the guns were on target. Even as the last round of the first barrage struck its target, the second barrage touched down a mere 500 yards to the north and slightly east.

Malcolm came running to Jesse's position and knelt next to him. Jesse peered intently through his field glasses at the second target. Malcolm said, "Damn, man, you're a little close to first platoon with that one."

Jesse took the glasses from his eyes, looked at Malcolm, and smiled. "Not with that one, Sir." About that time, missions nineteen and twenty found their targets. Mission twenty struck about 600 yards south. Mission nineteen landed 150 yards southeast. The ground shook and trembled as the 81mm. Mortar rounds threw dirt and trees into the air. Malcolm hugged the ground.

"Goddamnit, Indio, cease fire! Cease fire!"

"Can't. It's only an eight-round barrage. It's already fired," shouted Jesse over the exploding mortar rounds.

Suddenly, there was silence. Not even the sound of a rifle broke the stillness in the air. Jesse looked at Malcolm. "Permission to take a patrol out front, Sir?"

Malcolm made a visible effort to maintain control of his voice. "You damn near drop a mortar barrage right on top of us, and then you calmly ask permission to go chase the gooks as if you hadn't exceeded the damn safety margin by two or three hundred yards. I ought to lock your ass up."

"C'mon, Skipper, you know we got a few with that last mission. Let's go get 'em."

Despite his irritation Malcolm smiled. "One of these days I'm gonna scrape you out of a mortar crater. Okay. First platoon is on our front. I'll let 'em know you're on your way. Sweep the area south and east. You won't be going more than 500

Forever Patriots

yards out, nor more than 500 yards east."

Jesse smiled. "Thanks, Skipper. That beats nothin'."

The sweep by the first platoon netted eight bodies and two wounded prisoners. It was more than Jesse had expected, especially the two prisoners. The VC were almost as fanatical as the marines when it came to leaving dead or wounded behind. They just didn't do it. The captured weapons included a light machine gun and several automatic rifles, indicating the VC in this area were better equipped than originally thought.

Two days later Jesse found a small, red banty rooster. With the help of Huy, he located the rooster's owner in a thatch house at the edge of a tiny rice paddy. Not wanting to take another chance on Vietnamese cooking, Jesse choose to pay for the rooster and carry him back to camp alive.

At camp, a closer examination of the little rooster revealed he was quite thin. He wouldn't make even a poor meal for one man. It seemed a shame to Jesse that the bird should be killed when he wouldn't even provide nourishment for a single meal. For this reason the little red rooster was spared – at least until he could be fattened up.

Jesse tied a small piece of lightweight rope to the rooster's right leg and fed him C-rations. Within two days the rooster was the company mascot. Jesse called him Frank, for no particular reason other than it sounded right to him. At the time he named the bird he did not know the company gunnery sergeant's first name was also Frank. When this was pointed out to him, Jesse apologized but explained to the good gunnery sergeant that the little rooster liked his name and was used to it. To change it would break the rooster's heart, and he knew the gunny wouldn't want to be responsible for the little guy's death.

Almost a full week passed without an incident of any kind. Days were spent on patrol or ambush. Nights were long and tiring segments of perimeter duty or night ambush. There were no rivers close enough for bathing and the limited supply of water allowed for only an occasional "whore's bath", which consisted of washing under the arms and in the crotch and rectal area.

Time seemed to stand still, just like the war. Alpha Company licked its wounds, but recovery was slow. The C-rations provided the basic ingredients to sustain life, but did little to increase fat or muscle tissue. Jesse continued to lose weight. Frank, the rooster, seemed to be the only one to prosper in his new environment. He put on weight and his brightly colored feathers took on a lustrous shine.

Jesse approached Mud quickly. The company briefing had been short. "Pack it up, Mud. We're being lifted out of here in about five minutes. Some outfit west of us is in deep shit."

"What about Frank?"

"Take him with us. Hell, he likes to ride on your radio. If the chopper don't scare him off, he can go anywhere we do."

"Roj," replied Mud happily.

Shortly, the company was aboard the slow moving Choctaw helicopters and lumbering five hundred feet above the emerald green landscape as they proceeded on their Hawk mission. Jesse smiled as he inspected the M-60 machine gun

337

mounted on a crudely constructed swivel platform at the helicopter door.

Mud watched Frank walk amongst the gear splayed about the deck of the helicopter. The little rooster acted as though he had been trained all of his life to ride in the noisy, vibrating machine. He strutted from place to place, pecking at imaginary objects when it suited his whim, oblivious to the noise of the engine and the constant vibration. The men began to watch him intently, forgetting where they were or where they were going, their minds temporarily occupied with something other than fear.

As he strutted and pecked atop Lieutenant Malcolm's pack, the helicopter struck a pocket of dense air and lurched upward, causing the little bird to loose his balance and fall ungraciously to the deck.

"Damn, Skipper, what you got in that pack? A pair of your old socks?" asked the first sergeant.

Every man in the helicopter roared with laughter. It was a real laughter that comes from the genuine feeling of humor, a laughter not heard often in the line companies. It made every man feel good, if only for a moment. Some laughed so hard tears filled their eyes, others fought to catch a breath.

Somehow, Frank seemed to sense he was the butt of their amusement. He stood unsteadily and strode indignantly to a corner of the helicopter where he ruffled his feathers, sat down, and glared at the men surrounding him. The laughter was deafening. One of the men fell to the deck and laughed until he complained of pain in his stomach muscles. Not a man aboard was without tears of laughter in his eyes. Even the helicopter gunner couldn't contain himself.

The return to reality began slowly as the crawling Choctaw started its descent. The gunner leaned forward, tears of humor still streaming down his face, and addressed Malcolm. With a smile from ear to ear, he said, "You've got a hot LZ down there, Lieutenant."

Malcolm's expression became serious. He shouted above the drone of the engine. "We've got a hot LZ. Time to go to work. Prepare to debark. Sergeant Wilkes, you lead out."

"Yessir," replied Wilkes, grateful to be afforded the opportunity to exit the helicopter first.

The "hot LZ" was no more than a few stray rounds from afar, and turned out to be as close as Alpha Company got to the enemy during the Hawk mission. Not a man in the company made contact with the VC nor any semblance thereof. After two days of chasing shadows and one-hundred-percent alert at night, Alpha Company left the area the same way they had arrived.

The hills south and east of the Khe Trai looked almost like home as they touched ground. Frank, the rooster, had become an old salt and seemed to be in command of everyone and everything as he perched atop Mud's PRC-10 radio.

There was little doubt he was spoiled by the men as he showed no fear of anything or anyone. When he was hungry, he pecked and pestered whoever was in range. If he became irritated, he ruffled his feathers and strutted like a peacock, daring anyone to not heed his slightest wish.

Lieutenant Malcolm officially promoted Frank to "PFC in charge of mascots", in a brief but humorous ceremony. Several privates requested transfers to Frank's detail but all were denied on the grounds that the T.O. called for only one slot per company in that M.O.S.

Bathing details were sent to the Khe Trai in platoons. Most of the men were able to fully cleanse their bodies for the first time in almost two weeks. The elation

338

was toned down a bit by the discovery of large numbers of leeches in the river, but even those not inclined to frolic with the slimy little creatures managed to overcome their fear of the bloodsuckers when confronted with the possibility of another week or two without a shower. The human body can go only a short time without cleansing before it begins to cause discomfort on a large scale. These men were only too aware of that somber fact.

During the week following their first Hawk mission, Jesse roamed the hills with various patrols, designating several coordinates and marking them as H. & I. missions. Most were fired in the late evening hours to disrupt possible enemy movements against the company's position during the hours of darkness, but some he marked as daytime missions for various strategic reasons, none of which he could explain to Lieutenant Malcolm's complete satisfaction.

Contact with the enemy was rare and when it did occur it was usually at night in a hit and run attack by the VC, or by a lone sniper who fired from such a distance that the chances of being hit were mathematically impossible to calculate.

Mud went to Bangkok for six days of R & R and returned with a bottle of Jack Daniels which he gave to Jesse, who magnanimously shared it with JJ, Sandy, Faye, and several others.

Mud told stories of the most beautiful women in the orient and vowed he would return to Thailand before he grew too old to enjoy all of the "benefits" he had discovered while on his short respite.

During Mud's absence, JJ had acted as Jesse's radio operator, much to the contrary wishes of his new squad leader. Standard operating procedure required that Mud be replaced by an operator from the 81 platoon, but JJ had asked for the temporary assignment and, after a little persuasion from Jesse, Malcolm consented.

The six days passed without incident and JJ returned to his normal infantry duties upon Mud's return from his "six days of unabashed and unbridled sex and corruption" as he often described his experience. Aloud, Mud considered extending his tour by six months if they would give him two weeks in Bangkok. Three days after his return, the misery of field life brought him to the realization that two weeks in Shangri La would not be worth six more months of living like an animal in the hills and jungles of Vietnam. He opted to return to San Francisco in August if he should make it through the summer.

Rumors began to circulate that the battalion would join forces with other outfits for a large operation.

On the afternoon of May 3rd,1966 Jesse sat on a rock and listened to Lieutenant Malcolm as he briefed the platoon leaders and headquarters section.

"As most of you know, the hills around us are infested with the enemy. Maintaining a perimeter and having enough manpower to ferret them out is tough. Well, we're going to be getting some help. Tomorrow morning at 0500, we jump off from our present position. The rest of the battalion will be joining us as we move. Also participating in this operation will be the First Battalion, First Marines and the Third Battalion, Fourth Marines. We'll also have a battalion of ARVN in tow, so expect to carry more than your load if they happen to be on our flank."

Eyebrows raised and soft whistles emitted from the officers and NCO's present at the thought of three marine battalions on the sweep at the same time, in the same area. Maybe this was it – the beginning of the way it should be done. Maybe they could end the war in time for the World Series at home.

339

After his brief pause, Malcolm continued, "Our objective is to annihilate the enemy in this area."

Cheers broke out.

"Okay, okay. Hold it down." He paused again. "We will accomplish our objective in the following manner: one: we will attack at the slightest provocation with the knowledge that we have the strength to prevail if the enemy chooses to stand and fight; two: if attacked, we will hold our ground at all costs until we are reinforced. In other words, gentlemen, we will defend our position. Period. We will not give an inch of ground to the enemy unless it is to our advantage to find a more defensible position in the immediate area; three: if called upon, we will reinforce any other unit involved in this operation, at any time of the day or night, regardless of the circumstances; four: while in the brush, we will hide our movements as much as possible and get as close to the enemy as we can before we engage; five: after we have taken a position in the attack, we will withdraw immediately and continue on our mission. We will leave the mop-up to those assigned that duty."

Malcolm paused to let the information settle into the minds of his leaders. "This operation has been code named *Cherokee*, for those of you who like trivia.

"Just a few notes about the rules of the game: platoon leaders, make sure that full use is made of camouflage. Be especially careful around streams. Watch for the booby traps and ambushes. If we take sniper fire, keep moving. This is not a squad patrol. If a man becomes a casualty, all of his gear goes with him when he is taken out. While in the assault, do not stop for casualties. I know that can be a tough thing to do sometimes, but the success or failure of our mission depends on us reaching our objectives. If the enemy only has to hit one of us to take two or three out of action, it doesn't take a mathematics genius to figure the kind of manpower we'd need to pull off a successful assault against even a platoon-sized enemy position. See to it that all men have two meals in their packs." He looked at Jesse and smiled. "Except for Indio here. He doesn't own a pack.

"Delta Company will jump off at 0630 from Hill 51. Alpha and Bravo Companies will be on line, with Alpha on the left flank, sweeping. The other outfits will filter into the operation as the day progresses and you will be made aware of their positions.

"We expect very heavy resistance. G-2 reports the following enemy units to be operating in this area: 812th VC Battalion, 802nd NVR, 804th NVR, 800th NVR, 806th NVR, K105 H.C., and local VC. Those are regiment-sized units by the way, and they have full support: mortars, artillery, heavy machine guns, 75mm recoilless, rockets, and the big 120mm.

"D-day is tomorrow, Four May. I want comm up on the net at reveille. You will all be issued new maps for our area of anticipated operation and re-supplied with batteries for the radios as soon as we get resupply.

"Any questions?"

"Let's just get to it and get it over with, Sir. I wanta go home in time for the World Series," said Sergeant Wilkes.

CHAPTER FIFTEEN: CHEROKEE

The three battalions took their first steps on operation Cherokee at 1005 hours. A shortage of helicopters and several other logistical factors were blamed for the delay. There were no clouds in the sky and the sun fired its rays of heat unhindered by any earthly shield. The humidity made the air almost drinkable.

Jesse glanced behind him at Corporal Simms, forward observer of the 8th Artillery Battery. He was about ten paces behind Mud, who was ten paces behind Jesse. The arty F.O. had been in Vietnam four months and said he had never seen an operation the size of Cherokee. Hell, neither had Jesse. That was part of Jesse's dilemma. He glanced at the section of his map he had folded so that it could be read while on the march, then glanced back at Simms.

Immediately to the rear of Simm's radio operator was a Forward Air Controller and his radio operator. The FAC was a second lieutenant, so Jesse knew to look for nothing from him. Simms seemed to be studying the terrain but he didn't see the man refer to his map.

Jesse stepped to his right and waved Mud by. "I'll catch up, Mud. I just wanna check something out."

Mud nodded and continued forward without breaking his stride.

Jesse waited for the artillery FO to reach him. "Hey, Simms, how recent is your map?" he asked, falling in next to him.

"Hell, I don't know. Let me check. Whatchoo got?"

"I ain't sure but I'm hoping I have one of those old French map copies that are shot full of errors."

Simms unfolded his map as he marched. As he tried to read the legend he asked, "What makes you think you've got errors?"

"According to the way my map reads, we're not where we're supposed to be. That can't be right because there's at least three reinforced battalions on line out here. I know I'm good but I can't be the only one in four or five thousand to know we're out of position – so we must be in position. I just need to know for sure. I'd hate to call in a fire mission with the coordinates I'm coming up with."

Simms pointed to the legend on his map. Jesse looked at it and shook his head. "Same as mine. Oh well, I guess I must be readin' wrong, but I'd appreciate it if you'd just get a fix on our position and tell me where the hell we are on the map."

"Did you shoot an azimuth?" asked Simms.

"Not yet. I was just using topography. I'll get back in position and do my own fix, but I'd like your opinion too."

Simms nodded in the direction of the forward air controller. "You gonna

341

check with the FAC back there?"

Jesse looked at Simms and grinned. "What the hell for? He's a second lieutenant – or didn't you notice?"

Simms returned his grin and shook his head. Jesse moved at the double back to his position in front of Mud.

"What's up?" asked Mud as Jesse moved past him.

"I don't know for sure but I don't think we're where we're supposed to be on the map."

"No shit?"

"I'm not for sure – well, I *am* for sure actually, but I don't believe it. Hell, somebody should have noticed it by now."

"How far off are we?" asked Mud.

"I put us almost exactly one grid square due northeast of where we're supposed to be."

"That's almost a mile."

"Closer to two-thirds – but that's close enough."

"Shit, man, I just heard our FDC say that arty is about to fire an H & I barrage on our right flank."

"Damn!" said Jesse. About that time, he heard a rifle butt striking a canteen and turned to see Simms moving his way at a dead run, the butt of his rifle striking his canteen every time his left foot hit the ground.

Almost out of breath, Simms said, "Goddamn! You're right! We're two thirds of a mile too far to the northeast! Arty's fixin' to let go an H & I on the right flank of where they think we are. We gotta get to the company commander!"

"What frequency is arty on?"

"Twenty-five point six," answered Simms.

Quickly Jesse stepped behind Mud and adjusted the frequency knob on the PRC-10 radio. "Mud, give me the handset."

Jesse heard voices near the frequency and tuned in. As soon as the voices stopped, he keyed the handset. "Any station this net, this Pied Piper Whiskey Alpha. Over."

A crackly voice answered, "This is Tom Thumb Five One. Go ahead, Whiskey Alpha."

Simms said. "That's them but we can't stop an H & I. That's a prearranged shoot. We need the C.O. to stop it."

Jesse ignored him. "Five One, Whiskey Alpha. Cease fire H & I on all flanks. Do you hear me? Over."

There was a pause. Another voice entered the network. "Pied Piper Whiskey Alpha, this is Tom Thumb Five One. Identify yourself. Over."

"This is Pied Piper Whiskey Alpha Actual. Do not fire your H & I missions at this time. Do you understand? Acknowledge. Over."

"Whiskey Alpha Actual, you're on the wrong net. Do you understand? Over."

"I'm aware of what net I'm on and I say again, cease fire until further advised. Over."

"Negative, Whiskey Alpha. Report to the proper net. Over."

"Be advised, we have a problem out here. Cease fire until a coded message can be transmitted. Over."

The voice on the radio sounded annoyed. "Can you cipher message in thirty seconds? Over."

"Negative. Give us two or three minutes. Over."

"Negative on the two or three minutes, Whiskey Alpha. You've got twenty seconds and counting. Over."

Jesse keyed up the PRC-10. "Listen, you fuckin' idiot! You've got a whole damn regiment out of position because nobody taught the goddamned officers how to read a map. Go ahead and fire your chickenshit barrage but you better leave the country when you're done, 'cause the survivors on the right flank are gonna be lookin' for your stupid ass."

Simms winced as Jesse unkeyed the handset. "That was our major you were talking to."

Jesse handed Mud the handset. "An idiot is an idiot. Let's find Lieutenant Malcolm." He turned to Mud. "Mud, stay on arty's net and try to find out if they're gonna hold their fire."

Mud nodded. "Roger." There was no mistaking the smile on his face.

As the two forward observers rushed past Simms' radio operator in search of Malcolm, the radioman shouted, "I think the major's pissed."

"Advise him to call Pied Piper Alpha Actual and stand by," ordered Simms as he continued after Jesse.

They located the company commander almost one hundred yards to the rear of the forward air controller, who remained uninformed with regard to their exact position. As Jesse approached Malcolm, he waved a greeting.

"What's up, Indio?" asked Malcolm.

"Skipper, we're out of position by almost a grid square. If we don't move the whole operation to the left more skoshe, our own support is gonna tear us apart," Jesse panted.

Malcolm looked at Jesse, then to Simms. "Are you absolutely certain?"

Simms opened his map. Malcolm stepped out of formation, motioning his radio operator to follow suite as he knelt next to Simms and tried to follow the excited movements of the man's fingers as they traveled back and forth on the mud-stained paper. He looked up from time-to-time to compare terrain features, unable to believe that such an error was even remotely possible.

Suddenly he stood, reaching for his radio operator's handset. "Holy Christ!"

Jesse and Simms stood by as Malcolm contacted battalion headquarters. Within a matter of two or three minutes, Malcolm turned to his forward observers. "We're halting movement until we get this thing squared away. Indio, you reach the point with your radio and tell him to hold up. Corporal Simms, get back to your radio and notify the forward air controller. Arty's apparently somewhat aware of the situation and they're holding all H & I missions."

Simms and Jesse exchanged a quick, knowing glance. "Aye aye, Sir," said Jesse. In a snap, the two moved forward in the column to carry out their respective orders.

Thirty minutes later, Jesse smoked a cigarette and listened to Mud complain about the ignorance of the officers in charge of the operation. At the close of a particularly long soliloquy, Jesse looked up at him. "Mud, I'm afraid I'm going to have to take exception to that part about our officers being ignorant."

"And just how in the hell do you figure that they're not ignorant?" returned Mud indignantly.

"Because I know for a fact they've been taught better. Therefore they're not

343

ignorant. They're just plain, ordinary, everyday stupid. You know – like a second lieutenant."

Mud's eyes smiled. "Oh, I see what you mean now that you put it in clearly understandable terms. I stand corrected."

Mud's radio crackled. He put the handset to his ear. "Whiskey Alpha. Go ahead."

After a short pause he turned to Jesse. "Skipper wants to see you."

"Tell him I'm on the way."

Malcolm smiled as Jesse approached.

"You sent for me, Skipper?"

"As a matter of fact, I did. Did you happen to have a radio conversation with arty regarding H & I missions on the right flank?"

Jesse hesitated. He rubbed his chin between his thumb and forefinger. "I can't recall, Skipper."

Malcolm laughed. "I'm sure glad to hear that. Seems like someone used your call sign and cussed the major in charge of artillery pretty badly. He's fuming about it but he admits he held fire until he could verify troop locations. He swears nobody but a Marine could have said whatever was said. I guess we owe that imposter using your call sign a debt of gratitude."

"Yessir. Well, if I ever find out who the guy was, I'll pass along that information."

Malcolm pointed to the map spread on the ground before him. "Let's get this outfit back into position. See this river up here?"

Jesse nodded.

"Three-four is all bunched up on the right flank, and in order to move them into the proper position, they've got to cross this river. The rest of us can be in position in about an hour but it looks like it's going to take Two Nine the better part of three hours to make the crossing at this point."

"So, basically, we're not going to get a whole lot done today. Is that what it all amounts to?"

"It kind of looks that way at this point. My main concern is our position at nightfall. If we set our schedule back by three or four hours, we're going to be too close to this ville when we set in for the night." He pointed to a village on the map. "If Charlie hits us we could be in a whole lot of trouble. We won't be able to call in artillery or air because of our proximity to the ville. And our position with regard to the companies on our flanks limits our defense to bayonets unless we're hit from the direct front. What do you think?"

Jesse studied the map momentarily. "I think we should send an advance unit beyond the ville and graveyard and have them secure a position about here," he answered, pointing to a location on the map. "Then the rest of the company could continue the march a little after dark, if it became necessary, to reach the defensible position. That way we could string out on our flanks and still be linked with the other outfits and be able to use most of our resources after dark."

Malcolm glanced at the map then at Jesse. "If I send a platoon forward, I'll want an FO to go along in case they run into something."

Jesse smiled. "I thought you'd never ask, Skipper."

"Report back to your position. If I get clearance, I'll notify you on the radio."

"Aye aye, Skipper."

344

Forever Patriots

In thirty minutes, Jesse and Mud were on the move with the first platoon as an advanced unit. Their objective was simple: locate a defensible position west of the graveyard and secure the area for the rest of the company prior to dusk.

The young platoon commander in charge of the first platoon was a bit of a hot head but Jesse liked him. On operation Oregon he had gone to the battalion commander's Pagoda and informed Colonel Soliman that the M-14 was a "useless piece of shit". Though there was nothing Soliman could do about the status of the M-14, Lieutenant Parker had relieved his frustrations somewhat by raising his voice at his battalion commander. Because of this, Parker was virtually assured of remaining a second lieutenant as long as he remained under Soliman's command. Parker didn't really care. He liked being a platoon commander. More rank would most likely require a change in status and he enjoyed the status quo. In essence, he was able to raise his voice at the old man and be guaranteed the job he enjoyed most.

The sound of small arms fire in the direction of the point put Mud and Jesse to the prone position. Mud's radio crackled. Momentarily Mud held out the handset. "It's Lieutenant Parker."

Jesse crawled to Mud and accepted the handset. "This is Whiskey Alpha. Over."

"This is Alpha 1 Actual. What have you got up there? Over," said Parker.

"Appears to be a small element. I'll check and advise. Over."

A lance corporal approached them in a low crouch. "We've got about six or seven gooks ahead of us in a small tree line. We could flank 'em but that takes time. A little whiskey would be easier."

Jesse nodded at the lance corporal. He keyed up and spoke into the handset. "This is Whiskey Alpha. We've got small arms fire at about 245545. Appears to be about six or seven rifles. Request permission to send 'em to Ho Chi Minh in a box. Over"

"Permission granted, Whiskey. Advise me of results. Over"

"Roger. Out."

In a few minutes, the initial mortar round sailed overhead. Less than a minute later, several more rounds were hurled at the target. Mud knelt next to the radio while Jesse watched the impacting mortar rounds from a vantagepoint about twenty-five yards to his front. Several minutes after the rounds exploded, a PFC approached Jesse and a short discussion ensued. Jesse stood and walked back to Mud's position, took the handset and keyed up. "Alpha One Actual. Whiskey Alpha. Over."

"This is Alpha One Actual, go ahead."

"Be advised, Alpha One, you'll be needing five – I say again, five – Charlie KIA's evacuated. We have one prisoner. Advise S-2 of our location. We are leaving two men to guard the prisoner and the bodies and are continuing our mission. Over."

"Roger, Whiskey Alpha. Tango Yankee out."

Jesse looked at the handset with raised eyebrows as he handed it back to Mud.

"What's wrong?" asked Mud.

"Nothin'. It's just that Parker gave me the old 'Tango Yankee out', sign off."

"What's wrong with that? I do it all the time. It's just a way of sayin' thanks."

"You damn radio operators do a lot of weird things all the time. This guy's a

345

grunt second lieutenant. Most of 'em wouldn't have enough time in to understand the term, much less use it." Jesse shrugged. "Let's get movin'."

Mud stared at the bodies and body parts as they passed the row of dead VC. He shuddered involuntarily at the sight of a severed leg. "Jesus. Do you ever wonder what the hell we're doing all of this bullshit for?"

Jesse studied the grotesque arrangement of body parts. "Not so much what we're doin' it for, but why we're doin' it the way we're doin' it. That bothers me more than anything else." He waved at the bodies. "These guys are tryin' to kill us and we're tryin' to kill them but it seems to me that once somebody has died for somethin' there should be somethin' to show for it. But it ain't that way over here. Hell, we lose a third of our company on *Oregon*, and for what? We pull out in a few days and the gooks can move right back into that ville. To me, that seems like a criminal waste of life – theirs and ours both. It's stupid."

Mud reflected on Jesse's statement for a moment then said, "You don't really give a damn about how many gooks get killed do you?"

"You have anything personal against any one of those dead gooks back there?"

"Yeah. The little bastards were trying to kill me."

"Other than that?"

"How the hell could I? I don't know any of 'em personally."

"That's my whole point. Why are we killin' people we don't even know unless it's for a tactical or strategical reason? If you can find a justifiable reason for all the killin' and walkin' away from the conquered territory, let me know, 'cause I can't figure it out."

"You're over my head with all that strategical bullshit. All I know is that I wish to hell I was in San Francisco, working in my dad's clothing store, driving to Carmel on the weekends in my Studebaker Golden Hawk."

"You got a Golden Hawk? What year?"

They pushed onward, the dead VC temporarily forgotten. They had new things to think about: Studebakers and Carmel and clothing stores.

Shortly after dark, the combined regiment was in proper position. The only enemy contact of the day had been the encounter of Alpha Company's first platoon. The only casualty suffered by the marines was a sprained ankle by one of the men in H company of the Second Battalion, Ninth Marines.

Without the mix-up in reading the maps, the second day was even more uneventful than the first. By late afternoon the battalions dug in for the evening.

"Let's take a stroll over to the 'toon and see how they're doin'," suggested Jesse.

"Sounds like a plan to me," said Mud.

After securing permission from Malcolm, the two marched to the rear of Alpha Company's position. They encountered Tuleano about six hundred yards into their trek.

"Hey, Tule. What's goin' on?" greeted Jesse.

"Indio. Mud. What the hell are you two guys doin' back here – slummin'?" asked the big Samoan, grinning broadly.

"If the truth were known, Tule, we figured you guys could use a nanny to take care of you. We haven't decided yet whether Mud or I will get the detail. I guess it'll depend on how bad off you girls are."

"How you doin' with the grunts?"

Mud answered, "You wouldn't believe it, Tule. Hell, it's bacon and eggs every morning for breakfast, submarine sandwiches for lunch, and meat and potatoes for dinner every night."

Jesse looked at Mud. "Yeah, and while it's on my mind, Mud, remind me to complain to the chef. That submarine sandwich I had today had too damn much garlic in it."

"I've been meaning to talk to him about that myself. Thanks for reminding me."

Jesse smiled at Tuleano. "Wop chef. Always uses too much garlic."

"Fuck you both. What's happening?"

"Not much. Just thought we'd drop by and say howdy. Doesn't seem to be a whole lot goin' on in this operation. You guys had any contact?"

"Shit no. The only mission we've fired since this thing started was the one you called in."

"Thanks a lot by the way. The guys were right on target – and on time."

"We just put the dope on the guns. You call the shots."

"Thanks just the same. It's nice to know we've got someone who can run FDC, and gunners who know what the hell they're doin'."

"Where's Court?" asked Mud.

Tuleano pointed to a small stand of trees. "In there somewhere, losin' his ass at poker."

Jesse smiled. "Some things never change. He can't play poker worth a damn. Wish we could stay long enough to take some of his money."

"I'm gonna go see Court. I'll catch you later," said Mud, stepping off in the direction of the trees.

Tuleano lowered his voice. "Things are really gettin' chickenshit around here. You wouldn't believe it."

"Like what?"

"This new battalion commander. He thinks we're in garrison or something."

"What's he doin'?" asked Jesse.

"Listen to this. He wants us to shave every day, even while we're on this operation."

"Whose gonna carry all them razor blades?"

"Exactly. And he says no more bare backs. You gotta wear a t-shirt."

"That ain't so bad."

"Yeah, but it's gotta be a green t-shirt."

"Green? Hell, we've never been issued green t-shirts. I've never even seen one. Where you supposed to get green t-shirts?"

"Damned if I know. He says we'll be gettin' some pretty quick but we haven't seen 'em yet. And listen to this shit. He wants us to polish our boots! I mean polish, not saddle soap or anything dull. He wants polish!"

Jesse looked down at his muddy boots, then back up to Tuleano. "You gotta be shittin' me."

"I'm serious, Indio. The man's a fuckin' maniac. He thinks we're on parade back in the States or something. I never seen anything like it in all my time in the Crotch. Even the gunny and some of the staff are bitchin' about it. There's talk about a request mast."

"By the staff?"

347

Tuleano nodded.

"I wonder why I haven't heard about all this garbage in Alpha Company?"

"You will. Hell, you're attached. Maybe your company commander figures you're informed by 81's."

"Yeah, maybe so. Hell, I haven't had much time to pay attention to that kind of stuff lately."

"You'll be hearing about it soon enough, I guarantee it." Tuleano paused. "Oh yeah, one more thing."

"There's more?"

"You'll love this one."

"Try me," said Jesse dryly.

"They issued us flak jackets this morning. Said eventually that everybody in the Nam was gonna be issued one."

"Damn. Those things weigh too much. Hell, I don't even carry a pack because I don't want the dead weight."

"Well, get ready for it, 'cause you'll be gettin' one in the next few days."

"Jesus Christ, Tule, you got anything good to report?"

Tuleano smiled. "Yeah, less than four months to do in this shithole."

Jesse smiled. "Thanks a lot. Don't know what I'd have done without that information. Where's gun one?"

Tuleano pointed to a footpath. "Down that trail about fifty yards and a little to your right."

"I gotta go, Tule. I wanna visit with the guys for a few minutes before dark. It's good to see ya. Keep yer ass low."

"Same to you, Indio. I'll see you later."

That evening, as Jesse curled up in his poncho next to Mud, the latter whispered softly, "What do you think about all the shit that's comin' down from the new battalion commander?"

Jesse stuck his head under his poncho and quickly lit a cigarette. "I think it's stupid, but after *Oregon*, it's no less than I'd expect."

"I can't believe all the bullshit. Is that Colonel crazy or what?"

"Hell, Mud, he just wants to be sure you look nice with your clean-shaven face, in your green t-shirt, with your spit-shined boots, in your new flak jacket, when they ship your body home. Wouldn't want the folks back home to think we were fightin' a war or somethin' over here."

"Yeah, I guess you're right. G'night, Indio."

"G'night, Mud." Jesse took another drag from the cigarette under his poncho.

The third day of operation Cherokee began like the other two, with no one sure of where they were supposed to be, or what they were supposed to do. At least that's the way it appeared to Jesse. He couldn't imagine how there could be so much confusion without a dress rehearsal.

About mid-morning, Alpha Company took rifle fire from a ridgeline on the company's right flank. Lieutenant Malcolm asked for support from artillery and mortars. Jesse smiled at Simms when he informed his company commander that the mortars were on the way a full minute before artillery was ready to fire.

When artillery did fire, they were off target by more than 500 yards. Malcolm ordered a cease fire from the arty FO and allowed the mortars to fire the barrage. Simms was not pleased with Malcolm's decision.

That afternoon, as the company dug in for the coming night, Simms approached Jesse. "Hey, Indio."

"Yeah?" Jesse looked up from his cigarette.

"What the hell am I doin' wrong?"

"Hell, Simms, I don't know. You gotta admit, that first round was a mite close to our guys. I don't think the skipper was too happy about that. He likes to play it safe when it comes to killin' our own men. He's kinda funny that way."

Simms winced. "Shit, it wasn't that close. I'd have pulled it away on the next shot."

"Maybe he figured there wasn't much sense in firing both of us. No reason to waste a bunch of ammo on a few stragglers. Who knows?"

"How the hell did you hit that position on the first shot?"

"Lucky I guess."

"That's not what I hear. Malcolm thinks you walk on water from the scuttlebutt I've heard."

"I ain't the first. I heard tell there was another guy did it a couple thousand years ago."

"I just don't want the skipper losing faith in me because he's got you to score a hit on the first damn round."

"Don't sweat it. You'll get plenty of chances if things go the way they been goin' with this outfit. Don't even think about it. The skipper's a fair man. He won't think you're incompetent just because you didn't hit the target with the first round. Hell, one of these days I'm gonna screw up real bad by not using the bracket method. I've already been told by some of the staff in Alpha that I'm takin' too many chances with their guys' lives. The only problem is, I've never had any training for this job and I can't see any reason to bracket if you're sure of your position."

"Well, it can be tricky as hell if you make a mistake."

"True. I guess I'll just have to be sure that don't happen then, huh?"

Simms shook his head. "I guess it helps to be a little crazy too."

"Yeah, and a lot lucky."

"How come you drew the short straw and had to come out here as an FO if you haven't had any training?"

"It happened real sudden-like. I thought it was only a one-day assignment but it looks like I'm gonna be here until somebody discovers that I don't know what the hell I'm doing"

"You do just fine."

"Thanks, Simms. You're not so bad yourself. Smoke?"

"Naw, I'm gonna get back over to my radio operator. He gets nervous as hell if I'm not in his sight twenty-four hours a day. By the way, where's Frank? I didn't see him this morning."

"One of the guys in first platoon has him today. Swears he's gonna give him a bath before dark. That little rooster's liable to whip the hell out of him if he tries it, but that's the way it goes. I warned him that Frank can get a little touchy around water, but he won't listen, so he's on his own."

Simms laughed. "I'll catch you later, Indio."

"Later."

349

Stoney Livingston

The following day was overcast but it was one of those days when the overcast seemed to provide no shelter from the heat. It seemed hotter than it had been the day before. Even Frank, the rooster, appeared bedraggled as he sat atop Mud's radio. Jesse couldn't suppress a smile as he occasionally turned to see Mud swatting and cussing at the little banty, who had undoubtedly just pecked at him.

"Lighten up, Mud. He's littler than you are."

"The aggrivatin' little bastard just about gave me a haircut in two bites! He knows what the hell he's doin'. He only does it to piss me off. He's still madder'n hell about that bath yesterday. I told him I didn't have anything to do with it but he thinks I'm lyin' and he's bound and determined to get even."

Jesse chuckled softly and turned his attention back to the march.

The afternoon wore on. Uniforms darkened with perspiration and the men became weary. With less than an hour of daylight left, Alpha Company dug in for the night.

Jesse studied the terrain, marked coordinates, and he and Mud joined Lieutenant Malcolm and the headquarters group in the courtyard of the plantation house, which they occupied.

"Damn, Skipper, this is the most beautiful place I've seen since I've been in this country. What the hell is it?" asked Jesse.

"A tea plantation. It's run by the Catholic Church."

"Definitely European influence in the architecture. I didn't know they had this kind of stuff over here."

"Neither did I but It's good to see, isn't it?" said Malcolm.

"I can't believe this is Vietnam. It's so peaceful here. It's hard to imagine this place in the middle of a war. Kinda sad too."

Malcolm said, "It's worse than sad. It's tragic. If the Cong win this war, I'm sure they'll destroy this fine example of capitalistic decadence."

"Well then, we'll just have to see to it they don't win the war, Sir."

Malcolm smiled. "I almost forgot. We have a one-man regiment with us. How can we possibly lose?"

Jesse returned the smile. "We can't."

"Pick a spot to hit the rack. The priest in charge says the headquarters group can sleep inside."

Jesse glanced around at the large house with its many rooms and Spanish tile roof. "I'd just as soon sleep outside, Sir. I don't belong in there."

"It's dry."

"Yeah, with a roof like that, I imagine it is. I just don't wanna sleep inside. I'd feel better out in the open."

Malcolm shrugged. "Suit yourself. I'll be in the north wing of the building if you need me for anything."

"Thanks, Skipper. I'll find someplace near the north end to bed down. Anything else?"

"No, that's it for now. Get settled in for the night. See me at daybreak."

"Aye aye, Sir," said Jesse as he moved away to the north side of the large building, Mud close behind.

"Now why'n the hell did you go and do that? We had a chance to sleep inside an honest-to-God-solid building and you volunteer us for the great-goddamn outdoors again," said Mud.

"Hell, we probably couldn't stand the luxury," replied Jesse.

350

"Don't we owe it to ourselves to try, for chrisakes?"

"Quit yer bitchin, Mud. You know they wouldn't let Frank sleep in there."

Mud looked at Jesse, dumbfounded. "You mean to tell me we just missed out on a chance to sleep inside a real building because of this little bird-brained excuse of a rooster?" He looked at his left shoulder to see Frank staring at him from his perch atop the radio.

"You useless piece of shit. All you do is make my life miserable whenever you get a chance."

Frank promptly leaned forward and pecked Mud soundly on the nose. "Ow! Goddamn your scrawny little feathery ass! You went too far that time."

He took his radio pack off and set it on the ground, reaching for Frank as soon as his hands were free. Frank seemed aware of Mud's intentions, for he left his perch the instant Mud's hands moved in his direction.

Jesse couldn't hold in his laugher as Mud chased the little rooster about the courtyard. Several minutes later Mud gave up the pursuit, exhausted by his efforts. Frank strutted indignantly just out of reach.

"Careful you don't piss him off, Mud. He'll probably shit on your face while you're asleep," said a passing marine.

Mud glared at the little rooster. "I wouldn't put it past you, you chickenshit little bird -brain."

Frank stood just out of Mud's reach and glared.

Jesse almost doubled over with laughter.

Shortly after 2100 hours, Jesse heard the explosion. Even before he could roll out of his poncho, a second and third explosion followed in rapid sequence.

"Mud! Grenades on the south side of the house!"

Mud sat up, slowly coming to his senses. Shouts and screams emanated from the building. There was a short burst of rifle fire from an M-14 on full automatic, followed by a silence, broken only by a moaning sound, then shouts for a corpsman.

Malcolm called loudly, "Indio! Get us some light!"

"Roger, Skipper," he shouted toward the house, then turned to Mud, "Mission 102, Mud."

Without acknowledging Jesse's order, Mud spoke into his radio. "Whiskey Six, Whiskey Alpha. Fire mission. Over."

The radio crackled. "Go ahead, Whiskey Alpha."

"Fire mission. Mission one zero two. Over."

"Roger mission one zero two, Alpha. Stand by." A short pause, then the voice on the radio said, "On the way, Whiskey."

"Roger on the way. Wait."

Jesse remained in a crouch near Mud, M-1 at the ready, eyes straining in the almost pitch darkness, waiting for the illumination round to ignite overhead. He heard the distinctive *pop* of the canister, and suddenly the landscape was ablaze in the eerie, wavering light of one-half million candlepower.

"You see anything?" asked Mud tensely.

"Nothin' but our guys." Jesse stood. "Keep the lights on until the skipper calls for a cease fire. I'm gonna move around to the south side and see what I can find."

"Keep yer ass low."

Jesse moved to the south side of the courtyard at a dead run. Men rushed about in all directions. He looked closely at them, trying to make certain none were VC. It was difficult to be positive, even with the illumination round drifting downward almost directly overhead. A second illumination round ignited and identification became easier.

Sergeant Wilkes called to him as he approached the large wall on the south side of the courtyard. "Indio?"

"Yo?"

"Over here."

"What've we got?" panted Jesse as he stopped near Wilkes.

"The gooks tossed a few grenades through a window and hauled ass. We've got three wounded, two of 'em pretty bad. Can't find the gooks. They couldn't have gotten too damn far. The whole company was up in a second. Your illumination was here in less than a minute. The sneaky bastards are still around here someplace. I know they are."

"How are you conducting the search?"

"I ordered everyone back to their position except the corpsmen and first platoon. First platoon is gonna work in a widening circle around the house until we flush something out. If everyone holds his position, we'll catch 'em."

A scream from one of the wounded men pierced the night.

"This damn war sucks. That kid never had a chance. Goddamn grenade went off right between his legs on the rack."

Jesse winced. "Oh Christ."

"Hell, even if he pulls through, he'll never have much of a love life."

"If you don't need me on the sweep, I'm gonna report to the skipper."

"Go ahead. Just be sure you keep the lights turned on."

"We'll keep 'em burnin' all night if we have to." Jesse turned and moved into the house.

Malcolm spoke into his radio operator's handset as Jesse approached. "Affirmative. We have three Californias." He looked up at Jesse as he returned the handset to his operator. "I'm tempted to let you talk to these people at battalion. You seem to speak a radio language that gets faster results than the one they taught me. They find the gooks yet?"

"Nossir, not yet."

Malcolm turned to a corporal standing near. "Get me an up to the minute report on the wounded."

"Yessir." The corporal left the room on the double.

Malcolm said, "Well, Indio, I've got the whole damn regiment screaming that I'm exposing their positions with the illumination. They want me to cease fire if I can determine that we are no longer in any danger of attack. You've been out there. What do you think our chances of finding anybody are?"

"I think they're pretty good, Sir, but it may take a while. I wouldn't want to be in your shoes. It's pitch dark out there so, if we turn off the lights, the gooks are most likely home free."

Malcolm pondered his options. It was obvious he didn't like either choice. He was saved the burden of making a quick decision by the sound of small arms fire within a hundred yards of the plantation house. Every man in the room was instantly on the floor. Jesse crawled for the door, not wishing to remain inside the building any longer than was necessary.

As quickly as it had begun, the shooting stopped. Several minutes elapsed before the first squad, first platoon moved into view, carrying one body and herding a prisoner. The two men carrying the body dropped it unceremoniously in front of the large foyer of the house.

The sergeant in charge of the first squad, a wiry man about Jesse's size, said, "We blew one of 'em away before we discovered that neither one of 'em had any weapons, Sir."

Malcolm looked at the young sergeant with a smile barely perceptible on his lips. "With you cowboys from Arizona carryin' M-1's, and getting all this work done, maybe I should put in a request for two hundred Garands."

The young sergeant glanced at Jesse then back to Malcolm and smiled. "It wouldn't hurt anything, Skipper."

Jesse studied the young sergeant. He had heard of Sergeant Jim Kelly, the most famous man in the First Battalion, Fourth Marines. Everyone called him "Sergeant Thunder", or "Thunder", a nickname earned on *Operation Starlite*, the first major operation for the marines in Vietnam. Jesse wondered if *he* looked as out of place with his M-1 as Kelly did.

Malcolm called for Lieutenant Huy to interpret. Jesse remained for a moment before returning to his position. In that moment he saw the prisoner, a fourteen-year-old boy, frightened almost beyond physical control. He was no longer the tough jungle fighter he had been but a few minutes prior. He was just a kid from down the block, not a killer of men while they slept. Jesse shook his head and left the building, stepping over the dead VC carefully. He returned to Mud's position.

"That you, Indio?" Mud hailed. "What the hell is going on?"

"Yeah, Mud. It's me. Cease fire. End of mission. I'll tell you all about it."

Late the following afternoon, Alpha Company dug in near the base of a large round hill. Enemy contact during the day was light, consisting of one booby trap and one lone VC. No one at the company level seemed to be aware of the over-all results of the operation. Everyone was too busy coordinating the movements of their own units to be bothered with the larger-scale problems and effects of the entire operation.

Jesse sat on a small rock and opened a can of C-ration crackers. As he shared the contents of the olive drab can with Frank, Mud said quietly. "What the hell are we accomplishing with this bullshit?"

Jesse looked up from the cracker crumbs spread upon the ground. "I don't really know, Mud. For no more resistance than we've encountered, we'da been better off with squad patrols. Maybe the other outfits have been makin' a lot of contact."

"I hope to hell they've made enough contact to end this fine little police action that we're involved in. I'd like to get home before summer starts."

"Me too but I think we're both dreamin'. Hell, even if we win the war tomorrow, someone's gotta stay behind and occupy the place for awhile. You know who'll get that duty."

"Shit. I forgot about that. Christ. You sure know how to ruin a guy's day."

Suddenly Frank jumped straight into the air about five feet, flapping his wings. He completed a half-barrel roll and came crashing to earth in the inverted position. Jesse and Mud watched, mesmerized, as the little rooster scooted about in the upside down position, beating his wings against the ground and squawking loudly.

353

Stoney Livingston

Jesse broke out of his trance and scooped him up, holding the little rooster against his chest, stroking him gently. Frank relaxed almost instantly. Jesse looked at Mud, then to the rooster. Still stroking the quivering bird, he stooped and inspected the cracker crumbs lying at his feet. He found nothing out of the ordinary.

"What the hell you suppose got into him?" he said.

"Maybe the greedy little bastard choked himself," said Mud.

"Yeah, maybe so. Oh well, what the hell." Jesse released the quaking rooster and watched as Frank walked unsteadily for a few feet, then seemed to regain his composure and continued his eating.

Mud looked at Jesse quizzically. "Damn. That was weird. That had to be the worst case of heartburn I've ever seen."

"I gotta admit, he sure made it look pretty rough."

As the company dug in for the night, Malcolm briefed his command staff and forward observers on the next day's assignment. The forward air controller asked questions that Jesse expected a second lieutenant to ask, and the briefing was extended by ten minutes to satisfy the FAC's ignorance and lack of common sense.

"Any further questions, gentlemen?" asked Malcolm after answering an uncommonly stupid question from the FAC.

No one spoke but all eyes turned to the FAC in anticipation of yet another masterpiece of stupidity. None was forthcoming and the briefing was dismissed. As the men moved to their respective positions for the night, Simms mumbled to Jesse when he was safely out of the FAC's hearing, "I hate to admit it but you're right about this one. He's one dumb sonofabitch."

Jesse smiled in the growing darkness. "Hell, he ain't much different from any other second lieutenant I've ever known. Believe me, until they get rid of those gold bars, there ain't a stupider life form in existence."

"I couldn't believe that question about friendly troops in a target area. Shit, a little bit of common sense would help."

"That'll come when he gets rid of those gold bars. It doesn't seem to come much sooner for most lieutenants," said Jesse as he arrived at his position.

"See ya in the morning," bade Simms as he continued further down the hill.

*****

Frank jumped from atop Mud's pack, flailing his wings wildly and squawking loudly into the greyness that was dusk. Quickly Mud grabbed the little rooster, quieting him by stroking his feathers gently and speaking to him in a soothing voice.

Jesse moved close. "Now damn it, Frank, you've gotta knock this off. These hills are crawlin' with VC. I don't care if you want to get your own head blown off but don't take the rest of us with you." His voice was a loud whisper.

The little rooster cooed softly.

"I've never heard him do that before," whispered Mud.

"There's definitely something wrong with him but I'm damned if I know what it is. Hell, he was all right last night."

"Maybe Doc would know," suggested Mud, still stroking Frank.

"Yeah, maybe so. Keep him quiet. I'll look for Sandy." Jesse disappeared into the approaching darkness in search of the corpsman. He returned shortly with Sanderson, who performed to the limit of his capabilities but was unable to offer any

354

explanation for the little rooster's strange behavior. After spending thirty minutes with Frank, Sandy returned to his position, none the wiser concerning the cause of the bird's discomfort.

After an hour Frank seemed to be comfortable and breathing normally. Mud released his charge and lay upon his poncho, grateful that the ordeal with the company mascot seemed satisfactorily concluded. No sooner had he set Frank free than did the little rooster suffer a relapse of his malady.

It took several seconds for Mud and Jesse to contain the screeching bird and several seconds more to calm him down once in hand.

A runner from company headquarters found the FO team and the little rooster shortly thereafter. "Psst. Hey, Indio. Skipper wants to see you right away," he whispered into the darkness.

"I'm on the way." He left Frank with Mud and followed the runner.

Inside the small C. P. tent Malcolm looked at Jesse, sadness in his eyes. "I'm afraid you're going to have to destroy Frank. He's going to get us hit tonight if we let him go on squawking."

"He's okay if Mud or I hold him and stroke his feathers, Sir. If we can keep him quiet, can we give him another chance?" Jesse's tone was almost pleading.

"I don't want him killed anymore than you do. If you want to stay up with him all night, go ahead. But if he starts squawking, destroy him immediately."

Jesse smiled. "Thank you, Sir. Will that be all?"

Malcolm sighed. "Yes, that's all. Except that I hate to see you lose a night's sleep."

"It's worth it to me, Sir."

"Go to it then. Report to me at daybreak."

"Yessir. And thanks again, Skipper."

"Hell, don't thank me. I should thank you. He's one of my command, remember?"

Frank remained calm through the night and the worst seemed past by dawn. As Alpha Company moved out after morning chow, the little rooster perched casually upon Mud's radio, surveying the landscape as though searching for the enemy. Thirty minutes into the march he was again overcome by one of his unexplainable fits.

Mud picked the quaking rooster from the ground and stroked him gently as he continued to march. Frank was quivering. "Damnit, Frank, knock it off. Don't you understand, bird-brain? We can't let you keep makin' all that noise. You'll get us all killed." He appeared close to tears.

"That was it, Mud. We gotta get rid of him," said Jesse as he dropped back in the column to Mud's side.

"C'mon, Indio, we can give him one more chance," said Mud pleadingly.

"Believe me, Mud, if I thought we could, we would. But we can't."

"We don't have to kill him, do we?"

"Who said anything about killin' 'im? There's a village not too far from here, according to my map. We'll just kinda deposit ol' Frank on the outskirts as we pass by. If he gets over whatever is ailin' 'im, he'll be okay."

There were tears in Mud's eyes as he gently placed the little rooster upon the grassy soil. "So long, Frank, you little bird-brained piece of shit."

Frank lapsed into another frenzy as they turned and continued the

355

westward march. Neither could bear to look back. They fixed their moistened eyes to the front until they could no longer hear the ear-piercing screams of the little banty rooster.

In the early afternoon, the company received rifle fire from a tree line on their right flank. Jesse huddled with Mud behind a small mound as the latter contacted company headquarters on the radio.

A movement to the company front caused Jesse to shoulder his M-1. Sergeant Kelly stepped from the sparse underbrush, his own M-1 carried casually in one hand. He smiled. "Don't shoot. Hell, I'm on your side."

Jesse said, "You gotta be Sergeant Kelly."

Kelly took the time to bow slightly before he assumed the sitting position next to Jesse. "And judging from the looks of your artillery, you must be the infamous Indio, recently of the 81 platoon."

Jesse almost laughed. "Good news travels fast, huh?"

"The guys call me Thunder." He offered his hand to Mud.

"Believe it or not, they call me Mud."

"Damn good name. I like it," said Kelly.

Jesse liked the young sergeant immediately. "So what's goin' on in the tree line?"

"I think it's just a few snipers. That's what I came back to talk to you about. If you don't mind, I'd like to bring up the ONTOS instead of you calling in mortars."

"ONTOS? What the hell for?"

Kelly said, "Well, it's like this. I've got a buddy in ONTOS. He says they're always gettin' the shit details and the perimeter work. Tanks get all the glory. He asked me to let him shoot if I got a chance on this operation." Kelly paused. "I know it would be simpler just to call in your mortars but I sure would like to let the ONTOS have their day."

Jesse smiled. "Consider it done if the skipper gives us the okay."

"Thanks, man. I owe you one."

"You don't owe me anything. It's my pleasure." Jesse had always liked to watch the ONTOS in action. The small, tracked vehicles looked a little bit like a tank, bristling with six 106mm recoilless rifles, three on each side of its lightly armored chassis. They were faster and more agile than tanks and were designed as anti-tank weapons. Unfortunately, the new rangefinders on the Soviet tanks rendered them obsolete due to the fact that the ONTOS had no such equipment and relied on the old-fashioned line-of-sight method. If the ONTOS missed its target on the first shot it would not get a second chance. For this reason the army had declared them obsolete and removed them from their inventory. As a result, the Marine Corps had sole possession of this unique vehicle.

The approval from Lieutenant Malcolm was quick and, as they waited for the tracked vehicles to arrive at their position, the three men made conversation.

"Why are you packin' an M-1?" asked Jesse.

"Same reason your are, I'm sure. They're tough, accurate and dependable. And I got mine cheap – a dead ARVN soldier. Hell, he wasn't going to put it to much good use, so I borrowed it."

"Where you from?" asked Mud.

"A little town called Safford...."

"Safford?" interrupted Jesse.

Kelly looked at him. "Yeah, you heard of it?"

"Heard of it? Hell, I spent every summer of my life there – at my cousin's – until I was fourteen years old."

"No kiddin'? Who was the cousin? I bet I know 'im."

The two talked about home, the war almost forgotten. The creaking sound of a tracked-vehicle returned them to the present. From their position the three had a good view as the three ONTOS moved into a firing line. No sooner had the last vehicle formed the line than the air was shattered by the sound of eighteen 106 mm recoilless rifles.

"Jesus! I didn't think they were supposed to fire all six at the same time," said Jesse.

Kelly winced. "They're not. I'll bet Willy gets an ass-chewin' for that one. He does it every damn time he gets a chance to shoot."

The enemy tree line disappeared in a monstrous cloud of dirt and vegetation. Trees and pieces of trees filled the air.

Mud said, "Holy shit! I want one of those for Christmas."

Kelly said, "I gotta go. My squad is going into the tree line to see what's left. I'll see you later. Keep yer asses low."

"Same to you there, Thunder," replied Jesse as the young sergeant disappeared into the brush.

Mud looked at Jesse quizzically. "What tree line? The damn trees are probably closer to San Francisco than they are to this place."

"Just a figure of speech, Mud. He meant to say 'Where the tree line was'."

"I can't believe there's two of you crazy bastards runnin' around these jungles with M-1's, and both of you are from Arizona. There must be something in the water out there."

Jesse smiled. "I wonder where in the hell he ever got a handle like Thunder?"

"If he's anything like you, I'm afraid to ask," replied Mud.

Alpha Company encountered no further resistance for the remainder of the day and camp was set up an hour before sunset.

Later, Jesse lay wrapped in his poncho, looking at the clear sky and contemplating his encounter with Sergeant Kelly.

His mind wandered back to Arizona. He was in high school. Shannon was walking down the hall. He lost the image. He saw Rob and Mark and John. They were riding their motorcycles north of town in the Catalina Mountains. He tried to hold that image but his mind wandered to Okinawa and his old outfit. He saw the village of Henoko, then Masako. *God, Margie, I miss your smile and your little girl ways, and your depth of understanding – even if you do understand everything in Japanese.* Her image faded and Shannon reappeared.

Jesse rolled to his other side and continued to think. He wasn't really thinking, but he wasn't dreaming either. He saw Joe and Sergeant Ribbon. There was Will that day at the football field. Then there was Barbara and dinner and the mugging, the hospital, and her touch that night. When their lovemaking was over, her image became that of Shannon's.

Jesse sat up and pushed his poncho away. *Damn.* He looked again at the clear sky above, then to the darkness that was the jungle surrounding him. *This is absolute bullshit. This isn't real. There is no war. No such thing as a VC. This is a very long dream; that's all it is. I'm gonna wake up soon, in my own bed, in Tucson,*

Stoney Livingston

Arizona. I never went to the recruiter. There never was a Barbara. I never saw Will Hunt. Hell, he's probably still overseas with his parents.

He reached for his rifle in the darkness. He felt of the wood and the cold steel. *Damn, this is the most realistic dream I've ever had – longest too.*

Jesse puzzled over his thoughts of the night before as he moved through the heavy underbrush. He shook his head to clear his mind. *Damn good way to get killed, Stupid. Pay attention to what you're supposed to be doing.*

An explosion twenty-five yards to his right front jolted him back into the war. Shrapnel cut the air around him, whining and buzzing as it passed, leaving him untouched. As he hit the ground, he heard the screams.

"Oh, God! Oh, God! Corpsman! Corpsman!"

Quickly Jesse moved to the voice, shouting over his shoulder, "Mud, stay here!"

Mud remained in his position, face down, grateful for the order to do just that.

Jesse felt the bushes shaking as he moved toward the wounded man writhing about upon the soft jungle carpet.

"Oh, God, somebody help me! Please! Corpsman!"

Jesse knelt beside the fallen marine. "Hang in there, Faye. Hold still."

Faye stared at Jesse through unseeing eyes. One eyeball hung out of the socket, the other was covered with blood. Jesse couldn't tell if the covered eye was injured. The sight almost made him wretch. As bad as the facial wounds appeared, they were minor compared to the wound in the Faye's right leg. Blood gushed from the severed limb with each beat of his heart.

"Mud! Get us some help! We need a chopper and some blood!" Jesse felt himself losing control, heard his voice crack a bit. His breathing was quick and shallow.

"Roger," shouted Mud.

"Indio! Is that you, man? Is that you?" screeched Faye.

"Yeah, Faye, it's me. Hold still, man. Help's on the way. You got some bad wounds, Faye. I'm gonna patch you up, so be real still and relax." Suddenly, Jesse began to feel calmer, more in control. Faye was counting on him.

Jesse quickly removed Fay's belt and tied a tourniquet to the injured leg, just above the knee. Faye squirmed and screamed as the tourniquet tightened.

"Oh, God! I can't stand the pain, Indio. It's killin' me. Oh shit! What's wrong? I can't move my leg! Oh, God! What's happened to me?"

Jesse fumbled at the first aid pouch on his cartridge belt and finally got it open. He grabbed a morphine syrette and injected Faye in the arm. "Now listen to me, Faye. You gotta lie as still as you can, goddamnit, or you're gonna bleed to death. If you lie still, you'll be okay – you hear me?" He elevated Faye's leg and propped it up with the man's helmet.

"I hear you, Indio. I hear you." Faye said through clenched teeth. "But I can't stand the pain. I never felt this much pain in my fucking life!"

Jesse shouted over his shoulder, "Mud! Where the hell is that corpsman? Where's the goddamn chopper?"

"They're both on the way. The corpsman should be here any second."

The morphine was beginning to take effect. Faye's movements slowed. "How you feelin', you crazy-ass grunt?" asked Jesse, with a whole lot more bravado than he felt.

With a thick tongue, Faye replied, "A little better, man." He paused. "I'm gonna die, ain't I, Indio?"

Jesse looked at the blood-covered face, with its eyeball hanging slightly from one socket. He looked at the leg, almost completely severed at the knee. He fought to maintain control of his emotions. "I ain't no doctor, Faye. Hell, you're barely hit, and you start talkin' this dyin' shit. This is your free ride home. You'll be chasin' round-eyed women before any of us. I don't wanna hear anymore of this dyin' crap. You're gonna live to be a hundred years old, fer cryin' out loud. Why, hell you ain't hardly scratched. You'll be...."

"He's dead, Indio."

Jesse looked into the eyes of Sandy, then back down to Corporal Faye. He hadn't been aware of the corpsman's presence until he had spoken. "He ain't dead, Doc. I just gave him a shot of morphine. He'll be all right if we can get him back to a hospital in time." He spoke softly, as if he didn't want to wake Faye - as though the corpsman's words, if heard by Faye, would make them true.

Sandy put his arm around Jesse's shoulders and said, "He's dead, Indio. The blood loss and the shock to his body were too much."

Jesse rocked back and forth from his knees to his boots. "Sandy, I was just talkin' to 'im a second ago. He'll be okay. That morphine just put him to sleep is all."

Sandy looked at the lifeless body, then back up to Jesse. "You couldn't have saved him in an operating room, Indio. The man is dead."

Jesse looked at the body of Corporal Faye, then to Sandy. "Not Faye, Sandy. Shit. He's one of the best men in the outfit. Check him out one more time."

Sandy shook his head and leaned over Faye's body. He checked for a pulse and found none then looked up at Jesse. "He's dead, Indio. I'm tellin' ya, he's dead. Let it go, man." He stood.

Jesse remained in his kneeling position, looking at Faye's body. "I can't believe it, Doc."

Sandy put his hand on Jesse's shoulder. "C'mon, Indio, take a break. I'll take care of Faye. The skipper needs you, man. Don't fall apart on me."

Jesse stood and looked into Sandy's eyes. Sadly he said, "Don't worry about me comin' apart, Sandy. That's not gonna happen in your lifetime. It's just that it was such a waste. One lousy, stinkin' little booby trap and he's gone - you know what I mean?"

Sandy averted his gaze. "Yeah, I know, man. Now get out of here. I'll do my job. You do yours."

Jesse placed his hand on Sandy's shoulder. "Thanks, Doc. I'll see you up the trail."

"Keep yer ass low."

"You too, Doc." He turned his head and shouted over his shoulder, "Saddle up, Mud. We're movin' out."

"Roger." Mud's voice drifted through the heavy undergrowth.

The day ended with no further enemy contact. Jesse sat on the ground, his back to a tree, as Lieutenant Malcolm briefed his platoon commanders and headquarters personnel.

"Well, gentlemen, it looks like operation Cherokee is about over. One-Four and an artillery unit will remain in this area for tonight but the bulk of the operation is over and done with. Tomorrow we turn back to the east and cover a lot of the same

359

ground. Eventually we're going to end up in the area just west of Hue. When that time comes we will be given a new mission.

"On the way back, gentlemen, I want you to be even more careful than you were coming out. We lost a damn good squad leader in Corporal Faye today – to a booby trap." He paused for a moment to be certain he maintained his composure. "The trap that got Corporal Faye was of a design we haven't seen in this area. It was triggered by trees and vines, no wires anywhere. And it was a dual explosive set-up. There was a charge camouflaged as moss about head high on a tree, and another charge underground. Both were set off mechanically. The whole trap was almost impossible to detect."

Malcolm looked slowly at each of his leaders. "For tomorrow, Lieutenant Parker and the first platoon have got the point. Third platoon has the center, then headquarters, then second platoon. FO teams begin the march with headquarters."

"I want to see the platoon commanders for detailed briefing; all others, dismissed."

As the group broke up, Malcolm said, "Indio, I'd like to see you a minute before I talk to the platoon commanders."

Jesse stepped to Malcolm's side. "Yessir?"

Malcolm reached inside the map pocket in his utility jacket, and withdrew a piece of paper. "This is Corporal Faye's parent's address, and his girl's too. I thought you might want to write.

Jesse stared at the piece of paper. Slowly he reached out and took it from his company commander. "I don't know, Skipper. I don't know what to say. I don't know what he died for."

"You don't have to do it. I'll write to them myself but I thought you might want to."

Jesse looked into the eyes of the man from North Carolina. They seemed heavy with grief. "Yeah, I guess I will. Thanks, Skipper. Will that be all?"

"That's all until daylight."

The day following the loss of Corporal Faye was tense and nerve-wracking for the men of Alpha Company but there was no enemy contact. Fear was evident in every man's eyes, fear of the unknown, the unseen. It was well known that the VC used booby traps indiscriminately and had since long before Americans entered the war. But Corporal Faye had been one of the most experienced men in the platoon. If he could fall prey to the booby trap then, surely, no man was safe.

On the second day of the march east, Alpha Company secured movement in the early afternoon. Through Corporal Simms Jesse was aware that an artillery battery was located less than three miles from Alpha's line. He was further aware that the men in the artillery battery were recently supplied with fresh produce.

Jesse looked at Mud without seeing him as he contemplated a garden fresh salad. *Hell. I didn't use to like salad all that much before I came to this place.* "Hey, Mud, I think I'm gonna stroll down to that artillery position and steal a fresh salad. You wanna come along?"

"Not me, man. I'm not into any more walkin' than is needed to get the job done and, for me, the job is done for the day."

"Suit yourself. I'm gonna get permission from the skipper. I reckon he'll have you on the company net while I'm gone."

When Jesse arrived at the artillery position, he drew curious looks from the marines at the guns but was not challenged.

He wandered to the battery mess and put on his most woebegone look for the mess sergeant. "I sure am hungry, Sergeant. I don't need much. Maybe just a little salad if you've got any left."

"I haven't got anything left in the way of fresh chow." He pointed to a stack of c-ration cases. "You're welcome to some C's if you want. 'S'bout all I've got left."

Jesse's stomach growled. He was determined. "Anything but c-rations, Sarge. Even one fresh tomato and a leaf of lettuce."

The sweaty mess sergeant looked at his scrawny figure. "What outfit did you say you were with?"

"I didn't, but I'm with One-Four"

"You're a ways from home, ain'tcha?"

Jesse played his ace. "Yeah but, to tell you the truth, Simms from your outfit told me you guys had some fresh produce today. Said you were an okay guy, and if there was any way you could spare a little chow, you'd do it for a hungry marine."

"He said all of that, did he?"

"You bet he did," Simms had warned him of the cook's notorious reputation for hoarding food for officers.

"Well, I guess if you came all this way on Simms' say-so, I might be able to scrape up a little something." The mess sergeant was bloated with his power.

Jesse smiled. "I sure would appreciate it, Sarge. To tell you the truth, I don't know if I even have the strength to make it back to my outfit without your help." He wanted to take the sergeant into the bush and beat the living hell out of him.

"Well, we can't have that shit. Hang on, let me see what I can dig up."

Jesse waited expectantly while the cook retired to his mess tent. In three or four minutes, he returned with a small portion of wilted lettuce and one over-ripe, small tomato in the center of a field mess kit.

"Here you go. I know it isn't much, but that's all there is left. Enjoy."

Jesse accepted the meager offering. "Say, Sarge, you wouldn't happen to have any kind of dressing for this would you?"

"Plumb out of dressing. How about some salt?"

"Yeah, thanks."

The cook handed him a small c-ration packet of salt.

"Thanks. Appreciate it."

"Anything for you guys on the line."

Jesse salted the limp lettuce and wolfed the meager morsel down in three bites. Turning to the mess sergeant, he said, "Where can I wash the mess kit?"

"Just set it down there. I'll Take care of it."

"Thanks." Jesse turned and began the trek back to Alpha.

That evening as he sat next to Mud on his poncho, Jesse said, "You know, Mud, things ain't really like they should be over here."

"No shit, Sherlock."

"No, I mean with regard to the way they pass out the chow. Now you take that arty outfit. They get hot food almost every day. They got their own mess cook, and every once in a while they get fresh produce. The further back you go from the line, the better the food gets. It oughta be the other way around."

"It's always been that way. It ain't never gonna change."

361

"Yeah, I know that, but at least that clears my conscience."

"For what?"

"Well, I think someone oughta confiscate some of that food from arty. And I think I oughta be the one to do it."

"And just how in the hell do you propose to do that?"

"Those guys are set in for today and tomorrow. I've seen their position and I looked it over real good. Tomorrow, I take a squad of men through their position in broad daylight and we lift some of their chow."

Mud breathed a mock sigh of relief. "Oh, for a minute there I thought you were gonna do something risky. Now that I know it's a simple broad-daylight raid, no problem."

"I'm serious, Mud. It'd be easier than hell. I just need about a squad to carry the stuff back."

"Why don't you just ask the skipper? I'm sure he'd lend you a squad for such a worthy cause."

"Keep meat-mouthin' and I won't give you any of the loot," said Jesse.

"You're serious?"

"As a damned cornered dog."

"How the hell you gonna get a squad? Faye might have done it, but ..." Mud's voice trailed off.

"Yeah, I know, Mud." There was a lump in his throat as he thought of Faye. "Well, there's always Thunder."

"Oh no, not him! You two guys are so much alike it scares the hell outa me."

"Then who better to do the job? Besides, he said he owed me one."

"Yeah, and you told him he didn't."

"That was an oversight on my part."

The following afternoon, as Mud marched thirty yards behind the arty F.O. and his radio operator, Jesse stepped out of the brush on his right. "How's it goin', Mud?" asked Jesse casually.

"Where the hell you been? Where's the chow? What took you so damn long?" said Mud.

Jesse raised a hand. "We ran into a little snag but everything's okay."

"Where's the chow?"

"In due time, my good man. In due time."

"Don't give me that shit. Who's got the chow?"

"Hold your damn drawers on, Mud. Just wait and see. No sense involvin' you in this operation any more than you already are."

"Goddamnit, Indio, I oughta shoot your sneaky ass."

"Maybe but, if you did, you'd never know what happened to the chow, would you?" Jesse assumed his position in front of his radio operator as though he'd been there all day. The march continued without interruption.

The company dug in two hours before sunset.

Jesse smiled broadly as he studied their position. "Hang tight, Mud. I'll be back in a little bit."

"You're startin' to piss me off with all of this secrecy shit," said Mud.

Jesse smiled. "It'll be worth it. Just give me about thirty minutes. I won't be very far away. We only missed our guess by about three hundred yards."

"What the hell are you talkin' about?"

"You'll see in a little bit." Jesse disappeared into the brush.

Lieutenant Malcolm looked at Jesse questioningly. He knew what was in the wax-lined cardboard, flat carton. He just didn't know where it had come from.

"Steak?"

Jesse smiled a broad smile. "Yessir. Thick, juicy, delicious, U.S.D.A. choice. Nothin' but the best for our men in the field, Sir."

"Where in the hell did you find fresh steaks?"

"Sir, I don't really think that's so important right now. I think we should eat 'em before they go bad. The ice is about all melted. We've got enough for every man in the company, and that includes attachments. We even got some steak sauce if you like it that way. Me, I just want a plain old...."

"Whoa. Slow down. Where did all of this booty come from?"

"I'd rather not say just yet, Sir."

"And I'd rather you did."

Jesse looked long at his company commander. He wasn't sure which way Malcolm would go. "Well, Sir, we ...that is ...I, sort of confiscated them from somebody who didn't need 'em as bad as we do. Hell, they get hot food every day."

"And who might that be?"

Jesse spoke softly, almost under his breath.

"I'm sorry, Indio, I didn't quite catch that."

"Arty, Sir," Jesse raised his voice.

"Arty? They eat steaks?"

"They were going to tonight, Sir."

"But now they aren't, is that it?"

"I certainly hope not, Sir. We got their steaks."

"And just how in God's name did you walk out of their position with two hundred steaks?"

"And sauce."

"And sauce. I stand corrected."

"It was easy, Sir. We just walked in and picked 'em up. We almost got away clean but this one PFC stopped us. Rather than tie him up, I gave him a hundred bucks. He threw in the steak sauce and kept his mouth shut."

Malcolm smiled. "You mean to tell me that these goods were purchased from a representative of the artillery battery?"

Jesse returned Malcolm's smile. "Yes Sir, that's exactly what I'm tellin' you."

"I don't suppose you've distributed them to the men yet?"

"Well, actually, Sir, I did. Meat doesn't last too long out here, you know, what with the heat and all."

Malcolm laughed. "If I get out of Vietnam alive, no one will ever believe the stories I have to tell. Who was in on this with you?"

"I gave my word not to divulge that, Sir."

Malcolm mused aloud. "Let's see. First platoon had the point. Oh yes. What's that other fella's name who carries an M-1? Naw, he wouldn't have had anything to do with something like this. Well, I guess it'll just have to remain your secret. Where's my steak?"

Jesse opened the box. "There's only one left. You want sauce?"

Again Malcolm laughed. "Yeah. I believe I'd like to try some of that sauce."

Stoney Livingston

Handing Malcolm a bottle of steak sauce, Jesse shook his head. "You easterners never did learn how to eat steak."

Two days after eating fresh steak, and suffering the internal shock it created in the form of diarrhea, the men of Alpha Company basked in the warmth of the afternoon sun near the original starting point of Operation Cherokee. JJ Washington sat on the edge of a machine gun pit, legs dangling from atop the sandbag parapet.

Jesse was deeply involved in a stud poker game and doing very well.

"Call," said Markowicz.

Jesse laid his hole cards on the poncho. "Three points, Mark. How about you?"

Markowicz looked at the three aces and threw his cards onto the poncho. "Goddamn. One ace already out and he comes up with the other three. I'm suckin' the hind tit again with three queens."

"Keep up the good work, Mark. I need the money."

"What the hell for? You startin' a bank?"

"Nope. But if they ever let me go on R & R, I'm gonna live like a king for two weeks."

"R & R is only six days," said Markowicz.

Jesse glanced at him briefly. "Not when *I* go it isn't. I'm goin' for two weeks – period."

"Aren't you about due for R & R, Indio?" asked Thunder.

"Aren't you about due to rotate home?"

"Naw. I extended for six months. They're gonna give me two weeks in Okinawa at the end of my tour, then it's back to this shit."

"You extended for six months? Do you like this lifestyle or something?" asked Silverstein, a lad of eighteen and a new member of the company.

Thunder looked pensive for a moment, then answered, "Nope, but I don't feel like goin' home till we've won."

Jesse looked up from the cards. "You're liable to be an old man before that happens."

"Yeah, maybe, but I'm stayin' just the same. Six months at a crack, with two weeks in heaven at the end of each six months, until this puny little war is over."

"That don't sound too bad to me," agreed Jesse.

Mud looked up from the letter he was writing. "Sounds like shit to me. Are you guys crazy?"

"Where the hell is your patriotism, Mud?" asked Jesse.

"It starts at the Golden Gate and that's where it stays."

"Sounds to me like that's a little bit one way," said Thunder.

"Sounds to me like a sensible man talkin'," returned Mud.

"Deal the damn cards," ordered Markowicz.

"it's your deal, Mark," said Jesse.

A lone marine strode up to the poker game. "I might have known I'd find you at a poker game."

Jesse turned. "Cue, what the hell are you doin' here?" He stood.

"Looking for you."

"What the hell for?"

Cue looked around him.

"You're among friends here." Jesse turned back to the game and introduced

Forever Patriots

Cue to the players.

The introductions completed, Cue said, "We're dug in not too far from this arty outfit, see? And them guys been taking our dough for the last two days."

"Poker or blackjack?"

"Neither. The biggest damn crap game in the Nam."

"Dice? Why come to me? That's not my favorite game."

"Yeah but I've seen you play it some and I just thought I'd let you know. They got lots of money. I know, 'cause most of it came from 81's."

Jesse looked over to Thunder. "What d' ya think? Should we stroll down to arty and shake the bones?"

Thunder shrugged. "Might as well. Can't dance."

In thirty minutes Jesse was rolling the dice in a crowd of artillerymen. Everything seemed to fall his way. He won on side bets, against the steepest of odds, and when he got the dice, he ran roll after roll. In a span of twenty minutes, he was more than nine hundred dollars richer.

The approach of a flight of Choctaw helicopters would have gone unnoticed but for Cue.

"Pssst. Hey, Indio. The platoon commander's got a personal friend flyin' one of those choppers. He's bringin' in two sixteen-ounce cans of ice-cold beer. The lieutenant said he was gettin' one and the other was going to be auctioned off for the platoon beer fund."

Jesse raised an eyebrow. "I didn't know there was a platoon beer fund."

"I didn't either but that don't really matter. The second can of beer is goin' up for sale to the highest bidder."

Jesse looked at the faces of the crapshooters. He handed the dice to the man on his left. "Hate to leave such pleasant company but you heard what the man said. They're bringin' in that can of beer I requisitioned last month."

One of the players, a heavy loser, said, "Hey, man, you can't just walk away with all that money."

Without a backward glance, Jesse said, "Watch me." He strolled away from the angry group, M-1 slung over his right shoulder.

"Little touchy weren't they?" said Thunder as he struggled to keep pace with Jesse's brisk walk.

"A mite."

Cue laughed. "No shit. You probably won half the money in their outfit."

The resupply helicopters ascended. Cue picked up the pace. "C'mon. That can of beer won't last long in this heat."

The bid was at four dollars and moving up in increments of twenty-five cents when they arrived at the edge of the crowd. Two men were posted as sentries to guard the can of beer. Jesse waited until the bid hit five dollars.

"Ten dollars," he shouted.

His bid was followed by a short period of silence. "Who said that?" asked Tuleano, the acting auctioneer.

"I did and I've got the money in my hand," answered Jesse.

Tuleano's eyes registered recognition. He smiled. "The man with the M-1 says ten dollars. Do I hear more?"

"Eleven."

Jesse looked to his right in the crowd. A black lance corporal held his

365

money high in the air. Jesse didn't recognize the man but that was no matter.

"Twelve."

"Thirteen."

"Fourteen." Jesse was becoming irritated.

"Fifteen," said the lance corporal.

"Twenty," shouted Jesse.

"Twenty-one," answered the lance corporal.

"Twenty-five." He waited for an answering bid. None was forthcoming. He looked in the direction of the lance corporal. Thunder stood next to the man, the barrel of his M-1 tucked neatly under the man's armpit.

Tuleano looked the crowd of marines over carefully. "For twenty-five dollars. Going once. Going twice. Gone to the man with the M-1."

Few in the crowd dispersed as Jesse stepped forward to claim his beer. He could see the moisture beaded on the outside of the can. His mouth watered. He handed Tuleano the m.p.c. and took his can of Schlitz from the outstretched hand.

"Hey, Indio, aren't you going to share that thing with your friends?"

Without knowing who he answered, he said, "No friend of mine would even ask me to share a twenty-five dollar beer."

Laughter broke out from those who had heard Jesse's reply. Jesse found Thunder and the lance corporal still standing in the same position. Thunder casually placed his rifle butt on the ground and looked innocently at Jesse. By way of explanation he said, "I knew you were gonna get the beer anyway. Didn't see any need for things to get out of hand."

Jesse smiled and opened the can of beer. The men cheered and applauded as he offered the first drink to the lance corporal. The man smiled and took a short drink, offering it back to Jesse immediately. Jesse waved him back.

"You can do a little better than that. I figure you must have wanted it pretty bad to offer twenty-one bucks for one can of beer."

The man smiled and took a healthy drink. He handed the can back to Jesse. "That's even better than payin' twenty-one bucks for the whole can." He turned and looked at Thunder who gave him a quizzical look.

"All's well that ends well I always did say," said Thunder, offering his hand.

Once again, the lance corporal smiled. "You wouldn't have pulled the trigger anyway, would you?" He shook Thunder's hand.

Thunder nodded, "You bet I would've."

"Over a can of beer?" The lance corporal appeared uncertain.

Thunder picked up his M-1 and locked the operating rod to the rear. "It wouldn't have really mattered all that much. I didn't have a round in the chamber."

The tension completely gone, Jesse took a sip of his beer. He hadn't been so sure of Thunder either.

CHAPTER SIXTEEN: HUE

Jesse studied the outskirts of the city of Hue through his 7x50 field glasses. It was nothing like the villages and hamlets of his past experience. The buildings were substantial; made of stone, brick and concrete. This was no farm village.

He knew the standing order was to avoid any fighting in Hue even though it was considered a communist stronghold. Until he saw the city in its quiet beauty, he hadn't understood. But as he studied the mixture of European and Vietnamese architecture he began to hope that maybe there were some places off limits to war. Hue could be such a place. War had no business rearing its ugly head amidst such ancient beauty.

He longed to throw down his rifle and walk into the city as a civilian; to wander through the shops and markets; mingle with the people; just be a member of the civilized human race. On second thought, he decided he wouldn't mind keeping the rifle.

He turned to Mud, offering the field glasses. "Take a look. It's mighty peaceful lookin'."

Mud accepted the glasses and gazed upon the city for several moments. The tall shadows of dawn's first light outlined the buildings below Hill 102.

"How far is it to the closest houses?" asked Mud.

"'Bout four-hundred yards."

"How far to the Citadel?"

"Actually, those near hooches aren't part of Hue. That's the village of Ap Long Ho Ha. The Citadel is about five miles northeast of us - up there by that big bridge." Jesse pointed.

"It's hard to believe that the place is swarming with VC."

"Yeah, I know. It looks kinda like a big antique amusement park, don't it?"

"More like some kind of Shangri La."

Jesse smiled. "I didn't know you knew how to read, Mud."

Mud returned the glasses. "Screw you. I've probably read more books than you've seen."

"Damn, Professor, don't get your britches in a knot. Who peed in your cereal this morning?"

"I'm still pissed that you didn't even save me a sip of that twenty-five-dollar beer yesterday."

"Hell, Mud, you were busy writin' a letter. It's not my fault you didn't go with us."

"Yeah, I know, but I wanted to be able to say I tasted a twenty-five-dollar beer."

"Maybe next time."

"You mean to tell me you'd pay that much for a can of beer a second time?

Stoney Livingston

Hell, no can of beer is worth that much money – even if it *is* cold."

"Maybe not but the gesture was worth twice that."

"You know what your trouble is?" asked Mud.

"No but I got a feelin' you're gonna tell me."

"You're just a damn frustrated romantic."

"A what? What in the hell is that supposed to mean?"

"It's your cavalier attitude about...."

"Cavalier? Cavalier! What the hell did you do – stay up all night rehearsin' this speech? Where you comin' up with words like cavalier?"

"Screw you. Forget it. I'll get you drunk one of these days and take that musket away from you and whip your ass. Then you'll know where I come up with words like cavalier."

"Mud, I swear, you surprise me more every day. Not only do you own a Studebaker Golden Hawk but you also have more than a basic understanding of the English language. What in the hell are you doing in Uncle Sam's Mountain Climbers?"

Mud's look became serious as he stared into Jesse's eyes. "The same thing you are, Indio. I'm looking at one of the prettiest, most quaint cities in the world, and wondering why I can't walk down the streets with my girl instead of waiting to blow somebody's head off with a mortar barrage."

The smile left Jesse's face. "That's dangerously close to what I *was* thinkin', Mud."

They both looked again at the city of Hue, the large and gentle Huong River rolling lazily through its mid-section in the early morning light.

Jesse lit a cigarette. "It kinda reminds me of that tea plantation. Remember how peaceful and beautiful that place was?"

"Yeah – until it got dark."

Jesse looked wistfully at the rolling river. "Yeah, and it always gets dark sooner or later, don't it?"

"You got that right. Mostly sooner."

Jesse field stripped his cigarette and stood. "So much for fantasyland. Back to the real world. Let's get back to headquarters and report to the skipper." He signaled J.J. Washington to move his fire team to the rear and watched as the team moved stealthily through the heavy vegetation toward the company command post atop Hill 200 more than 1500 yards away. Suddenly the distant rattle of small arms fire penetrated the peaceful morning air. J.J.'s fire team froze in place.

"Mud, switch to Alpha's frequency and see if you can find out what's goin' on," said Jesse quickly as he moved out in JJ's direction.

Mud adjusted the frequency knob on his PRC-10 radio. JJ held his position until Jesse stood beside him.

"What the hell is goin' on, Indio? It sounds to me like it's comin' from every direction," said JJ, his eyes darting from left to right, then centering on Jesse.

"Don't know yet. We're tryin' to find out." He listened intently, trying to identify each sound and point of origin.

"Indio, I can't tell what's goin' on. There's so much garbage on the air it's hard to pick anything out," said Mud.

"Shhh! Not so loud, Mud. We don't know how many or how close they are," said Jesse.

Mud lowered his voice. "Sorry, man. I just couldn't understand a damn thing

368

on the radio."

Jesse and JJ moved to Mud's position on the double. Jesse took the handset and listened for a full minute. He turned to JJ. "Well, JJ, you wanted to see some gooks. It looks like you're gonna get your chance. From what I can understand, we have the gooks right where we want 'em. We can attack in any direction."

"What the hell does that mean?"

"JJ, you dunce," said Mud. He nodded at Jesse. "What he is diplomatically pointing out is the fact that we're surrounded."

JJ's eyes widened.

"It sounds like Alpha is being hit from the east, north and west," said Mud as he pulled the handset away from his ear.

"That means the gooks are between us and the company. Let's move forward and see if we can spot something. JJ, you mind if I take the point?" asked Jesse.

"Be my guest." There was an unmistakable note of relief in JJ's voice.

The six marines moved west, keeping just below the skyline on the north side of Hill 102. As they descended to the stream that marked the beginning of their uphill climb to Hill 200 Jesse signaled a halt. He motioned JJ forward.

JJ knelt beside him, panting. "Whatchoo got?"

"Look – up this hill about seventy-five yards and to our left. We damn near walked by a platoon or more of 'em. And just across the stream, about a quarter of the way up Hill 200, just a little north of our position, about three hundred yards north of a line between us and the company, there's a bunch more," Jesse whispered.

JJ looked in the direction indicated by Jesse. The enemy was ascending Hill 200.

"What the hell we gonna do?" said JJ, his voice almost cracking.

Before Jesse could reply, Mud closed on them. "We got VC comin' up behind us!" He whispered in a near panic.

"How many?" asked Jesse.

"I don't know but it sounds like a bunch," answered Mud, his voice urgent.

Jesse turned to JJ. "JJ, move your men as close to me and Mud as you can and find cover. I'm gonna call in some whiskey on top of us. Get 'em covered as good as you can. You only got about two minutes. Now go to it."

JJ nodded and disappeared into the foliage as Jesse pulled his map from his map pouch and frantically studied the terrain. He was aware of Mud adjusting his radio to the mortar frequency. "Mud, give me the handset," he whispered. Quickly Mud complied, catching his ear with the coiled cord and cussing softly as he offered the handset hurriedly.

"Whiskey Six. Whiskey Alpha. Over," whispered Jesse into the radio.

"This is Whiskey Six. Go ahead, Alpha."

Jesse recognized Cue's voice and wondered what he was doing on the radio. "Cue, this is Indio. We need help now. I haven't got time to adjust and set up a search and traverse. Can you get me ten rounds of HE on the west side of Hill 102? Start at 708185 and work north and south a hundred yards in each direction, and east two hundred yards. Do you understand? Over."

"Roger, Indio, I mean, Whiskey Alpha. You want us to fire when ready? Over."

"Sooner than that if you can – and I'm not kidding. Over."

"Roger. Out."

369

Stoney Livingston

Mud's face was as white as the trunk of an aspen tree. "Ten rounds? Jesus! We got a better chance with the gooks!"

Jesse handed Mud the handset. "Cut it back if you think it's too much. You got a bayonet for that pistol?" He nodded to the .45 in Mud's holster.

JJ's men were in position, all within twenty yards of the radio. The terrain they had stumbled upon was, perhaps, the best on the western slope of Hill 102 to provide protection from mortars but it would afford little help in the event of a direct hit.

Two minutes passed.

"Why the hell haven't they fired yet?" whispered Mud through clenched teeth.

The trees a mere thirty yards behind them rustled as the lead men from the enemy unit moved toward them. JJ fired his rifle at the point, missing the enemy soldier only twenty yards from where he lay. The VC, unaware of JJ's location, sprayed the area before him with his AK-47. The staccato sound of the high cyclic-rate of fire of the Soviet-made automatic weapon drowned out all other sounds.

Jesse fired his M-1, striking the man in the chest. He then jumped to his feet and charged into the trail, firing from the hip and bellowing a loud rebel yell. The next VC was felled immediately by the heavy 30.06 slugs from Jesse's weapon. A man following fired his rifle into the air as he fell, seeking cover.

Jesse continued his advance, stepping on one of the downed men as he ran forward in search of the third. He heard movement and fired his remaining three rounds into the brush at his right front, only fifteen feet from where he stood. His heart leapt to his throat as the empty clip ejected from his rifle with a resonant "ping". Still he ran forward, knowing his only chance was to kill the man hiding in the brush with a rifle butt. There was no time to reload. Fear was heavy in Jesse's chest as he charged into the brush.

The VC rolled to face him as Jesse smashed at his chest with the butt of his rifle. By bringing his weapon into the firing position, the enemy soldier partially absorbed the crashing blow with his forearm and rifle, but was unable to hold the rifle in his hands. It fell from his broken arm and bounced harmlessly on the ground. The little man struggled but was no physical match for Jesse.

As Jesse pressed his rifle stock against the VC's throat with the adrenal strength of ten men, the little man's body went limp. Jesse released the pressure on his throat and grabbed the VC by the front of his uniform and dragged him back down the trail. The distinct whoosh-whistle of descending mortar rounds sent a wave of fear to his bone marrow. He fell prone, holding tightly to his unconscious prisoner.

The mortar barrage lasted a short eternity. The ground shook and rumbled and seemed almost fluid as the high explosives disintegrated everything that was solid or semi-solid. The jagged shrapnel from the exploding rounds controlled every square inch of airspace more than six inches above ground.

Then there was silence except for the ringing in the ears of those who had survived the barrage.

JJ's voice drifted to Jesse over the ringing in his ears. "Oh no! Damn! Not you, Indio."

"Goddamnit, JJ, will you keep it down? Yer gonna get us all killed with that damn catterwallin'," Jesse crawled from beneath the fallen VC, wiggling one of his front teeth between thumb and index finger.

JJ half-smiled, obviously not certain as to just how relieved he should be.

370

"Where you hit, Indio?"

"Hell, I don't think I am." Jesse examined his prisoner.

"Where'd all the blood come from?" asked JJ.

Jesse pointed to the V.C. "Him, goddamnit. Shit, he's dead. I was hoping we could get some intelligence from him." Jesse stuffed a fresh clip into his M-1 and looked around him. "Everybody make it?"

"Yeah. Stumpy got a nosebleed is about all."

JJ and his team followed as Jesse returned to Mud's position.

"Mud. Fire mission. We've gotta hit the gooks on the east side of Hill 200." He turned to JJ. "JJ, set up a perimeter. I'm sure we're not the only ones who survived the barrage." He rubbed his front teeth with his tongue. "Damn mortars caused me to chip a tooth."

"Jesus, man, you okay?" asked Mud.

"If you don't count bein' pissed off, I'm fine. Stand by for the fire mission."

JJ disbursed his three men in a tight perimeter as Jesse plotted his fire mission. Mud called the mission to Whiskey-Six. They waited.

"Wonder what happened to Thunder and his squad? You suppose they got caught on the south side of the hill?" asked Mud.

"They may be fightin' like hell over there, but I don't see ol' Thunder gettin' caught with his pants down. That guy has eyes in the back of his head."

The first round exploded on the slope of hill 200. Jesse peered through his glasses. "Right one hundred. Add fifty. Ten rounds. Fire for effect."

Mud repeated the corrections into his radio handset.

As the mortar rounds found their targets on the slope of Hill 200, Jesse heard the small arms fire from their rear. He stood in a half crouch and moved towards JJ's position. "Sit tight, Mud. I'm gonna check things out."

"Rog," replied Mud nervously.

Jesse knew they were in serious trouble long before he reached JJ's position. Judging by the intensity of the small arms fire, the enemy force moving toward their position was at least four or five times their strength.

JJ fired aimlessly into the dense underbrush before him as Jesse approached from his rear.

"Damn, JJ. Save some of that ammo until you can see somethin'," ordered Jesse as he closed in.

Jesse's voice so startled JJ that he spun about and nearly pulled the trigger. Jesse dove for cover.

"Hey, Indio, I'm sorry, man. You scared the shit outa me is all." JJ's voice was high-pitched and edged with fear.

Jesse cautiously raised his head from the ground. "You didn't do a whole lotta' good for my pride either. Goddamnit, JJ, you gotta watch where you're pointin' that thing."

"It's okay, man. C'mon on."

Jesse moved to his side. "You got any ideas on what we got out there?"

"A whole damn bunch of gooks is all I can tell you," replied JJ, eyes wide with fear.

One of the marines shouted. A second voice reported momentarily. "JJ! Stephens is hit bad!"

Jesse moved to the injured man. "Get back to your post. I'll take care of Stephens." The man resumed his position and commenced firing into the brush.

Stephens suffered a wound high on his chest, near the right shoulder. The bullet had exited below the shoulder blade. Quickly Jesse applied his pressure bandage to the exit wound. He knew from his battle experience that Stephens needed blood and shock therapy as quickly as possible.

Using the fireman's carry, he removed Stephens to Mud's location and placed him gently in a semi-sitting position. The wounded man was unconscious. "Mud, find out from Whiskey-Six if there's any chance we can get some help up here. Stephens is hit pretty bad. He needs a chopper. When you're done with that, try to raise Alpha and find out if Thunder is still on the other side of our hill." He nodded at Stephens. Cover him with your poncho to keep him warm and keep the wound as high as you can. Don't let him lay down. Prop him up against something."

"Rog," replied Mud in his almost matter-of-fact tone.

Jesse returned to the perimeter. JJ and his two remaining men were pulling back, firing over their shoulders at the unseen enemy.

"Whoa, goddamnit, JJ. Where the hell you goin?" He grabbed JJ by the arm as the latter ran by him.

JJ spun around. "We gotta get the hell outa here. We can't hold!"

Jesse put his face only inches from JJ's. He spoke softly so the two marines kneeling twenty yards east would not hear. "JJ, you're supposed to be a goddamn team leader. We got no place to go. This is the most defensible position within our reach. Now, you turn around and tell your men to dig in and hold, or I'm gonna tell 'em for you, after I put a bullet between your eyes. Now turn around and be a goddamn leader – tell 'em!"

There was no doubt who JJ feared most. He turned to his team, and with more authority than Jesse had ever heard him use, said, "Dig in. We're gonna hold 'em here."

The VC were within hand grenade range when Thunder's squad moved down the slope at an oblique angle to their position. The ranks of the enemy force, though numerically superior to the combined forces of the Americans, were decimated. They were completely surprised by the onslaught of Thunder's men and, in the ensuing confusion, lost eleven men to American bullets and suffered a total of four captured. The surviving VC retreated in total confusion and rout. Thunder's squad suffered one casualty. One of his men tripped and broke his nose during the assault.

Two of Thunder's men guarded the four prisoners. The remainder joined JJ's fire team as they quickly formed a new perimeter.

Jesse smiled at Thunder as he took a deep drag on his cigarette. "We should have chased 'em all the way to Hanoi." His hands seemed to shake a little as he held the smoke loosely between his fingers.

"Maybe but I don't think they're gonna counter-attack. They're gettin' whipped pretty bad." He pointed to the 6 x 30 field glasses hanging around his neck. "Been watchin' 'em. I figured we'd wait a little bit until things die down on Hill 200 enough for us to break through without gettin' blown away by our own side."

"Sounds like a good plan to me, 'ceptin' for Stephens. And I just wish I could be so sure these guys we just ran off won't counter-attack."

"We left a few surprises for 'em back on up the hill."

An explosion almost drowned out Thunder's voice.

Jesse instinctively jerked at the suddenness of the sound. He looked at Thunder and smiled. "Son, you surprise me, stooping to usin' booby traps and what

372

not."

Thunder grinned from ear to ear. "Yeah, It's awful, ain't it?"
Another explosion rumbled down the hill.

Lieutenant Malcolm had just finished speaking to his gathered company when Jesse and the patrol, complete with prisoners, returned to Alpha Company's position. Reinforcements from Bravo and Charlie companies and a mortar barrage had saved them from being overwhelmed. He had praised them for their courage under fire and then had asked for complete reports from team leaders up through the chain of command.

He was about to dismiss the gathered troops when Jesse said, "Skipper, we need a chopper for Stephens. He's hit pretty bad. Then would you mind repeatin' that part about the mortar barrage that was fired in excess of safe limits and without clearance?"

Malcolm turned to face him and the rest of the men in the party. The four prisoners stood nervously in a tight group. Stephens was stretched out in a poncho.

"Corpsman!" shouted Malcolm. Instantly, a corpsman appeared and began checking Stephen's injuries.

As Stephens was carried away on a stretcher, Malcolm turned to the company gunnery sergeant. "Gunny, dismiss the men." He turned back to Jesse and his party. "Indio, you, Thunder and JJ stay here. The rest of you are dismissed."

The company gunnery sergeant turned to the men standing and kneeling behind him. "Get those reports to HQ more skoshe. Dismissed."

The men dispersed to their assigned duties.

Malcolm debriefed his dawn recon patrol.

During the week following the VC assault on Hill 200, Alpha Company knew no rest. Though the enemy did not again attack in force in broad daylight, they constantly harassed the rifle company with hit and run tactics and rocket and mortar attacks. The VC mounted a full scale assault one morning, shortly after 0100. The attack was poorly planned and even more poorly executed. The result was disastrous for the VC. Though their losses could not be confirmed, estimates placed the enemy dead and wounded at more than thirty. The marines on Hill 200 suffered a total of two wounded, neither of which required evacuation. The VC returned to the hit and run tactics with more even results.

*****

Lieutenant Malcolm briefed his officers and staff. The large sandbag bunker stunk of human perspiration and unwashed feet. Cigarette smoke fogged the air.

"Gentlemen, information received from one of the captured VC has apparently changed the thinking at battalion. Tomorrow at 0430 we jump off. We're going into Hue." He paused.

"What made 'em change their minds?" asked Lieutenant Parker.

Malcolm pointed to a contour map. "Right here, in this old French fort west of the city, the VC have a large cache of munitions. The place is a myriad of tunnels below ground.

"We will assault the fort from the high ground in regimental strength. Two company's, Echo and Foxtrot from the Second Battalion, Ninth Marines, have been assigned the job of neutralizing this blockhouse." He pointed to a position east and

373

north of the fort. "The remaining two companies from Two-Nine will move down this hill at 0600 from the north. At the same time, elements of the Second Battalion, Fourth Marines will assault down the south side of the same hill. The enemy will be caught in a pincer movement. The operation will have heavy ordinance support."

"Where are we on this operation, Skipper?" asked Parker.

Malcolm moved his finger eastward on the map five kilometers then north two kilometers. Jesse's mouth went dry as he gazed through the cloud of cigarette smoke at Lieutenant Malcolm's index finger.

"The western bridge. That's where we jump off, Gentlemen. We move to the road north of Hill102, about right here, board six-bys and ride up the road, around the big bend in the river, passing within five hundred yards of the old fort on the east side. Then we continue to the bridge. We debark the vehicles and sweep back west, along the river until we meet with friendly forces at the fort.

"Besides the intelligence about the munitions in the fort, S-2 has obtained information that the bulk of these munitions are coming in by water and being dropped in various houses along the river." He looked at his staff. "That does not mean, gentlemen, that everyone living along the river is a VC. There will be no harm to any civilians. Our primary mission is to disrupt the flow of enemy weapons. Do you all understand this?"

"How are we goin' to determine whose VC and who's civilian?" asked a voice from the rear.

Malcolm smiled. "The VC will be the one shooting at you."

"Sir, why did we draw this part of the mission? Seems to me that we're a little more qualified for the assault on the fort," suggested Lieutenant Parker. He was obviously irritated that his battle-hardened marines should have to stoop to searching houses for weapons while outfits he considered less qualified conducted the real war.

"I wasn't consulted on that matter, Lieutenant Parker, but it's my guess the powers-that-be decided to give us a break. We've had our share of the action this past month or two.

"This isn't going to be a picnic. We have a mission and I want it carried off successfully. Though we don't expect heavy resistance on our particular part of the overall mission, we could encounter some fighting. Should this occur, I can't over emphasize the importance of not killing innocent civilians.

"Now, another reason for our movement is to throw the enemy off guard. We are scheduled to roll by the area of the fort at precisely 0530. The sight of a battalion of marines moving down the road towards the city will cause concerns among the VC. S-2 expects them to deploy some of their forces to harass us in the partial protection of the city."

The marines in the bunker exchanged looks. Malcolm continued. "Under no circumstances are we to move east of Highway One. And above all, stay away from the Citadel. Do I make myself clear?"

No one spoke. "Hue is a communist stronghold. You won't find many friends there, so don't expect any. This is going to be a little different than what we've been doing. You're going to have to reach back to your Advanced I.T.R. days for house-to-house fighting. I'm counting on you all to instruct and control those in your command. Any breach of propriety or violation of the spirit of my orders will be dealt with severely. Any questions?"

The question and answer period lasted almost ten minutes, an unusually long time for these experienced marines, who normally listened to the briefing and knew immediately what was expected of them. At the end of ten minutes, most were still not sure of what to expect on the morrow.

Jesse spent a sleepless night. His two-hour watch on the perimeter ended at 0100, but he remained awake in the confines of his poncho, dreaming about the city of Hue in a peacetime Vietnam. He drifted into sleep fifteen minutes before reveille.

Nerves were tense as they bounced down the roadway past the fort only 500 yards to their left, but they drew no fire from the suspected enemy position. Apparently a battalion of marines was a little more than the VC were willing to attack conventionally.

The road curved from north to east and the column headed toward the heart of the ancient city. They crossed a bridge at the Sau River, where it emptied into the gently flowing Huong. There was no indication of any VC activity, though it was plain to see on the faces of the civilians that the Americans were looked upon as intruders. The hate and distrust was openly displayed in the eyes and on the faces of much of the populace.

Jesse watched the fishing boats in the Huong River. The six-bys were close enough to the water that any one of the boats near the shoreline was within hand grenade range. He shuddered at the thought and turned his attention to the graveyard on the left side of the road. It was huge and strangely beautiful as it lay nestled between the Sau and Huong Rivers. There was room for more graves, he thought, as the column left the expanse of the cemetery behind.

The road hugged the river's edge on their right and continued thus right up to the big bridge on the southwestern corner of the central city. On their left, the hateful stares of the citizens of Hue made Jesse aware that he was not liberating *all* of the Vietnamese. Some did not appear to appreciate his valuable assistance.

A main road intersected the column at ninety degrees on their left. The advancing marine unit ignored the road and continued into the city. Just past the intersecting road Jesse noticed a pagoda. Another seventy yards and an elaborate temple came into view. A hundred yards further and a large brick and stone building blocked the early morning sun..

"Hey, Mud. Take a look at that building. It looks like something from early Washington, D.C."

Mud stared at the massive building. "What the hell is it?"

"I ain't got the foggiest idea."

The column halted. Someone dropped the tailgate of the six-by and the marines poured out, scattering in prearranged directions, each man aware of his assignment.

Jesse looked in awe at the large steel bridge spanning the Huong River. The size of the bridge was not so awe-inspiring. It was relatively small by American standards – but the fact that it stood in the middle of all that seemed so primitive to Jesse made it seem out of place.

North of the bridge and just west of the central city, fifty yards from where Jesse stood, a temple glistened in the early morning sunlight. He moved up the well-traveled footpath, passing directly in front of the temple, Mud close behind him.

A fire team from Bravo Company entered the building north of the temple. Jesse and Mud remained outside, seeking cover momentarily at the corner of the stone structure. Their mission was to remain with Alpha Company's second platoon and be available in the event mortar fire was needed later in the sweep to the west.

Bravo Company was responsible for the houses within two hundred yards of the road. Charlie Company had the center, and Alpha Company had the northern area of responsibility in the battalion's sweep to the west, while Delta company held road security. Bravo conducted a slow and thorough search of the buildings next to the temple while Alpha and Charlie made a hasty dash to the north to get on line for the sweep to the west.

"What the hell we stoppin' here for? I thought we were supposed to stay with the second platoon?" asked Mud.

"We are. I just wanted to stop and look at all those footbridges across that canal leading into the city. That's about the neatest thing I've seen over here."

"If that don't beat anything I ever heard. Here we are in the middle of fifty billion unfriendly gooks and you gotta stop and admire the scenery."

"Tell me it ain't worth seein'."

"It ain't worth seein' now. How about some other time? Second platoon has the northernmost area. We better haul-ass."

Jesse glanced at him. "Damnit, Mud, we may never see this place again."

"We may never see anyplace again if we don't get our asses movin'."

Jesse shrugged. "Okay, have it your way. Let's move out."

They moved northwest on the dirt road paralleling the canal surrounding the central city. Most of Alpha Company was almost five hundred yards ahead of them as they hurried to catch up. A squad stopped and quietly peered into a pagoda. They continued on their way without incident.

The dirt road ended abruptly where the Sau river met with the canal surrounding the city. The second platoon commander, a sharp-tongued, ex-college football player from Detroit, named Hinkleman, advised company HQ that his men were in position. The sweep to the west began at 0630.

Second platoon's area of responsibility was sparsely populated in the first sector of the sweep and they were able to conduct a thorough search rapidly. No weapons were located but vocal opposition from some of the inhabitants was loud and long. Many were still chattering rapidly as the marines moved away from their homes to follow the Sau River west to the next group of houses located almost two hundred yards away.

The men in the second platoon followed the bend in the river to its temporary southward flow, where they too moved south, approaching the next group of houses with their hearts in their throats. The point man was a mere twenty-five yards from the nearest house to be searched when the firing began. It was intense and it caught the marines in a difficult position.

The terrain was flat and without cover. The small-arms fire was heavy and left the forward group of marines few options. Rear elements of the second platoon were able to retreat to the cover of the previously searched houses and take up defensive positions. Jesse and more than half of the platoon were not so fortunate. Their advance had taken them too close to the cluster of houses next in line to be searched. A retreat across the open ground to their rear was a far greater risk than digging in and laying flat on the ground.

Jesse sighted down the barrel of his M-1, keeping his head as close to the ground as his position would allow. He fired two rounds into the area from where the bulk of the enemy firepower seemed to originate. His body was rigid with fear as he pulled the trigger. The solid thump of the rifle into his shoulder settled him a bit and he turned to Mud.

"You okay, Mud?"

Mud, face down in the muddy soil twenty yards away, answered, "Yeah, how about you?"

"I'm okay." He paused. "This sounds like more than a little token resistance to me."

"How many you figure?"

"More 'n we're ready to handle in this position."

An automatic rifle tore up the mud a few yards away. An M-79 round exploded among the houses. A machine-gun opened up from the tightly grouped houses before them. Shouts for corpsmen and ammo were clearly audible above the din.

Lieutenant Hinkleman sent a fire team into the Sau River in the hopes they would be able to flank the VC unnoticed. The VC were waiting and, as the four-man fire team stood in waist-high water, the enemy opened up with a light machine-gun, cutting them down to the last man.

"Indio, Skipper wants to talk to you," shouted Mud above the sounds of battle.

Jesse crawled to Mud's position and took the handset. "This is Whiskey Alpha Actual. Over."

Lieutenant Malcolm's voice sounded worried. "Be advised that Alpha Two Actual has lost his radio. Are you in a position to call in whiskey? Over."

Jesse looked at Mud, then at the clump of houses hiding the enemy. "Roger, but be advised, the target is within four hundred yards of the central city and less than two hundred from our Alpha Two. Over."

There was a slight pause. Malcolm said. "Call in the whiskey. We are not in a position to assist. We have encountered resistance and you are cut off from our position. Do you copy? Over."

"Roger. I copy. Over."

"Fall back under cover of the whiskey and hold your position until we can get you some help. Do you copy? Over."

"Roger. I copy. Can you get us medical assistance and resupply? Over."

"Negative. Not at this time. Pull back and hold your position at the canal. We'll get you some help as soon as we can. Out."

The radio went silent. Jesse looked at Mud. "Skipper says to call in a fire mission. He says we gotta pull back to the canal and hold till we get some help. You stay here. I'm gonna contact Hinkleman and advise him of the situation. He's lost his radio so we're it as far as communications go until he can grab a prick-six that works from one of his squad leaders."

Mud nodded. Jesse scribbled some coordinates on a piece of his tablet and handed the paper to him. "These are the coordinates for the fire mission if something happens to me. Don't call 'em in until Hinkleman is aware of what's goin' on. Look for me on yer right flank. I think he's over there somewhere. I'll signal you when to call in the first round. Make it Willy Peter. We'll follow it with HE once we're on target."

Mud's eyes were wide but his reply was the standard, "Rog."

Jesse crawled to his right in search of Lieutenant Hinkleman.

Ten minutes later, when the mortar barrage impacted among the houses,

377

the second platoon moved to the rear, taking with them their dead and wounded, with the exception of those gunned down in the river. The bodies in the river had long since drifted west, to eventually float south to the much larger Huong River. In the rearward movement the platoon suffered three more casualties, two wounded and one killed.

As the survivors of Hinkleman's platoon gathered among the houses next to the canal he directed one squad to the southernmost group of houses. The remaining two squads took the northern area of their perimeter and dug in. Mud was relieved of his radio and he and Jesse were assigned to the squad with the southern group of houses.

The squad with the southern perimeter moved into position as Mud deposited his radio with Hinkleman.

PFC Dugan held tightly to an older woman's arm, dragging her through the front door of a substantial house. A younger girl was screaming and fighting, holding onto the woman's other arm, trying to pull her free of Dugan's grasp.

Jesse and Mud met Dugan just outside the door. "What the hell's goin' on in here?" asked Jesse.

"It's Bingo, Indio! He's gone nuts! I think he's rapin' a girl in the back room of the house. I couldn't stop him. He's out of it." Dugan averted his gaze.

Jesse ran into the house, Mud right behind him. He heard the sounds of a struggle and the moans and whimperings of a female voice. He stepped into the back room and knew instantly that Bingham was about to complete his vile act, judging from the movements of the large man's body and his heavy breathing.

With the butt of his M-1 he struck the larger man in the ribcage, toppling him from the girl. As Bingham rolled onto his back he ejaculated into the air, his body jerking and trembling with each surge of sperm.

Enraged, Jesse stepped in with a horizontal butt stroke to the large man's jaw. There was a dull crack as the jaw broke. Bingham thudded against the wall, his lower jaw hanging grotesquely to the right. Bingham raised his hands in a feeble effort to protect his face but the effort was futile. Jesse's rifle butt struck him square in the face, breaking his nose and knocking out two of his front teeth. Jesse jammed his rifle barrel hard into Bingham's stomach – so hard he thought the barrel might break through the man's back. That grotesque thought jarred him and he stopped.

He breathed heavily as he slowly pulled the rifle from Bingham's mid-section. He felt the muscles on his neck tightening as he backed away two or three steps. His body shook as he stared disgustedly at the grotesque figure propped against the wall.

He turned to the girl. She lay on the floor, her clothing almost entirely torn from her body, whimpering and crying softly, a welt plainly visible on her cheek; her neck showing the early signs of bruising. Jesse spun about and kicked Bingham savagely in the groin.

Slowly, he turned away from Bingham. Mud and Dugan, with the mother and younger child, stood behind him. No one spoke as Jesse took off his utility jacket and partially covered the crying girl. He picked her up and carried her to the front room of the house where he gently placed her on the sofa.

The only sounds in the room were the painful moans of Bingham, who lay on his back with his head propped up against the wall, and the almost inaudible whimpering of the frightened girl. The girl's mother watched silently, her mouth partially open, waiting for Jesse's next move.

Bingham attempted to stand but was unable to do more than sit with his back supported by the wall. He attempted to speak but his words were a gurgling moan.

Jesse glanced at him through the open door of the adjacent room then looked back into the eyes of the girl. She returned his look uncertainly. Softly he said, "You're okay now." He pointed to Bingham. "Number ten G.I. He won't hurt you anymore."

The girl looked at Bingham leaning against the wall, his jaw hanging to the right and his swollen nose covering most of his face. Her eyes narrowed.

Jesse stood from his kneeling position. Everyone in the room remained silent and motionless as he pulled his pistol from his left hip and pulled the slide to the rear. He released the slide, chambering a round, removed the magazine, emptied it, pushed it back into the handgrip and handed the pistol to Bingham's victim.

She stared at it, unmoving.

He pointed to the man against the wall. "He's all yours."

"Goddamn, Indio, you can't do that! I mean, I know he did wrong, but Jesus Christ, man, that's cold blooded murder," pleaded Dugan.

Quietly Jesse said, "You wasn't the one raped, Dugan."

The girl shook her head. Jesse stuffed a fresh magazine into the pistol and re-holstered it. He looked at Dugan. "Well, I guess she looks at it like you do, Dugan."

He knelt and looked into the girl's face. "I'd have shot him if it were me."

She smiled weakly.

Jesse turned to the girl's mother and pointed to his shirt. "Mama-San. Get her some clothes please."

The older woman didn't move, apparently unsure of the meaning of the American words. The girl on the sofa spoke quietly to her mother who quickly moved into another room.

Jesse knelt next to the girl and studied her face. "You speak English, don't you?"

She smiled a weak smile. "Some. As well as some French. Thank you for helping me. You are very kind."

Jesse nodded in Bingham's direction. "We're not all like him. I apologize for the whole United States." He paused, wanting to say more, but not sure how to do it tactfully. "I don't think he was able to ...er ...I mean ...I don't think ...aah ...Well, what I mean is, I don't think he was able to complete the act. I mean, you won't get pregnant."

She looked at him quizzically.

"Would you like to be checked by a doctor?"

The girl shook her head. "My father is a doctor. He will arrive here when it is safe. He is in the Citadel since early today."

The mother returned with a robe and an *ao dai*, the traditional silk tunic over pants. Jesse looked at Bingham then Dugan. He sighed, "You better get a corpsman over here – and bring a chaser. I think he's under arrest. If he's not, I'll shoot him myself."

Dugan looked about the room in a daze, apparently still trying to sort out the events of a few moments prior. The whole scene had occurred too quickly for him to

379

grasp it all. He left the house in search of a corpsman and Lieutenant Hinkleman. Bingham remained still, making gurgling sounds as he breathed through the blood in his nose and mouth.

Jesse and Mud entered the back room while the girl changed her clothing.

Dugan returned in ten minutes with Hinkleman, two chasers, and Corpsman Sanderson.

Hinkleman stared at the big man, still propped up against the wall. "Jesus Christ!"

Mud, who had been silent through the whole ordeal, said, "Things happened kinda fast, Sir."

"It looks to me like things happened kinda violent."

"Rape is a violent act, Sir," replied Jesse.

Hinkleman turned his attention to the Vietnamese victim. She was fully dressed and composed. Jesse was back in his utility jacket, and the house seemed to be in order.

Hinkleman said, "For someone whose just been raped, she looks awfully calm to me. Does she want a doctor?"

Jesse tensed. "She was raped, Sir. I caught Bingham in the act. Look at the front of the big bast ..." He remembered the girl's ability to speak English. "Look at the sperm all over his trousers." He pointed to the girl. "Her father is a doctor. I don't think she wants any more help from us."

"How do you know all of this?" asked Hinkleman.

Jesse nodded to the girl. "She speaks English."

As though startled by the thought that one of the Vietnamese could speak his language, Hinkleman said, "Are you sure?"

"Yes, Lieutenant, I speak English."

Hinkleman turned with a start to face the girl.

She continued, "The very big man pushed me into the room." She pointed. "He tore my clothes and forced his way into me." She spoke shamelessly, aware that everyone present could hear.

"That man, the one you call Indio." She pointed to Jesse. "He came into the room very fast and fought with the big man. The big man did not win the fight. The big man is very bad. Indio is very good. These other men are also very good. They help ...helped me."

"Well, I'll be damned. You speak English very well for a g ...Vietnamese," stammered Hinkleman.

Sandy looked up from Bingham's battered form. "Sir, it appears to me that Indio is tellin' it straight. There's sperm all over this man's trousers and on the floor, but if you want to keep him alive, we gotta get him medical attention." He glanced at Jesse and shook his head, perhaps remembering an old mama-san and a machine-gunner.

Hinkleman looked at Bingham's pitiful form. He spoke to the two marines acting as chasers. "Get that bucket of slime outa here. Now! And don't put him near any of the men wounded by enemy fire. I don't want them cheapened by the stench."

The two chasers quickly and roughly placed Bingham onto a stretcher and carried him from the house, Sandy in attendance.

Small arms fire erupted from the north side of the perimeter.

Hinkleman turned to Jesse. "I want a complete report when this thing is over." He looked at the girl. "I'll be back as soon as I can. We'll get to the bottom of

this before we leave. Indio, you, Mud and Dugan stay here and secure the house."
He turned and left the house on the double.

"Dugan, you take the southwest side of the house. Mud, you got the northwest. I'll take the southeast corner," ordered Jesse.

As Mud and Dugan left the room, Jesse looked at the girl. "What's your name?"

She smiled. "It is very difficult to say in your language."

"Try me."

"Thaoset."

"I see what you mean. Does it have an American meaning?"

"Not really. In VietNam, girl's names are like flowers but my English-speaking friends at the University call me Barbara. It is easier for them to say."

Stunned, Jesse slowly turned and left the house silently to assume his position on the southeast corner. His whole body trembled as he thought of that night in Southern California; the two men, the intent, the results. His mind left the City of Hue. He entered an unreal world of fantasy where events kept recurring, only the people changed. The names remained the same. Everything happened over and over with different people with the same names.

His stomach tightened with fear. He wondered if he was losing his mind. What was happening? *This is impossible. There can't be a girl named Barbara in Vietnam, and if there were, I would never meet her, and if I did, it wouldn't be under these circumstances. You're losin' it, Langley. You're really losin' it. You must have some kind of combat fatigue or somethin' What the hell is combat fatigue anyway?.*

He looked at the bright sun glaring almost directly overhead. He moved closer to the canal and looked at the city center on the other side. He turned and looked at the house behind him.

An explosion from the house slammed him to the ground. His ears vibrated with a high-pitched ring. He stood on shaky legs and looked at the house. A large portion of the south wall was missing. Smoke and dust hid most of the structure. Jesse returned to reality – fast – *Rocket!*

He ran into the house, unseeing in the heavy dust as he entered through the hole in the south wall.

"Barbara! Are you okay?" It felt odd to say that name.

A voice answered, "We are here. My sister is injured!"

Jesse moved to the voice. He ran into her in the dusty darkness that was the interior of the house. He slung his rifle. "You okay?"

"Yes but my sister is injured! She needs help!" She took Jesse's arm and guided him through the fine dust to the injured girl.

"Is everything okay in there?" shouted Mud.

"Hold your positions. I'll let you know." Jesse answered.

Jesse looked at the youngster in the clearing dust. He searched for blood and found a slight trickle low on her chest, slightly below her left breast. It appeared to be a laceration wound but he couldn't ascertain the extent of the injury. She also appeared to be suffering a head injury. A piece of the house had struck her in the temple as it careened upward from the force of the explosion. A gash, surrounded by bruised tissue, stood out prominently on her temple.

"We gotta get her a doctor. We've only got one corpsman with us and I'll bet he's too busy to take care of a go ... Vietnamese right now." He looked up into the eyes of the girl he called Barbara, embarrassed by what he had almost said.

381

Stoney Livingston

She did not appear to recognize his discomfort. "Perhaps I can find my father in the city."

Jesse looked at the injured girl lying on the floor, and her mother, who knelt over her. His eyes met those of the mother, the plea for help written plainly in her large almond-shaped eyes. He returned his attention to the Vietnamese Barbara. "I'll go with you."

He stood and re-slung his rifle over his shoulder.

"You cannot go into the city. It will be very dangerous for you. There are many who do not like Americans. They will kill you."

Jesse shrugged. "Sounds like fun. C'mon, let's go."

Once outside, she took the lead as they crossed the footbridge south of her home and entered the ancient city of Hue. With the canal behind them they ran north on the paved road, hugging the east side of the roadway. Two hundred yards north of the footbridge they crossed the inner canal via a concrete bridge supporting a paved road.

On the city side of the bridge she pulled him abruptly to the side of the building located on the southeast corner of the intersection just east of the bridge.

"Are you okay?" he asked, panting heavily from the long run and the surprise of her move.

She put her finger to her lips then quickly pointed through the building, to the east. "Many men are there. They will not be friendly even if they are not VC."

"Where is your father?" Jesse pulled a map from his map pocket. He knelt and spread it upon the ground. The Vietnamese girl knelt next to him and studied the map. Jesse pointed out their current position. She nodded and pointed to a schoolhouse on the map.

"This is the school where my father stays."

The building was a mere two hundred yards from where they hid from the crowds in the street but they would have to expose themselves as they crossed the road before them. Jesse pondered his options.

"You must stay here. I will bring my father. I am in no danger. It is you who must not be seen."

She was right. Reluctantly Jesse said, "Go ahead. I'll be in the neighborhood when you come back."

"I do not understand 'in the neighborhood'."

Despite all that went on around them, Jesse smiled. "I'll be here."

She turned and walked casually across the road. Safe on the other side, she strode briskly out of Jesse's sight.

He watched her disappear from view, her white silk pantaloons shining in the afternoon sun and her shiny red, silken tunic casting sharp rays of red light as it reflected the bright sunlight at odd angles.

Jesse moved to the south side of the building and peered eastward. He stared at the citadel a mere three hundred yards from where he stood. He could make out the large pond in the northwest corner of the square and he could see the wide diagonal pathway bisecting the square but there were two buildings obstructing his view of the ornate Citadel center.

Suddenly he realized he had failed to advise Mud of his movement. He became aware of the sounds of battle, some not more than four hundred yards from where he stood. He hoped the girl would return quickly with her father so that he could rejoin the second platoon. Mud was right; this was not the time to see the city.

There would be time enough for that when the war was over. He would return and visit the city without having to worry about being shot by the VC.

Where was the girl? *Is she turning me in to the VC swarming in the city? Am I going crazy? Why should I trust her?*

He was just about to retrace his steps to the house when he observed the girl returning to the concrete bridge with a man dressed in a white smock. She carried another smock over her arm. Quickly she introduced him to her father and, without asking, handed Jesse the smock and removed his helmet in one deft move.

"You must wear this. Put the ...hat under the coat. There are many gathering in the streets. They do not come this close to the river yet but they look this way. Some will see us as we cross the bridge. Many have weapons. They must not know you are an American."

"That makes me a spy. I can't conceal my uniform. A guy can get shot for that kinda stuff."

"They will surely shoot you if you do not do as she says," said the doctor calmly.

Jesse donned the smock. "I'm beginnin' to feel like I'm at home. Everybody speaks English all of a sudden."

The doctor smiled and said, "Many of us in the cities have learned several languages out of necessity."

With his rifle slung upside down on his right shoulder and his helmet tucked under his arm, Jesse stepped out in the direction of the bridge. The three walked casually across the concrete structure. As they crossed the footbridge into the second platoon's area Jesse quickly removed the smock and put his helmet on his head.

The small arms fire was sporadic and seemed indiscriminate as the three moved to the doctor's house. Dugan challenged them as they approached but apparently recognized Jesse and let them pass without incident.

Leaving the doctor and his daughter at the door, Jesse moved to Mud's side of the house.

"Damn, I'm glad to see you," he said as he saw his radio operator kneeling by a large tree.

Mud was obviously confused by Jesse's greeting. "Yeah, it's good to see you too, but don't you think you're goin' a little overboard? Hell, I just saw you a few minutes ago. Are you crazy or something?"

Jesse explained where he had been.

"You mean you left us exposed on the other side of the house?"

Jesse stared at the ground. "I was still east of the house."

"Are you okay, man?"

"Yeah. What've the gooks been doin'?"

"They just spray the area from time to time. Then, every once in a while, they fire a rocket our way. North end of the perimeter is catching most of it. They just throw something at us every once in a while to keep us honest and let us know they haven't forgotten about us."

"Any word on reinforcements?"

Mud shook his head. "Haven't heard a damn thing since I came out here. For all I know you been at your post the whole time. Better play it that way. I don't know about Dugan."

Jesse rubbed his chin. "Yeah, maybe you're right."

383

Stoney Livingston

Gunfire erupted from the city side of the canal.

Mud hugged the ground. "Damn, they're everywhere! I thought Hue was supposed to be sacred. Shit, Indio, we can't hold this position without some help."

"I'm gonna get back to my post. If it looks like they're comin' across the footbridges we're gonna pull back."

"I ain't gonna be much help with this forty-five. I need a rifle."

"If it comes to that we'll be headin' north," replied Jesse as he moved in a crouch to the southeast corner of the building. In short order he returned to Mud, carrying an M-14. He handed the rifle and four magazines to Mud.

"Here's your rifle. Dugan don't need it anymore. He took a stray round in the neck."

"Oh, shit, man. Let's get out of here."

"Let's get the people out of the house."

"Hell, they live here."

Jesse looked stupidly at Mud. "You're right. What the hell am I thinking?" He paused. "You go, Mud. I'll catch up."

"Bullshit. It'll take both of us to carry Dugan's body."

Jesse was having difficulty dealing with the reality of his situation. Finally, he shrugged. "C'mon, let's get Dugan and get the hell outa here." He moved to the southwest corner of the house, Mud right behind..

Gently they laid Dugan's body upon the moist ground. Lieutenant Hinkleman knelt. "What the hell happened?"

"The gooks are crossing the canal from the city. Must'a been a stray round. We saw fifteen or twenty of 'em crossin' the footbridge south of the house where the rape took place."

Hinkleman turned to a lanky corporal at his side. "Corporal Prescott, take a squad and form a perimeter to the south."

"The gooks have got those last three houses by now, Sir," said Jesse.

Hinkleman looked at Jesse then turned back to Prescott. "Set up at the Pagoda."

"Aye aye, Sir," replied Prescott. Instantly he called the names of the men for the southern perimeter to follow him.

Jesse moved to follow Corporal Prescott and his men.

"Where you going, Indio?" asked Hinkleman.

"With Prescott, to help stop the gooks, Sir."

"We can't hold 'em without help. If there's that many of them moving to our side of the canal we're going to need mortar support."

Jesse's heart gave a start. "But, Sir, there are civilians in some of those houses."

Hinkleman exploded. "Goddamnit, Marine, look around you. We're gettin' the shit kicked out of us. I haven't got half a platoon left. The rest of the company has got troubles of its own. We can't count on any help from anybody except ourselves. You wanna tell me again about those innocent civilians?"

Jesse looked at Hinkleman, then to Mud, who averted his gaze. "We'll need the radio, Sir."

Hinkleman pointed to the radio. "Keep it in my sight. It's all the contact we have with the company. Those little prick-sixes don't have the range and communication is spotty."

"Yessir."

Mud picked up his radio and found the mortar platoon's frequency. "Where you gonna put 'em, Indio?"

Jesse turned to Hinkleman. "Sir, I've gotta take the radio a little south so I can see the target for adjusting fire."

Hinkleman pondered his options. "Okay, but don't take it past Prescott's position."

"Yessir." He turned to Mud. "C'mon, Mud. Let's go."

Mud followed him in a crouch to the pagoda fifty yards south, where Prescott's squad waited.

Jesse looked though his field glasses at another pagoda five hundred yards south of his position. Almost directly east of the southern pagoda, armed men straggled across the footbridge from the city center. From time-to-time the M-60 machine gun attached to Prescott's squad fired a burst and the armed men retreated back across the bridge. Occasionally the machine-gunner would hit one of the figures and the injured man would fall into the canal, looking like a toy soldier in a mock scenario.

Jesse assumed the prone position beside the machine-gunner. "Give me a shot," he said, placing his M-1 to his shoulder.

As he took careful aim at the bridge, the gunner studied the distance and said, "No way."

Without taking his eye from his sight, Jesse replied, "Five bucks says I can."

"You're on."

The old M-1 bucked into Jesse's shoulder. A small figure toppled slowly into the water.

"Jesus! That's gotta be over six hunderd yards on a moving target." The gunner's mouth hung open.

"I couldn't resist takin' your money – but what I'd really like is to rent that gun for about ten minutes."

"Do what?"

"Rent your machine-gun. I'll give you a dollar a minute. You keep the time, and ol' Mud here will see to it that you stay straight."

The gunner looked at Mud. "Is this guy crazy?"

Mud looked at Jesse. "Indio, what the hell do you want this guy's M-60 for?"

Jesse, still in the prone position, looked over his left shoulder. "You know where our target is gonna be don't you?"

"Pretty close."

"Well, damnit, Mud, those people are still in that house. We gotta find a way to warn 'em."

Mud's jaw dropped. "You gotta be shittin' me. Indio. You've lost it, man. There ain't no way in hell! The gooks are all over those three houses down there!"

"I can't call in a mission on 'em, Mud – not if we can get 'em out of there."

"But we *can't* get 'em out of there, goddamnit!"

Jesse moved to Mud. "Here. You call in the mission." He handed Mud his map, compass and field glasses.

Mud shook his head. "Don't do this, man, not this time. There are too many guys countin' on us."

"I've marked the coordinates for the first round and written the magnetic azimuth to the target. After the first round hits, just adjust from your position. FDC will know how to figure the dope."

"C'mon, Indio, this is stupid. Jesus Christ. What do you owe those people that you don't owe us?"

Jesse's mind was made up but he had no answer for Mud. He turned to the machine-gunner. "I'll give you fifty bucks right now and I'll give you the gun as soon as I get back."

"Don't bullshit me. You ain't comin' back if you go down to those last three houses."

Jesse quickly reached into his left front pocket and pulled out a roll of brown ten dollar bills. "Fifty bucks – and four hundred more if I don't get back with your gun."

The man reached for the money.

"Uh uh. You get the fifty. Mud here holds the four hundred. If you don't get the gun back, he gives you the four hundred. You can just tell Hinkleman I ordered you to give me the gun. You're off the hook and four hundred bucks richer if I don't make it back."

Without further hesitation, the man grabbed the fifty dollars and handed Jesse the M-60.

"I want two more belts of ammo."

"You got it, Crazy Man," said the machine-gunner as he placed two one-hundred-round belts over Jesse's shoulder.

Jesse handed Mud his M-1. "Take care of old Betsy here, Mud. I'll be back to claim 'er. Give me three minutes then call in the mission. By the time they fire that first one, I should be at the house. If I got the coordinates right, the first round should land about fifty yards south of there. That'll give the gooks something to think about. By the time you've adjusted we should be outa there. Tell Prescott what I'm doin' after I split. I don't wanna be shot by our own guys."

Mud looked blankly at Jesse. In a voice devoid of feeling, he said, "I guess yer mind is made up?"

"Yeah, it is, Mud."

"Keep yer ass low."

"Thanks, Mud. Remember – three minutes." Jesse turned and moved to the canal, M-60 at the ready.

Jesse encountered no resistance in the confusion that is battle until he reached the northernmost of the three houses. He was among a group of four VC on the northeast corner of the building before he was discovered. He sprayed the vicinity of the enemy troops, unsure of how many, if any, were hit by his shotgun tactics. He ran south.

His wild charge was a blur in his mind as he fired the M-60 time after time at sounds and perceived movement. He was driven by fear, unaware of the results of his machine gun bursts. Twice he threw hand grenades. Several times he fell to cover, only to gain his feet and continue forward. He was on his second hundred-round belt of ammo when he arrived at the southernmost house.

Inside the structure he fell to the floor and fired at the two VC hiding near the large window facing north. They both fell, bodies leaking their existence. He became aware of screams from the back room of the house and charged blindly forward.

Inside the room stood the Vietnamese Barbara, fear on her face, a VC

386

holding her tightly. She pushed the small man from her and fell to the floor. Jesse fired a short burst from the M-60. The VC soldier was slammed into the wall by the force of the 7.62mm slugs. He fell limply to the floor, dead before his body lay prone.

Jesse heard the telltale sound of an 81mm mortar round as it fell earthward. "Barbara, You and your family have gotta get outa this house. We're fixin' to drop a mortar barrage right on top of it in less than two minutes."

"Why are you here? There are many VC," said the Vietnamese girl, her voice breaking with fear.

The mortar round exploded fifty yards south of the house.

"We don't have any time to talk. Let's get outa here."

Her father spoke. "My youngest daughter cannot be moved. Her head injury is much too serious. She will die if she is moved at this time."

Jesse shuffled his feet nervously. This wasn't going at all according to plan.

He spoke to the doctor. "But, Sir, you don't understand. The marines are gonna bomb this place into dust in about a minute. You gotta take the chance on movin' 'er."

"It is *you* who do not understand. My daughter will die if moved. I must stay with her. Please take my wife and oldest daughter – quickly."

His wife screamed. Jesse spun and fired point blank into the surprised face of a VC soldier. The man's skull and brain splattered against the wall.

Barbara looked at Jesse and said, "You must go. We will stay."

Frustrated, Jesse stomped and shuffled his feet and looked through a broken window at the landscape. He was afraid. He didn't want to be in the impact area of a mortar barrage again – not as long as he lived – however long that might be. He rubbed his chipped tooth with his tongue.

He looked at the sky through the window. "Damn!" He turned to the Vietnamese. "Damn! Damn! Damn!"

He looked about the room. To the doctor he said, "Cover your injured daughter with a mattress of some kind. The rest of you lay on the floor and cover up with anything that will provide some kind of protection.

Quickly the doctor repeated Jesse's instructions to his wife. She lay flat on the floor. Jesse turned the only sofa in the house upside down and placed it gently on top of her. He was grateful they were wealthy enough to afford such western decadence.

Barbara and her father covered the injured girl with a mattress and quickly took up positions on the floor, covering themselves with mattresses. Jesse stood inside the door of the house, listening for the deadly sound of falling mortar rounds, searching for VC. *What's takin' 'em so damn long? Get it over with.*

"Indio, why do you not seek protection?"

He turned to Barbara's voice in the other room. Though she couldn't see him, he smiled, very close to tears. "No more mattresses."

"There is room for you with me – please."

Jesse paused. *What the hell am I doin'? We're all gonna die in a minute and I'm almost lookin' forward to it.* He shook his head and entered the back room of the house. Gingerly he lay on the floor and crawled under the heavy mattress, keeping his machine-gun to the outside.

He became aware of his own body odor under the stifling mattress. In the dim light he turned his head and looked at the Vietnamese girl. He wanted to say something but could think of nothing intelligent. "I guess I must smell pretty bad, huh?"

She smiled a beautifully white smile. "You smell like a good man – an honest man. I am sorry you are an American."

He looked into her eyes for a moment then turned to face the door, placing his back to her as he waited for the whooshing sound of the mortars to announce their deaths. "I'm not."

Jesse grasped his M-60 tightly. He had no perspective of what was real and what was not. He was acutely aware of the girl at his back when he knew he should be thinking of other things – things like dying.

Two more minutes went by. Still they waited. Jesse looked over his shoulder at the girl. "I don't know what's takin' so long. Mud should have adjusted by now."

He crawled cautiously from under the mattress and moved into the other room. Still there was no *whoosh-whoosh* sound of a falling mortar round.

Intense small arms fire erupted from the north. Stray rounds whizzed by the house as Jesse ducked for cover. Soon he heard the sounds of marines in the assault: the catcalls, the rebel yells, the sarcastic insults, as they doggedly moved against an enemy. Jesse smiled.

What's goin' on out there? Those guys can't move into a mortar barrage. They must be crazy – or there isn't going to be a mortar barrage.

He remained at his position, waiting for a human appearance, not knowing if the first face he saw would be friend or foe. The small arms fire from the marines grew louder and the juvenile utterings of the young men etched themselves into Jesse's mind. He smiled as he picked some of the standard phrases out of the jumble of voices. Still he saw no VC.

A rifleman came into his field of vision. Jesse shouted, "Don't shoot over here. I've got this position secured."

The rifleman fell to the ground with a start. "That you, Indio?"

"Yeah. Who' 're you?"

"Peterson, second squad, third team leader." He stood and moved to the door of the house.

The young lance corporal looked at Jesse, a huge grin on his face. "I can't believe yer still alive!"

Ignoring the team leader's remark, Jesse said, "What's goin' on? What happened? There was supposed to be a mortar barrage."

The lance corporal guffawed. "Hell, Man. We didn't need a mortar barrage. The ones you didn't kill, you ran off. They musta thunk they was bein' 'tacked by a damn division. We saw 'em runnin' 'round, confused as hell, and Prescott notified Hinkleman. He saddled up the whole platoon and we hauled-ass after 'em befur they could figger out what wuz goin' on."

A pair of marines came into view. It was Mud and the machine-gunner.

"You crazy bastard," greeted Mud. He moved forward and hugged Jesse.

"I hate to admit it, Mud, but it sure is good to see ya."

Lance Corporal Peterson continued south with a wave goodbye. The machine-gunner approached Jesse. Jesse looked at him with a wry smile. He held the M-60 at arm's length. "She's a good gun. Thanks."

The gunner stepped forward and accepted his property. He eyed Jesse silently for a moment. "You're one crazy bastard." He paused for a short while, then stuffed five brown ten-dollar bills into Jesse's right breast pocket. "Hell, I'd pay fifty bucks to see that show anytime." He turned and moved south, a broad smile firmly rooted on his lips.

Mud stood smiling, looking like the proverbial cat who had just swallowed the unfortunate canary. He shook his head. Tears rolled down his cheeks. Jesse retrieved his M-1.

"You okay, Mud?"

For a full minute Mud didn't speak. When he did, his voice cracked slightly. "You saved the whole goddamned platoon, all by yore-goddammed-self, you crazy bastard. There musta been close to a hundred gooks around here. You tryin' to get yourself killed?" He moved forward and hugged Jesse again.

"Goddamnit, Mud. Quit it. You gone off the deep end or what?" Jesse turned his face to hide his emotions, only to find Barbara staring at him.

He wiped his eyes quickly. "You okay?" He asked the Vietnamese girl.

She nodded, not speaking right away. They looked into each other's eyes. Quietly she said, "Are you?"

Jesse looked over his shoulder at Mud, then back to her. "No, I'm not okay. You're not okay. Mud's not okay. Your family is not okay. Your house ain't okay. Nothin' is okay. This is all stupid." He looked at the dead VC in the house.

He examined the body of the man whose face he had blown away. The sight was grotesque. His stomach turned. He quickly looked away, his face an ashen white. He felt weak. His legs began to tremble, as though begging to be relieved of his body weight. Shakily he sat on the floor with his back propped against the wall. Barbara knelt next to him. She turned and called for her father in her native tongue.

Barbara continued to talk to her father as he knelt next to Jesse. The doctor spoke to Jesse in English. "Are you injured?"

Jesse looked weakly at the small Vietnamese man, then to Mud standing in the background with a concerned look on his face. He turned to gaze at the doctor. "Yes, Sir, I'm injured, but not the kind of injury anybody can do anything about, I reckon."

As the doctor took his pulse Jesse said, "Doc, I'm okay. If you can leave your daughter fer a little while, I'd appreciate it if you'd look at some of our wounded."

The doctor looked into Jesse's eyes, his own eyes narrowing momentarily at the request. "You suffer from a mild case of shock, Mister Indio." He turned to Barbara and spoke in Vietnamese. She left the room and returned quickly with a medical bag. He stood and accepted the bag. With a look down at Jesse he said, "Yes, I will attend to your friends. We owe you much."

"You don't owe me anything, Doc."

"It matters little. I will attend to your injured."

"Thanks."

Mud said, "You sit tight, Indio. I'll stay with the doctor."

He led the small Vietnamese man from the house.

Jesse watched them depart and knew he should rejoin the battle but he could hear only sporadic fire. He looked at Barbara with her long silken hair, jet-black, glistening in the afternoon sun to well below her waist. He sat on the floor and stared at her.

She became nervous under his stare. "Why do you look at me so ..." She searched for the English. "...strangely?"

Without a waver in his soft stare, he answered, "I was just thinkin' how beautiful you are and how much I wished our countries weren't at war. And I was

389

wonderin' what it would be like to go out on a date with you – a real date – like in my country."

"What means 'date'?" She sat next to him.

Jesse smiled. "It's when a guy and a gal go somewhere together to have fun."

"Where do they go?"

She looked into his eyes as he answered with tears rolling slowly down his cheeks.

"Anywhere they want."

When Lieutenant Hinkleman stepped into the house. Jesse sat with his back against a wall, M-1 standing muzzle-up on the floor, supported by his right hand. The Vietnamese girl sat next to him on his left, her head on his shoulder, asleep.

Jesse looked up at Hinkleman. "How many did we lose, Sir?"

Hinkleman said, "What are you doing with that woman?"

Barbara awakened. Jesse stared at the sharp-tongued Lieutenant from Michigan. "Don't read anything into it, Sir. This girl has had enough for one day."

Intuitively, Hinkleman seemed to realize the error of his question. "It's been a long day, Indio. I just don't want another incident."

Slowly Jesse rose to his feet. He looked the lieutenant straight in the eyes. "Sir, if I ever do anything over here to dishonor my country or my name, I'll hand you the rifle to shoot me with."

Before Hinkleman could reply, the girl stepped in front of Jesse. "No! You cannot shoot him! He is good!"

Hinkleman smiled. "No one is going to shoot him, though I ought to. He's number one crazy GI." He glanced at Jesse and said, "It looks to me like you've made a friend, Indio." To the girl he said, "I'm sorry. You can have him for a little while longer."

Jesse smiled. "How about the go ...er, VC?"

"They've dispersed. Third platoon is linking up with us now. As soon as we get choppers in for our dead and wounded, and re-supply, we'll be gettin' outa here. From what I can gather, Alpha caught more hell than the rest of the operation combined. The fort was taken without a shot being fired. The VC were all down here in Hue, keeping us busy."

"What do you want me to do, Sir?"

Hinkleman looked into Jesse's eyes for a moment, then to the Vietnamese girl. "Take a break. I know where you are. I'll be getting another radio pretty quick. When I do, you get yours back. Until you hear from me, you are responsible for this position. Don't leave your post until relieved. Understand?"

"Yessir. And thank you."

"Thank you, Indio, even though I should have your ass for risking that M-60 by doing what you did." He turned and left the house.

Confused, Barbara asked, "What did he mean?"

"He said we won the battle and that I must stay here and take care of you and your family until your father returns."

They moved into the back room where her sister lay unconscious, her mother keeping a silent vigil. They stood, Jesse and the Vietnamese girl, looking at each other in the dusty air of the stifling room. A peaceful sadness enveloped them both.

*****

In the hills west of Hue, Jesse looked down at the city through his field glasses. Two weeks had passed since that day he had discovered Bingham in the act of rape. Bingham was still in a hospital in Japan, awaiting court-martial as soon as he was released from medical treatment.

"It was weird, Thunder. I'd like to have known her better."

"Yeah, I heard about her from Mud. Said she was quite a looker. Said she spoke English better'n most of us. Too bad about this stupid war, ain't it?"

"Thunder, that's the understatement of the year." He looked wistfully at the city. "I'm glad we didn't stay the night down there. There was somethin' awful special about her. She reminded me of someone I knew in the States. Funny thing is, her name in American is the same as that girl's too. That whole deal is like some kind of twilight zone thing in my mind. I'm not sure it really happened."

"Oh, it happened all right. Between you runnin' into 'em and shootin' the hell out of the bunch of 'em, and Mud callin' in the wrong correction on his fire mission and...."

"What are you talkin' about? What wrong correction?"

"You didn't hear?"

"Hear what? What the hell are you talkin' about?"

Thunder laughed. "Hell, the correction Mud called in put the next round smack smooth on top of a pagoda on the map. Battalion wouldn't let 81's fire the mission. Hinkleman saw the gooks were confused as hell by your crazy-ass charge, so he ordered an assault. It wasn't until you guys retook the position that Hinkleman realized that Mud had called in the wrong coordinates. If he had known at the time he may have changed the coordinates and blew you and that girl's family plumb to hell."

Jesse put his field glasses to his eyes. He studied the city of Hue, wondering where she was and if he would ever see her again. He thought of Mud's "error" and smiled.

CHAPTER SEVENTEEN: PRAIRIE

Jesse cooked his C-ration chocolate with a single-mindedness of purpose, oblivious to the rest of the world. Carefully he added just a pinch of sugar from the small C-ration pack to his creation. He stirred the contents of the can slowly, carefully. A dash of powdered coffee gave it a special flavor.

"What the hell you makin', Indio, some kinda seven course dinner er sumpthin'?" asked JJ.

Without taking his eyes from his masterpiece, Jesse answered, "If I gotta eat this garbage from time to time, I want it palatable."

"What the hell makes it so good by all them slow-ass preparations?"

Jesse lifted the almost-boiling solution from the small chunk of burning C-3 explosive. Offering the can, he said, "For you, JJ – just a taste now. Don't get carried away."

Gingerly, JJ accepted the steaming can of hot chocolate. After first burning his fingers on the can, then his mouth with its contents, he carefully handed the can back to Jesse. "Jesus, that stuff is hotter'n hell! But I gotta admit, it's about the best I've tasted since I was a kid back in Alabama. What'd you do to it?"

Jesse squinted his eyes against the bright afternoon sunshine and smiled. "Basically, JJ, old man, you've just gotta have the touch. Without the touch, you can't make it taste worth a damn with all of the finest French cookbooks."

"Quit bullshittin' me, man. I'm serious. How'd you make it taste like that?"

"Well, the first thing you gotta do...."

A runner from company headquarters interrupted Jesse's dissertation "Hey, Indio, Skipper wants to see you," he panted.

Jesse shrugged. "Tell 'im I'm on the way." He glanced at JJ. "Remind me later, JJ." He picked up his rifle and moved up the hill toward company headquarters, sipping his hot chocolate.

In less than ten minutes, Jesse returned. "Saddle up, Mud. We're goin' on a combat patrol."

"Combat patrol? What the hell they want us to go on a combat patrol for? We ain't supposed to do the grunts' job."

"Just lucky I guess. C'mon, quit yer bitchin' and let's get movin'. We gotta meet up with Thunder's squad at the base of the hill."

"Oh shit, not him." Mud picked up his radio. "Goddamnit, every time you two get together it's a contest to see who's the craziest. One of these days you're gonna find out and neither one of you is gonna like the answer."

Jesse smiled. "But it sure is a lotta fun, ain't it?"

Mud shook his head as he moved down the hill. "Yer both crazy enough to win the nut-of-the-year award as far as I'm concerned.."

Jesse looked over his shoulder. "See ya in a couple a hours, JJ."

"Keep yer ass low, man."

"Yeah, thanks."

At the bottom of the hill, Thunder and his squad waited patiently with Lieutenant Huy.

"Huy. I thought you went back to that cushy job at division," offered Jesse with a smile and a handshake.

The little Vietnamese interpreter returned the smile as he offered his hand. "Lieutenant Malcolm say he need me to accompany you on your hunting trips. Can't spare me to division."

The entire squad laughed – more at the *way* Huy said it than what it was he said. Thunder picked his point man and the patrol moved out. Their mission was to ferret out VC suspected of operating out of a nearby village. The trip to the village was without incident and, though Jesse and Thunder were disappointed, Mud appeared quite pleased to find his walk uninterrupted by gunfire or booby traps.

The village was small, consisting of only eight thatch houses and a larger building used as a trading center. The larger building was a combination of the remnants of a French colonial plantation house and the patchwork construction of the Vietnamese. Through Huy, Thunder questioned the village leader, an old man with a crooked back and a straight beard. The old man denied any knowledge of VC activity in the area and asked the marines to leave, insisting that he feared reprisals from the hills. The squad conducted a thorough search of the village and surrounding area with negative results.

It was Mud who discovered the large black rooster with his feathers shining in the late afternoon sun. The big fellow strutted about proudly, leaving little doubt as to who ruled the henhouse.

Jesse shook his head. "I don't know, Mud. Jeez. He's twice the size of ol' Frank. I don't believe you could carry him around on your radio all day if we ever had to take him on an operation."

"Carry 'im? Who said anything about carryin' 'im? Hell, I'm gonna teach *him* to carry the damn radio."

Jesse Chuckled and turned to Huy. "Hey, Huy, make a deal for the big shiny rooster for us, will ya?"

"You wish to buy the rooster?"

Jesse looked at Mud and smiled. "Yeah, I reckon we do."

*****

Malcolm shook his head. "Wasn't Frank enough for you?"

"Well, Sir, Frank was a right fine mascot and if he hadn't taken sick he'd still be with us. Hell, you know as well as I do that he was good for morale." They stood near the Alpha Company CP, on the gentle slope of a hill.

Malcolm smiled. "What's this one's name?"

"Wellington, Sir."

"Wellington?" Malcolm raised his eyebrows.

"Well, he sure as hell don't look like a Frank. He's got that royal British look so we thought we'd give 'im a Limey-soundin' name. Seems like he took to it already."

Malcolm shrugged. "Okay, Wellington it is, but see to it he's kept quiet after dark." He studied the rooster strutting at the end of a long leash. "He's sure a big

393

one."

"Yessir, he is. If worse comes to worse, we could eat 'im."

Malcolm grinned. "Get the hell out of here, and take that black peacock with you."

Jesse smiled. "Aye aye, Sir. And thanks." He turned and moved down the hill, dragging Wellington behind him on the leash.

*****

Wellington rode atop Mud's radio, looking like a sorrowful sparrow as the rain plastered his beautiful black feathers to his body. Visibility was less than a hundred yards as the column moved up the muddy roadway. The early morning light, obscured by the torrential downpour, cast faint and strange shapes upon the landscape. For more than an hour the battalion had struggled to make progress on the slippery road. Footing was uncertain at best, and the company mighty-mite was unable to maintain a steady pace in the slick clay mud. Malcolm sent it to the rear in order to insure the company maintain its timetable.

Mud slipped and fell, sending Wellington to the slick clay in a flurry of feathers. The soaked rooster slipped and fell as he excitedly tried to regain his footing and escape from the short leash at the same time. Still in the prone position, Mud tugged at the leash. "Goddamnit, Wellington, you useless piece a' shit! Settle down before I make chicken soup outa yer ass."

Jesse stepped to the rear and helped his struggling radio operator to his feet. "Gimme the leash, Mud. I'll take him for a while."

Mud jerked the leash from Jesse's grasp. "I can handle it. I just lost my footin'."

"Okay. Okay. Jesus Christ, You're worse'n a damn woman ever since we got that struttin' peacock." Jesse moved forward and resumed his position, rain cascading from the lip of his helmet.

Mud picked up the struggling rooster and carried him under his arm, swearing and mumbling to the frightened bird for the next fifty yards. Tree branches near him fell, almost unnoticed until the falling was followed by the report of an automatic rifle. Once again he was on his stomach; this time by choice. Jesse grabbed him around the ankles and suddenly and, not at all gently, pulled him to the side of the trail and into the underbrush. He sat up and stared silently at Jesse.

"What the hell were you doin' out there on the road – takin' soil samples? Goddamn, Mud."

"What the hell's goin' on?" Mud replied.

"I don't know. Can't see or hear a damn thing with all this rain." Jesse peered into the wall of water toward the column front. A marine about fifty yards away, in the prone position, rifle at the ready, was pointing to the left flank.

"What the hell do we do now?" asked Mud.

"I guess we sit and wait. Whoever it was has stopped shootin'. Hell, I barely heard the shots, the rain is so heavy."

Mud looked down at Wellington, who shivered indignantly. He placed the rooster under his poncho. They waited. Several minutes passed without an audible sound, other than that of the falling rain.

"Damn. I could sure use a shot of sourmash whiskey."

In a loud whisper, barely audible above the din of the pouring rain, Mud said, "Whiskey? We could be killed any second – and you ask for whiskey?"

394

Jesse shrugged under his poncho. "Well, damnit, the thought crossed my mind and I just thought I'd share it with you."

"You sure as hell have a warped mind. Remind me to have your brain checked next chance we get. I wanna see if you have one."

"I'll be sure to do that. Remind me to remind you."

An uneasy moment of silence passed. Finally Mud said, "How long before we do something?"

"I don't intend to do anything until I run out of rations or they show themselves. What the hell you wanna do? You got any idea where they are?"

Mud shook his head. "No, but we can't stay here forever."

"Why the hell not? You got some kinda hot date or somethin'?"

"Hell, there could be a million of 'em out there, waitin' for the rain to quit so they can see us."

"Yeah. Maybe so, but what can we do? If we advance against a fortified position in this muck, they'd mow us down like fresh hay at harvest time. You got any brainstorms you wanna relay to the battalion commander? You got a radio ya know."

"I just thought you might have an idea or two. I've never seen you without an opinion on anything," said Mud.

"Oh, I got an opinion all right. It's my opinion that we oughta' sit tight and wait for them to make the next move."

Small arms fire erupted from the left flank. Bullets chopped the tree branches overhead. Wellington squawked loudly under Mud's poncho. Mud quickly soothed the frightened bird by stroking him gently and swearing softly at him.

"Well, goddamnit, they sure as hell don't seem to be afraid of our size," offered Mud as the firing died down.

"I noticed that."

"Maybe Thunder will come rollin' down the road with his squad of crazies and kick some ass," suggested Mud.

"Don't hold your breath."

The rain seemed to intensify. They heard the *whish-whish* of the sixty mm mortar just before the round impacted only thirty yards from where they hid. Clods of mud and debris flew overhead, causing little more than psychological damage, but the psychological damage caused was immediate and intense.

"Goddamn, I barely heard that sonofabitch!" shouted Mud.

"We gotta do somethin' now. If they rake the roadbed, they don't have to see us. They can just take potshots and rip us to pieces," said Jesse. "Keep an eye out and see if you can figure out where they're comin' from."

With water running from the lip of his helmet like a waterfall, Mud replied, "Sure! Hell yes! I'll just stand up and get a quick look at their little ol' sixty, then I'll pinpoint the location on the map for you." He paused. "Just how in the hell do you expect me to see anything underwater without a set of goggles?"

"Hell, I don't know. Give me the handset."

With great difficulty, Mud managed to extract the handset from under his poncho and keep the big black rooster under control.

Jesse accepted the handset and keyed up. "Pied Piper Alpha, this is Whiskey Alpha. Over."

Barely audible over the roar of the rain, a crackly voice answered, "This is Alpha. Go."

"Roger, Alpha. Put Alpha Actual on. Over."

395

"Roger. Wait one."

There was a short pause, interrupted by Malcolm's voice. "This is Alpha Actual. Over."

"This is Whiskey Alpha. Do you have any special instructions? Over."

After a short pause Malcolm said, "You're at home plate. I'm centerfield. Alpha One-One is moving to left field. Enemy suspected at five hundred yards beyond third base and two hundred yards into foul territory. Do you understand? Over."

Jesse paused for a moment then smiled broadly. "Can you hold One-One at the foul line and let me hit a few foul balls? Over."

"Stand by."

Thunder's voice came over the radio from his position in the brush, "I copied, Alpha Actual. Do you want me to remain in fair territory? Over."

"Roger, One-One. Remain in fair territory. Whiskey Alpha, you're at bat. Over."

"Roger, Alpha Actual. Goin' to Whiskey frequency for batting practice. Out."

He handed Mud the handset. "Switch to 81's frequency. We got a fire mission."

As Mud fumbled with the PRC-10 radio, Jesse pulled his map from the canvas map pouch and studied the terrain. He attempted to keep the map dry but it was an effort in futility. After a moment he cursed. "Goddamnit. I can't be sure where we are. I've gotta find a landmark to be sure."

"How the hell you gonna do that?"

"There ain't but one way. I gotta go find one. Gimme the radio. You stay here with Wellington."

Mud looked Jesse square in the eyes. "Not this time, by gawd. I'm goin' with you." He quickly tied Wellington's short leash to a small tree.

Mud's look and his voice were determined. "Lead off, godamnit. Whatchoo waitin' for?"

Jesse shook his head and ran clumsily across the clay mud road, slipping and falling head first as he tried to stop on the other side. He was just gaining his feet when Mud slid into him and bowled him over.

Once both men were again standing erect they moved to the rear of the column and deeper into the jungle growth on the upward slope of the hill, Jesse in the lead by a mere ten yards, almost hidden from Mud's view by a curtain of water. Jesse stopped under a conspicuously large tree and removed his poncho.

Mud moved close and whispered, "What the hell are you doin'?"

"The rain hittin' the poncho makes too much noise. If you stay about twenty yards behind me, you can keep yours on." He rolled his poncho as he spoke.

"Bullshit, I can hardly see you *ten* yards back!" Mud removed his poncho and rolled it, tying it to his cartridge belt. They continued stealthily forth, soaked through their clothing in less than five yards. An automatic rifle opened up a mere twenty five yards in front of them but the fire was directed at the roadway below.

Both crouched low in response to the initial burst of fire. With his mouth only inches from Jesse's ear, Mud said, "What the hell we gonna do now, toss a grenade?"

"No, we can't let the gooks know we're here. We gotta pinpoint our location. We'll have to sneak around 'em."

Mud's jaw dropped. "Are you crazy?"

396

"We ain't got a choice."

"Bullshit. Let's go back to the road. That's a choice. And a damn good one from my point of view," whispered Mud.

The sound of sixty mm mortar rounds exploding on the column below drifted up to them through the rain. Jesse looked at Mud. "You go right ahead. I'll take my chances with the gooks."

"No thanks. I'll just tag along if you don't mind."

They skirted the automatic rifle, both men well aware they were in among the VC troops firing on the column below. The climb became suddenly very steep. Soon they were unable to continue on their chosen path. A sheer rock wall, almost vertical for one hundred feet, blocked any further progress. Jesse sat and studied his soaked map. He had their location.

"That's gotta be it." He turned to Mud. "Fire mission."

Mud repeated the information to FDC as Jesse gave it to him. The request was for one round of white phosphorus and a "will adjust".

FDC reported the round on the way. Jesse pointed to a spot one hundred yards below and to the left as they faced the column. "It should hit over there somewhere."

"Jesus, could you get it any closer?"

"It's gotta be close enough so I can see it in this soup. How the hell can I adjust if I got nothin' to adjust from?"

"Why've you always got a goddamn answer for everything?"

"Just smart I guess. Now be quiet so we can be sure of where the round hits – just in case I'm off a little bit."

With a gentle *poof*, the white phosphorus landed, sending a beautiful white fountain of burning death symmetrically skyward, a bright orange glow at the center of the fountain.

"Right on target," said Mud, almost in a whisper.

Jesse pulled out his compass and shot an azmuth, which he quickly relayed to Mud. "Okay, Mud, eight rounds of H.E. Left four hundred. Add one hundred. Search and traverse. Search up fifty. Traverse left fifty. Fire when ready."

Mud dutifully repeated the command. After a long pause, FDC reported the barrage was on the way. Jesse turned to Mud and said, "The gooks may run this way. We might as well fix 'em up a surprise."

The two barricaded themselves behind a fallen tree with a clear field of vision of almost fifty yards to their front, the weather notwithstanding. Jesse removed his four hand grenades drawn earlier in the morning for the operation. He laid them neatly in a row next to fallen tree. Mud followed suit with his two grenades even as the mortar barrage exploded below their position. They lay in the wetness, shivering and waiting.

Mud switched frequencies and advised Malcolm the mortar barrage was ended. The company commander acknowledged the report and ordered the FO team to stand by.

Suddenly Mud and Jesse found themselves in the middle of an impact area as the marines on the roadway below fired M-79's and machine-guns at the ridge. Branches were cut cleanly from the tree overhead as the projectiles from the machineguns below cut a swathe through the jungle. A forty mm projectile exploded twenty yards in front of the fallen tree protecting them.

Shortly, the firing of rifles very close to their position added to the fear

397

churning inside both men. The origin and direction of fire was impossible to determine in the heavy rain. Visibility was still almost zero. The rain crashed to earth with the roar of Niagara Falls, drowning or distorting all other sounds.

Jesse peered over the fallen tree. He could see nothing but sheets of water falling from the sky. He rubbed his eyes and strained his every sense. The small arms fire intensified. He could hear voices shouting but the sounds were so garbled he was unable to determine the language spoken. He saw a form to his left front, a mere twenty-five yards from where he lay. *VC or marine*? He held his breath. The form moved into the jungle to his left.

A stray bullet struck the trunk of the fallen tree. Quickly Jesse retired behind his cover. He looked at Mud, then to his grenades lying on the ground. *What a mess. No one knows we're up here. We can't see ten feet in front of us – and there's bodies movin' all over the place right next to us.*

A Vietnamese voice on his left flank shouted a command. Jesse pulled the pin on one of his grenades and threw it as far as he could in the direction of the voice. Before it hit the trees and exploded, he had another in the air. He repeated the procedure until all four of his grenades were gone. Mud followed suit, throwing both of his grenades as quickly as he could pull the pins and get rid of them.

Both men fell behind the fallen tree trunk and waited. The small arms fire died down immediately after the grenades exploded. A new set of deeper voices could be heard. Soon they were able to pick out certain epithets. Definitely marines. Mud raised above the protection of the tree to hail the advancing marines.

A wall of hot lead slammed into the tree trunk and the surrounding area. Mud fell behind his cover.

Jesse shouted, "Mud, you okay?"

Mud nodded. "I think so."

A forty mm exploded almost on top of the tree trunk, sending chunks of wood and debris flying in all directions. M-14's on full automatic raked their cover.

"They're comin' in for the kill." Jesse's voice was even, almost resigned..

"Oh, shit! We're dead, Man! So long, Indio!"

Another M-79 round exploded only a few feet in front of the tree trunk, the concussion lifting both men a short distance off the ground.

Jesse shouted above the din of the rain and the roar of the automatic rifles. "Hey, you crazy bastards, we're on your side! Cease fire!"

The marines continued to pour it on as they flanked the hapless pair. Jesse's shouts went unheard in the crescendo of rain and gunfire.

Jesse grabbed the handset from Mud's radio. "Pied Piper Alpha. Whiskey Alpha. Over"

"This is Alpha. Go."

"This is Whiskey Alpha Actual. We are behind the enemy line and are being assaulted by our own troops. Call 'em off long enough for us to identify. Over."

"Stand by, Whiskey Alpha."

"Stand by hell! Call a cease fire!"

Even as he spoke, another M-79 round exploded only yards away.

Roughly, he pulled the radio from Mud's back and flung it to the ground. "Let's try a run for it to the south." He slithered on his belly in the slimy clay soil in an attempt to keep himself concealed until he was out of the range of visibility of the advancing marine unit. Mud followed so closely that twice he was struck in the face by Jesse's boots.

Forever Patriots

After an indeterminable time, Jesse stopped crawling and assumed a crouch position. "Let's go it on foot from here. Follow me."

Mud followed in a mad dash to the southwest. No shots were fired directly at them as they plunged headlong deeper into the jungle. They ran for almost three minutes without a rest. Jesse finally stopped beneath a large tree and motioned Mud to sit down.

"This is it. We're far enough back that they'll probably set up a perimeter below us. If they do come this far, they'll probably be movin' a lot slower and we'll have a chance to identify ourselves," gasped Jesse.

Mud had not the strength for conversation. He merely nodded and leaned his back against the large tree. The minutes ticked by like hours. Strength slowly returned to their bodies.

After a while, Mud spoke. "Sorry I got a little sentimental back there, man. But I thought we were goners."

Jesse smiled. "Hell, so did I. At least you had the courtesy to say goodbye."

"Well, we made it anyway," said Mud.

"We ain't outa the woods yet, but I gotta admit, I sure like our chances a lot better here than back there."

Mud smiled. "I bet there's a bunch of pissed-off grunts back there when they find out we got away."

"Yeah, that is kinda humorous, ain't it?"

They both chuckled softly.

A voice silenced them. It seemed to originate from the direction of the advancing marines. Jesse whispered above the sound of the falling rain. "I'll let 'em know way ahead of time that we're on their side. I'm not ready for another round with those guys just yet. You stay here and I'll move to that big tree over there and holler at 'em. I'll wait until I'm sure they can hear me, then I'll just holler at 'em and duck down until it sinks in that we're on the same team."

"Keep yer ass low," said Mud.

Jesse looked over his shoulder as he moved out. "Believe me, I intend to."

The voices had been much closer than either man had anticipated. Jesse had just reached the tree when a Viet Cong soldier walked casually from behind it, totally unaware of Jesse's presence. Jesse struck the man brutally in the chest with the barrel of his M-1. The VC's flesh exploded through the rear of his uniform as Jesse pulled the trigger while his rifle was imbedded in the man's chest.

Mud jumped to his feet and ran toward Jesse. Another Viet Cong appeared from the other side of the tree. Mud fired a wild shot from his pistol, nearly hitting Jesse in his haste. The Viet Cong soldier, his attention drawn to the charging Mud, pointed his rifle and fired from the hip. Before he could fire a second round, three bullets from Jesse's M-1, only five feet away, blew his intestines from his body. He fell, quivering and jerking in spastic movements, scattering his internal organs further from his body.

Jesse rolled away from the tree, pointing his rifle into the more dense undergrowth. Using the foliage as cover, he moved into the jungle, searching for more VC.

Mud took a position behind the tree and stared at the two Viet Cong on the ground. The one was most definitely dead. The other moved slightly, causing Mud to start. He moved closer to the fallen man, bending over him. The young Viet Cong soldier looked at him pleadingly. He appeared unable to move more than his facial muscles.

Mud removed his helmet and held it above the man's face, protecting it from the rain. Quite suddenly, the soldier vomited blood and died. Mud forgot about the war and his danger. He looked at the dead VC as the heavy rain washed the blood from his lips and neck, the lifeless eyes oblivious to the falling rain. Mud replaced his helmet on his head. He sat between the two dead men and waited for Indio's return.

It was almost ten minutes before Jesse returned with a squad of marines from Charlie Company. The squad leader looked from Mud to the two dead VC and back to Mud.

Jesse spoke to the squad leader. "Mud here is one helluva crack shot with that pistol. You shoulda seen 'im."

"You got both of these gooks with a pistol?" He asked Mud incredulously.

Mud stood and looked at Jesse. "Screw you." He turned to the squad leader. "If you check the bodies, I think you'll find thirty-ott-six bullet holes in 'em." He turned back to Jesse. "I don't want your reputation. Who the hell needs those kinda headaches? All I want is my radio and some dry clothes." He unstrapped his poncho and placed it over his soaked uniform.

A PFC. strolled up to one of the bodies and spat on the lifeless face.

"You do that again, bud, and yer gonna need an operation to remove my boot from your ass."

The PFC. stared at Jesse. "What the fuck's the matter with you, man? It's just a dead fuckin' gook."

Jesse looked contemptuously at the young PFC. "I don't think you'd spit in his face if he was alive, so you ain't gonna do it while he's dead."

"What's yer fuckin' problem, man?"

"Assholes like you – that's my problem. You feel like a badass, spittin' on a dead man? Does it make you feel like a big shot or somethin'? Why don't you spit on me, asshole?"

The corporal squad leader stepped between Jesse and the PFC. "All right, Ducat, knock off the shit." He turned to Jesse. "Sorry about the boot. I guess it makes him feel like a real hero."

Nervously, Jesse wiped his face to clear the water from his eyes. "Yeah, well, tell him it ain't necessary. Just bein' here is enough to be a hero."

A lance corporal approached from the bush and placed a radio on the muddy ground at his squad leader's feet.

Mud looked at his PRC-10. "Goddamn! Did you guys have to do that?"

The squad leader looked at the mangled metal and broken knobs. "Sorry as hell about that, but we thought you guys was gooks."

Disgustedly, Mud picked up what was left of his radio and slung it on his back. He looked at Jesse. "Well, what now?"

Jesse took a quick look at the bodies and shivered involuntarily. He closed his eyes and tried to erase the memory forever from his mind. He turned to the squad leader before opening them. "Can you guys take care of the bodies? We've gotta get back to Alpha Company and report to the skipper."

"Yeah, go ahead, but I need to know your name for the report."

"Langley. Jesse. Forward observer from 81's attached to Alpha One-Four. PFC Robert Whitman is my radio operator. And thanks. I owe ya one."

"What say we call it square?" smiled the lanky corporal.

"Later," said Jesse as he move into the brush, Mud close behind.

"Keep yer ass low."

"You too."

Mud and Jesse found their way to the muddy road where corpsmen attended to the casualties and leaders counted the survivors. They found Wellington somewhat indignant but not much the worse for wear. Mud untied the short leash from the tree and placed the soaking bird upon his battered radio. "That's all it's good for now is a goddamn perch for a hair-brained rooster."

Jesse laughed as Mud slipped on the roadway, sprawling on his stomach and sending Wellington screeching to the wet clay, their recent ordeal temporarily forgotten. He assisted Mud to his feet and they sloshed up the road in search of Lieutenant Malcolm.

Lieutenant Malcolm rested beneath a large tree in a futile effort to escape the downpour. Jesse smiled as he and Mud approached the company commander's position. "May we join you under your private tree, Skipper?"

Malcolm returned the smile. "Be my guest. I was wondering if Charlie Company missed you until I heard 'em screaming over the radio that they found your Prick-10 and no bodies."

Jesse continued to smile. "Well, Sir, I'll guarantee you they gave it one helluva try – makin' bodies out of us I mean."

"What the hell were you doing up there anyway?"

"To be honest about it, Skipper, I wasn't sure of our position and we were looking for a landmark."

"You must have found it. The guns were right on target. What the hell did you use for a landmark?"

"A cliff."

"A cliff?"

"Yessir."

"How in the hell did you know which cliff you were looking at in this soup?"

"I just figured that we had to be at the one I was lookin' at on the map. With this lousy rain, we couldn't have made it far enough west to be at any of the others."

Malcolm raised an eyebrow.

"What the hell? It worked," said Jesse.

Malcolm shook his head. "Next time you move out like that, notify comm before you get into the impact area."

"Yessir."

"Now that you know where in the hell we are, why don't you tell me, so I can tell battalion. You seem to be the only man in the battalion who has any idea which country we're in. If my memory serves me correctly, this isn't the first time this has happened."

Jesse shrugged. "Who's keepin' count? You got any dry cigarettes?"

Malcolm shook his head. "I haven't got anything that's dry."

Jesse pulled out his plastic cigarette pack carrier. He dug inside until he located a cigarette dry enough to light. "What's the scoop, Skipper? Did we win? Do we still have to make the first objective today?"

"Yes and yes. We suffered seven casualties, four of 'em were from Alpha, but we burned the VC for about ten or twelve."

"Is Thunder okay?" asked Jesse as he attempted in vain to ignite his cigarette.

"Not a scratch. He's about a hundred yards up the trail, on the left flank."

Jesse sucked hard on his moist cigarette. "How in the hell are we supposed to make the first objective in this weather, and stoppin' to fight the gooks?"

"That's what the old man wants, so that's what we gotta do."

"That figures. Why don't someone give him a toy soldier set so he can move 'em around without worryin' about the gooks and the weather?"

Malcolm lowered his voice so that none but Jesse and Mud could hear his words of chastisement. "He's your commanding officer, Indio, and these men here respect you. What you say carries a lot of weight. I don't want to hear that kind of talk from you again. Is that clear?"

Jesse spoke softly. "How about if I say it so no one else can hear it?"

Malcolm couldn't suppress a smile. "That's enough, you shitbird. You got my drift. Now, show me our position on the map."

The column moved tiredly forward as the rain continued to pour down and darkness crept upon the land without the lengthening of shadows. Jesse turned to Mud, who had shortened the distance between them to less than five paces.

"Goddamn, Mud, one grenade gets us all."

"I can't see a damn thing. How the hell is the whole battalion gonna stay together?"

"We ain't much longer. If they keep this up, we're gonna be sittin' ducks. Our only consolation is that we've only got about half a mile to go."

"Hell, it'll be pitch dark by then."

"Yeah, I know. We already passed up our best shot to stop for the night back down the trail about a mile. We can't stop here, and by the time we get to the objective we won't know how many gooks we're sleepin' with."

"Ain't there somethin' we can do about that ignern't battalion commander?"

"Yeah, we can surrender his ass to the gooks, but they probably don't want him either."

Mud looked at his hands in the fading light. "My goddamn hands look like white prunes – you know – like when you've been swimming too long."

"Yeah, I know. Just think of what your feet must look like."

"Shit, I gave up on my feet months ago."

Above the muffling sound of the rain, they heard the small arms fire. It seemed to emanate from the approximate position of the battalion point.

"Shit, here we go again!" shouted Mud as he made for the cover of the trees on his right.

They remained in the trees for a full fifteen minutes without hearing another shot. Finally, the word to move out filtered down the line and the column reformed in the semi-darkness, hampered by the torrential rain. The enemy had achieved his purpose; the Americans would arrive at their destination well after dark. Communication and continuity would be difficult. They would be susceptible to an attack.

"It's gonna be a long night, Mud," muttered Jesse as they stepped onto the slippery clay road.

Were it not for the rain, Jesse would have fallen asleep walking. The rain not only made that seemingly difficult task impossible, it also rendered breathing quite difficult.

"Jesus. Do you suppose this is the beginning of forty days and nights of rain?" Mud mumbled as they trudged through the slime.

"I don't think it would take forty days of this to get the job done. More like a week or two," answered Jesse.

A voice from the darkness in front of Jesse whispered, "Hold up and dig in. Pass it on."

Jesse turned and repeated the order to Mud, who in turn did the same to the man behind him. Soon the muffled sounds of entrenching tools striking the resilient clay soil filled the ridgelines with a dull thud, followed by a sucking, oozing sound as the elastic ground was pulled away from itself by the steel blades.

Jesse didn't carry an entrenching tool, nor was he inclined to dig in where ordered to do so.

"Save your strength, Mud. There's plenty of cover if we need it. If something happens, we're gonna have to move to the skipper's position to use his radio, so there ain't no sense settin' up housekeepin' here."

Mud nodded in the darkness. "Makes sense to me. Damn hole'd fill up with water faster'n you could bail it out anyway."

"I'm gonna move back down the trail and parlay with the skipper. I wanna make sure he's got the dope for illumination if we get hit. Be back in a few minutes."

Ten minutes later he returned and sat next to Mud in the darkness. He leaned close so that he wouldn't have to raise his voice to be heard over the rain. "Looks like another winner for our battalion commander. We got a hundred percent alert tonight and business as usual tomorrow."

"If I ever live long enough to be a civilian again and if I ever see that fuckin' Colonel, I'm gonna kick his ass clear up around his shoulders," offered Mud.

Before Jesse could form a reply the enemy opened fire. It became clear from the onset they were a large, well-armed force. As Jesse and Mud huddled behind a large tree, the unmistakable sound of a fifty-caliber machine gun was clearly audible above the rain and the clatter of other small arms, the heavy tracers pointing red beams of death and destruction at anything before them. Soon the night was filled with the explosions of mortar rounds. The ground shook and seemed to roll as the enemy rounds impacted inside the battalion.

"Shit – eighty-two's!" exclaimed Jesse as an exploding round covered them with debris. There was that damned ringing in his ears again. He raised his head to observe the tracers from the enemy's heavy machine gun. "C'mon, Mud, let's get to the skipper's radio."

Mud followed in the darkness as Jesse stepped out. Their progress was impeded by the explosions of the Soviet-made eighty-two mm mortar rounds as they exploded randomly on or near the dirt road.

It took only a few minutes to arrive at Lieutenant Malcolm's position.

"Skipper. It's Indio and Mud. Can we call in a mission?"

"I've got illumination on the way," answered Malcolm.

"I was thinkin' about HE, Skipper. I think I know where they've set up that fifty."

An illumination round burst overhead, casting its erie glow upon the landscape. Malcolm looked at his radio operator and nodded at Mud. "Give him the radio."

Mud knelt beside the radio operator and accepted the handset. Quickly he changed radio frequency and contacted the mortar platoon. Repeating Jesse's words, he called in the fire mission and waited. He lifted his mouth from the handset and reported, "On the way."

"Roger on the way. Wait." Jesse peered through his field glasses. The round impacted on the ridgeline, about seven hundred yards from his position. He turned to Mud, smiling broadly. "Cease fire. End of mission."

Malcolm raised an eyebrow. "You change your mind?"

"No, Sir. We got lucky. That first round landed right on top of him."

"How can you be so sure in this light?"

"He was firing a burst when the round hit. The tracers stopped and I actually saw a piece of the damn gun flyin' through the air, outlined by the flash of the explosion."

Malcolm smiled. "I can't believe it."

"Listen up for 'im, Skipper. You won't hear anymore from that gun tonight. And that's a guarantee."

Bullets cut through the trees around the kneeling and squatting marines at the company commander's radio position. The enemy mortars continued to wreak havoc along the hastily constructed line.

Lying flat on his chest in three inches of water, Jesse said, "When do we assault their position, Skipper? We got their fifty and, if we stay here much longer, their heavy mortars are gonna rip us up."

Malcolm hesitated only an instant before retrieving the radio handset from Mud. He shouted to his radio operator, "Get me battalion's frequency."

Malcolm spoke into the handset. "Pied Piper. This is Pied Piper Alpha. Over."

A crackly voice answered, "This is Pied Piper. Go ahead, Alpha."

"We have neutralized the enemy's fifty caliber gun. Suggest we display the colors," said Malcolm, using the operation's assigned code phrase for assault.

The voice on the other end of the radio wave hesitated. "Stand by, Alpha."

Another voice spoke. They all knew it was Colonel Soliman. "Alpha, this is Pied Piper Six. Negative on your last transmission. Do you copy? Over."

A mortar round exploded only fifty yards away as Malcolm keyed up to speak. When the noise faded into the night, he said, "Be advised, Pied Piper, that we have neutralized the enemy heavy machine gun and our position is untenable due to heavy mortar fire. Request permission to display our colors."

Quickly, Soliman's voice filled the airwaves. "Negative! Do you understand? Over."

Malcolm answered. "Roger. Alpha out."

As he handed the handset to his radio operator, he looked at Jesse and Mud and shrugged in the artificial light provided by the marine mortars. "The Old Man says we sit this one out."

Jesse was about to give his opinion of the colonel's order when voices carried down the line. "Fix bayonets! Here they come!"

The command was repeated over and over. The sounds of bayonets being jammed onto rifle barrels filled the night air, the distinctive clicks breaking the muffling effect of the rain momentarily.

"I don't even own a bayonet for this M-1," muttered Jesse.

Small arms fire erupted from the marine line. Pandemonium ensued. Forward in the column, Jesse could hear the shouts and curses of the marines as they met the enemy charge head-on. Grenades exploded and rifles fired in rapid succession. Then the rifle fire became only a few sporadic rounds. Jesse knew the marines forward of his position were engaged in hand-to-hand combat. He shivered involuntarily at the thought.

For what seemed like an eternity he waited while the enemy tried to break the center of the marine line. What appeared to be forever to Jesse and those near him, was in reality less than five minutes. Soon, the small arms fire began to increase. Voices shouted. "They're runnin'!"

"We beat 'em!"

"Corpsman!"

"Oh, God! Help me!"

"Watch the left flank! ..."

Jesse tensed, waiting for an assault on his position, but it didn't come. Instead, the enemy mortars opened fire again.

Malcolm's radio operator was slightly injured by a falling tree but held onto his radio and waved back attempts to check his ribs and chest for broken bones.

Jesse cursed. He didn't know which was worse, the incoming mortars or the prospect of a hand-to-hand encounter with the VC. He decided on the mortars.

Malcolm called his squad leaders for a casualty report as soon as it was practical to ascertain the information.

Jesse shouted above the roar of the incoming mortars. "Skipper, we gotta find out where those gook mortars are."

Malcolm nodded and spoke into his radio.

Mud looked desperately at Jesse. "What the hell we gonna do? Five billion troops on this operation and we sit here and let the gooks blow the shit outa us with mortars. That's crazy!"

Frustration and anger welled inside of Jesse. "I shoulda shot that bastard when I had the chance on *Oregon*." His reference was clearly to Colonel Soliman.

The incoming enemy fire ceased. Shouts to the rear of Jesse's position foretold another enemy attack. The scene of only a few moments earlier was repeated. The VC engaged the marines in hand-to-hand combat. Once again, Jesse and the Alpha Company center were spared contact. Once again the marines successfully repulsed the attack.

Malcolm motioned to Jesse. "Thunder's on the radio. He's got the gook mortars spotted. Talk to him and get their position."

Jesse crawled through the mud to Malcolm's outstretched hand and accepted the handset. He keyed up. "Hey, Thunder, where are they? Over."

Thunder's voice answered. "They're in the draw behind that ridge on the column's left flank. From your position figure about twelve hundred yards and three fingers to the right of due west from where you stand. Now, you figure out where that is on the map and let'er rip. I'll be standin' by to adjust. Over."

"Roger. Standby."

Jesse studied his map in the artificial light of the illumination rounds overhead. It wasn't the best light he could hope for but he wasn't about to use a flashlight. He turned to Mud and gave him the information needed for a fire mission. Mud called in the information to the 81 Platoon over Malcolm's radio and they waited. Mud switched to Alpha's frequency for a report from Thunder.

The round impacted. Thunder's voice crackled over the radio. "Indio. From your position, go left about three hundred yards and add about two hundred. Over."

Jesse repeated Thunder's instructions. "Roger left three hundred, add two

405

hundred."

Mud called in the change to FDC. Shortly the round impacted on the other side of the ridge and Thunder called in another correction. "We're close. Right one hundred, drop one hundred and let 'er rip."

"Roger, right one hundred, drop one hundred. Fire for effect," acknowledged Jesse.

The muffled sounds of the marine mortars exploding in the adjacent draw comforted Jesse and those around him. If the enemy mortars could be rendered out of service, the battalion would not suffer as many casualties, nor would the VC be so likely to attack without their mortar support.

Thunder's voice came over the radio. "I think we've hurt 'em. It looked like we were right on target. Advise Alpha Actual that I'm gonna hold this position until ordered to do otherwise. Over."

"Roger, One-One. Will advise. Whiskey Alpha out." Jesse turned to Malcolm and relayed Thunder's message.

The remainder of the night was spent on one hundred percent alert as the marines waited for the VC to attack. Dawn crawled from behind its curtain of darkness with little fanfare as the rain continued to pour down upon the jungle. For reasons known only to them, the VC had not attacked again that night.

Mud rubbed his eyes in the chalk-like dawn. He looked down at Wellington and then to Jesse. He spoke to the latter, "Say, Indio, would you mind puttin' in a requisition, in triplicate, for a pair of frog feet and some gills?"

Jesse smiled. "It's another glorious day in the Corps, Mud, ol' buddy. Quit yer bitchin'. Not everybody has the opportunity to serve their country in such a fashionable manner, you know."

"How in the hell do you keep from just sayin' 'fuck this shit'?"

"What good would it do?"

Mud thought about it a moment. "Yeah, I guess you're right. Nobody really wants to hear that crap anyway. You got any chow?"

Jesse pulled his cigarettes from his pocket and offered the plastic pack holder. Mud shivered. "No thanks. I'll wait for lunch."

Men moved about, up and down the column. Lieutenant Malcolm spoke to battalion over the radio. When he finished his conversation he turned to Jesse. "Indio, have Mud report to the rear. Choppers are bringing in another radio with chow. Just turn in the old one for salvage."

"Aye aye, Sir." He turned to Mud who nodded as he stood in ankle-deep water.

Mud handed the rooster's leash to Jesse, stepped onto the trail and walked to the rear.

Late that afternoon, as the battalion dug in for the coming night, Mud wiggled his toes in bright sunshine. His boots sat nearby, looking like relics of a bygone war, all curled up at the toes and brittle. The sun had made its presence known less than an hour before, amid cheers and shouts of hundreds of water-weary marines.

"Damn, that feels good," remarked Mud as he wiggled his toes again and again.

Jesse too had his boots off. He looked at a nearby ridge line as he exhaled his cigarette smoke. "You know what this means, don't you?"

Forever Patriots

"What what means?"

"Stoppin' this early in the day, so far from where we're supposed to be."

"Yeah, goddamnit, it means we get a break for a change."

"We'll pay for it tomorrow."

"What the hell are you talkin' about?"

Jesse took another drag. "Well, if Colonel Shithead stays true to form, he'll try to make up the lost distance tomorrow if the weather holds. You know he's not going to have the whole operation held up because of *his* battalion. He don't care if he kills every man in the outfit, so long as it doesn't look bad for him."

"How many you figure we lost last night?"

"Got no idea, but it was more than we should have, even if it was only one man."

Mud rubbed his chin and neck. "I sure could use a shave."

"It'll be easier to live with in a few more days. It's that first two or three days that's a real bitch."

Mud pondered Jesse's statement. "Yeah, that's the truth. I wonder why?"

"Probably 'cause the beard gets long enough so it doesn't stick you in the neck like a knife whenever you move your head. It kinda limbers up a bit I guess."

"What the hell, I guess I'll just grow a beard like one of them sailors on sea-duty until we get outa the bush."

"Dream on. Colonel Shithead will have us standin' inspection at high noon in dress blues in a day or two."

Mud turned pensive. "Indio, what the hell are we doin' out here? What are we accomplishin'?"

"I wish I knew, Mud."

"Maybe them protesters back home are right and we shouldn't even be here."

Jesse's eyes narrowed. "Those goddamn protesters are the biggest reason we aren't marchin' to Hanoi. The politicians are afraid of the long-haired hippie bastards. If it wasn't for the politicians controlling the generals, we'd probably be drinkin' Panther Piss in Hanoi, waitin' for a ride home. If you're gonna start talkin' treason to me, maybe you better go back to the 'toon. I'll get a radio operator I don't have to worry about goin' hippie on me."

Mud looked up at him, a combination of hurt and anger in his eyes, tears ready to fall. "Fuck you, you ungrateful bastard! I'll go back to the 'toon all right, but it won't be because I'm a hippie or a traitor or any of that bullshit! It'll be because you aren't worth my damn time!" He fumbled for his socks.

Instantly, Jesse was sorry for what he had said. He stood and walked the few feet to Mud, kneeling beside him. "Wait a second, Mud. You're right. I ain't worth your time, but the outfit needs a good FO operator. I didn't mean any of that stuff about you bein' a traitor or hippie. I just lose it when I think of those bastards back in the States bitchin' about the very thing that gives 'em the right to bitch. I did you wrong, Mud." He leaned forward, sticking out his chin. "Go ahead, man, take a shot. I owe you. I'm sorry. That was a dumb thing to say."

Mud looked through moist eyes. His voice broke as he spoke. "You sorry bastard. I oughta take you up on that."

"Go ahead. It's fair. Take a shot." He protruded his chin further.

"Piss on you. I'll take my shot when you're not expecting it. That'll be worth hangin' around for."

407

Jesse looked into Mud's eyes and felt his tears welling to the surface. He turned away. "Thanks, Mud." He stood and resumed his position by his soggy boots.

Mud said, "Nobody else would put up with your ass. And despite your lousy personality, yer not all that bad an FO. You need my guidance from time to time to keep you from blowin' yer own head off though."

Jesse was grateful for Mud's response but, knowing the man, he should have expected it. He stood and moved into the jungle near the trail. "I'm takin' a stroll. Holler if the skipper wants me."

"You goin' barefoot?" asked Mud, smiling.

Jesse turned and looked at him, then down at his feet. He had been so upset by their argument he had forgotten he was barefoot. No sense letting Mud know. He moved his gaze from his feet back to Mud. "Yeah, godamnit, I'm goin' barefoot."

In the pre-dawn darkness the marines moved out. Marching intervals were shortened until it was light enough for better visibility, but the battalion had to get an early start if it was to attain its objective for the day.

A fifty-percent alert during the night allowed most of the men at least four hours sleep and, while they could have used more, it was enough to renew their strength and determination, at least for another day.

The sun beat down upon the column like a blowtorch almost from the first ten minutes of daylight. The moisture in the air and on the ground only tended to add to the greenhouse effect. Most of the men experienced what was called "prickly-heat" as a result of the combined effects of the sun and humidity. The body felt as though a thousand white-hot needles were being jabbed into it in all areas of the anatomy, but especially in the crotch, armpits and around the waist. It was almost unbearable.

To make matters worse, the march was forced and, under the circumstances, almost at breakneck speed. Men loaded down with forty or fifty pounds of gear and ammo were forced to march with undo haste through enemy territory in a stifling heat that would wither the strongest of souls in much lighter clothing, without the added weight.

After four hours they took their first break – fifteen minutes – then onward to the objective.

Jesse spelled Mud carrying the radio several times during the course of the morning. As Mud walked behind Jesse, carrying only his pistol and Wellington, he muttered, "Who the hell can operate the point at this speed?"

Puffing under the load of his rifle, pistol, cartridge belt, map pouch, field glasses, and Mud's radio, Jesse grunted, "Nobody."

The marine in front of Jesse in the column began to waver. He staggered to the side of the trail and fell onto his face, unconscious before he hit the ground. Jesse knelt beside him. He removed the man's pack and helmet, opened the front of his utility jacket and poured water from his canteen upon the neck and chest of the downed man. "Corpsman! Corpsman up!" he shouted.

Marines were feeling the heat and lack of nourishment all up and down the column. The few corpsmen could not keep up with the demand for their services. Soon they too could scarce keep the pace. The column came to a ragged halt about eleven A.M. The men found what shade they could and prayed for rain or wind or helicopters or anything that would halt the forced march. The one thing they didn't pray for to cease the forward movement was an enemy attack.

First came the eighty-two mm mortars and recoilless rifles, then the V.C. The marines attacked the attackers and met them midway in their assault. Jesse joined in the assault, ordering Mud to remain with the headquarters section. He met Thunder and his squad as they charged headlong into the trees on the left flank. Adrenalin mixed with confusion as the opposing forces joined in close-in fighting. Jesse had no time to fear as he fired several rounds into moving bushes and dark uniforms on the run. It wasn't much of a contest. They met the V.C. with such a ferocity the enemy was repulsed in short order.

The marines suffered eight dead and tweny-four wounded in the assault, while the enemy suffered seventy-three dead, twenty-eight confirmed wounded, and fourteen captured.

Later, when Mud came upon Jesse, the latter was sharing one of his cigarettes with a wounded V.C. prisoner. The smaller man looked up at Mud's face fearfully.

"What the hell 'r' you doin', Indio? Givin' comfort to the enemy or what?"

Jesse looked up from the prisoner. "Howdy, Mud. This here is my prisoner. I didn't have time to reload, so I had to work him over pretty good with the rifle. I damn near killed him in the process. I guess you might say I'm just tryin' to show 'im there's no hard feelin's."

Mud shook his head. He scrutinized the battered enemy soldier. "Yeah." He smiled. "From the looks of 'im, I guess that's the least you could do."

The remainder of the day was spent digging in and collecting intelligence from the prisoners. Several weapons were captured. This, combined with the heavy enemy loss, was apparently sufficient to exonerate Colonel Soliman from any derogatory or snide remarks that may have been made by other ranking officers. He didn't seem quite so concerned with arriving at a specific location on the map at a certain time. The truth of the matter was that not a single unit involved in the operation was on schedule. Soliman's command had been closer than all of the others when they had made their counterattack.

An hour before dark, Jesse sat on a rock, writing in his tablet as Mud prepared a C-ration meal with the aid of some C-3 explosive. Lieutenant Malcolm strolled up to Jesse and stood, looking down at him.

"Plotting missions?"

Jesse looked up and smiled. "No, Sir. Just makin' up a menu."

"A menu?"

"Yessir, a menu. I'm gonna pull this thing out and order from it every time I have to eat chow. At least this way I can pretend I'm gettin' somethin' decent to eat."

Malcolm appeared interested. He knelt next to Jesse. "What do you have on that menu?"

Proudly, Jesse handed the handwritten menu to his commanding officer. Malcolm studied the extensive menu for several moments, then handed the document reverently back to its owner. "I can't order from your place. I didn't see any grits, or black-eyed peas, or corn bread."

Jesse shook his head with a disdainful look and turned the piece of paper over. He began to add items to his menu. "Jesus Christ. I've got the most extensive menu in the Nam and you complain. Okay, okay. I'll add some of that down home, southern cookin' to the cuisine."

Malcolm smiled. "Let me know when you're open for business." He patted

409

Stoney Livingston

Jesse on the shoulder and walked away.

Five minutes later,Thunder strode into view. "Hey, Indio. Mud. What's happenin'?"

Jesse looked up from his completed menu. "Not much around here. How'd it go with you this morning?"

"I can honestly say I've had more fun other places. I lost a damn good team leader."

"Who?" asked Mud.

"Wise. Damn good man."

Jesse winced. He knew Lance Corporal Wise, as he did most of the men in Thunder's squad. "How'd he get it?"

"Gut shot, then bayoneted. I came up on the little gook bastard while he was still stabbin', and dusted 'im, but it was too late for Wise."

"Sorry." Jesse became distant as he often did when he thought of the dead.

Thunder shrugged and quickly changed the subject. "Skipper tells me you didn't do too bad yourself."

Jesse lit a cigarette. "Depends upon your point of view I guess."

"Skipper says you got more confirmed kills than my whole squad."

"Hell, I can't say I got any kills for sure. He'd say anything to piss you off. You know how them Yankees are." They both knew Malcolm was from North Carolina.

Thunder laughed. "Yeah, I know how them Yankees are. He tells me you're makin' up a menu. Whatcha got good to eat on it? I'm starvin'."

"What d'ya want?"

"Chili and beans, Sonora style."

Jesse smiled. "Item number one on the menu." He tossed Thunder a can of beefsteak and potatoes. "Here, be my guest."

Thunder accepted. "I heard they're bringin' the New Jersey outa mothballs," he said as he broke off a small chunk of C-3 to heat his rations.

"What the hell for?" asked Mud.

Jesse answered. "If she'd a been sittin' off the coast last night, we coulda dug in and gone to sleep. Her sixteen-inchers woulda blown the gooks into Cambodia." He thought for a moment of a sailor named Lewis on the USS Breckinridge.

Mud nodded. "Oh. Hey, what else you got on that menu?"

"For you, Mud, straight from the better restaurants in San Francisco, we have Alaskan king crab and all the clams you can eat. May I suggest a bottle of Chardonnay to bring out the flavor?" He thought briefly of Barbara as he mentioned the wine.

"That sounds good to me. What are you havin'?"

"A New York cut with pinto beans and chili and a bottle of Jack Daniels."

*****

Jesse studied his menu as Mud rolled out of his poncho in the early morning light. Lieutenant Malcolm approached. "You got any specials this morning?"

With a broad smile, Jesse glanced at his menu. "Funny you should ask. Our special this mornin' is buttermilk biscuits, two eggs anyway you like 'em, smoked Virginia ham, grits, and a side of red-eye gravy."

"Stop – you're killin' me! I'll take one special."

410

Forever Patriots

Four days had passed since the menu was originated and already it was the talk of the company. Men searched Jesse out just to hear him rattle off the daily special, then they would open their C-rations and pretend to eat the meal so sumptuously described.

*****

At noon, the battalion was lifted out of the jungle by helicopter to the Phu Bai airstrip. As the battalion formed a column for the march to the Phu Bai encampment, Mud said, "Now, can you tell me why in the hell the choppers couldn't have put us down in Phu Bai instead of droppin' us out here so we have to walk for half an hour or more in this heat?"

Jesse hitched up his slung rifle. "That's a really dumb question, Mud. If you wanted to do things logically, you had three or four other branches of the service to choose from. Since you joined the Crotch, you gave up your right to having any question on logic answered."

Mud nodded. "Oh. Yeah, I almost forgot."

The battalion moved out.

Jesse studied the camp as the battalion marched in a column of two's through the compound. He noticed the large tent with a PX sign standing proudly in front of it. He stepped out of the marching column, speaking to Mud over his shoulder, "I'm gonna pick up some cigarettes. I'll catch up."

He walked away from the advancing column.

Inside the expanded PX tent, there were crudely built shelves containing items he had not seen for the better part of six months. There were radios, detergent soap, toiletries, towels, bags of sugar and candy, and row upon row of American cigarettes in cartons. He walked directly to the cigarettes and unrolled his poncho from his cartridge belt. After placing ten cartons of Camels onto his poncho, he carefully folded the corners, picked up his treasure and moved to the plank checkout counter. The starched corporal standing behind the counter looked disinterestedly at Jesse.

Jesse placed a brown ten-dollar bill on the counter. "Smokes still a dollar a carton?"

The corporal stared at him. "I need to see your ration card."

Jesse turned and looked behind him to see who the corporal might be addressing. Seeing no one, he turned back to the corporal. "You talkin' to me?"

"There's no one else in here," came the monotone reply.

"You got it wrong. I don't want any rations. I get more of those than I can handle. I'm just buyin' cigarettes."

"Not without your ration card you're not."

Jesse's confusion turned to impatience. "Okay, if I gotta check out rations just to buy cigarettes, give me a B-1 and two B-3's. Seems like a pretty stupid order to me, but what the hell do I know?"

"Look, buddy, I don't know what fuckin' rock you crawled out from under, but you're not gettin' those cigarettes until I punch your ration card."

Jesse's impatience made the transition to frustration then anger – almost that quickly. Deliberately he unslung the Garand and chambered a round. "Here's my ration card, asshole." He spun on his heel and fired four rounds into the shelves. When he turned to face the corporal, the man was laying on the wooden floor of the tent. Jesse stood on his toes and peered over the counter at him disgustedly, threw

411

Stoney Livingston

the ten-dollar bill onto the counter, re-slung his rifle, picked up his poncho full of cigarettes and said, "I'll be takin' my cigarettes now." His last vision of the interior of the PX tent as he stepped outside was the sight of liquid shampoo dripping into a broken bag of sugar.

In the bright sunlight not a soul was visible as he walked nonchalantly across the compound. A voice shouted, "Hey, Marine! VC in the compound!"

Jesse dropped to a knee, bringing his rifle to his side, his poncho falling to the ground. His eyes searched the compound. He saw nothing. He heard no gunfire. He suddenly realized that his rifle fire in the PX tent had probably been mistaken for enemy fire. "Damn." He re-slung his rifle, picked up his poncho, and walked briskly to the outer perimeter on the north, where he knew Alpha Company would be set up.

Twenty minutes into the poker game, the runner approached. "Hey, Indio, Skipper wants to see you in the CP tent."

Jesse folded his cards and moved out, determined to face the wrath of Malcolm. When he entered the small CP tent, he took note of the two MPs standing at either side of Malcolm's field desk. "You wanted to see me, Sir?" He watched the MPs carefully.

"You been to the PX, Indio?"

Jesse cleared his throat. "As a matter-of-fact, Sir, I did stop by just for a minute, to buy some smokes."

Malcolm shook his head. "Anything unusual happen?"

"Well, kinda. This corporal runnin' the place didn't wanna sell me any cigarettes at first but we came to an understanding and, in the end, he decided to let me have 'em."

Malcolm suppressed his need to smile. "Goddamnit, Indio, this isn't the bush. The base commander wants your ass hung on a flagpole. I've convinced him that you're not a nut case and that I need you in this outfit. We're pulling out of here tomorrow, so he's agreed to forget about the whole matter if you pay $207.50 in damages and apologize to the corporal."

"$207.50? Hell, the whole damn PX ain't worth that much. I just fired a few rounds to get his attention. They make it sound like a direct hit with a one-five-five."

"You got the money?"

Reluctantly, Jesse replied. "Yessir, I got the money. How about if I throw in another fifty bucks and we forget the apology to that rear echelon corporal?"

Malcolm turned his face slightly to hide the smile he could no longer suppress. He turned back to face Jesse, his lips showing his best stern look. "You get your ass down there and take care of this matter. These two MPs will accompany you to see that there is no further trouble."

Jesse looked at one of the MPs, then the other. "You really think two of 'em is enough?"

One of the MPs made a slight move toward Jesse then thought better of it and held his position. Jesse smiled. "Just kiddin'."

Malcolm held out his hand and snapped his finger and thumb. "Give me the rifle."

"Aw, Skipper...."

"Give it to me."

Jesse un-slung the Garand and slowly handed it to Malcolm's outstretched hand. He turned to leave.

412

"The pistol," said Malcolm in a monotone.

He removed his pistol and placed it on the field desk.

"The grenades," ordered Malcolm, still in monotone.

Jesse removed the hand grenades from his utility jacket. Laying them on the desk, he said, "Skipper, don't ask me to leave my knife. I give you my word there won't be any trouble from me, but I'm not leavin' my knife."

Malcolm looked into Jesse's eyes, then at the MPs, and nodded. "Okay. Keep your knife, but I don't want any trouble. We're only gonna be here a short while and I've got a lot of information to pass on. So do your duty and get back here. Your weapons will be on my desk."

Jesse left, an MP at each side, watching him distrustfully, but neither speaking.   The starched corporal looked with a start at the unshaven Jesse when he entered the PX, his first instant of fear replaced by an air of cockiness when he realized Jesse was unarmed and accompanied by two MPs.

"Well, if it ain't Mr. Bad-Ass," said the corporal.

Jesse looked at the soft and pale skin of the corporal. It was beyond his ability to take the verbal abuse silently. He motioned to the two MPs with a nod. "Let's make sure we both understand how this is. These two MPs here aren't what's keepin' me from kickin' your ass. I made a promise to my company commander. That's all that's savin' you. But he's an understanding man and, if you get too carried away, he'll understand why you got your ass kicked."

The corporal looked nervously at the MPs, then at the bone-handled knife on Jesse's hip. "You owe the U.S. government $207.50," he said.

Jesse found a small paper note for fifty cents and added the two hundred and seven dollars. He peeled off an extra fifty dollars and placed it on the counter with the rest of the money. "That's my apology. Take it or leave it.." He turned and walked through the tent flaps, the MPs right behind him, the corporal scooping up the money.

Thunder outlined the briefing Jesse had missed while taking care of business at the PX. He displayed his new ration card. "This is what that corporal wanted. Seems like some of the rear echelon poges was buyin' goods and sellin' 'em to the black market for a nice little profit. So now, when you buy something, they stamp it on your ration card. That way a guy can't buy a hundred cartons of cigarettes or a dozen radios and that kinda thing."

Jesse stared at the white card. There were certain items pre-printed on it, apparently those things in demand on the black market.

Thunder pointed to one of several CTN CIG on the edge of the card. "See. When you buy a carton of smokes, they punch the card.

"Great," said Jesse.

"That ain't the worst of it. This afternoon we're gonna be issued flak jackets."

Jesse's face took on a look of horror. "You gotta be kiddin'?"

"I wish to hell I was. But never fear. All is not yet lost. They don't have enough for the whole battalion yet. I figure you and me will be busy when they're givin' 'em out and, since we're leavin' for the field in the morning, they may never catch up with us."

Jesse smiled. "My-my, but you do have a devious mind my friend. Where we going tomorrow?"

413

Stoney Livingston

"They weren't real specific. We're just gonna go out in the field and stay there, runnin' patrols and kickin' ass, or gettin' ours kicked, until they decide to bring us back in."

"Sounds like a helluva plan. Who thought that one up?"

"Probably your friend and mine, Colonel Shithead."

"What other tidbits of good news you got?"

"We survey boots and uniforms this afternoon. This may be your last chance to get some new duds for a while." He reached into his map pocket and produced several letters. "Here. I picked up your mail at mail call. You were real popular today. Hell, I got a couple myself."

Jesse accepted his mail. "Thanks." He leafed through them. There was one from his mother. He read that one first as he sat in the bright afternoon sun, seeking no shade.

When he finished reading his mother's letter he looked up to Thunder who read his own mail ten feet away. "It looks like the protesters got my mother all fired up. She's fixin' to go into town and kick some hippie ass."

Thunder smiled. "Seems like my younger brother is of the same mind. He and some of his buddies are planning a trip to Berkeley. I'd hate to miss that one." He looked into the distance pensively. "You know, it's a real bitch when you gotta fight the enemy at home while you're doin' your damndest to fight 'em over here."

Jesse agreed. "I think the ones at home are worse than the ones here. At least the ones at home are enjoyin' a way of life these people can't even imagine. They oughta come over here and spend a few years. Let 'em see what Ho Chi Minh and his pals are doin' to these people."

"Hell, you can't tell those do-gooders anything. They already know it all. Just ask one of 'em."

"I wonder what it's like back in the World now. Things must have changed a lot." Jesse furrowed his brow,

"Makes me wanna stay over here. At least the average Vietnamese isn't out to have us leave the country," said Thunder.

"We as Americans can fix that. Americans can be the biggest bunch of jerks when they go to a foreign country. War only makes it worse. Pretty soon, all the Vietnamese will want us to leave 'cause they're tired of our 'holier – than – thou' attitude."

"Yeah, you're right. I wonder why the average American can't treat people with the respect they expect for themselves?"

"Never have been able to figure that one out. I've seen some real bad ones. You know – the kind of guys that are the shitbirds of an outfit – act like they own the world when they're in someone else's country? Hell, they couldn't get the time of day in the States, but if they go to Japan or the Philippines, they act like those people owe 'em an ass-kissin'," said Jesse.

"Yeah, I know what you mean. It makes me wanna puke."

"Hey, Thunder, when you gonna go on R&R?"

"Maybe when things slow down a little bit."

"The way things are going that may be never."

Thunder smiled. "Yeah, but think how much R&R they'll owe me."

"I think I could use some but I don't wanna walk out on the outfit until we're back in a place like Sherwood Forest."

"As long as we have this glory-hungry bastard for a battalion C.O., we're

414

Forever Patriots

never gonna see another permanent camp," said Thunder.

"I'm beginning to think you're right."

"Who else did you get mail from?" asked Thunder.

"My cousin Mike from Safford," answered Jesse as he folded the letter open.

Thunder moved closer. "He say anything about the copper mines moving in? I heard from Benny that one of the big mining companies discovered a whole bunch of copper around there. He says it may be bigger than Bisbee or San Manuel."

"No kiddin'?" Jesse read the letter aloud. There was no mention of the copper so recently discovered in the area.

"Who's Susan?" asked Thunder as he peeked at the letter.

"She's my first cousin on the Greenfield side."

"Greenfield? You mean Susan Greenfield is your first cousin?"

"Yeah, we almost grew up together. Why?"

"Why? Hell, she's only the best lookin' gal in the whole damn valley, that's why."

Jesse laughed. "I hadn't given it much thought, but you're right – she ain't all that bad lookin'."

"Jesus Christ, man – introduce me!"

"I haven't written to her since I've been here. I don't even remember her address." He paused. "I guess I could send her a letter through Mike."

Thunder was obviously excited at the prospect of writing Susan. "Do it, godamnit! What're you waitin' for? Here's my pencil."

"I've got my own pen. If I didn't know better, I'd say you had the hots for my cousin, you degenerate pervert."

"Me and everybody else in Safford, Thatcher and Pima, and all of the rest of Graham County. Jesus. She's Beautiful! Who the hell would ever believe that I'd have to go to war – ten thousand miles from home – to get introduced to the girl of my dreams."

"Susan?"

"You damn right, Susan."

"I mean, she's good lookin' and all of that, but don't think you're goin' overboard?"

"I suppose you're goin' with somebody who's twice as good lookin'?"

Jesse hesitated. "No, can't say that I'm goin' with anybody. Hell, how can anybody say he's goin' with anybody over here?"

"You know what I mean – a girl back in the States or somethin'."

"Naw, not really. Most of the gals I went to school with are up and married by now. I know a gal in Hawaii, but she ain't no steady or anything like that."

"Hawaii? I heard they was gonna make Hawaii an R&R stop. Mainly for officers and married men. Maybe you could get the skipper to see to it you got Hawaii on yer R&R, bein' as you know somebody there."

"Fat chance." Jesse thought about it for a moment. "Hell, I've got a buddy stationed at Camp Pendleton. He could probably find a way over there and we could raise all kinds a hell. That ain't such a bad idea, Thunder. If you haven't got your R&R by the time they get around to me maybe we could hit Pearl together."

"Not me. I'm not goin' back to the States until we've won this chickenshit war."

Stoney Livingston

"That could be awhile."

"I'm prepared to wait it out."

"The way I see it, it's a long way from over. Besides, we'd just be goin' to live it up a little bit. Nobody said anything about stayin'."

"You go. Tell me all about it when you get back. In the meantime, write that good-lookin' cousin of yours for me. Lie a little bit and say I'm okay."

Jesse looked at him. "You *are* okay."

Thunder looked at the flat terrain surrounding the base. "I wonder what kind of country we're goin' to tomorrow?"

"I'm sure it'll be pastoral and serene. Nothin' but a few thousand VC to interrupt your lazy days and nights."

"Hurry up and write that letter so we can go hide somewhere so we don't have to get those damn flak jackets."

Jesse tucked Will's unread letter into his map pocket and said, "I'll write that letter later. Let's get out of here now."

As Jesse and Thunder hid out on the perimeter to avoid the issuance of flak jackets, Jesse dug into his map pocket and pulled out Will's letter. Thunder had a pen and a pad of paper and was writing a letter. Jesse wondered what the hell he was doing here.

CHAPTER EIGHTEEN: THE TRAIL

The battalion was nestled in a large valley along the Hoa My Trail. The dirt road winding through the center of the valley looked small and insignificant when compared to the vastness that surrounded it. Battalion headquarters, with command and medical tents, sat on the south side of the roadway. The rifle companies ringed the hills surrounding the tents, ever watchful for the VC.

The hills were smooth and rolling, the vegetation providing cover for stationary troops but lacking density to hide movements of larger units, giving the marines a false sense of security as they manned their posts. This was more like conventional warfare; more like what most of them had envisioned war would be like. From their positions in the hills around the battalion center, the marines could see a long distance and, should the VC attack at night, mortars could restore vision to almost daylight quality with their illumination rounds.

*****

From his position atop Hill 31, Lance Corporal J.J. Washington surveyed the terrain. He looked down on the battalion aid tent four hundred yards distant as the hot afternoon sun warmed his dark face.

Jesse approached, the chinstrap on his helmet dangling on each side of his face. He squatted next to JJ. "What the hell you thinkin' so hard about, JJ?"

"You wouldn't believe it, man. I was thinkin' about my transfer to Thunder's squad. I'm kinda glad. If I'm ever gonna to win a medal and return to Alabama a hero, it'll best be done as a member of Thunder's squad of misfits. They're the best in the company when it comes to gettin' the job done."

Jesse took a drag on his smoke. "That's a damn sure fact."

" I was a little worried about Thunder's methods at first but, after only two days of working with him, my mind's at ease. These guys work as a team. It don't matter what color your skin is or what part of the country you came from. I think he's about the best damn squad leader in the Nam. It's weird that you and him are from the same part of the country. You're both a lot alike. I've known you longer than Thunder but he's about like you."

"Is that good?" Jesse grinned broadly.

"Could be worse."

"That's nice to know."

"I was just thinkin' how you and Thunder do things. I mean, like how you treat folks."

"How's that, JJ?"

"Well, y'all don't make a big difference outa the black dudes and the white dudes. It's like there ain't no difference."

"Hell, JJ, we both know there's a big difference."

"You do?" Disappointment crept into his voice.

417

Stoney Livingston

"You damn right. It's a well-known fact that darker skin gets hotter'n lighter skin. I bet your skin temperature is at least five degrees hotter'n mine right now." Jesse's grin grew into a large smile.

JJ returned his smile. "You shithead. You had me goin'."

"Speakin' a goin', when you goin' on R&R?"

"I don't know. Probably some time next month. How about you?"

"Don't have the foggiest. But I'm tryin' to talk ol' Thunder into goin' with me if we can swing it. Right now I can't convince 'im that it's the thing to do but, if you and I work on 'im together, I know we can convince 'im that the three of us could raise more hell together than a regiment of NVR. He couldn't pass that up. How about it? You wanna try and swing R&R together if we can pull it off?"

"Are you serious?"

"Is there something I'm missing here? Why the hell shouldn't I be serious?"

JJ pointed to his bare forearm. "You wanna go on R&R with me?"

"Is there something wrong with your arm? You keep rubbin' it with yer finger." He paused. "If the truth were known, I'd rather go with someone wearin' a skirt, but I figure we can find some of those once we hit the beach."

"I'm black, man. Or didn't you notice?"

"That make you a special case, or what?"

"No, man, I mean, you know what I mean. Shit."

"You're startin' to piss me off, JJ. Do us both a favor. Don't ever talk that racial bullshit with me again. If there's anything I can't stand, it's somebody tellin' me what's inside my head. If you wanna be a damn racist, go right on ahead, but don't drag me down there with you. I really ain't got the time for it. You gotta live with the color you were born with, just like me. You pull yer trousers up just like me and yer a man just like me. If we can't be who the hell we are and stay in each other's company, then let me know. I'll still cover yer ass, and I expect you to do the same fer me, but we don't have to talk if you're so dead set on bein' some kinda special case."

"I didn't mean nothin' by it, Indio. It's jus' that no white boy ever asked me to go anywhere with him before."

"I never shot a man till the first time either. So what? Think it over." Jesse stood and walked slowly away.

*****

Thunder approached Jesse and Mud with another man in tow. "Hey, Indio, you got any bacitracin ointment?"

Jesse looked up from his can of hot C-ration coffee. "Yeah, hang on a second." He unsnapped his first aid pouch and withdrew the small tube. "Whatcha got?"

Thunder pointed to the marine at his side. "Damn Cooper here scratched his arm in the bush on Prairie and didn't do anything for it. It may be beyond bacitracin now but I wanna get something on it right away. I'm takin' 'im down to sick bay right now."

Jesse moved to Cooper's outstretched arm and looked at the festering wound. He looked into Cooper's face. "You're in deep shit, Coop. I ain't no doctor, but it looks to me like gangrene." He put his nose next to the wound. "Whew!" He jerked his head away from the stench.

418

"That does it," said Thunder. "I knew it. That's two opinions, Coop. Did you hear me say anything to Indio about gangrene? He came up with it on his own, didn't he?"

Tears filled Cooper's eyes. "Godamnit, Thunder, I didn't wanna leave the squad fer no damn little scratch."

Thunder shook his head. "C'mon, let's get on down to sick bay." He turned to Jesse. "Thanks, Indio. I couldn't convince his sorry-ass that he was in serious trouble with his little scratch. Hell, he's all sick and feverish. Look at him. Bacitracin won't do him much good, I reckon. I think he's convinced now. See ya later." He returned the tube of bacitracin ointment.

Jesse and Mud watched as the two walked down the hill.

After a while, Mud said, "Jesus, the damn sickbay ain't five hundred yards away, and Coop doesn't do anything about a scratch until it turns to gangrene? That's crazy. They can't cure that shit, can they?"

"Only by cuttin' the infected part off," answered Jesse.

"You mean they may have to cut his arm off?"

"As bad as it looked to me, I'd say he was lucky if that's all they had to do." Mud shuddered.

PFC Cooper was lifted out by helicopter within one hour of his examination by the corpsmen at battalion sick bay. He lost his arm just below the elbow at Da Nang East Hospital. That was the last anyone heard from him.

In late May, Jesse and Mud were part of a hammer and anvil sweep, acting as members of the anvil. Simply stated, this is a sweep of an area where the enemy is pushed before the sweeping force into a waiting force. The enemy is caught between the moving force – the hammer, and the stationary force – the anvil. On this particular afternoon the temperature was well over one hundred-twenty degrees with a relative humidity of ninety-nine percent.

Jesse sat in the tall grass, feeling the heat and humidity bore through his skin into his inner flesh. He was used to heat. He had grown up in one of the hottest places in the United States. But this heat was almost unbearable. The tall grass was sufficient to hide him from visual contact by the VC but afforded no protection from the sun. There was not even the hint of a breeze to move the hot, thick air. He longed to be with Thunder in the hammer. At least they were moving.

Lieutenant Malcolm was on Jesse's right. A marine not twenty feet from Malcolm fell forward onto his face. Jesse watched the quiet activity as the unconscious marine was moved to the rear. Within a ten-minute period, five more men succumbed to the stifling heat. With only forty men in the anvil, the loss of six men to heat stroke was no small matter.

Malcolm contacted his first platoon commander on the radio to call off the sweep due to the extreme heat. Even as he spoke, Jesse saw the VC running before the hammer.

"Get ready, Mud. Here come the Indians," Jesse said calmly, grateful for any activity that would allow him to move a part of his body, even if it was only his trigger finger.

Ten yards to his left a marine fell with a muffled cry. The sharp crack of the stray VC bullet quickly followed. Almost in unison, firing erupted from the marines waiting in ambush, causing the enemy to turn momentarily to the rear.

On Jesse's command, Mud called in the pre-planned fire mission. There

419

was no adjusting fire. The pre-planned mission was right on target. From his vantagepoint less than three hundred yards from the impact area, Jesse saw bodies and body parts clearly as they flew in all directions, guided only by the force of the exploding mortar rounds. Of the twenty-five VC in the open field, only six survived; three of them were wounded. The remaining three were captured without further incident. Total marine casualties for the day consisted of seven men: six out of action for several days as the result of heat stroke and one killed in action by enemy fire.

Four days later, Alpha Company set out on a daylight combat patrol in the company of three Ontos. Neither the VC nor the North Vietnamese had used tanks in the war yet, but the Ontos was capable of other tasks with its six 106mm recoilless rifles. It was an awesome gun platform.

As the company walked the Hoa My Trail they received one round of sniper fire from a tree line four hundred yards off the right flank. The round missed its intended target and the company took cover while Malcolm decided on the next course of action.

Jesse crouched next to his company commander. "You want some whiskey, Skipper?"

He looked at Jesse, then down the trail to the leading Ontos. He nodded in their direction. "What do you think? It worked once before."

"Hell, I say let 'em have at it. It must be boring as hell to ride around in one of those ovens all day and never get to do anything but tour the country." He remembered Thunder's friend in the ONTOS who had fired on another tree line at a hiding sniper.

Malcolm turned and shouted down the line. "Ontos up."

The word was passed quickly down the line and soon the three Ontos were on line, facing the tree line four hundred yards away. In total disregard for the regulation, each Ontos on the line fired all six rifles simultaneously, in unison with one another. The blast was deafening. It was far worse on the lone sniper in the tree line.

When second platoon swept the area after the Ontos barrage they found only the twisted barrel of a rifle jammed six inches into the trunk of a large tree, a hand, one boot complete with foot, and a piece of rifle stock.

The marines took no more sniper fire that day.

When the moon allowed, Jesse slipped out of camp at night in search of food, but hunting was sparse and the VC were numerous. On at least two occasions he let game go for fear of alerting the VC to his presence. Malcolm learned of his night hunting trips and, despite Jesse's pleading, put an end to them by executive order.

Jesse continued to lose weight, as did most of the men in the battalion. In June, Alpha Company received twenty new troops, fresh from Camp Pendleton. Though the veterans were glad to have some relief on perimeter duty, the new men suffered the usual hazing that went with their status.

One of the new men stepped on a land mine his second day in the valley. He was still alive when evacuated but died before the helicopter arrived at Da Nang. His death had a sobering effect on the new men and shortened their hazing period for the most part.

Two days after the new man was lost to the land mine, a second replacement was lost to a Malaysian Gate. The big booby trap punctured the life out of the young man but he took almost an hour to die, suffering miserably the whole time. The patrol was in a canyon inaccessible by helicopter when the incident occurred and the men took turns carrying the wounded man to a relatively open area. Jesse and Mud were carrying him when his life left his body. He never made a sound. His body began to quiver and shake. Blood drooled from his mouth and he died.

Soon the stories of Jesse's and Thunder's exploits were known by the new men, and one of them, PFC Mitchell from Omaha, Nebraska, christened them the "Arizona Rough Riders". The term stuck, though it was most often shortened to "Rough Riders". Thunder's entire squad soon had the name attached to it and they wore the label proudly.

PFC Mitchell was the only new man assigned to Thunder's squad. He seemed to revel his new assignment until he realized the reputation was not given to Thunder or his squad for no reason.

Jesse was with a daylight combat patrol returning to camp one afternoon when Thunder's squad ran across a platoon of Republic of Korea troops operating in the area. The ROK soldiers had a reputation for being fierce fighters and haters of all VC. Based upon this reputation alone, most marines respected them and had no reason to believe them to be anything less than rumored.

Thunder's point man became aware of the Koreans before the patrol was discovered. Thinking it a fun thing to do, Thunder moved his men to the Korean perimeter undiscovered. Thunder shouted to the Korean sentry a mere twenty yards away. The Korean almost fired a panic round but was able to control himself in time to avoid a confrontation. After a few tense moments, the marines were invited into the ROK camp.

The captain commanding the Koreans was surprised to see Thunder and Jesse carrying M-1s. He offered them a supply of ammunition, which they gratefully accepted. Shortly thereafter, the marines were introduced to three prisoners.

All three were tied to the sunny sides of trees. It was obvious the Vietnamese had not been given any water for a long time. When Thunder questioned the Korean captain regarding the matter of his treatment of the prisoners, the man appeared indignant, and replied in broken English that the prisoners were VC with valuable information, who refused to cooperate. He informed Thunder that they were now in a weakened state and could easily be tortured to provide the information desired.

He invited Thunder and his men to watch the interrogations. Thunder thanked him for his invitation but explained that he must return to his own camp.

The marines bid farewell to their allies and walked slowly from the Korean camp to the screams of the tortured Vietnamese. Jesse couldn't believe Thunder was leaving the Korean camp without stopping the torture. He was about to say something to him when, twenty yards outside the Korean perimeter, Thunder called a halt.

"What the hell we stoppin' for, Thunder? I can't stand to listen to that screamin' much longer," said Lance Corporal Kerr.

"We ain't gonna listen to it much longer. We're goin' back in there and take those prisoners to battalion," replied Thunder.

"What if they don't want to give 'em to us?" asked Mitchell.

Thunder looked at his new man. "We're gonna make sure they want to give

421

'em to us, Mitch." He faced the rest of his squad. "Fix bayonets."

Mitchell's mouth fell open. "You're not serious? They're our allies. We can't just attack our allies and take their prisoners."

"Ain't nobody that treats prisoners like that is an ally of mine." He turned to Kerr. "How many did you count?"

"About twenty-seven or eight."

Thunder looked over his eleven-man squad and winked at Jesse. "That's about right. Okay, sling the rifles upside down so they don't notice the bayonets until we've got 'em covered. I'll lead. Kerr, you take the rear. We'll just walk right back in like we forgot somethin'. I don't want any killin' unless they ask for it, and I don't think they will. If they do – oblige 'em."

Mitchell fixed his bayonet and fell in line.

When Thunder returned to the battalion with his three grateful prisoners, the beginning of an international incident was on the roll. Though the Koreans had relinquished their prisoners without incident, they radioed their command upon Thunder's departure and the protests flowed forth to high places in I Corps.

Malcolm shook his head disdainfully as he listened to Thunder's story. When the young sergeant finished his tale, Malcolm spoke quietly. "Did you have to call the Korean captain a pussy? Did you have to add insult to injury?"

Thunder looked at the soil near his feet. "Yessir, I did. Any man who would do what he was doin' to those prisoners is a helluva lot worse than that. I was so damn mad, that was all I could think of at the time." He nodded at Jesse. "Indio here kept his head better. He offered to stake the captain out and cut his manhood off."

Jesse winced. "Damnit, Thunder, you promised you wouldn't tell that part."

"You know, between you and Indio, I'm gonna lose my commission. Were you guys both deprived kids or something? What the hell makes you two think you can do whatever in the hell you want to do, and it's okay with the rest of the world? Do you realize what the hell you've done this time?"

"Yessir. I've saved three men from bein' tortured to death," said Thunder.

Malcolm looked into Thunder's hazel eyes. "Is it worth a court-martial – even if they're VC?"

With no hesitation, Thunder answered, "Without a doubt."

Malcolm shook his head. "I don't know why I even asked the question. I knew what your answer would be."

"We had to carry one of the prisoners in, Sir," said Thunder. Jesse was doing his best not to speak.

"What was wrong with him?"

"The Koreans stuck a hot piece of steel in his ass and spun it around for effect. I think they fried part of this guy's intestine."

Malcolm grimaced. "Are you sure?"

"No question, Sir."

"If that's the case, I'll be right there with you if it comes to a court-martial."

"Thank you, Sir. I kinda figured you might."

No one in the company but Lieutenant Malcolm was aware of the large amount of paperwork required as a result of Thunder's action, but eventually the incident was written off as a "....misunderstanding as a result of the language barrier".

Forever Patriots

Shortly after the incident with the Koreans, the VC began to fire rockets and mortars into the battalion center during the hours of darkness. Extended perimeters and listening posts did not alleviate the situation. After suffering the shellings four nights in a row, the battalion commander assigned Alpha Company the task of removing the enemy mortars.

Based upon the previous shellings, it was determined the VC were operating from the hills north of the battalion position. The plan was simple: Alpha Company would move into the hills at sunset with sixty-mm mortars and throw counter-mortar fire upon the enemy position once it was discovered.

As Malcolm explained the order of movement at the pre-ambush briefing, he looked up at Jesse. "Lieutenant Parker will be in charge of the platoons on our perimeter. In the event something happens to me, Indio will be in charge of headquarters and, subsequently, the company, until we are out of the hills. Any questions?"

Jesse was the most surprised man at the briefing. He looked at Malcolm, then to the lieutenants and staff sergeants standing or kneeling nearby. Not a man offered an objection. But the small staff sergeant in the second platoon, Staff Sergeant Menenghello, looked at Malcolm, then to Jesse.

Menenghello was a seventeen-year veteran who had reached his plateau six years ago. He possessed neither the intelligence nor the drive to better his position. He was a whiner and one quick to point the finger if things went wrong. Jesse knew that Menenghello was hoping something would happen to discredit him with the company commander. He wished the small staff sergeant would be transferred to another outfit.

"Who's in charge of the sixties?" Menenghello asked.

Malcolm knew what the man was looking for, but gave him less. "You're in charge of the light mortars, Sergeant Menenghello. The normal responsibility of your command has not been changed. I've changed only the chain of command for this particular mission for reasons of my own that I don't want to discuss at this time."

Menenghello shuffled his feet. "Yessir."

Malcolm looked at the rest of the men at the briefing. "Anymore questions?"

No one spoke.

"If there are no further questions, you're all dismissed with the exception of Indio. Indio, I want to talk to you for a minute."

When the others were out of earshot, Jesse spoke. "Second in command? Me? Why, Sir? You've got a bunch of pretty good NCO's and officers in this company."

"Yeah, I do. And every last one of 'em is in a rifle platoon. The new company executive officer is straight out of O.C.S. I assigned him to second platoon for tonight's ambush so I wouldn't have to deal with him in the chain of command."

"But what about your staff NCO's?"

"The first shirt is on temporary assignment to battalion, and the company gunnery sergeant is on R&R. The rest of the staff isn't as qualified as you are."

"But my rank, Sir – I'm only a lance corporal."

"Hell, Indio, there aren't three men in this battalion who know what your rank is. Most of the men think you're some kind of general. The staff and officers all assume you're a sergeant."

"Yessir, but I'm not really into this command business. Nothin' is gonna happen to you anyway."

423

Stoney Livingston

"I don't expect anything will, but I'd be remiss in my duties if I let the normal chain of command run its course on tonight's show."

"Sir, I'm honest-to-god honored by the faith you're showin' in me, but I'd just as soon we went down the normal chain of command. I've never heard of a lance corporal being put in charge of a bunch of staff and officers, and I don't really wanta be the first."

Malcolm looked Jesse in the eyes. "You're the only lance corporal I ever met who I thought could pull it off if he had to."

Jesse shrugged. "Nothin' is gonna happen to you anyway. Why the hell are we making such a ruckus about the second in command of headquarters?"

"I feel it's necessary."

"Who would be next in line in the headquarters group right now?" asked Jesse as he tried to remember where all of the staff and officers were.

In a calm monotone voice, Malcolm answered, "Menenghello."

"Oh."

Malcolm waited for Jesse to expand his response.

Jesse shuffled his feet. He looked up at his company commander. "Just call me your second-in-command on this one."

Jesse sat in the bushes in a swale, sparse branches providing little cover from the suspected enemy, the small hills providing more comfort. Darkness would have to take up where the almost leafless plants left off. He waited silently for the last vestiges of sunset to disappear, grateful for the darkness to hide his miserable and suffering body from the VC.

Mud sat, his back leaning into the bare branches of the bush behind him, his radio standing before him on the ground. Staff Sergeant Menenghello and his men were setting up the two sixty-mm mortars only twenty yards away.

"Jesus Christ," whispered Mud. "It sounds like they're puttin' in a battery of one-five-fives,"

"I have heard quieter groups," agreed Jesse.

"Them dumbshits might as well put up a neon sign."

"He's a staff sergeant. Let 'em have his fun playin' war."

The company settled in and waited. The moon showed it's almost-full face shortly after sunset. From time-to-time the cheery mirrored light of the moon was obscured by the thin clouds wafting above the sparsely vegetated hills below. The land went from a ghostly-lighted landscape to a hole of blackness, and back, at the whims of the clouds.

At 2100 hours, a cloud covered the moon. It was thicker than the previous clouds, much smaller, and much closer to the surface of the earth.

"Jesus Christ, look at the mosquitoes! There must be a billion of 'em!" whispered Mud loudly.

Jesse reached his hand into the cloud of mosquitoes and clenched his fist. He felt the flying insects squish between his fingers. Rarely did he use his insect repellent for anything other than a novelty. He liked to watch the leeches disintegrate as he applied the smelly liquid to their slimy bodies. On this night however, he considered using the Government Issue insect repellent for its designed purpose.

Quickly he pulled the small plastic vial from his right breast pocket and applied the stinky substance to his exposed body parts in the hope that, if nothing else, the mosquitoes would find the smell too repulsive to endure.

424

For almost thirty minutes the cloud of mosquitoes hovered over the center of the headquarters group, feasting upon human flesh, gorging themselves. Then, as if on cue, they left, a dark heavy cloud of human blood, covered by the bodies of the satiated little insects.

Despite the large numbers of mosquitoes Jesse suffered but a few bites. He didn't know if it was the insect repellant or the lack of flesh on his bones that turned the hungry mosquitoes to other prey. He didn't concern himself with the reasons long. He was glad to have suffered so little. He breathed out hard through his nose, blowing out the last of the mosquitoes that had entered that private passage of his body. He moved his tongue around inside his mouth and lips and spit more mosquitoes into the dried bush.

Once again, the moon made Mud visible. He slapped his face and neck to rid his body of the lingering mosquitoes. "I don't believe this shit. I never saw anything like that in my life. I thought it was never gonna end. How bad they get to you?"

"Not too bad, considerin'," whispered Jesse.

"Considerin' what?"

"Considerin' I ate about two or three hundred of 'em."

"Ugh. I know what you mean. I was tryin' to forget about that. They feel funny as hell when you get a dozen or two of 'em in your nose and mouth at the same time."

"You can tell this one to your grand-kids and they'll look at you like you're the biggest nut that ever walked the face of the earth."

"I ain't tellin' this one to anybody. I don't even believe it myself. I came closer to dyin' tonight than I have since I been here. And that's sayin' a whole bunch, considerin' I hang around with you. Hell, I couldn't even breathe for a while there."

"Well, let's hope they find the VC next. It does my heart good to think of the VC swimmin' around in that cloud of mosquitoes."

"I ever tell you, you think of some of the weirdest things at some of the weirdest times?"

"Yeah, you've mentioned it once or twice before. Well, we might as well relax and wait for the gooks to put on a show."

"Yeah. Another glorious day in the Corps."

They fell silent and waited.

Twenty minutes later, Jesse was startled by a grunting sound emanating from Mud's position. Quickly he crawled to his radio operator's side and shook him roughly. Mud came awake slowly, mumbling.

"Shhh! You tryin' to get us killed or what? You're snorin' like a heavy saw. I don't care if you wanna catch a few Z's but do it without snorin', okay?"

Mud answered. "I'm sorry. I don't know what happened. I was just sittin' here and all of a sudden you're shakin' the shit outa me."

"Cool the snorin'." Jesse returned to his position.

He had barely resumed his crouched position when Mud's snore broke the still night air. He moved quickly back to Mud's location and shook him roughly. A voice twenty yards away said, "There they are!"

Jesse released his grip on Mud and searched the hills nearby. He heard the feint "thump" of a mortar round leaving a tube. The sound came from the south. He turned his attention in that direction and saw the flash of the VC mortars as they fired out their barrage.

425

"Shit!"

"What the hell's goin' on?" mumbled Mud, coming out of his deep sleep.

"They're in the hills southeast of the battalion. Get on the radio. Fire mission."

Jesse became aware of the sounds of Menenghello's men moving the sixty-mortar. He shouted down the trail. "Sergeant Menenghello, don't fire the sixty. They're out of range."

"Bullshit! I can see 'em as plain as day. They're only about a thousand yards away," returned Menenghello.

Jesse turned to Mud. "Hang on, Mud. I'll be back in a minute." He turned and strode furiously in the direction of the small mortars.

In the moonlight he could see one of the men placing a round up to the mouth of the tube on one of the guns as he approached. With no time to talk, he kicked the mortar tube sideways, laying it on the ground. He turned to Menenghello. "I told you they were out of range, godamnit!"

Menenghello's voice was challenging. "Who the fuck are you anyway? I been in this man's Marine Corps long enough to know when to fire a sixty and when not to."

"You ain't firin' it this time."

"And who the fuck's gonna stop me?"

"I am. The gook guns are out of our range but we're not out of theirs. You fire one round and we're all dead. They'll be on us like stink on shit with those big-ass 82's in less time than it'll take you to get the hell out of the way. I don't have anymore time to waste on this shit."

"I'll have yer ass for this!"

"Later, godamnit, I've gotta call in a fire mission."

"What the hell is goin' on up there?" It was Malcolm.

Menenghello spoke first. "Indio has kicked over one of my guns and won't let me fire on the gooks, sir."

Malcolm puffed up the hill. He looked at the overturned mortar in the moonlight and quickly summed up the situation. "Indio, what the hell's the problem?"

"The gooks are firin' at the battalion from the hills to the southeast. They're more than three times beyond the range of our sixties. If we fire our sixties, the gooks see the muzzle flash and blow us to hell with their big mortars and recoilless, Sir."

Malcolm looked at Menenghello and struck the final blow to the man's ego. "If Indio says don't fire the sixties – don't fire the sixties."

"Thank you, Sir. I've gotta get back to Mud and get a mission called in before the gooks get away clean." The enemy mortars exploded in the valley below as Jesse made his way back to Mud's position.

He knelt by Mud and spread his map carefully upon the ground. With his red-lensed flashlight, he determined the coordinates of the enemy guns and marked them on his map with an X. Mud called in the mission and Jesse adjusted from the first round to a twelve-round barrage on the second call.

Alpha Company abandoned their ambush and returned to their assigned perimeter positions.

Shortly after daybreak, Alpha's first platoon swept the area suspected of hiding the VC guns on the previous night. They found mortar baseplate depressions amid the pockmarks of marine mortar fire but could find no evidence that any of the enemy mortars had been disabled. The VC had been able to fire their barrage and retreat further into the hills before Jesse called in his mission. The extreme accuracy of Jesse's coordinates mattered little to Menenghello, who continued his attempts to have Jesse court-martialed for insubordination.

Thunder persuaded Menenghello to forget the whole matter. Thunder was very persuasive when he wanted to be. The exact methods employed were never known to any but Thunder and Menenghello, but they were sufficient to convince Menenghello that he wanted a transfer to a staff position at division headquarters. Menenghello was transferred within a week of the night ambush.

On the morning Menenghello boarded the helicopter for his last look at the Hoa My Trail, Malcolm quietly handed Jesse his promotion papers.

"Here. Congratulations. You're a full-fledged corporal now. I didn't present it in front of the others because most of 'em already think you're a damn general."

"Thank you, Sir. I can use the extra money. And thanks for not going public with this. I'd hate to be demoted from general to corporal."

"I asked for sergeant but they refused me. Suggested I put you in for a commission. I checked your G.C.T. scores. You're sure as hell eligible. What the hell are you doin' in the Marine Corps infantry with that I.Q.?"

Jesse smiled a broad smile and said, "Crazy?"

Malcolm returned his smile. "How about it? You want to go to O.C.S.?"

"Go through all of that bullshit and be demoted from corporal to second lieutenant? No thanks, Skipper. I appreciate the thought but you'll never see gold bars on my uniform. I can do more good where I am."

Malcolm appeared to think about Jesse's statement a moment. "Yeah, maybe you're right. We need guys like you to humble us once in a while. I just think you're capable of commanding a company right now. And with a little training, who knows? Maybe you could become another Chesty Puller."

"Not me, Skipper. I just wanna fight my share of this little war and go back home and become a civilian."

"Then what? Any plans?"

"Yeah. And none of 'em include the Crotch. Too many Menenghello's in the government."

"I can't argue with that." Malcolm knew the subject was dead. "What's on the menu today?"

Jesse reached into his pocket and extracted his weatherworn paper. "Lunch or supper?"

*****

Jesse's heart thumped hard, threatening to explode as he opened the letter from Shannon. Thunder sat in his fighting hole several yards away, on the side of the ridge, reading his own mail. In Shannon's letter, she expressed concern for his safety and said how proud she was of him for serving his country. She gave some news of her son and daughter, and a glimpse or two into her thoughts, and she wished him well. She signed the letter: "Always, Shannon"

"You okay, Amigo?"

He looked over to Thunder.

"I don't know," answered Jesse dumbly.

"You look like you're shell-shocked, man."

"Maybe I am, Thunder. Maybe I am."

427

Stoney Livingston

"Jesus. What's in that letter?"

"I don't know. I'm trying to figure it out, but I'm not sure."

"Sure of what?" asked Thunder.

"Whether she wants to hear from me again."

"Who?"

"Shannon."

"Shannon? That's a letter from Shannon?" Thunder moved and sat next to him. He knew about Shannon. Jesse had shared his thoughts about her with him on more than one occasion.

"It's not very personal, and yet it is. I honest to God don't know what to do, Thunder. If I write her back and tell her how I feel, it would ruin what little I have with her. I can't say those things to a married woman. If I write to her, I don't know if I can do it without sayin' 'em."

Thunder looked at him as a father might look at a foolish child. "Amigo, what you have with her is killin' you. If you share it with her, it might kill her. Why 'n-the-hell don't you just find another girl?" Without waiting for an answer, Thunder stood and walked up the hill.

Jesse sat for several moments as he watched Thunder disappear over the top of the hill. He opened his map pouch and withdrew his writing tablet.

Shannon,

Thank you for the letter. It was thoughtful of you to write. I'm sure the stories printed in the papers are overdone and probably represent the war worse than it really is. I don't mean to belittle it, for men are dying in this war as in all wars, but it is not something to dwell upon. I'm in a good unit and the men beside me are top notch.

The country of Viet Nam is a beautiful place. I wish you could see it under peacetime conditions. It would be a good place for a bunch of resort hotels (providing they had air-conditioning). The beach near Chu Lai is gorgeous.

Jesse felt himself wavering. He wanted to tell her – what? Knowing she would read his words was almost too much to bear. He could say anything he wanted and she would read it at least once. It would get to her.

The jungles are lush and green and full of exotic wildlife. I've even seen a panther. The rice paddies are works of art when located on gentle slopes. They look like patchwork quilts. The people are modest and hard working but very poor. And they live in constant fear. I hope someday they are able to live free of that fear. If that is accomplished, I'll feel like we did it right.

What was he doing? This isn't what he wanted to say.

I hear from Will now and again and I guess he's doing just fine. I never would have figured him for a marine. Just goes to show you what I know. I hope Jimmy and Jerrie are doing okay and I wish you the best of everything.

Jesse

He read and re-read the letter. It was short, blunt, and compared to what he had written for other men in the outfit, unfit to send. It said nothing he wanted to say.

428

He put it in an envelope and walked down the hill to the battalion mail drop.

*****

Jesse and Mud were on a routine daylight combat patrol when Wellington suddenly jumped from Mud's radio and fell to the ground flapping his wings and squawking wildly in much the same way Frank had done. The patrol halted while Mud tended to the big black rooster. In five minutes, Wellington was dead of an unknown malady. Quickly and with no ceremony, he was buried in a shallow grave and the patrol moved on.

*****

Alpha Company moved through the rice paddies like a long, disjointed worm, following the dikes and trails to avoid the stinking mud and ooze of the paddies. One man led the way, a hand-held minesweeper assuring him that all was well. It was the first time in Jesse's experience minesweepers had been used by Alpha Company. As a matter-of-fact, it was the first time he had seen one since Advanced Infantry Training at Camp Pendleton in 1962.

The cloudless sky did nothing to thwart the merciless rays of fire from the sun. The company had been in this sector before, but boredom and the lack of a real plan of action by the battalion commander led them once again to sweep the area. Jesse watched from one third of the way back in the column. He would be glad when they were out of the open and into the trees.

Mud, who marched ten paces in front of him, stumbled momentarily then quickly regained his balance. *If I had to carry that damn radio around all of the time, I'd volunteer for a suicide mission.*

Just as Mud appeared to get back into his stride, the ground under his right heel seemed to explode, throwing the wet soil in all directions and flipping him into the air much like a tossed coin.

For an instant Jesse thought Mud had stepped on a land mine, undiscovered by the minesweeper, but then he heard the crack of the bullet as the sound raced to catch the projectile, whizzing within inches of his right ear. Mud somersaulted through the air and landed with a splash in the rice paddy.

As Mud slapped at his side in the thick water, Jesse jumped into the paddy next to him. "Mud, where you hit?" The water was almost knee-deep. Mud lay on his left side, frantically slapping at his right hip.

"Hell, I don't know!"

"What the hell are you doin'?"

"I'm tryin' ta get my pistol out but the damn holster's covered with mud and I can't get the flap open."

Jesse turned and looked in the direction from which the bullet had originated. He looked down at the comical figure of Mud trying to remove his pistol from its muddy holster and laughed. "What the hell you gonna do when you get it out, throw it at 'em? The nearest tree line is four hundred yards away."

Mud ceased his battle with the uncooperative holster and raised up on one arm to peer toward the tree line. He looked back at Jesse and frowned. "Well, godamnit, how the hell was I supposed to know we wasn't bein' attacked?" He raised his foot from the slime of the paddy and examined his boot. "The bastard shot my heel off! That's too damn close."

"I don't wanna bust yer bubble, old friend, but he was aimin' for me. Bullet

429

Stoney Livingston

almost creased my ear. You okay?"

"Does injured pride count?"

"Not today."

"I guess I'm okay then."

Jesse pulled his field glasses from their case and studied the tree line. Malcolm approached in a low crouch.

"Should we call in some whiskey, Skipper?" asked Jesse.

Malcolm studied the tree line. "I don't know. It's pretty close to third platoon's position."

"Those guys on the 81's are good, Skipper. That's duck soup."

"Okay, go ahead, but give yourself a little leeway on that first round."

"Aye aye, Sir." Jesse turned to Mud. "C'mon, Mud. Get up and see if that radio still works. Fire mission."

Quickly Jesse studied his map. When he felt comfortable, he called for one round of white phosphorus with a "will adjust". When Mud gave him an, "on the way", he put his glasses to his eyes and waited.

He studied the tree line to the east, waiting for the fiery round to mark its own demise. He heard the dull pop of the round as it struck the ground and exploded but saw nothing within his field of vision. He searched left and right but still he saw no evidence of the exploding round.

"What the hell? I couldn't have been that far off. I can't even see it."

"Cease fire! Cease Fire! End the mission!" Malcolm's voice was filled with urgency.

As Jesse turned to the voice, he noticed the white smoke four hundred yards west of his position. He turned to Mud. "Cease fire. End of mission." To Malcolm he said, "What the hell is it doin' over there?"

Malcolm replied, "I thought you might be the one to give me that answer."

Jesse pulled his map from the map pocket of his utility jacket and studied it carefully. He turned to Mud. "Mud, what coordinates did you call in?"

Mud flipped the pages in his pocket notepad until he found the proper page. He repeated the numbers he had given to FDC.

Jesse looked at Malcolm, totally lost for an explanation. "I don't get it, Skipper. Those coordinates should have put the round in the tree line. Here, take a look for yourself." He proffered his map.

Malcolm studied the map. After much chin rubbing and terrain checking, he turned to Jesse. "It looks right to me. Maybe FDC got the numbers wrong." He glanced over to Mud and said, "Check with your FDC and see what they show as the coordinates."

Mud complied. FDC responded by repeating Jesse's coordinates.

"That does it. I don't know what in the hell's goin' on, but that's all the mortar support I want for today," ordered Malcolm. He turned to Lieutenant Parker, kneeling nearby. "You've got the sniper, Lieutenant. We'll give you covering fire."

Jesse sat silently in the muddy water of the rice paddy and watched as Parker's platoon flanked the tree line under covering fire. In fifteen minutes it was over. Second platoon suffered one wounded and the enemy sniper was killed as he ran from his cover.

The walk back to battalion was long for Jesse. He questioned his ability. He was certain of his location on the map and yet he had missed his target by almost nine hundred yards. Maybe he was going crazy. He spoke to no one, not even Mud, who limped along on his heel-less boot. He walked in the blazing sun, unaware of his surroundings or the heat.

Back at battalion, the company dispersed to the perimeter. Jesse walked to the mortar position. Outside the FDC tent Sergeant Tuleano smoked a cigarette. "Tule. Who the hell was runnin' FDC about an hour ago?"

Tuleano met his stare briefly. He jerked his thumb at the tent. "He's still in there. That's all I gotta say."

Jesse opened the tent flap and stepped inside. At the plotting table sat, Sergeant Simmons. Jesse held his fear and anger in check. He was not yet sure which was appropriate. "What happened on my last mission?"

Simmons raised himself from the plotting table. "I made a one-grid error."

Jesse stood for a moment silently, relieved that it was not he who was responsible for the errant round. He stared at the tall Canadian. "Just like that? You made a one-grid error? How in the hell do you make a one-grid error?"

Simmons started to explain how he had placed his plotter incorrectly on the map, but Jesse interrupted him. "Okay, okay, so you made an error. Why the hell didn't you notify me or Mud? We could have corrected and continued the mission."

Simmons replied, "I don't know."

Jesse waited. When it became apparent that Simmons had no intention of elaborating, he said, "You don't know? That's it?"

Sergeant Simmons stood quietly. Jesse hit him full in the mouth with his left hand. Simmons fell onto the plotting table, collapsing it to the ground. As he rolled over and regained his senses, Jesse stood over him. "Go ahead and get up, you stupid bastard! We had a man wounded today that should be in here kickin' yer ass instead of me, but I'm gonna be his goddamn stand-in! You got anything to say about that? Or don't you know about that either?" His hands were clenched fists, perceptibly held in check, so great was the effort not to strike another blow.

Tuleano stepped into the tent. "That's enough, Indio. It ain't gonna change anything."

Jesse breathed heavily. He looked from Simmons to Tuleano and stepped back. "Yeah, yer right, Tule." He left the tent silently and reported his findings to Lieutenant Malcolm.

In mid-June, the arrival of five marines with bolt-action rifles, telescopic sights and carrying-cases signaled a new phase of the war for Jesse. He was introduced to five members from a marine sniper platoon.

"Sniper platoon?" He smiled at the lanky corporal in charge of the five-man unit. "I never heard of such a thing. When did they start this shit?"

Corporal Newsome answered in his Philadelphia accent. "It's a new war, man. You gotta use new tactics."

Jesse looked at the bolt-action Remington 700 brandished by Newsome. "What's the scope for? How far away you guys shootin'?"

"A thousand yards is common," replied Newsome proudly.

Jesse wasn't sure he liked the man's attitude. "Yeah, I'll agree that a thousand yards is common, so what d'ya need the scopes for? Seems like a lot of extra weight to be carryin' around for common shootin'."

Newsome's face reddened. "Maybe you'd like to go with us on a mission or two? You can bring that relic with you," He nodded at Jesse's M-1 Garand, "and then maybe you'll appreciate the difference in our equipment."

Stoney Livingston

Jesse enjoyed irritating the sniper. He wasn't certain he liked anyone who killed from hiding. It seemed cowardly. He glanced at his old M-1, then up at Corporal Newsome. "Yeah, if it's okay with you, I'd like to tag along and see how you pros do it. Who knows? I might learn something."

Newsome smiled a knowing smile. "Clear it with your commanding officer. We're steppin' off at 0400 tomorrow."

"Consider it done. Where do we meet?"

"Right here."

"See ya' at 0400." Jesse walked to Alpha Company's CP tent.

Malcolm smiled as Jesse relayed his request. When his forward observer finished speaking, he said, "This guy must have really pissed you off."

"Not really, Sir. I could learn a lot about some of the new tactics they're teachin' back in the States."

Malcolm's smile broadened. "What did he do to piss you off so bad?"

Jesse could keep a straight face no longer. He returned Malcolm's smile. "Actually, Sir, the guy has a haughty attitude that needs a little adjustment. I don't know if I'm the guy to do it but I got nothin' to lose by tryin'. Besides, he insulted Ol' Betsy." Jesse tapped the barrel of his M-1.

"Okay, Indio, but go easy. Don't start an incident. I don't need anymore paperwork."

"Thanks, Skipper. I'll let you know how things progress."

Jesse participated in three sniper missions with the sniper platoon. The first mission was uneventful. Acting upon information supplied by S-2, the five-man unit moved into the hills north of the battalion position. They moved out at 0400 and returned at 1600 with no enemy contact.

Jesse suggested they search the area two miles south of the battalion on their next jaunt. Newsome took Jesse's advice and the team encountered an enemy patrol three hours after sunrise.

Jesse watched, amazed at the stealth and speed, as the marine snipers quickly and without commands, set up their positions in the trees protecting them from the enemy's view. Using a metal rod with a "Y" at its upper end, four of the snipers stuck their rods into the soil until they were satisfied with its aboveground height. They then positioned their rifles, placing the forearm stock into the "Y" of the rod. Sitting behind the rod, they adjusted the riflescopes.

PFC Miller, who did not set up his rifle, informed them that the wind was blowing at five miles per hour out of the south. Jesse wondered how he knew that. He had been so intent on watching the riflemen, he had paid no attention to Miller. After passing along the wind velocity and direction, Miller produced a telescope and mounted it upon a small tripod. As Jesse directed his attention to Miller, Newsome spoke to the other three men.

"The one with the field glasses – are we agreed?"

The others nodded their assent. They looked into their scopes and took up the slack in their triggers. Jesse peered across the long clearing to the VC camp on the edge of the tree line, almost nine hundred yards away. He jerked involuntarily as the marine rifles went off in unison.

When shooting relatively long distances with a rifle, the successful results are always eerie. Everything seems to happen in slow motion and delayed time. It

432

seems to take the bullet forever to reach the target and then, the report of the rifle long gone in the shooter's ears, the target falls silently to earth. Those nearby the victim look unsuspectingly at their fallen comrade, unaware he has been shot. Then the speed of sound catches up to the halted bullet and the survivors run for cover.

It happened so on this morning. To further add to the surreal effect, PFC Miller reported before the victim fell, "Three hits. In the chest." He looked up from his telescope and quickly folded the tripods and packed the fragile telescope into a case. Fifteen seconds after the rounds were fired, the team moved out for battalion headquarters, Jesse acting as rear guard, the VC having not fired a round.

After they put some distance between themselves and the ambush site, Jesse said, "How come all you guys shot at the same gook? Seems to me that if three out of four hit the target, that means four of you shootin' at four targets woulda hit three targets."

Newsome said, "He was the only one we could positively identify as an officer. It was more important that we get him than take a chance of missing him and gettin' three peons."

Jesse nodded. "Oh."

The following day, operating a mile further south and a little east of the previous day's kill, the team encountered two hootches. The VC had set up housekeeping in the otherwise abandoned structures. Jesse was operating as the point when he discovered the camp. The six marines huddled together.

Newsome looked at Jesse. "You found them before they found us. You wanna give it a try?" He offered his bolt-action, scoped Remington.

Looking at the match-grade Remington, Jesse answered. "Yeah, I'd like to give it a try." He didn't accept the Remington but moved to the edge of the trees with his M-1. "I'd like to give the guy a sportin' chance though." He lay in the prone position and adjusted the elevation knob on his M-1. He wet his finger and held it aloft then adjusted the windage knob two clicks to the right. He looked over his right shoulder. "Which one do you want me to take out?"

"Give us a minute to get set up in case you miss," offered Newsome.

"Don't bother. If I miss, then the guy should get another chance at life. It just ain't his day to die."

"It's almost a thousand yards," argued Newsome.

"That's about right," said Jesse. "Now which one do you want?"

Miller looked through his telescope. "Do you see the guy standin' by the northwest corner of the hootch on the left?"

Jesse squinted. "Yeah. Is that the one?"

"That's the one."

Jesse peered through the peep sight at the man, who appeared about the size of a grain of pepper. Jesse breathed deeply once, then two or three normal breaths. He partially released his breath and took up the slack in the trigger. The rifle slammed into his shoulder. He watched and waited for the man to fall.

Before the man fell, he heard Miller say, "Dead center in the chest."

The unsuspecting VC crumpled to the ground. Without another word the sniper team abandoned their site and headed for home.

That Jesse had gained the respect of the sniper team, including Newsome, there was no doubt. Once they felt safe from retribution by the VC they slowed their pace and Newsome spoke.

Stoney Livingston

"You ever think about joinin' the sniper platoon, me and the guys here could put in the word and you'd be in, no sweat."

Jesse wrestled in his mind to justify what he had just done. "I couldn't handle a steady diet of this. It ain't the way I like to do things. No offense, but I wished to hell I'd a' missed that gook back there."

They walked back to battalion in silence, no one rebutting Jesse's feelings.

*****

The battalion began to suffer severely as a result of the attrition rate. Replacements were not arriving as fast as casualties departed. Not all of the casualties were a direct result of enemy action. Many were caused by the conditions under which the marines labored. The long hours on one boring patrol after another, or the routine working parties, or the thirty-three percent security every night, or the filth, or the heat, or the mosquitoes, or the lack of fresh food – all took their tolls.

A full-strength battalion with minimum field attachments should have exceeded thirteen hundred men. In the summer of 1966, the First Battalion, Fourth Marines had less than six hundred and forty-five healthy enough to carry on the simplest of tasks. At one point, only eighty-four were considered by the battalion aid station as fit for full duty. Jesse was one of the eighty-four.

The roughest duties were assigned to those most fit to fight and, as a result, those men bore the brunt of the duties in the month of July. From time-to-time the ranks of the fit would swell to over a hundred but heat or enemy action would reduce the number until another man would become rested enough to perform to minimum standards.

Jesse weighed less than one hundred thirty pounds but he continued to perform, knowing that any day the battalion would surely be relieved and evacuated to Phu Bai or Da Nang or Chu Lai, or anyplace where there was hot food and showers; where they could sleep a full six or seven hours at least twice a week and maybe even listen to the Armed Forces Radio station.

Some of the men from the mortar platoon pulled combat patrol when the rifle companies needed help in filling their ranks. An outbreak of dysentery added to the problems of maintaining the perimeter and the patrols.

*****

Thunder smoked his cigarette and looked at his patrol. He was one of the few squad leaders to have a majority of his squad in fit condition. Of his original thirteen man squad, seven, counting him, were on the patrol. This particular patrol was beefed up by Jesse, Cue and Rich from the mortar platoon.

They had been out for most of the day and were resting before starting back for camp. Thunder looked at the sun, low on the horizon. "We better get started. We should get back just before dark. Preacher, you take the point on the way back. Don't lollygag just because we're on our way home. Mitch, you follow Preacher. The rest of the squad follow, except JJ. JJ, you got the rear guard. Cue, you in front of JJ, Indio in front of Cue, then Rich. I'll be in front of Rich. You all got it?"

They moved out, tired but anxious to beat the darkness into camp.

The hills stretched before them for yet another mile and a half to camp when they waded into the Khe Trai, a small river with its origins not a half mile south of where they crossed. Preacher took his time in the crossing as the rest of the patrol took cover in the hills. Once safely across the river he moved into the trees on the other side and assumed a defensive posture while the rest of the patrol waded through the knee-deep and swiftly moving water.

Jesse was in the water when the shooting erupted. The air around him was filled with flying lead and splashing water as he dove into the river to protect himself. He felt his body pummeled against the rocks in the riverbed by the force of the water. He drifted downstream forty yards before he was able to gain a foothold on the rear-guard side of the river. Still hanging onto his rifle, he crawled against the bank and drew air into his lungs.

The enemy fire came from the direction of the rear guard, so until the VC arrived at the river, he knew he was protected momentarily from their bullets. The shooting continued at what he judged to be a constant distance. *How many?* He tried to estimate the numbers but the return fire from Thunder's squad across the river made that task difficult. He looked over his shoulder in the direction of the bulk of Thunder's squad. A marine entered the water and fell victim to the heavy firepower of the VC. Another marine was able to pull the wounded man to the relative safety of the trees on the other side. It looked like Preacher but Jesse couldn't be certain in the fading light.

Where the hell are Cue and JJ? They had been behind him during the crossing.

The shooting slowed to intermittent pot shots by both sides. Jesse took stock of his position. He had drifted north and slightly east from the crossing and was in a position to be partially behind the VC if they were close to the river. He moved further downstream and exited the river, moving into the brush on the rear guard side. The sun was fading fast. Should he wait until dark? He couldn't. He didn't know the status of Cue and JJ. He moved in the direction of the rear guard.

As he crested the small hill separating him from Cue and JJ he observed a Viet Cong soldier slithering down the slope, intent on something below. He brought his rifle to his shoulder and fired. The enemy soldier jerked into a ball then straightened out. His body went limp. Jesse crawled the twenty-five yards to his fallen foe. His position was now known to the VC.

"Cue? JJ? You guys okay?" He shouted.

"Indio? Is that you?" It was Cue.

"Yeah, man. What's yer status?"

"JJ's hit bad. We gotta get 'im the hell outa here."

Jesse felt his stomach tighten. "You hang in there, JJ. You hear me?"

"He's hit too bad to talk but he heard ya," shouted Cue.

The VC fired upon Jesse's position. He lay on his stomach in the thick brush, nearing panic. Something had to be done quickly but he didn't know what he could do by himself. The size of the enemy force was unknown.

"Cue, I'm comin' in, man! Cover me! Now!" Without waiting for a response, he dashed headlong down the hill, missing Cue's position by ten yards. There was no covering fire from Cue, nor was there much in the way of shooting from the VC. Despite the lack of enemy fire Jesse threw himself prone and crawled to his left the required distance to Cue's position. He found Cue hiding among some large rocks, cradling JJ's head in his lap, his rifle held loosely in his right hand.

"I thought you were a goner when I saw you fall in the river," said Cue.

"Never mind that. Where's JJ hit?"

"In the gut, man."

Stoney Livingston

In the fading sunlight, JJ looked up at Jesse with glassy eyes and smiled a weak smile. He spoke softly, his voice barely audible. "I shoulda known you'd be here, you crazy bastard."

"Shut up, godamnit, JJ. Save your strength. Your gonna need it." Jesse glanced at the roughly dressed wound just above the belly button. Blood seeped through the thick battle dressing. He turned his face away, afraid JJ might see his expression.

He wondered where the VC were and why they had stopped firing. "Cue, who had the prick-six?"

"I did. When the gooks hit us I was just steppin' into the water. I lost it somewhere near the bank. I don't know if it hit the water or not."

"I'm gonna go look for it."

"They'll blow yer head off, man."

Jesse was already on his way to the river's edge. The VC firing erupted anew as he searched the rocks near the river's edge in vain for the lost radio, the ricocheting lead making whizzing sounds as they passed within inches of him. The marines on the western side of the river returned the VC fire with vigor as they attempted to provide cover. Jesse spent almost a full minute in his search before giving up. It seemed like an hour. He retraced his steps, panting heavily as he fell next to Cue and JJ. "I can't find the damn thing. We gotta get JJ outa here."

"How? They got us pinned to this side of the river. There ain't no way we're gonna make it across the water."

"Yer right, Cue, so we'll just have to wait a few minutes for it to get a little darker and move south into the hills till we can cross the river."

Cue looked at JJ. "How you feelin', JJ?"

Weakly, JJ replied, "Not so hot, man."

"Hang in there, JJ. You ain't gettin' outa here that easy. You hear me?" said Jesse, almost in a whisper.

JJ mumbled something inaudible. Jesse bent over him. "What'd you say?"

JJ replied weakly, "I said for you to get the fuck outa here, man. I'm hit bad and I'm dyin'. No sense bullshittin' each other. You and Cue get the hell outa here."

Jesse looked into JJ's face and saw the look of death. He had seen it enough to know it well. "We're gettin' outa this together, JJ, just like we came into it," he whispered.

JJ ignored him. "And, man, I'm sorry about that crack about you bein' white and me bein' black. Yer right – there ain't no difference. Now get outa here."

Tears rolled down Jesse's cheeks. He raised JJ up gently and hugged him tightly. "You hold on, JJ. You hear me? Just hold on." Gently he laid JJ's head back on Cue's lap. Tears flowed in rivers down his cheeks.

"Cue, we gotta get him out now. If you got the strength to pack him south, I'll go after the gooks."

"By-your-damn-self?"

"There ain't nobody else, Cue. We gotta go now. JJ ain't dyin' out here without a chance – not if we can give him that chance."

Cue looked down at JJ, who shook his head weakly in the negative. Cue looked back up at Jesse. "Let's do it."

Jesse readied his M-1 with a fresh clip. He picked up JJ's M-14 and checked the magazine. Quickly and carefully he removed the magazines from JJ's cartridge belt and tucked them into his waistband. He looked at Cue. "I'm gonna work my way to the left about twenty yards, then you're on your own. Give me a count of thirty then haul-ass. Good luck, Cue."

"Same to you, Indio. Keep yer ass low."

Jesse looked down at JJ in the last remnants of dusk. "Yeah, you too. JJ, don't you die on me. We're goin' on R&R together – remember?"

JJ smiled weakly. Jesse moved stealthily to the left.

Jesse let out a rebel yell and began firing both rifles as Cue moved south, carrying JJ piggyback as quickly as he could.

There was no doubt in Jesse's mind that he was going to die as he moved up the hillside in the semi-darkness but somehow it didn't matter as much as it used to. He was tired, tired of the dying and suffering all around him; tired of the filth and the vermin, and the hippies back home, and of the good guys like JJ gettin' their guts shot out while the politicians played to the tune of the protesters. He had no fear of dying on this day. He was angry, angry at everything. His biggest desire at the moment he opened fire was to kill as many of the VC as possible before their bullets found their marks on his body. He would be proud if Shannon found out how he died this time.

He ran up the hill, firing at nothing, from his hip, bellowing a rebel yell. He ran left to right, running into bushes and crashing through them. He heard the telltale *ping* of the ejecting clip on his M-1 as he continued up the hill, firing the M-14 until it too ran out of ammunition. He knelt and reloaded the M-1. From the protection of a large boulder, he fired eight rounds just as fast as he could pull the trigger, reloaded, and repeated the procedure. He paused and reloaded the M-14 and his M-1, then continued his wild charge, untouched by the enemy fire as it poured past him in a sporadic stream.

With both rifles empty, he crashed through a large bush, knocking a Viet Cong soldier to the ground in the early darkness. He dropped the M-14 and beat the hapless VC with his Garand until the enemy soldier was a twisted mass of broken bones and battered flesh. He attempted to reload the Garand and continue his charge but could not get the clip into the receiver. He dropped his rifle and found the M-14. He released the empty magazine and replaced it with a loaded one. Up the hill he moved.

Suddenly, he was on the down side of the hill. *What the hell happened? Where are the gooks?*

He stopped and squatted near a bush, listening to the crackling sounds of panic-stricken men crashing through the vegetation on the hillside below his position.

The sounds of men moving up the hill from behind him brought back the fear he had lost only a few seconds before.

He shouted to the approaching sounds. "You better be rough."

"Riders," came the reply from Thunder.

"You okay, Indio?" asked Thunder as he approached in the darkness.

"Hell, I don't know. How's JJ?"

"JJ? Hell, we thought he was with you. Where's Cue?"

"I sent 'im south. JJ is hit bad."

Thunder said, "Jesus Christ, you mean you took this goddamn hill by yourself with a frontal assault? Are you crazy?"

"Yeah. Yeah, I guess I must be. Let's get the hell outa here and find Cue and JJ. I gotta pick up my rifle. Somethin' was wrong with that last clip I tried. It wouldn't feed."

437

Stoney Livingston

Preacher stopped near his squad leader. "Praise the Lord, Thunder. Look at Indio's rifle. We found it next to a dead gook. It's all busted up."

Thunder accepted the M-1. "Thanks, Preacher. Let's find out how many more gooks we got splattered over this hill and mark 'em for pick up in the mornin'. We gotta find JJ and get him and Kerr back to battalion more skoshe."

"You got it." Preacher disappeared into the darkness.

Thunder handed the M-1 to Jesse. "Here. Maybe we can fix it in the morning."

Jesse slung the Garand and followed Thunder back down the hill.

They found Cue an hour later, sitting with his back to a tree, JJ's head in his lap. He sat silently as the patrol approached.

"That you, Cue?" asked Thunder in the darkness.

"Yeah, it's me. Me n' JJ."

Jesse moved to JJ's side and knelt next to him. "How is he, Cue?"

Cue wept softly. "He's dead, Indio."

"No!" screamed Jesse. He shook JJ roughly. "Wake up, JJ! C'mon, godamnit! Quit playin' around." He felt the coolness of JJ's body and recoiled. He stood and looked at the indigo sky. "No! You hear me? I said no, you sorry sonofabitch! Let 'im come back! Haven't you had enough, you bloodthirsty bastard?"

Thunder stepped next to Jesse and said softly, "Take it easy, Indio. There's still a lotta gooks out there somewhere."

Thunder's voice was like a kick in the chest. Jesse looked at him. "Carry JJ's rifle, will ya, Thunder?"

Thunder reached for the M-14. "Sure, man. You okay?"

"None of us are okay." He bent over and picked up JJ's body, positioning the dead man over his left shoulder in the fireman's carry. Not a word was spoken by a man in the patrol as they found their way back to camp. They waited for Jesse to stop and rest or ask for someone to spell him in carrying JJ's body, but neither occurred.

Malcolm was waiting for them on the perimeter when they arrived. Kerr, was assisted by Mitchell and Preacher, and Jesse carried JJ draped over his left shoulder, his broken M-1 slung on his right. Jesse walked by Malcolm without a word.. He continued, exhausted but determined, to the battalion aid station. Malcolm fell in next to him, studying his face, saying nothing.

At the aid station, Jesse gently placed JJ's body on a cot and flexed his cramped muscles. Corporal Sanderson had the duty. Jesse looked at the corpsman and said, "Is he really gone, Sandy? Is there anything you can do?"

Sandy looked at JJ's body. He checked for a pulse and felt the cold skin. He looked only briefly at Jesse. "He's gone, Indio. There's nothin' I can do. There's nothin' anybody can do. He's in his maker's hands now."

Jesse stared at JJ's body. "Fuck his maker," he said dully. To JJ he said, "So long, JJ." He turned and left the tent without speaking to Malcolm.

Shortly after daybreak Jesse reported to Malcolm and handed him a written report of the previous day's ambush. "I'm sorry I didn't report last night, Sir, but I was havin' a rough time with JJ's death. I figured you'd get the scoop from Thunder."

"How you feeling now?" asked Malcolm.

"Like hell – but I'll get by – just like you and Thunder and the rest of the guys. We'll all get by, unless we get an early out, like JJ."

Malcolm read Jesse's report. When he finished he looked up from the paper, an eyebrow raised. "This report differs a little bit from Thunder's. Are you sure it was JJ who charged up that hill singlehandedly? I don't have Thunder's written report yet but I was sure he said it was someone else last night."

"It was pretty dark when JJ assaulted that hill. Maybe Thunder couldn't really see well enough to make a determination, Sir. I think though, when you get his written report, you'll find out that he must have been confused last night. It was a pretty long day for all of us."

Malcolm raised both eyebrows. "I guess I'll just have to wait until I get Thunder's report to make a determination."

Jesse smiled weakly. "Yessir. If it's all the same to you, I gotta go on another patrol. Will there be anything else, Sir?"

"No, Indio. That'll be all. Thanks."

Lance corporal Jonathan James "JJ" Washington was awarded the Silver Star posthumously. His hometown newspaper ran a front page spread on JJ, and his family appeared in a photograph accepting the medal. Thunder looked up from the newspaper sent to him by JJ's family and smiled at Jesse. "JJ wanted a medal in the worst way. I guess his death wasn't a total waste after all."

"It's the pits. But I guess it could have been worse." Jesse took a drag from his cigarette,

Thunder folded the paper and stood. "Well, I guess it's time to see what kind of hell we can raise today. Let's check in with the skipper."

*****

Life for the First Battalion Fourth Marines on the Hoa My Trail continued as before. Amoebic dysentery took a heavy toll. Some of the men tried to hide the ailment but all were eventually discovered. For one man in Charlie Company the discovery came too late. He died of dehydration. The more fortunate were evacuated to Da Nang. The severe cases were flown to Japan or even the United States. To those who remained behind the workload became even heavier.

Jesse traded an Australian soldier out of a Thompson sub-machine gun with a hundred-round drum and three thirty-round magazines. He offered the Thompson to Thunder in return for his M-1 but Thunder would not give up his precious Garand.

On a two-company sweep with Delta Company Jesse was able to fire the Thompson at a group of VC at a distance of three hundred yards. There were no VC casualties. That same afternoon, as the platoon took a short break from the march, he attempted to talk Thunder into trading him on an every-other-day basis. Thunder steadfastly refused to have anything to do with the short-range Thompson.

"Damnit, Thunder, I'd have just as much luck with my knife as I would this Thompson."

"Why don't you carry an M-14 till you find another Garand?"

"I'd rather have the Thompson. That damn M-14 is about as dependable as a fart in a whirlwind."

Thunder smiled. "If you get any skinnier, you won't be able to tote a Garand around anyway. Hell, I believe you're about the biggest bag-a-bones I ever saw."

"It's all part of my strategy. Makes me a smaller target."

Thunder agreed. "You got that right. Hell, when you turn sideways, you

Stoney Livingston
disappear."

A corpsman walked down the trail of resting marines, passing out salt tablets. Thunder accepted his two tablets. "Thanks, Sandy."

Sandy eyed Jesse. Jesse shook his head. The corpsman moved down the line. Thunder buried his tablets in the soft soil.

"Why 'n the hell don't you just tell him you don't want the damn things?" asked Jesse.

"No sense hurtin' his feelin's. He's a damn good corpsman."

"Hell, Sandy wouldn't take it personal."

"Never can tell. And who knows – might need his services some day? No sense pissin' 'im off."

"Good point," agreed Jesse.

Thunder watched Sandy as the corpsman examined a marine two places forward in the column. "I wonder what the hell Preacher is doin', droppin' his drawers?"

Jesse turned his attention to the corpsman. Preacher was bent over, almost like he was trying to touch his toes. Sandy appeared to be pushing his fingers into the lanky man's rectum. "I'll be damned. I'm sure there's a medical explanation for this but I don't know what the hell it is."

Whatever Sandy did, he completed his task quickly, washed his hands with water from his canteen, and moved on to the next man in the column. Preacher pulled his trousers up and buttoned them expeditiously. Five minutes later, as Sandy returned to his proper place in the column, he passed Thunder and Jesse.

"Hey, Doc. What the hell is wrong with Preacher?" asked Jesse. "What was all that business with his drawers down around his ankles?"

Sandy looked first at Thunder then Jesse. He stepped closer. "That man has one of the worst cases of hemorrhoids I've ever seen. I gotta stuff 'em back where they belong every once in a while. I can't do much for him out here."

"That sounds painful as hell to me," said Jesse.

"You can bet on that. That guy shouldn't even be out here," agreed Sandy.

Thunder said, "Send him out, Doc."

"I tried once. He begged me not to do it. Said they really didn't bother 'im that much. I know he's lyin' but he wants to stay. If he wants to stay that bad he can have his way. I'm tellin' ya, that man has a ticket to the States right now if he wants it."

Thunder said, "When we get off this sweep, send 'im home, Doc. He don't wanna stay because he likes this shit. He just doesn't wanna leave us with that much more bullshit to do and fewer men to do it with. Send 'im home. I'll write 'im unfit if you don't. Guy like him oughta be home totin' a bible instead of over here with an M-14 in his hands. He hates this garbage even more than the average guy does."

"Okay, Thunder, I'll have him outa here by tomorrow afternoon."

"Thanks."

Sandy took his place to the rear of the unit.

"Jesus. Can you believe that guy?" said Thunder, nodding in Preacher's direction.

Jesse shuddered. "Not me. What the hell is his real name anyway?"

"MacIntire. But we all call 'im Preacher 'cause he's always spoutin' off some sort of religious phrase or some such thing. He's a good man under fire though. Can't really figure 'im out. Don't matter now. He's goin' home tomorrow."

440

"That's a good idea. Can you imagine livin' like we gotta live and havin' to put up with those hemorrhoid things? That guy's crazy."

Thunder looked back at Jesse and said, "Don't bullshit me. You wouldn't leave either. Not because you wanna be a hero, but for the same reason I'd stay and Preacher stays. None of us wanna leave the other guy here to suffer this shit alone. It's the guys we'd stay here for, not the damn war. This war is rapidly becoming a piece of shit as far as I'm concerned."

Jesse inhaled his cigarette smoke. "Yeah, yer right. Nobody wants out while we're in the bush. It'd be kinda like runnin' out. If we were back at Phu Bai, and I had Preacher's problem - whatever-in-the-hell it is - I'd leave in a New York minute."

"Yer right there."

Voices moved down the line. "Saddle up."

*****

Jesse and Rich Cummings talked quietly in the Gun One pit, neither expending a lot of energy. There wasn't much to spare. Mud lounged against the sandbag wall of the pit, speaking to Courtney, complaining of Jesse's crazy antics and unreasonable behavior; Courtney knowing all the while that Mud wouldn't trade his position for anything less than a transfer home.

Rich and Cue were the healthiest members in the first squad, being the only ones not on some sort of light duty. Sal and Courtney both suffered from a mild form of dysentery. Manny walked with a limp as the result of spraining his ankle in his mad dash to find cover during one of the VC shellings of the camp. Willis lay on his back in the shade of the bunker, recovering from heat stroke and a bad case of exhaustion. The corpsmen at the aid station had told him he would be fit for duty in three more days. He didn't believe it but was willing to give it a try. The rest were weak from the steady C-ration diet and the long nights without rest . Everyone's eyes were glazed and bloodshot. Jesse knew the only thing keeping them going was hope. They all knew they would be relieved soon. They had to be.

Rich said, "Too bad about JJ. He was a good guy. What a shitty way to get it."

"You know a good way?" asked Jesse.

"You know what I mean. A goddamn ambush, and him bein' the rear guard and all. It sure is strange."

"How many gooks you think it was that hit you guys that night?" asked Sal.

"Thunder figures between nine and twelve. I put it about the same," answered Jesse.

"It's a cryin' shame about JJ," repeated Rich.

"Yeah," replied Jesse.

"Rumor has it that we're gonna be pullin' outa here in a week or two," offered Cue.

"I don't know about all of that shit. I been hearin' that crap for a month or more," said Manny, still laying on his back in the shade.

Tuleano stepped into the gun pit and offered two envelopes to Jesse. "Here, you got a couple a letters that didn't get sent to Alpha Company. Whoever it is addressed 'em to the 81 Platoon. You really oughta give yer girlfriends the right address or Jody will start takin' care of 'em for ya."

Jesse accepted the letters and stuffed them into his map pocket. He would read them later. "Thanks."

Stoney Livingston

"You look like shit, man. A small wind'd blow you outa the country," offered Tuleano.

Jesse smiled. "Then let's all pray for a tornado."

"What d'ya hear with the grunts, Indio? Any word on us gettin' the hell outa here?" asked Rich.

"Hell, I'm never around long enough to hear anything. I come in offa patrol and I go out on a night ambush." He looked at Tuleano. "How's that damn order on the flak jackets holdin' up? They makin' you guys wear them things?"

Tuleano mumbled, "We wear 'em when we're firin' the guns but that's about all. How about the grunts?"

"Some of us never got issued the damn things. Those that did just leave 'em layin' around their holes. I ain't seen anybody wear one on a patrol yet. Some of the guys are takin' 'em on the ambushes but that's about it," replied Jesse.

"I don't think they're worth a pound of shit," offered Sal.

"I'm with you, Sal. Well, I gotta go. Got another one of those famous patrols in about twenty minutes. You guys take it easy." Jesse turned to Mud. "C'mon, Mud, you got voted in on this one."

"Shit," blurted Mud disgustedly as he followed Jesse from the gun pit.

*****

As the afternoon wore on, Jesse began to feel sick. His skin became dry and his head began to throb. He could feel his body temperature rise rapidly. He fought against it but was powerless to control the problem. He had lived long enough in the desert to know he was suffering from heat stroke. He knew too that heatstroke – sunstroke as he called it when he was a kid – was a killer. The patrol was returning from an uneventful afternoon of walking the hills. He gritted his teeth and continued to walk. With less than half a mile to go he was sure he could make it. No sense having two men carry him in. Every one on the patrol was weak and emaciated. They probably wouldn't get a hundred yards if they had to carry him in addition to their own gear.

His vision blurred as he tried to focus on the tents when they entered the outskirts of the battalion perimeter. With only a hundred yards remaining between him and the battalion aid station Jesse's trembling legs would support him no longer. He sank to the ground and sat unceremoniously, leaning on the Thompson for support. Thunder approached from the rear.

"You okay, Indio?"

"Not this time, Amigo. I think I've got heatstroke. I thought I could make it but now I'm too weak to stand, and my vision is blurry as hell."

Thunder put his hand on Jesse's forehead. "Shit!" He ripped Jesse's helmet off and emptied a canteen of water over his head. "Corpsman! Corpsman up!"

Jesse attempted to stand but staggered and was saved a fall only by Thunder's quick action. The young sergeant scooped him over his shoulder in the fireman's carry and shuffled to the battalion aid tent as fast as his legs would let him travel in their weakened condition, Jesse hanging on to his Thompson, feeling each jolt as Thunder's feet hit the ground.

Jesse was vaguely aware of Sandy pointing to a cot as they entered the tent. Thunder placed him on the indicated cot. Sandy took his temperature as Thunder and Mud stood by.

"Holy shit!" Sandy turned to the two junior corpsmen in the tent. "Get the

442

alcohol and any ice we have left - on the double! This man has a temperature of a-hundred-and-eight degrees! Get on it!"

As the corpsmen hustled about the tent, Thunder said, "Doc, are you sure about that temperature? I didn't think a person could be alive with that kind of temperature. Hell, he was walkin' only about a minute ago."

"I believe it, but I'll guarantee you, I ain't met anybody else that ever did it and can tell you about it. I don't have anymore time to talk right now. Here, hold this pan of ice water."

Thunder accepted the pan and held it as Sandy and the two junior corpsmen dipped rags into the cold liquid and bathed Jesse who had been undressed by one of them even as Thunder had been speaking to Sandy.

Jesse shivered and fought against the cold water treatment as it was applied to his genitals, neck and underarms first, then his chest and back. Over and over the ice water was applied. Sandy took his temperature again, "One-oh-six-point-seven. It's comin' down. We're low on ice." He turned to one of the corpsmen. "Get the alcohol." Turning back to Mud, he said, "Get on the horn and get a helicopter out here and have 'em bring some more ice, and tell 'em they'll be takin' one to Da Nang East Hospital."

"You got it," replied Mud.

Sandy and the others worked feverishly over Jesse as he fought them every step of the way. He cursed the damp coldness and anyone who might be responsible for his discomfort.

"Hey, Doc. We can't get a helicopter here for an hour or maybe two. They're all tied up on some damn operation," said Mud.

"Give me that damn radio," said Thunder, "I'll get a helicopter in here if I have to threaten the damn airwing commander's life."

"Take it easy, Thunder. His temperature is comin' down. If we can get it down, and it stays, he'll be okay. He's reactin' real good to the ice bath," said Sandy.

Thunder watched Jesse as his puny form writhed about on the soaked cot. "You call that a good reaction? It don't look too good to me."

"He may not like it but it's workin', and it's savin' his life," replied Sandy.

"You sure? What about brain damage and all of that stuff?"

"Too early to tell about brain damage. We'll just send him off to the hospital and let them follow up."

"What the hell you guys tryin' to do? Kill me? Jesus Christ!"

Sandy opened Jesse's eyes with his fingers and peered into them with the aid of a flashlight. "You feelin' better?"

Jesse shivered involuntarily. "Better than what - a frozen shrimp? Yeah, I feel better than a frozen shrimp, but not much else. Where in the hell did you get ice?" He shivered again as one of the corpsmen placed ice near his genitals. "Godamnit, that's kinda a personal area there, buddy. Be real careful." He turned his head back and twisted his neck. "Hey, Thunder, cover that guy will ya'? If he makes a mistake, take 'im out."

Thunder smiled, relieved that Jesse appeared to be improving rapidly. "You got it."

Jesse turned his attention back to Sandy. "How about it, Sandy - where the hell did you get ice?"

"We get it on resupply. Sometimes we have to get it from a larger ville, but we have to have some on hand for certain drugs and for heatstroke. I gotta tell ya,

443

man, it's a damn good thing we have what we've got, or you'd be a dead man right now."

"Think so?"

Sandy nodded. "No doubt about it. Now, how do you feel?"

"Like my head's got a bullet in it. I feel weak as hell but at least my vision is clearin' up."

While the two junior corpsmen continued their work, Sandy ran a few simple tests designed to check vision, memory and motor responses. When he had completed the tests he checked Jesse's temperature. "I'll be damned. I never saw anything like that in my life."

Thunder and Mud stepped forward, both concerned that Sandy had found some incurable something.

"What's the matter, Doc?" asked Thunder.

"Almost nothing. That's the problem. His damn temperature is down to a little over a-hundred degrees, and I think it's still fallin'."

"That's good, ain't it?" asked Mud, who seemed confused.

Sandy stepped back and studied Jesse for a short moment. "Yeah, that's good, I guess, but I've never seen anybody recover from heatstroke that fast. And sure as hell no one with a temperature of a-hundred-and-eight degrees. As a matter-of-fact, I never saw anybody with a temperature of a-hundred-and-eight degrees before."

Jesse, though weak, sat up and put his feet on the ground. "How about it, Sandy? Are you guys done with me? Can I go now?"

Sandy pushed him gently back onto the cot. "Not on your ass. You're going to the Hospital at DaNang."

Jesse sat up again. "What the hell for? I feel fine. Hell, if I went to the hospital in Da Nang now, it'd be like goldbrickin'. There ain't a damn thing wrong with me. You guys did a helluva job. Now let me do mine." He attempted to stand.

Thunder stood close to him, making it impossible for him to gain his feet. "Doc says you gotta go to the hospital, Indio. The man knows his job. You even said yourself he was one of the best damn corpsmen in the Crotch."

"Godamnit, Thunder!" Jesse fell back onto the cot. "That's true. But the fact-of-the-matter-is that I don't have need for a hospital, and I ain't goin' to one."

Sandy said, "I'll tell you what, Indio. You stay at battalion aid overnight and let us keep an eye on you and, if you feel okay in the morning, we release you back to your company on light duty. How's that?"

"Bullshit. I got a night ambush tonight with second platoon."

Sandy's voice became firm. "Either you stay here overnight or you go to the hospital. I'm not gonna bullshit with you anymore. You had a close call with the reaper, Indio. Now which way do you want it?"

"Damn, Doc, you drive a hard bargain."

Thunder smiled. "Hell, he's holdin' all of the cards."

Jesse gave up the argument. "Okay, Doc. One night in this stuffy-assed tent, then I go back to the company, right?"

"If you're up to it."

"I'll be up to it."

Late that afternoon, Jesse read his mail. In addition to the two letters given to him by Tuleano, Mud brought him two more. He answered letters to Charlotte,

Dave, his mother and Will Hunt.

In the letter to Will, he suggested that the two of them might be able to meet in Hawaii if he could possibly wrangle a leave from the legal office at Camp Pendleton. Though he wasn't certain when he would get his R&R, he knew it would be soon. Too bad Charlotte couldn't join them. He'd like to meet her in person someday. He explained what he could remember of his battle with heatstroke and signed off.

Jesse was up with the morning sun, asking for his release from sick bay. The corpsman on duty advised him that under no circumstances could he be released without Sandy's approval. Jesse waited impatiently while a runner summoned the senior corpsman.

After an examination Sandy looked into Jesse's eyes. "I don't believe it but I can't find anything wrong with you that two weeks of good food wouldn't cure. You're the healthiest undernourished specimen I've ever seen. I can't believe you weigh a hundred-and-twenty-three pounds."

"I'll be takin' care of that when I get my R&R. And I don't wanna hear any of this six-day garbage. That hardly makes it worth the trip. I'm takin' two weeks."

Sandy smiled. "I'll bet you do too."

"Count on it."

The following day, he received a letter from Shannon.

My Dearest Jesse,

Your letter (short as it was) did more for me than you will ever know. You have always been special to me, Jesse. Very special. The shame of my pregnancy was almost too much for me to share with you, but I did it. You have a special place in my heart, and you always will.

I worry about you and think of you often. I'm sorry things didn't work out differently for us but I still love you. You will always be my Cyrano.

Please take care of yourself and write when you can. Your letters mean so much to me.

I know this is very short, but it has taken a lot of nerve for me to say what little I have said. Please try to understand.

Always,

Shannon

After re-reading the letter several times, he took out his writing tablet.

Shannon,

I have just read your letter and am honored by your thoughts. I seem to live in a world where nothing is real — not even life itself — but you are very real to me and I hope everything goes well for you and you remain happy in this life.

Thunder walked up to his position and stopped, looking down at him. "Hey, amigo, you goin' on this patrol or not?"

Jesse looked up at him. "Oh. I forgot."

Thunder nodded at the writing tablet. "Shannon?"

Jesse smiled.

Stoney Livingston

He returned Jesse's smile. "I'll be with the rest of the squad down by the road when you're ready." He turned and walked down the hillside.

Jesse returned to his letter.

I have to go on a patrol right now and will write a better letter later. Please know that I think of you often and only with the warmest affection.

Jesse

Damn! He almost blurted it out. He couldn't do that. He would think of Shannon as a sister from now on. She was married. End of sentence.

CHAPTER NINETEEN: R & R

Jesse beamed as he debarked the old C-46 with Thunder and Cue. He had thought the helicopter ride from the Hoa My Trail to Phu Bai had been a joyous occasion but, when they had seen the old twin-engine C-46 on the loading ramp at the Phu Bai Airstrip waiting to take them to Da Nang, it had become a trip back in time. They had made a special celebration out of the ride in the ancient aircraft by pretending it was a B-17 bomber. They sang and laughed and joked for the duration of the short ride to Da Nang, each pretending to shoot VC from the ports on the old plane as it lumbered along at one-thousand feet above the ground.

At one point in the journey the starboard engine had coughed and seemed to sputter but it had little effect on the three, other than to add more adventure to their trip and a touch of realism to their childish game of pretend. They could not be dissuaded from their amusements. When the engine smoothed out, it had seemed almost a disappointment.

The plan to take R&R together had failed at the last moment but at least they would have one night in Da Nang before they went to their separate destinations. Cue was on his way to Hong Kong, while Thunder had opted to go to Okinawa to visit old friends. Jesse had landed the only slot open to Hawaii and he was sure it had happened only as the result of a major effort by Lieutenant Malcolm. There were no married men scheduled for R&R at the time so Jesse jumped at the chance to revisit Hawaii and perhaps meet Will Hunt. His bout with heatstroke of more than a week prior already forgotten, he was ready for R&R.

It was mid-morning when the three stepped onto the tarmac at the Da Nang airstrip. "How about we do a little recon?" asked Jesse as the bright sunlight struck him full in the face.

"Sounds like a real plan to me," agreed Thunder, barely able to contain his excitement.

"Jeez, this place has grown," said Cue.

"You got that right," agreed Thunder. "There must be five times the planes and four times the concrete there was when I saw this place last."

"That just means five times the fun. Let's go," said Jesse.

A voice brought them back to reality. "You marines over there – fall in for your briefing."

The three looked at each other quizzically. They shrugged in unison and formed a rank before the well-fed staff sergeant who had commanded their attention.

The staff sergeant cleared his throat. "As you are well aware, gentlemen, we are still in a combat zone."

The three looked around them at the modern facilities; the vehicles and aircraft; the solid buildings and the concrete taxiways. The smell of cooking food wafted to the large hanger from a not-too-distant mess hall.

"Give me a combat zone every time," said Jesse quietly. Cue and Thunder chuckled softly.

The staff sergeant continued. "It may look a little bit more secure than where you've just come from but, I promise you, there are plenty of VC within spittin' distance of where you're standing.

"There are a few rules you ought to know about for your own safety. You will be staying overnight, no matter what your R&R destination. This will not be counted as one of your six days."

"Two weeks," mumbled Jesse quietly.

Thunder shot him a knowing glance.

"You will be issued passes to the mess facilities and the clubs on base but you will not be allowed to pull liberty in Da Nang. Is that clear?"

Spirits were starting to fall a little bit. Jesse said, "We hear what you're saying, Sergeant, but why can't we pull liberty? Hell, if it's that tough in town, just issue us a rifle and a liberty card. We'll be back in time to make the airplane out of here."

The staff smiled. "I know how you feel but we've had bad experiences with the line companies coming in here and raising hell with the local populace. The next day you guys are gone but we have to stay and put up with the shit you've left behind. The base commander says no liberty for those personnel destined for R&R. I know you guys don't want to hear this but we've got some pretty good clubs on base, and they even let some of the Vietnamese women aboard to mingle. You may even run into an American nurse or two."

Prospects were picking up.

"Besides, several of the first groups through that were allowed liberty in town came up with a lot of the marines missin' their R&R. Once they got into town, they just stayed there and drank the gook booze and screwed their brains out until their money was gone. Then they'd drag-ass back to base and hitch a ride back into the bush.

"Speaking of money, you will be allowed to change a maximum of twelve-hundred dollars from MPC to foreign currency. The brass figures that even a marine doesn't need more than that for six days of hell-raisin'"

Jesse said, "What if you're going to Hawaii?"

"The rules do not apply to the United States or any of its possessions at this time." He cleared his throat. "You will be in my care for the next hour or two while we change currency, check medical records, brief you on your destination country, and generally lay out how this R&R thing works. We want you all to have a good time but we don't want anyone getting lost or missing their return flight – or getting into trouble while on R&R. Things are not the same in the bush as they are where you're going. You represent the United States Marine Corps and the United States itself. Do it with dignity and honor."

He paused. No one spoke. "If there are no questions, follow me."

That afternoon, Jesse changed almost four thousand dollars of MPC into U.S. dollars. One thousand of it was for Thunder, who figured he might need a little emergency money in the event his twelve hundred didn't last for one reason or the other.

By late afternoon, after receiving a bunk for the night, with instructions for the morrow, they were allowed to roam the expanse that was the Da Nang Airbase.

They were ejected from the first club they entered almost immediately for failure to meet the minimum requirements – they were not officers. Armed with

448

Forever Patriots

instructions to the E.M. and N.C.O. clubs, they left the officer's club indignantly.

An air force tech sergeant strolled by. Thunder accosted him. "Say, Sergeant, which is better, the NCO club or the EM club?"

The tech sergeant looked the scrawny marines over. "You guys goin' on R&R?"

"It shows, huh?" asked Thunder.

The tech smiled. "More than usual. Where the hell you guys from anyway?"

"This morning it was the Hoa My Trail, 1st Battalion, 4th Marines. We could sure use some good chow and a cool drink. We had chow in a mess hall at noon but we'd like to sit down somewhere and order up a meal like a big shot at a restaurant in the States," said Thunder.

The tech smiled a knowing smile and held out his hand. "Name's Riley."

A short round of introductions followed.

Riley said, "I think I know what the doctor ordered for you guys. Are those the best dungarees you've got?"

Jesse answered, "These are the *only* dungarees we got – except we call 'em utilities."

Riley clucked with his tongue. "They won't ever do in town. The shore patrol 'd pick you out in a minute."

"They won't give us a liberty card. Can you believe that?" said Cue.

"Yeah, I believe it, but I don't believe *in* it. You guys are out there bustin' yer asses and starvin' to death and these rear-echelon poges wanna keep all the food, beer and women to themselves. Don't worry about the liberty card. I've got some spares, and my men have the west gate to the base. I forgot to tell you, I'm in charge of a platoon of AP's."

"Oh shit!" said Cue.

Riley raised a hand. "Don't sweat it. I was in the old army air corps – waist-gunner on a B-17. I don't have a whole lotta use for the way you guys get treated back here." He paused for a moment, holding his chin between thumb and forefinger, thinking deeply. His eyes lit up. "I know where we can get you some dungaree ...I mean utilities. There's a marine supply sergeant who owes me more favors than he'll ever pay if he stays over here twenty years. Let's go get a drink and I'll get you guys what you need for a trip to town."

"Are you serious?" asked Jesse. This had all happened too fast for him to believe any of it.

"Don't worry about it. I've got six months left in this goddamn outfit and I really don't give a damn about a few marines havin' a little bit of hard-earned fun."

"Hell, I even take back some of the things I've said about the air force," said Cue.

"Don't bother. I don't. Meant every word I ever said about it – good or bad."

They all laughed as they followed Riley to the NCO Club. Later, with a good meal under their belts, phoney liberty cards, and brand new utility uniforms, they left the base in Riley's Jeep.

Jesse sat with his back to the wall, Thunder on his right, and Cue across from him at the small round table. A Vietnamese prostitute sat on Cue's lap, begging for more Saigon Tea, except she called it a drink. Cue didn't seem to care that he was paying two dollars for a small glass of colored water.

Sergeant Riley returned to the table with a Vietnamese woman. Jesse and

449

Stoney Livingston

Thunder nodded at their approach. Cue was aware of nothing but the Vietnamese prostitute on his lap.

"Guys, I'd like you to meet Susie. Susie, these are my marine buddies I told you about."

Jesse and Thunder rose. Cue turned his head and nodded.

"Nice meetin' ya, Ma'am," offered Jesse.

"Howdy, Ma'am," greeted Thunder. He waved to an empty chair.

Riley and Susie sat on Thunder's right. Cue and his prostitute scooted counter-clockwise to give them room. Susie was older than most of the women in the bar, though nonetheless prettier. Her skin was flawless and stretched on her face like a tightly-fitting surgical glove, giving the impression it was the tautness of her skin that had a flattening affect on the bridge of her nose.

"Guys, I been knowin' Susie here since the day I arrived in this little Shangri-la. She's taken good care of me and she sees to it that me and my men don't catch any flak from the shore patrol. I can only stay for a few more minutes, then I'm gonna leave you in her hands." He winked. "And I'm tellin' ya, those are *some* hands."

Thunder and Jesse both smiled an embarrassed smile. Cue continued to ignore everything but the girl on his lap.

While Thunder spoke with Susie and Riley, Jesse studied the small bar with its dim lights and ceiling fans. In a strange way it reminded him of Nick's bar in the movie *Casablanca*. There were many more people in the *Flak Jacket*, as the bar was named, and the smoke was thicker, but the ceiling fans made him think of that old movie.

There were about nine or ten girls working as prostitutes in the direct employ of the bar and three or four more about whom Jesse was uncertain.

He drank from his beer and smiled. *Life is really funny. All of these guys are gonna go back home some day, and I'll bet every damn one of 'em will tell of the horrors of war and how many VC they killed. And they won't even let the real VC killers in their posh bars. I guess they're right, some of that field shit might rub off. Can't be too safe, you know.*

"Hey, Indio, you with us or what?"

Jesse looked up from his blank stare at the table. "Sorry, Thunder. I was just thinkin'."

"That's bad fer ya, man. Listen, Riley here's gotta go."

Jesse leaned over the table to be heard above the crowd noise. "You really gotta go, Riley? Hell, man, the night's young yet."

Riley nodded. "Yeah, I got the duty tonight. You guys stay out of trouble and have a helluva time on R&R. It was nice meetin' ya. Stay cool and Susie here will take care of you." He stood.

Cue spoke, ignoring his female friend for the first time since she had landed in his lap. "Thanks, Riley. We won't forget it."

"My pleasure. See you guys." He turned and walked through the door.

As soon as Riley left the room, Susie said to Thunder, "Your friend want girl? I get him number one boom-boom in all Vietnam."

Thunder turned to Jesse. "Which one you want? Susie here says you got your pick."

"I like Susie." Jesse smiled wryly.

"Somehow I knew you were gonna say that. I'll tell you what I'll do. I'll flip

450

you for her."

"I was just kiddin'. I don't want anything right now. I just wanna sit here and tip a few drinks and feel good about bein' outa the bush. Thanks anyway. She looks like more fun than I could handle right now anyway." Jesse tipped his glass in a short salute.

Susie snapped her fingers at one of her girls who then approached the table rapidly. Susie spoke to the girl at length in Vietnamese. When she finished speaking, the girl moved to Jesse's side and pulled up a chair. She rubbed her stockinged leg against his as she moved her chair to the table.

Jesse leaned across the table toward Susie. "I appreciate it, Susie, but I don't really want any company right now. I'm not lookin' for any boom-boom yet. I'll let you know if I change my mind."

"No. I tell her sit next to you. Keep you company. If you buy her drink, she drink real whiskey, no Saigon Tea. You friend of Joe Riley. Susie treat you good. Li best girl in place. She pretty, smart, and drink real whiskey if I say okay."

Jesse relaxed a little. He couldn't stifle a smile.

"That much better. You see. Susie know. You buy her drink. She stay with you tonight. Longtime. No worry. You Joe Riley friend."

Jesse turned to the girl on his left. He had paid little attention when she had first sat next to him but now his eyes riveted on her face. "You're not Vietnamese."

"Yes, I am." She answered in English, thick with a french accent. "My father was French but my mother was Vietnamese."

"I didn't mean anything by it but you do look European."

"I have been told that many times before. You think it is true?"

"I sure do."

"Amen, brother," offered Thunder from across the table.

Jesse looked at the dark-haired girl at his side, suddenly aware that her leg was still touching his. "Would you like a drink?"

"Thank you. A gin and tonic please. What is your name?"

"Indio. What's yours?"

"Li."

"Nice meetin' ya, Li." Jesse ordered Li's drink from a passing waitress.

Cue stood. "If you guys are gonna be here for a while, I'm goin' for a little boom-boom. I can't stand it any longer."

Jesse laughed. "Go for it, Cue. We'll keep your back covered."

Cue walked away with his Vietnamese prostitute, disappearing in the thick smoke long before he reached the door leading to the rooms in the rear of the building.

"Do you want boom-boom with Li?" asked Jesse's companion as she took a sip from her tall glass.

Jesse boldly studied the prostitute at his side, something he would have been too shy to do only ten months prior. Oh, sure, he would most certainly have looked at her, but not in the careful and analytical way he did now. He looked at her face, with its slightly oriental eyes, and her long dark hair for which many nationalities could have claimed origin. He brazenly studied her small breasts as they pushed tightly against her form-fitting silken dress. He took note of the curvature from her small waist to her firm hips. His stare continued down her well-formed legs and ankles to her tiny feet.

"You like?" she said.

451

His eyes met hers and he smiled broadly. "Oh yeah, I like. As a matter-of-fact, I like a whole bunch. Only problem is, I don't think this is the time or the place for it to happen. I wanna break into things a little slower." Thoughts of Shannon danced through his head. How he wished he could go to California for his R&R. He didn't know what he'd do in California but he was back to where he was in 1962 – that's where Shannon was. Of course she was more like a sister now, Langley – remember?

Li appeared puzzled.

"I appreciate the offer, but tonight I just wanna take it easy and drink too much whiskey."

"Susie tell me to make you feel good. You friend of Joe Riley. Li make good boom-boom for Indio. Make Indio very happy."

Jesse raised an eyebrow. "Yeah. I'll bet you could." He had a fleeting vision of the girl's naked body on silken sheets. "Not tonight, Li. I just wanna sit here and drink a few drinks. Sorta like unwindin' after a hard ten months work. You know what I mean?"

"Li no understan'. You no like Li?"

"That's not it at all. It's just that tonight I want whiskey. Tomorrow maybe I want Li. Okay?"

"You no tell Susie you not want boom-boom with Li?"

"I won't tell."

Li smiled and sipped her drink.

Jesse drank his whiskey quietly and thought of another Vietnamese girl who spoke English in the City of Hue. He wondered if her younger sister had recovered from her wounds.

The three of them walked arm-in-arm down the roadway. Cue whispered. "Hey, Indio, how come you didn't go out back with that French girl? Hot damn! She was a looker."

"I don't know – not in the mood, I guess. She was nice and all, but I'm goin' where I know people. She probably had every disease known to man. If I'm gonna die over here, I'd rather it be from a bullet. Ya know what I mean?"

"Yeah, I know what you mean, but I'm tellin' ya, that little thing I was with was good. I mean, she had more moves than an Ohio State halfback."

"No shit," said Thunder. "We figured by the third time you went out back with 'er that she was at least passable."

They all laughed quietly.

"Indio, are you sure this is the way back to the base?" asked Cue, a small note of concern showing in his voice.

Jesse looked down the moonlit road. "Yeah. I think so. Hell. I don't know for sure. Let me take another pull of that bottle, Thunder, so I can be sure."

Thunder passed the bottle of whiskey. Jesse took a long swallow. He handed the bottle to Cue. "Yeah, we're headed the right way. Oughta be gettin' pretty close."

"What the hell time is it?" asked Thunder.

Jesse looked at his Zodiac SeaWolf watch in the moonlight. "'Bout one-thirty or so."

The metal sound of a machine gun bolt being pulled to the rear halted them. Even in their current state of intoxication, instincts prevailed. They separated and flattened out on the side of the road. A voice challenged them – a foreign voice.

Jesse spoke first. "We don't speak that shit."

There was a short silence as the three waited for the gun to open fire. A Vietnamese voice spoke broken English. "Who go there?"

"Friends," answered Jesse.

"How do I know this?" asked the voice.

"Jesus Christ," muttered Jesse under his breath. Louder, he said, "We're American marines. And I can tell you right now that the army or air force trained yer ass by the way you issued the challenge."

"Godamnit, Indio, don't piss the guy off. We ain't got any weapons, remember?" whispered Thunder, the liquor's effect rapidly disappearing.

The Vietnamese voice replied, "Stand and be recognized."

"Bullshit. I'll meet you halfway," replied Jesse.

"You wait. No move."

They waited. Thirty seconds elapsed.

"What the hell's goin' on?" whispered Cue, not yet sober enough to appreciate the gravity of the situation.

"Hell, I don't know," whispered Thunder. "I think we walked into an ARVN road block. At least I *hope* they're ARVN."

A voice broke the stillness, an unmistakably American voice. "Who the hell's out there?"

Jesse answered. "Three drunk 'n' pissed-off marines. Who the hell are you?"

The voice answered. "Is that you crazies from One-Four?"

Cue hiccoughed. "How the hell did he know that?"

Thunder ignored Cue and addressed the voice. "Is that you, Riley?"

The booming voice answered. "I should have known. Cue, Indio and Thunder, right?"

"You got a helluva memory," said Thunder.

"That's part of what I get paid for."

Jesse said, "Listen, if it's all the same to you guys, I'd rather bullshit somewhere else. This ground is wet."

Riley laughed. "It's okay. You guys can come in now."

Jesse, though inebriated, was cautious. "You sure? One a them ARVN's got an A-4 with a chambered round in it."

"I'm sure. C'mon in before we all wind up in the shithouse."

Three embarrassed marines stood and approached the roadblock. The three Vietnamese soldiers laughed and joked among themselves and with Riley as the marines staggered to their position. Jesse and Thunder greeted the ARVN soldiers while Cue remained silent behind them.

Thunder squinted and looked at Riley in the darkness. "I'm sure glad you were nearby. These guys had us pretty cold."

"I figured you three might be headed this way so I alerted them to that possibility. Any other time they'd a' shot first and asked questions later. This isn't the normal way back to the base. Anybody comin' this way at this hour is assumed to be a VC. I forgot to tell you to return through the main gate. I'm sorry about that."

"Great," muttered Cue.

They all laughed at Cue's remark, even the ARVN soldiers, who had no idea what they were laughing about.

Stoney Livingston

Riley transported the three to their quarters in a jeep and left them to get a few hours sleep before their departures in the morning. After Riley disappeared into the darkness, Jesse lay silently on his bunk.

"Yer thinkin' too loud, Indio," said Thunder. Cue snored loudly in the bunk below him.

Jesse took another pull from the bottle of whiskey and said nothing. A full minute went by.

"You gonna hog that bottle all night?" asked Thunder.

Slowly Jesse stood and moved to Thunder's bunk. Handing him the bottle, he said, "We almost bought it tonight."

Thunder took his turn at the bottle. "Yeah, we sure as hell did. If it hadn't a been fer ol' Riley we'd probably be wrapped in ponchos for the long ride home. I been kinda thinkin' about that myself. It *was* kinda dumb, wasn't it?"

Jesse retrieved the bottle from Thunder. "That's prob'ly the best thing it was. It was too close, Thunder. We haven't even had R&R yet. The government would'a' won again. They wouldn't 'a' had to pay for our R&R trip."

Thunder retook the bottle. He shook his head and laughed softly. "I'll be damned if you don't have a warped sense of humor."

"I earned it. But if the truth were known, every one of us that volunteered fer this shit has somethin' wrong with some spot in his brain. I think it must be the spot that controls common sense. Maybe we were all born brain-damaged."

Thunder handed Jesse the bottle. "I'll accept that as an explanation."

"On that note, I'm signin' off the net fer the night. See ya at reveille." Jesse stumbled to his bunk.

"See ya at reveille, Indio."

Cue continued to snore peacefully.

*****

As Jesse rode in the front seat of the taxi, he looked forward to his meeting with Claudia. True, she hadn't been home when he had called, but Katrina had indicated that she should be home in an hour or two at most. Katrina had sounded genuinely glad to hear from him and had asked for any news of Joe. He had related his meeting with Joe at the tail end of *Operation Oregon* to her in detail.

The taxi stopped in front of her house. Jesse had been so engrossed in his thoughts he had seen nothing of the city in his passing. He didn't worry. He would have time for that later. Maybe Claudia could be his tour guide. He felt good. He thought of Shannon for a moment and wished he could share Hawaii with her. It would be a fairy tale come true if he could meet her here.

"Hey, bub, you gonna sit there all day?"

He paid and tipped the driver and stepped from the cab in his new civilian clothes, freshly purchased from the PX. He had purchased the clothing by merely picking his old size, giving no thought to the fact that he was almost forty-five pounds lighter than he had been only ten months prior. The shirt was loose and the pants baggy but he didn't care. He would put on his weight again and the clothes would fit just fine.

Katrina greeted him at the door with a hug and a matronly kiss. She oohed and aahed about his weight loss and immediately led him to the kitchen where she insisted he eat at least one of everything in her cupboards and refrigerator. He did his best to comply with her wishes, halting only to answer her many questions.

454

Forever Patriots

Several times she apologized for asking so many questions but, forthwith, returned to the questioning to satisfy her insatiable curiosity.

He was so involved in his conversation with Katrina, he lost track of time. A quick glance at his watch reminded him of the few hours left in the day. "Holy cow. I've been here almost three hours. It's gettin' onto six o'clock. I wonder what's keepin' Claudia?"

"She'll be in shortly. If she had only known you were coming she would have been waiting at the door when you arrived."

"Maybe I'd better go check into my hotel room so they don't give it away."

"I suppose you know you don't have to spend money on a hotel room – but I guess it wouldn't be quite the same if you didn't. Where are you staying?"

"I appreciate the offer but I'll be stayin' at the Royal Palm."

Katrina raised an eyebrow and smiled. "You certainly know how to do things in style. That's the classiest place on the Island."

"I can't take credit for that. A colonel on the plane told me about it."

"It's nice. I've only been there a couple of times but it was dreamy. Joe took me there one time, right after it was built."

"Say, why don't you join Claudia and me for dinner tonight? That is, if she ever gets home."

"I'd love to but I'm not going to be the third man out. You kids don't need me to get in your way. You two just have a great time."

He persisted. He and Claudia would have plenty of time together. He wasn't even sure they would like each other's company anyway. "You sure wouldn't be in the way. I enjoy your company and I really appreciate the warm welcome you gave me. It was like comin' home. You make me feel comfortable, and to tell you the truth, I wasn't even sure I could talk to a civilized person anymore. You made it easy for me. Please have dinner with us. I'll have a lousy time if you don't. I'm serious."

Katrina O'leary Haliniak laughed a beautiful laugh with pearl-white teeth. "Jesse, I do believe you're the funniest guy I ever met. I'll tell you what I'll do: I'll wait for Claudia to get home and talk it over with her. If she can stand my company for a few hours this evening, I'll join you two for dinner. How's that?"

"Great. I'll grab a cab and get checked in. What time do you think I should make the dinner reservations for?"

"Dinner at eight sounds perfect. I know Claudia'll be home in time to make that. We'll meet you in the lobby. I'll drive you to the hotel and come back and wait for Claudia. You ready?"

Jesse took in the beauty that is Hawaii as he rode in Katrina's old Desoto to the Royal Palm. He enjoyed the old car and the kind sunshine of the Islands, and the clear sky and the beautiful woman who had mothered Claudia. He laughed softly.

"Did you see something funny?" asked Katrina.

"Yeah – in my mind. I saw a skinny marine enlisted man with the two prettiest women in the Hawaiian Islands, at the ritziest restaurant in town. Maybe we'll run into a lieutenant or two."

Katrina laughed with him.

*****

Jesse waited nervously in the grand lobby of the hotel, its richly mahoganied walls providing distraction enough to keep him from pacing the floor. He lighted a small, slender cigar, recently purchased, and, leaning back in the

455

overstuffed chair near the coffee table, he studied the ornate ceiling. He sipped his sour mash whiskey and waited for Claudia and Katrina. He checked his watch. Eight fifteen. He stood and walked to the shiny wooden registration desk.

"Any messages for Jesse Langley?"

The stiffly uniformed deskman searched the rows of slots behind him. He turned to face Jesse, studying him and his suit, two sizes too large for him. "No, Sir, Mr. Langley. Nothing."

Jesse felt a deep disappointment. It was beginning to look like one of his precious days of R & R was going to be less than perfect. When he thought of the Hoa My Trail his spirits lifted. At least he wasn't there. He looked again at his pretentious surroundings. He smiled as he spoke to the deskman. "I may be joined by two ladies. If they should inquire, would you please inform them that I'm in the main dining area?"

"Yes, Sir, Mr. Langley. Will there be anything else?"

Jesse's smile broadened. "Yeah. Tell 'em I got hungry."

He had been seated no more than five minutes when Katrina approached his table. He stood. He knew it was the polite thing to do but, at his age, he felt awkward, as though every eye in the room was on him when he stood. A closer look at Katrina and he knew with certainty that none of the male eyes would waste their time on him with her in the room.

She was dressed in a blue silk cocktail dress that hugged her supple frame tightly. One side of the hem was split to above her knee. The bodice was cut low enough to reveal only a tasteful amount of breast but it was more than enough to draw the attention of the many men in the room, even those in the company of the opposite sex, many of whom drew hostile stares from their companions.

"Where's Claudia?"

"May I sit down?" asked Katrina, smiling.

"I'm sorry. Please." He moved to her chair and assisted her awkwardly.

Both seated, Katrina explained. "Claudia must have come home while I brought you to the hotel. She left a note saying that she was going to one of the islands for the weekend. I tried to reach her by calling everyone I know who she hangs around with but I didn't have any luck. I almost called you and told you that she couldn't make it and I would have to beg out but that didn't seem right. I like this place and I think you're a good kid. Why shouldn't we have dinner together? Tomorrow I can take you to the island. The kids camp out on the beach. I think I can find them without too much trouble."

Jesse held his mixture of disappointment and relief in check. He looked into Katrina's large dark eyes and smiled. "I'm glad you came. What the heck, you look younger than I do. I'll just pretend you're my date. I'll probably be accused of robbin' the cradle."

They both laughed a comfortable laugh.

Katrina taught Jesse how to read the wine list and how to order what wines might be good with their entree. He thought briefly of Barbara and a restaurant in California. They chose a French Bordeaux to accompany their Chateaubriand. They had cocktails before dinner to accompany their talk of the Islands and the war and politics. During dinner a bottle of Bordeaux was consumed.

As they sat drinking cognac after dinner, looking at the Pacific Ocean through the large window near their table, Jesse said, "Katrina, this has been one of the best times I've ever had in my life."

She smiled. "I'd think that anything would be better than what you've been through."

"Oh, it could always have been worse I guess. It wouldn't matter anyway. This has been great."

"Do you dance?"

Jesse was embarrassed. "Not really. I've got two left feet. I never learned how to dance. I guess I never had the time for it." An image of Shannon in his arms flashed into his thoughts. He felt her gentle embrace. "A friend of mine's sister tried to teach me but that was a long time ago and I haven't danced since."

"It's easy. Let's go to the lounge. I'll have you dancing in thirty seconds like Fred Astaire." Without waiting for him to respond in the negative, she stood. Jesse followed her obediently to the lounge. She held onto his arm lightly as they entered the subdued atmosphere surrounding the dance floor.

During the course of the evening, Jesse had thought little of Katrina as other than Claudia's mother – a beautiful mother to be sure, and a person very fun to be around – but nothing more. That line of thinking ended abruptly when she pulled him close on the dance floor. He felt her body as it formed to match the contours of his own. He was at once self-conscious. He wanted to pull away from her but could not, instead he backed his head away from her and looked into her eyes, looking for a sign of what she might be thinking.

She looked like any young woman enjoying her date. He read nothing. He backed away from her slightly. "Why don't we sit down a minute and let me warm up to this? Would you mind?"

She smiled. "Okay, maybe we could wait for a better song."

Jesse didn't even know the band was playing. "Yeah, that's a good idea."

He found a table midway between the booths lining the wall and the dance floor. Katrina pulled him to one of the booths, "Let's be more comfortable. I can relax better in a booth."

He allowed himself to be gently pulled to the nearest booth. Katrina scooted to the rear of the rounded booth, tugging on his sleeve for him to follow closely. Jesse was grateful for the prompt appearance of a cocktail waitress. The effects of the wine and cognac were beginning to tell but he ordered another drink, more to occupy his mind and time than to enjoy the drink.

As the waitress slid smoothly away from their table, Katrina said, "She's pretty."

"Yeah, she is, but not near as pretty as you and you know it."

"Thank you. Anything close to a compliment at my age is deeply appreciated."

Jesse wanted to move away from the subject. "I wonder what Claudia's doin' right about now?"

"There's no telling with that girl. She's got too much of her mother in her." Again the soft laugh.

Jesse was acutely aware of her nearness. He felt her leg against his and flinched away. He hoped she hadn't noticed his jumpiness. He wasn't sure why he was so jumpy. It was probably a moral thing, he thought. His physical attraction to Katrina was rapidly becoming considerably greater than any he might have for Claudia but Katrina was Claudia's mother. He didn't understand how that figured into the equation but he was sure it figured in somehow.

457

Stoney Livingston

The waitress returned to their table, drinks perched precariously on her tray. Jesse watched her more closely this time as she wiggled away from their table. He raised his glass in toast. "To the glorious wiggle of our waitress."

They touched glasses and sipped of the contents. The band began to play a slow-moving tune from the early fifties. Katrina slid around the booth. "C'mon, let's give it a try."

Reluctantly Jesse stood, dreading, yet looking forward to the moment he would feel her body next to his again. They moved onto the dance floor and she pressed near him. They fit well together and, though Jesse moved his feet to and fro in unfamiliar motions, he felt as though he was dancing magnificently. Katrina's lightly perfumed hair made him lightheaded. He went to a place in time he could not remember, dreamily taking in the soft scent.

He moved his hand on her back, massaging it gently, unthinkingly. She placed her cheek on his chest for but a moment then moved her head so that they were cheek to cheek. Jesse felt good about where he was and who he was with. He had never envisioned such a happening. He kissed her gently on her cheek.

She pulled her head back and looked into his eyes. For an instant, Jesse thought he may have gone too far. "Oh! I'm sorry. I didn't realize ...that is ...I ...I mean I don't know what made me do that."

Her eyes sparkled and she said, "I hope it was because you wanted to."

They stood on the dance floor, oblivious to the music or the few people nearby. The liquor left Jesse no inhibitions. The time spent in the jungle had left him no doubt as to the temporary nature of life. He pulled her close and kissed her full on the lips. She responded with a kiss as passionate as she dared on a public dance floor.

"Wow!" exclaimed Jesse softly as they pulled apart.

Katrina looked at him as though she were making a decision that in reality had been made for her when she had responded to Jesse's kiss. She pulled him from the dance floor. "Let's go to your room, Jesse. We both need this."

In the richly furnished suite, Katrina undressed unashamedly and stood before him in the brightly-lighted room. Her body was that of a woman in her early twenties. There was neither excess nor softness to any portion of it. She was proud of her body and rightly so. She moved slowly and with the grace of a cat to Jesse who stood, mouth agape, fully dressed. She unbuttoned his shirt carefully. He offered no resistance, neither did he assist.

Jesse experienced a fleeting feeling of guilt as the thought of Claudia passed through his mind. They had never been intimate. Viet Nam and the insignificance of life passed through his consciousness. He looked at the near-perfect figure of Katrina, knowing he may never live long enough to experience anything like her if he didn't experience her now. That's why he came to Hawaii for R&R – to experience life – though admittedly not with Katrina. He was completely naked now.

Katrina kissed his neck and chest.

Jesse wrestled to rationalize his thoughts. Her nearness rushed into his awareness. He gave up on rationalization. He leaned into her and kissed her lips. She responded passionately.

He pulled her naked body to his, kissing her deeply and roughly at first but as the kiss lengthened, his mouth softened and became gentle. He was consumed with a desire for her body that would wait no longer. She was docile and submissive, yet learned and experienced. Suddenly they were in the center of the room. Neither Jesse nor she could wait any longer. They melted into one on the plush carpet.

Afterwards, Jesse lay on his back on the carpet, the lights in the room still burning brightly. He stared at the ceiling, one arm wrapped around Katrina, holding her to his chest gently.

Katrina kissed his breast. "What are you thinking so hard about, baby?"

He squeezed her breast gently and kissed her forehead. "I'm tryin' to figure out why I think I should feel so bad about something that felt so good."

"What do you mean?"

"You're Joe's girl and Claudia's mother. I betrayed both of them to be here with you and I'd do it again. I don't believe there ever was a war in Vietnam. I don't believe I was ever there. It's too unreal. How can people go around killin' each other when it would be so much easier to find something like what we just had. Even if I never have you again, it was worth whatever may come of it."

Katrina brought her face close to his and brushed his lips with hers. "Jesse, Joe and I aren't married and, even if he knew we were together tonight, I honestly think he would understand. He's over there now. He took his R&R in Japan. Do you think he didn't sleep with other women?"

Jesse shrugged.

She continued. "As far as Claudia goes, I would never tell her. She accuses me of trying to steal her boyfriends as it is. In your case, the circumstances are just right for what's happened. I don't feel I have to justify my actions to anyone."

She gently massaged his manhood. "And as far as you never having me again, forget it. I'm having you again right now." She brought her lips to his stomach and kissed him, moving downward in soft little pecks until she found him ready.

The morning sun fired rays of light through the lace curtains of his room when Jesse awakened to Katrina massaging his genitals. He was instantly aroused and they rolled about the bed wildly, not slowing, fondling roughly until the passion exploded.

It was only after three sexual encounters they ordered breakfast sent to the room. Wrapped in a towel, Jesse accepted the tray, while Katrina stood naked behind the open door, out of sight of the delivering hotel employee. Jesse tipped the man generously and closed the door. Katrina giggled and stripped him of his towel. Again they made love on the floor.

Jesse breathed heavily, still atop Katrina's limp body. "Whew! Don't you ever use the bed?" he asked, still short of breath.

"We will If it's close enough when the urge strikes."

He rolled from her perspiring body to the thickly carpeted floor. "Oh. That makes sense I guess."

She laughed. "You're something else, Jesse. For as frail as you look right now, you keep up better than any man I ever met. I think I'll lock you up in a closet and open the door whenever I need a fix."

"I do my best, Ma'am," he said mockingly. She stuck a piece of toast in his mouth.

He chewed the toast slowly, testing the flavor, and swallowed hard. "What was on that thing?"

"Marmalade," she answered, the corner of her eyes turned up in a smile.

459

Stoney Livingston

"Whatever it was, give me strawberry anytime. Ugh!"

They ate the toast and fruit Katrina had ordered from the kitchen. Jesse covered his manhood with a towel but Katrina remained as naked as the day she was born. As she sipped her coffee from the small English teacup, she said, "Have you always been so capable a lover?"

"What d'ya mean by that?"

"Well, you and I must have made mad passionate love at least ten times in the last twelve hours. In my experience I find that unusual. I guess I should have found me a younger man a long time ago," she answered half thoughtfully and half jokingly. "I can hardly wait until you get back to your normal weight. I'll bet I couldn't handle you."

"I'll bet you could." He laughed.

They didn't leave the room that day. Jesse couldn't believe the things Katrina could do to arouse his passion. Never in his life had he been with a woman with her combination of beauty, passion and experience. In his wildest dreams while in Vietnam, he had never envisioned anything remotely as perfect as the physical relationship he experienced with Katrina.

It was shortly after seven that night they donned clothing for the first time in almost twenty-four hours. Katrina had had her evening gown cleaned and pressed during the day and she looked radiant as they prepared for dinner. Jesse had just finished shaving when the phone rang.

He picked up the receiver. "Hello?"

"Jesse?" It was a male voice.

"Will? Where are you? Did you get the leave?"

"I'm in the lobby downstairs. They wouldn't give me your room number."

"Six-twelve. Get on up here. You need help with your bags?"

"Are you kidding? There's a platoon of bellhops here. I thought these kinda hotels were only in the movies. Man, you went first class this time!"

Jesse looked at Katrina combing her long dark hair next to him. He smiled at her as he spoke into the phone. "The hotel isn't bad but if you want to see first class, get up here. I got someone I want you to meet."

"I'm on the way."

The meeting at the doorway was emotional and long as the two hugged and shook hands. Will said, "My God, what happened to you? You musta' lost a hundred pounds."

"More like forty-somethin', but I'm puttin' it back on." Jesse realized the two bellhops were standing idly by. He tipped each of them generously.

Will saw Katrina for the first time while Jesse paid the tips. He stood silently, a broad smile on his lips.

Jesse turned. "Oh, I'm sorry. Katrina, this is Will. Will, this is Katrina. Will and I have known each other since junior high school."

"Pleased to meet you, Will." She extended a hand. Will shook it softly, apparently not certain if he should shake her hand or bow and kiss it.

The three of them went to dinner in a French restaurant only two blocks away, where they were joined within the hour by one of Katrina's friends – against Will's better judgement.

Though lacking Katrina's beauty, Ona was, at the very least, an attractive woman in her late twenties, of pure Hawaiian ancestry, who displayed impeccable

460

taste and grace. Her conversation was at once relaxed and gracious. By slipping the Maitre de a twenty dollar bill, Jesse had been able to obtain a table on the wharf overlooking the water. Katrina sat close to him as they engaged in small talk and enjoyed their cocktails.

After dinner, at Jesse's insistence and with Katrina as an ally, they went to the Cabana Club, an exclusive nightclub for the well to do and those who could at least afford to pretend they were. They secured an excellent table and listened to the band play the songs of the forties and early fifties. Though Will obviously would have preferred more modern music, he was getting along fashionably with Ona. As the evening lengthened, he even expressed a preference for the old music over the more modern songs.

As Jesse left the men's room shortly after midnight, he met Will entering the all-male sanctuary.

Will laughed and beamed broadly. It was the first time since his arrival he had been able to speak to Jesse in a position away from the women. "You did it right this time, pilgrim." He imitated John Wayne.

Innocently, Jesse asked, "What d'ya mean?"

"What d'ya mean, what do I mean? Jesus Christ, the fanciest hotel in the world, a French restaurant right out of a movie, dinner over the ocean, an exclusive club for the rich and snobby, and two of the classiest lookin' chicks in the world. What do I mean? Shit." He laughed loudly.

"I take it you're gettin' along with Ona?"

"You know it," Will beamed.

"How good are you gettin' along with her?" asked Jesse.

Will winked. The liquor was having an effect. "Pretty damn good."

"Good, then maybe you won't have to sleep in that hotel room all by yourself." He handed Will the key to his room.

"What about you?"

"Don't worry about me, old friend. I'll be just fine." Jesse smiled as he left the men's room.

*****

When Jesse and Katrina returned to the Royal Palm the following afternoon, they found Will and Ona at the swimming pool. Will shook his head and smiled as the two approached. "You two look pretty rested. You turn in early?"

Jesse returned the smile. "Yeah. Early this morning. Hi, Ona."

"Good afternoon, you two. You look happy," said Ona.

"Sometimes you *can* tell a book by its cover," smiled Katrina.

They enjoyed a late lunch around the pool. Ona owned a small motorboat, which they utilized, in the late afternoon for a trip to a private cove. There they snacked and drank cool drinks, taking in the late afternoon sun.

Jesse discovered Katrina was as irresistible in a swimming suit as she was unclothed. He found it a struggle to maintain his composure until they could be alone together. He made mental notes, admitting she satisfied him sexually more than had any woman in his life. There was that very short period of time with Barbara in California, and there was Masako. And there was always Shannon. But he had never experienced a sexual liaison with her. He tried to imagine Shannon and him in a lover's' embrace but couldn't get the image to focus. Image or no image, he would give up everything to be with her. He studied the sensuous curves of Katrina's body.

461

Stoney Livingston
I would even give up her.

As they rode the choppy water back to the marina, Katrina said, "You and Will would probably like to visit awhile alone. Maybe we can get together in a couple of days."

Jesse felt disappointment at her words. She kissed him quickly on the lips. Quietly she whispered, "You know my number. I'll be there. I just thought you two might want to talk about old times for a while. When you want me, just call. He's come a long way to be with his friend. You owe him that much. Believe me, I don't like the idea either, but it's only fair." She kissed him again, longer this time.

Jesse knew she was right. Will had come a long way for a visit. Of course it wasn't like he wasn't enjoying his time in Hawaii. But he *had* come to visit Jesse first.

*****

Will looked up from the pool table. "How serious is this thing with you and Katrina?"

Jesse took a sip of his beer. "Will, how can I be serious about anybody until this damn war is over?"

"I don't know. You looked pretty kootchie-coo to me."

"Will, it's kinda hard to explain unless you been there. Katrina is the first woman I've touched in so long I can't remember when. She's about all a man could ask for and then some. I imagine I'll go back to the Nam and Katrina will carry on with her life like it was before. I suppose you might classify our relationship as sexual. And damn near perfect in that category."

"How the hell did you ever meet her?" asked Will.

Jesse related the story, leaving nothing out.

"No shit?" asked Will incredulously as Jesse finished. "She's over forty years old? Bullshit. She don't look a day over twenty-three or four."

"There's nothing about her physically that's forty-plus, but she's old enough to be my mother."

"What a mother!" said Will.

"To tell you the truth, Will, I never gave it a thought. How's Shannon?"

Will placed his cue on the green. "You got more good-looking women after you than Casanova and you ask about my married sister? You're crazy, Jesse."

"I didn't ask you for her room number, Godamnit. I just asked how she was doin'."

Will smiled his broad smile and shook his head. "Fine. She's doin' fine. She told me to give you a big hug and a kiss, but you can forget the kiss."

Jesse smiled outwardly but the lump was in his throat as it always was when Shannon acknowledged his existence. "You mean she knew you were coming to Hawaii?"

"Yeah. You don't think I'd leave for a week and not let her know, do you — especially under the circumstances? She might think I shipped out to the Nam."

"When you see her again, tell her I said hello – and don't forget."

"I'll tell her." Will picked up his cue stick and scratched on the eight ball.

Jesse laughed. "Let's go find a place to sit down and shoot the breeze. It's really good to see ya, Will."

Will punched him playfully on the shoulder. "It's good to see you too, Jesse. Even if you do look like a walking skeleton."

462

Forever Patriots

Later in the evening, after the beer changed to bourbon and Jesse became loose and relaxed, he realized how right Katrina had been about him spending some time with Will.

Will looked up from his drink. "How bad is it over there, Jesse?"

Jesse screwed up his face and squinted his eyes. "Depends on what you mean."

"I mean everything. From the looks of you, you aren't getting a whole lot of chow. Your eyes are sunk in so bad they look like chambers on an M-14. And what about the gooks -- you ever kill one?"

Jesse took a sip of his whiskey. He sighed slowly. "Yeah, Will. I killed a few gooks. I honestly don't know the exact number. More'n my share though." He paused and looked up to the ceiling, then back to Will. "That's what it's all about, isn't it? We kill more of them than they kill of us?"

Will's face appeared concerned. "I don't know, Jesse. I'm askin' you."

Jesse lit a cigarette. "Damned if I know anymore, Will. I thought I knew when I went over there but things aren't working out the way I thought they would. I don't think it makes a tinker's damn how many of 'em we kill. There's too many of 'em. Stayin' in the south and killing gooks is never gonna win this war. We've gotta go to Hanoi. Until we do that, we ain't winnin' anything. We're just wastin' American lives."

"How do you feel about all of this shit?"

"What the hell kind of question is that? Do you mean am I ready to throw in the towel and join the hippies? The answer to that one is 'hell no'. If you mean do I want to win the war, the answer is 'the sooner the better'. The minute the first American was killed in this little 'police action' is the minute I decided not to ever give up. We can beat 'em, Will. We can beat 'em." Jesse clenched his glass tightly with his hand.

Will shook his head. "I sure hate to see you go through this shit. There's too many good times to be had back in The States."

Jesse raised an eyebrow. "Yeah, and you know whose buyin' 'em? It's the guys out there in those goddamn rice paddies and jungles. So the next time you have one of those good times, think about the guy that bought it with his damn life, or an arm or leg."

Will fell silent.

Jesse wanted to cry but couldn't let it happen. "I'm sorry, Will. I'm not jumping on your case. You know that. I guess I really don't want to think about that kind of crap right now."

"Forget it," Will said.

"Damn good idea. You 'bout ready for another drink?"

A young prostitute approached Will and sat next to him at their table. Jesse couldn't hear what was being said over the bar noise but he didn't have to hear to know. He smiled across the table to Will, who had apparently asked the girl to see his friend.

She left her seat next to Will and wiggled around the table, sitting beside Jesse, making certain her leg rubbed against his firmly as she pulled her chair up to the table. "Buy a girl a drink?"

Jesse smiled at her, then Will. "Whatcha drinkin'?" He winked at Will.

"Rum and coke," answered the prostitute.

Jesse signaled for a waitress and ordered the girl a drink. With the drink

463

safely in her possession, she gave Jesse her sexiest look. A strand of her bleached hair fell over one eye. "You wanna have a good time?"

"How much?" Jesse smiled.

"Depends on what you want. A straight lay is ten bucks."

"What about all night?"

Will moved closer so that he could hear the verbal exchange.

The prostitute looked at her watch. "Thirty bucks until daylight."

"Are you worth that much? It's pretty late already,"

She smiled demurely. "I'm worth a lot more than that, baby. You'll see."

"I'll tell you what. You see that marine over there with the Bronze Star and Purple Heart on his uniform?"

"What's a Bronze Star?"

"Never mind. See that marine over there by the door? The tall one."

"Oh, yeah. I see 'im."

"He's a good friend of mine and he's real bashful, and a little broke. I want you to spend the night with him. And I want you to give him the royal treatment. Nothing's too good for that guy. He's a reg'lar hero. Now, he won't go if he thinks I paid for it, so just pretend you like heroes. I want you to pay for the room and everything else involved in this deal." He reached into his shirt pocket and withdrew several twenty-dollar bills. He laid them on the table and counted them out. "I think you ought to be able to put on a pretty good performance for a hundred bucks. How about it?"

"Are you serious?" she asked, mouth agape.

"Don't I look serious?" Jesse smiled.

She picked up the bills and stuffed them into her bra. "Mister, your friend is going to get an academy award performance tonight."

Jesse touched two fingers to his forehead in a lazy salute. "I'll be askin' 'im tomorrow how it was. If he gives a good enough report, you may have another customer."

"I'm not worried, baby. I'm good." She walked to the unsuspecting marine.

Will laughed as he watched the young prostitute wiggle toward the tall marine. "You *are* crazy. You just blew a hundred bucks on somebody you don't even know."

"Yeah, I know 'im, Will. His name is JJ Washington, and Corporal Faye, and Bean, and Hymie, and Guy, and a thousand others."

"JJ Washington? Isn't that the name of the guy you said got blown away?"

"Let's go, Will. I just wanna go back to the room. I'm tired of this place. I wanna stand on the beach and let the wind blow in my face and drink a bottle of whiskey and get ripped and not have to worry that some damn gook is gonna blow me away while I'm staggerin' around."

"Sounds like a winner to me."

They sat on the beach, well above the water line, drinking from a bottle of Jim Beam. Will was almost fall-down drunk. His words were difficult to understand.

"'m tellin' y', that Ona w'snice."

"She seemed okay," agreed Jesse.

"K'trina w'snice too. But I got a seriousss queshion t' ask ya."

Though Jesse was feeling the effects of the liquor, he was still quite a distance from Will's state of inebriation. "What's that, Will?"

464

Forever Patriots

"Barb'ra. You ever gonna shee her 'gin?"

Jesse stiffened. "What the hell is this thing with Barbara? She's in my past now, Will. It was about the shortest part of my past that I can remember, but it's over. Hell, she's probably married by now. I don't really have any desire to see her anymore. Katrina is more than I need right now – and right now is all there is, pilgrim. Tomorrow may never get here."

"You fergot Barb'ra but not my shishter, right?"

"What the hell are you talkin' about?"

Will didn't answer. Jesse turned to see him sprawled face down in the sand. He laughed loudly and picked up his unconscious friend, throwing him over a shoulder in the fireman's carry. He stooped down and retrieved his bottle of whiskey and carried Will through the lobby of the hotel, whiskey bottle in one hand and Will over his shoulder, half-consciously waving to the hotel employees and guests alike as Jesse proceeded to the elevator.

In the room he placed Will's limp body on the large bed and removed his shoes. This task completed, he sat on the bed and drank the remainder of his bottle. In the darkness of the room he talked as though Will could hear every word and was a part of the conversation. "Will, Ol' buddy, if I get outa this one alive, I'm gonna change what little I can. Don't misunderstand me now, I ain't gonna preach about God and all of that bullshit. I know yer into that God business but I ain't. I'm just gonna tell the people I care about that I care about 'em."

He lit a cigarette and studied his sleeping friend. When he finished his smoke, he crushed it in an ashtray and moved to the center of the carpeted room where he stretched out, fully clothed, and went to sleep.

Will was still passed out on the bed when Jesse awoke. A glass of cold water poured slowly over his face remedied that situation. Will came immediately awake, sputtering and coughing.

"Wha ...What the hell?"

Jesse smiled down at him. "Rise 'n' shine. You're sleepin' your damn life away. We got the beautiful Hawaiian Islands outside our window. I thought today we could rent a boat and cruise around. Maybe go over to Pearl and visit the Arizona for a minute, then down to this place Katrina told me about where you just park your boat like it was a car. You get out of your boat and presto – a fancy restaurant with torches and all that fancy stuff."

Will was not impressed. His head hurt. "What the hell makes you immune to hangovers?"

"Good whiskey I guess."

"What time is it?"

"About noon."

Will jumped out of bed. "Oh, shit, I gotta get dressed."

"No kiddin'. That's what I been tryin' to tell ya. C'mon, let's go get that boat."

"I can't. I mean, I got somethin' else to do today."

Jesse smiled. "Ona?"

Will hesitated. "Yeah, that's it. Ona and I got plans for the afternoon."

"You sneaky office Pogue, why didn't you say so? Maybe I'll call Katrina and we can take the boat out and meet you at this place I was tellin' you about. I'm buyin'."

"What's the name of it?"

465

Stoney Livingston

"The Pago Pago."

"What time?"

"About eight."

"You got it. I'll see you there at eight." Will disappeared into the shower.

The balmy night air slapped gently at his face as Jesse docked the small outboard at the Pago Pago. He wished Katrina had been with him to see how expertly he had managed the docking but she had an appointment at four-thirty and she insisted that he take the boat out by himself and she would meet him at the Pago Pago at about eight. The torches outlining the restaurant and the open-air courtyard took him back in time two hundred years. He felt as though he were landing somewhere on the Barbary Coast, a buccaneer of grand stature, coming home to his haven of safety and comfort. The table in the courtyard did little to change his mood. Jesse felt good about life in general, his own in particular.

He sat at a table and ordered an Old Fashioned while he waited for Will.

Shortly, Will approached the table.

Jesse greeted him. "How you and Ona get along today?" asked Jesse.

"I don't know. Listen, Jesse, I got a problem. I never had a date with Ona this afternoon. Something came up and it's gettin' complicated."

"What are you talkin' about, Will? You're not makin' any sense at all."

"Are you and I friends?"

"What's eatin' you?" asked Jesse. Will appeared more nervous than he had ever seen him.

"I'll be back in a few minutes. I just wanted to let you know I was here."

"What's goin' on? Something happen between you and Ona?"

"No. Nothing like that. I can't explain it right now. I'll be back in a few minutes."

Jesse shrugged. "You want me to order you a drink?"

"Yeah. How about a rum and coke?"

"You got it."

Will turned and walked briskly out of sight.

Jesse wasn't going to let whatever was bothering Will to upset him. He lit a cigarette. As the smoke from his cigarette drifted upward in the balmy night air, he wondered absentmindedly what was on Will's mind. His friend seemed very troubled about something. Oh well, whatever it was, nothing was serious enough to linger upon on such a beautiful night. It would take another Pearl Harbor to shake him from the feeling of euphoria that Katrina and the Hawaiian Islands had so recently given him. His vison encompassed the wooden piers and the gentle swells of the Pacific Ocean. He drifted to another century. Tall sailing ships dominated the seas. Cannons roared. Swords flashed in the glow of burning timber.

He lit another cigarette and thought of the men in the eighty-one platoon and Alpha Company. He hoped they were off the Hoa My Trail. He shuddered involuntarily at the thought of the Trail and looked around him to make certain his surroundings were real and not just a figment of his imagination. How was it even possible that life could go from one extreme to another in so short a period of time?

His gaze lingered on a girl standing nearby under one of the burning torches. He thought, at first, she was one of the many waitresses working at the Pago Pago. Her soft cotton skirt billowed slightly in the evening breeze as she moved slowly in his direction. As she drew nearer, his memory triggered a remote

466

recognition. There was something familiar about her auburn hair and the way she walked – and those emerald-green eyes. Of course in the wavering light of the torches it was difficult to be certain of color – and yet ...

She was but five feet from where he sat when he looked into her eyes and experienced another Pearl Harbor. He knew he was going crazy. Vietnam had caused him to lose his mind. He turned away and took a sip of his Old Fashioned. He looked back in her direction, certain she would not be there, but there she was.

"Jesse?" said the voice from a thousand years ago.

Jesse looked at her stupidly. He studied her emerald eyes intently, deeply magnificent even in the unsteady light. "You can't be who I think you are. I'm not ready for the nut-house yet." He took another drink.

She touched his arm and he knew he wasn't crazy.

Slowly he stood until he reached his full height, his face inches from hers.

CHAPTER TWENTY: BARBARA

"How can ..." His voice trailed into silence. He smelled the clean smell of her body, even above the liquor on his breath. For several moments they looked into each other's eyes, neither speaking nor moving.

Jesse stared at hair the color of an Arizona sunset, his attention fixed on the softness of it until she blinked her eyes, drawing him to dark emeralds of a stormy Caribbean sea.

"Barbara, is that really you?"

Tears trickled down her cheeks. She nodded slowly. "Yes, Jesse Langley. It's me. And I love you no less today than I did when I last saw you."

Jesse's eyes moistened. Still he didn't move.

"Jesse. Hold me. Please ...just hold me."

He slowly put his arms around her and gently pulled her close. They stood in their silent and motionless embrace for several moments, Jesse thinking private thoughts, feeling an unfamiliar emotion that flowed through his body, not sure of what it was, not caring, knowing only that nothing in life was comparable. He wondered if he was losing his mind.

Jesse held the embrace, unmoving, feeling he knew not what. He wanted to run, to go where he would never be found by anyone who knew him and, yet, he wanted to stay. He thought briefly of Katrina and knew she would understand; probably better than he understood. He thought of her perfect, sensuous body and saw it pale in comparison to the feeling he got deep inside when he was with Barbara. He had left Barbara once because she wanted him to desert his country in time of war. *What a laugh! It wasn't even a decent war.* And yet he knew he would never desert, even if she should ask him to do so again. He knew too that she would not.

Slowly they separated until their eyes met.

"Barbara. I can't believe it's really you. How in the world did you ...."

She placed a finger on his lips and held it there gently. He watched the light from the flames play upon her auburn hair and said nothing. He was completely taken by her presence in Hawaii. Softly and gently he kissed her. He felt the universe disappear. He was lost in a world he had entered only briefly, many months ago. Slowly they pulled apart and he looked at her face and smiled. He tasted the salt from her tears on his lips.

Movement on his right turned his attention to Will and Ona as they approached the table. Will waived sheepishly. "I brought Ona with me as a witness in case you try to kill me." Will's smile covered his face.

Ona looked at Jesse. "Jesse, you've got one-in-ten-million. Don't you ever be foolish enough to let her go. I talked to her for a few minutes before she came to see you and I'm telling you – this girl is first cabin."

"But....Katrina...?" started Jesse.

Will said, "Ona and I both talked to Katrina today. Barbara met her. I didn't know how else to pull this off."

"How is she?" asked Jesse.

Ona said, "She's a grown woman, not a kid. She had no delusions, Jesse, and, once she met Barbara, she said to tell you that you'll never do better."

The four of them had dinner at the Pago Pago. Will told stories of some of Jesse's youthful adventures and from time-to-time Jesse caught a line or two of Will's conversation and laughed at the funny way Will told the story, but mostly he looked at Barbara. He did little else. He was mesmerized by her nearness. The sight of her next to him was more rewarding than had been his intimacy with Katrina. That, he found difficult to understand.

Barbara returned his stare. She made no move to make any physical contact. . He watched the torchlight sparkle on her eyes – eyes full of happiness and laughter.

They finished dinner at ten-thirty. Jesse and Barbara bid goodnight to Will and Ona and the two couples went their separate ways. Jesse walked Barbara to the motorboat parked at the dock. Still they didn't speak more than was necessary for basic directions. As the small craft slipped out into the bay, Jesse kissed her gently on the lips. His body tingled from every molecule at her touch. He turned his attention to navigating the boat just long enough to spot a place in the darkness that would allow them a safe haven. They put in at a small inlet where he threw the anchor into the sand.

"Let me just put my arms around you and look at the stars, Barbara. Is that okay?"

"Jesse Langley, just being with you is okay."

Jesse awakened with the first light to the gentle waves rocking the small craft softly to and fro. They had both fallen asleep fully clothed. Not even their shoes had been removed. Their bodies had been so exhausted from emotion that all strength had been sapped from every fiber and they had drifted into a deep sleep in each other's arms.

In the early morning light Jesse took in the beauty that was Barbara. A wisp of auburn hair over one closed eye and the smile upon her lips caused him to feel a pang of sorrow and happiness at once. He knew he loved this woman beyond any depth of reason known to him. He felt the emotion so strongly it almost choked him.

Barbara stirred.

"I love you, Barbara. I really love you. I love Katrina and Will and JJ and Thunder and all my friends but I love you in a special and separate way."

The sleeping Barbara responded to his voice by coming fully awake. "Jesse!" She sat up and reached for him.

He held her tightly and kissed her cheek and the tears in her eyes.

"Oh, Jesse, I thought at first it was all a dream – that I hadn't come to Hawaii and that I hadn't really seen you. But I did, and I have."

He kissed her upturned nose, then her lips. They both lost the rest of the world. In the grey morning light they made love slowly, then passionately, each not able to get enough of the other, each afraid they would awaken somewhere else and

469

be alone, and they *would* be alone if they were not together.

When their lovemaking ended Barbara cried softly, her face cradled in his neck.

"Why are you crying, Barbara?"

There was a short silence. "I'm so happy to be here and so grateful you didn't reject me last night."

"I couldn't have," said Jesse.

"I wasn't sure. I thought I was but I really wasn't." She rubbed his shoulders. "And you've lost so much weight. It must be awful over there."

Jesse stared at the sky. "It could be worse. There's plenty of C-rations. I guess it's not the government's fault I can't stand the things."

She watched his face as he looked, unseeing, at the sky. "I don't know what to say. We hear stories. We get some of the guys in the hospital at Beaufort. Every time I see one of them I think of you. I've thought of you a lot, Jesse."

He turned his gaze to her deep-green eyes. "I don't know what *I've* been thinking of, Barbara. I really don't. I never really knew for sure about you. That's honest. I thought of you from time-to-time but I tried to make myself think of you as that girl who tried to get me to desert my country." He shrugged. "I guess that only goes to show how stupid I am."

"Jesse, hold me – just hold me."

Later that afternoon they moved her belongings into Jesse's room, checking her out of the hotel room she had used only for a shower the night before. Barbara was taken with the opulence of the Royal Palm Hotel. Jesse enjoyed watching her marvel at the craftsmanship that had gone into the construction of the building.

"Don't get too used to it. We've gotta move out tomorrow night," he cautioned.

"Tomorrow night?"

"Just a precaution. My R&R is only for six days. I'm goin' back in two weeks. I told my company commander that when I left. I'm not sure he believed me but he told me to have a good time." He smiled. "Don't worry. I've found another place that's just as fancy."

Barbara placed her hands on her hips and looked at him sternly. "Jesse Langley, I don't care if we camp out in the hills. I just want to be with you. It doesn't matter where we are."

Jesse raised a hand and smiled. "No more camping out for a while, please."

She returned his smile and stepped into his arms.

The next twenty-four hours were spent re-learning each other's bodies. Jesse couldn't understand the overpowering physical attraction he felt for Barbara. It was more than physical, for he could not separate her physical being completely from those other things that made her who she was. Katrina was a much more accomplished lover and in her very special way, perhaps the most sensuous woman he had ever known. And yet his attraction for Barbara far surpassed his desire for Katrina. He could no longer imagine making love to any woman other than Barbara. No matter their physical appearance, he was sexually drawn to none of them. He struggled to find a reason for this unnatural feeling. Maybe with a little civilian time under his belt he wouldn't feel so strongly about her. He didn't think so.

Barbara slept in his arms, the contented, peaceful sleep of a young lover

470

Forever Patriots

whose happiness knows no bounds. He looked at the curves of her body rising and falling with each breath. She seemed so innocent and helpless, yet somehow he knew she was not. He fell asleep.

Will Hunt was leaving in the morning. Since Barbara's arrival two days prior, Jesse had not seen him. On this night before his departure, Jesse and Barbara joined Will and Ona for one final and superb dinner.

Much to Jesse's chagrin, Will related more boyhood stories of high school and some of the situations into which Jesse had managed to become entangled. The girls seemed to enjoy Will's tales of woe and glory, laughing at each and every one.

After the meal, as the men enjoyed small cigars and cognac while the women drank cordials, the talk turned to Jesse's return to Vietnam.

Jesse puffed on his small cigar slowly. "Maybe I won't go back."

Barbara kissed him on the cheek. "And maybe you will." She sat close to him, her right leg thrown over his left. He couldn't get close enough to her.

"Yeah, maybe I will."

She smiled and kissed his cheek again. "I shouldn't tell you this but you're the perfect guy for me."

"Now I know you're crazy." He smiled.

"Before you two have your first lover's quarrel let's have a toast," suggested Will.

Jesse raised his glass. "A toast."

Barbara and Ona lifted their glasses. Will spoke ceremoniously. "To the most perfect match of man and woman. May it always remain as it is today."

They emptied their glasses and placed them on the table as one. Jesse looked at Barbara intently, speaking to Will as he studied her face. "It will. I know it will."

Barbara looked into his eyes and held his gaze. "There has been only one man in my life since that night at the restaurant in California, and there will be no other."

He pressed an index finger to her lips gently. They were aware of no one in the room other than the object of their respective emotions. Jesse's chest ached with the love he felt for this woman. His inadequacy to articulate his true and exact feelings in the English language frustrated him. They were both lost in time and space as they looked into each other's eyes.

Will cleared his throat loudly. "Remember the rest of the world, you two? I hope you weren't thinking anything too risque, because it looked to me like whatever you were thinkin', you were gettin' ready to do."

Jesse and Barbara returned to the present. Jesse said, "Will, have I ever told you that your timing is, at times, slightly less than perfect?"

They lay on the beach, watching the gentle swells offshore, each lost in separate but equal thoughts. In the two days since Will's departure for the mainland, they had not been out of each other's sight for more than five minutes. The bond between them seemed to grow stronger by the hour.

"The ocean looks so big and frightening. It seems to go on forever. To know that you're going to cross it and be that far away from me is scary, Jesse."

"To tell you the truth, Barbara, I'm not all that happy about it, but I don't

471

have much more left on my tour. Sometime in November I'll be headed back home."

She looked into his eyes then moved into his arms. "I'm afraid, Jesse."

"It doesn't do any good to worry. Just remember the good times always and everything will be okay."

"I try, but I love you so much that if anything ever happened to you, I would die inside."

"Barbara, don't even say things like that. I don't want anything to happen to me, especially now that I've found you. But if it does, I want you to be happy the rest of your life, not bitter and sad. Remember and be happy. I don't know about you but I've already had more happiness in loving you than most people get in a lifetime."

"What do you mean, you don't know about me?" she asked, pouting.

He kissed her quickly on the cheek and laughed.

"Why do you always call me Barbara?" she asked.

"Two reasons. First, that's your name. And second, it's the most beautiful name I've ever heard. I love to say your name. It makes me happy. I've known other girls named Barbara but it was just another name until I met you. It has a whole new meaning to me now. Satisfied?"

"Quite," she smirked.

"I even met a girl in VietNam called Barbara."

She raised her eyebrows. "Do you meet a lot of girls over there?"

He laughed loudly. "Two or three a day."

Her pout grew.

He rubbed his hand from her knee to her stomach in a soft, light movement. Instantly she responded, opening her mouth to meet his. They rolled in the soft sand of the empty beach, miles from the nearest human. He removed the top to her two-piece swimming suit and exposed her white breasts to the afternoon sun. She made no attempt to restrain him as he removed the lower portion of her scanty attire. He stopped to survey his exposed work.

Barbara breathed heavily. "What are you looking at?"

"You, Barbara. I can't believe I have all of this. I can't get enough of your looks or your touch or your kisses, or anything else that's you."

He touched her erect nipples then kissed them gently. Barbara began to breath heavily and her body made small convulsive movements. "Oh, God, Jesse. What do you do to me?"

He stopped all movement and looked into her eyes. "I just love you, Barbara. That's all."

She reached for his trunks and with his help they were soon both laying naked in the sun. Using techniques only recently learned from Katrina, he brought Barbara to a height of passion. When she reached orgasm her body quivered and jerked in spasms for several long seconds. He reached his own climax at the time hers peaked. Then Barbara's body jerked only slightly and she fell limp and exhausted into the sand. Jesse pulled a beach towel over them to protect them from the rays of the sun and they fell asleep.

It was several hours before they awakened; the late afternoon sun cast its red rays upon the beige sand of the beach, turning it a salmon pink. Jesse carefully brushed the sand pebbles from Barbara's breasts and kissed and caressed them one at a time. Immediately the nipples grew and hardened and they were once again locked in a lover's embrace.

Forever Patriots

Jesse stood, fully dressed, his back against a large palm, smoking a cigarette in the early evening, the lights of Oahu barely visible from their island getaway. He turned to watch Barbara in the moonlight. She wore a summer dress with nothing beneath it. He smiled as her form passed between him and their campfire. He felt a stirring in his loins and shook his head slowly. "You know what?"

She turned to him. "No. What?"

"I can't get enough of you. I can't keep my hands offa you. I can't quit lookin' at you. It's like every time I see you it's for the first and last time. You know what I mean?"

She stepped into his arms and hugged him tightly. "Jesse Langley, you are a unique man. Yes, I know what you mean because I feel the same way. If we wouldn't be arrested, I would have you always at my side, with no clothes, so that when we wanted to make love we could, right away."

He looked into her eyes, sparkling from the flames of the fire. "And that's what it is, Barbara – making love. It's so much more than just sex – I can't believe the feeling. I feel sorry for those who never experience it."

"This island almost makes me feel like we're Adam and Eve. If I couldn't see the lights across the water, I'd know it," she said.

"Maybe we should be gettin' back before it gets too much later. I'm not familiar with the waters around here."

"Let's stay. We've got food and drinks left. And thanks to your ever-present readiness, plenty of clothing. It would be wonderful. We've got this whole island to ourselves. It's more than I could ever ask for."

Jesse looked at the lights across the water, then to the dense vegetation inland. His body tensed and he shuddered involuntarily. "Me too."

They made preparations for the night.

They kissed and touched and made love into the night, then talked of things young lovers speak of: love, the stars, life, thoughts, feelings, dreams. It was after two in the morning when they fell asleep, almost as a single entity.

Jesse awakened with a start. He heard a movement in the heavy vegetation inland. He knew there were no marines on that side of the perimeter. His heart leapt to his throat as he jumped to his feet and searched for his rifle in the moonlight. He was surprised to find he was undressed, something he never did on the Trail. He saw Barbara lying next to him in the sand. *What's she doin' here?* He scooped her into his arms and ran south, then west into the heavy brush.

Barbara came groggily awake. "What... "

"Shhh! VC!" he cautioned. Barbara fell silent as Jesse carried her quietly deeper into the heavy vegetation.

He stopped and placed her gently on her feet. "Jesse, what is it?" she whispered.

Jesse looked at her, unable to explain anything. "Barbara?" was all he could manage to say in answer to her question.

"Jesse, are you all right?"

His heart thumped wildly in his throat. He sat on the wet leaves beneath his feet. "I don't get it. What's wrong? Where's my rifle?"

Barbara cried softly. "Oh, Jesse. I'm so sorry."

"Barbara ...Where are we? What are you doin' here?"

"Oh, my love. It's okay. We're in Hawaii. You're on R&R, remember?"

473

"R&R?" His head began to clear slowly. "Oh yeah. Hawaii. No VC here." He covered his face with his hands and moved them downward in a wiping motion. He was back to the present. "I'm sorry, Barbara. I don't know what happened. I thought I heard a noise. I thought ...I thought ...I don't know what I thought. I must be losin' it. I'm sorry." He stood and held her hand as they walked back to camp.

"You don't ever have to tell me you're sorry, Jesse. It was my fault for suggesting that we stay out here. I should have known better."

"Why should you have known better? I grew up camping out. I don't know what happened but it sure wasn't your fault. I guess it must have been pretty scary to have some weirdo pick you up and carry you into the bushes."

Barbara put her hands on her bare hips. "That was no weirdo. That was the man I love. Don't call him names." She smiled at him in the darkness.

Jesse, though shaken, had regained his composure. "I didn't know you were such a tough guy."

"There are still a few things about me you don't know. Some I'm afraid to tell you, but I will. I love you, Jesse Langley, and nothing is ever going to change that. I knew who you were when I first saw you. I don't know how I knew but I did. I was right by the way."

They found the beach towels and lay together, each holding the other silently, thinking deep thoughts, reassured by the touch of the other's flesh. It was more than thirty minutes before Jesse broke the silence.

"You still awake, Barbara?"

She nuzzled him on the neck. "Umm, uh huh."

"I wanna go to the battleship Arizona in the morning."

She sat up and looked at him in the fading moonlight. "I don't care where you want to go. That's where I want to go too." She kissed him gently on the mouth.

He held her tightly and closed his eyes.

Jesse read the bronze plaque at the memorial to the battleship Arizona and felt goose bumps and chills as he stared into the shallow water where more than eleven hundred men remained entombed. The water was clear, and the silhouette of the old battleship was plainly visible as he squeezed Barbara's arm. He felt a kinship with the men who had died that December morning more than three years before he was born.

Barbara seemed to know what he was feeling and she held her silence.

As they left the memorial and walked along the docks of Pearl Harbor, Jesse said, "Ya know, that was the last war, maybe the only war, where the whole country was behind the guys in uniform."

Barbara said nothing.

Jesse continued, "What the heck. No sense thinkin' about things like that right now." He smiled at his girl and hugged her to his hip as they walked along the old wooden docks.

An aircraft carrier, too far away to be identifiable, caught Barbara's attention. "Have you ever been on an aircraft carrier?"

"A couple of times. I was on the *Princeton* twice and the *Enterprise* once. Why?"

"Don't they have marines stationed on board permanently?"

"Yeah. Seagoin' bellhops is what we call 'em in the infantry."

"Couldn't you be stationed on one of them instead of being in an infantry

Forever Patriots

unit in Vietnam?"

Jesse stopped in his tracks and turned to face her. It was obvious she was instantly sorry for speaking her thoughts but she spoke again, before he was able to frame his words. "I was only asking, Jesse. You've served long enough for most men. If you want to stay, then stay, but allow me my selfish thoughts."

He stared into her dark emerald green eyes and smiled. "I'm not gonna be as stupid as I was in California. I've found something in you that made me a wiser and happier guy. You got a right to your feelings, just like I have a right to mine. As a matter-of-fact, I should feel kind of special that you feel the way you do. But I'm where I belong for this war. It's kinda hard to explain, Barbara, but I don't really think I ever had a choice."

"What do you mean?"

"The guys – it's the guys. Not that they wouldn't survive without me but I think that some of 'em are better off with me there. It just seems like I was meant to be where I am – in the outfit I'm in. I wanted my old outfit at first but I wouldn't even think of leavin' One-Four now."

She looked at him with understanding and compassion. She seemed to know what he was feeling. The slight wind from the water rustled her hair.

"By the way. Have I told you how beautiful you are – in every way?"

She kissed him full on the lips. As they broke their embrace in the bright sunlight, she said, "Jesse Langley, I love you more than you will ever know."

He put his arm around her slender waist and they continued their walk. "I do know. I know because I love you at least as much, if not more."

"More?" She smiled. "That's a pretty big statement."

"I can handle it."

She squeezed his arm as they moved to a waiting taxi.

As the taxi moved slowly through the streets, Jesse said, "I hope you're not sorry that we used some of our time together to go to an old battleship."

"Jesse, why would I be sorry? I'm with you. That's what's important. That's all that matters to me. I honestly don't care where we are. I mean that. As long as we're together, I don't care where it is or what we're doing."

"I wonder how a person can feel that way? I feel exactly the same. Just bein' around you makes my whole life important and worth something."

Barbara placed her head on his chest. They rode in silence.

"This is Waikiki." The cab driver's voice brought them both back to Hawaii.

They exited the cab and walked the sandy beach, each absorbed in their own thoughts. Jesse drifted to his teen years. He experienced the emotion he felt for Shannon and wondered about that feeling. He was certain he loved her but now there was Barbara. He knew too that his love for Shannon was different. He would have given his life to keep her from harm and most likely still would. But wouldn't he do the same for his friends in Vietnam? He realized his feelings for the men in his outfit were not the same as those he held for Shannon but, in certain respects, there were many similarities.

"Why the strange smile?" Barbara's voice interrupted his reverie.

"Oh, I was just thinkin' about how really lovin' someone can change a person's whole outlook on life."

"I know. Believe me, I know. You've changed my whole life, Jesse. I never knew that life could be so beautiful."

Jesse stopped walking and gazed at Barbara's face, framed by the blue of

Stoney Livingston

the Pacific Ocean and the fire of her hair. "This whole thing seems like a fairy tale to me. As a matter-of-fact, every minute I've ever spent around you has been like a fairy tale. How long do fairy tales last, Barbara?"

"As long as we want them to."

"That could be a mighty long time."

"Not long enough for me." She leaned into him and kissed him softly on the lips. He felt his body tingle at her touch.

He broke the embrace and became lost in the emerald seas of her eyes. He smiled, "How many ways and for how many reasons can a man love a woman?"

Barbara pouted playfully. "An infinite number, to both questions."

He hugged her tightly to him as they continued their walk on the beach.

They sat quietly in a booth at the small restaurant, Jesse with his arm around Barbara's waist. As the last rays of sunset fired a bronze glow over the ocean outside the window, she said, "It *is* like a dream, isn't it?"

"I keep waitin' to wake up. How could I ever have been so close to you in California and not been up to see you every day? What a waste of time that was," said Jesse.

"Jesse, our time together is so precious, no matter if it lasts a hundred years, it won't be enough."

He was once again lost in the emerald seas of her eyes.

"Jesse. Are you okay?"

He blinked to break the trance. "Yeah. Yeah, sure. I'm fine. You've got the most beautiful eyes in the world." Again he stared into them. "They look like seas of emeralds."

"Jesse, I didn't know you were a poet."

"Poet? What's poet got to do with it? I just feel like I'm drowning when I look into your eyes. That's the truth."

"I'll never be bored with you, you know that?"

"I sure hope not," he said.

Barbara's eyes widened . She was looking at something behind him. Jesse felt the presence of someone near and turned to follow her stare. When his eyes found a gargantuan Samoan, he made no attempt to mask his fear. "Barbara, get out of here!"

"What? I don't understand."

The big man said, "Relax, Lady. Yer safe." He turned to Jesse. "You ain't!"

Jesse jerked his head backwards and was able to deflect some of the murderous blow thrown by the big man but the strength and power of the thrust were devastating, even at half dosage. Jesse fell over Barbara as she scrambled to get clear of the table.

Haliniak moved in, tossing the table and its contents out of his way as easily as a more mortal man might remove a napkin. Jesse attempted to gain his feet but the big man had him cornered. He had no place to go as Haliniak stepped into him with his large fists flailing.

Jesse's efforts at mounting a defense were short-lived as the big Samoan pummeled his ribcage, knocking the wind out of him on the initial assault. He fell to the floor, gasping for breath. Haliniak stood over him.

"Get up, punk!"

Forever Patriots

Slowly Jesse rose to his feet.

The manager of the restaurant stepped next to Haliniak. "Please, Mister Haliniak. These kids weren't causing any trouble."

Almost as an afterthought, Haliniak pushed the manager with the back of his hand, slamming him into a nearby table. "This punk hit me from behind with a four-by-four one night."

Jesse regained his breath. "Look, man, I'm sorry about that. I don't want any trouble. Just let us be. We'll go somewhere else."

"Yer ass! C'mon, Punk! Whatsamatter? Can't hit a man in the face? You want me to turn my back again?"

"I told you, I don't want any trouble."

Haliniak smiled. "I'll bet you don't – at least not with me, you chickenshit little bastard!" He swung.

Jesse parried the blow and countered with a right-left-right combination, striking the big man squarely on the jaw twice. He felt the flesh give and heard the mushy sound of his knuckles pushing meat to bone.

Haliniak shook his head as though the punches were mere nuisances. He moved in, pinning Jesse against the wall with blows to the rib cage. When he had his smaller opponent against the wall, Haliniak put his massive arms around him and squeezed the air from his body, his grip growing tighter as the escaping air deflated Jesse's frame.

Jesse knew it was over. He began to feel lightheaded. His face was beet-red. He hadn't the strength to escape. A piece of chair flew by his head. He heard Barbara's voice and, from the corner of his eye, saw her holding the back and seat of a chair, the legs destroyed when she had struck Haliniak. She moved in, striking the big man on the side of the head with the edge of the seat. He loosened his grip. A quick movement of the chair between Haliniak's legs from behind and the big man screamed in pain, releasing Jesse and falling to the floor.

Jesse fell over the big man and rolled into the aisle lest his opponent recover in time to renew his vise-like death grip. His chest burned like fire and his ribs hurt when he moved. He became aware of Barbara's voice.

"Jesse! Are you okay?"

"Yeah, I'm okay," he said through clenched teeth. "How 'bout you?"

"I'm okay. Let's get out of here!"

Haliniak writhed about on the floor, clutching his groin.

"I've called the police," offered the manager.

"Oh no!" Jesse turned to Barbara. "Let's get outa here!" He grabbed her arm and ran for the door, more afraid of the police than he was Haliniak. He didn't want his extended R & R cut short. He wasn't ready to leave Barbara yet.

Once outside, they turned the nearest corner and flagged a taxi sitting idly halfway down the next block. They gave the driver instructions to their hotel and held each other as the slow-moving cab negotiated the evening traffic.

Barbara had tears in her eyes. "Jesse, are you sure you're all right?"

He smiled at her. "My ribs hurt a little bit but I'm gonna make it. I didn't know you were so tough. Remind me never to get you mad."

"I don't know what happened. I thought he was going to kill you. I couldn't think of anything except to get us out of there. I'm a marine too – remember?"

"That's not the way I think of you, but you did good."

She buried her face in his chest. "Oh, Jesse. I would have killed him. I'm sorry. I don't know what came over me. I would have done anything to keep him from hurting you."

"It's okay. It's over now. Don't think about it anymore." He winced as he drew a breath.

"You're hurt!"

"This is gettin' to be a bad habit every time you and I get together," he smiled.

"What's wrong?"

"I think the human mountain may have bruised a couple of my ribs. It's not too bad – just enough to make breathin' a little uncomfortable."

Barbara looked at the cab driver. "Take us to a hospital please."

The thought of a hospital was not a welcome sight in Jesse's mind. "Disregard that, driver. Just take us to the hotel."

The driver shrugged. "The hotel it is."

Barbara expressed concern. "We've got to get you taken care of."

"I'm not takin' a chance of bein' found out by the MP's. I'd rather just take it easy for a while and not risk leavin' you before my two weeks is up. I'm okay. Really. A lot better than I would be if they packed me out of here before I was ready to go."

The driver stopped his cab in front of their hotel.

In the quiet and safety of their room, Jesse lay face up on the large bed, fully dressed. Barbara looked at him from her sitting position at his side. "I don't understand you sometimes, Jesse."

"How's that?"

"You won't run away from your duty and yet you refuse treatment at a hospital because you're afraid of being returned to Vietnam because you're not ready to go back yet. What's the difference between that and just running away?"

"I told everyone I was gonna be gone two weeks. It ain't like they didn't know it."

Barbara smiled. "Jesse Langley, you are truly one-of-a-kind."

"This is the closest I'll ever come to desertin' and I'm not about to go back early. I'm stayin' with you as long as I can, Barbara. I've only got a few days left and I'm not gonna lose 'em over a couple of bruised ribs." He paused. "I might not be such a good lover for a couple of days."

Barbara laughed softly. Tears streamed down her face. "Jesse, just being able to look at you and touch you and know you're with me is more than I ever thought I would have again. If you only knew."

"So tell me."

She took off her shoes and gently put her body next to his on the big bed. "How much do you want to know?"

"Everything you wanna tell me and not a thing more."

She snuggled carefully next to him. "Once upon a time there was a little red-haired princess."

"How little?"

"About five."

"Have I ever told you, you are the only person I ever heard with a Long Island accent that I thought was beautiful?"

"Thank you."

478

Forever Patriots

"Well, it's true. Now where were we?"

She continued, "There was this little five-year-old princess."

"And she had red hair."

"Yes, she had red hair. Well, sort of red anyway."

"The most beautiful red hair in the world. It would make any Irish Setter green with envy."

She kissed him gently on the cheek. "This little princess, who made all of the Irish Setters green with envy, was about five years old when she realized that there was something missing in her life. Something the other children seemed to take for granted: a Father. The little princess lost her father in the great crusade in Europe before she was born. Several years later, when the princess was about five years old, her mother married again.

"At first, the princess was happy to have a father of her very own, but one day ..."

Barbara Wheeler was born in Wantaugh, Long Island, New York, to a young couple who already had two children. She was the result of a night of passion on one of her father's brief leaves from the Army Air Corps during the Second World War.

Her father had been a dashing figure of a man, with his fiery red hair and mustache, and a pair of green eyes that could melt the heart of almost any woman. He loved his wife and family and had great plans for their future when the war was over, but the night of Barbara's conception was the last time he saw his wife. Two weeks later he was killed in a bombing mission over Nazi Germany.

In 1950, six years after her father's death, Barbara's mother, Mary, married a traveling salesman. He was kind to Barbara and the rest of the family in the beginning, but as things went wrong on his sales route, he began to vent his frustrations on Mary and her children – drinking and staying out late at nights – sometimes striking Barbara's mother in a drunken stupor as he stumbled into the darkened livingroom after a binge.

In 1953, at the age of eight, Barbara was molested by her stepfather. She lived in constant fear for two years as she was molested time and again by her mother's husband when he returned from his frequent sales trips. She wanted to tell her mother, but didn't know how. She was spared the task by her stepfather's premature death in an auto accident on the icy Hudson River Bridge in late 1955.

Her mother grieved over her husband's death for more than two years, never knowing the emotional trauma he had inflicted upon her daughter over a two-year period.

One evening, when Barbara was twelve years old, she told her mother the truth about her second husband. From that point forward in time, her mother's relationship with her youngest daughter deteriorated to one of detached hatred. She somehow blamed her beautiful twelve-year-old daughter for the acts committed by her previous husband.

In high school, Barbara remained aloof and detached from boys, always finding some excuse not to accept her many requests for a date. At the age of fifteen she got a job at a soda fountain not far from her home and worked until ten o'clock each night after school.

Try as she did, she was unable to get close to her mother. Her two older sisters, Nancy and Marilyn, became concerned about Barbara's relationship with her mother and the boys at school but were unable to find a suitable remedy for her

479

Stoney Livingston

problems.

When she was sixteen she met a boy at school who seemed different than the others and she went with him to a school dance, much to the surprise of her family. Her relationship with the boy lasted almost two months. It ended abruptly one evening in Central Park after a heavy petting session that lead her boyfriend to insist that she provide him with sexual relief. She refused but he forced her to fondle him until he ejaculated. She went home that evening and withdrew into herself, certain that males were filthy, forceful demons. She decided she would become a nun.

Her decision to enter the convent was short-lived. Two weeks after her encounter with her boyfriend in Central Park she was brutally raped as she left work shortly after ten P.M. Two men in their mid-thirties held her down in an alley behind the soda fountain and took turns raping her. They stuffed old rags into her mouth to keep her from shouting and they beat her as they took their perverted pleasures.

Unfortunately for her assailants she recognized them as regular customers of the soda fountain. Within hours of her ragged appearance at police precinct headquarters, both were arrested. Barbara vowed never again to allow men to violate her body or her beliefs as long as she may live. She testified in court and the men were found guilty. She sat in fear at the sentencing as both men were given three-year prison terms.

She completed high school without friends and without participating in any of the school activities. Within a year of her graduation she moved to California to live with her sister, Nancy, and her husband.

While in California, she made the decision to join the Marine Corps with the thought that she could become as tough as any man and never have to fear them again.

After her enlistment, and shortly before she was to report to boot camp, she met Jesse Langley while visiting Knott's Berry Farm with her friend, Cindy. From the very first minute he looked at her with his steel-grey eyes she felt something less than hatred for a man. She didn't know what it was but she knew she wanted to see him again.

Their dinner had been perfect and she knew before she left the restaurant with him that she had found a man she could trust. When the two men in the restaurant parking lot accosted them she saw her whole life pass before her eyes. It seemed to be a series of filthy men who wanted to use her for their own purposes, without thought, without any feeling other than animal lust. She would not be mistreated on that night. She would have died before she allowed that to happen.

Jesse Langley had spared her life when he had attacked the two. He didn't know it at the time, but there was no doubt in her mind that she would have died fighting had he not stepped forward. She remembered how she had grieved while he was in the hospital, fearful she would lose something she didn't yet have – wanting to tell him how she felt. When they made love later that night, Barbara, for the first time in her life, knew the joy and the ecstacy of real love, both the physical and the emotional. The act of physical contact with a man was no longer a degrading act of animal desires. It was something beautiful and fulfilling.

In her youth and immaturity, she had misjudged Jesse when she had asked him to desert his service and his country, but she had been afraid – afraid of losing her first real love to something as insignificant as a small war, in a small country no one had ever heard of.

480

Forever Patriots

When Jesse left, she had felt empty and alone. She had wanted to call him and tell him she was sorry, that she loved him, and that she would wait for him. But she couldn't.

After boot camp, she was stationed at the naval hospital in Beaufort, South Carolina. While at the hospital she met a young Navy doctor who treated her with respect and appeared genuinely interested in her as a person. She refused to go to dinner with him despite his repeated requests. Finally, after two months of denial, she agreed to accompany him to dinner at the finest Old South restaurant in Beaufort.

Dinner had been enjoyable but the feeling was not the same with the young doctor as it had been with Jesse Langley. She began to feel uncomfortable towards the end of the meal and she wished she had continued to refuse the young doctor's advances. When he asked her to his place for a nightcap, she politely refused, but he politely insisted, and she consented to a quick drink before reporting to her barracks.

Within minutes of pouring her drink at his plush bachelor's apartment, the suave young doctor kissed her. His kiss was not all that unpleasant to her but it lacked that special something she had felt when Jesse had kissed her.

Something inside her wanted the young doctor but she was at the same time reluctant. She didn't love this man but she did find him physically attractive. She allowed the doctor to continue his advances until she found herself half undressed in his living room.

Suddenly she wanted to run away and hide – to leave this place and this man and never be seen again by anyone – not even Jesse Langley. She felt cheap and worthy of no more than the respect shown her by the two men who had raped her so many years ago in New York. Jesse Langley was too good for her.

She turned to pick up her blouse, so carelessly tossed on the back of the sofa. The young doctor attempted to stop her with physical force and was rewarded with a knee to his groin. As the surprised young man doubled over in pain, Barbara retrieved her blouse and left his apartment, buttoning the garment as she stepped outside.

Once again she withdrew into herself and remained aloof from her co-workers, male and female alike. The young doctor made one feeble attempt at reconciliation but was abruptly snubbed in the presence of two nurses in the hallway of the hospital. He never approached her again.

When she could stand it no longer she wrote a letter to Jesse. She remembered and felt close to him as she wrote. It was her happiest moment in months. When she received his reply she was confused. Her biggest consolation was the fact that Jesse had not shunned her outright. She held onto his letter and carried it with her twenty-four hours a day, often stealing glances at his words on her breaks or even while sitting at her desk.

When Will Hunt contacted her about the possibility of Jesse going to R&R in Hawaii, her heart had leapt to her throat. She made plans and waited by the barracks phone every night for weeks, waiting for his call to confirm the rumor. She saved every penny she could, often going without meals, never spending a dime on anything but the barest of necessities.

When Will's call finally came, she was unable to obtain air transportation immediately. She was on the verge of panic when her request for air transportation was finally granted. She held many fears as she boarded the military KC-130, not

481

Stoney Livingston

the least of which was that she might not arrive in time to see Jesse before he returned to Vietnam. If she could just see him for a moment, she would know if this feeling she had for him was real. She could not live much longer if she didn't know in her heart that Jesse Langley was everything she thought him to be.

Barbara had talked of her life, leaving nothing out. Only when she had arrived at the Pago Pago in Hawaii did she stop.

During her discourse Jesse had said nothing. He had listened to her every word, feeling pain when she felt pain, happiness when she felt happiness. He had shared her fear and her elation, her sadness and her victories. When she had described him sitting at the table under the torchlight at the Pago Pago, she had described the fear that had welled inside of her as she approached the table. It was there her voice fell silent.

She looked into his eyes with her almond-shaped emeralds. Jesse said nothing as he kissed her full on the lips. Gently he caressed her lips with his own. He traced their outline with his tongue. He kissed her eyes and the tip of her nose. He kissed her cheeks, wet with her salty tears, and he kissed her neck from side to side.

"I love you, Barbara. I can't change what's happened in the past and, for a while, I won't have a whole lot of say about the future but, when I come back, if you still feel the same way about me...."

She put her finger to his lips. "Don't ever say 'if', Jesse. There is no 'if' with you. There never has been. I'm so afraid I'll never see you again. This is too good to last and, yet, I know it will if only you stay safe over there in Vietnam until I can hold you again."

"You see." He smiled. "You said 'if only'."

"Oh, Jesse, I'm so afraid. My heart almost stops beating when I think of you going back over there."

"Don't think about it, and before you know it, I'll be back and you'll have to make good on your promises."

Silence filled the room.

"It's not really so bad over there. It could be worse. Things are gettin' better every day. I expect that we'll win the war in a few more months. I may even get to come home early."

Barbara brightened. "Do you really think so, Jesse?"

He averted his gaze. "No. I was just lyin'. But it sounded good, didn't it?"

"Jesse, don't play with my feelings. This is important to me."

"I know, Barbara. I know. I was gonna lie to you but I couldn't. I don't think we're ever gonna win the war unless we change how we're doin' things. But that's no never mind. I'll be headed home in November – win or lose." He kissed her gently on the lips. The softness of her mouth and the smell of her body excited him.

Slowly and gently they made love, Barbara careful not to irritate his ribs. They both lost control as climax neared and injuries were forgotten.

As they lay apart on the big bed, Barbara expressed concern. "Are you all right? I lost control of my whole body. I'm sorry."

"So did I and I'm not sorry."

She smiled shyly and pulled the sheet to her shoulders. "Why did that big guy come after you, Jesse?"

"It's kind of a long story."

Forever Patriots

"You don't have to tell me if you don't want to."

"I don't mind tellin' you anything you wanna know. It all started when Joe and I went to this little bar called Nikki's..."

The morning sun blazed through the window of their spacious room as Jesse dressed. Barbara sat patiently on the sofa, drinking the juice of the passion fruit.

"You be careful about how much of that juice you drink. We may both get in trouble," said Jesse as he buttoned his shirt.

She smiled up at him. "I don't need passion fruit for you, Jesse. Just being around you does that for me." She paused. "I never thought I could talk to anyone, much less a man, about the things I talk with you about. It just seems so natural with you."

"That could be a sign of great things to come."

Silence followed his remark. He turned to see Barbara staring at him. "Tomorrow you've got to go back, don't you?" she asked.

"Tomorrow makes two weeks, Barbara."

Her eyes moistened. "I know you have to go, Jesse, but I can't come to terms with it. Not yet. I know I will, but I'm just having a hard time with it right now."

He knelt next to her and put his arm around her shoulders. "It's August now. I'll be back in the States in late November. That's only three or four months at the most."

She turned and put her arms around him. "I love you so much, Jesse Langley."

He kissed her full on the lips. They held the embrace for several moments, neither speaking, each savoring the other's touch. When they pulled apart he looked into her dark green eyes. "Would you mind living in Arizona?"

She squealed and jumped into his arms, knocking him to the floor. She kissed his lips and face through tears of happiness.

"Whoa! What happened to you? I told you not to drink too much of that passion fruit."

Barbara remembered his injured ribs of only two days prior. "Oh! Are you okay?"

He kissed her quickly on the lips. "Of course I'm okay. You couldn't hurt me if you wanted to."

They rolled on the floor. "Oh, Jesse, I'm so happy! You just asked me if I wanted to live in Arizona."

"I know it's a nice place to live, but don't you think you're overdoing it?" He smiled broadly.

During their time together they had spoken little of the future. They were too busy living the present to waste any of their precious time together talking about the future. But now separation was near.

Jesse hadn't thought of the institution of marriage, not that he made a conscious effort to quell the thought, rather he assumed that he and Barbara would always remain together, giving no further time to the details suggested by such a thought.

He looked into her eyes, corners turned up to match the smile on her lips. "We could both go to school when we get out of the service. I mean, I'd have to work and all, but we could make it."

483

"We'll both work." She was giddy.

Jesse raised an eyebrow. "I'm not so sure I want my wife workin'. I'd rather she went to school and studied full-time so she could become a rich scientist and support me in the manner in which I'd like to become accustomed."

Barbara stopped breathing. Her large emerald eyes became even larger and, to Jesse's way of thinking, more beautiful.

Jesse said, "Barbara, are you okay?"

Silently she looked at him, tears streaming down her face.

"Barbara? What's wrong?" he repeated.

She flew into his arms. "Jesse, you just called me your wife."

"A Freudian slip of the tongue," he said around her lips.

She stiffened.

He pulled away and smiled.

She returned his smile and hugged him tightly. "Oh, Jesse. I'm so in love with you."

He stroked her back, smelling the clean smell of her body, feeling the softness of her hair as it brushed against his cheek. "I'm crazy about you, Barbara, and I'm not gonna hide the way I feel. I don't care who knows it. But the most important thing to me is that *you* know it."

She kissed him passionately.

That afternoon, Jesse reported to Hickam Field and advised a captain in special services of his overdue return to Vietnam. Barbara waited nervously outside the captain's office.

Early in the afternoon, gusty winds had suddenly come up from out of the southwest. As the day wore on the winds intensified. Jesse stared beyond the captain's shoulder, through the window behind him, at a swaying palm.

The captain sat at his desk as Jesse told his story. When he ended his tale, the air force captain said, "So you planned a little two-week leave right from the start, huh?"

"Yessir, but my company commander knew about it."

"He did, huh?"

"Yessir."

"Well, if I let you off of the base tonight, how do I know you'll be here tomorrow to catch the plane?"

"Because I said so, Sir."

"Oh. Because you said so?"

"Yessir." Jesse began to have doubts. It didn't appear as though the captain wanted to let him leave the base. He pressed on. "Sir, there's a girl sitting outside your office right now that came all the way from South Carolina to see me. When I get back from Vietnam I'm gonna marry her. I won't do anything to further jeopardize my chances of getting an honorable discharge."

The captain wavered.

"Sir, I'll give you the number of my hotel room. You can reach me if you change your mind. I'll come back early. I'll report in at 0600 if you want me too."

The captain shuffled a sheaf of papers. "All right, Corporal. You can stay in town tonight. But I want the phone number."

"Yessir. Thank you. Will that be all, Sir?"

"That'll be all. Leave the number with the desk sergeant."

Forever Patriots

Jesse stood and crisply snapped to attention. He did an about face and fairly bounced out of the room, smiling broadly at Barbara as she jumped out of her chair.

They walked on the beach in the gusty wind, arm in arm, the prominent features of Diamond Head barely visible in the waning light. They walked silently, each savoring the nearness of the other, each wishing they could extend the parting just one minute beyond forever. They seemed oblivious to the sharply leaning palm trees or the small flying objects thrown about by the brisk wind. At length Barbara broke the silence between them.

"Jesse?"

He cut his stride and turned to face her. The wind blew her hair all about her face. "Yeah?"

"I'm not real religious but I know God brought us together."

"God? What's he got to do with anything?"

"It has to be God, Jesse. I never knew life could be this good. I don't think it can be without God."

He sat with his back to a palm tree. Barbara joined him in the soft sand. "Barbara, I don't believe in a God."

"Don't say that, Jesse."

"No real God would allow wars. No real God would allow men to be so greedy and full of lies and willing to turn against another man for no good reason."

"Please, Jesse."

He held his silence for a moment. "Okay, beautiful. Have I told you lately that I love you?"

"Hold me, Jesse."

They sat in the sand, two lovers on a deserted beach, the wind howling madly at them from the heavy sea. They watched the clouds roll into shore with the cresting waves. Both held their silence as darkness overtook the island, each hoping to hold back time as they sat quietly reminiscing about their time together.

The sound of a human voice in the distance broke the howl of the wind. It seemed to come from far away but it was difficult to judge distance in the wind.

"Did you hear that?" asked Barbara.

"Yeah. It sounded like someone screaming for help."

They strained their ears to pick up another sound. They could see nothing in the darkness that surrounded them. The sound of the voice reached their ears again.

"It's comin' from somewhere east of us, I think," said Jesse into Barbara's ear.

They both stood and moved quickly down the beach in search of the sound's origin. At the water's edge, a mere seventy-five yards from where they had been sitting, stood a large woman, barely discernible in the darkness. She screeched out to sea as they approached.

"What's wrong, Ma'am?" shouted Jesse above the roar of the wind.

"My baby! He's out there! I can't see him!"

"Are you sure?" asked Jesse. He strained his eyes in the darkness.

"What happened?" asked Barbara. Two small children stood at the woman's side.

"He ran into the water. A big wave took him from the shore. I can't see

485

Stoney Livingston

him! Help me! Please! Find my little one," she pleaded.

"How old is he?" asked Jesse, his eyes piercing the darkness.

"Four. Please! Help me!"

"Can he swim?"

"Yes but the water is too rough! Please! Do something!"

A feint voice drifted inland from the swelling sea. Jesse removed his shoes and ran into the water to Barbara's screams. "Jesse! Don't!"

He was swallowed by the crashing surf.

Jesse broke water, gasping for air as the big waved coughed him to the surface. He heard the gurgling pleas of a small voice nearby. He tried to swim against the strong current but made little headway. A small body smashed into his face. He reached for it and clung to the wet clothing, fighting to maintain full consciousness. The water dragged them both under.

Jesse felt Barbara's body strike his as he tumbled to the surface. "Barbara!" He screamed into the howl of the wind. "What are you doin'?" He swallowed a mouthful of salty water. The ocean spray, driven by the wind, struck him full in the face, feeling like pellets from a shotgun.

She grabbed the child and helped hold his head above the crashing water. "The same thing you are, Jesse Langley!"

A large wave made further conversation impossible as it drove them under. They surfaced together, both of them still holding the child, gasping for air. The sounds of voices screaming from the shore helped them both find their direction. With what strength was left in their arms they struggled for the sandy beach. They caught the crest of a large wave and rode it until it smashed them upon the sand, almost at the feet of the screaming woman and two other passers-by who had stopped to shout into the howling storm.

The woman screeched at the sight of her child and, rushing forward, scooped it from the grasp of the exhausted pair, who lay on the wet sand, thankful to be alive. They clung to each other in the darkness, oblivious to the presence of the others, kissing the salty water from each other's faces.

"Barbara, don't ever do anything like that again," said Jesse between kisses.

Barbara removed her lips from his face only long enough to reply. "I almost died when you ran into the water." She kissed his salty lips.

"Are you two okay?" asked a voice.

Still clinging to each other, they turned their faces upward as another wave crashed to shore, covering them. When the water receded they lay in each other's arms, smiling to the passer-by, who stood mutely ten yards away. "Yeah, we're okay. How's the kid?" asked Jesse.

"Thanks to you two, it looks like he's gonna be all right. You gonna stay out there in the water all night? We've got some towels here."

They stood and walked slowly inland to the man speaking to them from the darkness. The mother of the child ran to them, the child still in her arms. She tried to put one big arm around them both as she held her child in the other. "Bless you! God Bless you both! Thank you so much!"

Jesse felt the heat of embarrassment as he often did when praised. He was thankful for the darkness. "You're welcome, Ma'am. How's the boy?"

"He is fine! He is wonderful! And thanks to you two – he is alive!"

The wind continued to howl as the rain started. It came at a sharp angle

486

from the southwest. The mother of the child spoke again. "Would you please come to my house? It's not far and it is dry and warm."

Jesse studied the heavy-set Polynesian woman holding the recently rescued child. He turned to Barbara. "How about it?"

She smiled up at him and nodded. Jesse turned back to the woman. "Okay. Whenever you're ready. My name's Jesse and the one who swims like Esther Williams is Barbara."

The woman kissed their hands. "I am Mary Malaulu and I'm so grateful that God sent you to me tonight. Thank you again."

Jesse arched an eyebrow. "That's the second time recently I been linked to that guy."

Barbara pinched his arm lightly. He laughed softly in the raging wind and rain as they followed Mary Malaulu to her house.

The wind and rain raged outside as Barbara and Jesse sat on the sofa in Mary Malaulu's livingroom. Her three children played on the linoleum floor, the four-year-old recently rescued from the violent waters of the Pacific acting none the worse for wear.

Jesse was covered by one of Mary's robes that was more than ample to hide his frame. Barbara wore a kimono three times too large for her. They sipped warm tea as Mary told stories of her dead husband who had been lost at sea while on a fishing trip.

Mary insisted on feeding them and, without being rude, the two found it difficult to refuse. Caught up in the recent emotional ordeal of earlier in the evening and seeing the obvious affection between the two young people, Mary scurried around the house, searching until she was able to produce two large candles. She proudly placed them on the table and asked Jesse to light them for her. She found a dusty bottle of French Bordeaux and opened it carefully. They dined on shrimp and pork, cooked in the inimitable style of the Polynesians. It was like any meal Jesse had ever shared with Barbara – perfect.

During the meal, Jesse placed his left arm around Barbara while he ate with his right. They couldn't get much closer. Her leg was thrown over his. He felt the constraint of time weighing heavily upon his shoulders. Late in the meal he turned to Mary and said, "With your permission, I'd like to use this happy time to speak to my girl on a matter of utmost importance."

Mary nodded solemnly and stood to leave the table.

"Please. Stay. I'd like you to stay."

She seated herself.

Jesse turned to Barbara and raised his wine glass slightly. She joined hers with his briefly in a silent toast then they each sipped the contents.

Jesse started falteringly. "Barbara, ...you know I love you more than Cyrano loved Roxanne, ...more than the stars love the heavens, and more than life loves itself. I mentioned you bein' my wife earlier, but now I wanna make an official proposal. Would you bestow upon me the honor of your hand in marriage? I'm still gonna drink sour mash and smoke cigarettes but I'll try to get rid of my other habits that may bother you. I promise. And I promise you too that you will be loved like no other woman has ever been loved."

Barbara's eyes sparkled with moistness as she smiled at the half-clumsy, half-poetic proposal. She leaned into him. "Oh, Jesse. There is no one on earth like

487

Stoney Livingston

you. I love you for your uniqueness and your sometimes child-like ways. I love you for the fire in your eyes and the fight in your heart. I love you for your selflessness and your compassion. I'll drink sour mash with you until I'm too old to lift the bottle. I love you, Jesse Langley, for just what you are. I will marry you anytime, anywhere. Does that answer the question to your satisfaction?"

"Indubitably." He kissed her softly. When they pulled apart, he watched the candlelight play upon her face. He saw the shine of happiness in her eyes and could imagine no feeling on earth greater than what he felt.

They both became aware of Mary's forgotten presence in the room. She wept softly. "That was the most beautiful thing I ever saw," she sobbed.

Jesse handed her a napkin. She blew her nose unceremoniously. Jesse ignored the noise and kissed Barbara on the lips, tasting the wine that lingered there. He wanted to be alone with her but knew he must wait a little longer.

Mary scooted her children off to bed and turned all but one of the lights in the livingroom off. "I know you kids want to be alone. I have your clothes hanging in front of the stove. They should be dry soon. I'm going to bed now. Thank you both for saving my baby, and thank you for sharing your love in this house."

"Thank you, Mary, for sharing your food with us. We'll lock the door when we leave," said Jesse softly.

"Goodnight, Mary, and thank you," said Barbara.

She left them alone.

"Life is so beautiful with you, Jesse," said Barbara softly after Mary disappeared behind a corner.

"Beautiful?"

"Everything about life is beautiful with you. A near tragedy turns into the most wonderful evening of my life. We meet a nice lady with three happy kids, have a great dinner, and you propose marriage to me in a manner as eloquently as any man ever proposed to a woman." She sighed. "Life with you is never going to be boring, even if we just sit around and drink sour mash whiskey and read books." She snuggled into him.

He hugged her to him with one arm as he stared into the burning light. "I wish I had found you sooner but I'm glad I found you when I did. The time was better. I feel so peaceful inside. I don't know that I could have felt this way a year or two ago. We're still so young and we've got a long time to spend together. I hope I won't disappoint you."

"You won't, nor will I disappoint you. We'll work together and love together, and nothing will ever tear our love apart."

They sat silently on the sofa for another hour, neither speaking. At the end of the hour they put on their dry, warm clothes and stepped into the night, leaving behind the folded robe and kimono and a wet, wrinkled hundred-dollar-bill.

They walked the distance to their hotel in the pounding rain, their dry clothes soaked in less than a hundred yards.

Jesse awakened to the sound of the telephone. He reached over Barbara and picked up the receiver. "Hello."

The voice on the other end sounded crisp in his ear. "Corporal Langley?"

"Yes. Who's this?"

"Captain Donelly at Hickam."

"What time is it? I'm not late am I, Sir?"

488

"No, no. It's 0530. I just called to let you know that all flights are canceled today and tomorrow. The weather's too rough. Look's like someone up there likes you. Check in with me tomorrow morning to make sure there are no further changes."

"Yes, Sir. I sure will. What time?"

"0730."

"Yessir. Will that be all?"

"That's all, Corporal. Have a good time."

"Thank you, Sir."

The phone went dead.

Barbara looked at him. There was concern in her voice. "Do you have to go now?"

He kissed her neck and said, "Nope. That was the captain at Hickam. He said since I was such a good guy, I could take two more days of R & R."

Barbara said nothing. She studied his face.

"All the planes are grounded because of the weather – for two more days."

She leapt into his arms.

CHAPTER TWENTY-ONE: CAM LO

It was mid-morning when the Choctaw helicopter squatted down on the Phu Bai Airstrip. Jesse jumped from the vibrating old machine almost as it touched the ground, glad to be free of confinement. He spotted a mighty-mite on the edge of the LZ. Lance Corporal Larry Cannon sat behind the wheel in the blistering sun, a smile covering his face. Jesse walked to meet him, his freshly washed utilities smelling clean and unfamiliar.

"I thought you were kiddin' about the two weeks but I guess you weren't, huh?" greeted Larry.

"Almost sixteen days, but the last two weren't my idea. They had some kind of storm warning. All the planes were grounded. How's things goin', Larry?"

"Battalion commander is madder'n hell at you. The word is that you're gonna spend a little time at Portsmouth, makin' little rocks out of big ones. Captain Malcolm..."

"Captain?"

"Yeah, he's a full-fledged captain as of about a week ago. Anyway, Captain Malcolm is citing some regulation where he still has jurisdiction over your discipline, because you're still in his command. Just thought I'd let you know what's goin' on before you go see the old man."

"Appreciate it, Larry. Where'd you get the Mite? How come the chopper didn't just drop me on the Trail?" Jesse sat next to Larry in the small jeep and settled into the hard seat as they pulled away from the LZ.

Larry laughed. "Hell, we got lifted out of there the same day you and Cue went on R&R. Been stationed at Phu Bai ever since, eating hot chow and runnin' gun drill and playin' volleyball and stuff like that. The mite belongs to H & S headquarters section. Their driver is so damn lazy, he told me I could use it to pick you up as long as I didn't tell anybody."

"Oh damn, not Phu Bai. Have they got the same base commander they had when we were here last time?"

"Nope. Some new guy. I don't even remember his name. Whoever he is, he just lets the battalion commanders alone as long as we follow the camp rules."

The mighty-mite struck a hole in the road and bounced violently. "Damn, Larry, I don't feel like fixin' a flat out here." He reached into the back of the vehicle and picked up Larry's M-14.

"This area is pretty secure in the daylight," said Larry.

"Where's my Thompson?"

"I think Thunder traded it for a crossbow."

"Crossbow? Is he crazy?"

Larry smiled. "We all figured you both were."

"Where's my gear?"

"We got our seabags back. Your stuff is at H&S Company supply. Except

490

your poncho and seven-eighty-two gear. Thunder told me to tell you he took it with him when they moved Alpha out this morning."

"Where'd they go?" asked Jesse with more than idle curiosity.

"I don't know where it is, but it's someplace called Cam Lo."

"How do I get there?"

"I don't know that either. I think they've got a mail run this afternoon but I don't know what time the chopper leaves. So how was R&R in Hawaii?"

"You wouldn't believe me if I told you."

"That good, huh?"

"Better. It was worth comin' over here just to have that happen to me."

"Jesus, it musta' been good."

They rode the rest of the way to the camp engrossed in talk of the way things should be in life. Larry stopped the mite in front of the H&S company headquarters tent and Jesse retrieved his duffel bag and laid Larry's M-14 across the seat. "Thanks for the lift, Larry. I'm gonna try and catch up with Alpha before the battalion commander finds out I'm here."

"I'd say that was a damned good idea." He released the clutch and pulled away from the tent.

Inside the tent, Jesse was confronted by a clerk sitting in front of a field typewriter. "You looking for somebody?" asked the PFC in a Texas drawl.

Jesse didn't recognize him and could tell instantly by the baby fat still remaining on his cheeks that he hadn't been in Vietnam very long. "Yeah. My name is Langley and I'm lookin' for a ride to Alpha Company. You seen anybody around that can tell me how to get to 'em?"

The PFC stood and searched about the tent as though looking for help. He was alone. "The company commander wants to see you. He's been lookin' fer you fer more'n a week now."

"Well, tell 'im I'm back."

"I think he's at chow."

"What about the first-shirt?"

"Same."

"Where's eighty-ones?"

The PFC pointed east. "About a hundred-and-fifty yards. You'll see the signs."

"Signs?"

"Yeah. This is gettin' to be like a regular stateside base. We got a PX, movies, hot chow, showers – and signs."

Jesse nodded. "Thanks. Tell the first-shirt I'll be at the eighty-one platoon if he needs me."

"He'll be wantin' to see you, you can count on that," said the PFC as Jesse exited the tent.

Jesse's reunion with the eighty-one platoon was a joyful one as he opened his duffel bag and distributed some of the whiskey he carried.

"You're in deep shit, man," offered Ruddleston as he took a pull from a bottle of whiskey and passed it to Hill.

"Yeah, so I heard. Where's the First Section?"

"Dey pulled out dis mornin' wid Alpha," answered Hill, passing the bottle.

"Damn. Anybody know how I can get to Alpha?"

"Whatchoo wanna go out der wid dem guys fur anyway? I heard dat fuckin'

491

Stoney Livingston

Cam Lo is in da middle a' nowhere. And dey ain't got no cover er nuttin'," said Hill. "Dey be sittin' up right out in da open."

"The mail chopper is making a run in about fifteen minutes, Indio, if you're serious about getting to Alpha," said Ruddleston.

"Thanks, Rud. Now, where do I find the chopper?"

Rud stood. "C'mon. We ain't got much time to waste. It's a hoof to get to the LZ in time."

Jesse followed the tall black man from Pennsylvania as he stepped out briskly in the direction of the LZ.

At first, the pilot was reluctant to take on the unauthorized passenger but Jesse convinced him to do so by simply telling him what had happened regarding his R&R. The pilot, a young warrant officer from Omaha, Nebraska, thought the situation humorous and agreed to comply with Jesse's request without clearing through proper channels. Much to Jesse's delight, the old Choctaw lifted from the LZ right on schedule.

The helicopter crew chief pointed to the village of Cam Lo as the Choctaw began its descent. Jesse could see the beginnings of a marine position almost a half mile to the west of the village. He counted three tanks and four one-five-five howitzers in addition to the two 81mm. mortar positions as the helicopter dropped to the marked LZ.

As Jesse stepped from the helicopter he came face-to-face with Captain Malcolm. Malcolm's face registered surprise.

"Afternoon, Skipper. Congratulations on the railroad tracks."

Malcolm smiled broadly. "How you doin', Indio? I take it we had a nice visit?"

"It was great, Sir. Thanks for helping me get Hawaii."

Malcolm's troops had already emptied the helicopter of its contents and the ancient bird vibrated skyward, throwing a cloud of dust over the LZ. When the stirred air died, Malcolm said, "If you aren't hauled out of here before daylight tomorrow, I'd like to hear about it. In the meantime we've got bunkers to build and wire to lay, and not a whole lot of time to get the job done."

Malcolm spent almost five minutes briefing Jesse on the current status of Alpha Company. There had been almost twenty replacement troops entered on the company roster since Jesse's departure for R&R, and most of the veterans had regained their strength while the company rested at Phu Bai, but they were still under strength as a company, with less than a hundred and thirty men of the more than two hundred required by the table of organization.

Three tanks, one of them a flame tank; a battery of howitzers, also under strength, the First section of 81 mortars, including guns one and two, and Alpha Company, were assigned the mission of protecting the village of Cam Lo from VC harassment. Some of the village leaders claimed the VC were operating unafraid in broad daylight, stealing food and intimidating the people of the village.

When Malcolm finished his briefing, Jesse looked around the position and said, "If they hit us tonight, there's no way we can stop 'em if they're in strength. Whose idea was this? Colonel Shithead's?"

Malcolm winced. "Keep that kind of talk low. I hate to be in total agreement with you, but you're right. We don't have enough wire, even if we string everything we've got today. Battalion has promised more wire tomorrow, and some combat

492

engineers to lay out some mines. Charlie or Bravo may be out here in the morning but that doesn't help us tonight. We've got two eighty-ones but only one of them has a sight. The other one is broken."

"I've got an idea, Skipper."

"I'm almost afraid to ask."

"Let's just call up battalion and tell 'em to get us the hell outa here until in the morning when we can come out here in strength and with some gear to get the job done right. Don't this dumb-ass colonel ever get tired of screwin' things up?"

Malcolm shook his head. "From our point of view that's a damn good idea, but I don't think battalion thinks our situation is so critical. I've already asked for two more companies to get us through the first night and battalion has advised me that priorities won't allow any reinforcements tonight. They told me to dig in and hold the position until tomorrow."

"Kinda' makes me wonder what I was in such a hurry to get out here for," mused Jesse. He looked at Malcolm. "What d'ya want me to do first?"

"Pick up a map from Lance Corporal Cummings. He was acting as the FO and squad leader on your gun one. He'll brief you on what's going on with regard to the tanks and the arty battery. It's not a full battery but it's better than nothing. They'll mainly be firing H&I's during the night. You'll be the only real FO in the camp so, if something happens, get on the net right away."

"Yessir. Where's Mud?"

"Mud rotated home. He left you a letter." Malcolm turned to a map pouch and retrieved a letter. "Said to be sure you looked him up when you got Stateside." He handed the letter to Jesse.

"No kidding? He made it. I'm so used to him being with me, I forgot for a second he was due to leave while I was on R & R. Damn. He was a good man to have around the radio. He knew what to do without being told. It's hard to find a guy like him. Damn. I'm glad he made it home." Jesse felt a wave of emotion overcome him momentarily. He broke it by speaking. "So who's the new FO operator?"

"We don't have one yet. The FO radio is in Cummings's charge. You'll have to get one of the men from eighty-one's to fill in temporarily until they can assign somebody to the job permanently. I think they're a little short-handed and they need everybody they can find to operate the guns. We don't plan any assaults from this position, so you won't really need anyone to leave the mortar position. Just pick someone who knows a little about proper radio procedure. I'll give you a list of the frequencies.

"When you're all briefed, report to Thunder on the southwest side of the compound. We need sandbags filled and wire strung."

"Aye aye, sir. I'm gone." He unzipped his duffel bag and withdrew a bottle of Old Crow bourbon. "I almost forgot. Here."

Jesse's greeting at the mortar position was warm and filled with handshaking. He placed two bottles of bourbon in Rich Cummings's charge and advised him to save them until the following day. Tuleano briefed him on the prearranged Final Protective Line in the event they were in danger of being overrun. After a short visit, Jesse left to report to Thunder.

He found Thunder filling a sandbag with his E-tool. "Hey, Thunder, what's happenin'?"

Thunder looked up from his work. He dropped his combat shovel and

493

embraced Jesse. "You crazy mortarman. I thought you were a casualty of the easy life. Thought maybe you got to likin' it so well you decided not to come back to this land of warmth and sunshine."

"I did consider it but I chickened out at the last minute. I understand I'm not the battalion commander's favorite son right about now."

"Don't sweat it. Hell, I was gone ten days myself. All I got was an ass chewin' and a slap on the wrist. The whole thing only took about two minutes. The skipper never said a word to me, 'cept to ask me if I had a good time."

Jesse looked at the expanse of open terrain, then to the mountains southwest of their position. "It looks like not much has changed. We're only about fifteen hundred yards from those hills south of us. The gooks can hide their mortars and rockets real good up there. About two hundred yards north of us is Highway 9, which can be fortified to hold us in here until they pick us off with their big stuff. Yeah, this is great."

Thunder became serious. "We really are in a shitty position this time – one of the worst I can remember. If the gooks leave us alone tonight we'll probably be okay but, if I was a gook, I'd hit this place with everything I could muster tonight."

"Yeah, me too. I can't believe that a grown man with any experience at all would do something this stupid."

"You know what happens don't you? These damn colonels and generals get out all of these old manuals on warfare and study a bunch of historical battles, then they try to make one of 'em fit over here. It's just a big game to 'em. They get to move pins around on a map and everything – just like in the movies."

Jesse smiled, "I think you're right there but this one is so stupid that maybe the gooks will think we're tryin' to draw 'em into a trap and they'll leave us alone. I don't think even the gooks believe we're this stupid."

"Yeah, you could be right. I hadn't thought of that. If I was a gook commander, I'd have to look at this one real close. We're too obviously exposed. It almost has to be a trap. Hell, now you've got me convinced." Thunder retrieved his shovel. "Well, we'd better get some more sandbags filled. It could be a long night."

Jesse picked up a sandbag and held it open while Thunder filled it with the moist dirt. "Speakin' of a long night, I hear I have a new T.O. weapon."

"Oh, yeah. I was gonna surprise you with that one."

"From what I hear, it would have been one helluva surprise. I mean, goddamn, man – a crossbow? Do I look like Ghengis Khan or something?"

"I got a grease gun too."

"I didn't hear about the grease gun."

"Yeah," Thunder dropped a scoop of dirt into the sandbag Jesse held open. "You see, there was this guy in tanks that saw the Thompson. He had always wanted one, so he offered to trade his grease gun and five hundred rounds of ammo for it. I told him no at first but, when he threw in the crossbow, I couldn't resist. You oughta see this thing. Hell, you gotta crank it back with a lever to cock it. It'll go right through a man at fifty yards."

"Yeah, if you can hit 'im."

"You wouldn't believe how accurate this thing is," defended Thunder.

"But why the grease gun? And why all the extra ammo? Hell, it shoots forty-fives just like the Thompson, don't it?"

"Yeah but that was a tradin' strategy. Now you got more to trade with if you run across a good deal."

Forever Patriots

"Oh." Jesse concentrated on holding the sandbag open for a moment. "Thunder, did you destroy all your brain cells while you were on R&R? You know – too much whiskey and that sort of thing?"

"Wait'll you see this crossbow."

"I can hardly wait. You didn't trade my pistol did you?"

"Hell no. It's still on your cartridge belt, over there by that small hole. And that reminds me, I almost had to whip a lieutenant's ass to keep that thing. He said I wasn't T.O. with it and I told him it belonged to a forward observer who was on temporary assignment. He advised me that FO's didn't rate pistols either so I told him I thought you were a captain in the airwing but I wasn't sure. That shut him up."

"Who is this guy?"

New platoon commander. Second platoon. Name's Converse. He's a brown bar by the way – and he's so damn gung-ho, you won't believe it. He's got two or three gook barbers up here givin' haircuts by the numbers."

"Oh great. Now I got a boot camp brown bar after my Godamned pistol. What other good news you got?" groaned Jesse as he retrieved his cartridge belt, complete with pistol, two canteens, first aid pouch, Bowie knife, rolled poncho, and Garand pouches loaded with .45 caliber ammunition loosely snapped inside.

"That's about it for now." Thunder wiped the perspiration from his brow. "So tell me about Hawaii. Did that buddy of yours from the States make it? And what about that Claudia gal? You see her?"

Jesse found his old, dirty headband and placed it on his head. "Thunder, you won't believe what happened."

The marines worked well into the night fortifying the position. After darkness had fallen, two men were placed in a machine gun position three hundred yards southwest of the perimeter. With their machine gun, two thousand rounds of ammunition and a landline, they were to be the early-warning device for Thunder and his side of the perimeter.

Thunder had been apprehensive when he had left his briefing with Captain Malcolm. Putting two men in front of the wire with minimal protection was not his idea of how things should be done, but Malcolm ordered it and it would be done. He had no trouble securing volunteers when he had made it clear that it was the skipper's idea. Malcolm was respected and well liked by the men in Alpha Company. Jesse volunteered, but was immediately reminded by Thunder that Malcolm wanted him to remain inside the compound in the event his services as an FO were required.

Darkness filled the landscape as completely as it fills an endless cave. The moon was non-existent and a veil of thin clouds covered the stars. Jesse cupped his cigarette carefully under his poncho and exhaled slowly. "This is sure an eerie night," he said softly to Thunder, only a few feet away.

"It's gonna come tonight, my friend. It has to. This is like slappin' the gooks in the face with a wet noodle. We ain't got the gear to back this one up."

"Yeah, I think you're right. I don't know what else we can do. I had the guys string a bunch a' C-ration cans on the wire, and we've got grenades planted with trip wires out front. I wouldn't wanna be those guys out there on that M-60," said Jesse.

"You volunteered, remember?"

"That don't mean I wanted to do it. Someone has to and, if you didn't get anybody, I'd go in a minute."

"Even after all that stuff about Barbara? Don't you wanna go home, Indio?

495

Stoney Livingston

In one piece, I mean."

"You damn right I do, now more than ever before, but I can't be less than who I am when I go home. I wasn't chickenshit when I came over here and I'm not growin' feathers just because I got the girl of my dreams. Hell, that's all the more reason to kick ass and get it over with."

Thunder put his head under his poncho and took a drag on his cigarette. "Do you really think the politicians are gonna ever let us win this war?" he asked, exhaling the smoke into the black void that was the night.

"It don't look that way but I think we can do it by accident if we play it right."

"How's that?" asked Thunder.

"All we gotta do is put together enough guys who feel like we do and march to Hanoi."

"Oh shit, you had me goin' there for a second," admitted Thunder. "I mean, seriously, what the hell are we doin' over here? Look at this shit we're in tonight for example. What's the purpose? Why couldn't we have waited until tomorrow when we could jump off with a reinforced battalion? Then we could kick some ass and take some names and quit screwin' around. Instead, they put a few of us out here to sit around waitin' for the end to come. You and I both know this is not how to fight a war. A goddamned second lieutenant could figure that out, fer chrisakes."

Jesse said, "Why do suppose they're makin' us fight the war this way? I've thought it over a hundred times and can't figure it out. There's probably a million ways we could fight this thing and do better than what we're doing. Why don't we pick any one of 'em and proceed?"

"I wish to hell I knew. Did you hear any scuttlebutt in Hawaii?"

"To tell you the truth, Thunder, I was lost in a world I never even knew existed. I didn't give a damn about this little police action while I was there. Oh, there were a few times that I stopped to think about the guys and how they were doin', but I never really looked at the over-all picture. I just didn't give a damn. You know what I mean?"

Thunder sighed. "Yeah, I can understand that. I didn't exactly meet the girl of my dreams, but I can't say she was a nightmare either, and I had about the same thoughts you did about this place. If the real story was known, I didn't really care about how the war came out – more like how the guys came out of it."

"That's basically it in a nutshell. Who cares about this damn politician's war anyway? You wanna die over here for some smooth-talkin' politician, or do you wanna go home and watch the U of A kick Tempe's ass at the end of each season?"

Thunder smiled in the darkness. "If my memory serves me right, that ain't the way it's been lately."

"Times are gonna change. U of A is gonna have a new quarterback in a few years."

"Oh yeah? Anybody I know?"

"Why not? I ain't seen anybody else do the job since I was a kid."

"You got a point there. I think the last really good quarterback they had at the U of A was Wilson, wasn't it?"

"That's what I figure."

There was a moment of silence. Thunder broke it first. "There's only one thing wrong with all of this bullshit."

"Yeah, I know," said Jesse.

"Who wants to go home as the first serviceman to lose a war for the U.S.?"

496

"That's the kicker. Especially when we could win it so damn easy," agreed Jesse.

"That's the part that gets my gall."

"Yeah, me too, Thunder. Me too. Well, I guess I better try to find the mortars in this inkwell. I'll see ya' at reveille."

"Keep yer ass low, Indio."

"You too, Thunder." Jesse felt his way in the darkness in search of one of the mortar gunpits.

He found Cue on the gunwatch at gun one. After a weak challenge, Cue allowed him to enter the pit. "Where the hell you been?"

"Drinkin' whiskey and chasin' women. Who the hell died and made you my nanny?" said Jesse.

"Goddamnit, Indio, this sucks. Rich says he thinks this is even dumber than *Oregon*."

"Shhh. Not so loud. Even the gooks have ears, you know."

Cue lowered his voice. "I'm sorry, man, but what the hell we gonna do if the gooks hit us tonight?"

"Fight like hell, I reckon. You got any better ideas?"

"According to what we been told, there's more gooks out there than you can shake a stick at. Whose bright idea was it to move three tanks and four five-fives onto the perimeter with a half-strength line company?"

"Sounds to me like you been talkin' to someone who, unlike our illustrious battalion commander, may have read a book or two on infantry tactics," said Jesse.

"Tule was bitchin' about it earlier. It makes sense to me. Those tanks don't belong here as sittin' ducks, inside a compound that wouldn't hold out a sick fullback. And the arty damn sure doesn't belong here. If we get overrun, the gooks have got the best artillery in their whole damn army."

"Whoa. Slow down. Who said anything about being overrun? They gotta kill us to do that, and me, I'm not gonna take too kindly to that notion."

"Nobody said they would. I just said 'if'," defended Cue.

"'If' they do, I'll be dead, and I won't really give a damn," said Jesse.

"You know, Indio, you've got a way with words that just pisses me off sometimes."

"Speakin' of a way with words, you goin' to college when you get outa the Crotch?"

"Hell, I don't know. I'd like to but I don't know if I'll have the money. And I'm not so sure I'll be around to find out."

"Yer cryin' with a loaf of bread in your hands, Cue. We'll get through this. Alpha won't go down without a bigger fight than the gooks can handle. And the feds will come out with some kind of G.I. Bill. They always do after a war."

"Maybe. I hope you're right – on both counts."

"Go anyway, Cue, even if they don't come out with a G.I. Bill. You got the brains for it. Use 'em." Jesse had already dismissed the idea of the VC taking their position and preferred to think in positive terms about their future.

"Think so, huh?" asked Cue.

"Yep." Jesse paused. "So how was your R&R?"

Jesse awoke to the rattle of an M-60 in the distance. First there were two or three short bursts, then a steady stream of noise. He looked at his Seawolf. Shortly

497

after 0415, small arms fire joined the steady sound of the machine gun. The shouting of men barking orders or giving warnings drifted to him above the rattle of gunfire..

"They're inside the wire!"

The empty C-ration cans clanked as something disturbed the concertina wire.

The unmistakable sound of a bangalore torpedo broke the night air.

"They're blowin' the wire!" someone shouted.

"Bangalore!"

"Get us some light!"

"Fix bayonets!"

"They're all over the place!"

"I can't see! Where's the illumination?" The rest of the words were lost in the confusion.

The thump of a mortar round leaving the tube foretold the coming light. When the illumination round ignited, Jesse was not prepared for what he saw. He estimated on his initial glance that at least fifty of the enemy were inside the wire and charging wildly in all directions. He felt fear in the marrow of his bones.

He put his helmet on his head and ran to the gunpit where Rich steadied the tube on Gun One while Cue dropped illumination rounds.

"Rich," shouted Jesse. "Where's the radio?"There's still a bunch of 'em outside the wire! Let's try to drop some H.E. on 'em."

"Hell, I don't know. Last I saw it, Tule had it."

"Let's go it without FDC," said Jesse.

Rich nodded. "Cue. Get some H.E. and some Willie Peter." He turned to Jesse. "What charge and elevation, and what direction?"

Jesse pointed south and said, "That way. Charge zero. Elevation 1210. H.E. medium. Let 'er rip. Ten rounds."

Frantically the ammo carriers began removing charges from the high explosive rounds. A bullet ricocheted off the tube, whining as it penetrated deeper into the perimeter and canting the mortar to the right. Rich grabbed the gun and reset its position without a word.

"Damn! That was close," shouted Cue.

Loud shouts from gun two, only twenty-five yards away, turned their attention momentarily to the second squad.

"The gooks are in their gunpit! Rich, you, Cue and Sal and keep shootin'. The rest of you, come with me," said Jesse to the gun One crew as he charged from the gunpit without a backward glance, slipping his Bowie knife from its sheath as he cleared the sandbag parapet and running headlong toward the crowd of men fighting hand-to-hand in the second squad pit.

Jesse did not slow his pace as he jumped the sandbags ringing gun two and plunged his knife into an unsuspecting Viet Cong soldier. So hard was his charge that everyone in the pit was sent sprawling to the ground in addition to his victim.

In the pile of bodies, Jesse slashed repeatedly with his knife. He stabbed and cut and plunged, sometimes feeling the heavy steel blade strike bone. He almost had his knife wrenched from his hand when he stuck it into an eyeball and the Viet Cong soldier jerked his head violently, but Jesse hung on and twisted the knife away from the screaming man's ruptured eye and punctured brain.

Jesse was beyond fear as he fought to regain his feet in the jumble of

498

bodies tumbling all around him. He heard a voice above the sounds of battle. "Stand back, Goddamnit, or he'll probably rip youse wide open!" It was Ski.

Jesse looked up to see a ring of marines picking bodies up and throwing them out of the gunpit. Some of the VC still moved but were obviously in the final stages of life.

"All right, ya crazy bastard, dere ain't no more gooks in dis hole. You c'n stop cuttin' now," said Ski, almost calmly.

Jesse stood. "Where the hell are they?"

"Shit, da ones ya didn't kill wid dat damn butcher knife, youse scared da shit out of."

"How'd we do?" Jesse searched around him for downed marines.

"Nuttin' serious at dis point." Ski turned to his gun crew. "All right, Goddamnit, Let's get some more illumination up. Set da gun up and let's get it up dere."

With a quick glance at Jesse, whose face, hands and uniform were covered with blood, the crew quickly returned to their task, as though this were all part of a large training exercise. The Gun One crew returned to their own gun.

In the melee, just as Jesse was about to leave the gun two pit, a VC ran past the gunpit. P.F.C. Wilbur, holding his M-14 by the barrel and using it like a baseball bat, struck the man in the face with the butt. The stock of the rifle shattered but so too did the facial structure of the Viet Cong soldier.

"Goddamnit, Wilbur, is dat any way ta treat government property?" barked Ski, oblivious to the writhing VC soldier.

"What about him?" asked Wilbur, pointing to the downed enemy.

"What da fuck do youse tink? Shoot 'im and set some more illumination fuses, We got no time to fuck around." ordered Ski.

With no hesitation, Wilbur placed his broken rifle to the man's ear and pulled the trigger. The VC's head jerked violently with the impact of the slug. Wilbur jumped back into the gunpit and picked up a fuse wrench as though he was in competition gun drill.

Jesse jumped from the gunpit and returned to gun one at the double. He found Rich alone. "Where the hell is everybody?"

"I sent 'em out. They're helpin' the grunts. I can manage. I've got thirty or forty rounds in the pit with me. If we don't stop 'em before they get to the gunpit, it won't make much difference."

"You're a sittin' duck in here by yourself."

"I ain't by myself anymore."

"Where's your rifle?" asked Jesse.

"I told Cue to take it," answered Rich.

"Great. Me and you and one damn forty-five. Just like old times, right?"

"Indio, behind you!"

Jesse turned to see the advancing Viet Cong soldier, rifle poised before him, charging over the sandbag wall, led by a foot-and-a-half of bayonet. Jesse lifted the flap on his holster and removed the pistol by twisting his wrist and cocking hammer with his left thumb as he brought the weapon to bear on the charging man's chest, falling backwards as he did so in order to remain out of range of the bayonet.

The heavy forty-five discharged its duty faithfully and sent a slug into the VC's face, causing flesh, bone, eyeball and brains to explode into the air. The impact of the slow-moving slug stopped the slain man's head in place but his lower body

Stoney Livingston

continued to move forward another step, dragging the head with it as an afterthought.

Jesse fell to the floor of the gunpit as the VC's body crashed upon him, the rifle bouncing harmlessly against the sandbag wall.

Rich pulled the dead soldier from Jesse and threw him to the side. "You okay, man?"

Time seemed to standstill for Jesse as he looked at the mangled head of the enemy soldier and nodded in response to the question.

"That was about the fastest I ever saw anybody draw and shoot a forty-five automatic in my damn life. That was a hell of a shot."

Jesse answered, trance-like. "I was aimin' for his Goddamn chest."

"You okay?" asked Rich.

"Yeah. I'm okay. I'm gonna take a smoke break. I'll be with you in a minute." Jesse's legs felt like rubber.

Rich returned to his gun. "Goddamn, Indio, you pick the damndest times to take a smoke break."

Jesse ignored him. In fact, he ignored everything except the dead enemy soldier. He propped the man's body in a sitting position, back upright against the sandbag wall surrounding the gunpit. Carefully he straightened the man's uniform, ignoring the blood and brains that continued to ooze from the skull. Jesse removed his helmet and placed it upon the dead man's disfigured head. Sitting next to his most recent victim, he lit a cigarette.

He stood slowly at the sound of an engine laboring at high rpm and saw one of the tanks moving through the compound. *What the hell good is that tank inside the compound? It's gonna run over somebody on our side.*

"Indio, I need some help! Give me a charge zero on some of those rounds."

Quickly Jesse dropped his cigarette and retrieved his helmet, dripping with the remains of his former foe, and moved to Rich's side. "Sorry, Rich. I was just sayin' my final goodbyes to the dearly departed." He pulled the helmet onto his head.

"We're in deep shit! I wonder if there's anybody left alive on the southwest side of the perimeter?" said Rich.

"I don't know but, as soon as I get you a bunch of rounds charged, I'm gonna try to find the skipper and see about some reinforcements."

The M-60 that had first awakened Jesse still sounded from three hundred yards in front of the wire. He found it odd that the VC had not silenced the gun by this time. Pointing to several rounds with all eight charges removed, he said, "Rich, I'm gonna haul-ass. If I run across one of the guys, I'll send 'im over to help. In the meantime, I'll have Ski send over one of his men. I'll be back as fast as I can." Without waiting for a reply from Rich, he dashed from the gunpit.

Confusion reigned supreme as he made his way northward in the compound in search of Captain Malcolm. Of one thing he was certain: the VC were no physical match for the marines by any stretch of the imagination. It seemed everywhere he looked, the small bodies of the Viet Cong were being thrown about by the larger, stronger marines. He stopped on two occasions to assist but found he was only in the way.

His lungs ached from running and fighting and fear. Exhaustion was about to overtake resolve when he found Captain Malcolm in the melee, or more accurately, Malcolm found him.

"Indio!"

500

Jesse turned to the voice. "Skipper!" He ran the short distance between them. "What the hell, Skipper? We gonna get some help or are we on our own?" A stray bullet narrowly missed his head. Both he and Malcolm fell to their knees.

"We've got help on the way but they estimate arrival at near daybreak."

Jesse checked his watch. "When the hell is that, Sir?"

"About 0500."

Jesse groaned. "What the hell, if we've come this far, another fifteen minutes won't make that much difference I guess."

"How are you doing on the southern perimeter?"

"Not all that great but we have the advantage. All we have to do is pull the trigger. Odds are we'll hit one of 'em. They're thick as fleas. Can you spare a squad? If we threw another squad into the fight it might help. We need some help around the mortars. One of 'em almost fell to the Cong."

Malcolm pointed. "See Corporal Chapin. His squad is in reserve near the CP. Let him know what you want done, and keep me posted. Get your radio on the company net."

"I haven't seen the radio, sir, but if I find it I'll have it on the net." Jesse moved quickly in search of Corporal Chapin. He found Chapin and his men near the command post. He advised Chapin of the situation on the 81 mortar side of the compound and they stepped off in that direction. They were closing in on the mortar positions when Jesse saw Rich fighting off a VC with a bore swab. The enemy soldier fired his rifle at point blank range but missed due to a fast swing of the swab. Jesse knew it was over when a second VC jumped into the gunpit and entered the contest. He felt the fear bubble up into his throat as one of the small men was able to maintain a grip on Rich's right arm. Jesse was running for all he was worth, his adrenalin flowing freely, unaware of any bodily exertion. Rich struggled to free his right arm but could not. In the eerie light cast by the illumination rounds, Jesse clearly saw the look of hatred and glee on the face of the VC as the man lunged forward, bayonet aimed at Rich's chest.

He saw Rich stiffen his body to receive his deathblow and Jesse let out a loud, screeching rebel yell as he pulled the trigger on his forty-five. The skull of Rich's attacker exploded. Almost immediately, the other VC was struck by a marine from his left, his rifle slammed from its intended course, but not in time to cause it to completely miss its target. The bayonet tore the flesh on Rich's right arm. He broke free of the other VC's grip as the little man was pierced by no fewer than two marine bayonets.

Jesse picked himself from atop the fallen VC, his forty-five semi-automatic pistol still in his hand. He turned to Rich, "Sorry it took me so long, Rich. You okay?"

Chapin's squad removed the fallen VC from the gunpit.

"A helluva lot better than I thought I was gonna be."

Jesse tended the gash in Rich's arm, dressing it with Rich's own battle dressing. He worked quickly, ignoring a wince now and then when he became a little too rough. His work completed, he said, "Skipper says help is on the way. They should be here at first light, about ten or fifteen more minutes. Pass the word to anyone you see. We just gotta hold out a little bit longer. Two of the grunts are gonna stay in the pit with you until I can find some of the squad and get 'em back here. You okay to run the gun until I can find Cue or Sal?"

Rich nodded. "Yeah. Thanks, Indio. I mean, really thanks. I was dead, man."

"I gotta go. I'll get you an 0341 as soon as I run across one. You seen Tule or the radio?"

"I haven't seen shit since this bullshit started."

Jesse jumped from the gunpit. Chapin and all but two of his men followed. The sky was beginning to turn grey in the east.

Jesse and Chapin's men joined the fight on the southern perimeter at the edge of the wire. The concertina seemed to have been replaced by a wall of bodies. Whose side they represented, Jesse couldn't tell. He spotted Thunder, an eighteen-inch bayonet on the fighting end of his M-1. Even in the dim light, Jesse knew the darkness on Thunder's bayonet was not a result of the parkerizing process. The darkness dripped from the edges of the cold steel.

"Thunder, I brung you some help, Old Man."

Thunder looked around gratefully. "We can sure as hell use it. We got any more help comin', or do we have to whip these little bastards by ourselves?" He had to shout to be heard.

"Another ten or fifteen minutes and we're supposed to have all kinds of help."

The M-60 continued to fire from beyond the wire.

"How much help did you 'brung' me?"

"Chapin's squad, or most of it anyway."

Thunder shouted. "Hey, Chapstick. Over here. Let's talk."

From somewhere in the confusion, Chapin emerged. "Whatchoo need, Thunder?"

"My M-60 is still alive and well out there. We gotta get to 'em and get 'em back inside what's left of the wire."

Chapin glanced at the mass of bodies piled on the concertina. "Whew! That's a tall order, Thunder. There must be a million gooks here. We'd never make it."

"They'd never expect us to break to their front."

"That's because if we did, it'd be suicide."

"You don't have to go along. You just get your squad to hold my position. My guys'll do the rest. You just give us what cover you can without blowin' us away."

"That I can do, but I think it's crazy."

"You want the gooks to get their hands on that M-60?" asked Thunder.

"No thanks, brother. Where's your area of responsibility?" said Chapin.

Thunder pointed out the boundaries his squad held against the onslaught of Viet Cong. Chapin tried to replace Thunder's men with his own on a one-to-one basis but it couldn't be done for several reasons, none-the-least of which was attrition. Several of Thunder's men had been killed or seriously wounded and were out of the fight, and the continuing confusion made it impossible for Chapin to pick out a man and position him without first fighting off two or three of the enemy.

Thunder was able to muster five of his men who were yet able to fight and gather them near the largest break in the wire. Gathered there too was the largest concentration of enemy troops, still clamoring to enter the compound, their progress slowed by the remaining wire and mounds of bodies to impede their forward movement. Their problem was further compounded by the stubborn marines, who continued to deny the advancing Viet Cong by killing and wounding them en masse.

Jesse held his position at the break in the wire. Thunder approached with his five-man squad.

502

Forever Patriots

Jesse shouted above the roar that was battle, "Goddamnit, Thunder, I'll give you a thousand dollars for that M-1, and throw in an extra hundred for the bayonet."

Thunder smiled. "See me when this is over."

"When this is over, I'll steal one from somebody."

Thunder handed Jesse an M-60, complete with an eighty-round belt. "Lasovic don't need it anymore. I'm countin' on it. Will you cover us?

Jesse snatched the M-60 from Thunder's hand. "I'm comin' with you. I just wish it had a bayonet on the end of it."

"Not this time, Amigo. I need you to stay here, as close to the wire as you can get and keep us covered," said Thunder.

"Damnit, Thunder!" said Jesse.

"We need accurate covering fire. You're about the best I know with an M-60." He turned to Mitch. "Mitch, give Indio the rest of the ammo."

Mitch handed Jesse four one-hundred-round belts. "Good huntin', Indio."

Thunder took them all in with a quick glance. He handed Jesse his PRC-6 radio. "I'll use Chapin's. Stay in touch."

"Damnit, Thunder," repeated Jesse.

Thunder ignored him. He looked at the remnants of his squad. "Ready?"

Each man nodded quickly.

"Damned hero," smiled Jesse.

"Can't help it, Amigo. Some of us were just born to be great," replied Thunder.

Jesse pondered for a short moment why he felt so calm and in control, almost like this was only a movie and the script didn't call for him to be injured or killed.

Thunder turned back to face his squad.   "Let's go!"

Jesse stepped to his left and moved forward into the mass of moving flesh. He fired several short bursts and ran forward, taking a position near the wire. He dropped the bi-pod legs on the barrel to the ground and took up the prone firing position and fired a long burst at the moving bodies outside the wire.

The charge through the wire was over infinitely quicker than Jesse anticipated it would be. The squad was in the open, the grey light of the early morning casting a dull glow in contrast to the harsh light provided by the mortar illumination continually bursting overhead.

The concentration of enemy troops lessened and the marines broke into a dead run, heading straight for the machine gun outpost, shooting only occasionally as they dashed for the machine-gun pit. There weren't as many bodies to be concerned about.

The marines arrived one after the other, almost as fast as Jesse could count. All had made the charge unscathed.

Once in the machine gun pit, Thunder's squad fired at the enemy to their front. They didn't fire toward the compound for fear of hitting the marines. "Thunder's voice crackled through the PRC-6 radio, "Indio. Lee is slightly wounded in the shoulder and Whitey has got a bad chest wound but they're both still alive.

Jesse picked up the radio, keyed up and said, "Roger." He dropped the radio next to his gun and fired a short burst.

"Look! A plane!" shouted a marine on Jesse's right, pointing skyward.

"One of ours, I hope?" said another..

"I ain't seen a gook plane since I been here. I'll make book it's one of ours,"

503

said another..

As the aircraft closed upon the camp, one of the men said disgustedly, "It's an old C-47."

"Only one?" said another voice.

"Only one," came the answer..

"What the hell they gonna do with one C-47? Hell, you can't get more'n a squad of paratroopers and all their gear in one of those things."

"Maybe these are real bad paratroopers," shouted Jesse to the unknown speaker.

"They're gonna have to be if all they brought was one squad," came the prompt reply..

A platoon sergeant said, "Goddamnit, they promise us help and they send one squad of paratroopers?"

The silver, twin-engined aircraft lumbered over the field of battle at slightly more than one hundred miles per hour, circling the compound in a clockwise motion. The cargo door opened.

"Jesus Christ! They *are* gonna jump," shouted the sergeant..

The sporadic fire from the compound was suddenly drowned out by the roar of a Gatling cannon. The rate of fire was so fast as to make an almost continuous sound. The ground between the machine gun position and the compound seemed to explode from near the surface in a rapidly advancing wave from the east to the west. Any thoughts of assisting the paratroopers were instantly forgotten until the source of the Gatling cannon could be identified.

With his face against the side of the machine-gun butt, Jesse said, "Anybody see where the hell that came from?"

Before anyone could form an answer, the Gatling cannon spewed forth more of its explosive projectiles. The air was filled with flying dirt and pieces of metal. The screams of men wounded or dying could be heard even as the last sounds of the cannon echoed into the distance.

"Jesus Christ, It's comin' from the C-47!" said the man on Jesse's right.

Jesse raised his head slowly. He gazed at the cargo door. From where he lay, he could see what looked like a large black canister pointing out the door at the swarming VC troops below. Even as he watched, the cannon opened up again. He saw the bright white flashes of light as the heavy projectiles were thrown from the end of the multi-barreled weapon at the densely populated ground below.

"Jesus H. Christ!" he said, "I'm glad that fire-breathin' dragon's on our side."

"Goddamn! He's puttin' so much lead in the air – how can he control the shit?" Jesse could not identify the speaker..

Flying dirt fell between Jesse and the man on his right. "I ain't so sure he can,"

The VC were retreating. They were fleeing the compound like ants from a flooding anthill, trampling one another in their rout. The C-47 circled patiently overhead, waiting for another wave to put enough distance between them and the compound to fire another burst. As the VC population within the confines of the wire dwindled to manageable numbers, the weary marines cheered the fire-breathing C-47, their shouts audible only between bursts of the cannon in the belly of the old aircraft.

The men in the machine-gun pit hunkered down below the surface of the earth for fear of being the dragon's next victim. Soon the airborne cannon ceased to

Forever Patriots

fire and the silver craft circled slowly about the field of battle, surveying the results of its devastating fire.

Those in the aircraft above could see the carnage on the ground below but they could not hear the moans and the screams of men suffering from pain and fear. Jesse searched the field of battle with his eyes and gagged. VC lay in between the wire and the machine gun pit in numbers larger than he had ever seen before at any one time. He didn't attempt to count but he guessed there had to be at least two hundred within his field of vision. How many lay inside the wire, he had no way of knowing.

All firing ceased. The cheering also ceased. An eerie silence, broken only by those in pain and dying, and the drone of the C-47, covered the scene. For a long time no one spoke. They all watched the VC carefully, noting a movement here or there, but they said nothing, did nothing.

Only fifty yards from the machine gun pit, a VC attempted to stand and run away, but fell to his face when the leg that was no longer there would not support him. He died of blood loss within seconds of his fall. Nearby, an arm twitched and jerked, the fingers on the hand curling and extending as though begging to find the body to which the arm had once been attached. A bodiless head lay only thirty yards from Jesse, looking very much like a bloody soccer ball. He stared at the grotesque head, mesmerized by the thought that, only seconds ago, it had contained thoughts and life and dreams; now it was only meat and bone to rot in the humid heat that was Vietnam. He shivered involuntarily.

Farther from the wire, a badly wounded VC stood with rifle in hand and hobbled toward the compound, firing his rifle from the hip as he moved. A solitary shot from within the camp struck the man in the face, ending his life instantly. Again the moans and screams took possession of the battlefield.

The C-47 dipped its wings and departed to the east.

Jesse watched as the men in Thunder's squad stepped from the machine-gun pit, two of them carrying White. They walked softly and carefully, much like cats trying to keep their feet dry on wet ground. Slowly they made their way back to the compound, jumping at every move of a downed VC, not trusting the little men to be dead or incapacitated. Some of the marines picked up weapons as they moved through the field of dead and dying; others just kept a slow but steady pace, praying they would reach the wire before a bullet fired by a dying VC pierced their flesh.

The grisly sight of a man not yet dead, trying to stuff his intestines back into his body was more than Mitchell could stand. He turned his face but it was to late to avert the regurgitation already on the way. He vomited upon another VC, who lay breathing weakly, his right eye and part of his nose missing. As Mitchell saw the putrid fluid strike the injured man fully in his disfigured face, he was only further distressed. He wretched violently out of control. Thunder grabbed an arm and dragged him away from the inevitable fruits of war, struggling to control his own digestive tract.

The marines inside the wire cheered weakly as Thunder's squad re-entered the sanctuary of the compound and, yet, the victory seemed tainted in some way not a man among them could put into words. It was true they had held off a far superior force, undiscovered until inside the compound. But the battle ended up being decided not by bravery on the battlefield but rather the possession of a mighty weapon capable of destructive powers to that point undreamed of by the marines in Alpha Company. What if the VC had such a weapon?

505

Stoney Livingston

Malcolm stood at the edge of the perimeter as Jesse helped Mitchell through the cut and broken strands of barbed wire.

"How'd we do, Skipper?" asked Thunder as he released Mitchell's arm.

"Not all that great but, under the circumstances, I guess we did fairly well. First reports indicate fourteen dead and about twenty-two wounded. We've got to get the wounded out of here as soon as possible. Choppers are on the way. Bravo is being lifted in and should arrive with the choppers. Meanwhile, we collect the dead and tend the wounded VC. I need a body count – one for those inside the wire and another for those outside the wire." He turned to Jesse. "I'm putting you in charge of the bodies inside the wire."

"Me, Sir?"

"Yes, you. I want it done now, and I want it done right. Get to me with a complete report as soon as you've completed your mission." Without further comment, Malcolm turned to Thunder. "Thunder, I want all the live VC inside the wire tended to and guarded by your squad. Second platoon will be bringing the ones from outside the wire to you after they've been patched up. When all prisoners have been medically treated, a squad from third platoon will relieve you on prisoner watch until they can be evacuated. Any questions?"

Both Jesse and Thunder stared at their company commander. Jesse was astounded at his gruffness.

"No, sir." Thunder shrugged. He turned to what was left of his squad. "All right, you guys, let's go get the live ones inside the wire. We gather 'em up and patch 'em up and wait for relief from the third platoon. Let's go."

Jesse watched Thunder's back as he walked away. He turned to Malcolm. "Skipper, I didn't mean anything. Hell, I guess I can count bodies as well as the next guy. You'll have an accurate count, Sir." He turned to leave.

"Indio." Malcolm said softly.

Jesse turned to face him. "Yessir?"

"I was out of line. You and Thunder are two of the best troops in the damn Corps. I was just a little pissed at him for moving out to the machine gun. We lost enough good men today. I guess you two didn't do anything any differently than you usually do it, but today it just pissed me off."

"Yessir. We didn't want the gooks to get their hands on the gun. Will that be all, Sir?"

"That'll be all."

"Yessir." He turned away.

"They got Top this morning, Indio." Malcolm's voice was soft and seemed to waver.

Slowly Jesse turned to face his company commander. Jesse was not particularly close to First Sergeant Weber, but that was only because he had very little contact with the man. From the stories he had heard from the men who had served with the first sergeant any length of time, he was an intelligent, brave and honorable man. Jesse had always respected him.

"How bad is he, Sir?"

"He's dead, Indio," answered Malcolm, his eyes shining with moisture that threatened to spill.

Jesse knew there wasn't an officer in the company who rated as high on Malcolm's list as did his first sergeant. He had lived side by side with him through almost a year of always uncertain times. About the only thing certain for Malcolm

506

was the first sergeant's presence – that and his reassuring smile when the going got really tough. A single tear escaped the confines of one eye socket and found its way down his cheek.

"I'm sorry, Sir. He was a good man."

Malcolm composed himself. "He was more than that. He was a good marine."

"Yessir. Would you like some help?"

Malcolm's voice was soft. "No thanks, Indio. Carry on."

"Yessir." Jesse turned and walked toward the mortars.

He found a corpsman re-bandaging Rich's arm. "Is he gonna live, Sandy?"

Sandy turned and displayed an expression of relief. "Yeah. I see you made it through another one too."

"Another walk in the park, Doc," replied Jesse with false bravado. "Anybody else hurt?"

Rich peeked around Sandy's shoulder as the corpsman performed his duties. "Markovich bought it on gun two. You might wanna see Ski. I think Rawley got stuck with a bayonet. He's okay though."

Jesse paused. He had liked Markovich. His soft voice, accompanied by his guitar, gave most of the men a quiet kind of pleasure. He was a good kid with no enemies, other than the VC, and that was only because they didn't know him.

"Okay, I'm on my way, but first, I need everybody but you to help me on the dead-man detail. We gotta count and collect the dead gooks inside the wire. Rich, you stay on the gun, the rest of you follow me to gun two."

Ski's gun was intact, though the inoperable sight did suffer additional damage. The second squad stood mutely over Markovich's covered body as Jesse and the first squad approached. Jesse squatted next to the body and lifted the corner of the poncho. Markovich's short blond hair was matted with dried blood. Part of his left ear was missing and there was a deep, purple gash on the left side of his neck, made more prominent than it should have been by the paleness that comes with death.

Jesse looked up at Ski. "Bayonet?"

"Yeah. Da sunuvvabitch got him from behind. Mark never had a chance."

"You get the gook?" asked Jesse.

Ski pointed to a body at the edge of the gunpit.

Jesse lowered the poncho and said sadly, "So long, Mark." He turned to the others and said, "We gotta collect the dead gooks inside the wire and take 'em to a collection point. Ski, I guess you and Rawley better stay on the gun. I need the rest of your guys for the dead-man detail."

Ski, usually very vocal, merely nodded. Jesse and his detail left to carry out their unpleasant assignment.

As Jesse and the men from the mortar section hauled the VC bodies to a central collection point, Jesse found some of the marines wandering about the compound with no sense of purpose. Others sat dumbly and stared at the horizon. Some worked frantically at an assigned cleanup detail, while still others carried on about their duties as though nothing unusual had happened that morning. Some of them had wet crotches in their utility trousers, mute testimony that fear had caused them to lose control of their respective bladders, or that they had simply relieved themselves while in the process of fighting the enemy.

Corpsmen worked frantically over the wounded marines, knowing when

507

they were through with the friendly casualties there were many injured VC who would require medical attention. The morning sun began to heat the compound. The woeful cries of those wounded became weaker as the morning grew older.

Cue stared intently at two dead VC lying beside one another. "Holy shit!" He pointed to one of the bodies. "That's one of the barbers that was cuttin' hair in the compound yesterday!"

"You sure?" asked Jesse.

"Hell, he cut my hair. I oughta know."

Jesse bent over the body and searched the clothing. He withdrew a piece of paper from one of the dead man's pockets and unfolded it carefully. "No wonder they knew where the hell they were goin'. This guy's got a hand-drawn map of the whole damn compound."

The others present studied the map quickly. Jesse turned to Cue. "Cue, you take over. I'm gonna get this map to the skipper. Set the barber's body to the side in case someone else needs to look at 'im."

"Yo," replied Cue.

The first four helicopters arrived at 0930. They brought no replacements, only rations and ammunition. Later, more helicopters came and went, bringing in resupply and evacuating the wounded and dead. The surviving marines tended to their duties devoid of feeling. It was as though some giant force had sucked the energy and emotion from their bodies and minds.

It was during this time, Jesse found where Tuleano had been during most of the enemy assault. He spotted his section leader being attended by a corpsman. Tuleano smiled as Jesse approached. "How's it goin', Indio?"

"How ya doin', Tule?"

"I'll be good as new as soon as I get my hands fixed."

"What the hell's wrong with your hands?"

The corpsman answered for Tuleano. "The crazy bastard beat two gooks to death barehanded."

Jesse was beyond surprise. He smiled at Tuleano. "Were you just givin' 'em a fightin' chance, Tule?"

"I couldn't find my damn weapon. One of 'em grabbed the radio and I had to stop 'im. One thing lead to another."

Jesse grinned broadly at Tuleano's explanation. "I gotta go, Tule. I'll be talkin' to ya later."

It was after 1500 hours when the first fresh troops arrived at the compound. The men of Alpha Company were relieved to see the marines of Charlie and Delta Companies step from the Choctaws but they had neither the strength nor the emotion to form a cheer for a greeting. From some, the arriving troops received a casual wave or nod. From others they were greeted by blank stares.

Alpha Company was bunched together and reassigned to the southeastern quadrant of the compound. As the men gathered their gear in the more tightly packed area, a feeling of special camaraderie made its presence felt among those who had survived the ordeal of the early morning attack. Though true that Alpha had been one of the most active line companies in the Vietnam War to date, none had experienced such a feeling of terror before this early-morning attack. The completeness of the enemy surprise assault and their successful penetration of the wire was an encounter Alpha had suffered as a unit, an encounter that bonded the men with threads stronger than steel.

Jesse smoked a cigarette and studied the fresh troops as they improved the position. He wondered why Alpha Company had been thrown into Cam Lo without adequate time and provisions.

Rich spoke from his sitting position at the rear of the gunpit. "A hundred-and-ten gooks inside the wire. Not bad for a bunch of dumb grunts against Ho's finest."

"Shit, I tink Indio got half a' da bastards wit dat damn pigsticker a' his in gun two's pit," said Ski.

"I didn't hear about this one, Indio. Why'd you use the knife instead of your pistol?" asked Rich.

Jesse glanced at Rich and said, "Ski and his men would a' been in more danger than the gooks."

"What da hell ya talkin' about? Ya damn near got us all anyway when youse bowled everybody over," retorted Ski. He turned to Rich. "Ya shoulda seen dis crazy bastard. Dere must'uv been six or seven gooks in da pit, and here comes Indio, chargin' inta da pit, full speed, swingin' dat damn sword of a knife like he wuz cuttin' wheat. It wuz all I could do ta get da rest a' our side outa da impact area."

Those present laughed the first laugh of the day. It was a genuine laugh, and yet it was a laugh of relief that they were still alive to laugh about a very unfunny situation.

"Was that the final count? A hundred and ten?" asked Cue.

"That's just the ones inside the wire. I don't know how many they scraped up out there." Jesse pointed to the target area of the C-47's wrath.

"Does anybody know what the hell that thing was?" asked Sal.

"As far as I'm concerned, it was a friendly dragon," answered Jesse.

"No shit. That's it – Puff, the Magic Dragon." offered Cue. "Puff – no more gooks."

"Puff-the-Magic-Dragon, my ass," disagreed Piroge. "That was one bad fuckin' airplane. That's what the hell it was."

More laughter. Ski said, "Ya dumb mudderfucker. You can't call it 'one bad fuckin' airplane'. It needs a name dat sticks out. I like da name dat Cue came up wit. It's got kinda a ring to it."

"Whatever-in-the-hell it was, we'd be deader'n' hell if it hadn't showed up," said Rich.

The mood became sober. Willis remarked. "Ya know, Rich is right. Stop an' think about it. I mean, we'd no longer exist. It'd be like we never were. Dyin' is all around us and I still ain't sure what the hell it is. Where the hell do all the thoughts go that each one of us has in his head?"

"Don't get philosophical on us, Uncle Willie. When youse die, yur dead," said Ski coldly.

"Maybe so but I'd like to think that dyin' ain't the end of everything."

Jesse said, "Them guys we sent outa here in ponchos'll be real glad to hear that. When you're dead, you're dead, Willie. All we gotta' do is try to keep from gettin' that way."

"Don't you believe in God, Indio?" asked Manny.

Jesse looked at the young marine from Mesa, Arizona. "Worse'n that,

509

Stoney Livingston

Manny - I say, if there is a god, he's on the other side and I don't want anything to do with his sorry ass."

Manny moved nervously two or three feet away from Jesse. "Damn, man - be careful what you say out here. Just in case - you know what I mean?"

Jesse smiled and looked skyward. He extended his right hand to the heavens, center finger prominently displayed in a well-known American gesture of disrespect.

Even Ski, always a cynical man, was taken aback by Jesse's display. "Goddamn, Indio, it wouldn't hurt ta hedge yer bet by at least remainin' neutral."

Jesse looked Ski in the eyes. "Anybody who is supposed to be so omnipotent that would let this kinda' thing go on is a Goddamn asshole and I don't wanna be associated with 'im."

"Jesus Christ," said Manny.

"Him too," agreed Jesse.

"You're gettin' a little rough around the edges, Amigo."

Jesse turned to see Thunder standing beside him. "I don't need this religious crap, Thunder. If he's out there then let 'im show himself and tell us all how damn great he is; how all men are brothers and all of that other shit. Look around you. There's your brothers. Not the gooks, or the college punks, or the politicians, or the generals, or even your damn God. The only thing you can count on is your rifle and the guy in the hole next to ya."

He turned from Thunder to face the rest of the men. "When the shit gets deep, those of you who think I'm wrong, you call on God for help and see how fast you get it." He turned and walked from the group.

Evidence of the recent assault was everywhere. One of the tanks, though not damaged, had been blackened by an explosive device. Slightly, wounded marines sat or walked about with bandaged arms or faces. Some of the equipment smoldered in the afternoon sun, the ashes not worth the effort it would take to put them out. Jesse thought of the dead and wounded, and of the fear that had brought bile to his mouth.

Jesse stopped near the perimeter and studied the horizon. *Where the hell did the survivors go? Would they come screaming back tonight with more of their friends? Did they have the strength to assault three reinforced companies? How many were out there? And where were they coming from? Why didn't we take a company in pursuit earlier in the day? What kind of goddamn war is this anyway?*

His thoughts drifted to Hawaii and Barbara. It seemed so unreal now. Did it really happen? Maybe he had just dreamed it.

He shook his head to clear his thoughts.

"You got somthin' loose up there, amigo?" Thunder approached his position.

"I must have. I came back to this didn't I?"

"That don't say much for me. I came back sooner 'n' you did."

"The prosecution rests its case."

Thunder sat next to him and quietly lit a cigarette. The two smoked in silence for several minutes. Jesse spoke first. "You know, the thought has recently occurred to me that I might not make it outa this place alive. It's soberin' as hell."

"Yeah, I know what you mean. This kinda' shit can start a man to thinkin' some thoughts that he might have kept buried if it weren't made so blatantly clear that some thought on the matter is called for."

Jesse stared at the land beyond the concertina wire. "If I don't make it, I'm gonna be aggravated as hell. I got more reason than ever to make it home in one piece. That's what worries me. When I didn't give a damn, it didn't really bother me so much. As long as it didn't hurt too long, I wasn't afraid to die. Now I ain't ready to cash in at all – pain or no pain. I got a lot of livin' to do and I intend to do it right."

"I've got a thing or two I'd like you to take care of for me, if you make it and I don't. Nothin' real special, just a few little details that I'd rather not leave up to some asshole in rear echelon," said Thunder quietly.

Jesse looked at Thunder's face, still spattered with the blood of unknown dead and wounded, a bruise under his right eye. "We're both loosin' it, Thunder. It's no different now than it was last fall or winter. Why are we startin' to think like this?"

"Scared of dyin' with things undone I guess. Hell, if it's gonna happen, it's gonna happen, but it's a real bitch knowin' certain things won't be done afterwards." Thunder thought a moment. "The more I think about it the less I like the idea of puttin' you in charge of my affairs. Be my luck we'd both buy it on the same day."

Jesse smiled. "Thanks. I appreciate the vote of confidence."

"I didn't mean anything by it but you know what I mean. Hell, you're out there as much as I am. Do you know anybody in eighty-ones who could take care of a few details for us?"

Jesse pondered the question. "That makes sense to me. How about Cue? I think he'd take care of reasonable details."

"Cue it is." Thunder reached into his map pocket and withdrew a pint of Jack Daniels whiskey. "Here's to Cue."

Jesse laughed. "It was my idea. Doesn't that qualify me for the first drink?"

Thunder gave him a sober look. "Under normal circumstances, it would be appropriate for you to get the first drink, but these are not normal circumstances – and more important than that – I've seen you drink." He took a healthy pull from the bottle and handed it to Jesse who quickly imitated his action.

After receiving his half-empty bottle and screwing the lid down tightly, Thunder placed it into his map pocket. He looked over his shoulder at the fresh marines filling sandbags and building new fortifications. "I'd offer to help them guys but if I know the Crotch, they'll have us standing a hundred-percent watch tonight. I think I'll hit the rack. You okay, man?"

"Yeah. I'm okay. I'm just tired. Real tired."

"See ya' whenever it hits the fan again." Thunder walked slowly to his hole. Jesse watched him, feeling the whiskey warm his insides and reminding him of a not too distant time in the past.

After several minutes had passed Thunder returned, carrying a grease gun and a crossbow. "You forgot to claim your t.o. weapons."

Jesse smiled. "I swear, if I ever get out of this, I'm gonna write a book about the crazy stunts you pull."

Thunder squatted next to him. "Me? Hell, I been takin' lessons from you. I thought I was cool until I ran across your crazy ass."

Jesse inspected the grease gun. "Now I know why the tanker wanted the Thompson. You can have it. I'll take the crossbow." He handed the unwanted grease gun to Thunder and picked up the crossbow. "Who the hell will ever believe I used a crossbow in 1966?"

"I will."

"That's only because you gave me the damn thing."

511

Thunder smiled and stood. "I'm gonna get that sack time. See you later."

"Later," said Jesse as he inspected one of the small bolts lying on the ground next to his foot.

Jesse remained alone for the remainder of the day, not wanting company of any kind. Most of the blood on his uniform had dried but there were still areas of moistness. The blood was beginning to smell badly. He walked to a water buffalo, took off his utility jacket and rinsed it as best he could. He wiped his chest and arms and put the garment back on. It still smelled of death but at least the stench was not as strong as it had been. He tried to sort things out in his mind but there were too many unresolved questions, questions he had never before considered. Thoughts of Barbara entered his mind constantly, interrupting his train of thought, causing him to start at the beginning and continue forward until she again entered his mind to block out all else.

He looked at the M-14 he had picked up after the battle. "Useless piece of shit," he said softly. He longed for his old M-1. He lit a cigarette in the fading light and waited for the darkness to bring with it the fear and the gut-wrenching anxiety that would follow. The thought of nights was becoming more difficult to endure since Barbara. He wondered what she was doing and he thanked her in his mind for just being the person she was. Night folded around the camp like a heavy blanket.

Shortly after midnight, Jesse heard the voice. It came from the south, aided by a loudspeaker. He jerked involuntarily when the crackly voice said, "Men of the First Battalion, Fourth Marines. You have fought well but you all know the war cannot be won. Why do you persist in the useless sacrifice of human life for no cause? The people back home do not want you here. You do not want to be here. Why then do you remain? Your corrupt politicians grow fat from war profits while you suffer and die for a losing cause. Vietnam belongs to the People. The people do not want you here. Throw down your arms and show the politicians and the generals they can no longer wage such an unpopular war..."

Jesse ran to Captain Malcolm's bunker. He was standing near a sandbagged trench. Almost out of breath from the short run, Jesse said, "Skipper, I think I know where the gook is broadcasting from. Can I call in a mission?"

Malcolm said, "Where do you think he is?"

Jesse pointed to the southeast. "The speaker is over there somewhere. To run the wires to it they probably used the best protection to get 'em as close as they could with the least chance of detection." He pointed south. "The nearest protection from that point is the hill to the southeast. I'll bet he's sittin' right behind that hill."

Malcolm nodded. "It makes sense to me. Call in your mission. Don't use more than five rounds and I'll advise battalion what's going on."

"Aye aye, Sir." Jesse turned and ran for the first section guns.

Malcolm waited for the adjusting first round of the mortar fire mission, listening with half an ear to the almost perfect English of the Viet Cong spokesman. He heard the first round leave the tube with a 'thump-pow'. It was followed almost immediately by four more reports. He smiled.

The seconds ticked by slowly. The target was close enough that the marines inside the camp heard the *whoosh-whoosh* of the descending mortar rounds as they fell toward the target. As the rounds impacted on the far side of the hill it was silhouetted by the flash of the exploding projectiles. Indio was right on target with the

512

mission.

As the rumble of the exploding mortar rounds echoed into eternity, the men inside the camp listened for the voice. It was gone. So too was the crackly sound made by the speaker, though the speaker remained in place, somewhere to the south of their position. A full minute passed. No sound was heard.

"I'll be damned," muttered Malcolm under his breath. He turned to his radio operator who stood by his side. "Report to battalion that we appear to have eliminated the gook with the Oxford accent."

"Yessir," beamed the young radio operator.

Alpha Company remained at Cam Lo camp for three more days. Within two days of their return to Phu Bai, several medals were awarded to those who had participated in the defense of the young camp where an old flying machine had saved the day. PFC Lee, the outpost machine gunner was awarded the Silver Star, as was his assistant gunner, for remaining at their post in the face of overwhelming numbers of enemy troops. White's medal was announced at the formation but his medal was awarded at the hospital in Da Nang. Rich received a Bronze Star with a combat V for remaining at his post and providing both illumination and HE fire while the enemy overran the gun. Thunder added another to his long list with a Navy Cross for his actions in providing leadership and participating in the action to save the machine-gun. If one man deserved a medal, they all deserved one, Thunder succinctly voiced when notified he would be receiving a Navy Cross..

Two days after the awards ceremony, the battalion left Phu Bai for the DMZ.

Stoney Livingston

CHAPTER TWENTY-TWO: CHARLIE MED

Jesse looked warily at the winding trail ahead. He wasn't sure he liked the idea of the mortars marching in the middle of the Rifle Company. It wasn't so much that the rifle companies treated the mortarmen so badly – quite the converse was true – but when an entire battalion was on the march, it seemed prudent to Jesse for the mortars to march as a platoon. He would be with the Rifle Company and there was no sense in the mortars being in the middle of one if there was an ambush.

Jesse turned to his new radio operator. "You sure you got all the frequencies memorized, Charlie?"

"Yeah, I got 'em all up here, Indio." Charles Marr pointed to his temple. Jesse turned back to the front and continued his march.

The weary column halted for a short break at ten in the morning. As was the custom with the men of the eighty-one platoon, several groups indulged in a quick game of blackjack with limp, sweat-soaked cards, under a tree. On this operation, Jesse didn't join, nor would he allow his radio operator to do so. He called Marr aside and they found shade under a large tree.

"After we've worked together a while I won't worry about you, Charlie but, for now, I wanna make sure you know what to do, okay?"

Marr answered hesitantly. "Sure. I got no problem with that. I'm here to do a job, ain't I?"

Jesse studied him. "I don't know. Are ya'?"

Marr stared hard at Jesse. "I can handle whatever is thrown at me." There was an edge in his voice.

"Do yourself a favor, Charlie, don't break bad with me. We're supposed to be on the same side. My radio operator and I are a team. We work together, not against each other. I really don't give a damn how bad you think you are, or who you wanna impress. If you're worth a shit, I'll know it about ten seconds into a fight. Show me then, not now."

"I'm not tryin' to impress anybody," he said after a moment.

"Out here, you don't have to. Your chance will come. Now, let's go over a few situations." Jesse pulled a map from his map pouch and spread it upon the ground. "Where are we?"

Marr looked at the map for a moment. He turned his eyes upward to meet Jesse's. "I'm a radio operator not an FO."

Jesse spoke sternly. "We're on this operation, attached to Alpha. I've just been taken out of action by enemy fire. There are no arty FO's and no FAC's. The company is pinned down and the gooks are movin' in for the kill. You gonna tell the skipper you're no FO? You're it, man, at least temporarily. Now look at the map again." Jesse pointed to a location on the map. "See how close the contour lines are

514

at this point? That means you've got a fairly steep slope. See this..."

Jesse was in the middle of the stream when the mushroom erupted behind him. Then he heard the explosion. He fell face down in the stream with the M-60 machine-gun he carried held high above his head. The M-60 barrel broke the surface of the stream, followed by an arm, then a shoulder, then helmet and upper body. Jesse quickly splashed to the opposite shore and crawled into the heavy undergrowth.

A full minute passed with no movement. Jesse heard something being passed up the column. Behind him, Sergeant Tuleano stood and said, "Accidental discharge."

Marr turned to his front and repeated the phrase. "Accidental discharge." Jesse turned to his front and repeated the same words. Then he turned back to Marr. "Tell me that was a joke."

Marr answered. "You okay, Indio?"

Jesse stepped from the brush to the side of the stream. "I was, but now I ain't so sure. I think I need a corpsman. I'm bleedin' from just above the ass. Tail bone hurts like hell."

Marr turned in Tuleano's direction. "Corpsman! Corpsman up!"

As the battalion stirred to life, a young corpsman rushed forward to meet the casualty at the stream. When he arrived, Marr and Tule were attending Jesse's wound. "Where you hit?"

"Too close to the ass to suit my comfort," replied Jesse.

"You need something for the pain?" asked the corpsman.

"Yeah, a fifth of sour mash and two weeks R&R."

The corpsman examined the wound. It was a small puncture at the base of Jesse's tailbone. Bleeding was minimal. He cleansed and dressed the wound while Jesse stood with his trousers pulled down to his knees, M-60 machine-gun at the ready, a cigarette dangling from his lips.

Jesse spoke around the cigarette in his mouth. "And just what in the hell do you find so amusing, Tule?"

Tuleano's smile broadened. "What the hell you gonna do with that M-60, with yer trousers down around your knees – scare `em to death?"

Jesse returned his smiled. "It's a new tactical weapon I'm tryin' out. Whatd'ya think?"

"The gooks are in deep shit."

A second lieutenant approached, an M-79 grenade launcher slung on his right shoulder. He and the sergeant accompanying him crossed the stream and stopped about ten yards from Jesse and the corpsman. "I'm Lieutenant Rowe. I'm the one who had the accidental discharge."

The smile disappeared from Jesse's face. He stared at the young lieutenant, who looked about nineteen years old. "You wanna tell me how a lieutenant has an accidental discharge with a grenade launcher?"

Rowe spoke quickly and nervously, running his sentences together. "I'm short a grenadier. The only M-79 available was this one. It's got a faulty safety and I was carrying it loaded. I don't know what happened. I was just walking down the trail and it went off."

Jesse studied the young face with it's fear plainly evident. "No shit it went off. You know I'm inclined to shoot you to make it even, don't you?"

515

Stoney Livingston

"I don't blame you. All I can say is I'm sorry. It was an accident."

Jesse winced as the corpsman cleansed the wound roughly. He turned and said, "Goddamn, Doc, that ain't your girlfriend you're playin' with." He turned back to face Rowe. "Lieutenant, I'm not real proud to meet you under these circumstances. Could you just go away and come back some other time when I'm dressed for the occasion?"

Lieutenant Rowe and the sergeant moved back down the trail, splashing across the stream in humiliation.

The corpsman placed a small dressing over the wound. "I can get you a med-evac in about thirty minutes."

"For this?"

"It doesn't look like much but the risk of infection is high. You only took one small piece of shrapnel and I got it out and treated the wound with bacitracin, but it could use a little more attention. Your tail bone will probably be a little sore for a few days."

"After the sweep is over, Doc. Okay?" He pulled up his pants.

"Okay, but as soon as the sweep is over, you're going to sick bay."

"Okay, Doc. Thanks. You done for now?"

The corpsman nodded. "For now."

Within minutes the battalion was on the march, Jesse mumbling about second lieutenants and how the rank should be abolished. The pace grew faster as the day wore on and with the increased pace came the fatigue, but the marines held on, knowing they would soon reach the tall hill they were looking for. The hill stood out from others in the DMZ like a lone sentinel. Its steep slopes, almost vertical in places, and its rocky soil had already earned it the name of the "Rockpile".

In the late afternoon, less than a mile from the objective, the battalion was once again confronted with a stream crossing. This stream was almost a river. It was chest high at its deepest point in the fording area and the current was swift and powerful.

A human chain was formed by the leading elements to insure that none who followed would be swept downstream. As the marines moved slowly and cautiously across the stream, their gratitude for the respite waned rapidly. They cursed the strength of the water and the man who had chosen the direction of march. The water slammed those crossing into those forming the chain. Men clung to their weapons tightly for fear that the raging waters might snatch them from their grasps, only to leave them defenseless in the face of the enemy and, even worse, subject to court-martial for losing government property.

Within two hundred yards of the main stream crossing, a winding tributary joined the white waters. While not as deep, nor quite as strong, it had to be crossed twice in a hundred-yard span due to the fact that terrain features prevented circumvention.

Jesse was in the strong current of the first leg of the tributary, in water just above his knees, when the rifle grenade struck ten feet in front of him. The water erupted like a geyser and shrapnel whizzed in all directions. He felt the sharp sting of hot metal in his left thigh as one of the jagged projectiles penetrated his flesh. When the water pushed skyward by the explosion fell back into the river, Jesse remained standing in the knee-deep current, machine-gun held on his right shoulder, his arm draped over the barrel.

He looked calmly down at his thigh, at the small black hole in his trousers, no larger than a dime, smoke wafting gently from the seared edges. Blood ran freely down his leg. "I'll be goddamned," he said, almost casually. He took the machine-gun from his shoulder and held it at the ready, searching the trees in the surrounding hills with his eyes.

"Indio! Get to cover!" Ramirez shouted from somewhere nearby. Not a soul was in sight.

Jesse stood, daring the VC to shoot again, hoping for a small sign that would allow him to pinpoint his enemy. Nothing stirred. He continued across the small river and sat casually in the soil at its edge. From the bushes nearby came Ramirez, his K-bar knife in hand. He knelt next to Jesse and slit the trouser leg to expose the wound.

"Careful with that damn thing, Rosie. I got about twelve hundred dollars in that side pocket."

Ramirez examined the wound. He shouted over his shoulder. "Corpsman up! Corpsman!" He turned back to Jesse. "Shit, man, what the hell were you doin' out there in the middle of the river?" He removed Jesse's battle dressing from the pouch.

"Lookin' for the gook that just shot me. What the hell you think I was doin' – waitin' for an eclipse of the sun?"

"I was beginning to wonder."

The battalion began to stir. Shots were fired to the left front of Jesse's position. Then all was quiet.

A corpsman approached on the run. Jesse recognized him as the same man who had treated him earlier that morning. The corpsman fell to his knees next to him and quickly removed the battle dressing recently tied off by Ramirez. He made a quick assessment of the wound and turned to Ramirez. "Get a chopper in here. He's goin' out."

Marr, who remained on the other side of the tributary, shouted, "I heard. I'm making contact now."

Jesse winced as the corpsman cleansed the jagged edges of the wound. "Ow! Jesus Christ, Doc, anybody ever tell you your bedside manner leaves something to be desired?"

"Sorry. I gotta get this thing cleaned up and stop the bleeding as fast as I can."

"It ain't all that bad. Hell, it ain't no bigger'n a minute."

The corpsman replied, "I can't tell where the shrapnel went. It looks to me like it might be close to the artery."

"I don't think it hit the artery. It ain't bleedin' enough."

"Can't tell how close it came. If it's even close, any movement might cause it to rupture the artery."

"Just stick a pressure bandage on it and let me finish the walk. Hell, we been marchin' all day and we're almost there. Let me go in with the rest of the guys so I can at least see what this damn Rockpile looks like."

The corpsman was wavering. He rubbed his chin. "I don't know. I don't think you oughta."

"Just to the Rockpile, Doc, then I'll take the ride to the hospital."

The corpsman caved in. "Okay, we'll try it but, at the first sign of any blood on the outside of the bandage, you're going."

Jesse smiled. "You got a deal, Doc. Just give me one of those super deluxe

517

Stoney Livingston

bandages and I'm on my way. I hope this wasn't that Lieutenant Rowe again. I'd have to shoot him this time."

Tuleano spoke from across the stream. "It was a gook rifle grenade. Some of the guys on the flank spotted 'im but it looks like he got away."

"Great," said Jesse softly as he winced from an ungentle touch by the corpsman.

When the corpsman finished his work Jesse picked up his machine-gun and stood unsteadily. His left leg felt stiff and he experienced a sharp pain with his first steps.

"How's it feel?" The corpsman had a worried look on his face.

"Fine, just fine. I recommend it for everybody," quipped Jesse, hiding the pain as he stepped into the second leg of the tributary. He splashed and walked unsteadily on the rocky streambed beneath his booted feet. His strength seemed to drain away with each step. When he exited the water on the other side he looked down at his bandaged thigh. The bandage was already soaked through with blood. He sat upon the ground and muttered quietly. "Shit."

Marr exited the water behind him and knelt at his side, staring at the wet, blood-soaked bandage. "You gotta get to a hospital, man."

"Kinda' looks that way, don't it? Well, you're on your own, Pilgrim. Stay in line and get Tule to give you a decent FO. And stay outa the damn rivers. They don't seem to be what's happenin' today."

The column continued past as the corpsman stopped and redressed the wound. When the old bandage was removed Jesse watched, mesmerized, as blood ran from the small hole in a steady stream.

"Shit! Just lie back and elevate the leg," ordered the corpsman. "It sure is bleeding funny. Too much blood for what I see and not enough for an artery."

Jesse silently complied with the corpsman's request. As he waited for the helicopter to arrive he made mental notes of the nearest LZ. It wasn't too far, maybe a hundred yards. He passed his M-60 and ammunition to Tuleano for distribution.

Thunder walked by. He stepped out of the march, kneeling at Jesse's side. "How ya' feelin', Amigo?"

"Stupid. How many guys you know get hit twice on the same day – once by each side?"

Thunder studied the dressing. Blood was already beginning to seep to the outer layer of gauze. "I guess it just wasn't your day for a walk in the woods."

Jesse removed his holster and handed it to Thunder. "Take care of this for me, will ya'?"

Thunder accepted the pistol and holster with a nod and watched as Jesse removed his Zodiac SeaWolf watch.

"Here. You'll need this more than I will for a while. Of course I'll want it back when I rejoin the outfit, unless I can find one in a PX somewhere." He offered the watch to Thunder.

Thunder stepped back. "Uh uh. You keep the watch. I'll take it when you get outa here for good. Are you crazy? You'll be back."

"Yeah, I know but, in the meantime, we could swap watches."

"I'll wait."

Reluctantly Jesse returned his watch to his right wrist. The distant whop-whop of helicopter blades foretold the arrival of his transportation. He looked up at Thunder and said, "Keep yer ass low, Thunder."

518

"Don't get into no trouble with any of them round-eye nurses, Amigo."

The helicopter ride out of the DMZ was different for Jesse. He had never ridden in a helicopter lying down. It seemed he could feel every vibration of the old machine to the marrow of his bones as it labored skyward and struggled to maintain flight. He longed to watch the green land below as it passed by but couldn't with his leg propped up to lessen blood loss.

He was certain his stay at the hospital would be short, a day or two at most, but he would put up with it if it meant lessening the chance of infection. He knew only too well what infection and gangrene could do to the body. Who knows? Maybe he could find an ARVN soldier willing to sell him an M-1 Garand while he was in the rear echelon area.

The helicopter began it's slow descent. Jesse struggled to catch a glimpse of the ground below. He saw several tents in neatly dressed rows, separated by dirt roads or walk paths. The helicopter landed almost a mile from the tents.

Two marines picked up his stretcher and lifted him gently from the old helicopter. A familiar voice said, "Indio! What the hell are you doin' here?"

Jesse turned his head to view the speaker. "Sandy, you old rat. I wondered what happened to ya. How'd you rate this skatin' duty?"

Corporal Sanderson smiled. "They needed a good man to show 'em how things should be done at a field medical unit."

"Field medical unit? You mean this ain't Da Nang East Hospital?"

Sandy laughed. "Hell no. This is Charlie Med. Da Nang East is closer to the city, and it's a real hospital – you know – like the ones back in The World."

"That must mean that I'll be goin' back out to the field pretty quick, huh?"

"Maybe. Can't tell for sure until the Doc looks at you. What the hell happened?" Sandy studied the cut trouser leg and the blood-soaked pressure bandage.

"Basically, a gook sniper with a rifle grenade."

"You guys gonna talk all day or can we put him in the ambulance?" asked the marine at Jesse's feet.

Sandy opened the rear door of the olive drab chevy panel truck. "Yeah. Sorry about that. He's an old friend of mine."

The two marines placed the stretcher into the field ambulance and Sandy climbed in, closing the door behind him. Jesse insisted he really didn't need to remain in the horizontal position but Sandy, true to his training, insisted that he remain motionless and propped his injured leg up with a pillow.

At Charlie Med the ambulance was greeted by two stocky corpsmen, who quickly carried Jesse to a hardback tent for examination.

A medical doctor entered the tent. "What do we have here, Sandy?"

"Shrapnel puncture wound in the left thigh, Doctor."

Sandy remained with Jesse while the field surgeon removed the bandage and probed the purple puncture wound. Jesse attempted to focus on Sandy's conversation, but the pain created by the probing doctor made that task extremely difficult.

The flow of blood was not as strong as before but it continued to flow at a rate indicating potentially serious problems. The doctor "uhmmed" and "hmmmed" then turned to Sandy. "I need pictures. Get him to x-ray. Don't irritate the wound. I think we may have a cut artery."

Jesse attempted to stand but Sandy put a hand in the center of his chest

519

and held him down. "Not this time, Indio. You might have a serious problem here."

"How the hell serious can it be? It wasn't much bigger than a pellet."

The doctor threw Jesse an authoritative glance. "It could be one tenth that size. If it ruptured that artery, you could bleed to death in a matter of seconds."

Jesse smiled sheepishly. "Like I said; what are we waitin' for? Let's get some pictures there, Sandy."

Sandy carefully assisted Jesse into a wheel chair and pushed him to another tent filled with the latest in field x-ray equipment. In a few short moments they were back in the surgical tent. Jesse was placed on a table while the doctor read the x-rays. He could hear Sandy and the doctor discussing the negatives. The doctor turned from the lighted background of the x-rays and walked the two steps to the table.

"You've had a pretty close call. The shrapnel penetrated the muscle and came to rest between the femur and the artery."

"How did it do that? It was a head-on hit."

"It appears that it ruptured the arterial wall only slightly but, from the bleeding, it doesn't look like it got enough of it to kill you if it can be removed so that further damage to the wall doesn't occur."

"So I guess we gotta remove it, huh?"

Sandy gave a quick sidewards glance to the doctor.

The doctor nodded. "Now."

"Can I watch? I mean, after all, it *is* my leg."

"I don't have any problem with that as long as you don't get sick on me."

"I'll look the other way if I even feel like that might happen."

The doctor turned to Sandy. "Roll up some gauze, Sandy."

Sandy turned and began to roll a four-inch-wide strip of gauze while the doctor scrubbed and put on his surgical gloves. When the gauze roll was about as thick as a man's thumb, Sandy stepped to Jesse and said, "Put this in between your teeth."

"Say what?" Jesse looked up at him, searching for a sign he was joking. None was forthcoming.

"Put it between your teeth. We're out of drugs and we don't want you breaking your teeth."

Jesse was now certain Sandy was joking. "That's okay. I'll wait for the drugs."

"I'm serious, Indio. We're out of drugs. We've got just enough Novocain to deaden the epidermis, but it's not gonna take care of all of the pain." He offered the roll of gauze.

Jesse shook his head. "I don't believe this. You're serious?"

Sandy nodded.

"This is great. I really like this. Now I can really feel like a reg'lar hero. I appreciate you guys goin' through all this trouble just to make me feel macho, but I'm not really into it right now, so dig up some morphine or somethin'."

Sandy shook his head.

"Damn." Jesse resigned himself to the facts. "Let's try it without the gauze. If it gets too bad, I'll let you know."

"Okay. I'll have it right here." Sandy placed the gauze in a small stainless steel tray.

Jesse watched as the doctor moved in with a hypodermic needle to deaden

520

the pain near the surface of his wound. After several jabs with the needle around the edges of the ragged hole in his thigh, the doctor placed the empty needle and syringe in a tray. Sandy handed him a scalpel.

Jesse stared, fascinated, as the doctor made an incision straight across the center of the ragged hole in his thigh, enlarging the opening from a quarter of an inch to almost two inches. "Jesus Christ, Doc. I came in here with a little hole in my leg and you make it into a big one. Are you sure you're not in the Marine Corps?"

The doctor's eyes squinted as he smiled and handed Sandy the scalpel. "I've treated so many of you guys, maybe I'm beginning to think like a marine."

"Don't tell me that now."

The doctor turned to Sandy. "Probe."

Jesse felt almost like an objective observer as he watched the silvery steel instrument pushed into his thigh. His objectivity disappeared instantly as he felt a sharp pain. Involuntarily he jerked his leg slightly.

"Get two men in here to hold him down!" shouted the doctor.

Two large corpsmen appeared. Jesse wondered where they had come from.

The doctor looked at Jesse sternly. "This is for your own good. I can't take a chance on any more movement. That piece of steel is too close to the artery."

Jesse nodded his understanding. "Sorry, Doc. It just took me by surprise is all."

"You're not in a position for any more surprises."

"I'll be okay, now that I know what to expect."

"Maybe, but these two men will be my insurance."

"Okay, Doc, have it your way. It's your show."

Perspiration poured from Jesse's forehead and above his upper lip as the doctor probed into the wound. He stood the pain for almost three full minutes before he turned to Sandy and asked for the roll of gauze. For almost twenty minutes longer he withstood the pain as the doctor unsuccessfully attempted to remove the jagged piece of metal from his body. His jaw muscles hurt as a result of him clamping them tightly shut. Finally, he could stand the pain no more.

"Hey, Doc, whoa – hold up a second. I got a question."

The navy doctor looked up from his work. "I know this hurts like hell, but I can't get to it for fear of puncturing the artery."

"Well, that's what I wanna talk to you about. What the hell would it hurt to leave that thing right where it is. It's botherin' me a hell of a lot less than all that jabbin' around with that steel thing and your finger."

The perspiring doctor stood upright. "We could leave it where it is and you may never have a problem, but it could eventually work its way into your bloodstream and ultimately to your heart."

"Doc, at this point, I'm willin' to take that chance. If you keep on like this, I won't be any good to my outfit for two or three weeks."

"Okay. I'll send you over to Da Nang East in the morning."

"Da Nang East? Why can't you just sew it up and send me back to my outfit?"

Away from the doctor, Sandy turned his head and smiled.

"You're not going back to your outfit for at least a month or more," replied the doctor.

"A month?"

521

"Or more."

"What the hell for? Now that you ain't tryin' to mix oatmeal in my leg, I feel great."

"This type of wound can't be sutured until it has healed from the inside out. It has to be cleansed daily until the injured tissue has a chance to build layer upon layer until it gets close to the surface. Then and only then can it be sutured."

"But a whole month?"

"Or more," reminded Sandy.

"Shit."

The doctor said, "Bandage him up, Sandy." He turned to the two big corpsmen. "You two can go now." He followed the two as they left the tent.

Jesse looked at Sandy. "Did I do something to piss that guy off?"

"Naw. He's just a funny guy. I think he was a little pissed that he couldn't get the shrapnel after you went through all of that pain. He's an okay guy. Hang on, I'll put a bandage on your leg and get you a new pair of trousers."

Jesse sat patiently while Sandy bandaged his wound. As he pulled up his new trousers, he said, "Okay, Sandy, where's the booze?"

"Booze?"

"Yeah. Booze. I'm gonna take advantage of this bein' wounded business. I know swabbies and I know you guys have gotta have a club around here. Now, where is it?"

"Yeah, we got a club, but there aren't any patients allowed."

"Patients?" Jesse pointed to Sandy's collar. "You got any more of them things?"

"Damn, Indio. Yer puttin' me on the spot, man."

"Yeah, I know. I also know I'd do it for you. And besides, you don't have to walk in the place with me. Just get me that Caduceus thing or whatever you call it. I'll wait until it's full dark and we can meet inside."

"I don't know, Indio, you shouldn't be drinkin' with that wound. And you damn sure shouldn't be walkin' on it. You lost a lotta blood."

"I ain't gonna make a career of it – just two or three drinks."

Sandy gave in. "Okay. But if you get to feelin' woozy, you gotta promise me that you'll leave right away."

"You got it, my friend."

Sandy briefed Jesse on the layout of the tent serving as the club. The plan was simple: Sandy would be sitting at one end of the bar when Jesse walked in. Jesse would pretend to recognize an old friend and he would join him at the end of the bar where the light was weakest.

Sandy offered him a pair of crutches, which Jesse accepted with some hesitation.

"You'll need 'em, believe me."

"How do I get in the club on crutches?"

"You'll have to stash 'em alongside the tent just before you go in. You think you'll be able to make it from the door to the bar without limpin'?" Sandy looked a bit worried.

"How far is it?"

"About fifteen feet."

"No sweat. What time?"

"Eight o'clock."

Forever Patriots

"See ya there. Thanks, Sandy." Sandy helped Jesse into a wheelchair and pushed him to his quarters for the night in an adjoining tent.

Jesse glanced at his watch as he slid his crutches under the guy ropes on the side of the club tent. It was exactly eight o'clock. His leg had stiffened considerably as the afternoon had grown older and, with the passing of time, so too went the effects of the Novocain. He was in pain but it was still bearable so he had made the decision to keep his rendezvous with Sandy fairly short – booze or no booze.

He limped markedly to the front door of the large tent. In front of the door he stood erect and composed himself in anticipation of the fifteen-foot walk ahead of him. Slowly he opened the flap and stepped inside. The pain in his leg became almost unbearable before he had covered two steps. He was grateful the lights inside the tent were dim enough to help hide the pain he knew must be written all over his face. He stopped walking long enough to ease his pain and allow his eyes to adjust to the semi-darkness and spotted Sandy at the end of the bar.

He sauntered slowly to the bar and offered salutations as rehearsed. Sandy smiled a nervous smile as he offered to buy the first drink.

As the bartender moved away to fill the order, Sandy said, "You okay, man?"

Jesse smiled. "I've been better, but it's great to be able to sit down and sip a drink with an old friend. I never really thought we would."

Sandy reflected pensively for a moment. "Yeah. I guess you're right. Neither did I."

The bartender placed a cold beer on the bar in front of Jesse and left to attend to another customer.

Sandy raised his glass of beer in toast. "To the Hoa My Trail. May we never have to go through that again."

"Amen, brother." Jesse sipped from his beer.

The two men reminisced for an hour, Jesse sipping three beers during that period. At the end of the hour, Jesse said softly, "I think I better go, Sandy."

Sandy's look of concern turned to horror as he spotted the pool of blood under Jesse's barstool. "Jesus Christ! How long you been bleedin' like that?"

"I noticed it about thirty minutes ago. I was havin' such a good time, I didn't wanna bother you with it, but now I think I better get the hell outa here."

"Hang on, I'll get a stretcher."

"I'm not gonna blow your cover. I walked in here and I can walk out."

Sandy looked again at the pool of blood on the plank floor. "I don't think you better, Indio."

"I'll just pretend to be drunk and you can help me outa here. Just remember, I need you to take the weight offa' my left side."

Sandy appeared taken by surprise as Jesse began to mumble and slur his words loudly. Jesse stood unsteadily and staggered back against the bar. Sandy moved in to assist him with an apologetic look at the bartender. "He can't hold his liquor. I'll get him outa here." He turned to Jesse. "C'mon. I told you not to drink that damn gin before you came in here."

The bartender paid little attention to the two as they moved for the door.

Safely outside, Jesse smiled. "How was that actin' job?"

Sandy slapped him on the shoulder. "You shithead. You had *me* convinced

523

for a minute there. Where are your crutches?"

"Around the corner."

Sandy retrieved the crutches and assisted Jesse back to his tent where he removed the old bandage. "Holy shit!"

"Holy shit what?" said Jesse.

"Goddamn, man, you've lost a lotta' blood."

"No shit, Sherlock. They actually pay you for that kind of diagnosis?"

Sandy examined the blood-soaked bandage and tried to remember how big the pool of blood under the barstool had been. He shook his head. "Maybe I oughta get a doctor to give you some blood, Indio. This ain't right. Something's wrong." He worked quickly to re-bandage the injured leg.

"Don't try those scare tactics on me, Sandy. Other than bein' in a little pain and a bit weak at the knees, I feel fine."

Sandy felt of Jesse's forehead. "Shit! Your temperature is low."

"What the hell is that supposed to mean?" asked Jesse.

"You need blood, man. I'm gonna go get a doctor."

"If a doctor finds out I was in that club, you're in deep kimche."

"We're talkin' about your life, you hard-headed grunt!"

"I think I oughta know when I'm hurtin' that bad," said Jesse unconvincingly.

"Yeah, you oughta, but you got no damn common sense. I gotta go find a doctor. Keep that leg elevated and don't move." He propped a pillow under Jesse's injured leg and left the tent before Jesse could form a response.

Almost before Sandy was through the tent flap, Jesse jumped from the cot and grabbed his crutches. He headed straight for the club where he found a sympathetic corpsman to walk inside and buy him a bottle of Jim Beam. He thanked the corpsman and gave him a red five-dollar bill. Quickly he disappeared into the darkness on the perimeter of the camp.

He found a secluded spot and sat with his back against a large rock, his left leg elevated slightly with the aid of a small bush. Quietly he sipped his whiskey and reflected on his last year. He remembered sitting on a large tree trunk at Camp Pendleton, drinking bourbon. He had been a confused and bewildered youngster. Now he was no longer confused. He was totally mixed up. He felt more relaxed after the first two swallows.

He went over every detail of every minute he had ever been in Shannon's presence. *I wonder if I'll ever see you again, Shannon. Sometimes I'm not so sure. This damn war is sure crampin' my style.*

His mind drifted to Barbara. He was sure now that his experience with her in Hawaii had been a dream. Things like that didn't really happen in real life. *It was a damn good dream though*, he had to admit.

You know what's funny, Barbara? I'm tempted to desert now. Yeah, that's right. Now that I don't have a snowball's chance in hell of gettin' back to the States, I'm ready to pack it in. They don't really need me here – not for much more than a VC target anyway. I wouldn't mind so much if they'd let us win. I know you understand what I'm trying to say.

What the hell is wrong with me? Damn! Shannon, you'll always be first. That ain't exactly fair, you know.

He took another pull from his bottle. Suddenly the sound of an explosion in the distance, followed by small arms fire, caused his heart to jump into his throat. His hand rested on his bone-handled Bowie knife, his only weapon. When he realized the shooting seemed to be coming from the other side of Charlie Med's perimeter, he relaxed a bit.

Shouldn't have anything to worry about on this side. He took another pull at the bottle.

An illumination round from a large mortar lit up the compound. "Damn. Four-deuces. These guys go first class." He took another swig as the sounds of battle raged less than eight hundred yards from where he sat.

Sure hope you guys hold the line. I don't really feel up to fightin' gooks tonight. Now where was I? Oh yeah – Shannon. That's where I always am. But how in hell's name can I love Barbara? She's definitely the one. She has to be. He felt light-headed. *Maybe Barbara was real.*

The rocket attack by the VC lasted only a few minutes and did little damage, but it had the desired effect of placing the compound on full alert and irritating the sailors and marines within the camp.

Jesse had almost half of his bottle gone when he decided enough was enough. He felt as drunk as he had been at almost any time in his life. He knew he was in no position to be intoxicated but he didn't really care. He felt as lonely as he imagined a man could feel. Even worse than the feeling of loneliness was the feeling of helplessness. His wound, coupled with the heavy blood loss, his level of intoxication, and his lack of a rifle, all tended to impress upon him exactly how helpless he would be if confronted by even an unarmed VC. He cursed his stupidity.

This is no way to get back to The World, dummy!

His mind shifted to Okinawa and Masako. He wondered if it was wrong to miss Margie and wonder how she was doing.

But Barbara is special – real special.

A noise a few feet away startled him. He looked up to see a marine with an M-14 pointed at his chest.

"What the fuck are you doin' out here?" asked the marine, apparently surprised to see Jesse sitting calmly propped up against a rock, a bottle of whiskey in one hand.

Feebly, Jesse replied, "I could ask you the same thing, ya' know. This ain't exactly the safest place in camp. You oughta have better sense 'n ta be out here this time a' night."

The rifleman nodded at the half empty bottle of whiskey. "Where the hell you from, man?"

"First Battalion, Fourth Marines."

"You wounded or somethin'?" He gestured to the leg resting in the bush.

"I wish to hell it were 'somethin'', but it ain't. I got a piece of shrapnel in my left thigh."

"The swabbies know where you are?"

"What the hell do you think?"

"Your name isn't Langley by any chance?"

"Captured."

"Goddamn, man! They're turnin' Charlie Med upside down lookin' fer you. They told us there was a chance you might be bleedin' to death."

"Slim chance."

The rifleman moved next to Jesse and placed his rifle against the rock at his back. "Let me have a look at that leg."

Jesse's left trouser leg was dark with fresh blood. The sentry removed his bayonet from its scabbard and leaned over the leg to cut the trousers. He found himself looking at the shiny steel blade of Jesse's Bowie knife, held menacingly before him.

"Stay away from me with that bayonet," said Jesse.

The newcomer froze. "Hey, take it easy, buddy. I just wanna cut open the trouser leg and check the wound."

Jesse smiled. "Not with that damn ol' bayonet. Here, use a real knife." Deftly he shifted the knife so that the handle was extended toward the sentry. As the man reached for the knife, Jesse passed out.

He awakened to the sight of Sandy sitting next to his cot, eyes bloodshot.

"What's happenin', Sandy?" He smiled.

"How you feelin'?"

"Better. How 'bout you?"

"I feel like shit. We had to give you two units of blood. Your blood pressure was so low, we didn't think you were gonna make it."

Jesse sighed. "Well, unfortunately for the Crotch, I'm still among the living. What happens now?"

"The doctor wants your ass outa here at first light. He said until you're gone I'm not to let you outa my sight."

"I guess I really made an impression, huh?"

Sandy laughed. "You got that right."

"What time is it?"

"Almost oh-five-hundred."

"Where's the guy who found me?"

"Probably in the rack by now. You were lucky he didn't blow you away."

"Yeah. I know."

"What the hell were you doin' out there anyway?"

"Just thinkin'."

"You coulda' done that right here."

"I just wanted to be away from this, I guess. Hell, I don't know. This bein' wounded is for the birds. It ain't even a respectable wound and it's gonna keep me down for a month. It seems like goldbrickin' to me. I don't see why they can't make it heal faster than that. You know how short-handed we are out there. It don't seem right that this puny little wound should keep me out of action for so long. There's guys worse off than me out there in the bush."

"It's more serious than you think, man."

"It don't feel all that serious. The worst thing about this whole thing was the doctor workin' me over. I didn't feel so bad until he got to me."

"You'll get over it."

"Yeah, I guess."

There was a short pause then Jesse said, "Hey, Sandy, how long you been married?"

Sandy smiled. "Almost four years."

"What's married life like? I mean, do you still feel the same way about her as you did when you first got married?"

Sandy beamed. "Things are a little different, 'cause we've got a little girl now, but I think I got the best gal in the state of California."

"Would you do it again?"

"In a heartbeat."

"It must be kinda' tough on you, bein' over here for so long, and feelin' that way about your wife."

"Yeah, it's not easy, but it sure makes me appreciate her even more than I did before." Sandy went on to relate stories of his wife and child. Jesse listened intently to Sandy's enthusiastic discourse, heartened by the love Sandy had for his wife and the way he openly discussed the matter with him. It was comforting to Jesse to know that not all relationships were unreal, and he knew, from listening to Sandy, that at least one man was happy with his wife and that their love was real.

At oh-six-hundred a corpsman appeared with a tray of food. Jesse accepted the tray. He shared the contents with Sandy, who continued to talk of his wife and child, grateful to share his thoughts with another man who was genuinely interested in the subject.

Transportation to Da Nang East Hospital was delayed due to the lack of available vehicles. Even though Jesse was anxious to get to the hospital and begin his recovery, he was glad to spend the time with Sandy. When it appeared that Sandy might stop talking about his wife and family, Jesse encouraged him to continue, assuring the corpsman he was not bored by his friend's lengthy discourse.

Before the ambulance arrived at noon Jesse learned as much about married life vicariously as he had in the first twenty-one years of living. Almost always his knowledge had come from personal experience and, since he had never been married, he had little knowledge in that area..

When the two stretcher-bearers entered the tent to take him to the hospital he was saddened that he would miss that left unsaid by Sandy. The two friends said their goodbyes. Jesse felt a loss at the parting.

Jesse could see little of the city of Da Nang as the ambulance lumbered its way through the heavy military and civilian traffic. The hot stuffy air of the closed vehicle was stifling. He heard Vietnamese voices and tensed, waiting for a grenade or a bomb to end his journey. He was relieved when the ambulance stopped and the rear doors were opened, exposing him to the bright sunlight. Carefully the corpsmen carried him inside to an emergency room where he was placed on a Gurney.

A corpsman dressed in a white smock pushed him into an admitting room where Jesse dispensed the information requested of him by a stern looking major. His valuables were placed in a safe and he was issued a receipt. He wasn't so worried about his money but he made it clear to the corporal who issued the receipt that he wanted his knife left untouched. The corporal glanced at him nervously and assured him the knife would be safe.

After the short ordeal of admission, Jesse was wheeled into a ward and placed in a hospital bed with sheets. He met the stares of the curious as he was given a hospital gown. He removed his trousers and utility jacket and wrapped the gown around his body.

As he laid his head down upon his pillow a navy nurse walked into the room. A female navy nurse. A round-eye!

CHAPTER TWENTY-THREE: THE HOSPITAL

Jesse watched the nurse's every movement as she went from bed to bed, checking on each patient's condition, in her neatly pressed white smock. She was in her early twenties and had light brown hair, a tuft of which fell over one of her sparkling blue eyes. The smock didn't conceal the fact that she was a woman – an American woman. Jesse felt a mixture of self-consciousness about being in her presence in a hospital gown, and a closeness to his country that sometimes comes to those who fight wars and remain for extended periods so far from all that is familiar.

As he noticed the severity of some of the wounds in the ward, he thought less of the nurse and more about his own condition. He didn't belong in the same room with these men. There were arm-less and leg-less men in the room. There were those who had lost an eye, or were badly disfigured by fire or booby traps. He wondered what he was he doing in the company of men who had suffered so much more than he.

The nurse smiled as she approached his bed. "Good afternoon. Did you just arrive?"

"Yes, Ma'am," he answered sheepishly.

"My name is Hollingsworth. Judy Hollingsworth. I haven't seen your chart. Why are you here?"

"That's what I'd like to know. I took a small piece of shrapnel in the leg and you'd think I stepped on an anti-tank mine."

"Where did you get hit?"

She had pretty blue eyes. Of course, they weren't near as pretty as Shannon's or Barbara's, but they were pretty – for blue eyes. "In the left thigh."

"Let me have a look."

"I beg your pardon?"

"I said, let me have a look."

Jesse turned a light shade of red. He could see the color on his arms and felt the heat rise to his face. "If it's all the same to you, I'd just as soon not right now."

She smiled. "The first time I had a shy male patient, I was fresh out of nursing school and I embarrassed both the male patient and myself by insisting he submit to an examination. Experience has taught me that patience is the best course of action in these types of situations." She lowered her voice and put her face closer to Jesse's. "Not real crazy about a woman checking you out, huh?"

Jesse kept his voice low. "Not exactly. I'd rather have a male nurse if I could. No offense intended, Ma'am."

"I'm the only nurse on this ward on the day shift, except on Thursdays and Fridays. I'm afraid that, eventually, I'll have to look at the wound." She glanced at her watch. "The evening nurse will be on duty in about an hour. I guess we can wait that long today. But prepare yourself. Tomorrow, I'm not only going to have to check the wound, I'll be the one who cleans it."

Jesse said, "Yer kiddin'?"

She smiled. "For real."

"I can clean it by myself. I been taking showers for years."

"Eventually, you will clean it but, for the first two weeks, the nurses will take care of that matter."

"Any chance of you rotatin' back to the States by tomorrow?"

"'Fraid not. What did you say your name was?"

"No real sense gettin' to know one another. I don't plan on bein' here very long."

Her voice took on a stern tone. "What is your name, Marine?"

"Jesse Langley."

"Rank?"

"Corporal."

"Unit?"

"First Battalion, Fourth Marines. Eighty-one forward observer, attached to Alpha Company."

When she finished writing the information on her clipboard she looked up at him and smiled. "See? That wasn't so bad, was it?"

Jesse glanced at the gold second lieutenant bars on her white collar. "Speak for yourself – Lieutenant."

Judy Hollingsworth arched an eyebrow. She turned and moved on to the next patient.

The man in the bed on Jesse's right said quietly, "She ain't so bad. That guy they got workin' the midnight shift is a real sonofabitch."

Jesse looked at the man, who spoke through a facial bandage. "What d'ya' mean by that?"

"He's about as gentle as a bull rapin' a rat."

Jesse groaned. "Oh, great. I'm really lookin' forward to meetin' this guy. What the hell, it beats havin' a woman work you over."

"What's your name?" asked the bandaged face.

"Jesse Langley. The guys in my outfit call me Indio. How about you?"

"Colombo. They call me Wop for short."

"What happened to you?" asked Jesse.

"I was near an ammo bunker that got hit by a gook rocket, down by the airstrip. Damn Willie Peter hit me on the neck and chest. A little bit of it landed near my left eye. They tell me I'm gonna be able to see just fine when the bandage comes off. What are you in for?"

Jesse was almost embarrassed to answer. The large bandage on Wop's neck and chest had gone unnoticed a at first. "I picked up a piece of shrapnel from a gook rifle grenade."

"No kidding? Where'd you get hit?"

"Left thigh."

"That must 'of hurt like hell."

Jesse stared at his companion. "You gotta be kiddin' me! It was nothin' compared to what happened to you. I feel guilty even takin' up bed space in this place."

Colombo laughed softly. "You'll get used to it. It ain't so bad once you know your way around. They got a PX on the next wing. I heard you tell Judy what outfit you were from. From what I hear, the Brigade has more than earned its colors back."

"What outfit you from?"

"Supply Battalion."

"Supply Battalion?" repeated Jesse.

"Yep, a rear echelon outfit. I spent five months with Two-Three, in Fox Company then, one day, the company commander ups and tells me I've been transferred to Supply Battalion. Five months and I never got a scratch. Two months in the rear and I get fried by our own Willie Peter. Crazy war, ain't it?"

"What outfit did you say you were from originally?"

"Two-Three."

"I used to be in two-three back in 1963."

"No kiddin'?"

They talked about two-three until evening chow.

Jesse ate his meal heartily. It was served on the standard stainless steel tray of the stateside mess hall but, to Jesse, it couldn't have tasted better if served on fine china.

Shortly after the meal, the evening nurse made his rounds. A young doctor, who paid little attention to Jesse, accompanied him. The male nurse was a large black man in his early twenties with a booming voice and an ever-present smile.

"So, Mr. Langley, Nurse Hollingsworth tells me that you aren't real pleased with the thought of her playing doctor on your body. You don't look queer to me. Most guys would get shot just to see her smile. What's your excuse?"

Jesse liked the big man immediately. "Chicken, I guess."

The big man widened his smile. "My official title is Nurse Singleton, but that sounds like shit to me, so I prefer you call me Bill. You got any objection to that?"

"It'd be kinda stupid to have an objection, wouldn't it? I mean, you could make a guy's life miserable if you wanted to."

"I see you *are* an intelligent man. Now, let me remind you that Nurse Hollingsworth is in the same position as I."

"Damn, Doc, I could have gone all evening without hearin' that."

"Let me have a look at that wound of yours."

Jesse pulled down the covers of his bed and moved his hospital gown above the wound. Singleton removed the bandage quickly and efficiently. He produced a stainless steel bowl with Epsom salts and a small towel. For ten minutes he bathed the wound and talked to Jesse of things unrelated to battle or war. When he completed his work he deftly applied a new bandage and left the ward.

It was too early to sleep and Jesse did not feel up to writing a letter, not even to Barbara. He felt stupid and useless. He rested on his back and counted the lines on the ceiling. He was still awake when the midnight nurse came into the ward and stopped by his bedside.

"You awake, Langley?"

His dislike for the man was as immediate as had been his liking for Singleton. "Yeah."

The male nurse turned on the small light above Jesse's bed. "I'm Godfrey. I've got the midnight shift and, for a while, I'm gonna bathe your wound – about this time every morning."

"What time is it?"

"Two-hundred".

"Oh."

"Okay, let's get to it. Let me see the wound so we can get this unpleasant experience over with."

Jesse exposed his bandaged thigh. Without warning, Godfrey pulled the tape from his leg in a fashion, which appeared to Jesse, designed to inflict the maximum amount of pain.

"Ow! Hey, take it easy. That ain't a plastic doll, you know."

Godfrey ignored him and went to work on the leg. Jesse jumped at the touch of the cold water.

"I thought the water was supposed to be warm."

"I'm running behind schedule and didn't have time to draw hot water," answered Godfrey, irritation clear in his voice.

"It's okay with me if you wanna catch me later. I ain't goin' anywhere."

"I have other patients to attend to. Now just hold still. This won't take long." Godfrey worked roughly at the wound. He scrubbed harder and deeper than Bill had. Soon the irritated wound began to bleed profusely. He couldn't see to clean the tissue. The blood ran freely over Jesse's leg and onto the white sheets.

Jesse, who had deliberately held his tongue in order not to give Godfrey the satisfaction of knowing he was hurting him, finally said, "I think you better get a doctor in here. That's too much blood."

Godfrey ignored him and continued to scrub at the aggravated tissue. "And who made *you* into a medical expert, Langley?" He pushed against the bloody hole as he spoke Jesse's name.

Pain shot through Jesse's body from head to toe and back again. He kicked Godfrey with his good leg, striking him in the face. Quickly he picked up the bowl of cold, bloody water and threw it in the nurse's face. Godfrey was taken totally by surprise and fell from the edge of the bed where he had been sitting.

Jesse jumped from the bed and kicked him in the ribs. Godfrey shouted for help. Someone turned on the ward lights and, as the men in the room awakened, Jesse continued his assault on Godfrey. Blood spurted from his leg wound with each beat of his heart as he hit the nurse with the stainless steel bowl.

Several uniformed sailors appeared and restrained Jesse, pinning him to the floor. One of the sailors shouted. "Goddamn! This guy's bleedin' like a stuck pig! Get a doctor in here!"

A doctor had examined Jesse's wound and found the tissue rubbed raw. He had immediately relieved Godfrey of his duties and installed a female nurse to finish the night's work. After thirty minutes of feverish work by two over-worked doctors, Jesse's leg stopped bleeding. He was returned to the ward under sedation.

A tired-looking Nurse Hollingsworth entered the ward and made straight for Jesse. A wisp of hair hung loosely over one eye as she stopped near the edge of his bed. Evidence of the late night altercation had been eradicated by the changing of sheets and mopping the floor. Jesse opened one eye and looked at her without moving.

"I understand you had a busy night?" she said pleasantly.

Jesse didn't reply. He closed his eye and ignored her. He was tired of the hospital. Being out in the field was preferable.

Hollingsworth continued, "It looks like you're spared from me for another day. The doctor tells me we won't have to clean the wound until sometime late tonight."

Jesse opened one eye again. "Don't bother sendin' that Godfrey guy. He ain't gettin' near me." He closed his eye.

Hollingsworth looked over at Colombo, sitting on the edge of his bed. She shrugged. "If he needs anything call me, will you, Wop?"

Colombo nodded. "He's okay, Judy. You shoulda' seen what Godfrey was doin' to 'im. There was no excuse for it. Indio there didn't do anything to bring it on."

"Indio? I thought his name was Langley?"

"It is. The guys in his outfit call him Indio."

"Oh." She glanced back at Jesse and moved to her next patient quietly.

"Hey, Indio," whispered Colombo.

Jesse turned toward the voice. "Yeah?"

"Why'd you treat Judy so shitty? She never did anything to you."

"Hell, Wop, I didn't mean to treat her shitty. I just want outa this place. She ain't done anything to me. I just don't want her to get to thinkin' I've changed my mind about her workin' on my leg."

"She's a nurse, man. She's seen about as much of a man as there is to see."

"I don't care about all a' that. I can clean my own wound."

"Ya know, they called her out to stand the rest of Godfrey's duty. The least you could do is act civil."

"Damn. I didn't know she'd been up all night."

"And gotta work all day too. Course you had no way of knowing without talking to her."

"Touche."

"What?"

"Never mind. I'll apologize next time I see her."

"Might not be a bad idea. Besides bein' a nurse and a damn good one, she's about the best-looking woman in the hospital from what I understand."

"I got eyes. I know she's good-lookin'. There's a lot a' good-lookin' women out there. That don't have anything to do with what she really is."

"You'll find out if you live long enough. She's prettier inside than she is on the outside – and man – that's beautiful!"

"Maybe you're right, Wop. I'll put on some manners next time I see her."

The day passed uneventfully for Jesse. He remained on his back for most of the time, moving as little as possible. He was having a difficult time believing this whole thing started over such a small piece of metal in his thigh. Exhausted, he fell asleep at midnight.

He awakened in the darkness. Someone sat on his bed. The bandage had been removed from his leg. He could feel the air as it cooled the warm water being applied to his wound. He whispered in the darkness to the gentle touch. "Is that you, Bill? Why didn't you turn on the light?"

"No, it's not Bill, and I didn't turn on the light because I thought I could finish the job before you woke up."

Jesse tensed. "Nurse Hollingsworth?"

"Yeah. It's me, Indio. Your second favorite nurse."

His nickname sounded strange to his ears when spoken by an American woman. "How'd you get my nickname?"

"Your bunkmate, Colombo. I know a lot about you – a lot more than I know about most of the other patients anyway."

He reached up and turned on the light. His manhood was still discreetly concealed beneath the raised hospital gown.

Hollingsworth looked tired. Her blue eyes seemed to droop a little at the corners. She smiled. "I didn't peek."

Jesse liked her. "That's okay. Nothin' special there, I reckon. More like just personal."

"I understand."

"I apologize for acting like a jerk."

"I've seen a lot worse than you."

"That don't really make me that much better, does it?"

"Depends on how you look at it."

"That's the way I look at it." He paused for a moment, wanting to say something but not knowing what to say. "What makes a pretty woman wanna come to a combat zone?"

Her hands stopped moving over his wound momentarily. "What makes anyone go to war?"

"Ideas, I guess," said Jesse.

"Ideas?"

"Yeah, ideas. Ideas about what's right and what's wrong. Patriotism. Freedom. Little things like that."

She began to cleanse his wound again. "Is that why your company commander speaks so highly of you? Because you're a patriot?"

"Who you been talkin' to?"

She smiled tiredly. "I talked to a lot of people yesterday. I wanted to know who you were and how we should respond to your altercation with Godfrey."

"So, what's the verdict?"

"Depends on who you listen too. Some described you as a little unconventional. Others said you walked on water, but all of them expressed respect for you as a combat marine. Combat marine – those were their exact words."

"What does that have to do with that Godfrey guy?"

"It has some bearing. We've known for some time that Godfrey had a cruel streak. It's too bad because he's got the knowledge. But, getting back to you, I passed the information I received on to the doctor investigating Godfrey. I originally looked into it because I wanted to be sure that Godfrey was punished this time but, the more I talked to those marines out in the field, and the more I learned about you, the more you became a person with a history – just like all of the others – except I never took the time to find out about the others – never had any reason to. I don't think I could keep all of it in my head if I knew this much about every wounded man in the hospital."

"I think I know what you mean."

She looked him in the eyes. "No, I'm not sure you do but thanks for saying so."

There was an awkward pause. She broke the silence. "A Captain Malcolm spoke very highly of you. I never heard one man praise another like he did you. Maybe I shouldn't tell you that, but it's true."

Jesse smiled. "I'd do the same for him."

Hollingsworth put the bowl on the floor and bandaged his thigh. Her touch

533

Stoney Livingston

was gentle. She stood to leave. "Good night, Corporal Langley."

"What happened to Indio? I meant it when I apologized. By the way, that was a fine job you just did on my leg. Thanks."

Nurse Hollingsworth cried softly as she left the ward. Jesse sat with his back propped up with his pillow, watching her tearful departure, wondering what he had said to distress her so.

The days passed slowly for Jesse. His wound began to heal cleanly and he got along well with the new night nurse, a professional-looking little man with bifocal, horn-rimmed glasses. Male nurse Collier was an easy man to like. He did his job and showed consideration to others when he worked.

Nurse Hollingsworth continued to attend to Jesse's wound in the afternoons and Bill Singleton took care of him in the evenings. He felt self-conscious about all of the attention but each man on the ward received the same treatment. His was nothing special, though there were times when Nurse Hollingsworth seemed to be on the verge of confessing something personal to him.

He wrote letters to everyone he knew. He didn't mention the fact he was writing from a hospital. He wasn't really hurt that badly, so why alarm anyone? When he wrote to Barbara he talked of Hawaii and how much he loved her. He loved everything when he thought of her – even the VC. He only wished that there were some way he could teach the VC and the North Vietnamese that America meant them no harm; that all men were capable of better things than war.

Of course he would leave the hospital and go forth to kill them if they persisted in trying to kill him but it was not a thing he wanted to do. He wanted the war to end.

On his sixth day at the hospital two young American girls in their late teens or early twenties came into the ward pushing a large cart loaded with books. Many of the men appeared to be familiar with the girls as they greeted them with jokes and advances. The girls smiled to one and all and parried all attempts by the patients to become overly familiar.

"What the hell is that?" Jesse asked Colombo, who sat on his bed reading a magazine.

"Candy stripers. They get the name from their uniforms, I guess. They come by once or twice a week and visit the ward. They bring books and magazines. Sometimes they play cards with the guys, or just talk. The little blonde is okay but the ugly one is the nicest. She's from Brooklyn and she cracks me up with her accent."

"Those kinda broads don't belong here. They oughta be back in The World, goin' to school."

"So shouldn't we all," replied Colombo solemnly.

The brunette from Brooklyn approached Colombo's bed. "G'morning, Wop. How ya feelin' t'day?"

"Better, now that you came in to brighten up my life."

The girl looked at Jesse and shrugged. "Dis guy is such a Romeo."

Jesse smiled. "He says nice things about you too."

"My name's Denise. You want a book or a magazine?" she asked.

Jesse nodded. "They call me Indio. No, thank you, but if you have a spare deck of cards, I'd sure appreciate it."

She reached into the cart and withdrew a pack of playing cards. "One or two decks?"

"One'd be fine."

She handed him the pack of cards.

"Thanks."

"Youah welcome."

Jesse turned his attention to his cards as he opened the pack and shuffled them for a round of solitaire.

Colombo spoke to the brunette. "So, beautiful, when we goin' out?"

The girl ignored his remark. "I heah ya get ya bandages off tamarra."

"Yeah, that's what they tell me."

"What time?"

"About ten, I think."

"I'll try ta be heah."

"You don't have to do that. You may not like what you see."

"Don't be silly. I wanna be heah."

Colombo reached out and pulled a magazine from the rack. "I'll see you then."

The Candy Striper smiled and moved on to the next patient.

That afternoon Jesse received his first mail since leaving his outfit. There were three letters from Barbara, one from Will, Charlotte, and Rob Preston. He answered Charlotte's letter first, telling her all about Barbara and explaining that he would still like to meet her when he got home. He thought she was a great person and he would like her to meet Barbara.

Will's letter was full of jokes and cheer and he mentioned that Shannon seemed happy and she had asked him to say hello. Jesse felt the heart-stopping emotion he always felt whenever Shannon acknowledged his existence. He wondered why it was still that way, what, with Barbara in his life and all. He wrote Will a short, cheery letter.

The letter from Rob Preston disturbed him. While Rob did not openly state he supported the anti-war movements, Jesse feared his friend leaned in that direction. He loved Rob like a brother and it would be a difficult pill for him to swallow if his old friend were to take up sides with the opposition. Except for the small shadow of political doubt cast by the letter, it was enjoyable to read and Jesse was grateful for the news of his friends.

The letters from Barbara he saved until last. He savored every line and re-read them all until he had them memorized. Her letters were filled with both happiness and loneliness. But the loneliness was not expressed openly. Jesse knew only because he knew her. He answered all three of her letters, one at a time, with three of his own. No sense in her knowing that he received all three of them at once. She might think something was wrong.

Jesse watched anxiously as the doctor removed the bandages from Colombo's chest. He winced at the ugly scar tissue covering the man's chest where once there had been a bandage. *He was better off with the bandage*, thought Jesse, as he stared at the puffy scar tissue. He held his breath as the doctor moved to the bandage covering Colombo's face.

Jesse leaned forward in his bed as the last of the gauze disappeared and the facial tissue was exposed. He had expected worse, more like the chest, but the only scar visible on Colombo's face was in the corner of his left eye, a small scar, hardly noticeable.

Stoney Livingston

"Wop. Can you see out of both eyes?" he said through the doctor's back.

Colombo blinked and squinted his eyes several times, then smiled broadly. "Can I ever! It's a little blurry but I can see."

The doctor smiled. "Your vision should improve rapidly. You'll be released in a few days."

"Thanks, Doc. This is great!"

The candy striper from Brooklyn stepped forward and gave Colombo a big hug. "Youah one handsome devil, Wop."

It wasn't until later that day that Jesse noticed a change come over Wop as he began to think about the massive scar on his chest. The more thought he gave the matter, the more depressed he became. Jesse watched the change go from bad to worse and desperately tried to cheer him up, but without success. That afternoon, as Nurse Hollingsworth cleansed his wound, he voiced his concern about Colombo.

"Can you do anything to help the guy? I mean, he's always been so cheerful. Now he acts like a zombie. I think he's a candidate for the depression ward."

"I'll see what I can do." She bandaged his leg and moved on to her other duties.

The following morning, Colombo smiled as he ate his morning meal. He looked over his tray at Jesse. "Ya know what?"

Jesse said, "No. What?"

Colombo lowered his voice. "That Judy Hollingsworth is something else."

"Oh? What d' ya mean by that?"

"You won't tell a soul? Promise. She could get in big trouble if anyone found out."

"Damn, Wop. I like the woman. Why would I want to get her in trouble?"

"Okay, okay. I just had to be sure."

"So what happened?"

"Well, you know I been feelin' sorry for myself ever since I got to lookin' at the scars on my chest."

"So?"

"So, out of the blue, Judy comes in the ward late last night and sits down next to me and talked for more than an hour."

"About what?"

"Everything. But that's not the good part. Before she leaves, she plants a lip lock on me that would give a priest a hard-on. Jesus, can that woman kiss!"

"What the hell brought that on?" asked Jesse.

"I don't know. Maybe she's just lonely."

"With all the men runnin' around here, and her not exactly the ugliest thing in the country, I don't think that's too likely," said Jesse.

"Maybe she's tired of doctors and male nurses," offered Colombo.

Jesse smiled and shook his head. "So she took a likin' to you, huh?"

"I swear, man, I thought for a minute there she was gonna crawl in bed with me. She gave me her parents' address in the States and asked me to look her up when she gets back home."

"I'll be damned."

"All I know is that I was one surprised Wop. She's always been friendly but this was something else."

Forever Patriots

"Sounds like it. She's a fine lookin' woman, Wop. A man couldn't do too much better than her if he looked a hundred years."

"Tell me about it."

"You wanna play some poker?" asked Jesse.

Colombo smiled. "Not right now. I just wanna think about that kiss. It has to last me a long time and I wanna enjoy it."

Two days later, Colombo was released from the hospital and returned to his unit a happier man than he had been before he had been wounded – all because of one woman's kiss. Jesse gave much consideration to the abrupt change in Colombo. The pen may be mightier than the sword but it appears that there's something out there a whole lot mightier than the pen, he thought.

The days dragged on for Jesse as he watched the slow improvement in his leg. Nurse Hollingsworth seemed more detached than she had been before she kissed Colombo but she was still friendly and professional. The amputees came and went. They stayed only long enough to gain strength for the ocean crossing home. Most of the men on Jesse's ward would be returned to their units upon release from the hospital. The Candy Stripers came and went on their weekly rounds and, on one occasion, the brunette informed him that it was possible to make a call home from the hospital. Jesse waited with anxious anticipation for the day he could get his uniform back and go to the M.A.R.S. phone center and call Barbara.

The air-conditioned hospital gave Jesse the impression he was in the United States. Since he was never allowed outside, the impression was probably accurate. It had been a long time since his life had been so easy.

One night, shortly before dark, several orderlies and nurses arrived in the ward, pushing large carts containing mattresses.

Jesse's new bunkmate, PFC Porter, leaned towards him and said, "What's goin' on?"

Jesse watched the bustle of activity, ignorant of its meaning. "Hell, Port, I got no idea. This is a new drill to me."

Nurse Bill Singleton stood in the middle of the room and signaled for everyone's attention, his ebony skin prominent in contrast to the white uniform he wore. When the room became quiet, he said, "We've brought extra mattresses for cover in the event we're hit tonight. Intelligence info indicates the VC are going to hit the hospital tonight. We don't know where or when but, the word is, they *are* going to hit."

Complaints and groans from the injured filled the room. Singleton raised his hands to quiet the men. "We've got extra security on the perimeter, and the mattresses are just an extra precautionary measure. We'll be well protected."

Singleton paused for a moment. "Just before lights out we'll be placing a mattress on top of each of you whose wounds will allow it. In the event we are hit, the full staff is on standby to assist those of you who can't support a mattress because of your wounds. Any Questions?"

Jesse said, "Hey, Bill, how about givin' us rifles?"

Nods of assent and vocal agreement swept the room.

"No can do. The brass don't want a bunch of wounded tryin' to shoot rifles in a crowded ward."

"Give me some crutches and a rifle and send me to the line," said Jesse.

"It's not that bad, gentlemen. These are just precautionary measures. We may not even be hit. This is a big hospital."

537

Stoney Livingston

They prepared for the night. When the lights were turned out, Jesse lay quietly on his bed, the unfamiliar weight of the extra mattress above him. At oh-two-hundred, Collier came into the ward and cleansed his wound as he did every night. The extra mattress was removed and placed on the floor during the cleaning process, which lasted only ten minutes. Collier finished applying the new bandage and was lifting the mattress to cover Jesse when the rocket came through the wall.

The explosion was deafening, as were the screams and shouts of the wounded shortly afterward. The room filled with smoke and plaster dust and confusion. Jesse was thrown to the floor by the concussion of the blast. He crawled under the bed, wishing he had a rifle, or even his knife. But he had nothing – nothing but fear.

The dim light in the hallway outside the ward flickered and died. Another rocket slammed into the ward. There were more screams of fear and pain, more plaster dust, more smoke.

Jesse heard a bubbling sound on the floor next to him. He crawled in the thick darkness to meet the sound. Collier had been hit. He felt in the darkness for the wound. Blood was everywhere.

"Collier, where you hit?"

"I don't know! Can't breathe! Blood in my mouth and nose!"

Jesse reached up and pulled the top sheet from his bed. He wiped Collier's face, removing the blood from his breathing passages. Another rocket slammed into the wall. The room shook and vibrated with the explosion.

Collier breathed without the bubbling sound. Jesse searched in the darkness for the wound and found the flesh above the forehead was gone. He felt the exposed skull of the injured man.

"Shit!" He reached up to the bed and pulled his pillow to the floor. Carefully, he situated Collier so that his back was propped up by the wall, and placed the pillow behind his head for support. Frantically he tore his top sheet into bandages and feverishly tied them around the top of Collier's head. The rocket attack was over. The only sounds in the room were the moans and cries of the wounded and the shouts for help by those in a position of need.

The light in the hallway flickered twice then came on and stayed. The weak light rays penetrated the smokey atmosphere of the ward, allowing visual inspection of the damage caused by the VC attack.

Jesse surveyed Collier's head wound and searched for more damage to the man's body but found none. He improved on his bandage work with the aid of the hallway light, then turned to Porter's bed. "Hey, Port, You o ..."

Porter's body hung half off his bed, his head almost severed. Jesse stared, horrified, at the gaping hole that had once been the left side of his neck. His knee slipped in the pool of blood that had once been Porter.

The lights flickered on in the ward. Jesse turned his face to avoid the sight of Porter. He looked at Collier, who stared blankly at him.

"You okay, Indio?" asked Collier.

"Am *I* okay? For Christ sakes, Collier, forget about your job for a minute. Are *you* okay?"

"I've got a headache."

"No shit. That I can understand. You've just had your widow's peak eliminated, my friend. You're gonna need a wig, or you're gonna have one helluva high forehead."

Collier smiled weakly.

"I'll take over here, Indio." Singleton's voice relieved Jesse of his charge. He crawled under the bed and stayed out of the way while Singleton lifted Collier onto his broad shoulders and carried him from the ward. Jesse moved back into the space between his bed and Porter's. He attempted to get back into his bed but found it full of broken glass. He sat on the floor, his back to the wall, oblivious to Porter's blood surrounding him.

Jesse sat as two orderlies removed Porter's body. Nurse Hollingsworth found him twenty minutes later, sitting on the floor in a pool of blood, smoking a cigarette. He looked up at her as she stood over him.

"Howdy. Glad to see you're okay. How's Collier?" he asked.

Hollingsworth looked at the pool of drying blood surrounding Jesse's bare legs. "He's fine. Are you okay?"

"I didn't get hit, if that's what you mean."

"Let me help you up. We'll get your bed made up and get you to sleep." She moved in to assist him to his feet, slipping and falling in the blood on the floor. She landed awkwardly in Jesse's lap, breaking her fall with one hand only slightly as it slipped on the slick floor.

The impact of her body on his left him breathless for a moment but he held his composure. When he could again breathe, he smiled and said, "You didn't have to go to all of that trouble just to get my attention."

Awkwardly she picked herself from his lap. "I'm sorry. Did I hurt you?"

"Not much but, for a minute there, I could understand why Wop was so excited about you."

Hollingsworth blushed but said nothing.

Jesse smiled. "Your secret's safe with me. I won't tell anyone you're a woman. We'll let everybody go on thinkin' you're just a nurse."

Hollingsworth regained her composure and smiled. "C'mon. Give me your hand and let's get things back in order."

"Yes, Ma'am." He held up his hand.

The hospital staff worked through the night. The Sea Bees were called in to make structural repairs to the building and the hospital continued to operate as though nothing unusual had occurred during the night.

The healthy flesh continued to grow into Jesse's leg. He was able to cleanse the wound by himself and no longer needed the nurses for anything other than a quick inspection of the wound. Everyday he asked the nurses and doctors alike if it was time to suture it. Every day they told him no, but he persisted.

He had no news of his outfit and he wondered what they were doing. He feared for their welfare, especially Thunder's. A letter from Mud brightened his stay. Nurse Hollingsworth delivered it to him and remarked on his smile as he read the return address. "Good news?"

"Good friend. He was my radio operator for a long time out in the bush. He knew what to do, sometimes even before I did. He was a great guy. We'd laugh and joke and fight about some of the craziest things. We had this rooster once. We called him ..." Jesse's voice trailed off.

"Yes?"

He looked up at her. "I don't know why I'm rattling on to you. You didn't know Mud."

Stoney Livingston

"I know his friend."

"We don't know each other. This is boring to you. You're okay for a second lieutenant, but I don't think your duties have to extend to listenin' to some crazy jarhead reminisce about his days in the field."

"I don't mean to pry. I'm glad you got the letter from your friend. I'll be by before I go off duty to take a look at your leg." She walked briskly from his bed.

His thoughts returned to Mud's letter. He read of his leave in San Francisco and of his return to Camp Pendleton to serve out his remaining six months. He enjoyed the way Mud wrote – almost like he spoke. The letter returned him to the rice paddies of *Oregon* and he smiled a sad smile for Mud's safety.

The day following his receipt of Mud's letter his leg was sutured with heavy wire. When the doctor finished his work, the wires protruded a full inch from Jesse's leg.

"Damn, Doc, I could catch that on something in the bush and rip that leg wide open."

"You're not going to the bush for another week or so, Corporal. You've done well and I don't want you leaving here until we've removed the wire."

"Couldn't we just flatten the wires out and let me get back to my outfit?"

The doctor smiled. "'Fraid not."

Jesse was re-issued his cleaned uniform, bloody stain and all, and allowed the run of the ward and the small library facilities. He hobbled on his crutches from the PX to the library and back to the ward. He was allowed to take his meals in the mess hall with the other walking patients who were no longer required to remain on a strict diet.

He had no friends in the ward and he associated with no one in particular, nor did he ignore any of the men when they wanted to play cards or engage him in discussion.

His underarms became sore the first day he had his crutches. He fought the pain and continued to venture forth, enjoying his newfound freedom.

He found the telephone linked to the M.A.R.S. network and placed a call to Barbara early in the morning. He figured the time on the East Coast of the U.S. should be about two in the afternoon. A sergeant answered the phone and informed him Barbara was not in. She had to take a routine physical and would be back later. He hung up disappointed. By the time he could get another appointment on the M.A.R.S. network, he would be released from the hospital.

*****

As he stood in full utility uniform in front of the PX counter, waiting to pay for his candy bar, one of the men from his ward rolled his wheelchair into the PX at breakneck speed.

"Indio, you better get back to the ward! General Walt is on his way to give out Purple Hearts."

Jesse placed his candy bar back on the shelf and hobbled as quickly as he could back to his ward. He saw Nurse Hollingsworth frown at him as he bounced by.

A voice near the door said, "Here he comes!"

Jesse quickly placed his crutches under his bed and climbed between the sheets, boots and all. Nurse Hollingsworth smiled and shook her head at Jesse's antics.

Jesse watched out of the corner of his eye as General Walt moved from

540

bed to bed with his photographer and staff. Each man was presented a Purple Heart and a picture of the General making the presentation.

General Walt was a solid-looking man. His closely cropped hair, almost a perfect flattop, added to his military bearing. Jesse didn't know Walt but had heard good things about him from others. He was considered by many as the enlisted man's replacement for Chesty Puller, the most famous Marine of all time.

The General approached his bed and stopped next to the head. "Good morning, Marine."

"G'mornin', Sir."

The General eyed Jesse's sideburns conspicuously. "Where you from, son?"

"Arizona, Sir."

The General smiled, apparently satisfied the sideburns – though well in excess of regulation – were okay because of the geographic origin of the man. "I spent a lot of time in Colorado myself. You looking forward to gettin' out of this place?"

"Does a cat have an ass, Sir?"

One of the General's staff cleared his throat. The General smiled. "Well put, Marine. It was a stupid question. Where did you get hit?"

Jesse wasn't sure if the General meant where on his body or where in the country. He opted for the country. "In the DMZ, Sir."

The General fielded it well. "Is that anywhere near your nuts?"

"Oh, I'm sorry, Sir. I thought you meant what part of the country was I in. Left thigh – just a little piece of shrapnel."

Walt turned to one of his aids. "Don't let me ask these kinds of questions in the future. If my marines can't understand what the hell I'm talking about, how the hell can we expect to carry on a fight?" He turned back to Jesse. "What's your outfit?"

"One-Four, Sir."

The General arched an eyebrow. "Good outfit. You men have carried a heavy load since the beginning of the year. I hope to get you some relief soon."

"The biggest relief would be winnin' the war, Sir."

"To all of us, Marine. To all of us." Without further discussion, the General presented his Purple Heart while the photographer scrambled for the proper position to take his picture. There was a short but awkward pause after the presentation while the photographer waited for the black and white Polaroid picture to develop in the camera. At length he retrieved it from within the black box and handed it to Jesse. The General and his staff moved to the next bed.

Jesse looked at the opened little folding box, its medal showing off inside. He felt a strange kind of sadness for the recipients of Purple Hearts worldwide. It was one medal he would rather not have.

When the General and his staff left the room Jesse got out of bed and smoothed it over. He tucked in the edges and pulled them tight.

"You're going to make someone a wonderful wife someday."

He turned to see Nurse Hollingsworth standing behind him. "Sorry about the boots on the sheets. It was kind of an emergency situation."

She smiled at his explanation. "So, what did you think of the General?"

"I liked him. Can't really tell too much by a two-minute meeting, but he seemed like a real person to me. With a guy like him runnin' things up here in I

541

Corps, I can't understand why we haven't won the war already."

"Oh, Jesse, if only things were that simple." She turned and walked back to her station.

Her use of his first name didn't go unnoticed. Not since Barbara had a woman called him by that name. It almost didn't seem to be his name anymore. It belonged to someone in the past.

He fingered the medal and looked forward with gleeful anticipation to his departure from the hospital. He knew he would be leaving shortly, possibly as soon as four more days. He bounced up and down and winced at the pain he caused in his leg by the childish display.

Early that evening, Jesse left the confines of the ward in search of excitement. He knew there was a club on the hospital grounds and he thought he knew where to find it. Armed with his newly acquired captain's bars on his collar, he set forth in search of the club. He limped only slightly as he moved along without the aid of his crutches, quickly and with great effort, moving into a limpless gate whenever in the presence of others.

He found the club and, after a few nervous moments, seated himself to the rear of the room. He drank sour mash and reflected upon his situation. He looked around the room at the officers, men and women, all drinking mixed drinks or cold beer, acting unaware there was a war outside. He ordered more sour mash.

He looked at his watch and had to focus his eyes twice to read the dial. He had another hour before he had to report back to the ward. He wondered if he would make it.

"Good evening, Captain. May I join you?"

He knew that voice. Who was it talking to? He turned and looked up into the face of Nurse Hollingsworth. Feebly, he waved at the empty chair next to him. "Be my guest, Lieutenant. I guess I was just leaving anyway, huh?"

She sat in the indicated chair and said, "What's the matter, Captain? You don't want company tonight?" Her voice was teasing. He knew he was in trouble.

He turned to face her. "Okay, so I'm captured. Whattaya gonna do to me, send me back to a nice safe brig?"

Nurse Hollingsworth smiled. "How in the world did you get the captain's bars?"

"Secret."

"Oh."

"You wanna drink before I go to meet my fate?" he asked nonchalantly.

"What are you drinking?"

"Sour mash."

"I'll have one of those."

"Straight?"

"Isn't that what you said you were drinking?"

"Yeah, that's what I said *I* was drinkin'. I didn't say *you* were drinkin' it."

"I know. *I* said that."

"Oh."

The little Vietnamese waiter, who had made many trips to Jesse's table, took the order for two more. Jesse and Nurse Hollingsworth sat in silence until he returned with their drinks. When he left the table, Nurse Hollingsworth raised her shot glass. "To Captain Indio."

542

Jesse raised his glass and drained it. He placed the empty glass carefully on the table and said, "It was nice visitin' with you, Ma'am. Now, if you'll excuse me, I gotta go on some kind of helicopter mission or somethin'."

"Just like that?"

"You think I'm gonna stay here so you can turn me in when yer done playin' games?"

"I'm not going to turn you in, Jesse. You deserve a night on the town. Why would I turn you in?"

"You could get in trouble sittin' with me and not turnin' me in."

"I could. But if I'm willing to take the chance, that shouldn't be your concern."

"What is my concern is: why would you do it?"

"For me. Not for you, but for me."

"What are you talkin' about?"

"Jesse, every day I've worked here I've seen the marines come and go – all young men in their prime, just like you. Some left for the States with arms and legs missing. Others went in coffins. The others we patched up and sent back into the jungle to get blown away at some later date. I just wanted to get to know one of you before I became like the others around here."

"The others?"

"The doctors and nurses. They tend to the patients like one would fix a car. If it can't be fixed, send it to the junkyard. Then, when their shift is over, they come here and drink and play musical beds during the night. I don't want to be like that. I wasn't raised that way and this war is not going to make me into something I'm not."

Jesse squinted to focus his eyes. "That's commendable, Nurse Hollingsworth..."

"Judy."

"Judy. But why me? Why not Wop? He went nuts for you."

"To be honest with you, he was due to be released too soon for me to get to know him."

"Well, I ain't hangin' around here much longer." He looked at the tables around them.

"I already know more about you than I do about my doctor – the investigation over Godfrey – remember?"

"Oh, yeah. Whatever happened to him?"

"He was transferred back to the States."

"That's all?"

"That's all."

They ordered another round of drinks.

"So, what do you need to do to continue with your experiment to know an average marine?"

"I'm serious, Jesse."

"Stop callin' me Jesse."

"Isn't that your name?"

"Yeah, it's my name – back home. But it don't sound right comin' from the mouth of a pretty American woman, ten thousand miles from there. It has a tendency to make me think of other things. And I don't wanna think about those other things right now."

"What other things?"

543

Stoney Livingston

"Nurse Hollingsworth..."

"Judy."

"Judy. Damnit! I've got the most wonderful girl in the world back in the States. She's more than any man alive deserves. And when I sit this close to you, and you talk to me like a woman instead of a nurse, the thoughts runnin' through my head are anything but noble. Fergive me but that's the simple truth. There's gotta be more to lovin' someone than fergittin' 'em when they're outa sight."

"You're not forgetting her, Jesse. It doesn't have anything to do with that."

The liquor must have affected his thinking. He was at a loss for rebuttal. "Then what does it have to do with, Doctor?"

"You're just responding to a stimulus."

"Yeah, I know all about that stuff. Just like a spider to electricity, huh?"

"Sort of."

"Well, I've had about all of the stimulus I can stand. I'm gettin' outa here." He stood unsteadily.

She stood and assisted him, concern on her face. He limped to the door with her at his side. Once outside in the moonlight, Jesse felt better, but her closeness bothered him. The light scent of her perfume was more intoxicating than the liquor had been. He stopped to lean against the side of a building.

"You okay?" she asked, her face close to his.

"Yeah, I'm just great," he panted. He looked into her eyes for a moment. Gently he pulled her to him. She didn't resist but came into his arms willingly. They kissed a long and soft kiss. It was tender and moist. Jesse was acutely aware of her body pressed against his.

He broke the kiss as gently as it had started. His heavy breathing slowed and he said, "Judy, you are one fine woman and I can't imagine anything more inviting than spending a night with you, but, even if you were willin', I just found out I could never do it. I've got Barbara."

Judy Hollingsworth's heavy breathing tapered off. "So that's her name? Well, all I've got to say is, she is one mighty lucky woman. This is a first for me. I'm not that easy, you know."

"I never thought you were." He still held her closely.

"Oh, Jesse, why is life so cruel sometimes?"

"Maybe it's because we're so stupid." He felt her warm breath on his lips.

"I can't argue with that."

He traced the outline of her lips with his eyes in the moonlight. "Judy?"

"Yes?"

"I don't think Barbara would mind just one more kiss – if you wouldn't."

They stood against the side of the building, in the bright moonlight, bodies pressing tightly together, and kissed softly for a long moment.

When they both broke the tender embrace, Judy Hollingsworth spoke first. "I feel like you just made love to me."

"I guess I kinda' did, in a way."

"I've never experienced anything like that."

"It was the best thing that's happened to me in this country." Jesse stared at her face.

"I may live long enough to forget many men but I'll never forget you or this night, Jesse. May God always keep you safe from harm and deliver you back to your Barbara."

Forever Patriots

"Thanks, Judy. I won't be forgettin' you either." He looked around him. "I guess I'd better be gettin' back to the ward, huh?"

"I'll walk with you."

"No, I'd rather go alone. I don't know how strong I am and I don't wanna test myself anymore. The thought of you in my arms is kinda' overpowering."

Judy Hollingsworth bit her upper lip and nodded. "I understand. I'll see you tomorrow on the ward."

"Goodnight, Judy."

"Goodnight, Jesse."

As she approached his bed, memories of the night before danced through Jesse's head. She was a pretty woman and, on this morning, she seemed even prettier and more vivacious than she ever had. Her eyes twinkled as she stood at his bedside with a thermometer in her hand.

"Good morning, Nurse Hollingsworth."

The twinkle in her eye faded.

"May I call you Judy?" He asked.

The twinkle returned. "You're the only one around here who doesn't."

"Let's start over. Good morning, Judy."

"Good morning, Captain Indio."

Jesse shot a nervous glance at the man in the bed next to him. The man ignored them, absorbed in a magazine.

Jesse lowered his voice. "Gettin' kinda' brave, promotin' me to captain, aren't you?"

"Actually, I've promoted you to general but I don't want to intimidate the rest of the men on the ward." Her smile was genuine and beautiful. That ever-present lock of hair fell into her eyes.

"Do I get private quarters?"

"Definitely!"

"Maybe I'd better not. I like to live like my men."

Nurse Hollingsworth sat on the edge of his bed, her eyes opened wide. "Do you know how important last night was to me?"

Jesse thought the man next to him looked up from his magazine but he couldn't be certain. He whispered, "Judy, you've gotta work here. Don't let people start talkin' and makin' it into something it wasn't. Don't give 'em any ammo."

"I don't care about that, Jesse. They can't hurt me. I know you're going home to a girl you really love and I'm happy for you. I'm just so glad that I had that experience with you that I can't explain how I feel."

The man next to him sat, staring at them, his magazine thrown carelessly on his bedspread.

Jesse lowered his voice. "Judy. Are you crazy? These guys are gonna get the idea that you're going to bed with patients and they'll kill themselves linin' up."

She glanced at the marine in the bed next to Jesse's. "Okay, whatever you say. Open up. I've got to take your temperature."

Jesse remained apprehensive about Judy's actions for the remainder of the day. His concern was for her. Maybe he would never understand women. Maybe he was better off if he didn't.

Late that afternoon he waited in the property room of the hospital, standing

545

casually by, while the orderly checked his release slip.

"Everything seems to be in order here. Hang on a second while I get your property," said the orderly as he stood and stepped into the room behind him.

Jesse waited nervously until the man reappeared with his Bowie knife and money. He signed the proffered document and left the room quickly. He was out the hospital door and halfway to the road at its entrance when he heard Judy's voice.

"Jesse Langley, wait a minute!"

He turned to see her running gracefully towards him, her white smock flowing behind her.

She was out of breath when she reached his side. "Where are you going?" she panted.

"Back to my outfit."

"But you aren't due for release for three or four more days."

"I got an early release."

"An early release – from whom?"

"That Commander Dunn."

Judy looked at the Bowie knife on his right hip. "You're lying. He didn't give you an early release. You still have the wires in your leg." She pointed to the sharp bulges in his left trouser thigh.

Jesse stepped close. "Shhh! Okay, so I got my hands on a release slip and forged the good doctor's name. I've gotta get back to my outfit."

"But Jesse, you can't even walk without a limp yet!"

"Almost."

"Why are you doing this? Is it because of me? If it is, come back. I promise I won't even talk to you. Give it a few more days and let the leg heal. Please."

"I'm okay, Judy. I really am. I feel great. I left you a note by the way."

"A note? How could you do this, Jesse?" she scolded.

Jesse grinned sheepishly. "It seemed like the thing to do at the time."

"Like kissing me in the moonlight? Did that just seem like the thing to do at the time?"

"That's a low blow, Judy."

She looked into his grey eyes solemnly. "I'm sorry. I didn't really mean that."

"I sure hope not. I'm proud to know you, Judy, and don't make anything out of my leavin' other than what it is. I'm goin' back to my outfit. That's all. Nothin' more or less."

"I can stop you."

"Yeah, you can. But you won't."

"What makes you so sure?"

"I've gotta go, Judy. I've got a late start and I've gotta find out where my outfit is."

"Kiss me good bye, Jesse."

He put his arms around her and kissed her quickly, then turned without a word and limped down the path to the road, Judy waving goodbye as he turned the corner.

A Mighty-Mite pulled up next to him on the dirt road as he limped on the uneven shoulder. "Where you headed, Marine?"

He turned to face a lieutenant colonel and his driver. "I'm tryin' to find transportation to the DMZ, Sir. I just got out of the hospital and I gotta find my own way back."

The colonel mumbled to his driver, "Seems like a damned strange way of doing things to me." He turned to Jesse. "What's your outfit, Marine?"

"Alpha, One-Four, Sir."

"Hop in, I'll give you a lift to the ferry."

"The ferry, Sir?"

"Jesus Christ! Didn't they even tell you how to get to the airstrip?"

"Oh. That's right. The ferry. I almost forgot. Thank you, Sir." He climbed into the small jeep and sat behind the colonel.

When the colonel and his driver deposited him within a block of the ferry, Jesse felt alone and defenseless. The hour was late and he had only his knife as a weapon. He limped to the ferry only to find that it had recently left on its last trip of the day. His fear intensified.

In the lengthening shadows he searched for an American Marine or an ARVN soldier. He found neither. *Where the hell are the MPs when you need 'em?* Maybe it was his imagination but the stares of the Vietnamese seemed to take on a more hostile air as dusk deepened over the city.

He walked cautiously down the sidewalk of a large paved street, staying close to the buildings on his side of the roadway and peering at the rows of buildings opposite him as he continued his trek in search of shelter for the night.

"Pssst! Hey G.I. You come here."

He spun around, Bowie knife instantly in his hand. A Vietnamese woman stood inside the doorway of a large building. She jumped back a pace at his sudden move. "Who are you?" asked Jesse, eyes darting from side to side.

"No question. You come inside quick. Boo Coo VC!"

He could be walking into a trap but he felt his options were limited at this late hour. He stepped into the building and was awestruck by the spaciousness of the large room. "What is this place?"

The Mama-San did not seem to understand his words. "You stay. Come back." She disappeared down a large hallway. Shortly, a more elegantly dressed Vietnamese woman in her early thirties appeared in the hallway. She took in Jesse's appearance with a glance.

"You come for boom-boom?"

He had stumbled into a Vietnamese whorehouse.

"Yeah. How much all night?"

"How many girls?"

Jesse smiled. "Just one."

The woman seemed disappointed. "One only?" She patted the front of his trousers. "Big G.I. Need more one girl all night, longtime."

Jesse shook his head. "Only one. All night longtime. How much?"

The woman rolled her eyes. "For all night longtime, one girl, you give me twenty dollars."

"Twenty dollars?"

"Numba one boom boom. Little pussy. Sucky-fucky. You like shaved pussy?"

"I don't care." He handed her two brown ten-dollar bills, careful not to expose his large bankroll.

She stuck the bills into her bra and led him to a wicker sliding door. She slid the door open and motioned him inside. He shook his head. "I wanna see the girl

547

first."

She walked down the hallway and disappeared around a corner, returning shortly with a Vietnamese girl in her late teens. She wasn't that much younger than Jesse but, for some reason, he felt much older.

The house madam gestured to the young girl. "See? Numba one boom-boom."

"Okay." He stepped inside the room and gently pulled the girl behind him. Quickly he closed the door and latched the flimsy lock. When he turned around, the girl was already naked. She had simply let her silken robe fall from her body.

He looked at her nakedness and noticed that her crotch was shaved clean. Her small young breasts were taut and firm and her chest gave way to a slim waist and slender hips. He slapped himself in the face and looked at the ceiling. "Barbara, I hope you appreciate how much I love you." He motioned to the girl to put her robe on.

She remained naked, standing across the room from him. Again Jesse pointed to her robe. "It's okay. Put the robe on."

Jesse spent most of the night holding the girl to his body with one hand and holding his knife in the other. He knew he had erred in his decision to leave the hospital so late in the day but there was nothing he could do but play it through. The cards had already been dealt. The girl's body would offer some protection if the VC came after him, but he held no illusions about the final outcome should that event occur.

Just before dawn, he quietly left the bordello for the streets of Da Nang, leaving the girl one hundred dollars. She had been quiet and cooperative, unaware that her only function for Jesse was to provide a shield in the event the VC entered the building. For her innocence she should be paid something.

Jesse waited for the first grey of dawn then made his way to the ferry crossing. He waited as inconspicuously as he could until just before the first departure of the day, when he rushed to board the overcrowded ferry.

The crossing was short but tense for Jesse as he searched in vain for another American. Once safely ashore on the other side, he was approached by a well-dressed Vietnamese sporting a white suit and white hat.

"Hey, Marine! May we speak?"

Somewhat surprised by the man's apparent fluency in English, Jesse answered, "Go ahead."

The man moved close and whispered, "You want boom-boom?"

Jesse smiled. "It's a little too early for me, my friend."

"It won't cost you anything," whispered the man.

"Wait a minute. How do you make any money givin' away free boom-boom?"

The little man looked about nervously. "You go to PX. Buy for me a stereo. I give you two girls. One time each."

"Oh, I get it. I buy you a stereo and you let me have a couple of girls. How much is the stereo?"

"No! No! I give you the money to buy stereo. You no pay any money. You buy for me. I give you two girls. One time each."

"I'm gonna buy you a stereo, with your money, and you're gonna give me two girls?"

548

The little man nodded and smiled.

"How do you make any money on that deal?"

The little man frowned. "Sell stereo. Boo-Coo money!"

Jesse laughed. "Either you're underpaying your girls, or overchargin' for the stereo."

"You want boom-boom?" The little man's voice became impatient.

Jesse thought about the advantages of accepting the little man's offer. "How do I get to the PX?"

"I take you. We go now?"

"Yeah. Sure. We go now."

The Vietnamese motioned him into an old Renault.

The ride from the ferry to the PX at the Da Nang airstrip seemed long to Jesse, but he was sure the trip was lengthened in his mind by his feeling of helplessness. He occupied his mind by studying the buildings and the people as they progressed through the busy city. Once again, he was taken by the western architecture. It didn't fit, in his mind, with the dress of the Vietnamese people. Something seemed out of place.

The car pulled into a small drive and came to a stop. The little man exited the vehicle quickly and bid Jesse do the same. He followed the man in the white suit into a small building with several bamboo partitions. He knew that in each sectioned off area there was a bed of some kind on which the prostitutes could ply their trade.

A swarthy Vietnamese sat behind a badly worn desk in what appeared to be an office. He glanced up as the two approached. The little man in the white suit spoke rapidly in Vietnamese and the swarthy one left the room. The little man turned to Jesse. "My name is Joe. My friend bring girls for you to see."

"That's okay, Joe. I trust you. Just show me the PX, and I'll get you the stereo."

"No! No! You see girls. Joe is honest businessman. Maybe we do more business." He offered a bottle of beer. Jesse accepted. He was on his second swallow of beer when the swarthy one returned with two prostitutes. One was in her early thirties and had the tough look of extensive experience. The other appeared little more than sixteen years old. She looked young but Jesse was sure she too would someday have the hard look of the older woman.

Joe waved his arm proudly at the two girls. "You see? Numba one boom-boom."

"Okay, Joe. Numba one boom-boom. Now where is the PX?"

Jesse received instructions and money from the little man and left shortly after finishing his morning beer. The PX was only two blocks from Joe's office. Jesse was glad it was so close. His leg hurt when he walked.

Inside the large PX, Jesse glanced about nervously as he searched for the stereo he was instructed to purchase. At last he located the unit in one corner of the large building. Quickly he scooped up the two cartons containing the system and made his way to the front.

He felt a wave of relief as he crossed the street to Joe's office, the stereo system tucked safely under his arm. How silly he had been to harbor such unfounded fears. When he had presented his ration card to the clerk, the man had acted as though he sold a dozen stereos a day. Jesse whistled off-key as he entered Joe's office. The little man greeted him with a smile and relieved him of his burden. Immediately he called to his two girls, who responded by rushing into the office.

549

Jesse smiled and patted Joe on the shoulder. "No, thanks, Joe. It was worth it to me just to get the ride to the base."

Joe's face fell. "You no like girls?"

Jesse beamed. "I love girls. But I'm in a big hurry. Gotta go DMZ. Fight VC."

Joe pointed to Jesse's left thigh. One of the sharp ends of the wire had already worn a small hole in the material and the metal protruded into the open. "VC?"

Jesse nodded.

"You go kill VC now?"

Again he nodded.

"You have time for maybe one boom-boom?"

Jesse laughed loudly. "Not today, Joe. I've gotta go."

The little man shook his hand. "You come back. You have free boom-boom. Joe say so."

"Thanks, Joe." He waved goodbye and walked toward the base, only two blocks away, his leg indicating already that it had been used enough for the day.

An hour later, as he sat with his back to the wall of a concrete building, contemplating the foolishness of his early departure from the hospital, he was approached by an Air Force sergeant.

"You lost, Marine?"

Jesse looked up from his sitting position. He exhaled his cigarette smoke and answered the thin black man with the Air Force version of staff sergeant stripes on his dungaree collars. "Lost as hell, Sarge."

"What you lookin' for?"

"A ride outa this place – to my outfit."

"Where's your outfit?"

"I'm not really sure. Last I heard they were in the DMZ at a place called the Rockpile."

The sergeant stood over him, rubbing his chin. "Seems to me like the first step is to find out where your outfit is *now*."

"That sounds simple enough but I can't even find a chopper pad on this damn place, much less where a Marine Company is located out in the bush."

The Air Force staff sergeant glanced at his watch. "You hungry?"

"I could use a bite. I had a beer for breakfast several hours ago, but it isn't holdin' up too well. I don't think beer sticks to the stomach so good."

The tall black man smiled and extended his right hand. "I'm Walt Greenway."

Painfully, Jesse stood and accepted Greenway's hand. "Jesse Langley, recently of the First Battalion, Fourth Marines."

"You hurt, man?"

"I just got out of the hospital. I guess I'm not quite a hundred percent yet. I been on this leg since about five this morning and it's startin' to bother me a little."

"Let's go to the club and grab some lunch. We can find your outfit after chow. You want some help?"

"No, thanks. I can make it if you're not in a big hurry."

Greenway walked slowly to the NCO Club, Jesse struggling to keep up. Once seated inside the air-conditioned building, a Vietnamese waiter took their order and moved quickly away to fill their requests.

"This is unbelievable," said Jesse. "You guys live like this all the time or is this just something you can come to once or twice a month?"

Greenway smiled. "This is where I eat three times a day, every day."

"Nice touch."

"I know you marines got it tough out there."

"Oh, I didn't mean to imply that we got it so rough. I was just kinda' taken in by it all, I guess."

"No offense taken. The fact is, we live like kings over here while you guys are livin' like animals out in the bush. Hell, there isn't a stateside duty station as good as this one. Even with all the heat and humidity I've put on five pounds since I been here. There's all the booze and women you could ever want, and the duty hours are shorter because of the heat."

Jesse smiled and shook his head. "You make it sound almost like Shangri La."

"Hell, it is. I'm extending at the end of my tour. I'll stay here as long as the Air Force will let me. This is great duty."

Another black man approached the table. Jesse was introduced to the newcomer, a young sergeant from Kansas City, named Watson. Greenway explained Jesse's predicament and, at the end of his explanation, Watson said, "I'll get the info on your outfit right after chow."

"Can you do that?" asked Jesse.

"Hell, ol' Watt here works in logistics. If anybody can find out where your outfit is, he can," said Greenway.

Two more men joined them at the large round table. They all appeared concerned for Jesse's well being and each asked for stories of his combat experience. He generalized a few of his experiences and that seemed to satisfy them for the moment. Jesse had difficulty understanding why he was being so well treated by the airmen. There seemed to be no inter-service rivalry. He couldn't remember when he had enjoyed himself more while in the company of airmen than he did on this day.

Greenway excused himself an hour into lunch but left Jesse in the capable care of Watson. He remained at the table for the better part of the afternoon as the airmen came and went. At no time was Jesse without at least two airmen at his table.

Watson left the table to return an hour later. He sat down with a smile that covered his entire face. "I found your outfit, but if you'd a' gone lookin' for 'em in the DMZ, you'd a' come up empty-handed."

"Where are they?" Jesse asked anxiously.

"Up near Hue."

"Hue?" He thought of the Vietnamese girl and her family. That had been a long time ago. It almost seemed as if it hadn't happened. He wondered if he would be able to visit with them.

"Yeah. They're actually a little south and west of there." Watson read his watch. "I don't think you're gonna be able to get there yet today but you'll be able to hitch a ride on a Huey in the morning."

"A Huey? Army?"

"Naw. You Marines got Hueys. More and more, now that they're phasing out the UH-34," replied Watson.

"But I can't get out there until tomorrow?"

"That's it."

551

Greenway, who had just returned, spoke from behind Jesse. "Don't sweat a place to stay, man. We've got all kinds of room at my barracks."

"Barracks?"

"Yeah. Barracks. What do they call 'em in the Marines?"

Jesse laughed. "Barracks, I guess. Do you mean tents, or real barracks?"

"Tents." scoffed Greenway. "Get real, man. I'm talkin' 'bout an air conditioned building here."

"I appreciate the offer, but I'd really like to try to make it to my outfit."

"We'll try, man, but I'm telling ya', it looks mighty slim for today," said Watson. "I'll tell you what. Let me go talk to one other guy and I'll be right back." He left the table and Greenway sat in his chair.

Jesse began to feel as if he had been born in the chair in which he was sitting. He had been in it for several hours and wanted any excuse to get up and leave, but these men were treating him like a celebrity. He felt a camaraderie for the Air Force men that he was at a loss to explain.

As the afternoon wore on the drinking began in earnest. Though Jesse had more than ample money to buy drinks for the whole club, the airmen would not allow him to spend a dime. They oohed and aahed over his bloodstained trousers and flinched at the unsightly wires now protruding through the cloth on his left thigh.

Jesse came to the conclusion that there were two wars taking place in Vietnam, and he wished he were part of the second one. Of course, he couldn't become a part of it unless all of the men in his outfit were able to participate, so that seemed like an unlikely happening. What the guys in his outfit would give for just one cold beer, never mind the air-conditioned barracks or clubs where you ordered chow like in a restaurant back home, or the excitement of the city, or the relative safety of the large military complex at Da Nang.

He thought of how they had lived for so long. Even when they thought they had it good in Sherwood Forest or that short time in Phu Bai, they had nothing. He looked at the friendly faces at the table and knew without proof these men wouldn't survive a month what he and his outfit had endured for almost a year. He liked them but they were not marines. They would never understand. They would probably all go home and tell their friends how they had won the war almost single-handedly, while guys like Faye and JJ and Bean never got to tell anybody anything.

They didn't know what it was like to stay awake all night on the perimeter of a company position, surrounded by superior numbers of VC, drenched by torrential rains, without the hope of a hot shower or a dry building anywhere in sight. *Look at 'em. They've got spit-shined boots and shiny emblems. Targets for VC rifles.*

You're losin' it, Jesse. Not everyone gets to be a hero. Not everyone is stupid.

"You okay, man?"

Jesse looked blankly at Greenway for but a second. "Yeah. I'm okay. I was just thinkin' some dumb thoughts is all."

"You looked far away there for a minute, man."

"I guess I was. But I'm back now." He looked around the table. Extra chairs had been drawn up to accommodate the swelling numbers. "You guys ready for another round?"

Cheerfully those at the table voiced their assent. Jesse ordered drinks for everybody but, when the beer and liquor arrived, they would not allow him to pay. To be friendly was one thing but such overwhelming friendliness and generosity was

Forever Patriots

more than Jesse could comprehend. He turned to Greenway.

"You guys are great. I really appreciate it, but why are you treatin' me like a Goddamned king? Hell, you won't even let me buy one round of drinks."

The table fell silent. For a moment no one spoke. Greenway stared into Jesse's eyes and said, "I guess, the truth of the matter is, we're glad we got guys like you out there. We know it sucks. We don't know like you know, but we know. We see the marines comin' in all shot up, or wrapped in ponchos. We know that we've got it dicked here. You guys got the short end of the stick. We live like goddamn royalty while you guys are out there makin' it possible. I guess you might say we all feel we owe you guys somethin' – somethin' we ain't never gonna be able to pay – but we're gonna make small installments whenever we get a chance."

There was an awkward silence around the table. Jesse waited a moment for someone to speak. No one moved. He cleared his throat and smiled at Greenway. "Damn, Walt, you oughta be a politician. I'd vote for ya in a minute."

The men at the table burst into uproarious laughter.

Early the following morning, Jesse took a hot shower and dressed quietly before the barracks came alive. He left a note for Greenway and was gone before first light.

He met the Huey helicopter at the designated time and place, per Watson's instructions, and was on his way to the First Battalion, Fourth Marines at oh-seven-thirty. As he sat in the smooth-running ramjet helicopter, he was struck by the feeling of power and lack of vibration given off by the smaller craft. He held in check his impulse to ask the pilot's permission to take the stick, and waited patiently for some sign of friendly troops below.

CHAPTER TWENTY-FOUR: PRAIRIE II

Jesse exited the helicopter, helped set the mailbags on the moist ground, and stepped off in the direction of the headquarters tents. He stumbled by chance into a large tent that turned out to be the battalion armory. The memory of his first morning in Vietnam and his experience with the battalion armorer rushed into his mind as he saw the neat rows of M-14s stacked against the inside of the tent.

A sergeant stepped from behind a stack of ammo boxes. Jesse recognized him from somewhere but couldn't place him.

The sergeant smiled. "Finally got tired of the good life, huh?"

"Yeah. I couldn't stand the luxury anymore." Jesse still struggled for recognition.

The sergeant offered his hand. "Carpenter. I was with Lieutenant Rowe when he had the accidental discharge with that M-79."

"Oh, yeah. Whatever happened to the good lieutenant?"

"He got transferred to the rear. I guess they figured he was more dangerous to us than he was to the VC."

"That breaks my heart."

"I figured it might."

"While I'm here, what are the chances of drawin' a weapon?"

"What d'ya want?"

"I'd like an M-1, but I don't see any."

"You won't – ARVN gets 'em all."

"You got a spare M-60?"

"Damn. You like firepower, or what?"

"I feel naked with that damn M-14."

"You in the weapons platoon?" asked Carpenter.

"No. I'm the 81 F.O. for Alpha."

Carpenter turned to the only M-60 in the armory. He picked it up an placed it on the plank counter separating him from Jesse. "This is the only M-60 I've got that isn't really accounted for. I haven't had a chance to check it out yet but you're welcome to it until I find out who it belongs to."

Jesse smiled. "I'll take it. I'll be attached to Alpha if you need it back."

He signed for the machine-gun, less tripods, and left the tent with two one-hundred-round belts of ammunition draped over his shoulders, in search of the eighty-one platoon.

The platoon was a bustle of activity as he approached the FDC tent. He stepped inside and was greeted by Tuleano.

"Indio, what the hell you doin' here, man? You crazy? You oughta be takin' it easy with some round-eye nurse."

He thought briefly of Judy Hollingsworth. "I tried that, Tule. It didn't work out.

So how are you?"

"Short. Six weeks and a wake-up and I'm outa here."

"Congratulations." He paused. "What's all the activity? Looks like we're fixin' to mount out."

"We are. First thing in the morning."

"Where to this time?"

"We don't know yet. Word has it that we're goin' on an operation they're gonna call Prairie Two."

Jesse shook his head. "Not much imagination at top levels these days, is there?"

Tuleano smiled. "Hasn't been since the 'Old Corps'."

"How are the rest of the guys?"

"They're okay."

"All of 'em still here?"

"Yeah, 'ceptin' the ones that rotated home. There's been a little rearrangement in the sections, but nothing major. Bailey went home last week. Ramirez, Hill and Ruddleston are in the First Section now."

"How about Rich and Cue?"

"They're still here." Tule pointed to the machine-gun. "What the hell you doin' with that thing?"

"Nothin' yet, but I'm fixin' ta go huntin' VC."

Tuleano laughed. "You better get on down and see the guys. I'm sure Malcolm wants you back."

"Who's his FO?"

"Bailey was until he left last week. Since we been here, we haven't been attached. Rich is scheduled to move out with Alpha in the morning, but he's about the best gunner in the platoon since you aren't here. I'm sure he'll be glad to see you back. He's not lookin' forward to goin' out there with the grunts."

Jesse smiled. "It does take some gettin' used to. Well, I guess I better be goin, Tule. After I talk to the guys, I'll be reportin' to Alpha. Who's my radio operator?"

"Marrs."

"Where is he?"

"He's probably down on gun one with Rich. I know he was one happy sonofabitch when Bailey rotated."

"I can't imagine why," Jesse said dryly. "Well, I'll be seein' ya, Tule. Tell the platoon commander I'm back."

"Keep yer ass low out there, Indio."

"You too, Tule. You more than me – you're the short-timer."

Rich Cummings was cleaning his rifle as Jesse limped into the gunpit. They embraced and shared a warm reunion. Cue and the rest of the gun crew joined in and soon the rest of the section was congregated in the gun one pit. Several members of the other sections drifted to the pit during the course of the hour Jesse spent renewing acquaintances.

At the end of the hour, Jesse turned to Marr. "How about it, Charlie? You ready to go back out to the grunts with me?"

Marr smiled. "After Bailey and his damn book, I'd go anywhere with you or

555

Rich."

     Chuckles made their way around the gun pit.

*****

     Malcolm studied Jesse with a smile on his handsome face. "You sure are a hard man to get rid of." He moved forward and shook Jesse's hand. "It's good to see you, Indio."

     "It's good to see you, Skipper."

     Malcolm pointed to the bulge in the middle of Jesse's left thigh. "What the hell is that?"

     "It's just the stitches. Hell, they used balin' wire to sew me up."

     Malcolm squinted. "Did you get released from the hospital?"

     "It was boring as hell there, Sir. I used a phoney release form and got out a few days early – that's all. I feel great."

     "How's the leg?"

     "It's okay. It'll get stronger in a few days."

     "We're gonna be doin' a lot of walking in the next few days."

     "I can handle it, Sir."

     Malcolm shook his head, the smile still on his face. "Okay, but if you start hurting, let me know right away."

     "I will, Sir."

     That night Jesse rested without the responsibility of perimeter duty and his leg felt strong when he awakened just before dawn. The short walk to the trucks didn't bother him, nor did the bumpy ride to Highway One.

     He relived the battle of Hue as they drove through the city. He was able to glimpse the house where Bingham had committed his vile act. It appeared to have been repaired from his distant point of view. He felt a sadness that he could not stop and say hello to the girl and her family. He wondered if the younger girl was still alive or if she had succumbed to her head injury.

     He watched the City of Hue disappear behind them as the rumbling six-by continued towards the DMZ. He took one last look at the old capital.

     They debarked the trucks on the southern edge of the DMZ and marched west, then north and west. The pace was fast and the morning sun merciless as the battalion snaked its way along the well-worn trail. It seemed they had been marching for weeks when the battalion stopped for its first break of the day, just before noon.

     Jesse lit a cigarette, grateful for the respite. Marr sat against a boulder not far away, his radio still on his back, supported by an outcropping of rock.

     "Don't say anything to me about me takin' over after you've been hit. It wasn't such good luck last time," Marr panted.

     "Not a word," replied Jesse solemnly. He drew the cigarette smoke deeply into his lungs and exhaled slowly, searching the lush green hillsides with his eyes. His leg bothered him somewhat but it was not as bad as he had expected it would be. On several occasions the protruding wires had snagged on vegetation but only once did it cause a major discomfort. Mostly it was just an irritant to the ease of his progress in heavy growth.

     He scratched softly through his trousers at the skin surrounding the wires. *Damn things. The hospital was gonna take 'em out in two more days. Maybe I could get rid of 'em a day or two early.* The order to resume the march gave him no more time to think about his problem.

556

The terrain became more mountainous as the column moved further west. Every man was loaded down with ammunition and gear and the going was difficult. Jesse had yet to see Thunder since his return. The young sergeant had been on a patrol when Jesse had arrived at the company and, when he returned from the patrol, he had joined his platoon on perimeter duty.

In the early afternoon Jesse observed a flight of Marine A-4 Skyhawks bombing the hills before them. He watched as the nimble craft dove towards the ground then pulled skyward in a smooth arc. As they nosed upward, Jesse watched the barrels of napalm released by the pilots as the big drums tumbled upward for a short distance then fell silently to the ground to erupt into glowing orange balls of flame, quickly covered by thick black smoke.

The battalion struggled forward, their only resistance being that of the terrain and nature. The heat was stifling.

As Jesse climbed the steep slopes of a burned-out hill he stopped to help those behind him. His burden was heavy but the rest at the hospital had given him strength and put flesh on his bones. He made several trips up and down the hill, his own gear left at the top, as he struggled to assist others.

After a while he could make no more trips up and down the hill. He was exhausted. On his last trip to the top he handed an unknown PFC his rifle and said, "Keep movin'."

A marine stood next to him at the top of the hill, shouting words of encouragement to the men below who had yet to master it. Jesse wasn't certain who the man was but he had the look of a staff sergeant about him. He turned to the man, nearly out of breath from his previous efforts, and said, "They're about at their limit, Sarge. I don't think they're gonna make it much further at this pace."

The man glanced at him and said, "They're doing fine. We don't have much farther to go. If you can climb that hill as many times as you have, they can climb it once."

Jesse didn't want to go into the story of his rest and recuperation at the hospital. He shrugged. "I'm tellin' ya, these guys are about give out." He paused. "You got it covered here?"

The man nodded.

"I'm gonna try to catch up to my position."

"Go ahead. Thanks for your help and inspiration."

Jesse took one last glance at the man before he moved on. *Inspiration? Damn strange word for an NCO to use in the field.*

Two hours later, the battalion stopped for the day. Men sprawled upon the ground, relieving themselves of their burdens and gasping for oxygen. Word was passed down the line to test fire all weapons. Jesse waited patiently for his turn to fire the untried machine-gun.

When his turn arrived he winked at his exhausted radio operator and pulled the trigger. The gun fired twice then jammed. He cleared the breech and re-cocked the weapon. His second attempt was no more successful than his first. He repeated the procedure three times, checking the gun carefully in between each attempt. He could find nothing wrong but the gun would fire no more than two or three rounds before jamming. He sat disgustedly as the next man down the line test-fired his rifle.

Jesse looked at Marr. "I've been carryin' around a damn boat anchor all day long."

"Boat anchor?"

557

Stoney Livingston

"It ain't good for much else, is it? Hell, you can't even put a bayonet on the end of the damn thing." He sat silently, contemplating his next move. He would attempt to have the gun taken out on the next supply run.

No sooner had he made his decision to have the gun evacuated than a Huey landed at the base of the hill occupied by Alpha Company. Two men moved in his direction from higher up on the hill. They carried a man in a stretcher. He turned to Marr. "Did you hear about any activity up in front of us?"

"Not a peep. Somebody broke an ankle and is gettin' lifted out is all."

As the stretcher-bearers passed his position, Jesse recognized the injured man as a member of the weapons platoon attached to Alpha's first platoon. He jumped up and moved to him. "Danforth, what happened? You guys get hit?"

The marines carrying Danforth stopped their progress while he responded to Jesse's question. "Naw, goddamnit. I slipped on a fuckin' rock and fell about twenty feet. Broke my damned ankle."

Jesse noticed the M-60 on the stretcher beside Danforth. His eyes brightened. "Hey, Danforth, my M-60 is down. You mind if I swap for yours?"

Danforth smiled. "Why the hell would I mind? It ain't gonna do me any good. You're welcome to it. Just give me yours so I'll have something to turn in back at battalion."

The swap was made quickly and Danforth continued to the waiting helicopter. Jesse received permission to test fire the gun. He smiled mischievously at Marr upon the successful completion of three short bursts.

The battalion moved out shortly before dawn. The order of march was changed and Alpha Company now held the point. Mid-morning, as the company spread out over relatively gentle slopping terrain, Jesse froze in his tracks. He looked down between his legs and found the log he straddled was, in fact, a five-hundred-pound bomb. He felt a tingling sensation in his testicles as the thought of the bomb exploding ran through his mind.

"Charlie!" He shouted to his radio operator. "Freeze! I'm straddlin' a five-hundred-pound dud!"

"Oh, shit!" Marr's voice carried to him.

"Turn that radio off and back up about four hundred yards then turn it on and call the skipper. Tell 'im we need combat engineers up here to blow this thing."

"You got it."

"And, Charlie, don't key up till you got that four hundred yards. I don't know what kind of fuse this thing's got."

"Roger."

Carefully, Jesse lifted his leg over the live bomb and backed slowly down the slope. He held his distance at one hundred yards and waited for the engineers.

After Jesse's discovery of the unexploded bomb, and once it was rendered non-existent by the engineers, the battalion moved forth with more caution, afraid more of unexploded American bombs than they were the VC. A full day was added to the operational schedule due to the slower movement. The battalion dug in early that afternoon in a peaceful valley where the rifle companies could easily control the ridge lines. Jesse returned to the mortar positions to assist in the digging of gunpits in the hard clay soil.

With thirty minutes hard labor behind him Jesse put down his borrowed entrenching tool and turned to Rich. "You know, Rich, we ain't all that smart."

"No shit. So what's new?"

"I'm serious. Think about these gunpits for a minute. We been diggin' the better part of half-an-hour and we've hardly dented the surface."

"So?"

Jesse pointed an index finger to his temple. "Let's dig these gunpits with our brains instead of our backs."

Rich looked at the hard soil and the puny results heretofore attained. "I guess we couldn't do much worse than we've been doin' with our backs. So what devious plan in yonder mind lurks?"

"The combat engineers."

Rich's eyes lit up. "You think they'd blow the holes for us?"

"If they got clearance from the old man they would. And we all know what a chickenshit ol' Colonel Dumbshit is. If he thinks he can have the guns safely nestled in quicker, I'll bet he gives the okay faster'n you can say, 'Fire in the hole'."

"Hell yes. Let's go talk to Tule."

Fifteen minutes later the gun crews sat, watching, as the engineers placed their charges in the small holes drilled into the soil. Rich puffed grandly on his filter cigarette and beamed at Jesse as he leaned back against a large tree. "This is the only way to dig a gunpit."

"I agree with that shit," said Cue, sitting next to Rich.

There were smiles and nods among the gun crews.

Once the charges were all in place, the engineers casually ignited the slow burning fuses. One of them said, "Fire in the hole!" and the men watched contentedly as the smoke from the burning fuses worked slowly toward the C-4 explosive charges.

"Wonder why they didn't use det-cord and blow 'em all at once?" mused Jesse.

Cue said, "They were going to but they're runnin' short of det-cord and they've got plenty of fuse left."

"Oh."

"Dey'll be startin' ta blow in a second now anyways," said Ski.

"Oh, shit!"

"What's the matter, Rich?" asked Jesse.

Rich pointed to the horizon. "The resupply choppers are comin' in! They're gonna sit down right in the middle of the pits!"

Cue jumped to his feet, waving his arms back and forth across the front of his body. The three old Choctaws continued their approach, unaware of the imminent danger before them.

"Somebody throw a red smoke," ordered Jesse as he ran to Cue's side, waving his arms frantically. A wisp of red smoke appeared in the air above their heads as someone threw a smoke grenade as far as he could throw it in the direction of the advancing helicopters. Marr searched his radio frequencies furiously to find the inbound helicopters and warn them.

Jesse glanced at the nearest fuse. He grabbed Cue and threw him to the ground just as the charge ignited. The hard soil shook and vibrated as it tore away from itself and flew skyward.

A second explosion quickly followed the first, thirty yards distant. The leading helicopter angled sharply forward and flew at maximum speed through the exploding charges, its heavy frame at a sharp angle to the ground, the big rotor clearing the soil by inches. The two helicopters behind the lead ship averted disaster by veering to the flanks. The marines on the ground breathed a sigh of relief as the leading helicopter flew over the last charge just before it ignited.

Jesse and Cue stood, brushing themselves. Jesse laughed nervously. "I didn't know those ol' grasshoppers could fly that fast."

"I'll bet that pilot didn't either," said Rich with his own nervous laugh.

"You guys okay?" asked Ramirez as Jesse limped to his position and sat gingerly down on the ground.

"Yeah, I think so. But I think I got one of these wires twisted and jammed into my leg." Carefully he loosened his trousers and pulled them down to his knees.

"Holy shit, Indio, you need a corpsman," said Rich.

One of the wire sutures had twisted and buried almost an inch into his leg. He winced then replied in a tone filled with disgust. "No, I don't need a corpsman, I need somebody with a pair of side-cutters. It's time to remove the stitches it looks to me like."

"You *are* kidding?" asked Manny.

He ignored Manny. "Will somebody please find a wireman so I can remove this goddamn aggravation from my leg?"

Salsbury produced a pair of side-cutters.

"Thanks, Sal. What the hell you doin' with side-cutters anyway?"

"I borrowed 'em yesterday and haven't got around to returnin' 'em yet. They work good for holdin' your c-ration can while you're heatin' it with C-3."

"Thanks."

"You're welcome."

The recent plight of the helicopters forgotten, Jesse cut the ends of the steel wires with the cutting pliers. Slowly, and with gritted teeth, he pulled the wires through his flesh until they were free of his body. The entire operation lasted only two minutes.

Jesse breathed a sigh of relief as the last wire came free.

"You takin' up doctorin' now too, Amigo?" asked a calm voice behind him. He twisted his head to see Thunder smiling broadly at him.

"Thunder. Where in the hell have you been?" He stood, pulling his trousers up and advancing to meet his friend in one movement. His trousers properly buttoned, he shook hands with the young sergeant.

"Where have *I* been? Where the hell have *you* been? You get a little scratch and you milk it fer a month. Jesus Christ, I been carryin' this damn pistol and cartridge belt around fer so long, I was about to put in a homestead claim on it." He offered the cartridge belt and its contents.

"Thanks, Thunder. I didn't mean to be gone so long. Hell, I thought I'd be back in a day or two. Didn't work out that way. By the way, I ran into Sandy at an outfit called Charlie Med. He said to say hello."

"Thanks. How you doin'?"

"Better, now that I got rid of those damn stitches."

"You've got some bacitracin left in your first aid pouch. You best use it on that cut."

"Okay, Mama."

The helicopters returned, the confusion behind them, and the men in the eighty-one platoon unloaded the supplies with Thunder's help. With the supplies unloaded, the men went to work clearing the holes blown by the engineers. Thunder joined in as he visited with Jesse.

Later that afternoon, as they cooked their C-rations over the abundant C-3 supplied by their new friends in combat engineers, Thunder laughed and joked with the men in the mortar platoon as if he were one of them. They accepted Thunder. He was a damn good grunt, and he was a friend of Jesse's.

As they sat eating C-rations and drinking the powdered coffee, Thunder watched one of the men absentmindedly as the latter cooked his can of beefsteak and potatoes with gravy over a large chunk of C-3 explosive. Calmly Thunder turned to Jesse. "I knew you guys in eighty-ones liked to play with explosives but don't you think that guy down there is overdoin' it a bit?"

Jesse followed Thunder's finger. He studied the man in question. "He's a new guy. I met him yesterday. You're right though. Somebody oughta tell 'im not to use so much of that stuff. It's a shame to waste it. Who knows? We may need it to blow up a gook bridge someday." He turned his attention back to Thunder.

Suddenly Thunder jumped to his feet. "No!"

Jesse looked in the direction of Thunder's attention just in time to see the new man stomp on the large ball of C-3 burning brightly on the ground. The ensuing explosion lifted the young marine five feet into the air, flipping him three or four times like a rag doll. He thudded back to earth, screaming, his right boot gone, along with the foot that was in it. Blood gushed in spurts from the jagged stump of his leg.

"Corpsman! Corpsman up!" Someone screamed.

Thunder, who had fallen to the ground before the explosion, gained his feet and rushed to the man's aid. Jesse was right behind him. Ski and Cue held the injured man down while Jesse removed his web belt and fashioned a tourniquet. Thunder squeezed the injured man's groin, searching for the large artery, trying to stem the flow of life from the body. Rich mashed his hand against the bloody stub of the man's leg to do his part in stopping the flow of blood.

"Jesus Christ, where's the corpsman?" shouted Thunder, his body awkwardly twisted so that he might attain the best possible angle on the groin.

"He's on the way'!" screamed Sal.

The blood flow slowed. Jesse pulled the belt so tightly the meat inside the bulging skin appeared ready to burst free of its fragile confining shell. "Goddamn! Get that corpsman up here!" he shouted.

A tired and panting corpsman knelt quickly at the injured man's side. Another corpsman followed within seconds of the first. The marines backed away and let the corpsmen go to work.

Jesse moved to Marr's side. "Get a chopper in here to get him the hell out."

"Roger." Marr keyed up his radio handset.

Jesse returned to the injured man to see if he could be of any further assistance.

It took the helicopter almost twenty minutes to arrive but the young marine was still alive when he left the ground. The corpsmen told them he would probably survive, but the likelihood of him losing his leg up to the thigh was great. They never knew for sure. No one in the platoon knew him well enough to write and find out.

That evening, the combat engineers introduced a new weapon to the men of the First Battalion, Fourth Marines: the Claymore Mine.

"What da hell is dat ting?" asked Ski as he studied the odd-shaped object sitting on the ground before the group of marines.

"Looks like a miniature radar antenna to me," said Manny.

Stoney Livingston

"It sure as hell does," agreed Cue.

"Who the hell ever heard of puttin' a mine right out in the open?" asked Sal.

The engineer standing next to the strange-looking device cleared his throat. "That's the beauty of this mine, Gentlemen. It only goes after what you want it to go after." He pointed to a wire trailing away from the mine. "This wire here is connected to this small trigger." He held up a small electrical switch for them to see. "You flip the trigger and – bam! It's all over for whoever or whatever is in front of this thing."

"What we have here is your basic new version of the old-fashioned grapeshot-from-the-end-of-a-cannon trick, right?" asked Jesse.

The engineer agreed. "Basically, that's it. Except that the Claymore has a much wider area of impact. If you have one of these set up on a machine gun position, you can protect a full forty-five degrees with one mine."

Jesse walked away from the crowd with Thunder as the latter made to leave for his squad's position for the night.

"They keep comin' up with better and easier ways of killin', don't they?" asked Thunder as they moved out of earshot of the engineer and the men listening to his class on the Claymore mine.

"Yeah. Maybe someday they'll have so many fancy new weapons, we won't have to come – they can just send the damn weapons to the war."

Thunder laughed. "That's not such a bad idea. What about the other side? They just gonna send their weapons too?"

"Why not? Then we can play this game like the generals. They don't get hurt; we don't get hurt."

Thunder smiled. "Guess what?"

"I give up."

"I heard from Susan."

"My cousin?"

"Who else?"

"How's she doin?"

"She's one fine lady. She asked about you. Seems like you're her favorite cousin. She says you're really a pretty good guy. I got to wonderin' if I had the right Susan for a while there."

"Screw you, Thunder. Tell her I said hello next time you write."

"I already did."

"I guess Alpha's got the rear tomorrow, huh?"

"Yeah. I hate that shit on a movement this size. It seems like you're always runnin' to keep up. The guys in the middle bunch up, then they stretch out. By the time it gets to the poor bastard on the end of the line, he's goin' nuts tryin' ta keep up."

"I know what you mean. I'll be marchin' with the eighty-ones tomorrow. We'll be right in front of Alpha so, if you need some help, just holler."

Thunder looked into the sky at the approaching darkness. "Well, Amigo, I guess I'd better get back up into the hills. I'll be seein' you sometime tomorrow. Keep yer ass low."

"You too."

Dawn found the battalion on the march, winding its way through the rugged terrain, unhampered by anything other than the natural environment. The VC had yet to make their presence known. Even this early in the day the men knew the march would be hard. The pace was rapid, almost careless, the men near the rear of the battalion's movement struggling to keep pace as the long green column of men expanded and contracted like an earthworm on the move.

At ten hundred hours, after more than four hours of forced marching, the battalion was allowed a short break. As the weary men relieved themselves of their respective burdens and sprawled carelessly on the damp foliage and soil, Ski complained, "What da hell's da matter wid dese fuckin' people? Dey tryin' ta kill us before da VC get a shot, or what?"

Hill, out of breath and panting from the weight of the outer baseplate ring and three rounds of mortar ammunition, replied, "Shit, da ma'fuckas er jus' tryin' ta even things out fer da gooks, man. If dey do hit us, we'll be so fuckin' tired, we'll be on even terms wi' da little bastids."

"Whew. You got that right. I feel like shit," said Cue.

Jesse sat a few yards away from the men, silently smoking his cigarette. His leg was hurting and he didn't want to use even the small amount of energy required to carry on a conversation. The machine-gun and ammunition, in addition to his field glasses, map pouch, and seven-eighty-two gear, were almost more than he could handle.

He had never fallen out on any march, under any conditions, since he had been in the Corps. It was a quiet kind of pride he held in himself, to be able to go as far and as fast as any man, and to shoulder his load or more.

He remembered with a wry smile the forced march from Pickle Meadows to Camp Marguerita during a training exercise at Camp Pendleton in 1962. *That had been a forced march!* Or that time in 1963, while on Okinawa, when President Kennedy had come out with his physical fitness program and the men of the Second Battalion, Third Marines had marched fifty miles, loaded down with full combat gear, in a little over sixteen hours.

The pain in his leg brought him back to Vietnam. He winced and glanced around to be sure no one had seen his action. Rich approached him slowly, tiredly.

"You okay, Indio?"

"Yeah, how about you?"

"They better not keep this shit up all day or they're gonna get wherever they're goin' without the mortars."

"I'll spell some of the guys as the day goes on."

"Hell, that M-60 is as heavy as the outer ring of the baseplate."

"Yeah, but you forget, I had a month of rest. I'm probably stronger than most of the guys right now."

"I don't even see Charles Atlas carryin' a machine-gun and a set of bipods at the same time at this pace."

"I can hack it a little while."

Ruddleston sauntered slowly to the two and plopped his tall frame into the sitting position next to Jesse. "So, let me give you an official welcome back to the 'toon there, Indio. I know yore havin' a good time so I won't ask you how yore doin'."

Jesse smiled. "How's it hangin', Rud?"

"I've got it all figured out. By the time we get offa' this operation, we will have walked every square inch of the DMZ. Seems like we got about half of it done already and we haven't seen a fuckin' gook yet. If we don't see one by tomorrow that means we won the war."

"You reckon, huh?"

563

Stoney Livingston

"No question about it. Look at the ragged-ass way we're walkin' through the DMZ. Now, I ask you – if you were a gook and had any intention of winnin' this war – would you, or would you not, kick our ass? Keep in mind, you'll never have a better opportunity."

"You're probably right about not havin' a better opportunity but maybe I don't wanna attack now. Maybe I wanna wait for the monsoon to hit full blast or somethin'."

Ruddleston smiled. "Then you're one dumb fuckin' gook."

"Saddle up." The word filtered down the line.

They continued the march at the same hectic rate they had maintained earlier in the day. Jesse moved up and down the column, relieving a weary marine of his burden for ten minutes, moving on to the next man who appeared to be in need of assistance and repeating the process.

There was another short break at fourteen hundred hours while they ate chow and gathered strength for the afternoon march. The men talked little as they savored the respite. With four hours of daylight left, they knew there was more tedium ahead.

So rapid had been the pace that day, and so stretched out were the men, the rear elements of the battalion had only ten minutes to eat when they finally came to a stop, the forward elements having stopped and eaten long before the last man in the rear was even aware of the halt.

As the order to saddle up and move out was given, Ski threw his half-eaten can of ham and lima beans into the heavy jungle and complained bitterly aloud to himself and anyone else who was within earshot and cared to listen. Tempers were on the rise.

Though it seemed impossible to imagine, the pace of the march picked up. Within an hour of the two o'clock break men began to falter. Some sat down to take a rest, unconcerned that the battalion continued inexorably deeper into the mountainous terrain without them.

The stragglers rested a while then hurried to catch up but the energy required to catch up was more than they had recouped while resting and they often fell, exhausted and unconcerned about the operation, the VC, the Marine Corps, or anything else. Those who had the strength, picked what gear they could from the exhausted and spoke words of encouragement to their weary friends. This worked to keep the battalion together for a while but, eventually, those unable to continue far outnumbered those willing to tax their aching bodies beyond superhuman physical limits.

Jesse moved cautiously up the slippery, narrow trail, carrying a mortar tube in addition to his own gear. He wondered at the insanity of the march and couldn't imagine its purpose. He was beginning to tire to the point where he could no longer carry so much weight. His legs felt rubbery.

Behind him he heard a crash and the sound of small limbs breaking, mixed with the rustling of leaves. He turned and found Cue missing from his position behind Marr. He placed the mortar tube on the ground and ran to the empty spot between his radio operator and Rich.

"Jesus! Cue was walkin' along and he just collapsed and fell offa' the trail," said Rich as Jesse jumped into the heavy vegetation surrounding the trail. He found Cue, unconscious, the forty-one-pound mortar bipods lying across his chest. He removed the bipods and poured tepid water from one of his canteens onto Cue's neck and temples.

"C'mon, Cue. Hang in there. Only two more hours till dark. You can make it." He turned to Rich. "Rich. Can you handle his bipods for awhile? If you can get Sal to take the tube, I'll take care of Cue."

"What the hell you gonna do?"

"Carry 'im if I have to."

"You'll never make it."

"Maybe not, but eighty-ones is stickin' together. We're not leavin' 'im here."

"You got that right." Rich picked up the bipods and moved back onto the trail. Jesse heard him shout to Sal to pick up the tube and keep moving.

Cue became conscious. He mumbled incoherently and swung feebly at Jesse, who grabbed his wrist and said, "Whoa. I'm on your side, Cue. Take it easy, man."

Cue's eyes met Jesse's. The pupils were dilated. "We can't keep goin'." Mumbled Cue as he lapsed into unconsciousness.

Jesse gazed into Cue's face. "Damn, Cue. I wished you hadn't done that." He picked the unconscious man up, put him over his shoulder in the fireman's carry, and stepped back onto the trail. The machine-gun beat against his hip, tenderizing the skin there, as he moved slowly up the hill.

"Give me that gun."

Jesse turned to see Tuleano puffing up the trail. Gratefully, and without argument, he allowed Tuleano to relieve him of the weapon. He was descending the hill when Cue came full awake. He felt Cue's body stiffen and heard him say, "What the fuck's goin' on?"

He stopped and let Cue to the ground, his shoulder muscles cramping slightly as their burden was lifted. His chest heaved as he labored to gather oxygen. "You give out, comin' up the hill. Instead a' leavin' yer sorry ass for the Cong, I thought I'd bring you along." Jesse panted.

Cue stared blankly at Jesse for a moment then said, "Where's the bipods?"

"Rich's got 'em."

Cue turned just as Rich walked by with the equipment in question. "Hey, Rich, give me them damn things."

"You okay?" asked Rich.

"Yeah, damnit. Gimme the 'pods!"

Quickly Rich handed Cue the heavy bipods, who accepted them and struggled to catch up with the fast-moving column. "Thanks, you guys." He said over his shoulder.

Jesse stood, trembling from exhaustion as he waited for Tule to reach him. After a brief argument with his section leader, he was able to reclaim his machine-gun. Tule argued that Jesse was over-exerting himself but Jesse assured him that wasn't true as he picked the gun from the Samoan's broad shoulders.

Jesse moved forward at an increased pace in an attempt to overtake his radio operator as quickly as possible. The terrain flattened momentarily though the vegetation remained thick. Jesse's knees trembled. He gritted his teeth and pressed on. He pulled the machine-gun to low port arms and was tempted to fire a short burst to stop the forward movement of the column. He held back, certain for the first time in his life that he would not be able to endure.

Suddenly it appeared the column was bunching up. He spotted Marr sitting

Stoney Livingston

on the ground, propped up by his radio. The radio operator waved weakly to him. "We're stoppin'," he panted.

"No shit?" Jesse plopped to the soft grassy soil. From his sweat-soaked utility jacket he produced his plastic cigarette pack holder and withdrew a limp cigarette. As he puffed gently on the tobacco, he felt his strength returning but he held no illusions. If the battalion had not stopped when it had, he would have fallen out. It was a sobering thought.

At the end of a fifteen-minute break the marines went to work digging in and fortifying the position. Helicopters arrived with supplies and mail. Manny received a care package from home and shared its contents with the members of the First Section. Among the goodies in the large box was a large can of jalapeno chile peppers.

In the heat and humidity, Manny could find no takers for this prize, other than Jesse. Though he offered to share the contents with all, Jesse found no one willing to eat the hot peppers with nothing more than tepid water to cool the mouth. He ate the entire contents without assistance, mixing some of the peppers with his can of spaghetti.

He listened to the jokes from the rest of the section regarding future bowel movements as he put down the last fiery pepper and smiled knowingly at them. He had grown up on jalapeno peppers and pinto beans.

Shortly after chow, about the time the gunpits were completed, the order to saddle up and move out was passed down the line. Bravo Company would lead, followed by Alpha, then Charlie and Delta. Eighty-ones were ordered to follow Bravo.

Ski shook his head and swore loudly. "Are dey fuckin' crazy? Dere's only about t'irty minutes a' daylight left."

Silently, Jesse picked up his machine-gun.

They continued to march into the night, aided by a three-quarter moon, their pace seemingly unslowed by the reduced visibility. The battalion stretched and fragmented. No longer was it a functional unit.

"Hey, Indio," Marr whispered from behind him. "Malcolm wants to talk to you."

Jesse took the offered handset and keyed up as he continued the march. Physically, he felt much better than he had earlier in the day. Mentally, he wasn't so sure of what they were trying to prove with this march.

Malcolm asked that Jesse and his radio operator hold their position until he reached them. Within five minutes Malcolm stood at their side in the soft moonlight.

"Skipper, what in the hell are we doin'? This is crazy," said Jesse.

"I don't know what's going on. I do know that we've got men falling out in the bush and we're walkin' by 'em in the darkness. I want you and Charlie here to remain with Alpha for the night. The Old Man has stopped the forward elements and he's moving us to the point."

"We're with you, Skipper." They moved forward in the ghostly night, passing first the eighty-one platoon then Bravo Company, as they made their way to the point.

Once at the point, they continued forward without a rest, first platoon in the lead. Jesse wondered about Thunder and how he was holding up. No one spoke as the night dragged on. The energy would be better used to continue the march. There wasn't enough left to do both.

566

The attrition rate reached uncontrollable proportions in the late evening. Men fell to the side and disappeared in the darkness and jungle. Jesse had never experienced anything like this in his entire time in the military. He couldn't believe what was happening around him. If the VC or NVR were to attack with any semblance of order and strength, Jesse felt certain he would be involved in the first total annihilation of an American unit since Colonel Custer had died at the Little Big Horn.

Just before midnight, the point slowed. Jesse walked in a relatively open area. He could distinguish a thick row of large trees ahead, and surmised the point had encountered a stream or small river. He moved slowly forward, maintaining his distance with the rifleman to his front. He entered the tree line and found almost total darkness under a large canopy of vegetation. A smooth but steep angle to the stream caused him to stumble and right himself.

"You okay?" asked a voice in the darkness.

"Yeah. Where the hell's the water?"

"Right in front of you – about ten feet," answered the unfamiliar voice.

Jesse waded into the gently flowing stream, imagining all sorts of vile creatures in the murky water surrounding his body. He fought panic as the water reached the middle of his chest but felt relief as the angle moved upward and he began to ascend the bank on the far side. He stepped onto the opposite bank and continued to move forward for a few paces. Captain Malcolm's voice stopped him.

"That you, Indio?"

"Yeah, Skipper. Where are you?"

"Over here – to your right."

Jesse moved to the voice.

When he stood at the company commander's side, Malcolm said, "We'll be setting up here for the night. The rest of the battalion will be moving through and setting up to our front. I'd like you and your radio operator to stay at the river and see to it that everybody gets across. We've got a hell of a mess behind us. I understand that Bravo has lost contact with Delta and Charlie. They're trying to establish contact now, but Bravo can't find the lead elements of Delta. We've got stragglers all over the damn hills."

"You mean the back half of the battalion is lost?"

"That's putting it succinctly."

"Oh, shit."

"Give me a shout on the radio if you need anything," ordered Malcolm, as he walked from the small river and away from the tree line.

"Aye, aye, Skipper."

Jesse and Marr remained in the darkness of the canopy by the river's edge until shortly after oh-one-hundred, when the slow-moving flow of men stopped. Jesse spoke to the last man through the water: "What company you from?"

"Bravo," whispered the marine in the darkness.

"Is there anybody behind you?"

"Not that I know of. I haven't seen or heard from anybody behind me in more 'n two hours."

Jesse radioed the bleak news to Malcolm.

PFC Charles Marr strained his eyes in the darkness to see Jesse's face.

Stoney Livingston

"What now, Indio?"

"I don't know. If the two lost companies are together as a unit they may form a perimeter of their own and wait until daylight, or, we may have to send a scoutin' party back and try to lead 'em to our position. We'll just stand by for some word from the skipper for now."

They waited thirty minutes in the darkness. Messages from the battalion commander and Captain Malcolm came over Marr's radio, requesting to know if there had been anymore stragglers make it to the river. There had been none.

Jesse moved to Malcolm's physical location and suggested they light up the sky with mortar illumination and guide the lost companies to their position. Malcolm discarded the plan, saying the VC would also be drawn to their position. Jesse countered that if there were any VC within fifty miles, they were aware of their positions and of their situation. Malcolm couldn't argue with the logic of Jesse's statement but the battalion commander wanted no illumination fired.

Jesse and Marr returned to the darkness of the canopy near the small river. Shortly after oh-two-hundred, Jesse observed a green flare, south and east of his location, about a mile. He heard no small arms fire and couldn't determine the purpose of the flare. He stepped into the river in the direction of the flare.

"Where the hell you goin', Indio?" asked Marr.

"At least we know where some of 'em are. I'm gonna try to find 'em and lead 'em in."

"You think you should?"

"Hell, I don't know. It's late, and I'm gettin' tired a' this shit. I'll be back in about an hour or so." Silently he disappeared into the night.

Once in the moonlight on the south side of the stream, Jesse moved with stealth, his fatigue temporarily forgotten. His senses were keen and polished, searching for the first sign of danger. He was almost half way to the spot where he thought he had observed the flare when a sound caused him to crouch to the ground. He held his crouched position for several minutes, waiting for another sound or sign of another's presence. He heard nothing.

He held his breath to better hear the sounds of his environment. He attempted to smell the enemy in the night air. He peered through the night with a vision sharpened by fear.

Now what, Langley? Do you issue a challenge and get your head blown off if the noise was made by an enemy soldier, or do you just wait it out? Hell, even if it's another marine, he'd probably fire a panic burst. With the way your luck's been lately, he'd probably hit you right between the runnin' lights. What the hell are you doin' out here anyway? This goddamn battalion will survive – with or without you.

Still in his crouched position, his thoughts drifted from Vietnam to Hawaii, then California, then Tucson. He saw Shannon and Will and a ping pong table. He heard Fats Domino singing *I Want to Walk You Home* as Shannon tried to teach him to dance. He saw those brilliant golden-brown eyes and that beautiful smile. He could almost smell her. Without a noticeable transition, he was in Hawaii and Barbara was standing there in the torchlight of an outdoor restaurant. He would never forget that sight. He had almost lost control of his body. He had felt the most blessed man on earth when he had touched her.

He returned to the DMZ. How long had he been dreaming? Not long, maybe only a few seconds. There had been no more noise. The moon began to fall on his right. There were too many lost marines out there to save single-handedly in

568

the darkness. The risk of death at the hands both sides was too great. He turned to retrace his steps to the river before the moon disappeared below the horizon.

He was challenged by Marr and the sentry posted to guard the trail. There was that brief instant of fear at the initial challenge, then passwords were exchanged, and Jesse was allowed to enter the water and cross to the relative safety on the other side.

"Did you find anything?" asked Marr.

"Yeah. I found out how stupid I am. We're not gonna be able to link up without light."

"Skipper's been callin' for you for about five minutes. He wants us to report to him. He says he's about a hundred yards due north of this crossing."

"Stay close." Jesse turned to the sentry in the darkness. "Keep yer ass low."

"You too, Indio."

"Who the hell is that?"

"Mitch, from the Rough Riders."

"Goddamn, Mitch. I didn't recognize ya in the dark. Where's Thunder?"

"He's around here somewhere. I ain't worried about it."

"Take care, man. We gotta go."

"You too."

In two steps, Jesse and Marr were out of the man's sight in the ink that was the night. They stumbled into Malcolm, more by accident than on purpose. Marr was unaware of the lucky nature of the meeting and was impressed by Jesse's ability to navigate in total darkness and said something to that effect.

Jesse ignored him.

"Indio," Malcolm said. "Our position is untenable in the event we're hit. The Old Man wants you to take your gun to the battalion CP and guard the headquarters group until first light."

"What?"

"You heard me right."

"Set up a machine-gun in the center of our perimeter? That's not exactly maximum use of our firepower, Sir."

"I know, but there are sensitive documents and codes that can't fall into enemy hands if we get overrun."

"Beggin' yer pardon, Sir, but that's plain stupid. They'll have more time to destroy documents if they have the gun on the perimeter where I can use it if we're hit."

"Orders are orders, Indio."

"But me? Jesus Christ. Can I just give the gun to someone in headquarters and take a position on the perimeter?"

"Funny thing, but the request came through your FDC. They asked specifically for you. Said for you to pick out three men from eighty-ones and report to the sergeant major at the center of the clearing."

"You serious, Sir?"

"I'm too damn tired to joke about much of anything right now."

"Aye, aye, Sir. I'm on the way."

Somehow he found the eighty-one platoon in the dark, where he picked Larry, Cue and Ruddleston to man the M-60 for the night. The five of them, counting Marr, reported to the Battalion Sergeant Major after three attempts to locate him in

Stoney Livingston
the night.

"How are you doin', Indio?"

"Is that you, Sergeant Major?"

"It's been a long time since that night you came into my tent looking for a rifle."

Jesse sighed. He felt a sad kind of happiness in his tired mind. It was almost like a homecoming to hear the sergeant major speak to him. "Yes, Sergeant Major, it has."

"You've come a long way, son."

"Thank you, Sergeant Major."

"You've earned more."

Since the sergeant major seemed to hold no grudges, Jesse had to try. "Sergeant Major?"

"Yeah?"

"I hope this idea of settin' up a machine-gun in the center of our perimeter isn't yours."

"It isn't, but I don't wanna hear what you're gonna say next. The Old Man wants it done this way, and this is the way it's gonna be done."

"Aye, aye, Sergeant Major. Where do you want us?" Jesse gave up the fight.

The sergeant major showed Jesse the position. "Any questions?"

"From this position, Sergeant Major, am I given to understand that we are to fire only in the event the HQ is under assault?"

"You'll know when to fire if the need arises."

"Thanks, Sergeant Major."

The sergeant major retired for the remaining three hours of darkness. Jesse turned to his men. "Okay, who wants the first watch?"

Cue volunteered. The others fell asleep within seconds of spreading their exhausted frames upon the damp soil.

Jesse awakened to the first ray of light peeking over the green hills to the east. Cue was asleep, his shoulder draped over the butt of the M-60. Jesse remembered Piroge, and smiled sadly. *Poor Cue. He was give out long before we got here.* Quietly, he moved forward and shook Cue gently. He came awake slowly.

"Shh," whispered Jesse. "Just stay there and pretend you and I shared the watch all night. Let the other guys sleep a little while longer. I'm gonna scout around. I'll be back in a little bit."

Cue looked at him blankly. He knew of the incident between Indio and Piroge. Piroge had confessed it to him weeks after the occurrence. "Thanks, Indio."

"To hell with it, Cue. It was a long day." He moved from the clearing to the trees at its edge. The camp appeared dead. It was almost as if he were living a dream. Men slept all around the perimeter. For a full ten minutes he moved on the outskirts of the perimeter, waking dead-tired marines and advising them to pass the favor down the line.

At last, satisfied he had done enough to earn a morning cigarette, he paused under a large tree and lit up. He breathed deeply on his smoke and exhaled joyfully, glad to be alive, grateful for the beauty of the morning and the safety of the battalion, even if it was only half a battalion. A marine appeared fifty yards to his front, strolling casually in his direction. He recognized him as the staff sergeant on top of the burned-out hill the day before yesterday. *Or was it a week ago?* He had lost track of time.

"Good morning, Sergeant," the marine greeted him.

"Just call me Indio, Sarge. My rank is corporal, but don't worry about it. Captain Malcolm tells me most of the guys think I'm a damn general."

The marine smiled. "You're the first one who's thought me a sergeant in a long time. Most of 'em think I'm a damn major."

"Hell, I'd rather be a sergeant any day. What's yer handle?"

"Rogers."

"What company you with?"

"Headquarters."

"Headquarters? You don't look like an office poge."

"Recent assignment. Used to be with Delta."

"Who'd you piss off to get a poge job?"

Rogers smiled, "I don't know for sure." He paused. "I just wanted to let you know, I appreciate the job you've done this past few days. I'll be sure the Colonel knows about it too."

"Hell no, don't say anything about me to him."

"Why not? Hell, it can't hurt you to be on his good side."

"It's kind of a long story there, Rog. Just please don't mention my name around him, okay? Besides, I didn't do much of anything at all. Hell, we haven't seen a gook on the whole operation."

"Have it your way. Well, I've gotta get back to the CP. I just wanted to let you know that I appreciate your example. It's too bad you don't want the Old Man to know."

"Please, no."

"Okay. I'm sure we'll meet again."

"Never can tell. Keep yer ass low."

"Same to you." Rogers turned and left Jesse alone under the tree. *That was a strange meeting.* Jesse fieldstripped his cigarette butt and returned to his machine-gun.

After his breakfast of two more cigarettes and a cup of C-ration coffee, Jesse moved to the rear in search of Thunder and his squad. His efforts were rewarded when the young sergeant stepped from behind a tree at the small river's edge.

"'Mornin', Amigo. Heard you pulled another one of your famous stunts last night. What the hell was runnin' through your head when you started backtrackin' down the trail?"

"I had a crazy notion I could guide the rest of the battalion to our position. Kinda dumb, huh?"

"Kinda." He pulled out a pack of cigarettes and offered one to Jesse.

Jesse eyed the pack. "You wanna trade them Camels fer two packs of Winston?"

"Nope. But I'll trade you two packs of Salem and one pack of Pall Mall for one of your packs of Camels."

Jesse took the proffered smoke. "To hell with you. I'll take the free one and forget about the trade."

They smoked silently for several minutes. Thunder broke the silence. "Have you ever seen anything like this operation?"

"No one will ever believe it."

"Hell, I was a part of it and *I* don't believe it," said Thunder.

"I heard Charlie and Delta are on the move with the stragglers. Word has it that there's still two men missing," offered Jesse.

"I'm surprised it ain't a helluva lot more than two men."

"Me too."

Thunder fieldstripped his cigarette butt. "I think the Old Man went too far this time."

"He went too far on Oregon," said Jesse.

"Yeah, but his time he won't get away with it."

"I hope to hell you're right. He's gonna get a lot of guys killed if they don't get him outa the field."

They discussed the operation at length as they waited for the lead elements of Delta Company to come into view.

The battalion remained in the same position all day, recovering from fatigue and lack of sleep. Operation Prairie Two was effectively over. Not one shot had been fired at the enemy. There were no sightings of enemy activity, nor were any stores or supplies uncovered. There were sixty-two non-combat casualties, ranging from broken legs to malaria. There were also two men missing.

When Charlie and Delta companies arrived at the battalion HQ, and a final role call determined the two men were still missing, Thunder and his squad were picked by Malcolm to retrace the battalion's steps since dark the previous night. Jesse volunteered to accompany them and Malcolm consented. For reasons known only to him, Marr volunteered to remain with Jesse.

The search was made difficult by the terrain and lack of sufficient daylight to allow a thorough search at a reasonably slow pace. In the late afternoon, Thunder radioed for permission to remain in his position and return to battalion the following day. Malcolm reluctantly granted his request. The missing men had to be found. The patrol found nothing on the first day.

That evening, as they bedded down for the night, Jesse and Thunder sat together, their backs resting against the same tree.

"You sorry you extended, Thunder?"

Thunder looked pensively at the moon. "Naw. Not really. We haven't won anything yet. I can't go home until we do."

"That's bullshit. The way we're doin' things, this damn police action could last longer than World War Two," said Jesse quietly.

"You could be right. I could be an old man by the time this thing is over but, if that's what it takes, then that's what it takes."

"What about my cousin, Susan?" Jesse played his trump card.

"Yeah, I thought about that. I gotta admit, it's mighty temptin', but to see that woman, I've gotta be the conquering hero, not some asshole who came home with his tail between his legs."

"Baloney, you've already got more damn medals than Audie Murphy. What the hell you want? Fergit this shit and come on home when your extension's up."

Thunder ignored him. "Speakin' of goin' home, how's Barbara?"

"Fine, goddamnit," Jesse whispered. "Don't be changin' the subject on me either."

Thunder smiled, his teeth bright in the moonlight. "Yer a good guy, Indio. I appreciate your concern. I really do. I wish I could go home and believe I did what I could, but I can't."

"Damn you, Thunder. I've got a girl back home I'd give anything to see for just five minutes. She's important as hell to me. Don't make me stay over here and take care of yer sorry ass." He referred to Barbara but was thinking of Shannon. He wondered what was wrong with him.

"I'll manage for a while without your able help, Amigo."

"Why?"

"If you hadn't found Barbara, you'd do the same thing. I know you. You'd stay until the cows came home. Don't bullshit me." He paused. "I'm glad you found her, Indio. When you get outa here, you'll be a better man for a million reasons. You two will have a great life together and raise a passle a' kids and, one day, ol' Uncle Thunder will come visit you with Aunt Susan."

"The woman won't wait forever."

Again Thunder smiled in the light of the moon. "Obviously you don't know my powers of persuasion with the fair sex, Amigo. I've got her eatin' outa my hand already, and I'm ten-thousand miles away."

"I granted you she was pretty. I never said she was smart."

They fell silent and listened to the sounds of the jungle at night.

Dawn found the patrol combing the hills in search of the missing marines. It was Mitchell who discovered the injured man shortly after noon. His right leg was broken above the ankle and he suffered from a concussion as the result of his fall from the trail in the darkness. He was hungry, thirsty, and in pain. The patrol saw to his needs as best they could. They made a stretcher from a poncho and two tree branches Thunder hacked down with his machete.

Taking turns at carrying the injured man, the patrol began its return trek, two men on the stretcher, one on the trail fifty yards to the front, one fifty yards to the rear, the rest walking the flanks in search of the last missing man. It was late afternoon when Thunder called a halt from his position to the right and below the trail. He had found the second missing man.

Jesse stood by Thunder's side and looked at the grotesquely twisted body, the man's head smashed beyond any form of recognition by his fall to the rocks below the trail.

Thunder stared at the body. "There just wasn't any call fer this shit."

Marr stared, mesmerized, getting his first sight of a dead man in the war. He averted his face in order to prevent regurgitation. Jesse unrolled his poncho from his cartridge belt and wrapped the fruits of their tedious search tightly therein. He and Thunder carried the man's body up to the trail.

The patrol returned to battalion headquarters with the last rays of light.

The following day the battalion made an orderly march to the east until an hour before dark. They marked an LZ and waited for helicopters. The light Hueys picked them up in three waves, the last man boarding the helicopter just before dark. They arrived at their new camp just as the pink sky turned to dark grey.

Two days after the battalion's arrival at Dong Ha, Jesse was promoted to sergeant. The battlefield promotion was presented personally by the battalion executive officer, Major Jonathan Rogers, the man Jesse had thought to be a staff sergeant. Colonel Soliman was relieved of command, and the battalion took the perimeter of the northernmost airstrip in South Vietnam.

Stoney Livingston

CHAPTER TWENTY-FIVE: DONG HA

The settlement of Thi Xa Dong Ha rested comfortably at the junction of Highway Nine and Highway One, two of the largest paved roads in the northern part of South Vietnam. Highway One ran the length of the troubled country from north to south, while Highway Nine began its existence in the center of Dong Ha and trailed westward in the valley paralleling the Cam Lo River.

The land east of Dong Ha was flat and filled with a myriad of rivers and streams. Rice paddies and villages crowded the fertile landscape from Highway One to the three-mile strip of sand separating the ocean from the farmlands. This area of Vietnam was rich in the food resources desperately needed by the Viet Cong.

The inhabitants of Dong Ha and the ten-mile strip of rich farmland between the ocean and the city were not overly sympathetic to the cause of their VC brethren, nor were they openly antagonistic. The land produced much and, though they weren't pleased by the rice quotas seized by the VC, they found it wiser to live with less than to die for the excess.

In the many years since the Viet Minh had defeated the French, there had been an occasional farmer who had protested the amount of rice confiscated by the VC, but these brave farmers were simply murdered and their bodies displayed to the populace at large to remind them of the VC's power and quick methods of reprisal. The people of this region grew accustomed to sharing a portion of each harvest with their politically different brothers.

The old French airstrip, abandoned by its builders in 1954, sat almost due south of Dong Ha, less than one mile from the substantial city center. The runway ran from southwest to northeast and was nothing more than a dirt path graded free of large objects. It was short by modern standards, only a little over a thousand meters. Not enough for jet fighters but the KC-130s could utilize it's rolling runway by maximum braking and reverse thrust from the engines. Plans to level out the hills in the runway were under discussion that October of 1966 but nothing had yet been done. Due to the terrain features to the southwest, the runway could not easily be extended to accept faster craft, and extension to the northeast was made impossible by two man-made obstacles: the railroad, which currently butted the northeast end of the runway, and Highway One, less than two hundred yards east of the tracks.

A small U.S. Army unit occupied the permanent buildings on the north side of the runway. Their primary function was to provide security and maintenance services to the small craft flying out of the old facility. Until recently they had been more than sufficient in numbers to dissuade the VC from attack but, in the last week of September, the VC had tested the mettle of the mechanics and clerks stationed at the airstrip and had inflicted casualties on the non-combatants, including some of the few Air Force personnel on permanent duty status at the small installation. The

574

company of marines stationed at the base had repulsed the assault but casualties had been high.

The remnants of an old French fort stood majestically on the north side of the airstrip. It had been redone by U.S. Army and Air Force personnel into a club for officers and n.c.o.'s, for their respective branches only. The marines were relegated to hot beer once a week on the perimeter. From time-to-time, marine officers were allowed to utilize the club, but only on an invitational basis. After the arrival of the First Battalion, Fourth Marines all officers, including marines, were authorized access to the club. All enlisted marines, with the exception of the rank of sergeant major, were forbidden to enter the premises.

The newly arrived First Battalion, Fourth Marines took up the perimeter and dug in, making substantial improvements to the existing fortifications. All attachments were withdrawn to their own units. Once again Jesse found himself with the eighty-one platoon.

Jesse continued his policy of wearing no rank despite the fact they were in a semi-permanent position.

Two days after Jesse received his promotion, Captain Malcolm rotated back to the United States. It was a sad farewell for Malcolm and his men. They had been through much together. He paid special respects to Thunder before he left his command in the charge of Lieutenant Parker.

Prior to boarding the KC-130 for Da Nang he stopped by the mortar platoon and found Jesse engaged in a card game. His forward observer looked up and threw his cards facedown on the blanket serving as a table. "Deal me out," he said, standing and moving to meet Malcolm.

"How's it goin', Indio?"

"It's been kinda boring this past few days, Skipper. We goin' out again?" he asked, eager to be with Malcolm and Thunder once more.

"I'm headed home. I leave in about thirty minutes." There was a sadness in his eyes. Not that he didn't want to go home, but at the parting from men he loved and respected. Jesse knew Malcolm was torn.

Jesse smiled a broad, toothy kind of smile. He moved forward and hugged Malcolm tightly. "You made it, Sir. Congratulations." He stepped back and shook Malcolm's hand.

They left the tent and walked slowly in the morning sun. Malcolm pulled a pack of Camels from his pocket. He offered Jesse one. Jesse accepted. "I didn't know you smoked, Skipper."

"I don't." Malcolm put a cigarette between his lips while Jesse brought his Zippo lighter into range. He puffed on the smoke, careful not to inhale.

Jesse lit his own and said, "So what's the special occasion?"

"I just opened these damn things. There are only gonna be two cigarettes missing. I'm gonna bronze the pack and every time I look at it, I'll think of you and Thunder."

"Seems like a waste of good smokes to me."

Malcolm smiled as he puffed a thick cloud of white smoke from his mouth. "I just wanted to say thanks, and I'm proud to have served with you, Indio."

There was an awkward silence.

"Alpha won't be the same, Sir."

"They'll manage. Parker's a good man."

575

Another silence.

Jesse inhaled his cigarette smoke deeply. "I couldn't have had a better company commander, Sir. And I never said it but I appreciate all of the things you did behind the scenes to keep my ass outa trouble. Without your help, I'd probably be makin' little rocks outa big ones at Leavenworth or Portsmith."

"You were a little rough around the edges at first but you always came through, and I appreciated that." Malcolm smiled, curling the corner of his handsome lips. He handed Jesse a piece of paper. "My new duty station. I know you're busy but if you get time, jot me a line and let me know how everybody's doing."

"Yessir, I will."

"Well, I guess I better hit the trail. Thanks again, Indio – for everything."

"You too, Skipper." They shook hands one last time. "Keep yer ass low over there in The World, Sir."

"I will. You do the same here."

"Yessir. Goodbye, Captain." Jesse snapped to attention and saluted smartly.

Malcolm stiffened and crisply returned the salute. "Goodbye, Sergeant." He turned and walked north, toward his waiting aircraft. Jesse watched him silently, a sense of loss filling his chest – tears filling his eyes.

For several days, Jesse couldn't accept the fact that Malcolm had gone home. It had seemed as though they would fight the war to its conclusion together. *The damn war should have been over by now. We should all be going home together.* He and Thunder found solace in each other's company when duties would allow. They swapped stories about Malcolm and the Rough Riders and drank warm beer when they could get it.

One evening Jesse approached Thunder in the latter's tent with a set of captain bars and a set of first lieutenant bars, one pair in each hand. "What d'ya' wanna be, a captain or a first louie?"

"What the hell are you talkin' about?" asked Thunder.

"That damn Air Force club. We're gonna go to the club tonight."

"There's a mine field all the way around the place from the French days."

"We don't have to worry about details like that with these bars." Jesse rubbed the bright silver metal. "Besides, I heard there was a female war correspondent stayin' with the Air Force for the next few days – a little blond. Thought you might be interested in that."

"If she's a war correspondent what the hell's she stayin' with the Air Force for?"

"So she can learn about the rigors of war, man. What's the matter with you? Don't you know how rough them guys have got it over there on the north side? Hell, I heard they ran out of ice yesterday for almost two hours."

"No shit? Damn, that *is* rough." Thunder clucked sympathetically.

"Well, what d'ya' think? You goin' with me?"

"They'll have our asses if we get caught."

"No doubt. Probably hang us from the south wall of that ol' French fort."

"Count me in. When do you figure is the best time to make our entrance?"

"Well, I been studyin' the place and, the way I figure, if we make our move about..."

576

Thunder and Jesse approached the door of the club nonchalantly. They stepped through the heavy wooden door and found themselves in a solid building. There were several rooms in the building, one of which contained a small pinball arcade.

"Would you look at this," remarked Jesse, pointing to the pinball machines. "Damn. Things are rough on this side of the runway."

A specialist fourth class looked up from his pinball machine to the two marine officers standing in the doorway. "It wasn't always this good around here."

"Yeah, I imagine it was kinda' rough at first," replied Thunder. He turned to Jesse. "Let's get a drink and sit down."

"Good idea."

They found a table in another room and ordered whiskey and soda. For two hours they sat silently sipping on one drink after another, smiling all the while at the coup they had pulled off by entering the club. At twenty-one thirty, several officers entered the club, escorting a short, blonde female. They swarmed around her subserviently.

Thunder looked with a critical eye at the two marines in the group of two army captains and one air force major. "You brought me in here for that? Goddamn, I haven't been over here that long!"

Jesse winced. "So, she's a little on the homely side. I'm sure she's got a nice personality."

Thunder smiled. "I'll drink to that." He raised his glass. "Here's to a great personality." They drained their glasses and ordered another round.

Thunder looked up from his whiskey glass in a stupor. "Uh oh."

Jesse turned to follow Thunder's stare. Lieutenant Parker, the new Alpha Company commander, was heading straight for their table.

"We're dead," offered Jesse under his breath.

Parker stopped at their table and gazed down at the two enlisted men with the officer's rank on their collars. "Good evening, gentlemen. May I join you?"

Thunder and Jesse shared a quick glance at one another. "By all means," replied Jesse with a sweep of his hand.

Parker sat at the table and turned to Jesse. "Captain Indio of Eighty-Ones, isn't it?"

"At your service, Lieutenant. I think you know Lieutenant Thunder." He waved weakly at Thunder.

"I believe the lieutenant and I have met on occasion – out in the field."

"Evenin', Lieutenant," Thunder smiled. "What you drinkin'?"

"Seven-seven."

"Ugh. Rotgut," said Jesse spontaneously.

Thunder shot him a glance and stepped on his toe under the table.

"One seven-seven comin' up." Jesse stood and moved to the bar to order a round of drinks. When he returned to the table, the spec-four from the pinball machine was sitting between Thunder and Parker. The man's state of intoxication appeared even more serious than his or Thunder's. He was looking for trouble but the time was not right for Thunder or him. The place was most certainly not correct.

Jesse placed the drinks on the table and slid into his chair. "You wanna drink?" he asked the soldier.

"I can buy my own drink."

Jesse didn't respond.

577

Stoney Livingston

"You fuckin' marines are all alike. You think yer shit don't stink."

"What the hell brought this on? Did I miss something?" asked Jesse.

Parker turned to the soldier. "Listen, Soldier. You're speaking to officers of the United States armed services. I don't give a damn what branch a man is in, you don't speak that way to an officer."

"That's it, hide behind those damn bars! I should have expected it."

Jesse leaned across the table and spoke quietly to the antagonistic young soldier. "Listen here, asshole. If you can pour yerself outa that chair and drag yer ass outside, I'll be more than happy to take off these bars." He pointed to the bright captain's bars on his collar.

Parker grabbed Jesse's arm. "I don't think that will be necessary, *Captain*. It's getting late. Maybe we should be getting back to the tents now."

Thunder joined in. "Yeah, I believe yer right, Lieutenant. I've gotta get my men ready for a patrol at first light." He turned to Jesse. "With your permission, Sir?"

Jesse smiled at him. "Maybe yer right, Lieutenants. It *is* getting late." They stood as one and left the soldier sitting at the table.

Outside the door of the old building the three walked slowly down the lined path. A voice from behind them said, "Fuck the Corps!"

Jesse turned and with a broad smile said, "Don't fergit to eat the apple."

The soldier stared silently at the three for a moment, then stepped from the path and stooped under the barbed wire strung along its edge.

"Hey, man, don't cross that fence. There's mines all over the place out there," said Thunder.

The soldier ignored Thunder's warning and continued through the restricted area. The three marines held their breaths and watched as the soldier strolled casually through the old minefield. He was fifteen yards from exiting the field on the far side when he stepped on a mine.

There was a bright flash of white and orange flame as the explosive device threw the man into the air. He landed with a thud, his body smoking from the lower extremities. Officers and men rushed from the confines of the club, followed by the lady war correspondent. The upper part of the soldier's body moved in the brightness of floodlights but he uttered no sound. An Army rescue team was on the scene with a minesweeper, attempting to reach him in moments.

"Let's get outa here," Jesse mumbled softly. The three left the north side of the runway for the peace and quiet of the perimeter on the south side.

Within a few days of the soldier stepping on the land mine, Alpha Company was detached from the perimeter and moved to the sandy beaches thirteen miles east northeast of Dong Ha. They went without mortar support and, since they were out of range of the guns at Dong Ha, Jesse remained with the eighty-one platoon. While at the platoon he performed the dual role of section ammo corporal and forward observer, though there was little for him to do in the latter capacity. His days were busy with gun drill and weapons cleaning. He wrote letters and composed a song of sorts about how he felt about fighting in Vietnam. He couldn't quite figure out how to end the song but knew it would come to him with time.

One afternoon, as Jesse played blackjack with Ski's crew in gun two's pit, an F-4 Phantom jet circled the airstrip, losing altitude as it made its approach. The marines stared into the bright sky as the Phantom made its rapid descent.

"Dat guy's got problems. He's gonna land dat ting," said Ski calmly.

578

"If he tries it, he'll be in deep shit. Runway's too short," said Cue.

The jet was approaching the far end of the runway, up by Highway One. Black smoke trailed behind it.

"He can make it if he holds her tight," replied Ski.

Jesse pulled a brown ten-dollar bill from the stack before him and placed it on the ground at Ski's side. "Ten bucks says he runs out of runway."

Ski didn't take his eyes from the plane as he dropped a ten-dollar bill on top of Jesse's. "Yer on."

They watched, mesmerized by the dipping wings of the injured craft as it lingered on the verge of stall speed. It cleared the concertina wire at the far end of the runway by inches and plopped onto the dirt surface. They all held their breaths as the pilot fought to stop his fast-moving craft before reaching the far end of the short runway. For a moment it appeared he might accomplish his difficult task, but there just wasn't enough runway to get the job done. The plane skidded into the concertina wire at the southwest end of the runway and fell into the dry canal on the other side of the wire, coming to rest on the far bank.

The marines rushed to the aid of the two men aboard the fighter jet. When they arrived at the plane, panting and puffing from the exertion of running in the heat and humidity, they found the pilot and his navigator moving away from the craft. It had been split in the center of the fuselage by the impact on the far bank of the canal and, most likely would never fly again, but the two men appeared uninjured. Jesse detached a detail to assist the two flyers to the north side of the runway then returned to the gunpit where he stuffed Ski's ten-dollar bill into his pocket. "Deal the cards, Ski."

That week the first section lost several of its most seasoned veterans. They rotated back to the United States amid congratulations and hidden tears. Tuleano, Rich, Larry, Courtney, Sal, and others all left on the same day the platoon was deluged with reinforcements. Jesse was promoted to section leader – a job which he neither liked nor wanted – and given the task of whipping the First Section into shape as an effective fighting unit.

Jesse sat in the unfamiliar surroundings of the stuffy FDC tent, studying the names on his piece of notebook paper. Most of them were new, having arrived only the day before, and with Hill and Ruddleston being transferred to the third section, Jesse knew only three men in his twenty-three-man section. He made Lance Corporal Cusick his ammo corporal. Marr remained as the FO radio operator. PFC Manny Lopez moved up to first squad leader. The rest would have to be tested. Except for Lance Corporal Thomas, who he appointed to the position of second squad leader, all of the new men were privates or PFCs. Most had less than six months in the service. He shook his head and turned his attention to the plotting board and maps before him.

That afternoon he found out just how far from being a fighting unit his section was when he conducted gun drill from the FDC tent. He gave the information to the guns via the landline and waited for the ammo corporal to advise him when each gun was up. As he sat nervously in the tent, waiting for a response from Cue, he paced the earthen floor.

The first mission he gave to the guns was a small deflection and elevation change from the standard setting. He sat through more than two minutes of silence before the first gun reported that it was ready to fire. The second mission he gave to his ammo corporal was a large deflection change. After more than five minutes had elapsed with no response from the guns, he left the FDC tent, informing Lieutenant Smith he would return only when he had trained a gunner who could get his mortar operational in something less than two week's time. Smith smiled as his new section leader exited the small tent.

Both gunners were frantically turning cranks and moving bi-pods as Jesse approached the pits. He shouted to Cue. "What the hell's goin' on out here? Somebody order chow call or what?"

Cue stared at the ground. "They need a little practice."

"A little practice?" He turned to face the two mortars. "All right, Goddamnit, hold it wherever-in-the-hell you are. Step away from the guns and don't touch 'em. I gotta see for myself what in the hell you guys are doin'."

Shyly the new gunners and assistant gunners backed away from the guns.

Jesse stepped into gun one's pit and moved to the sight. He checked the settings and looked up at PFC King, the new gunner. "You've got more time in the Crotch than anybody in this section and you can't even put the right goddamn dope on the sight? Where the hell you tryin' to shoot – to California?"

King was a tall thin man in his mid twenties. He was shy and retiring by nature, and easily intimidated. Jesse overwhelmed him. King said nothing.

"Goddamnit, King. Where did you get the dope that's on that sight?"

"I thought that's what Cue said." King finally spoke.

"Did you repeat the dope as it was given to you?"

"Some of it."

"Some of it? *Some of it?* What the hell's the matter with you? You can't shoot the damn gun with just *some* of the goddamn dope! Look at gun two. Couldn't you have figured out that one of you two guys were fucked up when his gun is pointin' one way and yours is pointin' another?"

King remained silent.

"There are guys out there countin' on you to put the round where it's supposed to be." He paused for a moment. "I'll tell you what, King. If you ever fail to repeat the dope aloud again, I'll beat yer damned head in with your own pistol. Do you understand me, goddamnit?"

"Yes," replied King timidly.

"What? Say it so the whole goddamn section can hear you."

"Yes," shouted King.

"Yes, what?"

"Yes, I will repeat the dope aloud at all times," shouted King.

Jesse stared into the thin face. "You damn right, you will," he said quietly as he stepped away to inspect gun two.

PFC Hanna, a short, stocky man with baby fat on his cheeks, stood next to his gun. Jesse inspected the sight. The settings were correct. He glanced at the odd angle of the bi-pods with respect to the rest of the gun. The cross-level and elevation bubbles in the sight were buried in one end of their respective vials.

Jesse pointed to the bi-pods. "What the hell is this? Is this some new kind of way to fire the eighty-one?"

"The ground isn't level there."

"Oh?" Jesse picked up the bi-pods and turned them perpendicular to the longitudinal axis of the tube and placed them firmly into the ground. He looked through the sight, turned the traverse handle one-half turn and the elevation crank

580

handle a full turn. He checked the bubbles in the sight and peered through the aperture to see that the crosshair was properly positioned on the left side of the aiming stakes to the front of the gun. He stepped away from the gun and quietly said, "Gun two up."

Hanna looked at the mortar in disbelief. Jesse had taken no more than six or seven seconds on the gun. He checked the crosshair and the bubbles. Perfect. Silently, he backed away from the gun.

"You wanna tell me again about the uneven ground, Hanna?"

"Well, I thought it was uneven, I guess."

"Bullshit. You were makin' excuses. Excuses are like assholes - everybody's got one. Don't waste 'em on me, and don't justify your lack of ability with 'em." He turned to Cue and said, "Cue, get 'em all over here in gun two's pit."

"Yo," came Cue's reply.

When the nervous shuffling and jockeying for position was over, Jesse looked at the group of young men before him. Many were older than his twenty-one years but he somehow felt older than any man there. "I'm gonna tell you guys this one time and one time only. I've got friends out there in those rifle companies, damn good friends. If one of 'em is ever injured as a result of your ineptitude with the mortar, the corresponding injury will be inflicted upon your own body by me personally. If you think I'm bullshittin', try me. Maybe a quick example would put everyone's mind at ease."

Nobody moved, nor did anyone speak. He continued, "I don't know why you're here. I only know that you *are* here. And while you're here, you're gonna do your job, and that job is to supply supporting fire on demand - not six goddamn months later or whenever you feel like gettin' around to it. Today we're gonna do gun drill until we find us some gunners. If we have to stay here until next week, here's where we'll be." He turned to Cue. "Cue, draw some rations. The First Section will be livin' on the guns until we know how to operate 'em." To the rest of the section he said, "Everybody get your ponchos and seven-eighty-two gear and report back to the guns in five minutes."

The First Section remained on the guns for forty-eight hours, sleeping in shifts, eating their cold C-rations when they could find time between mock fire missions. Jesse remained awake the entire time, shouting words of encouragement or chastisement as dictated by each situation. At the end of the second day Jesse dismissed the section to normal duty status with the exceptions of King and Hanna, who he worked for several more hours before letting them retire to their tents.

Of the four sections in the eighty-one platoon, Jesse's was by far the least experienced. Somehow, in the shuffle, he had ended up with twice the number of new men as any of the other sections. Lieutenant Smith expressed concern over Jesse's lack of trained personnel and offered to rearrange the sections but Jesse said he didn't want to give his problems to someone else. He continued to run gun drill a minimum of six hours a day.

Within a week of their arrival, the new men in the First Section showed a marked improvement in their ability to handle the mortar. In five more days they issued a challenge to the rest of the platoon: First Section was the best and the fastest. Pure and simple.

The other section leaders were quick to accept the challenge thrown at them by Jesse's men. Under the scrutinous eye of Lieutenant Smith, the competition

Stoney Livingston

gun drill began at oh-eight-thirty one sunny morning. By the time it was over at noon the First Section had proven its ability with the mortar. While it was true they had lost some of the drills, they nevertheless came out the overall winners of the competition.

Lieutenant Smith was impressed with the results of Jesse's work. It was no longer necessary for Jesse to threaten anyone in the section in order to get something done. He merely made a simple request and whatever he wanted done was done – right now.

Jesse was playing cards with some of the men in his section when he heard the shot, originating from somewhere near the Third Section tent. Quickly men dropped their cards and grabbed their personal weapons. Several minutes ticked off the clock while they waited, crouching by sandbag bunkers or in one of the gunpits. Shortly, the word was passed down to the guns that there had been an accidental discharge in the Third Section tent. Jesse and the others resumed the card game.

Ten minutes later Jesse was summoned to Lieutenant Smith's tent. He reported straightaway to his platoon commander and received news that Lance Corporal Ruddleston had been shot in the neck by Private Hill. Ruddleston had been evacuated to the hospital ship *Hope,* sitting offshore.

Jesse was given instructions to investigate the incident, first by reporting to the Third Section tent, then by following up with a visit to the hospital ship to check on Ruddleston's condition and taking a statement from the injured man if he was able to make one.

Jesse remembered his return from R&R and how Ruddleston had led him to the mail chopper in time to get aboard for the ride to Cam Lo.

Inside the Third Section tent Jesse sat next to Hill. "Okay, Hill, what the hell happened?"

"I shot da' Mu'fucka, whatchoo think happened, man?"

"Well, damnit, was it an accident or did you do it on purpose?"

"He said ah wuz cheetin' a' Pinochle. Ah picked up mah M-14 an' put it to his t'rote. Da dumb nigga' dared me t' pull da trigga', so ah did."

Jesse studied Hill carefully, his chest muscles tightening. "You shot him in the neck because he dared you to do it?"

"Said ah di'n't have da balls t' pull d' mu'fuckin' trigga'. Ah guess he won' be talkin' dat shit no mo'."

Jesse picked up Hill's rifle and sniffed the receiver. He smelled the recently burned gunpowder. "I'm takin' your rifle and you to the platoon commander."

"You betta' bring a lunch, Mu'fucka'!"

Jesse feared Hill. The man was big and powerful. Apparently he was also remorseless and cruel. "If you won't go walkin', you'll go in the prone position, Hill. I'm not gonna screw around with you. I'll shoot you once between the runnin' lights and drag your body to the lieutenant."

Hill tensed. Fear crept into Jesse's throat. Those inside the tent behind Hill moved to the left and right. Those behind Jesse did the same. The air was thick enough to cut with a knife. Jesse held Hill's rifle casually at port arms, trying to appear relaxed and confident, wanting to run away from the big man.

Hill shrugged and stood. "Okay, mu'fucka'. No sense you 'n' me gettin' it on. You got a job ta do."

"I appreciate that, Hill." He remained ready to spring into action, not trusting any man crazy enough to shoot one of his buddies over such a trivial matter. Several members of the Third Section accompanied them to Lieutenant Smith's tent. Three of the men remained while Jesse explained what he knew of the incident.

Hill was placed under arrest and flown to Da Nang for further action, pending completion of the investigation. Late that afternoon Jesse was flown to the *City of Hope* to question Ruddleston. Initial reports had indicated that Hill's bullet had just missed the large artery in Ruddleston's neck and that recovery was almost certain.

The clean white lines of the *Hope,* with its bright red crosses, came into view from the port window of the Huey. Jesse remembered reading about this ship. He had seen pictures of her in magazines when he was a kid. He was excited about the thought of boarding this piece of history but his excitement diminished as he remembered the reason for his visit.

The Huey sat down on the gently rolling landing pad near the stern of the ship and Jesse debarked with a wave of thanks to the pilot and crew. He approached an orderly standing at the edge of the landing pad and asked for directions to Ruddleston's location. The man didn't have the information but appeared eager to help the marine with his untucked shirt and M-1 cartridge belt. Jesse knew he looked like a relic from the past to the brightly polished young man in his shiny white clothes.

As they walked through the passageways of the busy ship and Jesse encountered more people like the young orderly, he became self-conscious for the first time in a long time. He tucked his headband further into his helmet and brushed his uniform. He didn't carry a rifle but his pistol was conspicuously reversed on his left hip. The bone-handled Bowie knife hung loosely from his web belt. In some of the narrower passageways his canteens clanked against the bulkhead, adding to his feeling that he was out of place.

The ship was like a small American city, bustling with the activities of many different occupations. Most of those aboard were in civilian dress. Jesse wanted to crawl into a hole and hide from these civilized people. He didn't belong here with his dirty uniform and instruments of war.

The young orderly stopped at a small office amidship and motioned him inside. "This is Doctor Patterson's office," said the orderly cheerfully. "She's in charge of the section your buddy's in, I think."

"She?"

"She," repeated the orderly. "She's on her way down from O.R. right now. Just have a seat. I've gotta go."

"Thanks."

Jesse sat uncomfortably in the small leather chair indicated by the orderly, careful to move his canteens and knife to the side so they wouldn't damage the leather. Shortly, a large matronly-looking woman stepped into the room, smiling. "You must be Sergeant Langley." She offered her hand. "I'm Doctor Patterson."

His title sounded strange to his ears. No one called him *Sergeant Langley* back in the jungle. He stood and timidly shook her hand. "Yes, Ma'am. I'm here to see Rud ...er Lance Corporal Ruddleston."

Doctor Patterson seated herself behind the small steel desk in her office. "Yes, I know." She paused. "There's been a slight complication and I'm afraid you won't be able to see him until in the morning."

Jesse leaned over her desk. "Is he gonna be all right?"

"Yes, yes. He's a strong young man. But his blood loss was great and the doctor in charge has specified no visitors until tomorrow morning at the earliest."

Jesse breathed a sigh of relief. "I guess I'll just have to find a way back here in the morning. I didn't even know this ship was out here."

"Be glad you didn't. The ones who find out about us aren't usually very happy about being here."

Jesse liked this matronly woman with her grey hair and straight back and eyes of wisdom. He became more comfortable with his dress. "Well, thank you, Doctor Patterson. I'll be back in the morning if I can catch a ride."

"We have room on board if you would like to stay, Sergeant. Besides, I don't think you are going to find a way back to your base yet this evening. As far as I know, there aren't any more scheduled runs to shore today."

Jesse thought of Cue and Manny alone with his section of new men. "I've gotta try, Ma'am. We sometimes get pretty busy at night."

"I doubt you will meet with much success. Here, let me try for you." She picked up her desk phone and placed a call. After several minutes of conversation she hung up the phone and said, "There is nothing coming or going for the rest of the day unless we have a casualty come aboard."

"I'll need to find a way to contact my outfit so my platoon commander will know what's goin' on."

She picked up the phone and handed it to him.

He chuckled. "I don't think you understand. There aren't any phones where we are."

She smiled. "We can patch into your radio frequency through the ship's radio."

"You can do that?"

"We do it everyday. That's how I knew you were coming aboard."

"Oh."

She made the connection for him and appeared not to listen as he spoke to Lieutenant Smith.

Even though he spoke into a telephone, he made an effort to remember he was in reality communicating via radio but the phone brought out the civilian in him. "Yessir. I'm supposed to be able to see him in the morning. No, Sir, I won't get used to the good life." He felt the heat rise to his face and lowered his voice. "I'll be careful, Sir. No, I haven't seen any nurses wearing mini-skirts. I think that must be another one of those rumors, Sir."

Doctor Patterson cleared her throat.

"I've gotta go now. Whisky One out." He handed the phone to Patterson.

She smiled a knowing smile and placed the phone on its receiver. "You young marines – I don't know what I'd ever do if you changed your attitudes about women. I guess I'd probably jump overboard." She laughed warmly.

After being shown to a large room on C Deck with several beds covered by white sheets, he was allowed to pick an empty bed for the night and roam the ship at his own discretion, with the exception of the clearly marked restricted areas.

He reported to the mess hall and stood in line with the crew, his helmet and headband left on his bunk for the night, along with his seven-eighty-two gear. His utility jacket was tucked in and he felt more at ease, though not completely. He was still somewhat of a freak in his uniform in the midst of the men and women of the *Hope*.

Forever Patriots

The evening meal was so delicious, he felt guilty eating it as he thought of his section at Dong Ha. He ate it anyway. Several people sat at his table as he stared into his tray and tried to avoid conversation. Perhaps if he didn't look at them, they wouldn't feel compelled to make conversation. The plan didn't work. A male nurse across the table from him said, "You a marine?"

Jesse chewed a bite of his meatloaf and nodded. The man persisted. "Boy, you guys got it rough out there."

"It's only temporary." He took a bite of his mashed potatoes.

"How long you been here?"

"'Bout a year." The corn was delicious.

"You must be about due to go home."

"Three or four more weeks." Real milk.

"What kind of job you do?"

"Infantry." The lettuce is fresh and crisp.

"Actually, Murdock, he's a forward observer for a rifle company."

Jesse swallowed his bite of salad without chewing. He knew the voice. Slowly, he elevated his eyes to the woman standing next to the inquisitive male nurse. "Good evening, Nurse Hollingsworth. How've you been?"

"You know this guy?" asked Murdock.

"Yes, I met him at the hospital in Da Nang. You're sitting across from a real hero, Murdock. He's been wounded twice, so treat him with respect." She turned her attention to Jesse. "May I join you?" She walked to his side of the table.

Jesse scooted to his right to make room, his appetite gone.

"How are you, Jesse?"

"Pretty good. What are you doin' on this ship?" She looked clean and wholesome and pretty – like the girl next door.

"They send some of us out here once in a while for training, and a break from the country. I'm out here for a week, then it's back to Da Nang."

"You look well." She looked better than that but it was the best he could do.

"I feel well, especially now that I know you're still alive. Why didn't you answer my letter? I thought something had happened to you when you didn't write." That wisp of hair fell over her eyes.

He smiled. "I did write. I just never mailed it. It's kinda hard to explain. No good reason, I guess."

She placed her hand on his arm. He flinched involuntarily at her touch. She shook her head and removed her hand. "Oh, Jesse, life is so funny sometimes."

"Yeah. It's a real barrel of laughs."

Judy Hollingsworth ate half of her meal as she talked to Jesse at her side. She suddenly became quiet and stared blankly at the grey bulkhead. She smiled weakly. "You want to walk on deck for a while?"

"Me and you?"

"Is there something wrong with that?"

Jesse glanced over at Murdock. "Well, Murdock and I were gettin' along pretty good. It'd be kinda rude to exclude him." Jesse didn't want to be alone with her. He wanted to be near her – but not alone.

Murdock looked at Jesse, eyebrows arched. "Naw, you two guys go ahead. I got the duty in about thirty minutes."

Jesse bit his tongue.

Stoney Livingston

They walked the deck in the light of a full moon. It was a beautiful evening that discouraged sadness and promoted romance. It was the kind of evening a travel agent would order for his best clients on a sea cruise.

Jesse lit a cigarette and leaned on the railing with his forearms. "It's a mighty pretty night, Judy."

"It's beautiful. It's even more beautiful that I can share it with you."

"Yeah, I guess you're right. It seems kind of unreal though – don't it? I mean, there's people dyin' right over the horizon, and here we are, fat, dumb and happy, pretending that it's not happening."

"I'm not pretending that it's not happening, Jesse. I know it's out there – and you're very much a part of it – but we can't think about it *all* the time."

He turned to face her. "I don't think about it *all* the time. But when I stand here on this fancy ship, next to you, I think about how lucky I am. And I reckon I just feel a little guilty that I should have so much when so many of the guys out there have nothin'. Just bein' this close to someone like you and talkin' to you is more than most of those guys are even hopin' for until their tour is up or until they get a few days of R&R."

"You always think of your buddies, don't you?"

"No, not always. Right now, I'm thinkin' that makin' love to you would probably be like steppin' into heaven. But I know it's not going to happen, even as bad as I want it to happen – even if *you* wanted it to happen. I know there's a biological thing about men and women, but something has to separate us from the other animals on this planet. I have a girl back in the States who means more to me than anything I've ever known. I could never betray that feeling."

"I don't think I've ever wanted anything more, but I'm like you. I know it's not going to happen. Maybe if it did, I wouldn't think as much of you as I do – knowing about Barbara and all. So, as badly as I want you, Jesse, I won't let it happen either."

He gazed at the moon, suddenly comfortable with her nearness, and put his arm around her. She moved close and placed an arm around his waist. "I think you're the first honest-to-God male friend I ever had, Jesse. I wish it could be more but I'm happy with what I have."

He squeezed her tightly in the moonlight. They stood, silently gazing at the ripples of the South Pacific dancing in the glow of the cool light, each wondering what tomorrow would bring.

Jesse sat next to Ruddleston's bed as the big Lance Corporal spoke softly to him, the large bandage on the left side of his neck making movement all but impossible. He confirmed what Hill had told him about the shooting incident and asked after Hill's well being. Jesse explained Hill's predicament and Ruddleston expressed regret at the outcome. Jesse wished Ruddleston well and left his ward.

On deck, he waited for the arrival of the helicopter. He wanted to say goodbye to Judy but knew she had the duty and didn't want to take her from tending to those who needed her services far worse than he.

The Huey landed softly on the pad and unloaded its cargo of wounded. Jesse turned to the sound of Judy's voice, just in time to see her snap the shutter of her Brownie camera. She moved forward and hugged him tightly.

"In case my memory fails me, I wanted a picture to remind me of what you looked like. Take care, Jesse. Please make it home to your Barbara."

"You take care too, Judy. I'll drop you a line and let you know how things

586

are goin'."

"Please."

"I will." He released her and boarded the waiting helicopter.

Lieutenant Smith read his report as Jesse stood casually next to the small field desk inside the stuffy C.P. tent. "So Rud doesn't want us to prosecute ol' Hill, huh?"

"Not really, Sir."

"That's too bad. That shitbird is gonna have the book thrown at him." Smith looked up at his section leader. "You haven't said anything. What's your opinion?"

"Hill wasn't especially useful in combat situations. He was lazy and unreliable. He was hard to command, and he couldn't run a gun worth a damn. They oughta just let him plea to something and give him an undesirable discharge and be done with it. If Rud doesn't want him prosecuted, why go through the expense of a court-martial and a long prison sentence?"

Smith shook his head. "I wish it were that simple. The Uniform Code of Military Justice is a little different than civilian law. We don't have all the options the civilians do."

"Seems like a waste of time and money to me, Sir. You ain't never gonna change Hill. What's the point?"

"It's not my choice. I'll pass along your recommendations but don't hold your breath."

Later that same day Thunder stopped by the gunpits as Jesse conducted gun drill at the mortars.

"Thunder, what the hell you doin' here?" asked Jesse upon seeing Thunder's ever-present smile.

"One of my guys went nuts this morning and I had to accompany him back here."

"Went nuts? Who was it?"

"You didn't know `im. He was a new guy in the second squad."

"Second squad? You in charge of the second squad now?"

"Parker gave me the whole first platoon. Made me a damn platoon sergeant."

"All you wanted was a little more responsibility, right?"

"Right. I heard you got screwed too. No more free an' easy life as an FO, huh?"

"I've got the First Section now. Things are changin', aren't they, Amigo?"

"Yeah. Almost makes a guy wanna go home and forget about this damn war. Hell, half of the kids they're sendin' over here don't know shit about combat trainin'. I think all they're doin' anymore in boot camp is teachin' `em how to march and shoot a rifle and sendin' 'em over here as cannon fodder."

"At least they know how to shoot. You should see what they sent me for mortar gunners."

"Pretty rough, Huh?"

"Whew! You wouldn't believe it. I hoped like hell Alpha wouldn't need mortar support for about a week or two there."

"Can they handle it now?"

Jesse smiled with pride. "They can handle it now. And they're gettin' better everyday."

"That's good. Never know when we'll need 'em."

"You guys gettin' much activity out there?"

"Hell no. It's a picnic. We go swimmin' in the ocean everyday, and we've set up a shower. The guys can go into the ville almost everyday. We've got hootches like grass huts. You wouldn't believe it."

"So what's to gripe?"

"We ain't winnin' the damn war this way. It'll drag on for years at this rate."

"Yeah, I see what you mean." He turned to Cue, smoking a cigarette nearby. Gun drill had ceased when Jesse had begun talking to Thunder. "Take over, Cue."

Cue nodded and ordered the men back to gun drill as Thunder and Jesse walked away from the guns.

"You stayin' in camp tonight?" asked Jesse.

"Yeah. They won't miss me out there on Caruso's Island. You got room?"

"We'll make room."

The two visited the remainder of the afternoon. Jesse learned news of his family through Thunder's correspondence with his cousin, Susan, who wrote his friend newsy letters filled with country charm and wit. Thunder shared the letters with him and they both laughed at many of the passages. Jesse missed the summers he had spent in the sleepy little town of Safford when he was younger.

Jesse looked up from one of Susan's letters. "There's a part in here that's kinda personal."

"It don't matter. You can read it. She's your cousin, and I ain't got any real secrets from you."

"Looks to me like you oughta be thinkin' a' goin' home for a spell."

"I've thought about it. Susan could sure change a man's mind if any woman could. But I figure, once we quit screwin' around and start fightin', we can win in a few months. I'll go see her then. And then I won't be comin' home with my tail between my legs."

"You figure that's what I'm doin?"

"Naw, not you, Indio. You done your share over here. We all know that."

"And you ain't?"

"It's different with me. You got Barbara. You got something really important waitin' for you."

Jesse held up Susan's letter. "Susan's not important? That's my cousin yer talkin' about."

"It's just a letter. Words come easy on paper. It's a nice letter, but it's still a letter. What if we don't even like each other face to face? Hell, I didn't speak two words to her in high school."

"That was a long time ago. You hardly knew one another."

"I'll wait till the war's over."

"You shithead," Jesse smiled. "How's Parker doin' as a company commander?"

"Pretty good. Of course it isn't his fault we sit around and play on the beach, but I can't help but think Captain Malcolm would have us doin' somethin' by now."

"He was a helluva guy. I wonder how he's doin'?"

Thunder reached into his map pocket and pulled out another letter. He handed it to Jesse. "He wrote this letter to all of us. Asked me to pass it around to as many of the guys as I could."

Forever Patriots

Anxiously, Jesse opened the letter and devoured its contents. Malcolm spoke of the trip back to the States and his short leave. He told of the easy life in their homeland and of his new assignment at Camp Pendleton. He was part of a new unit, the Twenty-Sixth Marines, that was forming to rotate to Vietnam. He gave thanks to all those who served under his command, and made special mention of Thunder and Jesse.

"He's comin' back?" asked Jesse as he returned the letter to Thunder.

"Kinda looks that way. The Twenty-Sixth Marines! Can you imagine? Those numbers are sure gettin' big," said Thunder.

"I never heard of the Twenty-Sixth Marines."

"I don't think there's been any such outfit since the end of the Second World War or Korea, or something like that."

Jesse motioned Thunder to follow him to his tent. Once inside, he opened his willie-peter bag and withdrew a letter. He handed the letter to his friend and said, "Since we're sharin' personal stuff, read this one."

Thunder noticed the return address. "Who the hell is Judy Hollingsworth?"

"Just read the damn letter." Jesse fell silent while his friend read the letter, line by line, pausing often to reread certain passages. It was a three-page letter, and it took Thunder a full ten minutes to read it to his satisfaction.

He looked up at Jesse as he lowered the letter and said, "A fella sure gets some strange mail over here. That's the strangest thing I ever read. She sounds like one helluva gal to me. I don't even know 'er and I like the hell out of 'er. You met her at the hospital I take it?"

Jesse nodded. "I saw her again yesterday on the hospital ship off shore."

"Did she stick to that part about no whoopie?"

"Like a trooper."

"Damn, if that don't beat all! Here we are, in the middle of a combat zone, and you find a woman in a million, who's crazy about you, and we could all die tomorrow, and you both blow it off. What the hell did I miss? How do you get all these women to go crazy over you?"

"I'd a' been in bed with her in a minute if it weren't for Barbara," admitted Jesse.

"Jesus Christ, man! You ain't married. Barbara would understand fer cryin' out loud!" Thunder leaned forward to chastise his friend. "Now, wouldn't you feel like shit if you got blown away and never got to see Barbara again, and you went to Valhalla never knowin' about this other girl – this Judy?"

"Believe me, I used to feel the same exact way you do until Barbara and I met in Hawaii. I never thought I could walk away from something like Judy."

"So who wants to?"

"I like the relationship we have."

"It's weird."

"It's kinda cool."

"Weird. Yer a disgrace to the Crotch."

Jesse hung his head in mock sorrow. Thunder slapped him on the shoulder. "What say we stroll over to the old French fort?"

"I try to stay away from the rough side of town."

Thunder shrugged and lit a cigarette. "You guys ever get any beer around here?"

Jesse reached under his cot and pulled out a bottle of Jim Beam whiskey.

589

Stoney Livingston

Thunder's eyes lit up. "Where the hell did you come up with that?"

Jesse beamed. "One of the guys brought it back from R&R. He sold it to me fer twenty bucks. He never could walk by a dollar."

The following morning, as Jesse and Thunder washed their mess gear, Thunder looked to the north, at the dirt road that lead from the inner settlement of Dong Ha. A long dusty column moved south, in their direction, leaving clouds of thick dust overhead as it slithered down the unpaved road.

"What the hell is it?" asked Thunder.

"Can't tell for sure, but it looks like every tank in the Marine Corps is droppin' in for a visit."

Thunder strained his eyes in the early morning light. "Them's the funniest-lookin' tanks I ever saw. Something weird about 'em."

They stowed their mess gear in Jesse's tent and walked to the end of the runway to get a better look at the new arrivals.

"It's the goddamned Army! What the hell are they doin' up here? I thought the Crotch had I Corps," said Thunder.

Jesse turned to him. "Maybe this is it. The big push. Maybe we're gonna take the fight to the gooks and we can all go home together in a few weeks."

"Maybe." Thunder was skeptical. "But what the hell do we need the army for?"

"Look at the tanks. We don't have that many tanks in the whole damn Corps!"

"Yeah, look at them tanks. They don't even look like our tanks. Must be somethin' new the army's testin' out for us to get after they've declared `em obsolete, like the ONTOS."

As the lead elements of the army column passed within a hundred yards of where they stood, Jesse said, "Those aren't tanks – they're self-propelled guns."

"Ain't that just like the army? All of that money to move a gun around," snorted Thunder in disgust at the waste of taxpayer dollars.

"Let's go back to my platoon commander's tent. Maybe he knows what's goin' on."

Silently Thunder followed him from the dusty column of tracked vehicles.

Lieutenant Smith was unable to shed any light on the sudden appearance of the army's self-propelled guns but he promised to check into the matter before day's end. Thunder left for Alpha Company, curious but in ignorance, as he had to leave before an explanation of the guns was obtained.

Life at the airstrip returned to normal within hours of the army units' passage. Lieutenant Smith's explanation that evening of the army's appearance was simple: the areas of responsibilities were being shifted by the top brass.

For several days, Jesse felt as though he were on garrison duty at Camp Pendleton. With the exception of two hours of liberty in Dong Ha, the duties carried on by the eighty-one platoon could just as easily be taking place on a base in the United States. There was no enemy contact. The biggest problem faced by Jesse and his men was boredom.

One of Jesse's more mundane tasks was a weekly foot inspection of the men in his section. Every week the men removed their boots while Jesse looked for signs of jungle-rot or some other form of fungus.

PFC Mackay was sent to Da Nang for mule driver's school. PFC Cromer

590

broke a leg attempting to run from the MPs on his return from an unauthorized trip into Dong Ha. He was out of action at Da Nang for at least six weeks. PFC Yeager developed a serious case of dysentery and was evacuated. His estimated time of absence was ten days. PFC Tursack injured his chest in a fall from the edge of the gunpit during a night gun drill and was sent to Da Nang for a period of no less than two weeks. Private Zadura was diagnosed as having a serious back problem and was sent back to the United States. PFC Darnell came down with a foot problem and was placed on no duty status for five days.

The problems went on and on. Jesse began to understand the myriad of things that could come about to render a unit ineffective, exclusive of combat. He couldn't remember these kinds of things in his isolation as a forward observer. It was always understood that you were hurting from one ailment or another but you didn't report it. You just gritted your teeth and kept going.

The eighty-one platoon was relocated to a newer row of tents, closer to the mortars. Delta Company moved into the 81s old habitat and when PFC Coleman returned to his old tent to pick up his forgotten willie peter bag, he discovered his pistol missing from the bag.

An investigation into the matter by Jesse and Lieutenant Smith was unsuccessful in turning up the pistol. The men from Delta Company living in the tent denied seeing it at any time. Coleman was put on report for losing government property and issued another pistol.

Jesse shook his head as Lieutenant Smith discussed Coleman's woes. "It ain't like it used to be, Sir. Seems like the petty shit is takin' over our lives. We pay more attention to our uniforms than we do to winnin' this war. What happened?"

"Speaking of uniforms, have you ever drawn a flak jacket? I've never seen you wear one."

"C'mon, Lieutenant, I'm talkin' serious here. Screw that flak jacket. What are we gonna do, sit around with our flak jackets on and pretend that we're doin' a great service to our country by just bein' here and lookin' tough?"

"I'm sure things are going to change here pretty quick." Neither his words nor his tone of voice were convincing.

"You've been sayin' that for almost a month now, sir. Can't we go to the battalion commander and volunteer to go kick some ass or somethin'?"

"I thought you'd been in long enough to know better than to volunteer for anything."

"I have. That's how damn bad things are gettin' around here," said Jesse.

"You should be getting orders for home any day now, shouldn't you?"

"Yessir, but that doesn't mean I wanna spend my last month sittin' on my ass, waitin' for orders home."

"I'm transferring you to the Third Section."

"What the hell for?"

"We're sending First Section out to join Alpha tomorrow and I don't want to have to try and get you transportation back in the next day or two. If you miss your ride to the States, it would be my ass."

"I've got a good friend out there, Sir. I'd like to see 'im. Besides, the Third Section don't need me, they've got two sergeants and two corporals. Hell, my guys need more supervision than Lassiter can give them by himself."

"I'll transfer half of the damn section then. I don't want you out there on the damn beach with only two or three days left in the country."

Stoney Livingston

Jesse considered Smith's objections. "How about if I just went along with Lassiter and helped him set things up? I could return the next day. C'mon Lieutenant, gimme a huss. After all, I trained those guys. They weren't worth a damn when they got here. Besides, I promised to give my watch to Thunder when I left."

The lieutenant hesitated. "Okay, Indio, but I don't wanna hear any bullshit about you having to stay an extra day or two to finish up any details."

"When do we leave?"

"I might as well call Lassiter in here and brief you both at the same time."

The briefing was short. There wasn't much that needed said, as both Lassiter and Jesse were veterans of many such movements. The big surprise came when Smith informed them they would be traveling by Mike boat. Since Alpha was regularly re-supplied by Mike boat, the battalion commander thought it best to maximize his resources. Besides, a Mike boat could carry a lot more mortar ammunition than two or three Hueys.

After the briefing, Jesse retired to his tent and informed his section of the move, and of the subsequent change in command. Lassiter was not especially liked by many of the men but, more importantly, they did not want to lose Jesse a day earlier than they had to.

He ignored them as they complained bitterly of their fate at the hands of Lassiter. He dug out his letter-writing gear and jotted a quick note to Judy as he had promised. With that task behind him, he wrote Barbara and Will. He knew in the next few days he would have little time to take care of these matters and he wanted to be ready when his orders arrived sending him back to the States. The thought of seeing Barbara again sent a warm feeling through his entire body.

CHAPTER TWENTY-SIX: GOING HOME

Jesse sat on the sandbag parapet surrounding gun one, absentmindedly surveying the silvery shadows of the landscape, his mind thinking a thousand thoughts. He exhaled his cigarette smoke with a sigh and stared at the moon, low on the horizon. He reflected on the past thirteen months of his life and asked himself what he had accomplished. What had any of them accomplished? *Nothing.* Was the only answer that came to mind.

"You want some company?" Manny stepped into the gunpit and sat next to him on a damp sandbag.

"Oh, hi, Manny. I guess I was thinkin' so hard, I didn't hear you approach. Be my guest."

"Whatcha thinkin' so hard about?"

"You and Cue are gettin' the short end of the stick."

"How's that?"

"The section isn't ready. They're still too green. If you have to go through another Oregon, or Hue, or Cherokee, or Prairie, you'll never make it with this group. They're about as squared-away as a soup sandwich."

"Don't sweat that shit, Indio. We'll make it. It won't be as easy without you to kick-ass and take names, but Cue and I can lean on Lassiter. I know he's kind-of an asshole, but he's been in a long time."

"Yeah, he's a little tough to get to know, but he does know what he's doin'. Don't forget that, okay?" said Jesse.

"We won't. Don't worry about us, man. You're goin' back to the World. Forget about this bullshit."

Jesse took another deep pull on his smoke. "I thought it would be the happiest day in my life, the day I left this place, but it's fast turnin' to crud."

"What the hell you talkin' about?" Cue stepped into the pit.

"Nothin', I guess. None of this garbage makes any sense to me. You been here a long time, Cue. What the hell have we accomplished? What did Faye, and Franks, and JJ, and Bean, and all the others die for?"

"We must be winning. Hell, they haven't beat us at anything yet."

"That's the real ass-kicker. They have yet to whip us on the field of battle and, yet, what have we won? What new ground have we conquered? Have the VC given up? Hell no. They've just been reinforced by the NVR. I expect any day now to see the Chinks join in, like they did in Korea. Why the hell not? The more, the merrier. At least we'd have a better excuse for not winning the war."

"You sound like you aren't wanting to go home yet," said Cue.

"Oh, yeah, I want to go home, believe me, but I don't think I can."

"What the hell do you mean by that?" asked Manny.

"Thunder extended his tour by six months. I thought about it for a while. At

593

the time, I decided it was a stupid thing to do. I'm not so sure now."

"You're talking crazy, Indio. Hell, man, you're getting out of here in a couple of days," said Cue.

"I've still got almost nine months left on my enlistment. What the hell am I gonna do – polish brass in the States? I think I can serve my country a helluva lot better over here in a line outfit. Besides, they'll give me a couple of weeks leave. I can get a taste of the good life, whip a few hippies, and come back and help you guys win this little police action."

Cue said, "Serve your country? Serve your country! Jesus Christ, Indio, you been reading too many comic books. You been through more shit than everybody in the eighty-one platoon combined. I think you've done your share. Knock-off that 'serve your country' shit.

"Remember Hill 76, and those little gook kids? Remember Hue and your crazy-ass charge into those houses? What about Oregon? What about Cam Lo for Chrisakes? Shit, man, a man's luck only goes so far. Don't start talking that extending bullshit, or me and Manny will tie your ass up and put you on the plane ourselves." He turned to Manny. "Right, Manny?"

"We sure as hell will. You're gettin' combat fatigue or something, Indio. Sleep on it. You'll change your mind when you see those orders for the States."

"Yeah, but it won't make any difference. I'm going out to Alpha with the section tomorrow and, when I get back, I'm extending for six months. If we haven't won the war by then, I'll go home and to hell with it."

"Sounds stupid to me," offered Cue.

"Thanks, Cue. I knew I could count on you to understand."

"When you gonna tell Lieutenant Smith?"

"As soon as I get back from Alpha's position."

"Why not before we go?"

"The way I figure it, I'll come back to camp, extend for six months and get my leave. You guys will be in position with Alpha and I'll be back before you move out. If I tell him before we go, he might make me stay behind and do the paperwork. I wanna be out there when the section sets up."

"Sounds to me like you got it all figured out," said Manny.

"Everything but the details," smiled Jesse in the moonlight.

The First Section sat at the river's edge in the afternoon sun. The Mike boat was several hours overdue and Jesse was concerned about the late hour. It was a long trip by water to Alpha Company's position and he didn't look forward to arriving after dark, even at a relatively secure position.

Cue spotted the large Mike boat first. "Here she comes."

"It's about damned time," said Manny.

The men shuffled about, picking up their gear and making last-minute adjustments to weight distribution as the grey, flat-bottomed boat approached the landing. Several men stood-by the ammo boxes, ready to carry them aboard the slow-moving craft, once beached.

The bow of the boat lurched against the soft sand at the river's edge and the ramp splashed into the water. Quickly, the First Section jumped into action.

"Let's go! Move it out! We ain't got all day," shouted the marine lieutenant from the stern of the boat as the First Section scrambled onto the craft, carrying and dragging their gear with them.

594

Jesse took an instant disliking to the man. "We've been here for more than three hours, Lieutenant. Seems like you could wait one minute for us to get our gear aboard."

The lieutenant signaled to the bosun's mate to raise the ramp, even as the last ammo box was being carried aboard, and stepped up to Jesse. With his face inches from Jesse's, he said, "What's your fucking name, Marine?"

Coldly, Jesse returned the man's hard stare. He caught the strong scent of alcohol on the lieutenant's breath. Quietly and sternly he answered, "My fucking name, Sir, is Langley. What's yours?"

The lieutenant continued to stare into Jesse's cold grey eyes. Jesse held his gaze. The lieutenant wavered and stepped back. He said, "I've seen your kind before. You think you're a big, bad-ass hero and you can talk shit to anybody you want. Well, I'm here to tell you, you picked on the wrong man this time. I eat punks like you for breakfast everyday."

"I didn't mean to start trouble, Lieutenant, but if you haven't had breakfast yet, have at it – if yer hungry enough."

There were snickers from Cue and Manny, standing nearby.

Lassiter stepped in front of Jesse. "Take it easy, Indio. You're too short for this kinda shit. Let it go. We'll be offa this boat in a few hours and the whole thing will be forgotten."

The lieutenant took advantage of Lassiter's intervention. "You heard him threaten me, Sergeant."

Lassiter turned to face the scrubby officer. "To tell you the truth, Sir, I didn't hear anybody threaten anybody."

The lieutenant turned to face the men in the First Section. One by one, they looked away from him. Frustrated, he walked to the rear of the flat-bottomed boat. "You just stay the hell up there and we'll get along fine," he said as he carelessly sat on a seabag.

Jesse sat on the metal deck, his back to the bulkhead, trembling from the sudden and unexpected build-up of adrenalin in his body.

"Damn, man, that was close," said Lassiter, sitting next to Jesse.

"You don't know how right you are," said Jesse quietly, eyeing the lieutenant through squinted eyes.

"It isn't worth it, man," offered Manny, kneeling against a bulkhead next to them.

"Yeah, I know." Jesse felt the adrenalin levels subsiding. His trembling stopped. He thought about the lieutenant a moment. "Ya know, Manny, it's guys like him that get guys like us killed. Somebody oughta take him out before he gets a good man hurt."

"Damn, Indio, them's pretty strong words for no more contact than we've had with the man," said Lassiter.

"How much contact you need with a turd before you know it's a turd?"

Manny laughed. "He always did have a way with words."

The engine in the old boat rumbled and vibrated as the large flat-bottomed craft negotiated the Bo Dieu. Where the Bo Dieu merged with the larger Thach Han, and the two rivers became the wide Viet, the vintage craft put in at the large Village of Gia Do, complete with small wharf.

"Now what?" asked Jesse as the boat pulled up beside the wooden dock.

The two-man Navy crew brought the boat quickly and expertly to dock and tied it to the moorings. The lieutenant jumped from the port side onto the dock and spoke to three Vietnamese merchants waiting for him on the worn planks. They conversed for several minutes, the lieutenant shaking his head in the negative three or four times during their discourse. The conversation terminated when the marine nodded in agreement with whatever the oldest of the three men said. He jumped back aboard the Mike boat.

The men in the First Section stood-idly-by while the lieutenant and the two sailors threw several seabags onto the dock. The Vietnamese complained loudly that the bags should be handled with greater care. The Americans ignored the smaller men and continued to carelessly toss the full seabags ashore.

"I wonder why he's givin' those seabags to the gooks? And what's in 'em?" asked Jesse quietly.

"The bastard's dealing in the black market. No telling what's in 'em," answered Lassiter.

"Pretty damn brazen about it, ain't he?"

"He probably figures nobody gives a damn enough to fink on 'im. Besides, we don't know what's in the bags."

"What about the bags themselves?"

"You think some crook in supply is gonna look into the disappearance of fifteen or twenty seabags?"

Jesse thought of Colombo. "I've got a friend in Supply Battalion who might."

"I wouldn't count on it."

"Maybe not, but when I come back in tomorrow, I'm gonna find out," said Jesse.

Several Vietnamese converged on the stack of seabags and carried them away. The lieutenant went with the three merchants to a small office at the end of the dock and the marines sat in the Mike boat, unprotected from the rays of the blistering sun, while the lieutenant remained in the small building a full thirty minutes.

Cue and Manny had some of the newer men deeply involved in a game of blackjack before the lieutenant was out of sight. Jesse joined in when he was able to control his impulse to leave the boat and drag the lieutenant back aboard. He tried to use the game to take his mind from the lieutenant but it didn't work.

The lieutenant returned to the boat, stumbling slightly as his feet touched the slippery steel surface of the deck. "Let's move it out," he shouted to the bosun's mate.

The lines were hauled in and the big boat backed away from the dock. The marines were grateful for the slow-moving air as it helped to cool their sweat-soaked bodies.

The old, weathered boat chugged downstream as the marines peered watchfully at the shoreline. Jesse fingered the M-60 at his side. "I don't believe I'd care for this duty on a regular basis."

Cue looked at a Vietnamese woman on the bank of the river only fifty yards away. "I don't know. It has its advantages."

"Wow! Would you look at that!" shouted Manny as the woman raised her peasant dress to test the water.

All eyes in the boat remained glued on her as they moved slowly downstream. Catcalls and wolf whistles echoed across the water.

A sandbar on the starboard side of the craft jutted out into the river, narrowing it by a hundred yards. The bosun deftly steered to port. Past the sandbar, the river widened and split into several tributaries. Instead of turning to the left to remain on the Viet, the bosun continued due east. Jesse pulled his map from his utility pocket and studied it briefly.

"This sure is the long way to Alpha," he whispered to Lassiter on his left.

Lassiter searched the map. He looked in the direction of the sun, which had long since passed its zenith. "We're not gonna make it before dark at this rate."

They watched anxiously as the large village of Duong Xuan drifted by on their port side, the village children running to the river's edge, shouting for cigarettes and candy. Even had the marines been inclined to respond favorably to the pleadings, the distance to shore was far too great at seventy-five yards to allow the dry transfer of the requested items.

At a large junction with another tributary the boat turned north for a moment, then put ashore on the northern edge of the village of Tuong Van. There was no dock, but that posed no problem for the Mike boat. The bosun gently nosed the flat-bottomed craft to the sandy shore and lowered the front ramp. The remaining seabags in the rear of the boat were quickly deposited on the sand and once again the lieutenant disappeared with a pair of Vietnamese.

Jesse studied the seabags lying on the sand as the Vietnamese picked them up and carted them to the shade of the palm trees further inland. He turned to Lassiter. "I'm gonna find out what in the hell is in those seabags."

"Let it be, Indio," said Lassiter.

"Bullshit." He stepped onto the ramp of the boat and walked ashore.

"Hey, Marine, where the hell do you think you're going?"

Jesse turned to face the bosun, the M-60 slung at his hip. "Any-fucking-where I want."

The bosun watched nervously as Jesse approached the dwindling stack of seabags on the beach.

Jesse waved the Vietnamese away with his machine-gun as he stooped to inspect the contents of the bags. He unhooked the top of a bag and opened it slowly, peering inside. Turning to face the Mike boat and his section, he said, "You know what this asshole's doing?"

No one in the boat spoke.

Jesse picked up the opened seabag and turned it upside down, spilling the contents onto the sand. "He's got a nice selection of stuff here, gents. What would you like? Let's see, we've got a forty-five pistol, several pairs of boots, a few hand grenades, about a case of C-rations, a few wrist watches – brand new government issue by the way – a brand new pair of 7 x 50 field glasses..." He paused as he reached into the stack and pulled out a carbine stock. He dropped it on the ground and pulled out a barrel and receiver, then a trigger assembly. He stuck his hand into the stack one more time and pulled out a small olive-drab drum. He held it aloft.

"Any of you guys know what the hell this is?"

The marines said nothing.

"I'll tell you what it is. It's a goddamned infrared scope. When's the last time you got to use one of those? Hell, I haven't even seen one of 'em since I been here. It looks to me like the good lieutenant is trying to even things out a bit – you know – provide the gooks with a little bit of help so the war won't be so lopsided and all."

He looked at Lassiter. The senior staff sergeant said nothing. Jesse faced Cue and Manny. "Cue, Manny, get the guys to round this shit up and load it back aboard the boat."

597

"With pleasure," said Cue. He turned to the section. "Let's get it done."

The section debarked the boat and moved inland to retrieve the bags already deposited there by the Vietnamese. Several of the Vietnamese chattered loudly but none offered physical resistance. Shortly the seabags were neatly stacked in the stern of the boat.

When the lieutenant returned to the boat, he was clearly intoxicated. He tripped on one of the small ribs on the ramp as he walked unsteadily into the boat. He fell within inches of Jesse's machine-gun but Jesse made no move to help him to his feet. Awkwardly, the lieutenant gained his feet and made for the stern.

He stood unsteadily before the mound of seabags and turned to face the marines. "Who the hell is responsible for this?"

Jesse stepped into the center of the boat. "I am, lieutenant."

"I should have known. Who the hell authorized you to countermand my orders?"

"I don't think you want to talk about it right now, Sir. Maybe tomorrow. Right now, we're gettin' this boat on the water and gettin' to Alpha Company."

"We'll move out when I say we move out, Marine."

"Then you better say it, Sir, cause we're goin' now. You're under arrest for theft of government property and aiding the enemy, and whatever else you been doing. I won't take a man's weapon in a combat zone, so you can keep your carbine, but remember, all of us know what's in those seabags, not just me. Now tell the navy to get this thing moving before we take over their boat."

The lieutenant looked to Lassiter for support. Lassiter averted his gaze by looking at his feet. The Lieutenant knew he was beaten. He turned to the bosun. "Let's move it out."

In the early twilight the boat pulled away from the shore and continued northward. None of the marines spoke. They waited and watched the lieutenant. He was armed with a carbine and they weren't certain he wouldn't use it against them.

It was fully dark when the bosun lowered the front ramp into the sand, five hundred yards west of where the Viet River emptied into the Gulf of Tonkin. Thunder and his platoon were there to meet them in the darkness.

The lieutenant in charge of the Mike boat cursed loudly at the night and voiced his anger at being forced to remain with Alpha Company until daylight. Earlier he had given little thought to time as he had carried on his daily business of stealing from his government to fatten his pockets.

Thunder and Jesse shared a warm greeting as the lieutenant's complaints fell on deaf ears.

"You're gettin' mighty short to be out runnin' around after dark, Amigo," smiled Thunder.

Jesse smiled back in the early moonlight. "Hell, I wouldn't have missed this trip for the world. I've gotta go back in the mornin' but I figured the least I could do was come out here and say adios. I still owe you my watch when I leave, remember?"

"I guess I'll take you up on that in the mornin'. You still carryin' that damn M-60?"

"Until I can come up with an M-1, and it don't look like that's gonna happen at this late date."

"You be sure and say hello to Susan for me, okay?"

"I'll do that."

Thunder turned his attention to the mortar ammo momentarily while he issued orders to his platoon. His men assisted the mortarmen with the ammo boxes.

"Hey, Thunder," whispered Jesse.

"Yeah?"

"C'mere. I gotta fill you in on this lieutenant."

Thunder stood close to him as Jesse related the story of the seabags. When he finished, Thunder looked into his eyes. "You gotta be shittin' me?"

"I swear. Take a look into one of those seabags."

"No, hell no. I believe you. Christ, what a low-life bastard."

"No kiddin'. Somebody's gonna have to watch him all night until we can take him back in the morning."

"I'll watch the sonofabitch myself."

"Since it's me he'd most likely want to blow away, I think I'll keep you company – if you can stand it that is."

"Hell, we got a lot to talk about anyway."

"Yeah. Oh, by the way, the watch is only a temporary loan."

"Damned Indian giver. What the hell are you talking about?"

"When I get off my leave, I'll bring you a brand new one from the States."

"What do you mean, you'll *bring* me a brand new one?"

"I'm extending my tour by six months."

"Are you crazy? What about Barbara?"

"Barbara already understands. I know she does, because she's Barbara."

"Why in the hell would you want to extend?"

"You did it."

"So what? You've got Barbara."

"And you've probably got Susan from what she says in her letters."

"So? It's not like it is with you and Barbara."

"So, I've got just as much right to march into Hanoi as you do, Amigo. Hell, we both know that we'll win the war for sure within the next six months. If I stayed in the States, I'd probably end up getting a court-martial over something. By coming back here, I get to march into Hanoi with you, and I might even end up with an honorable discharge to boot."

Everyone was loaded down with what he could carry. Mitch moved forward and advised Thunder they were ready to move out.

Thunder raised his voice to Jesse. "We've only got about five hundred yards to go. I'll lead. You can follow, the lieutenant behind you, then the rest of your men. My guys will bring up the rear, got it?"

Jesse nodded, "You're the boss."

The lieutenant shouldered his carbine and muttered something unintelligible.

"What was that, Sir?" asked Thunder.

"I said. Who the hell put you in charge of me?"

"I'm not in charge of you, Sir. I was just givin' the order of march to my men and thought you might wanna fit in somewhere. You're welcome to take the point if you like. This is a pretty secure area."

The rear echelon lieutenant nervously cleared his throat. "What's your name, Sergeant?"

"Kelly, Sir. But most of the guys call me Thunder."

Stoney Livingston

"I don't give a shit what most of the guys call you! I'll call yer ass grass if you get smart with me again. I'll take the order of march you suggested but I don't want you thinkin' you're gonna be tellin' me what to do."

"That thought never crossed my mind, Sir," replied Thunder, his sarcasm lost on the lieutenant.

Thunder left a squad to guard the boat, and the procession moved out in the direction of Alpha Company's position.

The platoon was only two hundred yards from the river's edge when firing broke out from somewhere on the far side of Alpha's perimeter. There were two short bursts then silence.

"That's just our guys, testin' the gun on the point," explained Thunder, not breaking his stride. "They fire a burst then move the gun. Just a little trick to keep the gooks on their toes."

Just as the guns fell silent to their front, a single rifle fired several times from the right and to the rear of Jesse as the platoon continued its march.

Men took cover in the sparse vegetation dotting the sand as Jesse turned and brought his machine-gun to bear on the muzzle flashes behind him, dark splotches of blood already marking his utility jacket. A pain and awareness not yet experienced flashed through Jesse.

He squeezed the trigger and his M-60 roared into the night, bright flashes from the muzzle marking each bullet's departure from the barrel. He staggered toward his foe, who had fallen with the first round out of the machine-gun barrel. Still Jesse held the trigger to the rear as he moved to within ten yards of the fallen man, the tracers from his bucking machine-gun slamming into the body, churning up bone and flesh.

The machine-gun bolt slammed forward on an empty chamber. Jesse's eighty-round belt was expended. He dropped the M-60 to the bloody sand at his feet and whipped his Bowie knife from its weathered sheath. With the knife held before him he advanced to the fallen man. Two steps from the lieutenant, he fell, his arm outstretched, reaching for the dead man with his knife, all strength gone from his body. The knife blade buried to the hilt in the sand only inches from the lieutenant's body.

The night became silent.

"Jesus Christ! What the hell's goin' on up there?" shouted a voice from the rear. It sounded far away, muffled. Jesse felt a dizziness, a nausea, a drowning sensation. He couldn't breathe. A liquid warmth flowed from his mouth but he wasn't vomiting.

Thunder was kneeling next to him. "Indio! Hang in there, Indio! It's gonna be okay! It's gonna be okay – you hear me?" He felt Thunder's strong grip as his friend rolled him face up. Jesse was unable to help. He seemed to have lost all control over his muscles.

Thunder tore Jesse's shirt open and lifted his torso, exposing the dark holes in his back. "Oh Shit! Corpsman! Get me a Goddamned Corpsman up here! Indio's hit bad!" he shouted. The only sound Jesse heard was Thunder's heavy breathing as he struggled to stop the bleeding. He placed Jesse carefully on his side.

Jesse was faintly aware of wetness. Wetness on his chest and back, his arms. The knees of Thunder's trousers were wet too. It wasn't water. Too dark for water, even in the moonlight. Blood. Was Thunder hit? No. it was his own blood.

A corpsman fell to his knees next to them, splashing thick, wet sand onto

Jesse's utility jacket.

"Make him right, Doc, goddamnit. Make him right. That's Indio. He ain't dyin' in this shithole. Not him."

Jesse was only vaguely aware of the corpsman's presence. Thunder would need the SeaWolf now. With every fiber in his body he willed his left hand to move to the right wrist and remove the watch from his arm. He experienced the greatest moment of triumph he had ever known when he felt the watch in his left hand, free of the wrist. The hand and watch fell into the soft sand.

A vision of a burning torch and a beautiful girl with auburn hair standing in its glow flashed before him. Barbara! Suddenly the vision was gone. He was in Will's front yard. A girl with gold-flecked eyes wearing a cotton blouse and a pair of shorts was washing a car. She had a garden hose in her hand. She gestured toward the house with the hose. Jesse watched the end of the hose as it moved toward him. He had seen this before but the other time the water had struck him on his chest. This time the stream hit him full in the face. He couldn't breathe.

"Shannon." He heard his voice whisper her name

EPILOGUE

It's been almost twenty years since that night in Early December of 1966 that a bunch of young marines were present when one of the greatest American patriots I have ever known paid the ultimate price for our country's freedom. Among the many sad things surrounding the death of the man we all called Indio was the senselessness of his premature demise. I had seen Jesse Langley survive through some of the most unbelievable predicaments, time and again – until I almost thought he was invincible – and yet he lost his life on a mission that should have been as routine as a barracks inspection. For those of you who never had the honor of knowing the man, the irony may well escape you but, to those of us who served with him, that irony was not lost.

Though many years have passed between me and my tour of duty in Vietnam, I can see Indio's smiling face as clearly as though he was sitting in this room with me tonight. I can hear his voice as he calls in a fire mission, or cracks a joke, or makes a cynical remark to an officer. I can see the fire in his eyes as he sees an American treating a Vietnamese peasant with less than the proper amount of deference, or as he looks at the officer who gives what Indio thinks is a stupid order. I see the bottomless sorrow in his eyes as looks at the dead, both Vietnamese and American, but especially the Americans. I think he died a little bit with each G.I. who fell in battle. Indio's compassion for others seemed boundless and yet he was unsurpassed in battle by any man I ever had occasion to meet.

Every one of us who served with him was deeply touched in some way. We may not have known it at the time, but those of us who survived the ordeal have come to appreciate his teachings more with the passing of years. He was as tough as any man who ever lived but, at the same time, he was the biggest softy in the world. He loved animals and children with the same intensity he hated injustice and tyranny. He was a storybook kind of guy.

There were several of us in the battalion who were fairly close to Indio, but none of us were as close as the friends he grew up with or had known for a long period of time. Maybe in some ways we were closer because of what we shared under combat conditions but, in things that most of us consider real friendship, we didn't qualify in his book. That's not to say we wouldn't someday but he was very slow to call a man friend for, once he did, you were a friend for life.

I have to make one exception to this statement and that was Thunder. Jim Kelly and Indio hit it off from the very start and it was almost like they were able to communicate with nothing more than thought waves at times. To say Indio's death deeply disturbed Thunder would be an understatement of the nth magnitude. It devastated him almost to the point of self-destruction. It wasn't so much Indio's death – for he understood the rules of war – but rather the senseless way it happened that disturbed him most. Thunder was eventually able to overcome his depression and, in my humble opinion, was second to no one in a battle.

Next to Thunder, I think Jesse missed Mud the most. I often heard him wish

602

aloud that he and Mud were still together and out with Captain Malcolm and Thunder's squad of misfits. Despite their many differences, Indio said that Mud was the kind of guy who knew him well enough to know what he wanted done, sometimes even before he knew himself, and that was what defined teamwork and trust.

In the years since Indio's death I have lost contact with most of the men in our old outfit but, for a while, I maintained contact with several of them. I corresponded with Thunder off and on for almost six years after I left Vietnam. He remained in Southeast Asia and fought for years. When one tour was up, he would extend his time and remain in country after an extended R & R in some exotic place. He wrote of his vacations in Hong Kong, Taipei, Tokyo, Manila, Bangkok, Melbourne, and several other places the average American would consider quite exciting.

During the course of our correspondence over the years, I saw the change in him reflected in his letters. He had vowed to stay in Vietnam until we won the war. In early 1972, I received my last letter from my old friend. In it, he admitted the U.S. had no intention of ever winning the war but he would not come home a loser. He mentioned Indio's name, as he always did, and closed by wishing me well and advising me that he would not write again until he was on his way home – and that day would come only when we had won the war. He said Indio's SeaWolf watch was still on his wrist and working like a charm, though the crystal was so scratched it was difficult to tell the time unless there was plenty of light.

Jim Kelly was true to his word. I never heard another thing from him. I have no idea whatever happened but his name does not appear on the Vietnam Memorial in Washington, D.C., nor have I had any news from the few men in our old outfit with whom I still maintain correspondence. I almost expect any day to hear that the communist regime in Vietnam has fallen. Thunder was that kind of guy.

Of the many others who knew Jesse Langley closely, Mud, or Robert Whitman, still corresponds regularly with me and we have become close friends over the years. He lives in San Francisco and operates his father's clothing store quite successfully. Though he long ago sold his Studebaker Goldenhawk, and often wishes he still had the faithful old car, he admits the wedding ring he purchased from the proceeds of the sale has withstood the test of time far better than even his old Studebaker could have. Many times he has told stories of Indio while his wife and two young sons listened intently, certain he was making them up, but enjoying them just the same.

I was assigned the duty of sorting out Indio's possessions the morning following his death when I was returned to Dong Ha. In the process, I found Barbara's address. I wrote, telling her that Indio had fallen in combat. She replied to my letter, wanting to know all of the details, which I would not tell her. She arranged a meeting with me when I returned home and, I must say, I was dumbstruck with her quiet beauty. She exuded an inner beauty to match the physical.

My fiance and I joined Barbara for dinner. We talked of Indio and the war in Vietnam. Even though I knew it was painful for her, she asked me to tell everything I could remember. Well, I did – tearfully. She thanked me and we parted company friends. We keep in touch at least once a year at Christmas.

Just before Barbara ended her four-year enlistment in 1969, she married a drill instructor at M.C.R.D. San Diego. A year later, he left the service and they moved to Ohio. They now have two children: a boy and a girl.

I wrote to Judy Hollingsworth of Indio's death and she replied, wanting to

Stoney Livingston

know all of the details. She said she couldn't believe it. She sent me a copy of the picture she had taken of Indio just before he had departed the *Hope*. Indio stood in front of a Huey on the *Hope*'s landing pad. His utility blouse was untucked, his pistol holstered backwards on his left hip, his helmet chin strap unbuckled and hanging loosely on both sides of his face, a bone-handled Bowie knife hung from his right hip on his web belt. That's the way I remember him. Judy and I corresponded for about a month or two, then I heard no more from her.

I also wrote to Rob, Melvin and John, Indio's high school friends. We all carried on a correspondence for a while.

Rob went to work for Standard Oil Company and is currently a manager in operations. He is married, with two children, living in Tucson, Arizona. His asthma has improved to the point where he rarely has to use his inhaler.

John served a tour of duty with the Army then moved back to his home state of Michigan and started his own business. He is married, with one child, and doing quite well, keeping ponds and pools clean of insects and other vermin. He is an avid hunter and has an impressive den, full of treasures.

Melvin served four years in the Air Force and ended up stationed in Tucson where, after his release from active duty, he took a job with Hughes Aircraft as a machinist. He is married with three children.

Will Hunt served his three-year hitch at Camp Pendleton and returned to civilian life as a court reporter. He did well financially but suffered through two bad marriages. When troubles began in his third attempt at matrimony, he became lost in a world of drugs. He died of an overdose of methamphetamine on Christmas day, 1983.

Shannon remained married to Chuck until 1985. He left her for a twenty-three-year-old woman who worked with him. Shannon fell into a deep depression and, the last I heard, is dependent on anti-depressant drugs.

In one of my last letters from Thunder, I learned that Indio's cousin, Susan, had married a miner and was expecting a child. I've heard nothing new since then. That was more than thirteen years ago.

Captain Malcolm returned to Viet Nam in 1967. Christmas of that year, I received a card and letter from Mitch of the old "Rough Riders." In the letter he told me that Captain Malcolm was killed by friendly mortar fire during a sweep in a remote village in I Corps. The irony did not escape me.

Manny and I have stayed in touch regularly since our rotations back to the States at the end of our tours. He became a police officer in a little town in central Arizona, called Gilbert. He's a sergeant on that department now, with a wife and three kids, all girls. When we talk on the phone, we often reminisce of our days in Viet Nam and the men we knew then.

Me? I took Indio's advice and went to college. I was graduated from U.C.L.A. in 1974 with a degree in accounting. Today I run a very successful accounting firm in Los Angeles, California, am happily married, and have three great kids. They've all heard my stories of Indio and our old outfit. They didn't believe me at first. They thought it was just good old Dad, telling his war stories. But from time to time I would have nightmares, as many veterans of my era are wont to have. They suffered through them with me for many years until they came to know that my light-hearted stories were not only real but also not as light-hearted as I tried to make them in the telling.

One night, not long ago, I had my last nightmare. I know it was my last for

Forever Patriots

reasons that will become obvious.

I was on the patrol where J.J. Washington was killed. I saw everything in perfect detail even though it was dark. I heard the VC closing in on me and I knew this time they would kill me. Suddenly Indio jumped from the bush with that old M-1 Garand. He fired over and over again and never reloaded. When the dust settled in the moonlight, he turned to me with a smile, the M-1 slung on his right shoulder, a cigarette dangling from his lower lip. I smiled back at him and wondered how he could shoot so many bullets from an eight-round clip without reloading. As if my thoughts were audible, he widened his grin and said, "Don't sweat it anymore, Cue. Be at peace. I'll take care of all the bad-asses in yer mind. You take care of yer civilian life. Leave the war to me and the rest of the guys. Why the hell you think we're still over here -- me 'n Faye, 'n JJ, 'n Bean, and the other guys? It's so the rest of you can go on with your lives. Now get to it! I don't wanna see yer sorry ass in my world fer a long time yet. You'll get here in due time, but you got a lot of livin' to do first." He paused for a time.

"Sorry it took me so long to get around to ya, Cue. There was others in worse shape. It ain't easy, is it?"

I shook my head.

"Thunder sends his greetings. Say hello to Shannon for me; Barbara too." He paused for a short time. I said nothing. Indio finally said, "I guess it's best it worked out the way it did. So long, Cue. I gotta go." He turned and disappeared into a dark fog.

I know it wasn't a dream. It had to be – but I know it wasn't. He's still out there with an old rifle that never runs out of bullets and a pack of cigarettes that is never empty. He's getting around to all the guys who lived through that crazy little war, to free them from their fear, horror and guilt. I think he's waiting for Shannon or Barbara. Who knows? Maybe they will be together again someday. For now, he will touch all veterans of that war if he can.

I've given much thought to Indio's meeting with me. In his mention of Thunder, he as much as told me that our old friend was dead and he was showing his respect for the man. Like I said, Indio and Thunder were close. I guess they still are. I don't know for sure about those things yet but I know my turn will come.

The more I think about it, the more I've got to believe that all of the guys who died over there, and in all of the wars our country has fought, are Forever Patriots, for they will always be out there, looking after the men who suffer through wars. The suffering never goes away but perhaps seeing the spirits of our comrades helps us, in some small way, to understand that which is difficult to completely comprehend.

James B."Cue" Cusick
Los Angeles, California
December, 1986